THE BEST SCIENCE FICTION
OF THE YEAR

T0056953

Also Edited by Neil Clarke

Magazines
Clarkesworld Magazine—clarkesworldmagazine.com
Forever Magazine—forever-magazine.com

Anthologies
Upgraded
The Best Science Fiction of the Year Volume 1
Galactic Empires
The Best Science Fiction of the Year Volume 2
More Human Than Human
The Final Frontier (forthcoming 2018)
Not One of Us (forthcoming 2018)
The Best Science Fiction of the Year Volume 4 (forthcoming 2019)

(with Sean Wallace)
Clarkesworld: Year Three
Clarkesworld: Year Four
Clarkesworld: Year Five
Clarkesworld: Year Six
Clarkesworld: Year Seven
Clarkesworld: Year Eight
Clarkesworld: Year Nine, Volume 1
Clarkesworld: Year Nine, Volume 2
Clarkesworld Magazine: A 10th Anniversary Anthology (forthcoming 2018)

THE BEST
SCIENCE
FICTION
OF THE YEAR

VOLUME 3

Edited by Neil Clarke

Night Shade Books
NEW YORK

Copyright © 2018 by Neil Clarke

All Rights Reserved. No part of this book may be reproduced in any manner without the express written consent of the publisher, except in the case of brief excerpts in critical reviews or articles. All inquiries should be addressed to Night Shade Books, 307 West 36th Street, 11th Floor, New York, NY 10018.

Night Shade books may be purchased in bulk at special discounts for sales promotion, corporate gifts, fund-raising, or educational purposes. Special editions can also be created to specifications. For details, contact the Special Sales Department, Night Shade Books, 307 West 36th Street, 11th Floor, New York, NY 10018 or info@skyhorsepublishing.com.

Night Shade Books® is a registered trademark of Skyhorse Publishing, Inc.®, a Delaware corporation.

Visit our website at www.nightshadebooks.com.

10 9 8 7 6 5 4 3 2

Library of Congress Cataloging-in-Publication Data is available on file.

ISBN: 978-1-59780-936-8

Cover illustration by Chris McGrath
Cover design by Jason Snair

Please see page 609 for an extension of this copyright page.

Printed in the United States of America

Table of Contents

INTRODUCTION:
A State of the Short SF Field in 2017

Neil Clarke

With two prior volumes in this series under my belt, I still haven't settled on a routine approach to writing these introductions. Some years will write themselves and others, like this one, require extra work. By and large, 2017 was a relatively stable year within the short SF field. It was the first full year without a monthly print magazine—*Asimov's* and *Analog* having switched to bi-monthly at the start of the year—but that doesn't appear to have had an immediate impact on quantity or quality. It's too early to say whether or not this has impacted readership. The ground ceded to the monthly digital and online publications doesn't appear to have changed the landscape at this time.

Perhaps the biggest and most personally exciting news was the announcement by Penthouse Global Media (PGM) that they were resurrecting *Omni Magazine* with Ellen Datlow returning as fiction editor. *Omni* was the first science fiction magazine to which I subscribed and it will always have a special place in my heart. There weren't a lot of stories in each issue, but I always enjoyed them and its quirky side held a special appeal in my youth.

However, over the last few years, there's been some debate as to who actually owns *Omni*, with Jerrick Media launching the now-defunct *Omni Reboot* online magazine in 2013 and, more recently, selling the back catalog of the original *Omni* as ebooks on Amazon. PGM has since taken Jerrick Media to court over this and other intellectual property issues. Meanwhile, *Omni* has published its first new (original content) print issue since the 1990s and plans to continue as a quarterly publication. This first print issue might be a bit of a challenge to locate these days but it is worth seeking out. Digital issues are available via Zinio. You'll find Nancy Kress's *Omni* story in this collection.

At a recent science fiction convention, I was interviewed alongside a well-established novelist. One of the questions they asked him was what he thought about the state of short fiction, and he declared it dead or dying. Naturally, I couldn't let that go unchallenged. It's disheartening to still be hearing this sort of statement echoing from corners of the field, but it typically comes from comparison to the heyday of genre magazines and a time where the subscriber counts for most magazines were artificially inflated by the impact of Publishers Clearinghouse.

For some time, genre magazine subscriber numbers were in freefall, but that "dead or dying" viewpoint ignores the digital explosion of the last decade. Not only were new market opportunities created, but the old print stalwarts were basically reinvigorated by the sales of their digital editions. Perhaps I am too close to this—my entire career is a result of these changes—but the turn-around saved and brought new life into the field.

Are things as healthy as they should be? No. I've addressed that in previous introductions. The number of new readers coming into short fiction is increasing, but not at the rate it needs to to adequately support the number of new markets being created. That said, the market adjustment I've been expecting hasn't yet materialized to the level I feared. (We're not out of the woods yet, friends.) While more than a few markets have shuttered in the last two years and some are still employing questionable business models, that sort of churn isn't terribly unusual for the field even in the best of times. What I haven't seen is a high-profile closure or recent "save market X" campaigns. That sign of stability is good. You need that before you can grow.

Through the small press and crowdfunding efforts to publish anthologies or support individual authors, we continue to see diversification in where stories are coming from and how they reach their readers. These little islands create a very fractured map of short fiction, but help charge innovation in the field. I have no doubt that some great things will rise from this and help improve the overall landscape. When you look at the state of the short SF community, you can't just look at numbers, you have to find places like this and project forward. It's amusing to have to point this out in science fiction.

Another big opportunity for growth in short fiction is international. The majority of what is published by US publishers originates from the United States, United Kingdom, Canada, and Australia, but there's a much larger audience beyond. It's not uncommon for works to be republished in other countries and often translated to other languages. Years after the digital explosion, the industry is still focused on regional instead of global marketing and distribution. For the online magazines, the internet makes that easy, but for digital and print, the distribution systems are complicated or nonexistent. In the EU, VAT fees are also an issue. In parts of Asia, books and magazines are sold at far lower prices than they are here. Adjustments need to be made and creative solutions discovered if we are to enter an age of an international science fiction community.

That said, this cannot be viewed as a one-way exchange. Opening the doors to the rest of the world also means letting others in. It's no secret that I've spent a lot of time over the last few years seeking out translated works for *Clarkesworld*. Through a relationship with Storycom in China, I've been able to publish many fantastic Chinese authors. We've also published translations from South Korea, Italy, and Germany. In the last few years, the short fiction community—publishers and readers—has become increasingly more open to works in translation. I've seen first-hand how these efforts can build an audience for both US authors abroad and for foreign authors at home.

Through these experiences I've learned a lot about the science fiction communities in other parts of the world. While some regions might still equate science fiction with children's literature or worse, others, like China, appear to have culturally embraced the genre at the highest levels of business and government. In November, I had the opportunity to visit China and participate in a number of events and conferences. It's a much younger community than ours is here, very enthusiastic, and growing fast. It's highly likely they'll continue to have increasing role on the global SF stage in the years to come.

Though its impact reaches far beyond just publishing, there was at least one crowdfunding issue that triggered some serious concern for a portion of the short fiction community in late 2017. Many authors and online magazines, mine included, utilize Patreon to connect with fans and generate revenue. You could describe what they offer as a cross between traditional subscriptions and crowdfunding. For example, a magazine or author can set up an account that allows you to make a monthly financial pledge, and in exchange you might get a digital issue from the magazine or a short story from the author. You can quit at any time. (It can get a lot more complicated than that, but I'm trying to keep it simple.) Over the last few years, the number of people using Patreon has grown significantly, and it's had a significant financial impact on the genre short fiction community. Some of the authors using Patreon include Tobias S. Buckell, Kameron Hurley, Sean McGuire, N.K. Jemisin, and Catherynne M. Valente. Magazines include *Clarkesworld, Fireside, Apex, Uncanny,* and more.

In December, Patreon announced that they would be making a change to the way they processed fees. They planned to pass along the credit card processing fees to the patrons, their term for the people who support "creators" on their site. The reason most people don't know about these fees is that it they are typically paid by the business where you use your card. Up until this point, they were being paid by the creators. The new model was met with almost universal opposition and made worse by poor communication from Patreon. Over the next few days, many supporters reduced or deleted pledges. By the time Patreon announced their intention to cancel the fee changes, many creators had lost a significant amount of monthly revenue. Some patrons returned, but the damage had already been done, namely to the trust that had built up over the last few years.

As we make our way through 2018, it will be interesting to see how Patreon recovers from this PR failure and how the community adjusts moving forward. In many ways, their timing couldn't have been much worse. Just a couple of months earlier, crowdfunding giant Kickstarter unveiled Drip, Patreon's first serious competitor. Drip is presently invite-only but anticipated to open to a broader audience in 2018.

In previous introductions to this series, I've described the process by which the stories are evaluated. Something I didn't spend much time on was how eligibility was determined. In most cases, it's fairly straightforward. If the story appears for the first time in English in 2017, it was eligible for consideration. However, there are some edge cases. For example, like most Year's Best editors and award rules, I treat a magazine or anthology with a January 2017 cover/publication date to be a 2017 publication, even though copies might have reached subscribers in December 2016. Basically, we're honoring the intent of the publisher.

Sometimes, a story can become detached from an issue/book and published separately. For example, a story from an anthology might be released online in December as marketing for the book. In that case, that particular story is considered published in 2016, while the other stories are from 2017. If you're lucky, best of the year editors have been told about this in advance and can consider the story for their 2016 volume. If you're not, the story/stories can fall between anthologies and fail to get some of the recognition they deserve.

One such case happened this year. Late last year, I was informed that the January 2017 issue of *Wired* would contain several science fiction stories, and I added them to my list of works to be considered for this book. Unfortunately, *Wired* decided to also publish the stories individually on their website mid/late 2016, making them ineligible in 2017. By the time this was discovered, it was too late to consider them for the previous volume. It's a shame, as it's likely one or more would have made it at least as far as the recommended reading list. However, since the stories are still online, you can check them out for yourself at www.wired.com/magazine/the-scifi-issue.

The twenty-six stories that did get selected for this year's volume came from thirteen different venues. I had hoped that would have been more, but some of the better stories from some of the other markets were more fantasy-oriented than appropriate for this anthology. Ten of the stories came from online magazines, six from print magazines, and ten from anthologies. This includes two novellas, eleven novelettes, and thirteen short stories. Overall, a stronger than average showing from the small press this year.

As always, I like to wrap things up with some of the people and things I'd like to draw special attention to for their work this year. The quantity and categories may change from year to year, but such is my nature. Before I start, I would also like to include a special thank you to friend and colleague Sean Wallace for his assistance and support with this anthology.

Best Anthology

Sadly, the larger publishers aren't producing many original science fiction anthologies these days. I only saw a handful in my reading this year. However, the small press has been actively trying to fill that void, and this was one of the years they had the upper hand. Of the ten stories selected from anthologies, seven came from small press projects. The best original anthology of 2017 was *Extrasolar,* edited by Nick Gevers and published by PS Publishing. At this time, the only edition of this fantastic anthology is a somewhat expensive UK hardcover. I'm hoping that there will be a trade paperback or ebook edition released in the future so more people can enjoy it.

Best New Writer

Of all the categories, this is my favorite and a great note to end on since the state of short fiction can be best defined by the quality of its new voices.

Some years, it might be someone who's been steadily publishing good stories but has recently risen to a new level. Other years, like this one, it will be an author eligible for the Campbell Award for Best New Writer—someone whose first professional sale was in the last two years. The opening story in this anthology was Vina Jie-Min Prasad's first professional sale, and she has since landed other fine stories at *Uncanny* and *Fireside Magazine*—one of which you'll also find in my recommended reading list at the end of this book. Although hardly an expansive catalog of stories, this category is very much about quality over quantity. Trust me, this is a writer you'll definitely be hearing more about in the future.

Thanks for reading my thoughts on the state of the short SF field in 2017. Now, go read some of the best stories published that year!

Vina Jie-Min Prasad is a Singaporean writer working against the world-machine. Her short fiction has appeared in *Clarkesworld, Fireside Fiction,* and *Uncanny Magazine.* You can find links to her work at vinaprasad.com.

A SERIES OF STEAKS

Vina Jie-Min Prasad

All known forgeries are tales of failure. The people who get into the newsfeeds for their brilliant attempts to cheat the system with their fraudulent Renaissance masterpieces or their stacks of fake checks, well, they might be successful artists, but they certainly haven't been successful at *forgery*.

The best forgeries are the ones that disappear from notice—a second-rate still-life moldering away in gallery storage, a battered old 50-yuan note at the bottom of a cashier drawer—or even a printed strip of Matsusaka beef, sliding between someone's parted lips.

Forging beef is similar to printmaking—every step of the process has to be done with the final print in mind. A red that's too dark looks putrid, a white that's too pure looks artificial. All beef is supposed to come from a cow, so stipple the red with dots, flecks, lines of white to fake variance in muscle fiber regions. Cows are similar, but cows aren't uniform—use fractals to randomize marbling after defining the basic look. Cut the sheets of beef manually to get an authentic ragged edge, don't get lazy and depend on the bioprinter for that.

Days of research and calibration and cursing the printer will all vanish into someone's gullet in seconds, if the job's done right.

Helena Li Yuanhui of Splendid Beef Enterprises is an expert in doing the job right.

The trick is not to get too ambitious. Most forgers are caught out by the smallest errors—a tiny amount of period-inaccurate pigment, a crack in the oil paint that looks too artificial, or a misplaced watermark on a passport. Printing something large increases the chances of a fatal misstep. Stick with small-scale jobs, stick with a small group of regular clients, and in time, Splendid Beef Enterprises will turn enough of a profit for Helena to get a *real* name change, leave Nanjing, and forget this whole sorry venture ever happened.

As Helena's loading the beef into refrigerated boxes for drone delivery, a notification pops up on her iKontakt frames. Helena sighs, turns the volume on her earpiece down, and takes the call.

"Hi, Mr. Chan, could you switch to a secure line? You just need to tap the button with a lock icon, it's very easy."

"Nonsense!" Mr. Chan booms. "If the government were going to catch us they'd have done so by now! Anyway, I just called to tell you how pleased I am with the latest batch. Such a shame, though, all that talent and your work just gets gobbled up in seconds—tell you what, girl, for the next beef special, how about I tell everyone that the beef came from one of those fancy vertical farms? I'm sure they'd have nice things to say then!"

"Please don't," Helena says, careful not to let her Cantonese accent slip through. It tends to show after long periods without any human interaction, which is an apt summary of the past few months. "It's best if no one pays attention to it."

"You know, Helena, you do good work, but I'm very concerned about your self-esteem, I know if I printed something like that I'd want everyone to appreciate it! Let me tell you about this article my daughter sent me, you know research says that people without friends are prone to . . ." Mr. Chan rambles on as Helena sticks the labels on the boxes—Grilliam Shakespeare, Gyuuzen Sukiyaki, Fatty Chan's Restaurant—and thankfully hangs up before Helena sinks into further depression. She takes her iKontakt off before heading to the drone delivery office, giving herself some time to recover from Mr. Chan's relentless cheerfulness.

Helena has five missed calls by the time she gets back. A red phone icon blares at the corner of her vision before blinking out, replaced by the incoming-call notification. It's secured and anonymized, which is quite a change from usual. She pops the earpiece in.

"Yeah, Mr. Chan?"

"This isn't Mr. Chan," someone says. "I have a job for Splendid Beef Enterprises."

"All right, sir. Could I get your name and what you need? If you could provide me with the deadline, that would help too."

"I prefer to remain anonymous," the man says.

"Yes, I understand, secrecy is rather important." Helena restrains the urge to roll her eyes at how needlessly cryptic this guy is. "Could I know about the deadline and brief?"

"I need two hundred T-bone steaks by the 8th of August. 38.1 to 40.2 millimeter thickness for each one." A notification to download t-bone_info. KZIP pops up on her lenses. The most ambitious venture Helena's undertaken in the past few months has been Gyuuzen's strips of marbled sukiyaki, and even that felt a bit like pushing it. A whole steak? Hell no.

"I'm sorry, sir, but I don't think my business can handle that. Perhaps you could try—"

"I think you'll be interested in this job, Helen Lee Jyun Wai."

Shit.

A Sculpere 9410S only takes thirty minutes to disassemble, if you know the right tricks. Manually eject the cell cartridges, slide the external casing off to expose the inner screws, and detach the print heads before disassembling the power unit. There are a few extra steps in this case—for instance, the stickers that say "Property of Hong Kong Scientific University" and "Bioprinting Lab A5" all need to be removed—but a bit of anti-adhesive spray will ensure that everything's on schedule. Ideally she'd buy a new printer, but she needs to save her cash for the name change once she hits Nanjing.

It's not expulsion if you leave before you get kicked out, she tells herself, but even she can tell that's a lie.

It's possible to get a sense of a client's priorities just from the documents they send. For instance, Mr. Chan usually mentions some recipes that he's considering, and Ms. Huang from Gyuuzen tends to attach examples of the marbling patterns she wants. This new client seems to have attached a whole document dedicated to the recent amendments in the criminal code, with the ones relevant to Helena ("five-year statute of limitations," "possible death penalty") conveniently highlighted in neon yellow.

Sadly, this level of detail hasn't carried over to the spec sheet.

"Hi again, sir," Helena says. "I've read through what you've sent, but I really need more details before starting on the job. Could you provide me with the full measurements? I'll need the expected length and breadth in addition to the thickness."

"It's already there. Learn to read."

"I *know* you filled that part in, sir," Helena says, gritting her teeth. "But we're a printing company, not a farm. I'll need more detail than '16–18 month cow, grain-fed, Hereford breed' to do the job properly."

"You went to university, didn't you? I'm sure you can figure out something as basic as that, even if you didn't graduate."

"Ha ha. Of course." Helena resists the urge to yank her earpiece out. "I'll get right on that. Also, there is the issue of pay . . ."

"Ah, yes. I'm quite sure the Yuen family is still itching to prosecute. How about you do the job, and in return, I don't tell them where you're hiding?"

"I'm sorry, sir, but even then I'll need an initial deposit to cover the printing, and of course there's the matter of the Hereford samples." *Which I already have in the bioreactor, but there is no way I'm letting you know that.*

"Fine. I'll expect detailed daily updates," Mr. Anonymous says. "I know how you get with deadlines. Don't fuck it up."

"Of course not," Helena says. "Also, about the deadline—would it be possible to push it back? Four weeks is quite short for this job."

"No," Mr. Anonymous says curtly, and hangs up.

Helena lets out a very long breath so she doesn't end up screaming, and takes a moment to curse Mr. Anonymous and his whole family in Cantonese.

It's physically impossible to complete the renders and finish the print in four weeks, unless she figures out a way to turn her printer into a time machine, and if that were possible she might as well go back and redo the past few years, or maybe her whole life. If she had majored in art, maybe she'd be a designer by now—or hell, while she's busy dreaming, she could even have been the next Raverat, the next Mantuana—instead of a failed artist living in a shithole concrete box, clinging to the wreckage of all her past mistakes.

She leans against the wall for a while, exhales, then slaps on a proxy and starts drafting a help-wanted ad.

Lily Yonezawa (darknet username: yurisquared) arrives at Nanjing High Tech Industrial Park at 8.58 AM. She's a short lady with long black hair and circle-framed iKontakts. She's wearing a loose, floaty dress, smooth lines of white tinged with yellow-green, and there's a large prismatic bracelet gleaming on her arm. In comparison, Helena is wearing her least holey black blouse and a pair of jeans, which is a step up from her usual attire of myoglobin-stained T-shirt and boxer shorts.

"So," Lily says in rapid, slightly-accented Mandarin as she bounds into the office. "This place is a beef place, right? I pulled some of the records once I got the address, hope you don't mind—anyway, what do you want me to help print or render or design or whatever? I know I said I had a background in confections and baking, but I'm totally open to anything!" She pumps her fist in a show of determination. The loose-fitting prismatic bracelet slides up and down.

Helena blinks at Lily with the weariness of someone who's spent most of their night frantically trying to make their office presentable. She decides to skip most of the briefing, as Lily doesn't seem like the sort who needs to be eased into anything.

"How much do you know about beef?"

"I used to watch a whole bunch of farming documentaries with my ex, does that count?"

"No. Here at Splendid Beef Enterprises—"

"Oh, by the way, do you have a logo? I searched your company registration but nothing really came up. Need me to design one?"

"*Here at Splendid Beef Enterprises,* we make fake beef and sell it to restaurants."

"So, like, soy-lentil stuff?"

"Homegrown cloned cell lines," Helena says. "Mostly Matsusaka, with some Hereford if clients specify it." She gestures at the bioreactor humming away in a corner.

"Wait, isn't fake food like those knockoff eggs made of calcium carbonate? If you're using cow cells, this seems pretty real to me." Clearly Lily has a more practical definition of fake than the China Food and Drug Administration.

"It's more like . . . let's say you have a painting in a gallery and you say it's by a famous artist. Lots of people would come look at it because of the name alone and write reviews talking about its exquisite use of chiaroscuro, as expected of the old masters, I can't believe that it looks so real even though it was painted centuries ago. But if you say, hey, this great painting was by some no-name loser, I was just lying about where it came from . . . well, it'd still be the same painting, but people would want all their money back."

"Oh, I get it," Lily says, scrutinizing the bioreactor. She taps its shiny polymer shell with her knuckles, and her bracelet bumps against it. Helena tries not to wince. "Anyway, how legal is this? This meat forgery thing?"

"It's not illegal yet," Helena says. "It's kind of a gray area, really."

"Great!" Lily smacks her fist into her open palm. "Now, how can I help? I'm totally down for anything! You can even ask me to clean the office if you want—wow, this is *really* dusty, maybe I should just clean it to make sure—"

Helena reminds herself that having an assistant isn't entirely bad news. Wolfgang Beltracchi was only able to carry out large-scale forgeries with his assistant's help, and they even got along well enough to get married and have a kid without killing each other.

Then again, the Beltracchis both got caught, so maybe she shouldn't be too optimistic.

Cows that undergo extreme stress while waiting for slaughter are known as dark cutters. The stress causes them to deplete all their glycogen reserves, and when butchered, their meat turns a dark blackish-red. The meat of dark cutters is generally considered low-quality.

As a low-quality person waiting for slaughter, Helena understands how those cows feel. Mr. Anonymous, stymied by the industrial park's regular sweeps for trackers and external cameras, has taken to sending Helena grainy aerial photographs of herself together with exhortations to work harder. This isn't exactly news—she already knew he had her details, and drones are pretty cheap—but still. When Lily raps on the door in the morning, Helena sometimes jolts awake in a panic before she realizes that it isn't Mr. Anonymous coming for her. This isn't helped by the fact that Lily's gentle knocks seem to be equivalent to other people's knockout blows.

By now Helena's introduced Lily to the basics, and she's a surprisingly quick study. It doesn't take her long to figure out how to randomize the fat marbling with Fractalgenr8, and she's been handed the task of printing the beef strips for Gyuuzen and Fatty Chan, then packing them for drone delivery. It's not ideal, but it lets Helena concentrate on the base model for the T-bone steak, which is the most complicated thing she's ever tried to render.

A T-bone steak is a combination of two cuts of meat, lean tenderloin and fatty strip steak, separated by a hard ridge of vertebral bone. Simply cutting into one is a near-religious experience, red meat parting under the knife to reveal smooth white bone, with the beef fat dripping down to pool on the plate. At least, that's what the socialites' food blogs say. To be accurate, they say something more like "omfg this is sooooooo good," "this bones giving me a boner lol," and "haha im so getting this sonic-cleaned for my collection!!!," but Helena pretends they actually meant to communicate something more coherent.

The problem is a lack of references. Most of the accessible photographs only provide a top-down view, and Helena's left to extrapolate from blurry videos and password-protected previews of bovine myology databases, which don't get her much closer to figuring out how the meat adheres to the bone. Helena's forced to dig through ancient research papers and diagrams that focus on where to cut to maximize meat yield, quantifying the difference between porterhouse and T-bone cuts, and not *hey, if you're reading this decades in the future, here's how to make a good facsimile of a steak.* Helena's tempted to run outside and scream in frustration, but Lily would probably insist on running outside and screaming with her as a matter of company solidarity, and with their luck, probably Mr. Anonymous would find out about Lily right then, even after all the trouble she's taken to censor any mention of her new assistant from the files and the reports and *argh she needs sleep.*

Meanwhile, Lily's already scheduled everything for print, judging by the way she's spinning around in Helena's spare swivel chair.

"Hey, Lily," Helena says, stifling a yawn. "Why don't you play around with this for a bit? It's the base model for a T-bone steak. Just familiarize yourself with the fiber extrusion and mapping, see if you can get it to look like the reference photos. Don't worry, I've saved a copy elsewhere." *Good luck doing the impossible,* Helena doesn't say. *You're bound to have memorized the shortcut for 'undo' by the time I wake up.*

Helena wakes up to Lily humming a cheerful tune and a mostly-complete T-bone model rotating on her screen. She blinks a few times, but no—it's still there. Lily's effortlessly linking the rest of the meat, fat and gristle to the side of the bone, deforming the muscle fibers to account for the bone's presence.

"What did you do," Helena blurts out.

Lily turns around to face her, fiddling with her bracelet. "Uh, did I do it wrong?"

"Rotate it a bit, let me see the top view. How did you do it?"

"It's a little like the human vertebral column, isn't it? There's plenty of references for that." She taps the screen twice, switching focus to an image of a human cross-section. "See how it attaches here and here? I just used that as a reference, and boom."

Ugh, Helena thinks to herself. She's been out of university for way too long if she's forgetting basic homology.

"Wait, *is* it correct? Did I mess up?"

"No, no," Helena says. "This is really good. Better than . . . well, better than I did, anyway."

"Awesome! Can I get a raise?"

"You can get yourself a sesame pancake," Helena says. "My treat."

The brief requires two hundred similar-but-unique steaks at randomized thicknesses of 38.1 to 40.2 mm, and the number and density of meat fibers pretty much precludes Helena from rendering it on her own rig. She doesn't want to pay to outsource computing power, so they're using spare processing cycles from other personal rigs and staggering the loads. Straightforward bone surfaces get rendered in afternoons, and fiber-dense tissues get rendered at off-peak hours.

It's three in the morning. Helena's in her Pokko the Penguin T-shirt and boxer shorts, and Lily's wearing Yayoi Kusama-ish pajamas that make her look like she's been obliterated by a mass of polka dots. Both of them are staring at their screens, eating cups of Zhuzhu Brand Artificial Char Siew Noodles. As Lily's job moves to the front of Render@Home's Finland queue, the graph updates to show a downtick in Mauritius. Helena's fingers frantically skim across the touchpad, queuing as many jobs as she can.

Her chopsticks scrape the bottom of the mycefoam cup, and she tilts the container to shovel the remaining fake pork fragments into her mouth. Zhuzhu's using extruded soy proteins, and they've punched up the glutamate percentage since she last bought them. The roasted char siew flavor is lacking, and the texture is crumby since the factory skimped on the extrusion time, but any hot food is practically heaven at this time of the night. Day. Whatever.

The thing about the rendering stage is that there's a lot of panic-infused downtime. After queuing the requests, they can't really do anything else—the requests might fail, or the rig might crash, or they might lose their place in the queue through some accident of fate and have to do everything all over again. There's nothing to do besides pray that the requests get through, stay awake until the server limit resets, and repeat the whole process until everything's done. Staying awake is easy for Helena, as Mr. Anonymous has recently taken to sending pictures of rotting corpses to her iKontakt address, captioned "Work hard or this could be you." Lily seems to be halfway off to dreamland, possibly because she isn't seeing misshapen lumps of flesh every time she closes her eyes.

"So," Lily says, yawning. "How *did* you get into this business?"

Helena decides it's too much trouble to figure out a plausible lie, and settles for a very edited version of the truth. "I took art as an elective in high school. My school had a lot of printmaking and 3D printing equipment, so I used it to make custom merch in my spare time—you know, for people who wanted figurines of obscure anime characters, or whatever. Even designed and printed the packaging for them, just to make it look more official. I wanted to study art in university, but that didn't really work out. Long story short, I ended up moving here from Hong Kong, and since I had a background in printing and bootlegging . . . yeah. What about you?"

"Before the confectionery I did a whole bunch of odd jobs. I used to sell merch for my girlfriend's band, and that's how I got started with the short-order printing stuff. They were called POMEGRENADE—it was really hard to fit the whole name on a T-shirt. The keychains sold really well, though."

"What sort of band were they?"

"Sort of noise-rocky Cantopunk at first—there was this one really cute song I liked, *If Marriage Means The Death Of Love Then We Must Both Be Zombies*—but Cantonese music was a hard sell, even in Guangzhou, so they ended up being kind of a cover band."

"Oh, Guangzhou," Helena says in an attempt to sound knowledgeable, before realizing that the only thing she knows about Guangzhou is that the Red Triad has a particularly profitable organ-printing business there. "Wait, you understand Cantonese?"

"Yeah," Lily says in Cantonese, tone-perfect. "No one really speaks it around here, so I haven't used it much."

"Oh my god, yes, it's so hard to find Canto-speaking people here." Helena immediately switches to Cantonese. "Why didn't you tell me sooner? I've been *dying* to speak it to someone."

"Sorry, it never came up so I figured it wasn't very relevant," Lily says. "Anyway, POMEGRENADE mostly did covers after that, you know, Kick Out The Jams, Zhongnanhai, Chaos Changan, Lightsabre Cocksucking Blues. Whatever got the crowd pumped up, and when they were moshing the hardest, they'd hit the crowd with the Cantopunk and just blast their faces off. I think it left more of an impression that way—like, start with the familiar, then this weird-ass surprise near the end—the merch table always got swamped after they did that."

"What happened with the girlfriend?"

"We broke up, but we keep in touch. Do you still do art?"

"Not really. The closest thing I get to art is this," Helena says, rummaging through the various boxes under the table to dig out her sketchbooks. She flips one open and hands it to Lily—white against red, nothing but full-page studies of marbling patterns, and it must be one of the earlier ones because it's downright amateurish. The lines are all over the place, that marbling on the Wagyu (is that even meant to be Wagyu?) is completely inaccurate, and, fuck, are those *tear stains*?

Lily turns the pages, tracing the swashes of color with her finger. The hum of the overworked rig fills the room.

"It's awful, I know."

"What are you talking about?" Lily's gaze lingers on Helena's attempt at a fractal snowflake. "This is really trippy! If you ever want to do some album art, just let me know and I'll totally hook you up!"

Helena opens her mouth to say something about how she's not an artist, and how studies of beef marbling wouldn't make very good album covers, but faced with Lily's unbridled enthusiasm, she decides to nod instead.

Lily turns the page and it's that thing she did way back at the beginning, when she was thinking of using a cute cow as the company logo. It's derivative, it's kitsch, the whole thing looks like a degraded copy of someone else's ripoff drawing of a cow's head, and the fact that Lily's seriously scrutinizing it makes Helena want to snatch the sketchbook back, toss it into the composter, and sink straight into the concrete floor.

The next page doesn't grant Helena a reprieve since there's a whole series of that stupid cow. Versions upon versions of happy cow faces grin straight at Lily, most of them surrounded by little hearts—what was she thinking? What do hearts even have to do with Splendid Beef Enterprises, anyway? Was it just that they were easy to draw?

"Man, I wish we had a logo because this would be super cute! I love the little hearts! It's like saying we put our heart and soul into whatever we do! Oh, wait, but was that what you meant?"

"It could be," Helena says, and thankfully the Colorado server opens before Lily can ask any further questions.

The brief requires status reports at the end of each workday, but this gradually falls by the wayside once they hit the point where workdays don't technically end, especially since Helena really doesn't want to look at an inbox full of increasingly creepy threats. They're at the pre-print stage, and Lily's given up on going back to her own place at night so they can have more time for calibration. What looks right on the screen might not look right once it's printed, and their lives for the past few days have devolved into staring at endless trays of 32-millimeter beef cubes and checking them for myoglobin concentration, color match in different lighting conditions, fat striation depth, and a whole host of other factors.

There are so many ways for a forgery to go wrong, and only one way it can go right. Helena contemplates this philosophical quandary, and gently thunks her head against the back of her chair.

"Oh my god," Lily exclaims, shoving her chair back. "I can't take this anymore! I'm going out to eat something and then I'm getting some sleep. Do you want anything?" She straps on her bunny-patterned filter mask and her metallic sandals. "I'm gonna eat there, so I might take a while to get back."

"Sesame pancakes, thanks."

As Lily slams the door, Helena puts her iKontakt frames back on. The left lens flashes a stream of notifications—fifty-seven missed calls over the past five hours, all from an unknown number. Just then, another call comes in, and she reflexively taps the side of the frame.

"You haven't been updating me on your progress," Mr. Anonymous says.

"I'm very sorry, sir," Helena says flatly, having reached the point of tiredness where she's ceased to feel anything beyond *god I want to sleep*. This sets Mr. Anonymous on another rant covering the usual topics—poor work ethic, lack of commitment, informing the Yuen family, prosecution, possible death sentence—and Helena struggles to keep her mouth shut before she says something that she might regret.

"Maybe I should send someone to check on you right now," Mr. Anonymous snarls, before abruptly hanging up.

Helena blearily types out a draft of the report, and makes a note to send a coherent version later in the day, once she gets some sleep and fixes the calibration so she's not telling him entirely bad news. Just as she's about to call Lily and ask her to get some hot soy milk to go with the sesame pancakes, the front door rattles in its frame like someone's trying to punch it down. Judging by the violence, it's probably Lily. Helena trudges over to open it.

It isn't. It's a bulky guy with a flat-top haircut. She stares at him for a moment, then tries to slam the door in his face. He forces the door open and shoves his way inside, grabbing Helena's arm, and all Helena can think is *I can't believe Mr. Anonymous spent his money on this.*

He shoves her against the wall, gripping her wrist so hard that it's practically getting dented by his fingertips, and pulls out a switchblade, pressing it against the knuckle of her index finger. "Well, I'm not allowed to kill you, but I can fuck you up real bad. Don't really need all your fingers, do you, girl?"

She clears her throat, and struggles to keep her voice from shaking. "I need them to type—didn't your boss tell you that?"

"Shut up," Flat-Top says, flicking the switchblade once, then twice, thinking. "Don't need your face to type, do you?"

Just then, Lily steps through the door. Flat-Top can't see her from his angle, and Helena jerks her head, desperately communicating that she should stay out. Lily promptly moves closer.

Helena contemplates murder.

Lily edges towards both of them, slides her bracelet past her wrist and onto her knuckles, and makes a gesture at Helena which either means 'move to your left' or 'I'm imitating a bird, but only with one hand'.

"Hey," Lily says loudly. "What's going on here?"

Flat-Top startles, loosening his grip on Helena's arm, and Helena dodges to the left. Just as Lily's fist meets his face in a truly vicious uppercut, Helena seizes the opportunity to kick him soundly in the shins.

His head hits the floor, and it's clear he won't be moving for a while, or ever. Considering Lily's normal level of violence towards the front door, this isn't surprising.

Lily crouches down to check Flat-Top's breathing. "Well, he's still alive. Do you prefer him that way?"

"Do *not* kill him."

"Sure." Lily taps the side of Flat-Top's iKontakt frames with her bracelet, and information scrolls across her lenses. "Okay, his name's Nicholas Liu Honghui . . . blah blah blah . . . hired to scare someone at this address, anonymous client . . . I think he's coming to, how do you feel about joint locks?"

It takes a while for Nicholas to stir fully awake. Lily's on his chest, pinning him to the ground, and Helena's holding his switchblade to his throat.

"Okay, Nicholas Liu," Lily says. "We could kill you right now, but that'd make your wife and your . . . what is that red thing she's holding . . . a baby? Yeah, that'd make your wife and ugly baby quite sad. Now, you're just going to tell your boss that everything went as expected—"

"Tell him that I cried," Helena interrupts. "I was here alone, and I cried because I was so scared."

"Right, got that, Nick? That lady there wept buckets of tears. I don't exist. Everything went well, and you think there's no point in sending anyone else over. If you mess up, we'll visit 42—god, what is this character—42 Something Road and let you know how displeased we are. Now, if you apologize for ruining our morning, I probably won't break your arm."

After seeing a wheezing Nicholas to the exit, Lily closes the door, slides her bracelet back onto her wrist, and shakes her head like a deeply disappointed critic. "What an amateur. Didn't even use burner frames—how the hell did he get hired? And that *haircut*, wow . . ."

Helena opts to remain silent. She leans against the wall and stares at the ceiling, hoping that she can wake up from what seems to be a very long nightmare.

"Also, I'm not gonna push it, but I did take out the trash. Can you explain why that crappy hitter decided to pay us a visit?"

"Yeah. Yeah, okay." Helena's stomach growls. "This may take a while. Did you get the food?"

"I got your pancakes, and that soy milk place was open, so I got you some. Nearly threw it at that guy, but I figured we've got a lot of electronics, so . . ."

"Thanks," Helena says, taking a sip. It's still hot.

Hong Kong Scientific University's bioprinting program is a prestigious pioneer program funded by mainland China, and Hong Kong is the test bed before the widespread rollout. The laboratories are full of state-of-the-art medical-grade printers and bioreactors, and the instructors are all researchers cherry-picked from the best universities.

As the star student of the pioneer batch, Lee Jyun Wai Helen (student number A3007082A) is selected for a special project. She will help the head instructor work on the basic model of a heart for a dextrocardial patient, the instructor will handle the detailed render and the final print, and a skilled surgeon will do the transplant. As the term progresses and the instructor gets busier and busier, Helen's role gradually escalates to doing everything except the final print and the transplant. It's a particularly tricky render, since dextrocardial hearts face right instead of left, but her practice prints are cell-level perfect.

Helen hands the render files and her notes on the printing process to the instructor, then her practical exams begin and she forgets all about it.

The Yuen family discovers Madam Yuen's defective heart during their mid-autumn family reunion, halfway through an evening harbor cruise. Madam Yuen doesn't make it back to shore, and instead of a minor footnote in a scientific paper, Helen rapidly becomes front-and-center in an internal investigation into the patient's death.

Unofficially, the internal investigation discovers that the head instructor's improper calibration of the printer during the final print led to a slight misalignment in the left ventricle, which eventually caused severe ventricular dysfunction and acute graft failure.

Officially, the root cause of the misprint is Lee Jyun Wai Helen's negligence and failure to perform under deadline pressure. Madam Yuen's family threatens to prosecute, but the criminal code doesn't cover failed organ printing. Helen is expelled, and the Hong Kong Scientific University quietly negotiates a settlement with the Yuens.

After deciding to steal the bioprinter and flee, Helen realizes that she doesn't have enough money for a full name change and an overseas flight. She settles for a minor name alteration and a flight to Nanjing.

"Wow," says Lily. "You know, I'm pretty sure you got ripped off with the name alteration thing, there's no way it costs that much. Also, you used to have pigtails? Seriously?"

Helena snatches her old student ID away from Lily. "Anyway, under the amendments to Article 335, making or supplying substandard printed organs is now an offence punishable by death. The family's itching to prosecute. If we don't do the job right, Mr. Anonymous is going to disclose my where-abouts to them."

"Okay, but from what you've told me, this guy is totally not going to let it go even after you're done. At my old job, we got blackmailed like that all the time, which was really kind of irritating. They'd always try to bargain, and after the first job, they'd say stuff like 'if you don't do me this favor I'm going to call the cops and tell them everything' just to weasel out of paying for the next one."

"Wait. Was this at the bakery or the merch stand?"

"Uh." Lily looks a bit sheepish. This is quite unusual, considering that Lily has spent the past four days regaling Helena with tales of the most impressive blood blobs from her period, complete with comparisons to their failed prints. "Are you familiar with the Red Triad? The one in Guangzhou?"

"You mean the *organ printers?*"

"Yeah, them. I kind of might have been working there before the bakery . . . ?"

"What?"

Lily fiddles with the lacy hem of her skirt. "Well, I mean, the bakery experience seemed more relevant, plus you don't have to list every job you've ever done when you apply for a new one, right?"

"Okay," Helena says, trying not to think too hard about how all the staff at Splendid Beef Enterprises are now prime candidates for the death penalty. "Okay. What exactly did you do there?"

"Ears and stuff, bladders, spare fingers . . . you'd be surprised how many people need those. I also did some bone work, but that was mainly for the diehards—most of the people we worked on were pretty okay with titanium substitutes. You know, simple stuff."

"That's not simple."

"Well, it's not like I was printing fancy reversed hearts or anything, and even with the asshole clients it was way easier than baking. Have *you* ever tried to extrude a spun-sugar globe so you could put a bunch of powder-printed magpies inside? And don't get me started on cleaning the nozzles after extrusion, because wow . . ."

Helena decides not to question Lily's approach to life, because it seems like a certain path to a migraine. "Maybe we should talk about this later."

"Right, you need to send the update! Can I help?"

The eventual message contains very little detail and a lot of pleading. Lily insists on adding typos just to make Helena seem more rattled, and Helena's way too tired to argue. After starting the autoclean cycle for the printheads, they set an alarm and flop on Helena's mattress for a nap.

As Helena's drifting off, something occurs to her. "Lily? What happened to those people? The ones who tried to blackmail you?"

"Oh," Lily says casually. "I crushed them."

The brief specifies that the completed prints need to be loaded into four separate podcars on the morning of 8 August, and provides the delivery code for each. They haven't been able to find anything in Helena's iKontakt archives, so their best bet is finding a darknet user who can do a trace.

Lily's fingers hover over the touchpad. "If we give him the codes, this guy can check the prebooked delivery routes. He seems pretty reliable, do you want to pay the bounty?"

"Do it," Helena says.

The resultant map file is a mess of meandering lines. They flow across most of Nanjing, criss-crossing each other, but eventually they all terminate at the cargo entrance of the Grand Domaine Luxury Hotel on Jiangdong Middle Road.

"Well, he's probably not a guest who's going to eat two hundred steaks on his own." Lily taps her screen. "Maybe it's for a hotel restaurant?"

Helena pulls up the Grand Domaine's web directory, setting her iKontakt to highlight any mentions of restaurants or food in the descriptions. For some irritating design reason, all the booking details are stored in garish images. She snatches the entire August folder, flipping through them one by one before pausing.

The foreground of the image isn't anything special, just elaborate cursive English stating that Charlie Zhang and Cherry Cai Si Ping will be celebrating their wedding with a ten-course dinner on August 8th at the Royal Ballroom of the Grand Domaine Luxury Hotel.

What catches her eye is the background. It's red with swirls and streaks of yellow-gold. Typical auspicious wedding colors, but displayed in a very familiar pattern.

It's the marbled pattern of T-bone steak.

Cherry Cai Si Ping is the daughter of Dominic Cai Yongjing, a specialist in livestock and a new player in Nanjing's agri-food arena. According to Lily's extensive knowledge of farming documentaries, Dominic Cai Yongjing is also "the guy with the eyebrows" and "that really boring guy who keeps talking about nothing."

"Most people have eyebrows," Helena says, loading one of Lily's recommended documentaries. "I don't see . . . oh. Wow."

"I *told* you. I mean, I usually like watching stuff about farming, but last year he just started showing up everywhere with his stupid waggly brows! When I watched this with my ex we just made fun of him non-stop."

Helena fast-forwards through the introduction of *Modern Manufacturing: The Vertical Farmer*, which involves the camera panning upwards through hundreds of vertically-stacked wire cages. Dominic Cai talks to the host in English, boasting about how he plans to be a key figure in China's domestic beef industry. He explains his "patented methods" for a couple of minutes, which involves stating and restating that his farm is extremely clean and filled with only the best cattle.

"But what about bovine parasitic cancer?" the host asks. "Isn't the risk greater in such a cramped space? If the government orders a quarantine, your whole farm . . ."

"As I've said, our hygiene standards are impeccable, and our stock is purebred Hereford!" Cai slaps the flank of a cow through the cage bars, and it moos irritatedly in response. "There is absolutely no way it could happen here!"

Helena does some mental calculations. Aired last year, when the farm recently opened, and that cow looks around six months old . . . and now a request for steaks from cows that are sixteen to eighteen months old . . .

"So," Lily says, leaning on the back of Helena's chair. "Bovine parasitic cancer?"

"Judging by the timing, it probably hit them last month. It's usually the older cows that get infected first. He'd have killed them to stop the spread . . . but if it's the internal strain, the tumors would have made their meat unusable after excision. His first batch of cows was probably meant to be for the wedding dinner. What we're printing is the cover-up."

"But it's not like steak's a standard course in wedding dinners or anything, right? Can't they just change it to roast duck or abalone or something?" Lily looks fairly puzzled, probably because she hasn't been subjected to as many weddings as Helena has.

"Mr. Cai's the one bankrolling it, so it's a staging ground for the Cai family to show how much better they are than everyone else. You saw the announcement—he's probably been bragging to all his guests about how they'll be the first to taste beef from his vertical farm. Changing it now would be a real loss of face."

"Okay," Lily says. "I have a bunch of ideas, but first of all, how much do you care about this guy's face?"

Helena thinks back to her inbox full of corpse pictures, the countless sleepless nights she's endured, the sheer terror she felt when she saw Lily step through the door. "Not very much at all."

"All right." Lily smacks her fist into her palm. "Let's give him a nice surprise."

The week before the deadline vanishes in a blur of printing, re-rendering, and darknet job requests. Helena's been nothing but polite to Mr. Cai ever since the hitter's visit, and has even taken to video calls lately, turning on the camera on her end so that Mr. Cai can witness her progress. It's always good to build rapport with clients.

"So, sir," Helena moves the camera, slowly panning so it captures the piles and piles of cherry-red steaks, zooming in on the beautiful fat strata which took ages to render. "How does this look? I'll be starting the dry-aging once you approve, and loading it into the podcars first thing tomorrow morning."

"Fairly adequate. I didn't expect much from the likes of you, but this seems satisfactory. Go ahead."

Helena tries her hardest to keep calm. "I'm glad you feel that way, sir. Rest assured you'll be getting your delivery on schedule . . . by the way, I don't suppose you could transfer the money on delivery? Printing the bone matter costs a lot more than I thought."

"Of course, of course, once it's delivered and I inspect the marbling. Quality checks, you know?"

Helena adjusts the camera, zooming in on the myoglobin dripping from the juicy steaks, and adopts her most sorrowful tone. "Well, I hate to rush you, but I haven't had much money for food lately . . ."

Mr. Cai chortles. "Why, that's got to be hard on you! You'll receive the fund transfer sometime this month, and in the meantime why don't you treat yourself and print up something nice to eat?"

Lily gives Helena a thumbs-up, then resumes crouching under the table and messaging her darknet contacts, careful to stay out of Helena's shot. The call disconnects.

"Let's assume we won't get any further payment. Is everything ready?"

"Yeah," Lily says. "When do we need to drop it off?"

"Let's try for five AM. Time to start batch-processing."

Helena sets the enzyme percentages, loads the fluid into the canister, and they both haul the steaks into the dry-ager unit. The machine hums away, spraying fine mists of enzymatic fluid onto the steaks and partially dehydrating them, while Helena and Lily work on assembling the refrigerated delivery boxes. Once everything's neatly packed, they haul the boxes to the nearest podcar station. As Helena slams box after box into the cargo area of the podcars, Lily types the delivery codes into their front panels. The podcars boot up, sealing themselves shut, and zoom off on their circuitous route to the Grand Domaine Luxury Hotel.

They head back to the industrial park. Most of their things have already been shoved into backpacks, and Helena begins breaking the remaining equipment down for transport.

A Sculpere 9410S takes twenty minutes to disassemble if you're doing it for the second time. If someone's there to help you manually eject the cell cartridges, slide the external casing off, and detach the print heads so you can disassemble the power unit, you might be able to get that figure down to ten. They'll buy a new printer once they figure out where to settle down, but this one will do for now.

It's not running away if we're both going somewhere, Helena thinks to herself, and this time it doesn't feel like a lie.

There aren't many visitors to Mr. Chan's restaurant during breakfast hours, and he's sitting in a corner, reading a book. Helena waves at him.

"Helena!" he booms, surging up to greet her. "Long time no see, and who is this?"

"Oh, we met recently. She's helped me out a lot," Helena says, judiciously avoiding any mention of Lily's name. She holds a finger to her lips, and surprisingly, Mr. Chan seems to catch on. Lily waves at Mr. Chan, then proceeds to wander around the restaurant, examining their collection of porcelain plates.

"Anyway, since you're my very first client, I thought I'd let you know in person. I'm going traveling with my . . . friend, and I won't be around for the next few months at least."

"Oh, that's certainly a shame! I was planning a black pepper hotplate beef special next month, but I suppose black pepper hotplate extruded protein will do just fine. When do you think you'll be coming back?"

Helena looks at Mr. Chan's guileless face, and thinks, well, her first client deserves a bit more honesty. "Actually, I probably won't be running the business any longer. I haven't decided yet, but I think I'm going to study art. I'm really, really sorry for the inconvenience, Mr. Chan."

"No, no, pursuing your dreams, well, that's not something you should be apologizing for! I'm just glad you finally found a friend!"

Helena glances over at Lily, who's currently stuffing a container of cellulose toothpicks into the side pocket of her bulging backpack.

"Yeah, I'm glad too," she says. "I'm sorry, Mr. Chan, but we have a flight to catch in a couple of hours, and the bus is leaving soon . . ."

"Nonsense! I'll pay for your taxi fare, and I'll give you something for the road. Airplane food is awful these days!"

Despite repeatedly declining Mr. Chan's very generous offers, somehow Helena and Lily end up toting bags and bags of fresh steamed buns to their taxi.

"Oh, did you see the news?" Mr. Chan asks. "That vertical farmer's daughter is getting married at some fancy hotel tonight. Quite a pretty girl, good thing she didn't inherit those eyebrows—"

Lily snorts and accidentally chokes on her steamed bun. Helena claps her on the back.

"—and they're serving steak at the banquet, straight from his farm! Now, don't get me wrong, Helena, you're talented at what you do—but a good old-fashioned slab of *real* meat, now, that's the ticket!"

"Yes," Helena says. "It certainly is."

All known forgeries are failures, but sometimes that's on purpose. Sometimes a forger decides to get revenge by planting obvious flaws in their work, then waiting for them to be revealed, making a fool of everyone who initially claimed the work was authentic. These flaws can take many forms—deliberate anachronisms, misspelled signatures, rude messages hidden beneath thick coats of paint—or a picture of a happy cow, surrounded by little hearts, etched into the T-bone of two hundred perfectly-printed steaks.

While the known forgers are the famous ones, the *best* forgers are the ones that don't get caught—the old woman selling her deceased husband's collection to an avaricious art collector, the harried-looking mother handing the cashier a battered 50-yuan note, or the two women at the airport, laughing as they collect their luggage, disappearing into the crowd.

Alastair Reynolds is the bestselling author of over a dozen novels. He has received the British Science Fiction Award for his novel *Chasm City*, as well as the Seiun and Sidewise awards, and was shortlisted for the Hugo and Arthur C. Clarke awards. He has a PhD in astronomy and worked for the European Space Agency before he left to write full time. His short fiction has been appearing in *Interzone*, *Asimov's*, and elsewhere since 1990. Alastair's latest novel is *Elysium Fire*.

HOLDFAST

Alastair Reynolds

1.

*W*e were in trouble before we hit their screens. What was left of our squadron had been decelerating hard, braking down from interstellar cruise. Three hundred gravities was a stiff test for any ship, but my vessels already bore grave scars from the maggot engagement around Howling Mouth. A small skirmish, against the larger picture of our war—it would be lucky if my squadron warranted a mention in the Great Dispatches.

But nonetheless it had bloodied us well. Weapons were exhausted, engines overloaded, hulls fatigued. We felt the cost of it now. Every once in a while one of my ships would vanish from the formation, ripped apart, or snatched ahead of the main pack.

I mourned my offspring for a few bitter instants. It was all I could give them.

"Hold the formation," I said, speaking from the fluid-filled cocoon of my immersion tank. "All will be well, my children. Your Battle-Mother will guide you to safety, provided you do not falter."

An age-old invocation from the dawn of war. Hold the line.

But I doubted myself.

From deep space this nameless system had looked like the wisest target. Our strategic files showed no trace of maggot infestation. Better, the system harboured a rich clutch of worlds, from fat giants to rocky terrestrials. A juicy superjovian, ripe with moons. Gases and metals in abundance, and plenty of cover. We could establish a temporary holdfast: hide here and lick our wounds.

That was my plan. But there is an old saying about plans and war.
I would have done well to heed it.

2.

The last wave of decoys erupted from my armour. An umbrella of scalding blue light above. Pressure shock jamming down like a vice. My knees buckled. The ground under me seemed to dip, like a boat in a swell. My faceplate blacked over, then cleared itself.

"Count."

"Sixth deployment," my suit answered. "Assuming an Eight-Warrior configuration, the adversary will have used its last suit-launched missile."

"I hope."

But if there had been more missiles, the maggot would have fired them soon after. Minutes passed, an iron stillness returning to the atmosphere, the ground under my feet once more feeling as secure as bedrock.

Then another bracket flashed onto my faceplate.

Optical fix. Visual acquisition of enemy.

The maggot leapt into blurry view, magnified and enhanced.

It was an odd, unsettling moment. We were still twenty kilometres apart, but for adversaries that had engaged each other across battlefronts spanning light-years, in campaigns that lasted centuries, it might as well have been spitting distance. Very few of us were gifted with close sight of a maggot, and our weapons tended not to leave much in the way of corpses.

Neither did theirs.

We stood on two rugged summits, with a series of smaller peaks between us. Black mountains, rising from a black fog, under a searing black ceiling. So deep into the atmosphere of the superjovian that no light now reached us, beyond a few struggling photons.

The maggot was quite brazen about presenting itself.

It must have known that I had used up my stock of missiles as well. The enemy knew our armaments, our capabilities.

I wondered if the maggot felt the same sting of loss and shame that I did. From a fully intact squadron, to a few ships, to just my command vessel, and finally just me in a suit, with the buckled, imploded remains of my ship—along with my children, still in their immersion tanks—falling into the deeper atmosphere.

Loss and shame? I doubted it.

The alien was a silver-grey form crouching on too many legs. It had come to the edge of its rock, poised above a sheer cliff. I counted the legs carefully, not wanting to make a mistake. From this angle a Ten-Carrier or a Six-Strategist looked almost alike. The difference could be critical. A Ten-Carrier would be rugged and determined, but also ponderous and lightly armed. They were shaped for moving logistics, munitions and artillery. A Six-Strategist, or a Four-Planner, could be viciously armed and clever. But they were averse to close-combat, all too aware of their high tactical value.

In my heart, though, I'd already known what I was dealing with. Only an Eight-Warrior would have pursued me so relentlessly, so mechanically.

And an Eight-Warrior was going to be very hard to kill.

The alien squatted lower, compressing its legs like springs, hugging its segmented body close to the rock. Then leapt off from the summit, a squirt of thrust from its suit aiding its flight, sailing out over the cliff, beginning to fall along a gentle parabola. I watched it wordlessly. Terminal velocity was very low in seven hundred atmospheres, so the alien seemed to float downwards more than fall, descending until it had passed out of view behind the furthest intervening summit.

I stood my ground, certain of the maggot's plan, but needing confirmation before I acted. A minute passed, then five. After ten a metallic glint appeared over the crest of the summit, a mere seventeen kilometres away. The maggot had leapt off one rock, touched down on some ledge or outcropping of the next, climbed all the way to the top.

With my suit-missiles depleted I only had one effective asset at my disposal. I unshipped the mine from its stowage point under my chestplate. It was a self-burrowing cylinder, angled to a point at one end so that it could be driven into the ground. Multimode selector dials: variable yield, fuse delay timer, remote trigger.

Being ahead of the maggot was my one advantage. I hefted the mine, wondering if this was the place to embed it, setting a trap for the alien. At full yield it would shatter the top of this mountain, so the maggot wouldn't need to be following in my exact footsteps. But we were only at seven hundred atmospheres now. Such a pressure was well within the tolerance factor for my suit, and doubtless the same was true for the maggot. If it caught the edge of the blast, it might survive.

But if I led the maggot deeper, pushed both our suits to the limit of crush depth . . .

Well, it was another plan.

3.

I reached the next mountain and climbed to its summit, then made my way over the crest and down a gentle slope. Nine hundred and fifty atmospheres—well into the danger margin.

Good.

I paused and for the second time unshipped the mine. This time I entered its settings, armed it, knelt to the ground—my suit lights created a circle of illumination around me—and pushed its burrowing end into the terrain. The mine jerked from my glove, almost as if it were eager to get on with destroying itself. In a few seconds it had buried itself completely, invisible save for a faint red pulse which soon faded into darkness. I checked my suit trace, confirming that it was still reading the mine, ready to send a detonation signal as soon as I gave the order. I had locked the yield at its maximum setting, deciding to take no chances.

Having done all I could, I rose to my feet and set off. The maggot could not be far behind now, and I imagined its quick metal scuttling, the hateful single-mindedness of its thoughts as it closed in on its quarry. I had timed things so that the alien would be ascending the far face of the nearest mountain as I laid the mine, screened from a direct line of sight, but that meant cutting my advantage to a very narrow margin. Everything depended on the next few minutes.

I scrambled my way down to my next jump-off point. Beyond the void was another, smaller mountain, and I was confident I could reach its upper flanks with the remaining propellant in my tank. It was lower than this one, though, and the increase in pressure would push my suit close to its limits. Once there, I would feign slowness, encouraging the maggot to cross ground more hastily.

Perhaps I would not need to feign it.

My suit was already beginning to warn of low power thresholds. Locomotion and life-support would be the last to go, but in the meantime I could help matters by shutting down as many non-essential systems as I dared. I blanked down my faceplate readouts, then dimmed my suit lights, the darkness rushing in from all sides. My suit already knew where I wanted to jump; being able to see where I was going would serve no purpose until I was nearly at the other mountain.

I had known many kinds of darkness in my military career. There is the darkness of deep space, between systems. But even then there are stars, cold and distant as they may be. There is the darkness of the immersion tank, as the lid clamps down and the surge gel floods in. But even then there are faint glows from the inspection ports and medical monitors. There is the darkness of the birthing vats, before we are assigned our living roles. But since we have known nothing but darkness until that instant of awakening, it is light that sparks our first understanding of fear.

This was not the same kind of darkness. When the last of my lights had faded the blackness that surrounded me was as total and unremitting as if I had been encased in ebony. Worse, I knew that this darkness was indeed a solid, crushing thing. It was the unthinkable pressure of all the layers of atmosphere above me, still more below. Air becoming liquid, then a kind of metal, denser and hotter than anything in my experience.

Slowly my eyes adapted—or tried to adapt. I did not expect them to see anything.

I was wrong.

There was a glow coming out of the ground. It was so faint that I had stood no chance of seeing it until this moment, and even now it was much harder to make out by looking directly at it, than by catching it in my peripheral vision. Nor was it continuous. The source of the glow was a loose tracery of yellow-green threads, branching and rejoining in a kind of ragged net. It was either growing on the surface, or shining through from a layer just a little below it.

I was careful not to assume too much from this one glimpse. It might be a living organism, and that would have been worth an annotation or two in any report I ever managed to file back to my superiors. But it could also have been the result of some mineralogical process, owing nothing to metabolic chemistry. Interesting either way, but only a footnote, albeit a curious one.

I committed to my jump and sailed off into the void.

4.

In darkness I watched the maggot crawl into my trap. We were a mountain apart, but within each other's line of sight. I was labouring up a slope, hardly needing to fake the slow failure of my suit's locomotive systems. Thermal overload warnings sounded in my ears, forcing me to halt for long minutes, allowing the systems to cool down to some acceptable threshold. It gave me all the time I needed to track the maggot. I had removed all my faceplate notifications apart from a marker showing the mine's location, and a dim pulsing bracket signifying the alien's moving position. Everything else—the larger mass of the mountain, the shape of its summit and plunging flanks—I trusted to memory.

Now the maggot had surmounted the summit and was working down to the same area where I had implanted the mine. Moving quickly, too– even for an Eight-Warrior. I wondered what it made of my painful, halting deliberations. Confusion or some faint flicker of alien contempt? Both our suits must be struggling now, though, even though the maggot had a temporary advantage. I was at one thousand and sixteen atmospheres, already over the thousand-atmosphere design limit for this type of suit.

"Come on . . ." I breathed, urging it forward.

I had been still for some while. Even with the symbols in my faceplate, I became aware that there was a tracery of yellow-green threads around my position. They seemed brighter and thicker than before, more apparent to my eyes, and as I leaned back from the slope I could trace their extent much more readily. The threads wormed away in all directions, forming a kind of contour mesh which gave shape and form to the mountain.

It was not a mountain, of course. Mountains have foot slopes and bedrock. They are anchored to continents. This was a floating mass, suspended in the air. In our hurried race for shelter, there had been little time for theorising. But since I was obliged to pause, I allowed my mind to skim over the possibilities.

Nothing like this could ever have formed as a single entity, intact and whole. Nor could the mountain have fallen from space and somehow bobbed down to an equilibrium position in the atmosphere. It would have burned into ash at the first kiss of air, and if a few boulder-sized fragments made their way into the depths, they would have been moving far too fast to ever settle at these levels.

More likely, I thought, that the mountain had grown into this form by a slow process of accretion. Tiny particles, dust or pollen sized, might be borne in the atmosphere by normal circulation patterns. If those grains stuck together, they might begin to form larger floating structures. Provided the density of the accretion was less than the volume of atmosphere they displaced, they would not sink. But floating at a fixed altitude demanded some delicate regulatory process. If living material infested the whole of the mountain, not just its visible crust, then perhaps what I stood on was better thought of as a creature or colony of creatures that had incorporated inanimate matter into its matrix. Biological processes–the ingestion and expulsion of gases, organic molecules, other airborne organisms, could easily provide the means to regulate the mountain's altitude.

So: perhaps more than a footnote. But it would be of only distant interest to my superiors. Simple organisms often did complex things, but that did not make them militarily useful. If a discovery could not be weaponised, or in some way turned to our advantage, it would be filed away under a low priority tag. A useful tactical data point, no more than that.

My suit had cooled down enough. I turned sharply back to the rock, and in that instant of turning a pulse of animation flowed through the glowing threads, racing away in all directions.

I had not imagined it.

The network had responded to my presence. I froze again, watching as the tracery returned to its former quiescence, and then moved again. Ripples of brightness raced through the threads, surging and rebounding. And even as I watched, new veins and branches seemed to press out from the ground. Perhaps they had been there all along, but were only now being activated, but it was impossible to avoid the sense that I had stimulated a spurt of growth, a spurt of interest.

It was aware of me.

My heart raced. Much more than a footnote, now. A reactive organism, capable of some low-level of information processing. And completely unknown, too. Had the maggot fleet not decimated ours, not forced our flight to this system, had their pursuit phalanx not chased us into this atmosphere, not whittled our fleet down to a few crippled survivors, and then just the one ailing ship . . .

Slowly my gaze returned to the mountain beyond this one. I should have seen nothing of it, across the void of darkness. But there was a faint glowing presence, something I could not possibly have missed earlier. The surge of activity in this living network had drawn an echo from that in the other mountain.

Call and response. Communication.

The maggot was as close to the mine as it was going to get. This was my chance, my only chance, to destroy the maggot. All I had to do was voice the detonation command.

5.

We regarded each other.

The alien's head was hidden inside a flanged metal helmet that had no faceplate or visible sensors, but still I felt the pressure of its attention, the slow tracking of its gaze as it studied me at close range. Even now, our theorists assured us, the maggots knew a lot more about our armour and weapons than they did about what was inside our suits. We had been careful not to give them the luxury of prisoners, or too many intact bodies. But exactly *what* they knew—the hard limits of their knowledge and ignorance—no one could be sure of that, except the maggots themselves.

But now something scratched across my faceplate. It was a flash of colour-less light, emanating from a point just under the Eight-Warrior's head. I squinted, but the flash was much too dim to be a weapon discharge. And it was organising itself, forming into a pattern of symbols that my brain could not help but imprint with meaning.

Why?

"Why what?" I mouthed back, almost without thinking.

Why did you not kill?

"You weren't worth the cost of a mine." Then I blinked in irritation and confusion. "Wait. Are you understanding any of this?"

You create sounds. I read the sounds through your glass. I know your tongue. All Eight-Warriors know your tongue. You call us Eight-Warriors. "Yes," I answered. "But you're not meant to understand us. No one said you could do that."

It is not an advantage we advertise.

It was just words, spraying across my faceplate. But it was impossible not to read a kind of sardonic understatement into the maggot's reply.

"No, you wouldn't, I suppose. Just as we wouldn't want you to know if we could read your comms. You'd change your encryption methods and we'd have to . . . I don't know, learn a new language or something. But you shouldn't have told me, should you? Now I know."

You know but you cannot report. Your signals will not penetrate this atmo-sphere, and even if they did there is nothing out there to hear them. Your fleet is dust. You will not see your kind again. Nor I mine. So there need be no secrets between us.

"You might be planning to die here, maggot. I've got other plans."

Have you? I should like to hear them. Your squadron was destroyed. You are the last survivor of the last ship—as I am the last of my pursuit phalanx. We are alone now, and our suits are both failing us. We have no weapons, no means of harming each other. We cannot go deeper, and we cannot ascend. Our only fate is to die here.

"So what, maggot? You were made to die."

And you were not?

"I was born. I have a name, a family. I am Battle-Mother . . ." But whatever I had hoped to say beyond that point died somewhere between my brain and my mouth. I had a name, I knew. I had been given one. But it was so long ago it was like some ancient blemish that had almost faded from sight. "I am

Battle-Mother," I repeated, with all the conviction I could find, as if that were indeed my name. "Battle-Mother. At least I have that. What are you, but an Eight-Warrior?"

I am Greymouth. And you are right, Battle-Mother. I was made for war.

But then which of us was not?

"We're not the same."

Perhaps. But you have still not answered my question—at least not to my satisfaction. You set the mine. I found it, of course, but by then it would have been much too late for me had you detonated it remotely. The blast would have destroyed me. So: why did you not kill?

"You know why."

You learned of the native organisms. You realised that destroying me would damage them. But it was just one of these floating mountains. No great harm would have been done to the rest of the ecology.

"I couldn't be sure."

And if you had been sure, Battle-Mother? Would that have changed things?

"Of course. I'd have taken you out. I'd been trying to kill you all along. Why would I have stopped?"

Because we are all capable of changing our minds.

"I'm not. We're not alike, you and I. We're different, Greymouth. I'd kill you now, if there was a way. After all the things the maggots have done to us, I wouldn't hesitate."

Crimes of war.

"Yes."

We know well of those, Battle-Mother. Very well indeed.

6.

We had been silent for a while. When Greymouth asked me if I had noticed the changes I took my time answering, not wanting the maggot to think I was in any hurry for conversation. But the question nagged at me, because I had been making my own observations and a part of me had been wondering when I was going to get around to asking something similar of the alien.

"The glowing threads have developed. They seem to be concentrating around us, growing and branching near our bodies. Near us, I mean."

Speak of bodies, Battle-Mother. It will soon be the truth. But I am glad we agree about the threads. I have been monitoring them, as best as I am able. They are definitely responding to our presence. We have made a discovery, then—the two of us.

"Have we?"

I think so. This is a more complex organism than we initially suspected.

"Speak for yourself." But my answer was peevish and I forced myself to admit that the maggot was not entirely wrong. "Fine; there's more to it than just some glowing infestation. It's reactive, and obviously capable of fast growth when the need arises."

Whatever the need might be.

After an interval I asked: "Have you encountered anything like this before, Greymouth?"

They do not tell Eight-Warriors everything, Battle-Mother. We learn only what we need. Doubtless it is different for you.

"Yes," I answered, reflexively. But I hesitated. "What I mean is, we're educated. We have to be, all the responsibility given to us. But I don't know that much about planetary ecologies. If I could get back to my ship, my fleet, I could submit a query to . . ."

Yes, I could ask questions as well. To a Four-Planner or a Three-Strategist, or even a Two-Thinker, if my question were deemed vital enough. But like you I would need to return to my ship, and therein lies a slight difficulty.

"Neither of us is going anywhere," I said.

No. That we are not.

Yellow light licked at the edge of my attention. I rotated my head, to the extent that I was able. My suit was stiffening up as its power levels faded. Around me the threads were branching and cross-weaving in a steadily thickening density, forming a sort of clotted, blurred outline of my form. The organisms" glow throbbed with strange rhythms, the colour shifting from green to yellow, yellow to green. The same process was happening to the maggot, with fine threads beginning to creep up the sides of Greymouth's armour, concentrating around the seams and joints, almost as if they were looking for a way to get inside . . .

"You spoke of crimes," I said, pushing aside the thought that the same process of infiltration must be going on with my own suit. "I won't pretend that we haven't hit you hard. But let's not pretend that we chose this war. It was a maggot offensive, pushing into our space, broadcasting your militaristic intentions ahead of your fleets. If you'd kept to your sector there'd have been no war, no crimes of war . . ."

Even though I had altered the angle of my head, the maggot's light was still able to splash across my faceplate.

We were pushed out of our homeworlds, Battle-Mother. Usurped by an adversary stronger than either of us. We fought back as best we could, but soon it became clear that we would have to move just to survive. But we did not wish for war, and we knew that our encroachment into your sector might appear provocative. Ahead of our evacuation fleets, we transmitted what we hoped would be recognised as justifications. We showed recordings of how valiantly we had struggled against the adversary, proving that we had done our utmost to avoid this encroachment. We thought that the nature of our entreaties would be plain to any civilised species: that we sought assistance, shelter, mutual cooperation. Slowly, though, we learned that our transmissions had been wrongly interpreted. You saw them as threats, rather than justifications. We attempted to make amends—modified our negotiating tactics. But by then the damage was done. Our evacuation fleets were already encountering armed opposition. Merely to survive, we had to shift to a counter-offensive posture. Even then our intention was to hold you at bay long enough for our peaceful intentions to become apparent. But they never did.

"You can say that again."

We were pushed from our homeworlds . . .

"It's a figure of speech, Greymouth. It means that I'm concurring with your words, while emphasizing that there's a degree of understatement in what you say."

Then you do agree. That is something, is it not?

"You've been told one story, one version of events. Maybe it's true, maybe it isn't. Obviously I don't hold you personally responsible for the things your side did to mine . . ."

That is a relief.

"I'm serious."

Then I will extend you the same courtesy, Battle-Mother. I do not hold you personally responsible. There. All our differences settled in one stroke. Who could have thought it could be so simple?

"It's simple because we don't matter."

If we have ever mattered. I am not so much. For every Eight-Warrior that falls, a billion more are waiting. I suppose you were much more important to your war effort.

"My children looked up to me. That's the point of a Battle-Mother." I brooded before continuing. "But there were always more above me. Layers of command. Superior officers. They gave me a squadron . . . but it was just one squadron."

Which you lost.

"Which you took from me."

We have both suffered much. We have both known sadness. Shall we agree on that?

"What does a maggot know of sadness?"

A warning icon sprang up on my helmet. I turned my eyes to it with dull expectation. Hermetic breach, the icon said. Foreign presence detected in suit.

I thought of the glowing tendrils. They had pushed their way through my suit's weak points. But the crush and heat of the superjovian's atmosphere was still being held outside, or else I would be dead by now. The organism, whatever it was, had overcome my suit's defences without compromising its basic ability to keep me alive and conscious.

Battle-Mother?

"Yes."

There is something inside my suit now.

"I'm the same."

What do you think it means to do with us?

"I don't know. Taste us. Digest us. Whatever superjovian rock creatures do when they're bored. We'll find out in a little while. What's wrong, Greymouth? You're not frightened, are you?"

I have never been very good at being frightened. But you are wrong about us, Battle-Mother. A maggot can know a great deal of sadness.

7.

Before long it was in my suit, glowing and growing. It had burst through in a dozen places, infiltrating and branching, exploring me with a touch that was both gentle and absent of thought. A blind, mindless probing. The yellow-green glow was both inside and outside now, and I knew that it must be the same for Greymouth. For all our differences, all the many ways in which we were not alike, we had this much in common. The superjovian had bested us. Our suits were not made for these depths, nor for keeping out this determined, pervasive alien presence.

Us, I thought to myself. That was how my perception had shifted now. The maggot was no longer as alien to me as this thing that was fighting its way into both of us. The maggot was Greymouth, a soldier just as I was. An Eight-Warrior and a Battle-Mother. Both of us lost now, both of us doomed. All that was left was to bear witness, and then to die.

The glow had washed out any chance of reading Greymouth's words. I knew it was out there, almost close enough to touch, that the threads surrounding our two bodies were probably cross-mingled, interconnected. I wondered if it was still trying to communicate with me. Could it still understand my voice, even if there was no way of responding in kind?

"Greymouth," I said. "Listen to me. I don't think you can answer me now, but if you're still out there, still hearing me . . . I'm sorry for the things that happened. I can't know if any part of that was true, what you said about the evacuation fleets, about the messages being misinterpreted. But I choose to believe that it happened the way you said. A terrible mistake. But there's hope, isn't there? Not for either of us, I know. But for our two species. One day they'll realise the mistake, and . . ." I trailed off, repulsed by the shallow platitudes of my words. "No. Who am I kidding. They'll just go on making more of us. More Battle-Mothers. More Eight-Warriors. More fleets, more phalanxes, more holdfasts. More war-fronts. They'll run out of worlds to shatter and then they'll turn to stars, and nothing that happened here will ever have mattered. I'm sorry, Greymouth. So sorry."

There was no answer, but then again I had expected none. We had been distant enemies, then closer enemies, and for a short time we had been something other than enemies, although I suppose it would be stretching a point to say that we had become friends. Allies in adversity, perhaps. Two unwilling souls pitched into the same crushing predicament.

I thought about fear, and wondered how it was for Greymouth. Fear was a strange thing. You might think that a fearless soldier would be the best soldier of all, willing to accept any hazard, even the likelihood of certain death. But a fearless soldier knows no restraint. A fearless soldier will throw themselves into the fray without a moment's consideration, even when their actions are militarily valueless. A fearless soldier is a weapon without a safety lock.

No. Our leaders—our Battle-Queens and Two-Minds—must surely have come to the same independent conclusion. Fear is useful. More than useful: necessary. Spice your soldiers with a little fear and they make fewer mistakes.

Greymouth felt it. So did I.

"Yes."

It was the soundless expression of an idea, but it was not at all like the inner voice of my head. The word had bloomed sharp and bright as if a small mine had just gone off inside my skull, lighting it up from within.

"Greymouth?" I asked.

"I think we sense each other, Battle-Mother. How odd it is to have your thoughts flowering inside me."

"How is this possible?"

"I do not know. But if the native organism has penetrated both our suits, both our bodies, and formed a connective network between our nervous systems . . ." Greymouth's chain of thoughts quenched out.

"It's all right. I don't have a better theory. And I think you must be right. But if that's the case then the network must be doing a lot more than simply wiring our minds together. It must be processing, translating idiosyncratic representations from one internal schema to another. Bridging vast gulfs of mental representation. How is it doing that? More to the point, why? What possible evolutionary pressure could ever have selected for this capability?"

"It is happening, Battle-Mother. Perhaps the wisest thing would be to accept it. Unless, of course, you are merely a figment of my own terrified imagination."

"I don't feel like a figment. Do you?"

"Not really."

"I was thinking about being alone," I went on. I was speaking, for now, but I had the sense that before very long even speaking would be superfluous, as the network extended its consolidation of us. "I didn't like it. It was better when we were able to talk."

"Then it is very fortunate indeed," Greymouth said, "that one of us did not kill the other."

8.

My faceplate displays were nearly all dimmed-out, locomotive and life-support power nearly drained. In a very short while the struggling refrigeration system would fail and the atmosphere's heat would lance its way through to me.

I hoped it would be fast.

"We will die here," Greymouth said, his thoughts bursting into my head like a chain of novae, each flare stained with a distinct emotional hue. Acceptance, regret, sadness, a kind of shivering awe. To die was a strange enough thing, even for a soldier. To die like *this*, in the black crush of a superjovian, on a tomb of floating rock, one enemy bound to the next by a glowing tracery of living matter: that was a strangeness beyond anything we had been prepared for.

"Maybe they'll find us some day."

"Maybe they will not." But after a silence that could have been minutes or hours, for all that I had any clear grasp on time's passing, Greymouth added: "I hope that they will. I hope that they will find us together here and think of what became of us. Your side or mine, I do not think it will matter. They will see us and realise that we chose not to kill. We chose not to destroy. That we chose this better path."

"Do you think that'll change their minds?"

The nova flare conveyed a prickle of emerald green, what I had begun to think was wry amusement, or bitter irony. "If minds are capable of changing."

"Do you think they are?"

"Ours have changed."

"Yes," I said softly. "They have."

"Then there is hope, Battle-Mother. Not much, but more than we had any right to expect."

"Greymouth," I said. "Can you still move? Just a little?"

"Not much of me. And any movement will only draw power from my central reserve."

"I know. It's the same here. I'm down to my last few drops. We're very different, aren't we? But put two soft-bodied creatures inside metal armour and drop them into a thousand atmospheres, and we're more alike than we knew."

"I do not see how moving will be of much benefit to either of us," Greymouth said.

More systems faded from my faceplate. What remained was a litany of dire warnings, and even those were faint and flickering. It seemed warmer than only a few moments before. Had the thermal regulation already failed?

"It won't be of any benefit to us," I said. "Not at all. But I'm thinking of those who come after us—those who'll find us."

"If they find us."

"They will. I believe it. Call it an act of faith, whatever you wish. But this system's too useful for either side to be left alone for long. They'll come, and they'll probe this atmosphere again, and they'll find the floating mountains, and they'll find traces that don't belong. Metallic echoes, technological signatures. Two bodies. Greymouth and Battle-Mother."

"Next to each other. Dead and gone. They will know nothing of our thoughts, nothing of what has passed between us."

"They won't need to."

I moved my arm. It was sluggish, my suit barely responsive. I felt as if I was using all my own strength to fight the metal prison in which I lay. Only a few faint symbols remained on my faceplate. An ominous silence now filled my suit, where before there had been the labouring of the overloaded life-support system. It was done, expired. Each breath I took would be staler and warmer than the last.

Still I reached. I stretched.

"Greymouth," I breathed.

"I am reaching. It is hard, Battle-Mother. So hard."

"I know. But do it anyway. For both of us."

"They will wonder why we did this."

"Let them."

I had almost nothing left to give. I *have* almost nothing. For a few moments I can still hold the chain of events in my head, can still remember what it was that brought me to this moment. The war, the battle, the flight, the shield, the decimation, the loss of my squadron, my ship, my crew, all my glorious children. I think that if I hold these things with enough clarity, some trace of them may escape me, some part of Greymouth's story as well, and between us we might leave some imprint of our memories in the living glow of the rock.

But I cannot be sure, only that it is better to die with a good thought in one's head than a bad one.

That is what I am thinking when Greymouth touches my hand, and my fingers close.

And we holdfast.

Nancy Kress is the author of thirty-three books, including twenty-six novels, four collections of short stories, and three books on writing. Her work has won six Nebulas, two Hugos, a Sturgeon, and the John W. Campbell Memorial Award. Her most recent work is *Tomorrow's Kin* (Tor, 2017), which, like much of her work, concerns genetic engineering. Kress's fiction has been translated into Swedish, Danish, French, Italian, German, Spanish, Polish, Croatian, Chinese, Lithuanian, Romanian, Japanese, Korean, Hebrew, Russian, and Klingon, none of which she can read. In addition to writing, Kress often teaches at various venues around the country and abroad, including a visiting lectureship at the University of Leipzig and a recent writing class in Beijing. Kress lives in Seattle with her husband, writer Jack Skillingstead, and Cosette, the world's most spoiled toy poodle.

EVERY HOUR OF LIGHT AND DARK

Nancy Kress

1668

Delft, shrouded in rain, was uniformly gray. Hunched against the cold and wet, the artist walked from Oude Langendijk along the canal to his patron's house. Much as he hated this sort of occasion, inside the house would be warmth, food, wine. And quiet. His own house, crowded with children, was never quiet.

"You are welcome," said his patron's wife shyly as a servant took his cloak. "Pieter will be glad to see you."

Johannes doubted that. This celebration was not about him, nor one of his paintings, nor even the newly acquired Maes painting being shown for the first time. This celebration was about the patron: his wealth, his taste, his power. Johannes smiled at his pretty wife, another acquisition, and passed into the first of many lavishly furnished rooms, all warm from good fires.

In this room hung one of his own paintings. Johannes glanced at it in passing, then stopped abruptly. His eyes widened. He took a candle from a table and held it close to the picture. *Lady Sewing a Child's Bonnet*—he had painted it four years ago. Catharina had been the model. She sat, heavily pregnant, on a wooden chair, the light from an unseen window illuminating the top of her fair hair as she bent over her work. A broken toy lay at her feet, and what could be seen of her expression was somber. On the table beside her were her work basket, a glass of wine, and a pearl necklace, tossed carelessly as if she had thrown it off in discomfort, or despair. On the wall behind her was a painting-within-a-painting, van Honthorst's *Lute Player*. The painstaking detail in the smaller picture, the hint of underpainted blue in Catharina's burgundy-colored dress, the warm light on the whitewashed walls—how long it took to get that right!—all shone in the glow from Johannes's candle.

But he had not made this painting.

Inch by inch, he examined it, ignoring guests who passed him, spoke to him. *Lady Sewing a Child's Bonnet* was the most skillful forgery he had ever seen, but forgery it was. Did Pieter know? Presumably not, or the picture would not still be on the patron's walls. How had it come there? Who had painted it? And—

What should Johannes do about this?

The decision came swiftly—he should do nothing. He owed money all over the city. He had hopes of Pieter's commissioning another painting from him soon, perhaps tonight. The original could not have been switched with the forgery without Pieter's consent, not in this well-guarded house, and Pieter would not welcome attention drawn to whatever scheme he was participating in. Say nothing.

"Ah, Johannes!" said a booming voice behind him. "Admiring your own work, you vain man?"

Johannes turned to face the guest of honor, Nicolaes Maes. "No," he said. Maes waited, but Johannes said nothing more.

Not now, not ever.

2270

Cran is working on clearances at his console when Tulia bounces into the Project room. "Cran! They chose it! They really chose it!" She grabs his hands and twirls him in circles.

"Careful! You'll hit the Squares!"

She stops moving and drops Cran's hands. He hears his own tone: sour, disapproving, a cranky old man. He sees that Tulia understands immediately, but understanding isn't enough to erase the hurt. Torn between them, she chooses hurt.

"Aren't you happy for me?"

"Of course I am," he says, and forces a smile. And he is happy, in a way. How could he not be—Tulia is him, or at least 32 percent of her genes are. It's the other 68 percent that prompts this terrible, inexcusable jealousy.

She says softly, "Maybe next cycle the Gallery will choose one of your pictures."

It is the wrong thing to say; they both know that will never happen. Cran does not have Tulia's talent, has perhaps no talent at all. How does she do it, produce art that is somehow fresh and arresting, after working all day at the Project's forgeries? How? Sometimes he hates her for it. Does she know this?

Sometimes he loves her for it. She knows this.

Cran says, "I am happy for you. But I need to work."

Her eyes sharpen. She, after all, is also part of the Project. "Do you have something?"

"An ancient Egyptian vase, on Square Three. Go look."

She looks, frowning. "We cannot reproduce that."

"Doesn't matter. It's inside a tomb. We can Transfer a lump of rock and no one would ever know."

We could Transfer one of my sculptures, which are just as dreadful as my paintings.

"The tomb was never opened before—"

"No." No one ever names the Madness, if naming can be avoided. Even in a deliberately rational society—legally rational, culturally rational, genetically rational to whatever extent the geneticists can manage—superstitions seep in like moondust in airlocks. No one says the word aloud.

"Well, that's wonderful!" Tulia says. "Has the Director vetted it? Have you done the clearances?"

"Yes, he did, and I'm completing them now. When . . . when is your Gallery presentation?"

"Tuesday. I'll go now. I just wanted to tell you about . . . about my painting."

"I'm glad you did," Cran says, lying, hoping she doesn't realize that. Sixty-eight percent foreign genes.

Tulia leaves. Cran de-opaques the window wall and stares out. The Project is housed in its own dome, and sometimes the bleak lunar landscape calms him when he feels equally bleak. Not, however, this time.

On the horizon, the lights of Alpha Dome are just visible below stars in the black sky. Alpha was the first, the only dome to exist when the Madness happened on Earth. Six thousand lunar colonists, half of them scientists. They had the best equipment, the best scientific minds, the best planners.

Earth had those who could not qualify; Earth had too many people and too many wars; Earth had the ability to create genetically boosted bioweapons so powerful that when the Madness began as just another war, it quickly escalated. In three months everyone on Earth was dead. How could they do that, those Terrans of two centuries ago? Those on Alpha watched in horror. There was nothing they could do except what they did: shoot down both incoming missiles and incoming, infected escapees.

He was not there, of course. He's old, but not that old. How long does it take for guilt to evaporate? Longer than two hundred years. Alpha Dome grew to sixteen more domes. If he squints hard, he might be able to see the robots constructing Sigma Dome on the western horizon, or the sprays of dirt thrown up from the borers digging the connecting tunnels. But through all the construction, all the genetic tinkering, all the amazing scientific progress, the guilt has not gone away. We humans murdered our own species. Thus, the Project.

Or perhaps, Cran thinks, that's wrong. There is, after all, a strong but polite political faction—all Luna's political factions are polite, or else they don't exist—that says the Project should be discontinued and its resources committed to the present and the future, not to rescuing the past. So far, this has not happened.

It takes Cran nearly an hour to finish the complicated clearance procedures for the Egyptian vase. He finds it hard to concentrate.

The clearances are approved almost immediately. They are, after all, only a formality; the Director, who is the Project's expert on art of the ancient world, has already inspected the image glowing in Square Three. Cran has worked a long day and it's late; he should go home. But he likes working alone at night, and he has the seniority to do so. He gazes at the vase, this exquisite thing that exists in dark beneath tons of rock in a buried tomb a quarter-million miles and three millennia away. A core-formed glass vessel, three inches high, its graceful, elaborately decorated curves once held perfumed ointment or scented oils. Perhaps it still does.

The Project room is lined with Squares, each a six-foot cube. Some of the Squares are solid real-time alloys; some are virtual simulations; some are not actually there at all—not in time or space. The Project is built on chaos theory, which says that the patterns of spacetime contain something called "strange attractors," a mathematical concept that Cran doesn't understand at all. He is, after all, a Project technician, not a physicist. A senior, trusted technician who will never be an artist.

Why Tulia? Why not me?

One of those questions that, like the Madness, has no answer.

2018

The guard at the National Gallery in Washington, D.C., made his early morning rounds. He unlocked each room, peered in, and moved on. He had worked there a long while and prided himself on knowing exactly what each exhibit held at any given time.

He unlocked a gallery, glanced in, and stopped cold.

Not possible.

This room held the Gallery's five Vermeers. At present, two were on loan. The other three should be on the off-white walls in their protected frames. They were.

But—

"Oh my God," the guard said under his breath, and then very loudly. His hands shook as he pressed the alarm on his pager.

2270

The Transfer happens, as always, blindingly fast. One moment Square Three holds a small stone. The next it holds a delicate purple vase trimmed in gold.

Cran doesn't touch it. He follows protocol and calls two members of the Handler Staff. Despite the hour, they both rush to the Project room. Marbet Hammerling's eyes water, an extravagance that Cran deplores even as he understands it.

Salvaging anything from the past is a slow, difficult, emotional triumph. Humanity's artistic heritage lay decaying on a deserted and contaminated Earth; nothing can be brought from the present without bringing contamination with it. But thanks to the genius of the Rahvoli Equations and the engineers who translated them to reality, some things can be saved from the past. Only things less than six cubic feet; only things deemed worthy of the huge expenditure of energy; only things non-living; only things replaced in Transfer by a rough equivalent in weight and size; only replacements that will not change the course of the timestream that has already unfolded. Otherwise, the Transfer simply did not happen. The past could only be disturbed so much.

Marbet whispers, "It is so beautiful." Reverently she lifts it from the faint shimmer of the Square.

Cran is permitted to touch it with one finger, briefly. Only that. The vase will go into the Gallery and thousands will come to view and glory in this rightful human inheritance.

The Handlers bear away the vase. Cran paces the Project room. It's well into the artificial lunar night; the lights of Alpha Dome have dimmed on the horizon. Cran can't sleep; it's been several nights since he slept. He's old, but it isn't that. Desire consumes him, the desire of a young man: not for sex, but for glory. Once, he thought he would be a great artist. Long ago reality killed the dream but not the gnawing disappointment, eating at his innards, his brain, his heart.

Tulia has a painting chosen for the Gallery.

His own work is shit, has always been shit, will always be shit.

Tulia, people are beginning to say, is the real thing. A genuine artist, the kind that comes along once in a generation.

Cran can't sit still, can't sleep, can't lift himself, yet again, from the black pit into which he falls so often. Only one thing helps, and he has long since gotten past any qualms about its legality.

He takes the pill and waits. Ten minutes later nothing matters so much, not even his inadequacy. His brain has been temporarily rewired. Nothing works optimally, either, including his hands and his brain, both of which tremble. Small price to pay. The gnawing grows less, the pit retreats.

A flash of color catches his eye. Square Two lights up. The endlessly scanning Project has found something.

2018

"*How?*" James Glenwood said. And then, "Is anything missing?"

Of the National's five Vermeers, *Girl with a Flute* and *Girl with the Red Hat* were on loan to the Frick in New York. *Woman Holding a Balance* and *Lady Writing* both hung on the walls. So did *Lady Sewing a Child's Bonnet*. Below that, propped against the wall in a room locked all night, sat its duplicate.

A fake, of course—but how the hell did it get there?

The guard looked guilty. But Henry had worked for the museum for twenty-five years. And naturally he looked upset—suspicion was bound to fall on him as the person who locked this room last night and opened it this morning. Glenwood, a curator for thirty years, remembered well the 1990 brazen theft of Vermeer's *The Concert* from the Isabella Stewart Gardner Museum in Boston. The picture had never been recovered.

Except this was not a theft. A prank? A warning of thefts to come—*Look how easily I can break into this place?*

Every other room in the National would now have to be meticulously checked, and every work of art. Security would have to be reviewed. The police must be called, and the Director. The curator pulled out his phone.

Only—

Phone in hand, he knelt in front of the painting that had so mysteriously appeared. Glenwood had studied seventeenth-century art his entire life. He had thousands and thousands of hours of experience, honed to an intuition that had often proved more correct than reason. He studied the picture propped against the wall, and then the one above it. His cell hung limply at his side, and a deep line crinkled his forehead.

Something here was not right.

2270

Cran has never seen anything like the picture whose image floats in Square Two.

The Squares seems to capture more three-dimensional objects than paintings, and only eleven have been Transferred since the Project began. Three Picassos, two medieval pictures that ignore perspective, two "abstracts" that seem to him nothing but blobs of paint, a Monet, a Renoir, a Takashi Murakami, and a faded triptych from some Italian church. None of them are like this.

The light! It falls on the figure, a woman bent over some sort of sewing. It glows on her burgundy gown, on the walls, on a pearl necklace lying on a table. Almost it outshines the soft glow of the Square itself. The woman seems sad, and so real that she makes Cran's heart ache.

He stares at the picture for a long time, his mind befuddled by the drug he's taken but his heart loud and clear. He must have this picture.

Not the Gallery. Him. For himself.

Not possible.

Unless . . .

He stumbles to his console and says, "Forgeries by Tulia Anson, complete catalogue, visual, at ten-second intervals."

The screen—not a Square, just a normal holoscreen—flashes the forgeries that Tulia has completed so far. Each awaits a Square's tracking the original somewhere in time. The catalogue is not random; curators and physicists have collaborated to estimate what periods and artworks have the greatest chance of appearing in the Squares. Cran does not, and has never tried to, understand the equations involved, those mysterious mathematical convolutions that make strange attractors out of chaos. He only knows that these are the pictures most likely to appear.

Several landscapes in various styles appear and disappear on the screen. Some portraits. More hideous abstracts. Tulia, the Project's best forger, works hard, and quickly. A bunch of still lifes, with and without fruit. And then—

"Stop catalogue!"

There it is. *Lady Sewing a Child's Bonnet*, by Johannes Reijniersz Vermeer, 1664. What a mundane name for such perfection. Cran *knows* this woman, knows her from the sad tilt of her head, the bonnet she sews for her unborn child, the broken toy at her feet, the pearl necklace she has flung off. He is sure that her unseen eyes are filled with tears. She is deeply unhappy; her life has not turned out as she hoped. Cran knows her. He is her.

How many pills did he take?

No matter. This is his painting, meant for him. And Tulia, who is 32 percent his genes, has completed a superb forgery. That, too, proves that what he is going to do was meant to be.

Yes.

He does not bother with clearances. Actually, he cannot. There must be no traces. Clean and quick. The universe, which has denied him so much, owes him this.

The Vermeer hangs on the silk-covered wall of what looks in the Square like a private house, although it's hard to be certain. Vermeer's house? A patron? It doesn't matter. Cran works quickly, calling for a 'bot to bring Tulia's painting from storage, erasing the bot's memory record, hoisting the forgery into the Square. Setting the controls. His hands fumble in their eagerness. It all must be done manually, to leave no record.

He makes the Transfer.

Tulia's forgery vanishes. Nothing appears in Square Two.

Nothing.

"No!"

Data flashes on the console below the Square. A mechanical voice says calmly, "Error. Error. Transfer malfunction."

And then, "Danger. Deactivate this Square."

"No!" Cran gasps, unable to breathe. The Square blinks on and off, as he has never seen a Square blink before. But he knows what this means; spacetime is being affected in what could be a permanent way if the Square is not deactivated immediately. Fingers trembling, he enters and speaks the commands.

The Square goes dark.

The console data still glows. Cran stares at it. He shakes his head.

TRANSFER 653
Transfer Date: Saturday, Decade 28, 2270
Transfer to Past:
    Planned Transfer: From present to March 16, 1668
    Achieved Transfer: From present to March 16, 1668
    Status: Transfer Successful
Transfer to Present:
    Planned Transfer: From March 16, 1668 to present
    Achieved Transfer: From March 16, 1668 to Unknown Time
    Status: Transfer failed
Reason for Failure: Incomplete Data Entry (Clearances 60–75)

Cran wills the data holo to change, to say something else. It does not. Because he did not complete the clearances, which were not merely the stupid bureaucracy he had assumed, the Transfer has failed. Tulia's forgery has gone to 1668, replacing the original on some silk-covered wall. The real Vermeer has not come all the way forward in time. Where is it? Cran doesn't know. All he knows is that Transfers send forgeries to where there is a similar article, which always before has meant the original being brought forward to 2270. That's how the strange attractors formed by the mathematics of chaos theory work—they *attract*. Only, due to Cran's haste—or possibly his intoxicated fumbling—Tulia's forgery has gone to some other attractor of Vermeers. Are there now two of the paintings on that silk-covered wall in 1668? Or has the original stopped somewhere else in time, snagged on a strange attractor someplace/sometime?

He doesn't know. And it doesn't matter where the original has gone—he cannot retrieve it.

Cran slumps to the floor. But after a few minutes, he staggers again to his feet. Why did he panic so? No one knows what happened. No one knows why the Square malfunctioned. All he has to do is erase the record—a task well within his skills—and report a malfunction. The Squares are a machine; machines break. No one ever has to know. All he has to say is that it spontaneously broke before he made any Transfer. That way, no one will blame him for an anomaly loose somewhere in the past.

Unless someone discovers that Tulia's forgery is missing from storage.

But why would they look? The only reason to call up a forgery is if the original appears in a Square. Only—

He can't think. He is afraid of what he has set loose in the timestream. He needs to get out of here. But he can't, not yet. At his console, he carefully composes a report of spontaneous Square malfunction while not engaged in Transfer operations.

In his mind, he can still see the glowing light of his lost Vermeer.

2018

The two paintings sat on easels at the front of the room. Guards stood outside. All cell phones had been collected and stored in a lockbox. Everyone had been scanned for cameras and voice recorders, a procedure that at least half of those present found insulting. A few said so, loudly. But no one was protesting now. They were too enraptured.

Side by side, the two paintings of *Lady Sewing a Child's Bonnet* looked identical to anyone but a trained observer. Half the people in the room were trained observers, art historians. The other half were forensic scientists.

Glenwood listened to one of the scientists' summary of his long-winded analysis. He'd barely looked at the paintings, consulting only his notes. "This painting," he said, gesturing vaguely in the direction of the Vermeer that had hung in the National since being privately donated sixteen years ago, "shows aging commensurate with having come from the mid-1600's. As I explained, carbon dating is not particularly accurate when applied to time spans as short as a few hundred years. But the frame, canvas, and pigments in the paint are aged appropriately, and nearly all of them are ones that, you have told me, Vermeer habitually used. That has been verified by both Atomic Absorption Spectrophotometry and Pyrolysis-gas chromatography-mass spectrometry."

"Almost all?" Glenwood said. "Some of the pigments are not from Vermeer's historical period?"

"No," said the expert from New York's Met, "but they could have been added later during restoration attempts. After all, the provenance of this painting is clearly documented, and it includes several dealers throughout the centuries, some of whom might have tried to clean or repair the Vermeer for resale. And, of course, it *has* a provenance, which your newcomer does not."

The New York expert had already made her position clear. She thought the "newcomer" was a clear forgery and Painting #1 the real thing. Glenwood was not so sure. He thought scientists, and even art experts, oversimplified.

Really skillful forgeries were notoriously hard to detect, and Vermeer's art had been plagued by imitators. At one point, "experts" had attributed seventy paintings to him. Today the number was thirty-four, with more in dispute even under scientific analysis. Vermeer's *Young Woman Seated at the Virginals* was considered genuine until 1947, a fake from 1947 to 2004, and then genuine again, with some disagreement. Science could only go so far.

A craquelure expert spoke next, and scornfully. "I don't know, ladies and gentlemen, why we are even here. Painting #1 is clearly the real thing. Its pattern of surface cracking is completely in keeping with an age of 354 years, and with the Dutch template of connected networks of cracking. The 'newcomer' has almost no craquelure at all. Furthermore, look how bright and new its colors are—it might have been painted last year. Its total lack of aging tags it as a forgery to anyone actually *looking* at it. Dr. Glenwood, why *are* we here?"

Everyone looked at Glenwood. He pushed down the temper rising in response to the craquelure expert's tone.

"We are here because I, and not only I, am bothered by other differences between these two paintings—differences that were not obvious when we had only Painting #1 and could not compare them side by side. Now we can. Look at the pearl necklace in the second painting. Vermeer painted pearls often, and always they have the sparkle and luster of the second painting, which the first mostly lacks. The second also contains far more tiny detail in the painting-within-a-painting on the wall behind the woman sewing. That sort of painstaking detail is another Vermeer trademark. Look at the woman's gown. Both versions feature the underpainting in natural ultramarine that Vermeer did beneath his reds to get a purplish tinge—but in Painting #2, the result is crisper. And Painting #2—I regard this as significant—was revealed by the X-ray analysis to have underlying elements that the artist painted over. Vermeer was obsessive about getting his pictures exactly right, and so very often he painted out elements and replaced them with others. Painting #1 shows no overpainting. I think Painting #2 is the original, and the picture we have hung in the National for sixteen years is the forgery."

A babble of voices:

"You can't believe that!"

"Perhaps a young artist, not yet proficient in his craft—"

"We have a clear chain of ownership going all the way back to Pieter van Ruijven—"

"The scientific evidence—"

"The lack of aging—"

In the end, Glenwood's was the only dissenting voice. He was a Vermeer expert but not a forgery expert, and not the Director of the National Gallery. The painting that had mysteriously appeared would be banished to basement storage so that no one else would be fooled into paying some exorbitant sum for it. And the one that had hung in the museum for sixteen years would continue to hang there. It had been declared the real thing.

2270

The physicists spend six days trying to fix the Square. Finally they give up, because they can't find any indicator that it is actually broken. Cran, who knows that it is not, insists over and over that the Square simply went dark. For six days, he holds his breath, not knowing what might happen. There are now two versions of the Vermeer loose in the timestream—what if that turns out to be so significant that something terrible happens to the present?

Nothing does.

Scientists and engineers wait for something—anything—to appear in Square Two. On the sixth day, something does: a crude Paleolithic figurine. Everyone goes crazy: this is the oldest piece of art the Squares have ever found. The expert on Stone Age art is summoned. The Director is summoned. The stone figurine is replaced with a lump of rock. No Transfer this early will disturb the timestream, not even if it's witnessed; the Transfer will just be attributed to gods, or magic, or witchcraft. The fertility carving is reverently taken to the Gallery. Toasts are drunk. The past is being recovered; the Square works fine; all is well. Cran's chest expands as he finally breathes normally.

As he leaves, the chief physicist gives Cran a long, hard look.

A few days later Cran goes to the Gallery to attend the presentation of Tulia's painting. It is so beautiful that his heart aches. The picture is neither abstract nor mimetic but, rather, something of both. What moves Cran so much is the way she has painted light. It is always the use of light that he cares about, and Tulia has captured starlight on human figures in a way he has never seen done before. The light, and not their facial expressions, seems to indicate the mood of each of her three human subjects, although so subtly that it does not feel forced. The emotion feels real. Everything about the painting feels real.

A woman behind him says, "Pretty, yes—but actually, it's just an exercise in an archaic and irrelevant art. Flat painting in a holo age? I mean, who cares?"

Cran wants to slug her. He does not. He congratulates Tulia, forcing words past the tightening in his throat, and leaves.

At home, he can't sleep. He is agitated, dispirited, depressed. No—he is jealous, so jealous that his skin burns and his head feels as if it might explode. He hates himself for his jealousy, but he can't help it. It drives him to pace, to almost—but not quite—cry out in the silence of his room. He can't sit still. In the middle of the night he takes the underground tram to the Project dome.

No one is here. Constant attendance isn't required; when a Square glows, it keeps on glowing until someone makes a Transfer. One of the Squares is glowing now. Inside is the image of *Lady Sewing a Child's Bonnet*.

Cran is not really surprised. Previously, the Square had found, through the obscure mathematics of chaos, a strange attractor linked to this Vermeer. Once found, there was a strong chance it would find it again. But which picture is this—the original or Tulia's forgery?

It is the original. He *knows*. The judgment isn't reasoned; it doesn't have to be. Cran knows, and he is prepared.

From a closet he takes one of his own pictures. The same size and shape as the Vermeer, it's a portrait of Tulia, painted from memory and so bad that no one else has ever seen it. The Vermeer in the Square is surrounded by a wooden crate in darkness. Someone has, for whatever reason, boxed it up and stored it. Maybe it will be missed, maybe not. It no longer matters to him. All his movements are frenzied, almost spastic. Some small part of his mind thinks *I am not sane*. That doesn't matter either.

Only once before has he felt like this, when he was very young and in love for the first and only time. He thought then, *If I don't touch her, I will die*. He doesn't think that now, but he feels it deeper than thought, in his very viscera. This must be what Vermeer felt when he painted the picture, alone in his studio, consumed from the inside.

It is the link between them.

Cran makes the Transfer. His dreadful painting disappears. Cran lifts *Lady Sewing a Child's Bonnet*—not an image, the real thing—from the Square. For a long time he just holds it, drinking it in, until the painting grows too heavy and his eyes too dimmed with tears.

His plan is to box it into the same container in which he brought in his own painting. Cran has done research in the library database. He was careful to have a printer create four of Vermeer's signature pigments—natural ultramarine, verdigris, yellow ochre, lead white—and that is what the security scanner will identify and match with the package he brought in. He will have the Vermeer in his own room, where no one ever goes, not even Tulia.

He has done it.

The door opens and the Director comes in.

"Cran! You couldn't sleep either? Such a wonderful presentation of Tulia's *Life in Starlight*. It made me want to come over and see what else the Project might have—Good Lord, is that a Vermeer?"

The Director, whose specialty is Tang Dynasty pottery but of course has a broad knowledge of art history, squints at the painting. All the frenzy has left Cran. He is cold as the lunar surface.

The data screen behind him says:

TRANSFER 655
Transfer Date Tuesday, Decade 29, 2270
Transfer to Past:
    Planned Transfer: From present to March 31, 2018
    Achieved Transfer: From present to March 31, 2018
    Status: Transfer Successful
Transfer to Present:
    Planned Transfer: From March 31, 2018 to present
    Achieved Transfer: From March 31, 2018 to present
    Status: Transfer successfully completed

"Yes," he says, "a Vermeer. It just came through, from the twentieth century. I sent back a forgery. But I think this one is a forgery, too. Look—does it appear aged enough to you?"

A commission is assembled. They examine the painting, but not for very long. *Lady Sewing a Child's Bonnet* was painted, the database says, in 1664. If it had come naturally through time to 2018, it would be 354 years old. Scientific examination shows it to be less than ten years old.

Yes, Cran thinks. Four years from 1664 to 1668, plus a few weeks spent in 2018. Yes.

On the scientific evidence, the painting is declared a forgery. A skillful copy, but a copy nonetheless. It isn't the first time the Project scanners have targeted a forgery. Previously, however, that had only happened with sculptures, particularly Greek and Roman.

"We already tried once for the original," says the Director, "and got this. It would be too dangerous to the timestream to try again, I think, even if the original turns up in a Square. Given the math, that might happen."

The head physicist stares hard at Cran. Cran has already been removed from the Project for failing to file clearances, which he has explained with "the memory lapses of age—I'm getting them more frequently now." He will never be allowed near a Square again.

A handler says, "What shall I do with this forgery?"

The Director is bleak with disappointment. "It's useless to us now."

Cran says humbly, "May I have it?"

"Oh, why not. Take it, if you like fakery."

"Thank you," Cran says.

He hangs the Vermeer on the wall of his room. The sad lady sewing a bonnet, disappointed in her life—the broken toy, flung-aside pearls, drooping head, of course she is disappointed—glows in unearthly beauty. Cran spends an entire hour just gazing at the painting. When there is a knock on his door, he doesn't jump. The picture is legitimately his.

It is Tulia. "Cran, I heard that—"

She stops cold.

Cran turns slowly.

Tulia is staring at the picture, and she knows. Cran understands that. He understands—too late—that she is the one person who would know. Why didn't he think of this? He says, "Tulia . . ."

"That's not a forgery."

"Yes, it is. A skillful one, but . . . they did forensic tests, it's not even ten years old, not aged enough to—"

"I don't care. That's not a copy, not even one by a forger better than I am. That's the original Vermeer."

"No," Cran says desperately. But Tulia has stepped closer to the painting and is examining every detail. Seeing things he cannot, could never learn to see. She knows.

He debases himself to plead. "Tulia, you're an artist. The real thing. For centuries to come, people will be collecting and cherishing your work. I am nothing. Please—leave me this. Please."

She doesn't even look at him. Her eyes never leave the painting.

"I'm an old man. You can tell them the truth after I'm dead. But please, for now . . . let me have this. Please."

After an aeon, she nods, just once, still not looking at him. She leaves the room. Cran knows she will never speak to him again. But she won't tell.

He turns back to the Vermeer, drinking in the artistry, the emotion, the humanity.

1672

Johannes walked through the Square beside the Hague, toward the water. In a few minutes, he would go inside—they could wait for him a few minutes longer. He studied the reflection of the stone castle, over four hundred years old, in the still waters of the Hofvijer. The soft light of a May morning gives the reflected Hague a shimmer that the actual government building did not have.

He came here to judge twelve paintings. They originally belonged to a great collector, Gerrit Reynst, who'd died fourteen years ago by drowning in the canal in front of his own house. Johannes couldn't imagine how that had happened, but since then, the collection had known nothing but chaos. Parts of it had been sold, parts gifted to the king of England, parts bequeathed to various relatives. A noted art dealer offered twelve of the paintings to Friedrich Wilhelm, Grand Elector of Brandenburg, who at first accepted them. Then the Grand Elector's art advisor said the pictures were forgeries and should be sent back. The art dealer refused to accept them. Now they hung in the Hague while thirty-five painters—thirty-five!—gave learned opinions on the pictures' authenticity. One will be Vermeer.

He was curious to see the paintings. They were all attributed to great masters, including Michelangelo, Titian, Tintoretto, Holbein. Vermeer, who had never left the Netherlands, would not have another chance to see such works.

If they were genuine.

Opinions so far had been divided. It was sometimes difficult to distinguish copies from originals. Consider, for instance, his own *Lady Sewing a Child's Bonnet* . . .

He hadn't thought about that picture in years. Always, his intensity centered on what he was painting now. That, and on his growing, impossible debts. He was being paid for this opinion, or he could not have afforded the trip to give it.

A skillful forger could fool almost everyone. Johannes, who seldom left Delft and so had seen few Italian paintings, was not even sure that he would be able to tell the difference between a forged Titian and an original, unless the copy was very bad. And a good forgery often gave its owners the same pleasure as an original. Still, he would try. Deceivers should not be able to replace the real thing with imitations. Truth mattered.

But first he lingered by the Hofvijer, studying the shifting light on the water.

Matthew Kressel is a multiple Nebula Award and World Fantasy Award final-ist. His first novel, *King of Shards*, was hailed as, "Majestic, resonant, reali-ty-twisting madness," from NPR Books. His short fiction has appeared or will soon appear in *Clarkesworld, Lightspeed, Tor.com, Nightmare, Apex Magazine, Beneath Ceaseless Skies, Interzone, Electric Velocipede*, and the anthologies *Mad Hatters and March Hares, Cyber World, Naked City, After, The People of the Book,* as well as many other places. His work has been translated into Czech, Polish, French, Russian, Chinese, and Romanian. From 2003 to 2010 he ran Senses Five Press, which published *Sybil's Garage*, an acclaimed speculative fiction magazine, and *Paper Cities*, which went on to win the World Fantasy Award in 2009. His is currently the co-host of the Fantastic Fiction at KGB reading series in Manhattan alongside Ellen Datlow, and he is a long-time member of the Altered Fluid writers group. By trade, he is a full-stack software developer, and he developed the Moksha submission system, which is in use by many of the largest SF markets today. You can find him at online at www.mat-thewkressel.net, where he blogs about writing, technology, environmentalism, and more. Or you can find him on Twitter @mattkressel.

THE LAST NOVELIST
(OR A DEAD LIZARD IN THE YARD)

Matthew Kressel

When I lift up my shoe in the morning there's a dead baby lizard underneath. It lies on its back, undersides pink and translucent, organs visible. Maybe when I walked home under the strangely scattered stars I stepped on it. Maybe it crawled under my shoe to seek its last breath while I slept. Here is one leaf of a million-branched genetic tree never to unfurl. Here is one small animal on a planet teeming with life.

The wind blows, carrying scents of salt and seaweed. High above, a bird soars in the eastern wind. I scoop up the lizard and bury it under the base of a coconut tree. Soon, I'll be joining him. I can't say I'm not scared.

"All tender-belly spacefarers are poets," goes the proverb, and I'm made uncomfortably aware of its truth every time I cross the stars. I ventured out to Ardabaab by thoughtship, an express from Sol Centraal, and for fifty torturous minutes—or a million swift years; neither is wrong—gargantuan thoughtscapes of long-dead galaxies wracked my mind, while wave after wave of nauseating, hallucinogenic bardos drowned my sense of person-hood, of encompassing a unitary being in space and time. Even the pilots, well-traveled mentshen them all, said the journey was one of their roughest. And while I don't hold much faith in deities, I leaped down and kissed the pungent brown earth when we incorporated, and praised every sacred name I knew, because (a) I might have met these ineffable beings as we crossed the stellar gulfs, and (b) I knew I'd never travel by thoughtship again; I'd come to Ardabaab to die.

I took an aircar to the house, and as we swooped low over bowing fields of sugarcane, her disembodied voice said to me, "With your neural shut off you have a small but increased risk of injury. Ardabaab is safe—we haven't had a violent incident in eighty-four years—but the local We recommends guests leave all bands open, for their safety." She sounded vaguely like my long-dead wife, and this was intentional. Local Wees are tricky little bastards.

"Thanks," I said to her. "But I prefer to be alone."

"Well," she said with a trace of disgust, "it's my duty to let you know."

The car dropped me off at the house, a squat blue bungalow near the beach set among wind-whipped fields of sugarcane and towering coconut palms. Forty minutes later I was splayed on the empty beach while Ardabaab's red-dwarf sun—rock-candy pink at this late hour—dipped low over the tur-quoise sea, the most tranquil I had ever seen. For a station-born like me, it was utterly glorious.

The wind blew and distant lights twinkled over the waters. I smiled. I had arrived. With pen and paper in hand, I furiously scribbled:

Chapter 23. Arrival.

When Yvalu stepped off the thoughtliner, she bent down and kissed the ground. Her hands came up with a scoop of Muandiva's fertile soil, which she immedi-ately swallowed, a pinch of this moment's joy that she would carry in her body forever. Thank Shaddai. She was here.

A lizard skirted by. Strange people smiled and winked at her. She beamed and jumped and laughed. Ubalo had walked this world, perhaps had even stepped on the same dark earth still sweet on her tongue. Ubalo, who had brought her to Silversun, where they had watched the triple stars, each of a different shade, rise above the staggered mesas of Jacob's Ladder and cast blossoming colorscapes of ever-shifting rainbows across the desert. Ubalo, who had traveled to the other side of the galaxy to seek a rare mineral Yvalu had once offhandedly remarked she liked during an otherwise forgettable afternoon. Ubalo, whose eyes shone like Sol and whose smile beamed like Sirius. For him she would have suffered a trillion mental hells if only to hold his hand one more time.

I wrote, and wrote more, until I ran out of pad. And when I looked up, the sun had set, and new constellations winked distant colors at me. Ardabaab has no moon. I had been writing by their feeble light for hours.

Early the next morning, after I bury the lizard, I head for Halcyon's beachside cafe with a thermos of keemun tea and four extra writing pads tucked deep into my bag. While hovering waiterplates use my thermos to refill cup after cup, I churn out twenty more pages. But when a group of exuberant tourists from Sayj sit nearby, growing rowdy as they get intox, I slip down to the beach.

I return to last night's spot, a private cove secluded from all but the sea, and here I work under the baking sun as locals, identified by their polydactyl hands and violet eyes, offer me braino and neur-grafts and celebrilives, each on varying spectra of legality.

"I got Buddhalight," a passerby says, interrupting my stream. "Back from zer early days, before ze ran out of exchange."

I grit my teeth in frustration. I was really flowing. "Thanks, but I prefer my own thoughts."

"Alle-roit," she says, swishing off. "You kayn know 'less you ask."

I turn back to my pad and write:

But no matter who Yvalu asked, none had heard of a mentsh named Ubalo. And when she shared his message with the local We, the mind told her, somewhat coldly, "This transmission almost certainly came from Muandiva. But I have not encountered any of his likeness among my four trillion nodes. It's plain, Yvalu, that the one who you seek is simply not here."

"Then where is he?" she said, verging on tears. "Where is he?"

And the local We responded with words she had never heard one speak before: "I am sorry, Yvalu, but I have no idea."

I finish a chapter, and a second, and before I begin a third, a shadow falls across my pad and a sharp voice interrupts me. "What you doing?"

"Not interested," I say.

"Not selling."

I look up. A child stands before me, eclipsing the sun. Small in stature, her silhouette makes her seem planetary. She has short-cut dark hair and six elongated fingers. And though the sun blinds, the violet glare of her eyes catches me off guard and I gasp. I raise a hand to shade my face, and sans glare, her eyes shine with the penetrating violet of a rainbow just before it fades into sky. I'm so taken by them I've forgotten what she's asked. "Sorry?"

"What you drawing?"

"This isn't drawing."

"Then what is it?"

"This?" It takes me a second. "I'm writing."

"*Writing*." She chews on the word and steps closer. "That's a *pen*," she says, "and that's *paper*. And you're using *cursive*. Freylik!" She laughs.

It's obvious she's just wikied these words, but her delight is contagious, and I smile with her. It's been a long time since I've met someone who didn't know what pen and paper were. Plus there's something in her voice, her cascade of laughs, that reminds me of my long-dead daughter.

"What you writing?" she says.

"A novel."

"A *novel*." A wiki-length pause. Another smile. "Prektik! But . . ." Her nostrils flare. "Why don't you project into your neural?"

"Because my neural's off."

"Off?" The notion seems repulsive to her.

"I prefer the quiet," I say.

"SO DO I!" she shouts as she plops down beside me, stirring up sand. "Name," she says, "Reuth Bryan Diaso, citizen of Ganesha City, Mars. Born on Google Base Natarajan, Earth orbit, one gravity Earth-natural. Age: ninety-one by Sol, two hundred ninety-three by Shoen. Hi!"

For a moment I pretend this girl from Ardabaab has heard of me, Reuth Bryan Diaso, author of fourteen novels and eighty-seven short stories. But it's obvious she's gleaned all this from public record. I imagine wistfully what it must have been like in the ancient days, when authors were renowned across the Solar System, welcomed as if we were dignitaries from alien worlds. Now mentshen revere only the grafters and sense-folk for sharing endless arrays of vapid experiences with their billion eager followers. No, I don't need to feel Duchesse Ardbeg's awful dilemma of not knowing in which Martian city to take her afternoon toilet, thank you very much.

"My name's Fish!" the girl says exuberantly, snapping me from my self-in-dulgent dream.

"Fish." I test out her name. "I like it. Nice to meet you, Fish." I hold out my hand, not sure if it's the local custom.

She ignores me and turns to the sea. "Here they come," she says.

In the sky above the waters an enormous blowfish plunges down from space, a massive planet-killing meteor, trailing vapor and smoldering with reentry fire. A crack opens in its face, a gargantuan mouth opening as it falls, as if it were a beast coming to devour us all. I grab Fish's arm, readying to run, when I remember: this is no monster. This is a seed.

The blowfish slows as it swoops down, and the air thunders with its decel-eration. For an instant it skims the surface, then eases its great mouth into the waters, scooping up megaliters, stirring up goliath waves. Now, belly full, it screams as it arcs back to the sky, mouth sliding closed, while cloud and spray and marine life flicker-flash in long tails behind it as everything that missed the cut tumbles back into the sea.

The blowfish wails as it speeds away, shrinking rapidly, off to the hell-bar-dos of thoughtspace and the Outer New, off to seed life on some distant planet's virgin seas. The ship recedes until it's too small to see, and when I awake from my stupor, Fish is gone. My hand holds not her arm, but a crum-pled towel. Beside me, a dozen small footprints lead into the sea.

A creature has dug up my grave. A rat, a bird, a monkey, it's hard to say. But, whoever it was, they left the lizard behind. Small red ants have gone to work dissecting it, and in the hot morning sun, its skin has turned to leather. I contemplate burying it again, but these local animals seem to have a better idea of what to do with it, so I leave it be.

Fish surprises me on the beach that afternoon. "I don't get it," she says.

I look up from my pad, unexpectedly happy to see her. "What don't you get?"

"Why write novels at all? You could project your dreams into a neural."

"I could. But dreams are raw and unfiltered. And that always felt like cheating to me. With writing, you have to labor over your thoughts."

My words seem only to perplex her more. "But you could *dictate* your story. Why make it so hard?"

"You mean, why use a pen?"

She sits beside me, her violet eyes boring into mine. "Exactly."

"Here," I say, handing her a spare. I pull out an empty pad from my pack. "Try it, and tell me what you feel."

She holds the pen like it's a sharp knife; a long time ago, all pens were knives. "I don't know what to do," she says.

"Just press the tip to the page, and swirl it around."

She gives it a try. Her eyes go wide. "Ooooooh, this is fun!"

"You've never scribbled?"

"Not with a pen."

I let the sounds of her drawing and the gentle breaking waves mesmerize me into a memory: my daughter sitting in our kitchen one sunny morning, scribbling on paper; my wife, sanding down her wooden figures in the next room; me, listening to them work, feeling full, feeling complete. Eventually, I wander back to my pad and write:

Once, when they had lain beside each other on Oopre's sparkling beaches to watch a parade of comets cross the sky, Ubalo had said something that had stuck with her across the ever-broadening gulfs.

"Can you imagine," he'd said, "what the first person to come upon a grave must have felt? When he saw the disturbed earth and smelled the fresh loam? When his human curiosity led him to the inevitable discovery of a body intentionally laid to rest? Did he understand what he'd just found? Was this the first time a human knew the sadness of the whole race, that despite all our lofty, endless aspirations, we are finite, we have an end?"

I reread what I've written and hate it. It's too cerebral. It doesn't drive the story. I tear off the page, crumple it, and toss it into the sea. Beside me, Fish has drawn the likeness of the blowfish gulpership on her pad.

"Wow, Fish!" I say. "That's amazing!" I'm not just flattering her. She's fantastic. Her detail is astounding.

"Nah," she says, tearing off the page. She throws it into the sea.

"Hey! Why'd you do that?"

"I don't know. Why you throw *yours* away?"

"Because . . . it wasn't perfect."

She squints at me, her violet eyes shining like lasers. Then she stands, drops the pad onto the sand, and hands me the pen. "I gots to go." And before I can stop her, she saunters off down the beach.

An ankle-high wave washes her crumpled paper toward me, and I wade into the water to fetch it. The ink has bled, but the core remains.

Back at my bungalow, I spread Fish's drawing on my kitchen table to dry. To my surprise, the running ink actually enhances the image, makes it seem as if the blowfish is leaping off the page into space.

Later, because I'm a masochist, I check my health. Five weeks, if I'm lucky. I'd better get cracking. Instead, I get drinking.

I was well into my cups last night before bed, so when someone knocks on my door just after sunrise, it takes me a while to rouse. When I finally open the door, Fish darts in and immediately gets a blood orange from the maker, plops on the couch, and says, "You made all them books by hand?"

"Still do," I say, fetching keemun from the maker. I'm not yet caffeinated enough for conversation.

"But that's so much work."

"It's also a ton of fun. I love the physicality of it, the smell of the pages, the feeling I get when I hold a book I've made in my hands."

"But you set every letter and print each page *by hand*?"

"I do."

"And everything else too?"

I take a large sip of tea. "Not everything. I have a maker build the printing press and the movable type. But, yeah, I've typeset, pressed, and bound every single copy of my books."

"But . . ." She seems as if she might explode. "I still don't understand *how*!"

If there is one thing that has defined writers throughout history, it's our endless capacity for procrastination. I need to finish my book soon—in a matter of weeks—but the thought of Fish becoming my apprentice excites me more than anything has in decades.

"Fish," I say, "if you'll let me, I'd love to show you."

Across her face, as broad as a gulperfish, a smile.

Fish is a sponge, and that's not meant as a joke. If I show her something once, she remembers it forever. And she's not using her neural. When she's with me, she shuts it off. She says she wants to know what it feels like to be a writer.

In the past I've waited until I've finished my book before typesetting it, but besides the obvious issue of time, this project delights me too much. We remove the beds from the bungalow's spare room and I have the maker set up the large printing press there. Its wood and iron frame smells delightfully ancient. The wall underneath the room's tall windows becomes our workspace. And though Fish had never seen cursive handwriting before mine, it takes her less than a day to memorize the patterns, even accounting for my awful penmanship, and before Ardabaab's pink sun has set she's transcribed twenty pages of my scribbled words into her own neat hand using a fountain pen she's had the maker craft for her.

"Yvalu and Ubalo are stellar in love with each other," she says.

"Yes, they are."

"Have you been in love, Reuth?"

"A few times."

"What's it like?"

I pause to consider. There are a thousand answers and none of them true. "What's your favorite thing in all the universe?"

She answers instantly: "Watching from my undersea bedroom the way the fish change colors as the sun rises."

I have a vision of Fish beside her window, eyes glowing in the morning light, watching Ardabaab's abundant sea life swim by. It makes me smile. "Being in love is like seeing that beauty every moment in the one who you love. But it also hurts like hell, because love always fades, and life after love is gray and lifeless."

"Oh," Fish says, hanging her head. "Oh."

"I'm sorry," I say, shaking my head. I feel like a schmuck. "I shouldn't have said that."

"No," she says, raising her head. "I's not afraid of truth. I want to know everything."

And I want to tell her. I want to tell her how it's not the big things you miss, but the small ones, like the peck on your cheek your daughter gives you before bed, or how your wife left pieces of stale bread on the windowsill so she could watch the sparrows come and eat them. I want to tell her how much their deaths still hurt, even now, all these decades later, how I still dream of my wife sleeping next to me and how I always wake up gasping. Instead I say, "You've got time enough for that," and walk over to inspect her work.

On her pad, beside my transcribed words, she's drawn a woman with wavy dark hair, large curious eyes, a glittering gem in her nose, the same gem Ubalo had crossed light-years to fetch.

"That's Yvalu?"

"You recognize her?" she says.

"This is fantastic, Fish."

"You think?"

"Fish, I have another idea. Do you want to illustrate my book?"

"*Hill-a-straight*?" Wiki-less, she seems confused.

"I want you to draw pictures of some scenes. We could have the maker convert them to lithographs and we can print them alongside the text."

"But I'm not any good."

"No, you're not good. You're amazing. With your permission, I'd like to use this picture of Yvalu on the cover so it's the first thing people see."

She stares at me, her violet eyes boring into mine. Then she breaks eye contact. "But," she says, almost a whisper. "Who will see it?"

I feel a pang of dread. Another fact she's gleaned from my wiki is that my readership has steadily declined over the years, so that the last person to request one of my printed books was an Earth antiquities dealer on Bora, who carefully sealed my book in plastic and placed it in storage, where it would serve as an example to future generations of what paper books had been like. As far as I could tell, the dealer had no intention of ever reading it. That was twelve Solar years ago.

Fish turns back to me. "Reuth, I'd love to *hill-a-straight* your book."

And at this we both laugh.

We get to work. Each day, Fish comes by just after sunrise and we use the mornings to set type. It's a laborious, slow process, but I love every aspect of it. I show her the right way to hold the composing stick, why she should let the slug rattle a bit, and how to use leads to add spacing between each line of type. I show her how to swipe her thumb to keep the type in place as she adds each letter, and I explain why it's imperative to have snug lines and why it's wise to start and end each line with em quads.

We press a few test signatures, adjusting here, correcting there, as our hands and faces become stained with ink. In the afternoons, after a break and a light lunch, Fish retreats to the corner to ponder my novel and draw new scenes, while I churn out more pages on my pad. Fish loves everything about the process and laughs easily, even when we make mistakes. And her joy is contagious. I haven't been this happy in a long time, and for no reason at all I find myself smiling too.

Fish draws: the cascading light of Jacob's ladder spilling across the desert; a close-up of Ubalo's eyes, fearless and sad, creased by time; a thoughtliner tearing through a hell-bardo, trailing the disturbed dreams of its passengers; a parade of glowing comets crossing the starry sky; Yvalu's desperate hand, reaching for a falling leaf. More than once, I catch Fish writing words of her own, but before I can look she always tucks her pad away.

Meanwhile, my words flow better than they have in decades. I write:

And after days of thought and deliberation, Yvalu knew there was only one rea-son why Ubalo had called her across the gulfs, why he himself could not be here to welcome her. There was only one reason why he had erased all evidence of himself

*from the planet's records. He had called her out here not to bring her toward him,
but to move her away from something else.*

He had sent her here to protect her.

I reread my words and a warm feeling fills my heart. There are moments as
I'm writing when I think this might be my best work yet, my magnum opus.
By now I should be suspicious of such thoughts, but the feeling is hard to
shake. If only I can finish it in time.

The afternoon is hot as Fish and I work from opposite ends of the room, deep
in creative flow when the voice startles us. "Dolandra! Oh, thank Mitra!"

A woman stands outside the window, and even from across the room, the
glare of her violet eyes shines brighter than the sun. She has the same shape
of face, the same nose as Fish. "I been looking for you all day!"

"Moms!" Fish says, dropping her pad. She leaps to her feet.

I walk to the front door to let the woman in, but she gives me a look as
if I'm a demon come to eat her soul and stays put. "DOLANDRA!" she
shouts.

Fish sprints around my legs, outside and onto the grass. Her shirt and
hands are stained black as she stands beside her mother, head hung low, and
I can't help but feel guilty even though I know I've done nothing wrong.

"Why you shut your neural?" her mom says, eyeing me. "What the bones
and dreck, girl?"

"I's . . ." Fish says. "I's drawing, Moms."

The woman stares lasers at me. "I got your number," she says. "You stay
the fuck away from my daughter, or I show you *real* Ardabaabian justice."
She grabs Fish by the shirt and yanks her away, down the path toward the
sea. Before they turn around a bend of sugarcane, Fish looks back.

I wave goodbye, because I have a feeling I'll never see her again.

The bungalow is quiet without Fish's exuberance. I try to write on the porch,
but find myself scribbling random shapes on the page, which pale in comparison to her art. I try the beach, seeking the inspiration I found on my
first days here, hoping Fish might return to plop beside me. But I meet only
wind and floating gulls and the occasional ship drifting slowly across the sky.
To jar my inspiration I buy a neur-graft of Gardni Johnner and experience
her famous BASE jump on Enceledus, the one where she tore her suit on a
rock and nearly died. But this just leaves me shaken and craving solid earth.
At night I drink and stare at Fish's drawings, following each delicate line,

wishing she were here. And still my words do not flow. I'm as dry as a lizard carcass in the sun.

The baby lizard still sits in the yard, just leather now. Even the ants have departed for tastier shores. The rain and wind have tossed it about, but the carcass lingers always near, as if it's trying to tell me something.

"I know," I tell it. "I know."

It's been six days since Fish has left, and I've written a sum total of negative three thousand words (I have scrapped two chapters) when I activate my neural for the first time since I arrived. I request a skinsuit from the local We, and after it instructs me on the standard safety precautions—using my dead wife's voice again, the bastard—I walk down to the beach.

I've found the address of one Dolandra Thyme Heurex in the local wiki, and my neural guides me to her home. While the hot sun slowly rises over the placid waters, I wade into the turquoise sea. I've swum in a skinsuit before, but my heart still pounds as I fully submerge. Fins grow from my feet and hands, and black-and-yellow striping appears on my body to mimic a local species.

And there are many. Their sheer number and palettes of bright colors make me gasp. It's as if some ancient god let her creative spirit loose on the canvas of the sea. Crimson and gold fans of coral wave like bashful geishas of old. Barracudas peer curiously at me before swimming off. Schools of fish flash in the sun as they dart from my grasp. In the distance, a pair of bottle-nose dolphins inspect a sponge on the sea floor.

Fish's house is set among a group of blue-gray domes in twenty meters of water. I swim up to the door and try the chime.

"Who's there?" I recognize the voice of Fish's mom.

"Havair Heurex? It's Reuth Bryan Diaso. I'd like to speak with you about your daughter."

"I warned you!" she says.

"Look," I say. "I did nothing wrong and won't apologize. Your daughter is a supremely talented artist. She was illustrating my book. I'm an author—"

"A what?"

"An author."

A wiki-length pause. "Go on."

"The truth is, Havair Heurex, your daughter and I have become friends. I respect your decision to keep her from me—you don't know me at all—but I wanted you to know what a talented artist she is, and I hope that you'll encourage her to pursue it in the future, that you won't keep her from her art."

The channel is still open, but I hear only silence.

"Anyway, that's all I wanted to say. Good-bye, Havair Heurex."

A beep. The connection closes. I'm just about to swim off when the side of the dome shivers and a panel slides open. A door, for me.

I swim in, the panel closes, the water drains, and the pressure equalizes. My skinsuit, sensing air, melts away. The inner door opens into a spacious and tidy living room. The outside of the dome was opaque, but from within the walls are transparent. The sea and its colorful fish surround us. Fish's mom stands in a wavering sunbeam, violet eyes flickering. "Why you write novels if no one reads them?"

Pads and scraps of paper are spread across the living room, each covered with a different drawing. Fountain pens lie everywhere. "The same reason," I say, "that Fish continues to draw. I can't stop."

"Her name is Dolandra."

"She told me her name was Fish."

"We moved under the sea because of her. Every day she gets up before dawn to watch the fish in the sunrise."

"It's her favorite thing."

"I know." Havair Heurex flares her nose at me, an expression that reminds me of her daughter. She turns to her kitchenette. "Would you like some tea?"

"I'd love some, thank you."

She pours me a cup and it's better than anything I've had in a long time. "No one shuts off their neural round here," she says. "When I found you with my daughter that day, I got nervous."

"I don't blame you. You were only being a mother."

"I looked you up. Not your public wiki. I . . . I used some favors. I got the local We to glean some of your private data."

I hold back my anger. Yet one more reason to hate the local Wees. "Oh?"

"You're dying?"

I nod. "Decades ago I drank Europan sea water. It's loaded with—"

"Microorganisms." Eyes wide, she retreats from me a step.

I hold up my hand. "Don't worry, I'm not contagious. But those microorganisms are loaded with genetic material similar to—but different enough from—our own that over fifty Solar years they've altered my biochemistry to the point that one day soon I simply won't wake up. If they'd discovered this forty years ago, they might have fixed me. But the genetic damage is too far gone now. I guess it's my punishment for one stupid night of hallucinogenic bliss."

Havair Heurex sighs deeply. "So you've come to Ardabaab to die?"

A school of rainbow parrotfish swims past the window. "It just seemed like the right place. Also, I came here to finish my last novel. Fish . . . she's been a muse of sorts. She reminds me a bit of my daughter. Is she here?"

"She's with her uncle on the other side of the planet."

"Well," I say, standing. "Thank you for your hospitality, Havair Heurex, but I should be going if I'm to finish my book before . . ."

"Yes," she says. "Good luck and all."

"Thank you," I say, heading for the door. But I pause. "Does Fish know?"

"That you're dying?"

"Yes."

"I haven't told her."

"Then if it's all the same, please keep it that way." I look around the room at her many drawings. "She seems to be doing just fine without me."

"So you're the last one?" she says, and I know what she means.

"Goodbye, Havair Heurex."

I swim away from her underwater home, and when I arrive back at the bungalow that afternoon, I surprise a green monkey while it's inspecting the dead lizard. The monkey leaps away, leaving the carcass behind.

I press every page of my book, inserting lithographs of Fish's drawings throughout the text. But my novel is incomplete. I have the final chapters yet to write. And as each day comes to a close and I look at my hastily scrawled words that make no sense I worry that I won't finish this before I die.

"Moms says I can see you again, long as I keep my neural on."

Fish stands above my bed, the morning light slicing my bedroom in half.

I sit up. "Fish! Hello!"

"I's at my uncle's," she says. "But I's back now. Get up you loafing fool, 'cause we gots work to do!"

I laugh, and it's as if a switch has been flipped and an engine turned on. My words flow as easily as water again. I will finish this after all.

Fish comes by every day now. In the mornings, she studies the art of book-binding. In the afternoons, she creates new illustrations. She says we have too many, but I tell her there's always room for more art.

She draws: Yvalu's transport ship landing in heavy rain; a flock of migrating sea birds on Muandiva silhouetted in the bright sun; a pine forest reflected in the glassy lake of Naa; Yvalu and Ubalo, da Vinci-like, reaching for each other's hand, galaxies swirling behind them; Yvalu tasting the dirt of Muandiva. And sometimes, she inks words, which she will never let me read.

I write:

"Yes, I's seen him," the street vendor said to Yvalu as she showed the woman a holo of Ubalo's likeness. "On Suntiks, he sat over there in the shade, throwing back lagers, listening to them steel drum bands."

"You sure?" Yvalu said, her hopes rising. "You certain?"

"Absolute," the woman said. "Certain as Shaddai makes the sun rise and the stars turn." She made the namaste gesture and bowed. "This mentsh, he were here, same as you stand now."

I pause to laugh.

"What is it?" Fish says, eyes flashing as she looks up from her pad.

"I've figured it out!" I say. "I know how my book will end."

"Don't tell me!" Fish says. "I want it to be a surprise."

"Okay," I say, smiling. "Okay."

Later, when the sun dips low, Fish goes home, and I head out to the porch to relax in the cooling afternoon. The early stars emerge, their constellations familiar to me now. The sugarcane bends in the breeze. The crickets chirp in the grass. High above, a ship, bright as a star, moves across the sky and vanishes. I take a deep breath. I'm so tired. So damn tired. But all is good, all is good.

I search the yard, but the lizard is gone.

"Reuth Bryan Diaso, citizen of Ganesha City, Mars. Born on Google Base Natarajan, Earth orbit, one gravity Earth-natural. Died on Ardabaab, Eish orbit. Age: ninety-one by Sol, two hundred ninety-three by Shoen."

So says Reuth's wiki now. In the morning, I's coming to see him, but he wasn't in bed. *Why don't he answer my call?* I thought. *Where's he at?*

I found him under a coconut tree, flat on the grass. He get real intox and pass out? The ants were on him something bad.

Moms and I buried him in the sea. We thought he'd like that, being with all them colorful fish. His wife and kid died a long time ago, I learned. And that crazy fool left everything to me!

Mornings are stellar quiet without the sounds of his pen on paper and the clink of setting type. There ain't no more words to press. Moms don't like it, but I sit out back in his bungalow, drinking tea, watching the gulls cross the sky, just like him.

A baby lizard skitters 'cross the deck and pauses to gaze at me. I pick up my pen and write:

"Don't you worry, Ubalo!" Yvalu shouts to the stars. "I's confused before, but not no more. I know where you at, and I's coming to get you!" Yvalu walks freylik down to the sea, cause that's where the most beautiful fish swim, specially in mornings, when the sun comes up and turns them bright rainbows. "I know you hiding under there, waiting for me, Ubalo, so you best be shiny. I got such a kiss waiting for you, it'll make stars shine, it'll make universes."

Vandana Singh was born and raised in India and currently inhabits the Boston area, where she is a physics professor at a small and lively state university. Several of her science fiction short stories have been reprinted in Year's Best volumes, and shortlisted for awards. For the wider context in which "Shikasta" was written, see the original anthology at csi.asu.edu/books/vvev/. For her essay on the multiple inspirations and challenges of writing this story, see her blog at vandanasingh.wordpress.com. Her second short story collection, *Ambiguity Machines and Other Stories,* is out February 2018 from Small Beer Press.

SHIKASTA

Vandana Singh

Chirag:

This is the first time I am speaking to you, aloud, since you died.

I've learned by now that joy is of two kinds—the easy, mindless sort, and the kind that is earned hard, squeezed from suffering like blood from a stone. All my life I wanted my mother to see her son rise beyond the desert of deprivations that was our life—she wanted me to be a powerful man, respected by society—but so much of what she saw were my struggles, my desperation. So when the impossible happened, when our brave little craft was launched—the first crowdfunded spacecraft to seek another world—the unexpected shock of joy took her from illness to death in a matter of months. She died smiling—you remember her slight smile. You were always asking her why she didn't let herself smile more broadly, laugh out loud. "Auntie," you'd say, "smile!" That made her laugh, reluctantly. You were always pushing at limits, including those we impose on ourselves.

For months after you were killed, I would wake up in the morning, wondering how I was going to live. But we kept going—your absence, a you-shaped space, was almost as tangible as your presence had been. And now, nearly 12 years later, we celebrate in your name the arrival of our spacecraft on another world. A homemade, makeshift craft, constructed on the cheap with recycled materials by a bunch of scientists and scholars from the lowest rungs of a world in turmoil, headed to a planet that of all the nearby habitable worlds had the least chance of finding life.

It was soon after the time of launch, over a decade ago, that our moment of fame got eclipsed. The world's mega space agencies' combined efforts found life on Europa. Suddenly ice algae were the thing. Six years ago the discovery of complex life on the water world of Gliese 1214b had the international press in a frenzy. Those of us who had dreamed up our space mission, and made of the dream a reality, were forgotten, and almost forgot ourselves. The wars and the global refugee crises took their toll. Now the first signals from our planet have catapulted us once more into public view, although some of the news reporting is critical. Why spend so much time and effort on a planet like Shikasta 464b, when the water worlds appear to be teeming with life? Yes, Shikasta 464b is a lot closer, about four light-years away, but it is a hell of fire and ice. A poor candidate for life—but we are dreamers. We want to think beyond boundaries, to find life as we *don't* know it.

You helped me see that I could be more than I'd imagined. You took my bitter memories of classmates laughing at my poor English, my ignorance, my secondhand clothes, and gave me, instead, Premchand and Ambedkar, Khusrau and Kalidasa. You taught me that a scientist could also be a poet.

So we are making this recording, for you and for posterity.

Sometimes, I practice a game I used to play when I was younger. I pretend to be an alien newly arrived on Earth, and I look at Delhi with new eyes. The dust-laden acacia trees outside the windows, the arid scrubland falling away, the ancient boulders of the Aravalli Hills upon which the squat brick buildings of the university perch like sleeping animals. In the room is the rattle of the air conditioner, the banks of computer monitors. That slender, dark woman in the immersphere—she is here, and she is not here. She is in this room, the modest control room for the mission, and she is four light-years away with her proxy self, the robot you and I named Avinash, or Avi for short. She *is* Avi. Despite the light delay time, she is there now, on that hellish world. The immer's opacity clears, and I can see her face. For just a moment her eyes are alien, unfocused, as though she does not see me. What does she see? If I speak to her she will become the Kranti I know, but before that she is, for just that moment, a stranger.

Kranti:

I will describe the planet to you, because you will never see it through Avi's eyes. It is a violent place. Imagine: a world so close to its sun that they face each other like dancing partners. That's how Annie first described it to me, when her group found it. The light curve signature was subtle but it was there. Shikasta 464's only known planet, a not-so-hot Jupiter, had a tiny sibling. Two Earth masses, a rocky world too close to its sun to be in the habitable zone. But between its burning dayside and the frozen night, there was the terminator, the boundary.

Nobody actually believed we would get there. I say "we" but really I mean the spacecraft, the *Rohith Vemula*.

How hard were those early years! Now we have our reward: the signals, first from the spacecraft, and then from Avi! I can see through his eyes, as *you* should have been doing right now. I know what he knows, even though the knowledge is more than four years old. My grandfather is in Bhubaneswar, celebrating with palm beer. He says that because I am a kind of famous person now, all will work out for our people. But I know and he knows it is not that simple.

From faraway Arizona, Annie is looking at the pictures on her screen. The substellar side of the planet, always facing its dim red star, is all lava seas. But in the terminator, what you called the Twilight Zone, the temperatures are less extreme, and the terrain is solid rock. For this reason you and Chirag designed our proxy to be a small, flat climbing robot, with very short legs, There he is, up on the cliff face, like a crab.

I am used to boundaries. Ever since my exile from my people's ancestral home, I have lived in in-between places. Living on a boundary, you know you don't belong anywhere, but it is also a place of so much possibility.

Through Avi's eyes, the planet's terminator has become more and more familiar.

Annie:

For my people the number four is sacred—four directions, four holy mountains. It always felt right to me that this project began with the four of us on a rock, stargazing. We're still figuring out what it means to be together again after all this time, without you.

Let me begin with the old question: How do you know when something is alive?

I grew up on the rez. Red dust and red rock, mesas and buttes against the widest sky you've ever seen. I grew up lying on boulders with my cousins, watching the constellations move across the sky, and the stars seemed close enough to touch. During the winter, when the snow still fell, we little ones would huddle inside the hogan, listening to our elders tell the stories of how Coyote placed the stars in the sky. My plump fingers would fumble as I tried to follow my grandmother's hands deftly working the string patterns—with one flick of the wrist, one long pull, one constellation would turn into another. The cosmos was always a part of our lives; even in the hogan there was Mother Earth, Father Sky. Now we live in boxes like white people. My uncle is a retired professor and a medicine man. He says our rituals and ceremonies keep us reminded of these great truths, even in this terrible time for our people.

Growing up, I thought I'd follow his footsteps—my Uncle Joe, the professor of Futures Studies at Diné University. But I took freshman geology to fulfill a science requirement, and ended up hooked. I remember the first time I realized that I could read the history of the Earth in the shapes and striations of the rocks, the mesas, and the canyons. I ended up going to the State University as a geology major, hoping to do something for the Navajo economy, which relied at that time on mining operations. I was naïve then. Luckily I got distracted by exoplanet atmospheres—late-night homework session, too much coffee, my boyfriend at the time—so here I am, planet hunter, all these years later, looking for biosignatures in exoplanets.

I've been looking at the images and puzzling over a few things. After several thousand exoplanets, we still don't really understand how planetary atmospheres originate. Earth is such a special case that it only tells us of one narrow band of possibilities. With the exception of the noble gases, nearly all the gases in our atmosphere are made by life. I'm thinking about my grandmother's story of the holy wind—life is breath, breath is life, literally and in every other way.

Shikasta 464b is too close to its star to do more than graze its habitable zone. Which is why it is last on everybody's list for habitability. But my argument is that (a) the thin atmosphere (only 0.6 atm) is nevertheless more than what we'd expect of a planet that ought to have lost much of its atmosphere long ago, so what's causing it to persist? Could be geology, could be life. And (b) the terminator between the magma pools of the dayside and the frozen desert of the nightside is actually relatively temperate in places, with temperatures that might allow for liquid water. There are trace amounts of water vapor in the upper atmosphere, but—let's not get excited—likely not enough to create oxygen by photolysis—nah, if you want an oxygen atmosphere you have to look elsewhere. There is hydrogen, methane, and carbon dioxide, but that is hardly surprising on a world with active geology.

So Kranti and I have been going back and forth about how we would actually know something is *alive*. We decided that since we both come from tribal cultures we should ask our elders the question. My Uncle Joe, who is a *hatałii*, says that life is a property arising from connectedness; the universe, being whole, is therefore alive. *Don't dissect things so much*, he says, professor and medicine man all at once. *See the entirety of things first. It is only through the whole that the parts come into being.* Kranti's grandfather comes of a hill people of lush tropical forests—they call themselves the People of the Waters—and he says that rocks, stones, and mountains are alive, they are gods.

Anyway, getting back to the point about the terminator—all those years ago some of us broached the idea that there are worlds where life is (a) different from what we recognize as life, (b) not widespread over the planet; in fact the planet might well have only a few habitable regions on it, and (c) it is theoretically possible to find pocket regions even in such inhospitable places as Shikasta 464b where some kind of life thrives, and (d) that life could well be complex life if the pocket habitats are (despite the name) deep enough, large enough, last long enough to have these forms of life evolve. Which is one reason I like red dwarfs—Shikasta 464 is a beauty, brighter and heavier than average, but still, a red dwarf: small, resilient, and very, *very* long-lived (as I, too, hope to be). Long-lived enough to up the possibility of life on one of its planets. I hope.

Our little rock is quite a mystery. It shouldn't have as much atmosphere as it does, tenuous though it is. Considering how close it is to its star, the solar wind ought to have stripped much of it away. Plus the frozen antistellar side is so cold that some of the gases in the atmosphere should have rained out as snow. So why so much atmosphere? Perhaps outgassing—Shikasta b is a happening place, lots of active geological processes churning up the surface—but our models don't give us the numbers we need. So—life?

I like it when we are surprised by the universe.

Chirag:

It began from a single discussion in a certain university in Delhi. The four of us—Annie, Kranti, myself, and you—talked all night.

You were witness to the great shaking-up of civilization in the 2020s—the wars and civil strife, the wave upon wave of refugees fleeing the boggy, unstable tundras, the unbearable heat of the tropics. You saw the anoxic dead zones of the ocean—you hung the "I can't breathe" banners over the bodies of the refugees floating among the silvery carcasses of dead fish, the photograph that made you briefly famous. From the shaking of the world arose little groups that came together the way sand gathers in the nodes of a banging drum: fiery intellectuals and dispossessed tribals, starving farmers and failed businessmen. We saw it grow—little groups around the world, islets of resistance, birthplaces of alternate visions, some of which became the solidarity circles from which our dreams emerged. We witnessed the collapse of things as we knew them, saw the great world-machine sink to its steel-and-chromium knees, threatening to drag us all down with it. We saw the paradox of life carrying on through the mayhem, in the big cities and small towns, even as our peoples fought the killing machines all around the globe—the small rituals of breakfast on the table, sleepovers for one's children, bringing your lover chocolates on her birthday.

It was a mad idea, in the midst of all this, to dream up a crowdfunded cheap space program, to send an experimental robot as explorer on another world. So many friends left us in outrage, accusing us of turning our backs on the real struggles. Those of us who remained launched the worldwide solidarity circles, the crowdfunding. Dissent was the spice and oil that moved us forward. The circles formed offshoots, generated ripples of their own, they birthed art movements, films, new university departments, even the growth of independent city-states around the globe, as long-existing boundaries wavered and re-formed. Then, during the spacecraft's journey, we scattered, were lost, some claimed by strife, others by the sweeping pandemics of the last decade. It is a miracle then that some of us have been able to return to the project, now that the signals are coming in thick and fast.

But of the four of us who first talked the whole thing into being, that night on the boulder under the unusually clear Delhi sky—only you have not come back. You gave yourself to this perhaps more than any of us, and then you were taken down, flung back into the earth from which you rose. I can still see your hands caressing the chassis that was to be Avi, muttering your strange AI spells, the grin lighting up your face as the robot came alive. You had no defense against the pain the world inflicted on us—you were Annie's uncle dying of radiation poisoning in the Navajo desert, you were Kranti's younger cousin shot by the police, you were my newborn sister laid outside a school in the hope that someone could feed her. Ultimately they came for you, and you knew in that moment what it was to be all the peoples of the world who have lived in hell. Each time I think of what you must have gone through, I die with you and for you, and I live for you, again and again.

I live for what the four of us represent. We are the idea of the destruction of caste, class, and race come alive. Together we are walking alternate paradigms, irrefutable counterarguments to the propaganda of the powerful, to the way of life that is accepted as the norm. We live in dangerous times, and because people like us threaten the established order, we are dangerous, and therefore in danger. I don't really know who the men are who guard us, but it is part of S.R.'s promise to me. S.R. approached me himself with the offer of protection for our project. Accepting it made me feel uncomfortable because his god is Money. Money, he says, is what will set Dalits free, and indeed it has freed him. So much that he can walk the streets (that's a euphemism for his armored car) surrounded by bodyguards and impunity. I am grateful for his protection, and for his support, although we only took a small fraction of what he offered. But his is not the kind of freedom I seek. I am uncomfortable around power, I suppose. Or maybe I am more of an idealist than I admit to Kranti and Annie.

You see, I remember what it was like when I was a child. Before we came to Delhi, my mother cleaned houses in Patna. She always pushed me to go to school, and she would ask me to repeat my lessons to her in the evenings, so she could learn to read too. I remember her repeating the letters after me, and sometimes she would be so tired, she would fall asleep before I had finished. Once when I came home crying because the teacher had pushed me to the back of the class for being a Dalit—she told me why she had named me Chirag. I remember her eyes burning in her face, saying, *in the darkness of my life, you are the light. What use is suffering if it doesn't make you stronger?* Much later I came across the poetry of Om Prakash Valmiki, who could have been speaking in my mother's voice. Here's how I translated his words for Annie.

> *That wound*
> *Of the hammer-blow*
> *On the rock*
> *Births sparks*

That night in Delhi, we started thinking about how we would explore space, and why. We were in a climate funk—the West Antarctic ice shelf had collapsed faster than predicted. Sea walls had been breached in Miami and Mumbai and Boston; fish were swimming in the streets of Kolkata. We'd thought to escape from grim reality by going to a movie, but they showed one from the tweens that pissed us off, called *Interstellar*. Lying on the cooling rock, you said, suddenly: "Trash, burn and leave. Yeah, I'm going to be a space colonizer now. That's my motto. Having fucked up the only world we have, I'm going into space to fuck up a few more." You laughed, bitterly, and started singing "Trash, burn and leave" to the tune of some pop number I don't even remember. "Shut up," said Kranti and Annie together. "Or at least sing in tune," I said. We laughed, drank a little more, and wept a little too. That was the start of one of those passionate discussions you have in college that goes on all night: How would *we*—those on the other side of colonization—do it differently? We couldn't have known then that the answer to the question would take our whole lives.

We look for life on other worlds because we want to deepen what we mean by human, what we mean by Earthling. As our own atmospheric and oceanic oxygen levels fall and species go extinct like candles winking out, year after year, we want to bring attention to the wonder that is life, here and elsewhere. It is an extension of our empathy, our biophilia. Build your approach, your business model, your way of thinking around that paradigm, and you've already built in respect for every human regardless of race or class or caste, connection between all life, and an enhancement of the collective human spirit. Back in the early years of the twenty-first century, one of my people—Rohith Vemula—was driven to sacrifice his life for a vision of a better world. I had suffered from depression for some of my college years, and in the days following that first late-night conversation, I reread what he had written before he died, how he'd wanted to go to the stars. It felt as though he was speaking to me across time and history, urging me to live and dream, reminding me who I was, "a glorious thing made of stardust." *I can live for this*, I told myself that night.

Now I wish I could tell him: Brother, you did it! You took us to the stars.

Kranti:

I've been spending more and more time exploring Shikasta b. Chirag tells me that it is not wise to spend so much time immersed. But I can't help it. When I am in the immersphere, I feel all relaxed, all tension goes away. I explore the Twilight Zone in Avi's little body, sampling data. It is becoming a place to me. Every night we look at the images, locate features on a grid, and name things.

Here's the description Annie posted on our Citizen Science website:

Shikasta b's sky is clear and filled with stars. Looking sunward, the star Shikasta 464 is a dull red sphere, bathing the planet with its inadequate light. Most of its radiation is in the infrared. Avi is standing at the eastern edge of the terminator, atop a cliff some 10 kilometers high. The view of the dayside is spectacular. Here the ground falls away in sheer vertical walls down to a redly glowing plain, where large pools of magma hundreds of kilometers across are connected by lava rivers. Near the cooler terminator region the surface lava in the pools crusts over, and enormous bubbles of noxious gases break through it at irregular intervals, popping like firecrackers that would be louder if the planet had much of an atmosphere. Fine droplets of molten rock rain down from these explosions. Behind Avi the top of the levee is a cracked and fissured plain, dark and shadowed, with a few odd rock formations. On the nightside the images beamed from our orbiting satellite show a frozen terrain cut through by fissures and canyons on a much larger scale. Perhaps deep in the cracks tidal friction from the interior warms the place enough for life to have a tenuous hold. We don't know yet. But the terminator between the two extremes is our best bet.

Today Avi has begun exploring a small canyon that we have named Shiprock. It is a maze of narrow gullies between jagged rock walls about 40 meters in height. Avi has already mapped it from the air; now he is methodically mapping details from the surface level, moving up the walls, along the canyon, poking his antennae into holes and cracks.

I am remembering, as I clamber up and down the terrain with him, the time I spent with my grandfather during summer holidays in my final year of college. He had returned to our tribal lands the year before. The refinery had ruined the land in the 20 years of his exile, and now the mining company wanted to extend the open-cast mines. My grandfather's village, my people, were all scattered by the initial displacement, but they had come together to fight for their land. The police brought the company goondas with them, looking for the agitation leaders. This is what they call an "encounter killing"—cold-blooded murder that is reported as a killing in self-defense. Four people, including my cousin brother Biru, were killed the week before I arrived.

I can't talk about it still. I have been insulated from the troubles of my people for so long because my mother took us children away when the refinery displaced us. Most of my childhood was spent in Bhubaneswar. I was good at studies, so she got me admitted to a Corporation school, even though my grandfather was against it. They had such arguments! But my mother won. She had seen too much violence and death in the war against our people; she wanted me to be safe, to get a modern education. My grandfather didn't speak to her for three years. Then he was forced to come to Bhubaneswar to find work. It proved my mother's point, that we could no longer live the way we had for thousands of years, so why fight and be killed? When she realized my grandfather was still active in the struggle she shook her head and said he was a fool. I never paid attention to all that, only to my studies. Only when I went to Delhi for university I realized what it meant to be Adivasi. I was so integrated into modern life that I had forgotten my native language and customs—but with my black skin and different features I was seen as backward, someone who had come to a top university because of the reservation system. I joined an Adivasi resistance group, and slowly began to unlearn the Corporation propaganda and learn again the language and history of my people.

That summer I went back to Odisha to see my grandfather. I still remembered the green hills and the clouds that would sit on top of them, and the plain, which used to be crisscrossed by small rivers and streams. But so much had changed. I stood in the dust and heat of the foothills and hugged my weeping aunt, as the bodies of the "junglee terrorists" lay before us. Biru lay on his side as though sleeping. Blood had seeped from the gunshot wound on his head into the ground. That day I understood for the first time the reality of being on the receiving side of genocide.

In the terrible days that followed the raid, our relatives, the hill tribes, hid us from the police. I went with the fugitives into the cloud forest. The narrow trails were filled with the calls of unfamiliar birds and beasts. Up there under the shadow of the mountain god, eating wild mangoes from the trees while a light rain fell, I had a strange experience: *belonging*. I looked at my grandfather's face, lined and seamed from decades of suffering, and laughing so defiantly despite all our sorrows, and I finally understood why he fought for what was left of our home.

In those days my head was filled with all kinds of grand ideas. I was a budding intellectual, all the worlds of knowledge were opening before me. I was writing a thesis on extensions of Walker Indices, which are a set of parameters that try to tell how alive something is, from a rock to a mountain goat. My grandfather was proud of me, and always wanted to know what I was studying. In his village he had been a man of wisdom and power; in the city he was an activist by night, and a gardener for hire by day.

But he was the one who taught me to see in a different way. My vague ideas of semiotics grew sharper and more vivid during that time in the forest. I didn't put it all together until some years later in my first academic paper—but what the forest taught me was that Nature speaks, that living and nonliving communicate with each other through a system older than language. In fact, physical law is only a subset of the ways in which matter talks to matter. When my grandfather went foraging for medicinal plants for the injured people, I saw him come alive to all the life around him. I had never seen him like that. I realized there is a way of being alive that we have lost by becoming civilized. I published my first paper in my final year—a very technical one on extensions of Kohnian semiotic theory—but the basic ideas, they all come from that trip.

What I am trying to do now—immersing myself in this alien environment—is because of those long-ago forest treks with my grandfather.

Whenever I used to ask him how he knew something about the forest, he would say that he just paid attention. At first I used to get irritated. Now I understand better what he meant. He practices a kind of radical observation, in which he opens all his senses to information flow without preconceptions, and simply waits until something crystallizes. This sounds ridiculous to Chirag: "just the kind of mumbo-jumbo that people associate with the 'mystical savage,'" but I think this radical, unfiltered immersion can lead to alternative ways of understanding the world. For example, all the emerging discoveries of animal language—the monkey species in Australia, the bowhead whale in the Arctic—the scientists in each case spent so much time with the animals, getting to know them, listening to their recordings day and night.

That is what I am doing here, on Shikasta b. And I want to understand Avi, whose Walker Index is 7.8, in between life and non-life. This is the first time he has been on active assignment in an alien world. He can learn. On an AI scale, he is a genius. In what ways will Shikasta b change him?

Annie:

This radical observation thing of Kranti's—as she says, it's nothing new—indigenous people have been practicing it for millennia. She was afraid Chirag would scoff—but I think she has a point. She thinks we should go even deeper. Let's tell ourselves Shikasta b's stories, she said, stories about this place. Maybe in assuming everything is alive, and giving each thing a certain agency, different degrees of aliveness will become apparent. What she's saying, I think, is that if you are looking for a pattern and don't know what it is, it makes sense to invent patterns of your own, semi-randomly. This Monte-Carlo-like shaking up of patterns and paradigms can throw up notions that you might not have reached through logic alone. This goes against conventional wisdom, which says—hey, we humans like patterns, so *beware*: the patterns we find are likely simply in our heads, as opposed to *real* patterns. The thing is, when it comes to "real": what we recognize as patterns and connections are neither purely cultural (or anthropomorphic) nor purely "natural." As Kranti says, "What is culture but a specific kind of contextualizing with the rest of one's environment?"

Well, it could all be a waste of time. But we have that—time, I mean. What's to lose?

Actually Chirag didn't scoff when we suggested it. He was about to—I know the signs well: the way his left eyebrow starts going up, and the deep sigh—but his poetic side saw an opportunity. It was funny how his face changed, you could see that internal struggle. He has declared himself the official scribe, collecting our story ideas and rewriting them.

Once there was a planet too close to its star. They shared a vast and complex magnetic field, and their proximity made a beautiful world of extremes, separated by a circular boundary. In the boundary world it was neither too hot nor too cold, but it was always windy. Various species of hot beings lived on the dayside, and they wanted to know what it was like on the other side of the world, where the star's heat and light did not fall. So the forces that shaped them—heat and pressure and magnetic forces—turned them into huge molten balls that rose from the lava seas and were flung at the sheer walls of the boundary, where they fell apart, crashing back down into the molten ocean. But the tiniest of them cooled and solidified into lava dust motes, and were able to ride the wind.

The Great Eastern Highlands, where Avi is exploring, is my favorite place on this planet. Imagine looking down into the magma pools of hell from such a height. I've never had vertigo—spent most of my childhood clambering up cliffs—but the vids from the edge of the great levee make me nervous and excited. I can hear the wind blowing at Avi's back, a constant dull, muted roar—the cold surface current from the frozen nightside. Higher up, hot air from the substellar side swirls in the opposite direction.

We've gridded off the highland plateau on top of the levee. The dramatic temperature difference at the terminator makes for a fissured, tortured landscape. Lots of crevasses, passageways, mazes, all bathed by the dim, angry grazing light from the red dwarf star. Avi has made progress on his ground-based survey of Shiprock Canyon, which winds between sheer basalt walls on the plateau. His headlights reveal a maze of passageways, rocky arches, and bridges. At first I thought there was something wrong with his optics, because when he looked up, the stars didn't look so clear at about 30 degrees around the zenith. Dust? The atmosphere is very thin, but I can imagine solidified lava bits from the molten rock fountains in the plains below, being swirled around by the wind.

Could there be dust devils on Shikasta b? Kranti's message read. And as I sipped my coffee in the glowing sunrise of the high Arizona desert and looked at the newest image, I thought: *Nilch'i.* I remember my grandmother explaining to me when I was very little that the whorls on my finger pads and the little vortex of hair on my head were signs of the holy wind that animates us. There's *Nilch'i* on another world, raising dust into a vortex, making this being, this *Dusty Woman.* Now that I know what to look for, I can see her form, faint but discernible against the backdrop of rock and sky, a dust devil composed of lava dust. She is whirling along the canyon like a live thing.

Dusty Woman danced through the narrow passageways of Shiprock Canyon,
shaking her skirts and looking into the caves and hollows.
"Who is tugging at my skirts?"
But the wind took her voice away, and when it died she had to lay down to rest
and wait until the wind picked her up again.

Kranti is making up a story about Saguaro, a creature that lives in the fissures and passageways of Shiprock Canyon. Chirag declares we are silly, but has joined the fun: his contribution is Balls of Fire (the semisolid glowing lava balls that are sometimes hurled up from the magma pools, hitting the levee wall with a splosh). We also came up with lindymotes (after my sister Lindy) for the little solid bits of lava that are blown over the magma pools toward the great cliffs. These have left their mark on the tops of the canyon walls, which have been roughened over millennia of constant battering by these windborne particles.

You should see Avi scuttle after the lindymotes like a little dog. He's been doing some odd little dancing steps. There's something we can't yet see or sense that he can. It occurred to me that we should plot his movements, just in case they give us some kind of clue. Avi's certainly been behaving weirdly. I wish you were here to see this, because more than anything, he is your baby.

Our pictures are being analyzed the world over by scientists and amateurs and nutcases via our Citizen Science Initiative. We hope someone will find something. But the far more exciting pictures from a major mission to a water world are eclipsing ours. As is, need I mention, the latest cluster of wars.

Still, we have some traffic. When we discover something it immediately goes to our site, becomes global and public. Our reports are clear and contextual—they lack the aloofness of scientific papers, but they're plenty rigorous. Then the world gets to dissect, shred, and analyze what we have to say. Like our finances, everything is public, everything is transparent. I like to think we are changing the culture of science, from the margins, a fringe bunch of scholar-activists in little circles around the world. I've realized after all these years that what's bothered me about Western science is that there is no responsibility. No reciprocity. You just have to be curious and work hard and be smart enough to discover something interesting. The things you discover, you have no relation to, no responsibility for—except through some kind of claim-staking. I grew up in two worlds—the world of conventional science, and the world of the Navajo. I used to think there was an insurmountable wall between them. But looking through Avi's eyes, I'm beginning to see whole. I'm feeling more complete.

Of course, there really is no such thing as a complete person. That's another Western concept, isn't it? We are open systems, we eat, we excrete, we interdepend. We feel your absence like a three-legged chair.

Chirag:

The lindymotes did not belong here. They had been forged in the lava beds, and here it was cold, so cold! Some of them were swept by the currents past the great cliffs of the boundary into the fabled nightside, where they nucleated tiny snowflakes as gases condensed around them, snowing on the frigid, tortured landscape. But others managed to stay in the boundary lands—flung against the canyon walls, they left their tiny footprints on the surface, only to slide down into sheltered gullies. Here they found that the wind was not as strong, and they could perceive the twists and turns of invisible pathways, magnetic field lines. They felt the pull and tug of these, and aligned themselves so. The invisible pathways changed, sometimes slowly, sometimes at random, but the lindymotes followed them like little flocks of sheep across a meadow.

I know metals and money. I went into metallurgy because I wanted to see if there was a way around extractive industries like mining. And I went into money because I wanted to kill that god, Money. Nothing against money, but Money? No. I know what it does to people.

Actually I wanted to jump-start an economy based on retrieving metals from waste, so that we didn't have to destroy lands and peoples for ore. In our college days, I promised Kranti on more than one drunken night that I would change the world. But I've been sober since, drunk only on the tragic poetry of life.

And here we are, on the verge of discovery. Kranti suspects that we have discovered a form of life so alien that we can barely recognize it. She gave me some technical stuff about orthogonal Walker Indices and negative subzones of phase space—but what it boils down to is that there are, possibly, at least two life-forms on Shikasta b.

One is Avi, or what he has become.

How to explain Avi? It is a task nearly as impossible as explaining you. To explain Avi—and Bhimu—to explain them is to go back in time to you and me, but where to begin? Perhaps it should be the time you lent me your battered copy of Jagdish Chandra Bose's *Response in the Living and the Non-Living*. It was somewhere between Ambedkar and Darwin, I think—you had been pushing books on me, my English and Hindi were both improving, my head was singing with ideas, a magnificent incoherence within which my slowly awakening mind wandered, intoxicated. From my mother's simplistic

dreams for me, which I had unconsciously adopted—a good job and reasonable wealth, freedom from want, your usual middle-class unexamined life—
from that, you took me to a place that whispered, "the universe is larger than
this." I remember the exact moment I opened the book and Bose's dedication
leapt out at me, "to my fellow countrymen," as though the great scientist had
himself touched my hand across time. I knew already that he was anti-caste,
that he had the ability to walk away from fortune, and that his contributions had only been recognized decades after his death. But it was because
of that book that I got really interested in metals. I decided then to go into
metallurgy, even though the engineering program's chief objective was to
produce mining engineers. Why not get to know the monster intimately?
My real interest was in the mining of landfills, in reclamation of metals from
electronic waste—but what caught my poetic imagination was the possibility
that metals were alive, in some metaphorical sense, if not the literal. Bose's
experiments on plants and metals under stress elicited similar responses—
he had made some conceptually audacious suggestions that were laughed
off or politely dismissed. Only in recent times, with the greatly increased
understanding of plant sentience and communication—man, he would have
loved mycorrhizal networks—have some of his ideas gained credence. But
metals—we know that metals are not alive in the usual sense. Metals in their
pure form allow for flow, just as living systems do. That we are all electrical
beings, that life is electricity, is true enough, but not all electricity is life.
Still, when I first started to learn about metals, I saw in my imagination the
ions studded in an ever-surging sea of valence electrons, the metallic forms so
macroscopically varied, silver and pale yellow, sodium, soft as butter against
the hardness of steel, the variations in ductility and malleability, the way
rigid iron succumbed to softness under heat—I saw all this and I wanted
to know metal, to know it for its own sake as much as for its practical use.
That's how you really know anything, anyway.

Between your mind and mine—yours trained in artificial intelligence, mine in metallurgy—Avi's predecessors were born, starting with
Kabariwallah, made to find metal waste in trash dumps. Celebrating over
daru, we began to argue about ethics—Frowsian models of value emergence
in technological development, if I remember correctly. Somehow the notion
came up of AI sentience, hotly debated for over a decade before us, as network
intelligences started to pass the lowest-level Turing tests. The AI Protection
Clauses started to be invoked and applied. You said, "to restrain a being, any
being that is capable of sentience, is to put a baby in a maximum-isolation
prison cell because you are afraid it will grow up a criminal." I argued that

artificial intelligence was not like the baby, not human at all. It was alien, despite its human parents. Wasn't that why there were laws against the development of free AIs? For any AI system there must be a balance between the freedom of complexity and the necessity of control. You looked at me with that intent, dark gaze and sighed. "Don't you get it? The restraint protocols are about slavery, not ethics. The question is not whether or not we should build free AIs. The challenge is—having built one, how do you teach *it* how to be ethical? For whatever we mean by 'ethical?'"

Thus Avi's precursors came about: experiments in the university's frigid AI development labs while the air burned outside. Finally you came up with the idea that an AI capable of learning could only acquire an ethical compass the way children do. So you and I became parents to the robots that would eventually give birth to Avi. The final development took us from pre-Avi-187 to Avi and his conjoined twin Bhimu. They were our babies. But you were the one who took Avi-Bhimu home with you every night, took them to work, to classes, to demonstrations, to children's birthday parties.

Avi-Bhimu's Walker Index earned each of them an Electronic Person identity chip, but an EP is only the lowest common denominator among the top-class AIs. What we've done, what you did, really, is to create a new class of artificial intelligence altogether: an ultrAI. Whether ultrAIs are sentient in the way we understand it, we don't yet know. They are free to learn and grow, yet grounded in years-long ethical training resulting from close contact with the same group of humans. There are only two ultrAIs in the entire universe, Avi and Bhimu. You might say the great worldnet AIs, the distributed Interweb intelligences, are just as complex and unpredictable, but Avi and Bhimu are so much closer to us, bound as they are in their metal-ceramic bodies, with bioware networks rather like our nerves. AIs are indeed alien; we know now we cannot download human consciousness into an AI because the physicality matters—but I have to admit that one of the reasons I can't spend more time in immer with Avi is because every step he takes up a rock wall makes my heart jump like an over-worried parent.

Now—I say *now*, despite the four-year time lag—Avi's been behaving oddly. The reports he sends back are cryptic and terse. He is sending us images and data, but he's stopped chatting, and his tone has changed. No explanation as to the odd dancing steps, no streaming feed of his thought process as he makes hypotheses and tests them, which he's designed to do. I can't quite put my finger on it but it feels as though he is preoccupied. His neural activity is faster and more intense than we've ever recorded, which means he's learning at a prodigious rate. We've sent queries of course, but we won't have the answers for another eight years. So we must draw our own conclusions.

I wish we had Bhimu with us to help us understand him.

Kranti:

Have we really discovered life on Shikasta b?

One thing we know about life is that living things have a larger phase space of possibilities. A stone falling down a cliff is limited by gravity. But a mountain goat can step to the side, he can go up or down.

That is why one of the things Avi has been doing is looking for apparent violations of physical law. This is not at all easy. He has found crystalline formations inside some of the caves and tunnels—but you cannot look at entropy alone. Order is also found in nonliving things. In my field we say information inscribes matter. But when something is alive, the information flow is top-down causal. So we need to see whether flow of information becomes—*alive*—when its causal structure is determined by the largest scale on which it can have a distinct form.

What Avi found was a mat of lindymotes, the lava dust that—now we know to look for it—is everywhere in Shiprock Canyon. The recurring dust devil we call Dusty Woman leaves layers of dust on the rocky surfaces as she dances. The dust is everywhere, even in the caves and tunnels. It is basically silica dust, crystalline fragments with hydrocarbons mixed in.

Avi found a mat of this stuff on the base of some of the rock formations. During a lull in the wind, it moved up a rock face, very slightly. That could just be some small-scale atmospheric vortex, but he's recorded the same thing multiple times, in different wind and weather conditions, from dead still air to gales. The vortex event was the strangest. I was there, looking through Avi's eyes, and I saw the Dusty Woman start dancing. Avi was recording the wind speed and gradient, and I saw the Dusty Woman pause—yes, pause, in the middle of the dance. Imagine it, in the light of Avi's headlamps: the wind still blowing, but the dust formation holding.

There are so many possible non-life scenarios for this phenomenon. The first thought in my mind was liquid helium II—in spite of its peculiar behavior, it is not alive. So we can't discount the possibility of a non-life explanation.

We have been discussing all this nonstop until we get tired. In the evenings we sit with bottles of beer or cups of chai and watch the city skyline. There are the searchlights arcing through the polluted air. In the distance are the Citadel towers like multicolored candles. Chirag plays our stories back to us.

The lindymotes lay on the rock face to rest. They felt the stirrings, small and large, and rearranged themselves. They were flung into a dance by great vortices of air, and they went whirling. When the whirling stopped as the wind died, the lindymotes felt the magnetic field lines shift and change, and held their place for a moment before falling slowly down on to the surface.

"We are playing!" said some of the lindymotes.

"We are being played with," said others in wonder.

"We are becoming something," said some of the lindymotes.

"We are making something," said others.

And so they knew they were themselves, tiny and separate, but together they were Dusty Woman.

One of the things I learned from my grandfather is that you cannot separate life from its environment. Understand an environment well enough, and you will understand what kind of life might arise there. Environment is the matrix that works with the life force to generate life-forms. That is how the environment becomes aware of itself, when it intra-acts at different scales. So I try to keep my mind open to possibility, even when my imagination comes up with something fantastic, so later on I can apply the constraints that are needed. Imagination has an even larger phase space of possibility than life. Sometimes in the immersphere I feel I am slipping away from Earth itself. It is scary but also exciting.

Annie:

Today I am a little shaky. I was stopped by a cop last night. I was walking back through campus at close to midnight when it found me. Its swiveling eyes locked on me, and the voice, gravelly and machine-like, said: *Stop. Do Not Move.* It scanned me top to bottom with the blue light. The cops can make mistakes. But it found me in its database and I was released. Some of my friends are convinced that the so-called mistakes are deliberate, used as a cover-up to kill leaders of the resistance. My colleague Laura was one of the "mistakes." Nobody was punished for her death. The AI tribunal pronounced the cop guilty of an interpretation error, and it was wiped. And that was the end of it. I've heard drone killings are better because they are swift—you have no time to be afraid. The drones are so small that you only notice them, if at all, when you are about to die.

Okay, deep breath. *I am alive, I am alive.* And what about life on Shikasta 464b?

I think a non-life explanation is the most likely. Magnetism is the most obvious thing to consider. Shikasta 464b has a roughly octupolar magnetic field that doesn't do much to protect it from its star's solar wind. The peculiar magnetic field, I believe, is due to the extreme heat of the dayside, which causes magma to upwell from the interior onto the surface, dragging with it denser magnetic minerals in long wisps and tendrils. This also causes the local variations in the magnetic field in both space and time.

I've looked at Avi's analysis of the dust fragments. Lots of silica and basalt grains, and—magnetite crystals! Not surprising that the dust moves around in response to the variations in the local magnetic field. There is so much magnetic material churning close to the surface of Shikasta b that the local fields must be shifting all the time. This would result in magnetic dust moving in weird ways, like Avi has observed. A relatively mundane non-life explanation for Dusty Woman's behavior. Of course, as Kranti points out, the environment shapes the possibilities for life. It would hardly be surprising that if life exists on this world, it would take advantage of the peculiar magnetic field distribution.

So. How would life adapt to magnetism, especially to complex and ever-changing magnetic fields? We have magnetotactic bacteria on Earth, and birds that migrate based on the little crystals in their skulls. But navigation wouldn't be much use when the magnetic fields are so weirdly distorted, when they change all the time.

The three of us have been talking about a new idea that is beginning to take shape. Our old questions: (a) What separates life from non-life? (b) Why is it that so many indigenous cultures regard the universe itself as alive? I think of my grandmother's string games during winter nights. Her fingers working. The constellations shifting from one to another. My favorite is Two Coyotes Running Away From Each Other. Her fingers and the strings between them hold the cosmos in a way I can't articulate.

This is what we are thinking: that there is no clear boundary between life and non-life as biologists define it. The answer to "what is life?" depends on your context. My people, like Kranti's people, knew long ago that the universe is connected, every bit linked with every other bit, and even the bits changing form and purpose all the time. This is not mere mysticism—it is consistent with science. If science had not started as a reductionist enterprise through an accident of history, this idea would be familiar. Over the last few days the three of us have been mapping "information channels" or "communication pathways," although we are not certain these are the same thing. We started with a diagram of a human—there are stabilizing negative feedback loops within each organ for homeostasis, but from organ to organ these pathways connect, forming even larger meta-loops.

But because humans are open systems, the pathways connect outside us, to the biosphere itself. They connect with the negative and positive feedback loops of the ocean (breathable oxygen, thank you, phytoplankton) and climate as a whole, as well as human-human interactions. Zoom out beyond the biosphere and the density of connections thins out, but the threads are still there—solar irradiation providing light and heat, cosmic rays influencing mutations, magnetic fields, gravitational fields reaching out through space between planet and star, planet and planet. Zoom in, into the human body, down to the cells, down to the protons and neutrons in atomic nuclei, and the pathways are there, tangled and dense. There may be some kind of fractal self-similarity governing the scale change. If we draw this "loop diagram" for a part of our biosphere, what do we see? The densest loops are those within living organisms, because they must have stabilizing feedbacks to allow for steady states, for homeostasis. "But even rocks have these," I told Kranti and Chirag exultantly. Rocks "communicate" through the laws of physics and geology—they sense gravity, they are subject to heat and pressure, they participate in cycles at long and short scales, from weathering to the carbonate silicate cycle, for example. "Their loops are just not as dense."

So then what is life, and what is not-life, depends on what cutoff choice you make in communication loop density. There is no a priori distinction between life and non-life.

Still, it would be nice to have life that will talk back to us! Or at least to Avi. If we truly find life on Shikasta 464b, Avi's position will become delicate. He will no longer be a highly sophisticated measuring instrument, but an alien communicating with potential native life-forms. We have spent years talking about the ethics of the situation, considering how we represent peoples at the receiving end of colonization. You designed Avi's protocols for what he should do if we were to find life. But you also put in enough leeway for Avi to develop in his own way—I am beginning to recognize some of your fierce independence in Avi's strange behavior.

Of course we wonder about Bhimu all the time. The twins, one on Shikasta 464b and one on Earth, each developing according to his environment. You took Bhimu away for safekeeping; it's what cost you your life.

I'm taking advantage of the armistice and a plane trip voucher to fly out to Delhi. But first I'm going home to Window Rock for a few days. There are places where life on the rez has become impossible because of the heat and the advance of the sand dunes, but we've found pocket habitats, we've learned to adapt. The coal mines have closed. We are working toward 100 percent renewable energy. Life is rough and difficult, due to the long drought in an already dry land, but adversity has brought the old ways to the surface again. The heat madness has not erupted among us as much as in the world outside our borders. The Southern Federation wants us to join them but many of our people are resisting. There have been incursions from the west, skirmishes on the borders. Refugees coming in from the south, they say, tore down the old Wall between the United States and Mexico with their bare hands. With bleeding hands they moved up in a wave through El Paso, and were turned back with gunfire.

It's been a year since I visited, and in that time so much has changed. Cousin Phil is involved in the Resistance, working on disabling drones. He tells me his DADS can get several of them in one sweep. They drop from the sky like flakes of ash, he says. Uncle Bill's new wind farm is taking off. Lindy's working on a desert farming project. I need to see them; I need a Blessing Way ceremony. I need to remember what it means to call a place home, before I leave.

Kranti:

Are you listening? Are you listening?

I hear that voice in a dream. Like a bird calling, again and again. *It is me. Are you listening?* I cannot remember if I have dreamed that dream again and again, or if it is just a memory of the first time. Who is speaking to me? Is it you, or someone else? What is it I have not listened to?

There is so much I do not know. I feel awkward when people praise me. Actually sometimes I feel angry. It is like they are saying, how surprising that you know so much, Adivasi girl. An embarrassed laugh—I thought Adivasi girls could only be maids. Very good ones, no offense. But a Ph.D. scientist. Well, genius can appear at random, anywhere. Besides, she went to a Corporation school. They should put all tribal children in those schools. Look at what the illiterate terrorist junglees are doing . . . .

They used to hold me up as an example of what a good Adivasi should be like. They stopped when I started supporting my people's fight against the corpocracy. Then I was called ungrateful, hypocritical, and worse names. But there are more interesting things in the world than angry, ignorant people, so I turn away from them and I think: everything in Nature communicates, whether through language, or signs, or signals. Even matter, dead matter speaks through physical law, the interrelationships of variables. I have tried to listen, that is why I wonder about the dream. What is it I have not listened to? Is it Avi speaking to me? Is it you?

When I told Chirag and Annie about my dream, Chirag was quiet for a bit. Then he said:

"Do you think it was Bhimu?"

I was surprised. Bhimu, calling me in a dream! Chirag looked embarrassed, then admitted *he* has had recurring dreams that Bhimu is calling him. In the dreams he is wandering through mountains and deserts, following her voice, convinced she will lead him to you. When he is awake he thinks of her lying in pieces deep inside some forest, her bioware torn apart.

"Just as likely," Annie says, "that she is growing up somewhere in the hills, or in a desert among nomads, perfectly safe." We have been waiting, listening for Bhimu, all these years.

Some weeks ago, Annie and I had made up a story about Dusty Woman writing in dust on the canyon walls—Shikastan graffiti. Recently we have been seeing dust patterns, both dynamic and stationary, that seem to be telling us something. I know humans can deceive themselves—hubris is powerful. So I learn humility; as the indigenous peoples have always known, humility before Nature tempers our delusions. We junglees don't have a word for Nature—that is a foreign word, a separation word. But you know what I mean.

What is Shiprock Canyon telling us? Its shapes and passageways, its corridors and caves are all mapped now, and we are getting a sense of how strongly the winds blow over it, and the thin vortices that form in certain areas. There are dust ripples like writing on sloping walls, what Chirag calls "the calligraphy of the wind." This inorganic material cannot by itself be alive.

Avi has also been doing flybys. He will rise suddenly over the canyon, turning slowly, scanning and sensing the magnetic fields, wind speed, visibility. I have realized that he has been increasing the range with each flyby, mapping the larger terrain within which Shiprock Canyon is embedded. And the data he's collecting—if we are right—could mean something spectacular.

Saguaro lived deep beneath the canyon, in the darkest places. He was slow, sleepy with the years. Time flowed for him like cooling lava. He could not see, but he had visions. He sensed rivers and pools of fire, and the deadly cold beyond. The heat below and the cold above fed his body, which was shot through with long cables of exobacteria, sipping electrons and passing them along. The passageways in which he lay had been shaped by magnetism and geological forces, so the biocables that were artery and vein, nerve and sinew for him, were likewise arranged in response to the ambient magnetism. He lay and dreamed.

Annie:

What we are beginning to notice is that superimposed on top of the ambient magnetism are smaller-scale variations, like signals riding a radio wave. Where are those variations coming from? Here, up high on the great terminator ridge, the subsurface temperature is too low for rocks to melt, and it is too far for the dense, ionized heavy metals to extend from the planet's core. We expect spatial variations due to the way magnetic ore is distributed, but we don't expect the magnetic field to vary in time so delicately. It's as though there are magnetic beasts in the subterranean caverns and passageways of Shiprock Canyon that, through their movements, create these fine magnetic signatures, ever-changing with time. The response of the magnetic dust is consistent with this hypothesis. So Dusty Woman twirls, the wind dies down suddenly and the dust, for a fraction of a second, changes pattern in a way inconsistent with the fluid dynamics. Now that we are thinking along these lines, we can see in Avi's data the gap between the observed motion of the dust and what we'd expect with only the wind and the ambient magnetic fields as factors.

Maybe Saguaro, or something like it, really does exist in the depths of the canyon. I can't avoid thinking that Dusty Woman is not merely a dust devil. We're going a little nuts, I think.

Amid all the excitement we are trying something new. Outside the mission room is a small patch of arid scrubland dotted with acacia trees. It slopes up to the observation post on top, where there's a sentry. But on the way up there is a side path into a bunch of trees. It leads to a small clearing, ringed by large boulders. Rainwater forms a small pool here, and the trees are hung with the woven nests of baya weaver birds. This is a nice little place to sit. You can barely see the city spread out below us, due to the haze. The air is warm and thick, and the little birds sing and dart about. An ecologically impoverished place, but one where we can practice the idea of radical immersion.

Chirag has the greatest difficulty with this. He is not used to sitting still; he says it makes him nervous. Chirag is letting his determination get in the way—have you ever seen anyone *pushing* themselves to relax? But he'll get there, once he stops trying so hard. As for me, all I have to do is to hold my corn pollen bag in my hand, and take myself back home in my memory. I hear the singing, I smell the corn. I see the dancers, feel their rhythms in my bones. Uncle Joe's voice in the background, deep and slow. As I breathe myself into receptivity, I become aware of the world around me—there's a flash of bright yellow, a little male weaver bird darts from the top of a rock to the hanging nest, an insect in his beak. There's the water gleaming, a muddy brown in the afternoon light. A ripple breaks the surface; a tiny frog, whose pale throat goes in and out as it breathes. We breathe together and I smell moisture in the air, just a hint, as though the monsoons may be sending us some rain after all. The weavers go chit-chit in the underbrush. Clouds pass overhead in small flotillas. Later, when I've come out of this, I will remember that I forgot myself in my immersion. I forgot my separateness, I became part of the cosmos, from the frog at the edge of the water to the clouds and beyond. Inside the control room, I say the *Hózhó* prayer, the word so inadequately translated as "beauty," and everything seems touched by the sacred, even to opening the fridge to get my lime soda. Later Chirag will ask me what it was like. His imagination fills in for experience, and he will give me his poet's words to speak into the recorder.

Kranti is already in the immersphere, going straight from this world to Shikasta 464b. I don't know what she sees when she practices immer— immer on this world, I mean. She never talks about it.

Chirag:

Avi is increasingly following his own ideas. Of course we can't send him commands and expect him to comply immediately—we are separated by four light-years, after all. But he has a communication protocol that is clearly being violated. He is modifying his own algorithms, ignoring, for example, the need to add commentary to his reports, or to explain what he is doing. I have seen him move lumps of magnetic debris in a way that looks like an attempt at communication with whatever it is he thinks he sees here. I think he has crossed the blurry boundary between non-life and life. We are estimating that Avi's Walker Index is probably around 8.3.

There's one more strange thing. It's to do with Bhimu. When she and Avi were separated, literally made two, they had already laid the foundations of a new communication system. A private language analogous to what identical twins sometimes make up, but one that makes no sense to us. I've started to look at their old transcripts again. In the patterns I am finding similarities to some of the signals from Avi. In Avi's transmissions, what seems like random noise overlaying the signals is revealing regularities astonishing in their subtlety. Am I deceiving myself, seeing what I want to see? Or is this a hint that Avi is trying to reach Bhimu—that perhaps she is still—alive?

We have been listening for Bhimu all these years in vain. It is strange that Avi's twin, who was to stay with us on Earth, was the one we lost. After the raid you escaped with her. For her safety you didn't tell us where. They captured you—but not Bhimu—in a remote region of the eastern Himalayas.

You were at their mercy how long, none of us can bear to think. How long before the picture of you was circulated, lying on the forest floor with gunshot wounds to your chest? They dressed your body in the uniform of one of the insurgent groups, and circulated your picture as a triumph of the progressive state versus the terrorists. Allegedly you had been hunted down after days of tracking you through the forest, yet the uniform was recently ironed, with its creases intact. Later we tried to find Bhimu among the tribals of the Northeast, and then, among the new hunter-gatherer anarchist groups. There are so many of the new groups, so many different philosophies: in the West, the gun-toting Savagers and the peace-loving Edenites, and here in India the Prakrits of MadhyaBhum and the Asabhyata movement's adherents in the East. I hope that wherever she is, Bhimu is well. And that she'll forgive us for separating her from Avi.

If Avi's Walker Index is up to 8.3, what might Bhimu's be? We have no way of knowing.

And if Avi is talking to the aliens—what is he saying?

Kranti:

Living things, always they contextualize. That is what adaptation is, a constant conversation with the surroundings, a contextualization intended to maintain life as long as possible. Ancient systems of medicine like Ayurveda talk of life force, what we call prana. It is called chi by the Chinese, holy wind by the Navajo. There are complex paths through which the life force flows in the body, and in Ayurveda the prana flows are part of a greater network, the cosmic prana. Could it be that life force inside living beings is a kind of metaphor for the communication channels? With the difference that in living beings beyond a Walker Index of 8, the information flows are top-down causal, shaped by the constraints and demands of the highest scale at which an organism exists . . . .

Living things have boundaries and sub-boundaries. But there is no absolute boundary because we are all open systems. In that sense what you define as life depends on the cut you make. Ancient peoples, forest dwelling people, desert tribes, they have always made different cuts in the world than scientists. Sometimes I make the cut as a scientist, sometimes as an Adivasi. I can slip from one world to another very quickly.

Chirag:

Kranti's not being concrete, of course. Her mind has always moved faster than her words can keep up with. What she is trying to say is that if this is a life-form, it is communicating via local magnetic fields, and it may actually be morphologically distributed. She is saying that perhaps its body is here, there, and everywhere. Maybe the universal constructor, the control unit, is distributed too. Either that, or we have a superorganism of some sort. There is, after all, no a priori way of telling the difference between an individual and a community of individuals. And there are life-forms on Earth, Kranti points out, like slime molds, that can exist as individuals as well as collectives. Those survey flybys that Avi did, if we are interpreting them correctly, are like the view you get when you rise up in an airplane over a city at night. You see nodes and structures, grids and symmetries. What he's seen—what we've seen through his eyes, converted to visuals—is absolutely breathtaking. Magnetic field lines swirling and shifting, field variations that are too dynamic and too widespread to be explained by mere geology (that's Annie scoffing at me in the background for using "mere" and "geology" in the same breath). In the dark spaces between the glowing lines, in the gradations, there are suggestions of long, sinuous shapes that move, and starfish-shaped exclusions that rotate slowly in place. Something lies deep within the fissures and canyons of the terminator plateau. Through its magnetic senses it knows the high escarpment, and the magma seas far below. And—another speculation here—since the magnetic fields of planet and star are constantly interacting with each other, how astonishing if this beast—if it is a beast indeed—is also sensing the storms and moods of its parent star!

Saguaro lived deep beneath the canyon, in the darkest places. He was old and wide, branching like the forks in a tree. Lying nearly still, he sensed the deep, fiery places beneath him, the pulls and tugs of the magnetized lava surging below, rising up like incandescent lace. Overhead he sensed the great cold, the more distant, yet larger, grander pull of something unfathomable, enormous beyond comprehension. The tugs from the star surged and varied, so although he could not see the red dwarf, he came to know its moods, its storms and meditations. He felt the tugs mediated by cold rock, the rock within which he lay like a many-armed god, but above that he had a sense of space, of motion. Here, in this tenuous region, he sensed the flow of magnetized material as dust, smaller bodies that moved differently, as though free of the grasp of the earth below. And a longing rose up in him to stretch toward that intermediate space between the star and the planet, neither of which he could see. But he knew their deep hearts, their veins of fire. Stretching, moving, he sensed he could make the lindymotes (for that was what the dust was) move in response. Through their resistance he knew the wind, and he thought: there is someone other than me in that clear space above the rock. I must speak to it, he said, and in that moment of recognizing another, he also knew loneliness. So he shifted his massive, coiled, many-branched body, and the wind, through the motion of the lindymotes, knew him too. So he danced with the wind, and Dusty Woman said: who is shaking my skirts?

Annie:

Kranti had a sort of breakdown last week. I don't know what to call it. She collapsed just after a session in the immersphere. We got her through the barricades to the university hospital. Chirag and I were terrified. She is stable now, somewhat annoyed at all the fuss, which is heartening. I'm so glad I'm here with the two of them. Together we four are something that deserves a name of its own. So far Chirag's only come up with AKCX, which is kind of clunky.

Kranti's mother and grandfather came to be with her. Her mother is a stern woman, very focused on the care being given to her daughter. Her grandfather is a character. He's very old, wiry and thin, with a bright and irreverent gaze. He reminds me of my great-uncle Victor. I could stay up trading stories with him all night. Grandfather, as we call him, tells us how his foothill tribe is trying to create a hybrid lifestyle, an alternative economy based on their old ways but "internet-savvy." If only the rest of the world would let them be! They are sitting on huge veins of bauxite, which are needed to feed the world's demand for aluminum, and for staying on their land they are treated like terrorists, under attack by drones and paramilitary forces. And they still have not given up. Listening to Grandfather's somewhat broken English, I am homesick suddenly, for the high plateau.

Update (a): Kranti's been told that she can get back to work in a couple of weeks. She's not sick in any way we understand—but I think it is a lot to take: all those hours spent looking through Avi's eyes! The neurologists tell us her EEG shows irregularities that were not in her baseline data. Chirag has this wild idea that the apparent irregularities are actually patterns, similar to the so-called noise in Avi's signals, which bears a remarkable resemblance to the as-yet-undeciphered private language of the twin ultrAIs. If it's happening with Kranti, is it a matter of time before this process, whatever it is, starts to happen with Chirag and me? What are we becoming? Could ultrAIs like Avi can achieve a connection across the gulf of space-time, resulting in the formation of a being that is morphologically distributed over such vast distances? Maybe I'm being fanciful.

Update (b): We received a message on a secure channel today. Point of origin not yet traced. Chirag ran his decrypting program and the result was a scramble of pairs of numbers. We had the brilliant idea that these were (x,y) coordinates. We got a plot that didn't make sense—a fuzzy pattern rather than a recognizable function. Then I happened to see the printout from a distance. "It's a picture," I said, and Chirag looked and said, "That's Avi." Why would there be a picture of Avi on a secure channel, and a pointillist one, for heaven's sake? Then it hit us both. *Bhimu.* It was a fuzzy picture of Avi's twin, but with sharp protrusions like wings. *Wings?*

That got us excited, and scared. The only ultrAI left on Earth, the one that got *you* killed. Is the message from her? From her protectors? Where is she? Chirag's trying to trace the point of origin of the message. It can only be from someone in our inner circle (which includes Bhimu)—unless security's been breached.

In Kranti's hospital room we had a whispered consultation. But there is nothing really we can do but wait, and make sure security, cyber and otherwise, is as tight as hell.

Later the tension got a bit too much for us. Chirag and I went off to the old campus and found the boulder on top of the hill where we used to stargaze as college students. We lay there talking and drinking tea from a local tea shack. After we had exhausted the subject of Bhimu, we were silent for a while. This is where it all began, all those years ago.

After a while Chirag said, "You know we are shaped by the cosmos. Cosmic rays are raining down upon us right now. Causing mutations in our cells, affecting evolutionary pathways. All those distant cataclysms light-years away, determining whether I end up a monkey or a man!"

"Can't tell the difference," I said, expecting a rude retort, but he just sighed. Chirag the poet. But the mood had taken me over too. I couldn't see Shikasta 464b's dim old sun with the naked eye, but I knew what he meant. I thought back to the old stories I'd heard as a child. When the nights were mild, we would sit around a campfire and look up at the constellations as the elders told the stories. Every once in a while a coyote would call from the sagebrush, as though joining in. Through all the years of my scientific training, I lost that feeling of belonging in a great old universe. Modern science is a shattered mirror—you see bits and pieces in each shard, sometimes in great detail, but never the whole. I nearly gave up the old way of knowing for the new way. But I've felt it more and more lately, and under that sky I felt it again.

Kranti:

I came back from the hospital just in time for the evening newscast—two more official mammal extinctions as of today. The strangest is a species of whale that was only discovered three years ago. They found the bodies on the beaches of Siberia. When the sea ice went, ice algae went also. That caused a catastrophic ecosystem collapse, leading to anoxia, which killed all the fish. Now this whale is extinct. I think of the forest I would have grown up in that also is no longer there. I am filled with so much sadness.

On the positive side, we have received two more messages on the secure line. They are almost the same as the first one. But when we plot them, the images are larger and larger.

Chirag says that Bhimu is coming home.

If she comes home, if we all survive, it will be very interesting to see how far she has come. AI intelligence is quite different from that of animals, and so it must evolve differently. How will an ultrAI on Earth interact with other Earth species? We are only just starting to figure out Avi's interaction with Saguaro on a planet four light-years away. Humans have learned to communicate with three other animal species. We can speak a little bit of Gibbonese, and a very rough Bowhead, and some dialects of Dolphin. What Bhimu could contribute to our increasing therolinguistic abilities, we don't know.

Even with the heat madness and the terrible things people do to one another, and the long lines at the refugee service centers, the old solidarity circles are coming up around the world. Like small ecosystems, they are emerging wherever new ideas and old ones have the freedom to develop. People are meeting in their houses, solving their problems together, discussing alternatives. Even some *bastis* have developed their own currency. What is the critical density of these kinds of pocket ecologies, beyond which we can have system change? When will we change our ways en masse, in time to immer inside our own biosphere, so we can heal with the Earth systems that maintain life on this planet?

When our project first started, I had a lot of arguments with my cousins. They said: why don't you raise money to help our people? I did not have a good answer to that and still that is so—but actually our crowdfunding initiative ended up putting money into the community. Annie is funding an alternative school on her reservation, and Chirag has started a scholarship for Dalit scientists. My part of it has helped the tribe hire the best lawyers for the big fight. And you gave us the DADS, Drona's Apology Defense System, the most intelligent drone-destroying system ever designed, keeping us safe from Arizona to Indonesia. But I know that we would not have collected so much money if the projects had only been about community transformation. People are much more willing to fund space exploration projects.

We have a dream, the three of us—no, the four of us, because you are here in your own way—a dream for an alternative university, one distributed across the world, that includes the best of indigenous knowledge practices and explores a new kind of science, just as rigorous as the one we know, but it goes beyond the shattered-mirror model, the one Annie described.

Another thing our way has shown us is that our practices, like radical immersion, allow certain values to emerge that then feed back to affect the practices, illuminating Frowsian value dynamics in a new way. See, how you practice science is a function of your values. Normally, you design experiments or observations based on distance and so-called objectivity. But you lose information in the process. When you change the practice, it also changes what you value. Chirag always says I am too idealistic. Probably that is true.

We are the shadow people, the broken people emerging from the cracks in the collapsing structures of the world. For so many generations, we have been told we are primitive, backward, in need of help, in need of uplifting. Sometimes we have even been invited to what Chirag calls "the smashing, burning, drinking mega-party that is modern civilization." We have been pushed from one world to another, wondering who we are, where is our place, never really able to move out of the shadow zone. And now we know: we have something necessary to give the world, we have visions of how we might live differently. We have answers to the destructive loneliness of modern civilization.

Ultimately our aim in starting this project was not to escape from Earth. The big space agencies justify their existence by saying it is natural for humans to wander and explore. That is true. But it is also true that only a tiny percentage of the world's people have left their homes through much of Earth's human history. People also like to belong someplace. Trash, burn, and leave is not our way, as you said so many years ago. I am thinking of the pictures the first astronauts beamed back to us: the Earth seen from space, the pale blue dot. We should always look back toward home, no matter how far we go.

I come from a people who know how to belong in a way that civilization has forgotten. I feel a need to return to the terminator of Shikasta 464b, where Avi has gone native—life beckons to life, and to mystery, too—but I also have another deep desire: to practice immersion among the green hills, the cloud forests of my people. There are things we still have to discover about life here, life on Earth. There are things Bhimu will help us learn, if she comes out of hiding. What we find will not leave us unchanged, and that is how it should be. I have always walked in multiple worlds. What is one more?

Message received on secure channel, encrypted.

Message Extract:

Calling AKCX. Are you listening?

As I made the being aware of the universe beyond its planet and its star, I became aware myself. I send this to let you know that although I can't come home, I am home. Here, and there with you and Bhimu.

Prepare to receive data file with magnetic field map in real time. Somebody has a message for you.

Sarah Pinsker is the author of the 2015 Nebula Award–winning novelette "Our Lady of the Open Road." Her novelette "In Joy, Knowing the Abyss Behind" was the 2014 Sturgeon Award winner and a 2013 Nebula finalist. Her fiction has been published in magazines including *Asimov's, Strange Horizons, Lightspeed, Fantasy & Science Fiction*, and *Uncanny*, among others, and numerous anthologies. A collection of her stories is due out in 2019. She lives in Baltimore, Maryland, with her wife and dog. She can be found online at sarahpinsker.com and twitter.com/sarahpinsker.

WIND WILL ROVE

Sarah Pinsker

There's a story about my grandmother Windy, one I never asked her to confirm or deny, in which she took her fiddle on a spacewalk. There are a lot of stories about her. Fewer of my parents' generation, fewer still of my own, though we're in our fifties now and old enough that if there were stories to tell they would probably have been told.

My grandmother was an engineer, part of our original crew. According to the tale, she stepped outside to do a visual inspection of an external panel that was giving anomalous readings. Along with her tools, she clipped her fiddle and bow to her suit's belt. When she completed her task, she paused for a moment, tethered to our ship the size of a city, put her fiddle to the place where her helmet met her suit, and played "Wind Will Rove" into the void. Not to be heard, of course; just to feel the song in her fingers.

There are a number of things wrong with this story, starting with the fact that we don't do spacewalks, for reasons that involve laws of physics I learned in school and don't remember anymore. Our shields are too thick, our velocity is too great, something like that. The Blackout didn't touch ship records; crew transcripts and recordings still exist, and I've listened to all the ones that might pertain to this legend. She laughs her deep laugh, she teases a tired colleague about his date the night before, she even hums "Wind Will Rove" to herself as she works—but there are no gaps, no silences unexplained.

Even if it were possible, her gloves would have been too thick to find a fingering. I doubt my grandmother would've risked losing her instrument, out here where any replacement would be synthetic. I doubt, too, that she'd have exposed it to the cold of space. Fiddles are comfortable at the same temperatures people are comfortable; they crack and warp when they aren't happy. Her fiddle, my fiddle now.

My final evidence: "Wind Will Rove" is traditionally played in DDAD tuning, with the first and fourth strings dropped down. As much as she loved that song, she didn't play it often, since re-tuning can make strings wear out faster. If she had risked her fiddle, if she had managed to press her fingers to its fingerboard, to lift her bow, to play, she wouldn't have played a DDAD tune. This is as incontrovertible as the temperature of the void.

And yet the story is passed on among the ship's fiddlers (and I pass it on again as I write this narrative for you, Teyla, or whoever else discovers it). And yet her nickname, Windy, first appears in transcripts starting in the fifth year on board. Before that, people called her Beth, or Green.

She loved the song, I know that much. She sang it to me as a lullaby. At twelve, I taught it to myself in traditional GDAE tuning. I took pride in the adaptation, pride in the hours I spent getting it right. I played it for her on her birthday.

She pulled me to her, kissed my head. She always smelled like the lilacs in the greenhouse. She said, "Rosie, I'm so tickled that you'd do that for me, and you played it note perfectly, which is a gift to me in itself. But 'Wind Will Rove' is a DDAD tune, and it ought to be played that way. You play it in another tuning, it's a different wind that blows."

I'd never contemplated how there might be a difference between winds. I'd never felt one myself, unless you counted air pushed through vents, or the fan on a treadmill. After the birthday party, I looked up "wind" and read about breezes and gales and siroccos, about haboobs and zephyrs. Great words, words to turn over in my mouth, words that spoke to nothing in my experience.

The next time I heard the song in its proper tuning, I closed my eyes and listened for the wind.

"Windy Grove"
   Traditional. Believed to have traveled from Scotland to Cape Breton in the nineteenth century. Lost.
   "Wind Will Rove"
   Instrumental in D (alternate tuning DDAD). Harriet Barrie, Music Historian:

The fiddler Olivia Vandiver and her father, Charley Vandiver, came up with this tune in the wee hours of a session in 1974. Charley was trying to remember a traditional tune he had heard as a boy in Nova Scotia, believed to be "Windy Grove." No recordings of the original "Windy Grove" were ever catalogued, on ship or on Earth.

"Wind Will Rove" is treated as traditional in most circles, even though it's relatively recent, because it is the lost tune's closest known relative.

The Four Deck Rec has the best acoustics of any room on the ship. There's a nearly identical space on every deck, but the others don't sound as good. The Recs were designed for gatherings, but no acoustic engineer was ever consulted, and there's nobody on board with that specialty now. The fact that one room might sound good and another less so wasn't important in the grander scheme. It should have been.

In the practical, the day to day, it matters. It matters to us. Choirs perform there, and bands. It serves on various days and nights as home to a Unitarian church, a Capoeira hoda, a Reconstructionist synagogue, a mosque, a Quaker meetinghouse, a half dozen different African dance groups, and a Shakespearean theater, everyone clinging on to whatever they hope to save. The room is scheduled for weeks and months and years to come, though weeks and months and years are all arbitrary designations this far from Earth.

On Thursday nights, Four Deck Rec hosts the OldTime, thanks to my grandmother's early pressure on the Recreation Committee. There are only a few of us on board who know what OldTime refers to, since everything is old time, strictly speaking. Everyone else has accepted a new meaning, since they have never known any other. An OldTime is a Thursday night, is a hall with good acoustics, is a gathering of fiddlers and guitarists and mandolinists and banjo players. It has a verb form now. "Are you OldTiming this week?" If you are a person who would ask that question, or a person expected to respond, the answer is yes. You wouldn't miss it.

On this particular Thursday night, while I wouldn't miss it, my tenth graders had me running late. We'd been discussing the twentieth and twenty-first century space races and the conversation had veered into dangerous territory. I'd spent half an hour trying to explain to them why Earth history still mattered. This had happened at least once a cycle with every class I'd ever taught, but these particular students were as fired up as any I remembered.

"I'm never going to go there, right, Ms. Clay?" Nelson Odell had asked. This class had only been with me for two weeks, but I'd known Nelson his entire life. His great-grandmother, my friend Harriet, had dragged him to the OldTime until he was old enough to refuse. He'd played mandolin, his stubby fingers well fit to the tiny neck, face set in a permanently resentful expression.

"No," I said. "This is a one way trip. You know that."

"And really I'm just going to grow up and die on this ship, right? And all of us? You too? Die, not grow up. You're already old."

I had heard this from enough students. I didn't even wince anymore. "Yes to all of the above, though it's a reductive line of thinking and that last bit was rude."

"Then what does it matter that back on Earth a bunch of people wanted what another group had? Wouldn't it be better not to teach us how people did those things and get bad ideas in our heads?"

Emily Redhorse, beside Nelson, said, "They make us learn it all so we can understand why we got on the ship." She was the only current OldTime player in this class, a promising fiddler. OldTime players usually understood the value of history from a young age.

Nelson waved her off. " 'We' didn't get on the ship. Our grandparents and great-grandparents did. And here we are learning things that were old to them."

"Because, stupid." That was Trina Nguyen.

I interrupted. "Debate is fine, Trina. Name-calling is not."

"Because, Nelson." She tried again. "There aren't new things in history. That's why it's called history."

Nelson folded his arms and stared straight at me. "Then don't teach it at all. If it mattered so much, why did they leave it behind? Give us another hour to learn more genetics or ship maintenance or farming. Things we can actually use."

"First of all, history isn't static. People discovered artifacts and primary documents all the time that changed their views on who we were. It's true that the moment we left Earth we gave up the chance to learn anything new about it from newly discovered primary sources, but we can still find fresh perspectives on the old information." I tried to regain control, hoping that none of them countered with the Blackout. Students of this generation rarely did; to them it was just an incident in Shipboard History, not the living specter it had been when I was their age.

I continued. "Secondly, Emily is right. It's important to know why and how we got here. The conventional wisdom remains that those who don't know history are doomed to repeat it."

"How are we supposed to repeat it?" Nelson waved at the pictures on the walls. "We don't have countries or oil or water. Or guns or swords or bombs. If teachers hadn't told us about them we wouldn't even know they existed. We'd be better off not knowing that my ancestors tried to kill Emily's ancestors, wouldn't we? Somebody even tried to erase all of that entirely, and you made sure it was still included in the new version of history."

"Not me, Nelson. That was before my time." I knew I shouldn't let them get a rise out of me, but I was tired and hungry, not the ideal way to start a seven hour music marathon. "Enough. I get what you're saying, but not learning this is not an option. Send me a thousand words by Tuesday on an example of history repeating itself."

Before anyone protested, I added, "You were going to have an essay to write either way. All I've done is changed the topic. It doesn't sound like you wanted to write about space races."

They all grumbled as they plugged themselves back into their games and music and shuffled out the door. I watched them go, wishing I'd handled the moment differently, but not yet sure how. It fascinated me that Nelson was the one fomenting this small rebellion, when his great-grandmother ran the OldTime Memory Project. My grandmother was the reason I obsessed over history, why I'd chosen teaching; Harriet didn't seem to have had the same effect on Nelson.

As Nelson passed my desk, he muttered, "Maybe somebody needs to erase it all again."

"Stop," I told him.

He turned back to face me. I still had several inches on him, but he held himself as if he were taller. The rest of the students flowed out around him. Trina rammed her wheelchair into Nelson's leg as she passed, in a move that looked 100 percent deliberate. She didn't even pretend to apologize.

"I don't mind argument in my classroom, but don't ever let anyone hear you advocating another Blackout."

He didn't look impressed. "I'm not advocating. I just think teaching us Earth history—especially broken history—is a waste of everybody's time."

"Maybe someday you'll get on the Education Committee, and you can argue for that change. But I heard you say 'erase it all again.' That isn't the same thing. Would you say that in front of Harriet?"

"Maybe I was just exaggerating. It's not even possible to erase everything anymore. And there's plenty of stuff I like that I wouldn't want to see erased." He shrugged. "I didn't mean it. Can I go now?"

He left without waiting for me to dismiss him.

I looked at the walls I'd carefully curated for this class. Tenth grade had always been the year we taught our journey's political and scientific anteced-ents. It was one of the easier courses for the Education Committee to recreate accurately after the Blackout, since some of it had still been in living memory at the time, and one of the easier classrooms to decorate for the same rea-son. I'd enlarged images of our ship's construction from my grandmother's personal collection, alongside reproductions of news headlines. Around the top of the room, a static quote from United Nations Secretary-General Confidence Swaray: "We have two missions now: to better the Earth and to better ourselves."

Normally I'd wipe my classroom walls to neutral for the continuing edu-cation group that met there in the evening, but this time I left the wall displays on when I turned off the lights to leave. Maybe we'd all failed these children already if they thought the past was irrelevant.

The digital art on the street outside my classroom had changed during the day. I traced my fingertips along the wall to get the info: a reimagin-ing of a memory of a photo of an Abdoulaye Konaté mural, sponsored by the Malian Memory Project. According to the description, the original had been a European transit station mosaic, though they no longer knew which city or country had commissioned it. Fish swam across a faux-tiled sea. Three odd blue figures stood tall at the far end, bird-like humanoids. The colors were soothing to me, but the figures less so. How like the original was it? No way to tell. Another reinvention to keep some version of our past present in our lives.

I headed back to my quarters for my instrument and a quick dinner. There was always food at the OldTime, but I knew from experience that if I picked up my fiddle I wouldn't stop playing until my fingers begged. My fingers and my stomach often had different agendas. I needed a few minutes to cool down after that class, too. Nelson had riled me with his talk of broken his-tory. To me that had always made preserving it even more important, but I understood the point he was trying to make.

By the time I got to the Four Deck Rec, someone had already taken my usual seat. I tuned in the corner where everyone had stashed their cases, then looked around to get the lay of the room. The best fiddlers had nabbed the middle seats, with spokes of mandolin and banjo and guitar and less confi-dent fiddlers radiating out. The only proficient OldTime bass player, Doug Kelly, stood near the center, with the ship's only upright bass. A couple of his students sat behind him, ready to swap out for a tune or two if he wanted a break.

The remaining empty seats were all next to banjos. I spotted a chair beside Dana Torres from the ship's Advisory Council. She was a good administrator and an adequate banjo player—she kept time, anyway. I didn't think she'd show up if she were less than adequate; nobody wants to see leadership failing at anything.

She had taken a place two rings removed from my usual seat in the second fiddle tier. Not the innermost circle, where my grandmother had sat, with the players who call the tunes and call the stops; at fifty-five years old, I hadn't earned a spot there yet. Still, I sat just outside them and kept up with them, and it'd been a long time since I'd caught a frown from the leaders.

A tune started as I made my way to the empty chair. "Honeysuckle." A thought crossed my mind that Harriet had started "Honeysuckle" without me, one of my Memory Project tunes, to punish me for being late. A second thought crossed my mind, mostly because of the conversation with my students, that probably only three other people in the room knew or cared what honeysuckle was: Tom Mvovo, who maintained the seed bank; Liat Shuster, who worked in the greenhouse—in all our nights together, I never thought to ask her about the honeysuckle plant; Harriet Barrie, music historian, last OldTime player of the generation that had left Earth. To everyone else, it was simply the song's name. A name that meant this song, nothing more.

When I started thinking that way, all the songs took on a strange flat quality in my head. So many talked about meadows and flowers and roads and birds. The love songs maintained relevance, but the rest might as well have been written in other languages as far as most people were concerned. Or about nothing at all. Mostly, we let the fiddles do the singing.

No matter how many times we play a song, it's never the same song twice. The melody stays the same, the key, the rhythm. The notes' pattern, their cadence. Still, there are differences. The exact number of fiddles changes. Various players' positions within the group, each with their own fiddle's timbral variances. The locations of the bass, the mandolins, the guitars, the banjos, all in relation to each individual player's ears. To a listener by the snack table, or to someone seeking out a recording after the fact, the nuances change. In the minutes the song exists, it is fully its own. That's how it feels to me, anyway.

Harriet stomped her foot to indicate we'd reached the last go-round for "Honeysuckle," and we all came to an end together except one of the outer guitarists, who hadn't seen the signal and kept chugging on the last chord. He shrugged off the glares.

"Oklahoma Rooster," she shouted, to murmurs of approval. She started the tune, and the other fiddles picked up the melody. I put my bow to the strings and closed my eyes. I pictured a real farm, the way they looked in pictures, and let the song tell me how it felt to be in the place called Oklahoma. A sky as big as space, the color of chlorinated water. The sun a distant disk, bright and cold. A wood-paneled square building, with a round building beside it. A perfect carpet of green grass. Horses, large and sturdy, bleating at each other across the fields. All sung in the voice of a rooster, a bird that served as a wake-up alarm for the entire farm. Birds were the things with feathers, as the old saying went.

It was easy to let my mind wander into meadows and fields during songs I had played once a week nearly my whole life. Nelson must have gotten under my skin more than I thought: I found myself adding the weeks and months and years up. Fifty times a year, fifty years, more or less. Then the same songs again alone for practice, or in smaller groups on other nights.

The OldTime broke up at 0300, as it usually did. I rolled my head from side to side, cracking my neck. The music always carried me through the night, but the second it stopped, I started noticing the cramp of my fingers, the unevenness of my shoulders.

"What does 'Oklahoma Rooster' mean to you?" I asked Dana Torres as she shook out her knees.

"Sorry?"

"What do you think of when you play 'Oklahoma Rooster'?"

Torres laughed. "I think C-C-G-C-C-C-G-C. Anything else and I fall behind the beat. Why, what do you think of?"

A bird, a farm, a meadow. "I don't know. Sorry. Weird question."

We packed our instruments and stepped into the street, dimmed to simulate night.

Back at my quarters, I knew I should sleep, but instead I sat at the table and called up the history database. "Wind Will Rove."

Options appeared: "Play," cross-referenced to the song database, with choices from several OldTime recordings we'd made over the years. "Sheet music," painstakingly generated by my grandmother and her friends, tabbed for all of the appropriate instruments. "History." I tapped the last icon and left it to play as I heated up water for soporific tea. I'd watched it hundreds of times.

A video would play on the table. A stern looking white woman in her thirties, black hair pulled back in a tight ponytail, bangs flat-cut across her forehead. She'd been so young then, the stress of the situation making her look older than her years.

"Harriet Barrie, Music Historian," the first subtitle would say, then Harriet would appear and begin, *"The fiddler Olivia Vandiver and her father, Charley Vandiver came up with this tune in the wee hours of a session in 1974 . . . ."* Except when I returned, the table had gone blank. I went back to the main menu, but this time no options came up when I selected "Wind Will Rove." I tried again, and this time the song didn't exist.

I stared at the place where it should have been, between "Winder's Slide" and "Wolf Creek." Panic stirred deep in my gut, a panic handed down to me. Maybe I was tired and imagining things. It had been there a moment ago. It had always been there, my whole life. The new databases had backups of backups of backups, even if the recordings we called originals merely recreated what had been lost long ago. Glitches happened. It would be fixed in the morning.

Just in case, I dashed off a quick message to Tech. I drank my tea and went to bed, but I didn't sleep well.

"Wind Will Rove"

Historical reenactment. Windy Green as Olivia Vandiver, Fiddler:

"We were in our ninth hour playing. It had been a really energetic session, and we were all starting to fade. Chatting more between songs so we could rest our fingers. I can't remember how the subject came up, but my father brought up a tune called "Windy Grove." Nobody else had ever heard of it, and he called us all ignorant Americans.

He launched into an A part that sounded something like "Spirits of the Morning," but with a clever little lift where "Spirits" descends. My father did things with a fiddle the rest of us could never match, but we all followed as best we were able. The B part wasn't anything like "Spirits," and we all caught that pretty fast, but the next time the A part came round it was different again, so we all shut up and let him play. The third time through sounded pretty much like the second, so we figured he had remembered the tune, and we jumped in again. It went the same the fourth and fifth times through.

It wasn't until we got up the next day that he admitted he had never quite remembered the tune he was trying to remember, which meant the thing we had played the night before was of his own creation. We cleaned it up, called it 'Wind Will Rove,' and recorded it for the third Vandiver Family LP."

My grandmother was an astronaut. We are not astronauts. It's a term that's not useful in our vocabulary. Do the people back on Earth still use that word? Do they mention us at all? Are they still there?

When our families left they were called Journeyers. Ten thousand Journeyers off on the Incredible Journey, with the help of a genetic bank, a seed bank, an advisory council. A ship thirty years in the making, held together by a crew of trained professionals: astronauts and engineers and biologists and doctors and the like. Depending on which news outlet you followed, the Journeyers were a cult or a social experiment or pioneers. Those aren't terms we use for ourselves, since we have no need to call ourselves anything in reference to any other group. When we do differentiate, it's to refer to the Before. I don't know if that makes us the During or the After.

My mother's parents met in Texas, in the Before, while she was still in training. My grandfather liked being married to an astronaut when the trips were finite, but he refused to sign up for the Journey. He stayed behind on Earth with two other children, my aunt and uncle, both older than my mother. I imagine those family members sometimes. All those people I have no stories for. Generations of them.

It's theoretically possible that scientists on Earth have built faster ships by now. It's theoretically possible they've developed faster travel while we've been busy traveling. It's theoretically possible they've built a better ship, that they've peopled it and sent it sailing past us, that they've figured out how to freeze and revive people, that those who stepped into the ship will be the ones who step out. That we will be greeted when we reach our destination by our own ancestors. I won't be there, but my great-great-great-great-great-great-grandchildren might be. I wonder what stories they'll tell each other.

This story is verifiable history. It begins, "There once was a man named Morne Brooks." It's used to scare children into doing their homework and paying attention in class. Nobody wants to be a cautionary tale.

There once was a man named Morne Brooks. In the fourth year on board, while performing a computer upgrade, he accidentally created a backdoor to the ship databases. Six years after that, an angry young programmer named Trevor Dube released a virus that ate several databases in their entirety. Destroyed the backups too. He didn't touch the "important" systems—navigation, life support, medical, seed and gene banks—but he caused catastrophic damage to the libraries. Music gone. Literature, film, games, art, history: gone, gone, gone, gone. Virtual reality simulation banks, gone, along with the games and the trainings and the immersive recreations of places on Earth. He killed external communications too. We were alone, years earlier than we expected to be. Severed.

For some reason, it's Brooks' name attached to the disaster. Dube was locked up, but Brooks still walked around out in the community for people to point at and shame. Our slang term "brooked" came from his name. He spent years afterward listening to people say they had brooked exams and brooked relationships. I suppose it didn't help that he had such a good name to lend. Old English, Dutch, German. A hard word for a lively stream of water. We have no use for it as a noun now; no brooks here. His shipmates still remembered brooks, though they'd never see one again. There was a verb form already, unrelated, but it had fallen from use. His contemporaries verbed him afresh.

It didn't matter that for sixteen years afterward he worked on the team that shored up protection against future damage, or that he eventually committed suicide. Nobody wanted to talk about Dube or his motivations; all people ever mentioned was the moment the screens went dark, and Brooks' part in the whole disaster when they traced it backward.

In fairness, I can't imagine their panic. They were still the original Journeyers, the original crew, the original Advisory Council, save one or two changes. They were the ones who had made sure we had comprehensive databases, so we wouldn't lose our history, and so they wouldn't be without their favorite entertainments. The movies and serials and songs reminded them of homes they had left behind.

The media databases meant more to that first generation than I could possibly imagine. They came from all over the Earth, from disparate cultures; for some from smaller sub-groups, the databases were all that connected them with their people. It's no wonder they reacted the way they did.

I do sometimes wonder what would be different now if things hadn't gone wrong so early in the journey. Would we have naturally moved beyond the art we carried, instead of clinging to it as we do now? All we can do is live it out, but I do wonder.

I don't teach on Fridays. I can't bounce back from seven hours of fiddling, or from the near-all-nighter, the way I did at twenty or thirty or forty. Usually I sleep through Friday mornings. This time, I woke at ten, suddenly and completely, with the feeling something was missing. I glanced at the corner by the door to make sure I hadn't left my fiddle at the Rec.

I showered, then logged on to the school server to see if any students had turned in early assignments—they hadn't—then checked the notice system for anything that might affect my plans for the day. It highlighted a couple of streets I could easily avoid, and warned that the New Shakespeare and

Chinese Cultural DBs were down for maintenance. Those alerts reminded me about the database crash the night before. My stomach lurched again as I called up "Wind Will Rove," but it was there when I looked for it, right where it belonged.

The door chimed. Fridays I had lunch with Harriet. We called it lunch, even though we'd both be eating our first meal of the day. She didn't get up early after the OldTime either. Usually I cut it pretty close, rolling out of bed and putting on clothes, knowing she'd done the same. I glanced around the room to make sure it was presentable. I'd piled some dirty clothes on the bed, but they were pretty well hidden behind the privacy screen. Good enough.

"You broke the deal, Rosie," she said, eyeing my hair as I opened my door. "You showered."

"I couldn't sleep."

She shrugged and slid into the chair I'd just been sitting in. She had a skullcap pulled over her own hair, dyed jet black. Harriet had thirty years on me, though she still looked wiry and spry. It had taken me decades to stop considering her my grandmother's friend and realize she'd become mine as well. Now we occupied a place somewhere between mentorship and friendship. History teacher and music historian. Fiddle player and master fiddler.

I handed her a mug of mint tea and a bowl of congee, and a spoon. My dishware had been my grandmother's, from Earth. Harriet always smiled when I handed her the chipped "Cape Breton Fiddlers Association" mug.

She held the cup up to her face for a moment, breathing in the minty steam. "Now tell me why you walked in late last night. I missed you in the second row. Kem Porter took your usual seat, and I had to listen to his sloppy bow technique all night."

"Kem's not so bad. He knows the tunes."

"He knows the tunes, but he's not ready for the second row. He was brooking rhythms all over the place. You should have called him out on it."

"I wouldn't!"

She cradled the mug in her hands and breathed in again. Liat and I hadn't been a couple for years, but she still brought me real mint from the greenhouse, and I knew Harriet appreciated it. "I know. You're too nice. There's no shame in letting someone know his place. Next time I'll do it."

She would, too. She had taken over the OldTime enforcer job from my grandmother and lived up to her example. They'd both sent me back to the outer circles more than once before I graduated inward.

"I'll tell you when you're ready, Rosie," my grandmother said. "You'll get there."

"You know Windy would have done it," Harriet said, echoing my thoughts.

The nickname jogged my memory again. " 'Wind Will Rove'!" I said. "Something was wrong with the database last night. The song was missing."

She pushed the cups to the side and tapped the table awake.

"Down for maintenance," she read out loud, frowning. She looked up. "I don't like that. I'll go over to Tech myself and ask."

She stood and left without saying goodbye.

Harriet had a way of saying things so definitively you couldn't help agreeing. If she said you didn't belong in the second row, you weren't ready yet. If she said not to worry over the song issue, I would have been willing to believe her, even though it made me uneasy. Hopefully it was nothing, but her reaction was appropriate for anyone who'd lived through the Blackout. I hadn't even gotten around to answering her first question, but I wasn't really sure what I would have told her about Nelson in any case.

I went to pick up my grandchildren from daycare, as I always did on Friday afternoons, Natalie's long day at the hospital. If anything could keep me out of my head, it was the mind-wiping exhaustion of chasing toddlers.

"Goats?" asked Teyla. She had just turned two, her brother Jonah four.

"Goats okay with you, too, buddy?" I asked Jonah.

He shrugged stoically. He didn't really care for animals. Preferred games, but we'd played games the week before.

"Goats it is."

The farm spread across the bottom deck, near the waste processing plant. We took two tubes to get there, Jonah turning on all the screens we passed, Teyla playing with my hair.

I always enjoyed stepping from the tube and into the farm's relatively open spaces, as big as eight rec rooms combined. The air out here, pungent and rich, worked off a different circulator than on the living decks. It moved with slightly more force than on the rest of the ship, though still not a wind. Not even a breeze. The artificial sun wasn't any different than on the other decks, but it felt more intense. The textures felt different too, softer, plants and fur, fewer touch screens. If I squinted I could imagine a real farm, ahead or behind us, on a real planet. Everything on every other deck had been designed to keep us healthy and sane; I always found it interesting to spend time in a place dedicated to keeping other animals alive.

The goats had been a contentious issue for the planners in my grandmother's generation. Their detractors called them a waste of food and space and resources. Windy was among those who argued for them. They could supplement the synthetic milk and meat supplies. They'd provide veterinary

training and animal husbandry skills that would be needed planetside someday, not to mention a living failsafe in case something happened to the gene
banks. It would be good to have them aboard for psychological reasons as
well, when people were leaving behind house pets like cats and dogs.

She won the debate, as she so often did, and they added a small population of female African Pygmy goats to the calculations. Even then there were
dissenters. The arguments continued until the Blackout, then died abruptly
along with the idea the journey might go as planned.

She told me all of that three weeks after my mother left, when I was still
taking it personally.

"Have you ever tried to catch a goat?" she asked.

I hadn't. I'd seen them, of course, but visitors were only supposed to pet
them. She got permission, and I spent twenty minutes trying to catch an
animal that had zero interest in being caught. It was the first thing that made
me laugh again. I always thought of that day when I brought my grandchildren to pet the goats, though I hoped I never had any reason to use the same
technique on them.

I had wrapped up some scraps for Jonah and Teyla to feed the nippy little
things. Once they'd finished the food, the goats started on Teyla's jersey, to
her mixed delight and horror. I kept an eye on goat teeth and toddler fingers
to make sure everybody left with the proper number.

"Ms. Clay," somebody said, and I glanced up to see who had called me,
then back at the babies and the fingers and the goats. They looked vaguely
familiar, but everyone did after a while. If I had taught them, I still might
not recognize a face with twenty more years on it, if they didn't spend time
on the same decks I did.

"Ms. Clay, I'm Nelson's parent. Other parent. Lee. I think you know Ash."
Ash was Harriet's grandkid. They'd refused to play music at all, to Harriet's
endless frustration.

Lee didn't look anything like Nelson, but then I recalled Harriet saying
they had gone full gene-bank. The incentives to include gene variance in
family planning were too good for many people to pass up.

"Nice to meet you," I said.

"I'm sorry if he's been giving you any trouble," Lee said. "He's going
through some kind of phase."

"Phase?" Sometimes feigning ignorance got more interesting answers than
agreeing.

"He's decided school is teaching the wrong things. Says there's no point
in learning anything that doesn't directly apply to what will be needed

planetside. That it puts old ideas into people's heads, when they should be learning new things. I have no idea where he came up with it."

I nodded. "Do you work down here?"

Lee gestured down at manure-stained coveralls. "He likes it here, though. Farming fits in his worldview."

"But history doesn't?"

"History, classic literature, anything you can't directly apply. I know he's probably causing trouble, but he's a good kid. He'll settle down once he figures out a place for himself in all this."

Teyla was offering a mystery fistful of something to a tiny black goat. Jonah looked like he was trying to figure out if he could ride one; I put a hand on his shoulder to hold him back.

"Tell me about the Blackout," I say at the start of the video I made while still in school. Eighteen-year-old me, already a historian. My voice is much younger. I'm not on screen, but I can picture myself at eighteen. Tall, gawky, darker than my mother, lighter than my father.

"I don't think there was anybody who didn't panic," my grandmother begins. Her purple hair is pulled back in a messy bun, and she is sitting in her own quarters—mine now—with her Cape Breton photos on the walls.

"Once we understood that the glitch hadn't affected navigation or the systems we rely on to breathe and eat, once it became clear the culprit was a known virus and the damage was irreparable, well, we just had to deal with it."

"The 'culprit' was a person, not a virus, right?"

"A virus who released a virus." Her face twisted at the thought.

I moved back to safer ground. "Did everyone just 'deal with it'? That isn't what I've heard."

"There are a lot of people to include in 'everyone.' The younger children handled it fine. They bounced and skated and ran around the rec rooms. The older ones—the ones who relied on external entertainments—had more trouble and got in more trouble, I guess." She gave a sly smile. "But ask your father how he lost his pinkie finger if you've never done so."

"That was when he did it?"

"You bet. Eighteen years old and some daredevil notion to hitch a ride on the top of a lift. Lucky he survived."

"He told me a goat bit it off!"

She snorted. "I'm guessing he told you that back when you said you wanted to be a goat farmer when you grew up?"

No answer from younger-me.

She shrugged. "Or maybe he didn't want to give you any foolish ideas about lift-cowboys."

"He's not a daredevil, though."

"Not anymore. Not after that. Not after you came along the next year. Anyway, you asked who 'just dealt with it,' and you're right. The kids coped because they had nothing to compare it to, but obviously the main thing you want to know about is the adults. The Memory Projects."

"Yes. That's the assignment."

"Right. So. Here you had all these people: born on Earth, raised on Earth. They applied to be Journeyers because they had some romantic notion of setting out for a better place. And those first years, you can't even imagine what it was like, the combination of excitement and terror. Any time anything went wrong: a replicator brooked, a fan lost power, anything at all, someone started shouting we had set our families up for Certain Death." She says "certain death" dramatically, wiggling her fingers at me. "Then Crew or Logistics or Tech showed them their problem had an easy fix, and they'd calm down. It didn't matter how many times we told them we had things under control. Time was the only reassurance.

"By ten years in, we had finally gotten the general populace to relax. Everyone had their part to do, and everyone was finally doing it quietly. We weren't going to die if a hot water line went cold one day. There were things to worry over, of course, but they were all too big to be worth contemplating. Same as now, you understand? And we had this database, this marvelous database of everything good humans had ever created, music and literature and art from all around the world, in a hundred languages.

"And then Trevor Dube had to go and ruin everything. I know you know that part so I won't bother repeating it. Morne Brooks did what he did, and that Dube fellow did what he did, and all of a sudden all of these Journeyers, with their dream of their children's children's children's etcetera someday setting foot on a new planet, they all have to deal with their actual children. They have to contemplate the idea the generations after them will never get to see or hear the things they thought were important. That all they have left is the bare walls. They wait—we wait—and wait for the DB to be restored. And they realize: hey, I can't rely on this database to be here to teach those great-great-great-grandchildren."

She leans forward. "So everyone doubles down on the things that matter most to them. That's when some folks who didn't have it got religion again. The few physical books on board became sacred primary texts, including the ones that had been sacred texts to begin with. Every small bit of personal

media got cloned for the greater good, from photos to porn—don't giggle—
but it wasn't much, not compared to what we'd lost.

"Cultural organizations that had been atrophying suddenly found themselves with more members than they'd had since the journey started. Actors
staged any show they knew well enough, made new recordings. People tried
to rewrite their favorite books and plays from memory, paint their favorite
paintings. Everyone had a different piece, some closer to accurate than others.
That's when we started getting together to play weekly instead of monthly."

"I thought it was always weekly, Gra."

"Nope. We didn't have other entertainments to distract us, and we were
worried about the stories behind the songs getting lost. The organized
Memory Projects started with us. It seemed like the best way to make sure
what we wanted handed down would be handed down. The others saw that
we'd found a good way to approach the problem and keep people busy, so
other Memory Projects sprung up too. We went through our whole repertoire and picked out the forty songs we most wanted saved. Each of us
committed to memorizing as many as we could, but with responsibility for
a few in particular. We knew the songs themselves already, but now people
pooled what they knew about them, and we memorized their histories, too.
Where they came from, what they meant. And later, we were responsible for
rerecording those histories, and teaching them to somebody younger, so each
song got passed down to another generation. That's you, incidentally."

"I know."

"Just checking. You're asking me some pretty obvious stuff." "It's for a
project. I need to ask."

"Fine, then. Anyhow, we re-recorded all our songs and histories as quick as
possible, then memorized them in case somebody tried to kill the DBs again.
And other people memorized the things important to them. History of
their people—the stuff that didn't make it into history books—folk dances,
formulae. Actors built plays back from scratch, though some parts weren't
exactly as they'd been. And those poor jazz musicians."

"Those poor jazz musicians? I thought jazz was about improv."

"It's full of improv, but certain performances stood out as benchmarks for
their whole mode. I'm glad we play a music that doesn't set much stock in
solo virtuosity. We recorded our fiddle tunes all over again, and the songs are
still the songs, but nobody on board could play 'So What' like Miles Davis
or anything like John Coltrane. Their compositions live on, but not their
performances, if that makes sense. Would have devastated your grandfather,
if he'd been on board. Anyway, what was I saying? The human backup idea

had legs, even if it worked better for some things than others. It was a worst case scenario."

"Which two songs did you memorize history for?"

"Unofficially, all of them. Officially, same as you. 'Honeysuckle' and 'Wind Will Rove.' You know that."

"I know, Gra. For the assignment."

"Windy Grove"

Historical Reenactment: Marius Smit as Howie McCabe, Cape Breton Fiddlemaker:

Vandiver wasn't wrong. There was a tune called "Windy Grove." My great-grand-father played it, but it was too complicated for most fiddlers. I can only remember a little of the tune now. It had lyrics, too, in Gaelic and English. I don't think Vandiver ever mentioned those. There was probably a Gaelic name too, but that's lost along with the song.

My great-grandfather grew up going to real milling frolics, before machines did the wool-shrinking and frolics just became social events. The few songs I know in Gaelic I know because they have that milling frolic rhythm; it drives them into your brain. "Windy Grove" wasn't one of those. As far as I know it was always a fiddle tune, but not a common one because of its difficulty.

All I know is the A part in English, and I'm pretty sure I wouldn't get the melody right now, so I'm going to sing it to the melody of "Wind Will Rove":

We went down to the windy grove
Never did know where the wind did go
Never too sure when the wind comes back
If it's the same wind that we knew last.

Nelson's essay arrived promptly on Monday. It began "Many examples of history repeating itself can be seen in our coursework. There are rulers who didn't learn from other ruler's mistakes."

I corrected the apostrophe and kept reading. "You know who they are because you taught us about them. Why do you need me to say them back to you? Instead I'm going to write about history repeating itself in a different way. Look around you, Ms. Clay.

"I'm on this ship because my great-grandparents decided they wanted to spend the rest of their lives on a ship. They thought they were being unselfish. They thought they were making a sacrifice so someday their children's children's children to the bazillionth or whatever would get to be pioneers on a planet that people hadn't started killing yet, and they were pretty sure wouldn't kill them, and where they're hoping there's no intelligent life. They made a decision that locked us into doing exactly what they did.

"So here we are. My parents were born on this ship. I was born here. My chromosomes come from the gene bank, from two people who died decades before I was born.

"What can we do except repeat history? What can I do that nobody here has ever done before? In two years I'll choose a specialty. I can work with goats, like my parents. I could be an engineer or a doctor or a dentist or a horticulturist, who are all focused on keeping us alive in one way or another. I can be a history teacher like you, but obviously I won't. I can be a theoretical farmer or a theoretical something else, where I learn things that will never be useful here, in order to pass them on to my kids and my kid's kids, so they can pass them on and someday somebody can use them, if there's really a place we're going and we're really going to get there someday.

"But I'm never going to stand on a real mountain, and I can't be a king or a prime minister or a genocidal tyrant like you teach us about. I can't be Lord Nelson, an old white man with a giant hat, and you might think I was named after him but I was named after a goat who was named after a horse some old farmer had on Earth who was named after somebody in a book or a band or an entertainment who might have been Lord Nelson or Nelson Mandela or some other Nelson entirely who you can't teach me about because we don't remember them anymore.

"The old history can't repeat, and I'm in the next generation of people who make no impact on anything whatsoever. We aren't making history. We're in the middle of the ocean and the shore is really far away. When we climb out the journey should have changed us, but you want us to take all the baggage with us, so we're exactly the same as when we left. But we can't be, and we shouldn't be."

I turned off the screen and closed my eyes. I could fail him for not writing the assignment as I had intended it, but he clearly understood.

"Wendigo"
   Traditional. Lost.
   Harriet Barrie:
   Another tune we have the name of but not much else. I'm personally of the belief "Wendigo" and "Windy Grove" are the same song. Some Cape Bretonians took it with them when they moved to the Algonquins. Taught it to some local musicians who misheard the title and conflated it with local monster lore. There's a tune called "When I Go" that started making the rounds in Ontario

not long after, though nobody ever showed an interest in it outside of Ontario and Finland.

If we were only to play songs about things we knew, we would lose a lot of our playlist. No wind. No trees. No battles, no seas, no creeks, no mountain-tops. We'd sing of travelers, but not journeys. We'd sing of middles, but not beginnings or ends. We would play songs of waiting and longing. We'd play love songs.

Why not songs about stars, you might ask? Why not songs about darkness and space? The traditionalists wouldn't play them. I'm not sure who'd write them, either. People on Earth wrote about blue skies because they'd stood under grey ones. They wrote about night because there was such a thing as day. Songs about prison are poignant because the character knew something else beforehand and dreamed of other things ahead. Past and future are both abstractions now.

When my daughter Natalie was in her teens, she played fiddle in a band that would be classified in the new DB as "other/undefined" if they had uploaded anything. Part of their concept was that they wouldn't record their music, and they requested that nobody else record it either. A person would have to be there to experience it. I guess it made sense for her to fall into something like that after listening to me and Gra and Harriet.

I borrowed back the student fiddle she and I had both played as children. She told me she didn't want me going to hear them play.

"You'll just tell me it sounds like noise or my positions are sloppy," she said. "Or worse yet, you'll say we sound exactly like this band from 2030 and our lyrics are in the tradition of blah blah blah, and I'll end up thinking we stole everything from a musician I'd never even heard before. We want to do something new."

"I'd never," I said, even though a knot had formed in my stomach. Avoided commenting when I heard her practicing. Bit my tongue when Harriet com-plained musicians shouldn't be wasting their time on new music when they ought to be working on preserving what we already had.

I did go to check them out once, when they played the Seven Dec Rec. I stood in the back, in the dark. To me it sounded like shouting down an ele-vator shaft, all ghosts and echoes. The songs had names like "Because I Said So" and "Terrorform"; they shouted the titles in between pieces, but the PA was distorting and even those I might have misheard.

I counted fifteen young musicians in the band, from different factions all over the ship: children of jazz, of rock, of classical music, of zouk, of Chinese opera, of the West African drumming group. It didn't sound anything like anything I'd ever heard before. I still couldn't figure out whether they were synthesizing the traditions they'd grown up in or rejecting them entirely.

My ears didn't know what to pay attention to, so I focused on Nat. She still had decent technique from her childhood lessons, but she used it in ways I didn't know how to listen to. She played rhythm rather than lead, a pad beneath the melody, a staccato polyrhythm formed with fiddle and drum.

I almost missed when she lit into "Wind Will Rove." I'd never even have recognized it if I had been listening to the whole instead of focusing on Nat's part. Hers was a countermelody to something else entirely, the rhythm swung but the key unchanged. Harriet would have hated it, but I thought it had a quiet power, hidden as it was beneath the bigger piece.

I never told Nat I'd gone to hear her that night, because I didn't want to admit I'd listened.

I've researched punk and folk and hip-hop's births, and the protest movements that went hand in hand with protest music. Music born of people trying to change the status quo. What could my daughter and her friends change? What did people want changed? The ship sails on. They played together for a year before calling it quits. She gave her fiddle away again and threw herself into studying medicine. As they'd pledged, nobody ever uploaded their music, so there's no evidence it ever existed outside this narrative.

My grandmother smuggled the upright bass on board. It's Doug Kelly's now, but it came onto the ship under my grandmother's "miscellaneous supplies" professional allowance. That's how it's listed in the original manifest: "Miscellaneous Supplies—1 Extra-Large Crate—200 cm x 70 cm x 70 cm." When I was studying the manifest for a project, trying to figure out who had brought what, I asked her why the listed weight was so much more than the instrument's weight.

"Strings," she said. "It was padded with clothes and then the box was filled with string packets. For the bass, for the fiddles. Every cranny of every box I brought on board was filled with strings and hair and rosin. I didn't trust replicators."

The bass belonged at the time to Jonna Rich. In my grandmother's photo of the original OldTime players on the ship, Jonna's dwarfed by her instrument. It's only a 3/4 size, but it still looms over her. I never met her. My grandmother said, "You've never seen such a tiny woman with such big, quick hands."

When her arthritis got too bad to play, Jonna passed it to Marius Smit, "twice her size, but half the player she was." Then Jim Riggins, then Alison Smit, then Doug Kelly, with assorted second and third stand-ins along the way. Those were the OldTime players. The bass did double duty in some jazz ensembles, as well as the orchestra.

Personal weight and space allowances didn't present any problems for those who played most instruments. The teams handling logistics and psychological welfare sparred and negotiated and compromised and re-compromised. They made space for four communal drum kits (two each: jazz trap and rock five-piece), twenty-two assorted amplifiers for rock and jazz, bass and guitar and keyboard. We have two each of three different Chinese zithers, and one hundred and three African drums of thirty-two different types, from djembe to carimbo. There's a PA in every Rec, but only a single tuba. The music psychologist consulted by the committee didn't understand why an electric bass wasn't a reasonable compromise for the sake of space. Hence my grandmother's smuggling job.

How did a committee on Earth ever think they could guess what we'd need fifty or eighty or one hundred and eighty years into the voyage? They set us up with state of the art replicators, with our beautiful, doomed data-bases, with programs and simulators to teach skills we would need down the line. Still, there's no model that accurately predicts the future. They had no way of prognosticating the brooked database or the resultant changes. They'd have known, if they'd included an actual musician on the committee, that we needed an upright bass. I love how I'm still surrounded by the physical manifestations of my grandmother's influence on the ship: the upright bass, the pygmy goats. Her fiddle, my fiddle now.

I arrived in my classroom on Thursday to discover somebody had hacked my walls. Scrawled over my photo screens: "Collective memory =/= truth," "History is fiction," "The past is a lie." A local overlay, not an overwrite. Nothing invasive of my personal files or permanent. Easy to erase, easy to figure out who had done it. I left it up.

As my students walked in, I watched their faces. Some were completely oblivious, wrapped up in whatever they were listening to, slouching into their seats without even looking up. A few snickered or exchanged wide-eyed glances.

Nelson arrived with a smirk on his face, a challenge directed at me. He didn't even look at the walls. It took him a moment to notice I hadn't cleaned up after him; when he did notice, the smirk was replaced with confusion.

"You're wondering why I didn't wipe this off my walls before you arrived?"

The students who hadn't been paying attention looked around for the first time. "Whoa," somebody said.

"The first answer is that it's easier to report if I leave it up. Vandalism and hacking are both illegal, and I don't think it would be hard to figure out who did this, but since there's no permanent damage, I thought we might use this as a learning experience." Everyone looked at Nelson, whose ears had turned red.

I continued. "I think what somebody is trying to ask is, let's see, 'Ms. Clay, how do we know that the history we're learning is true? Why does it matter?' And I think they expect me to answer, 'because I said so,' or something like that. But the real truth is, our history is a total mess. It's built on memories of facts, and memories are unreliable. Before, they could cross-reference memories and artifacts to a point where you could say with some reliability that certain things happened and certain things didn't. We've lost almost all of the proof."

"So what's left?" I pointed to the graffitied pictures. "I'm here to help figure out which things are worth remembering, which things are still worth calling fact or truth or whatever you want to call it. Maybe it isn't the most practical field of study, but it's still important. It'll matter to you someday when your children come to you to ask why we're on this journey. It'll matter when something goes wrong and we can look to the past and say 'how did we solve this when we had this problem before' instead of starting from scratch. It matters because of all the people who asked 'why' and 'how' and 'what if' instead of allowing themselves to be absorbed in their own problems—they thought of us, so why shouldn't we think of them?

"Today we're going to talk about the climate changes that the Earth was experiencing by the time they started building this ship, and how that played into the politics. And just so you're not waiting with bated breath through the entire class, your homework for the week is to interview somebody who still remembers Earth. Ask them why they or their parents got on board. Ask them what they remember about that time, and any follow-up questions you think make sense. For bonus points upload to the oral history DB once you've sent your video to me."

I looked around to see if anyone had any questions, but they were all silent. I started the lesson I was actually supposed to be teaching.

I'd been given that same assignment at around their age. It was easier to find original Journeyers to interview back then, but I always turned to my grandmother. The video is buried in the Oral History DB, but I'd memorized the path to it long ago.

She's still in good health in this one, fit and strong, with her trademark purple hair. For all our closeness, I have no idea what her hair's original color was.

"Why did you leave?" I ask.

"I didn't really consider it leaving. Going someplace, not leaving something else behind."

"Isn't leaving something behind part of going someplace?"

"You think of it your way, I'll think of it mine."

"Is that what all the Journeyers said?"

My grandmother snorts. "Ask any two and we'll give you two different answers. You're asking me, so I'm telling you how I see it. We had the technology, and the most beautiful ship. We had—have—a destination that reports perfect conditions to sustain us."

"How did you feel about having a child who would never get to the destination?"

"I thought 'my daughter will have a life nobody has ever had before, and she'll be part of a generation that makes new rules for what it means to be a person existing with other people.' " She shrugs. "I found that exciting. I thought she'd live in the place she lived, and she'd do things she loved and things she hated, and she'd live out her life like anybody does."

She pauses, then resumes without prompting. "There were worse lives to live, back then. This seemed like the best choice for our family. No more running away; running toward something wonderful."

"Was there anything you missed about Earth?"

"A thing, like not a person? If a person counts, your grandfather and my other kids, always and forever. There was nothing else I loved that I couldn't take with me," she says, with a faraway look in her eyes.

"Nothing?" I press.

She smiles. "Nothing anybody can keep. The sea. The wind coming off the coast. I can still feel it when I'm inside a good song."

She reaches to pick up her fiddle.

There was a question I pointedly didn't ask in that video, the natural follow-up that fit in my grandmother's pause. I didn't ask because it wasn't my teacher's business how my mother fit into that generation "making new rules for what it means to be a person existing with other people," as my grandmother put it. If I haven't mentioned my mother much, it's because she and I never really understood each other.

She was eight when she came aboard. Old enough to have formative memories of soil and sky and wind. Old enough to come on board with her own small scale fiddle. Fourteen when she told my grandmother she didn't want to play music anymore.

Eighteen when the Blackout happened. Nineteen when she had me, one of a slew of Blackout Babies granted by joint action of the Advisory Council and Logistics. They would have accepted anything that kept people happy and quiet at that point, as long as the numbers bore out its sustainability.

My grandmother begged her to come back to music, to help with the OldTime portion of the Memory Project. She refused. She'd performed in a Shakespeare comedy called *Much Ado About Nothing* just before the Blackout, while she was still in school. She still knew Hero's lines by heart, and the general dramatists and Shakespeareans had both reached out to her to join their Memory Projects; they all had their hands full rebuilding plays from scratch.

The film faction recruited her as well, with their ridiculously daunting task. My favorite video from that period shows my twenty-year-old mother playing the lead in a historical drama called *Titanic*. It's a recreation of an old movie, and an even older footnote in history involving an enormous sea ship.

My mother: young, gorgeous, glowing. She wore gowns that shimmered when she moved. The first time she showed it to me, when I was five, all I noticed was how beautiful she looked.

When I was seven, I asked her if the ocean could kill me.

"There's no ocean here. We made it up, Rosie."

That made no sense. I saw it there on the screen, big enough to surround the ship, like liquid, tangible space, a space that could chase you down the street and surround you. She took me down to the soundstage on Eight Deck, where they were filming a movie called *Serena*. I know now they were still triaging, filming every important movie to the best of their recollection, eight years out from the Blackout, based on scripts rewritten from memory in those first desperate years. Those are the only versions I've ever known.

She showed me how a sea was not a sea, a sky was not a sky. I got to sit on a boat that was not a boat, and in doing so learn what a boat was.

"Why are you crying, Mama?" I asked her later that evening, wandering from my bunk to my parents' bed.

My father picked me up and squeezed me tight. "She's crying about something she lost."

"I'm not tired. Can we watch the movie again?"

We sat and watched my young mother as she met and fell in love with someone else, someone pretend. As they raced a rush of water that I had already been assured would never threaten me or my family. As the ship sank—it's not real, there's no sea, nothing sinks anymore—and the lifeboats disappeared and the two lovers were forced to huddle together on a floating door until their dawn rescue.

When I was sixteen, my mother joined a cult. Or maybe she started it; NewTime is as direct a rebuttal to my grandmother's mission as could exist. They advocated erasing the entertainment databases again, forever, in the service of the species.

"We're spending too much creative energy recreating the things we carried with us," she said. I listened from my bunk as she calmly packed her clothes.

"You're a Shakespearean! You're supposed to recreate." My father never raised his voice either. That's what I remembered most about their conversation afterward: how neither ever broke calm.

"I was a Shakespearean, but more than that, I'm an actress. I want new things to act in. Productions that speak to who we are now, not who we were on Earth. Art that tells our story."

"You have a family."

"And I love you all, but I need this."

The next morning, she kissed us both goodbye as if she was going to work, then left with the NewTime for Fourteen Deck. I didn't know what Advisory Council machinations were involved in relocating the Fourteen Deck families to make room for an unplanned community, or what accommodations had to be made for people who opted out of jobs to live a pure artistic existence. There were times in human history where that was possible, but this wasn't one of them. Those are questions I asked later. At that moment, I was furious with her.

I don't know if I ever stopped being angry, really. I never went to any of the original plays that trickled out of the NewTime; I've never explored their art or their music. I never learned what we looked like through their particular lens. It wasn't new works I opposed; it was their idea they had to separate themselves from us to create them. How could anything they wrote actually reflect our experience if they weren't in the community anymore?

They never came back down to live with the rest of us. My mother and I reconciled when I had Natalie, but she wasn't the person I remembered, and I'm pretty sure she thought the same about me. She came down to play with

Nat sometimes, but I never left them alone together, for fear the separatist idea might rub off on my kid.

The night I saw Natalie's short-lived band perform, the night I hid in the darkness all those years ago so she wouldn't get mad at me for coming, it wasn't until I recognized "Wind Will Rove" that I realized I'd been holding my breath. Theirs wasn't a NewTime rejection of everything that had gone before; it was a synthesis.

"Wind Will Roam"
Historical Reenactment: Akona Mvovo as Will E. Womack:
My aunt cleaned house for some folks over in West Hollywood, and they used to give her records to take home to me. I took it all in. Everything influenced me. The west coast rappers, but also Motown and pop and rock and these great old-timey fiddle records. I wanted to play fiddle so bad when I heard this song, but where was I going to get one? Wasn't in the cards.

The song I sampled for "Wind Will Roam"—this fiddle record "Wind Will Rove"—it changed me. There's something about the way the first part lifts that moves me every time. I've heard there's a version with lyrics out there somewhere, but I liked the instrumental, so I could make up my own words over it. I wrote the first version when I was ten years old. I thought "rove" sounded like a dog, so I called it "Wind Will Roam," about a dog named Wind. I was a literal kid.

Second version when I was fifteen, I don't really remember that one too well. I was rapping and recording online by then, so there's probably a version out there somewhere. Don't show it to me if you find it. I was trying to be badass then. I'd just as soon pretend it never existed.

I came back to "Wind Will Rove" again and again. I think I was twenty-five when I recorded this one, and my son had just been born, and I wanted to give him something really special. I still liked "Wind Will Roam" better than "Wind Will Rove," 'cause I could rhyme it with "home" and "poem" and all that.

(sings)
The wind will roam
And so will I
I've got miles to go before I die
But I'll come back
I always do
Just like the wind
I'll come to you.
We might go weeks without no rain
And every night the sun will go away again

Some winds blow warm some winds blow low
You and me've got miles and miles to go

I wanted to take something I loved and turn it into something else entirely.
Transform it.

The next OldTime started out in G. My grandmother had never much cared
for the key of G; since her death we'd played way more G sessions than
we ever had when she chose the songs. "Dixie Blossoms," then "Down the
River." "Squirrel Hunters." "Jaybird Died of the Whooping Cough." "The
Long Way Home." "Ladies on the Steamboat."

Harriet called a break in the third hour and said when we came back we
were going to do some D tunes, starting with "Midnight on the Water."
I knew the sequence she was setting up: "Midnight on the Water," then
"Bonaparte's Retreat," then "Wind Will Rove." I was pretty sure she did it
for me; I think she was glad to have me back in the second row and punctual.

Most stood up and stretched, or put their instruments down to go get a
snack. A few fiddlers, myself included, took the opportunity to cross-tune to
DDAD. These songs could all be played in standard tuning, but the low D
drone added something ineffable.

When everybody had settled back into their seats, Harriet counted us
into the delicate waltz time of "Midnight on the Water." Then "Bonaparte's
Retreat," dark and lively. And then, as I'd hoped, "Wind Will Rove."

No matter how many times you play a song, it isn't the same song twice.
I was still thinking about Nelson's graffiti, and how the past had never felt
like a lie to me at all. It was a progression. "Wind Will Rove" said we are
born anew every time a bow touches fiddle strings in an OldTime session
on a starship in this particular way. It is not the ship nor the session nor the
bow nor the fiddle that births us. Nor the hands. It's the combination of
all of those things, in a particular way they haven't been combined before.
We are an alteration on an old, old tune. We are body and body, wood
and flesh. We are bow and fiddle and hands and memory and starship and
OldTime.

"Wind Will Rove" spoke to me, and my eyes closed to feel the wind the
way my grandmother did, out on a cliff above the ocean. We cycled through
the A part, the B part three times, four times, five. And because I'd closed my
eyes, because I was in the song and not in the room, I didn't catch Harriet's
signal for the last go-round. Everyone ended together except me. Even worse,
I'd deviated. Between the bars of my unexpected solo, when my own playing

stood exposed against the silence, I realized I'd diverged from the tune. It was still "Wind Will Rove," or close to it, but I'd elided the third bar into the fourth, a swooping, soaring accident.

Harriet gave me a look I interpreted as a cross between exasperation and reprobation. I'd used a similar one on my students before, but it'd been a long time since I'd been on the receiving end.

"Sorry," I said, mostly sorry the sensation had gone, that I'd lost the wind.

I slipped out the door early, while everyone was still playing. I didn't want to talk to Harriet. Back home, I tried to recreate my mistake. I heard it in my head, but I never quite made it happen again, and after half an hour I put away my fiddle.

I'd rather have avoided Harriet the next morning, but canceling our standing date would have made things worse. I woke up early again. Debated showering to give her a different reason to be annoyed with me, then decided against it when I realized she'd stack the two grievances rather than replace one with the other.

We met in her quarters this time, up three decks from my own, slightly smaller, every surface covered with archival boxes and stacks of handwritten sheet music.

"So what happened last night?" she asked without preamble.

I held up my hands in supplication. "I didn't see you call the stop. I'm sorry. And after you told me I belonged in the closer circles and everything. It won't happen again."

"But you didn't even play it right. That's one of your tunes. You've been playing that song for fifty years! People were talking afterward. Expect some teasing next week. Nothing else happened worth gossiping about, so they're likely to remember unless somebody else does something silly."

I didn't have a good response. Missing the stop had been silly, sure, but what I had done to the tune didn't feel wrong, exactly. A different wind, as my grandmother would have said.

"Any word on what went wrong in the database the other day?" I asked to change the subject.

She furrowed her brow. "None. Tech said it's an access issue, not the DB itself. It's happening to isolated pieces. You can still access them if you enter names directly instead of going through the directories or your saved preferences, but it's a pain. They can't locate the source. I have to tell you, I'm more than a little concerned. I mean, the material is obviously still there, since I can get to some of it roundabout, but it really hampers research. And it gets me thinking we may want to consider adding another redundancy layer in the Memory Project."

She went on at length on the issue, and I let her go. I preferred her talking on any subject other than me.

When she started to flag, I interrupted. "Harriet, what does 'Oklahoma Rooster' mean to you?"

"I don't have much history for that one. Came from an Oklahoma fiddler named Dick Hutchinson, but I don't know if he wrote—"

"—I don't mean the history. What does it make you feel?"

"I'm not sure what you mean. It's a nice, simple fiddle tune."

"But you've actually seen a farm in real life. Does it sound like a rooster?"

She shrugged. "I've never really given it much thought. It's a nice tune. Not worthy of a spot in the Memory Project, but a nice tune. Why do you ask?"

It would sound stupid to say I thought myself on a farm when I played that song; I wouldn't tell her where "Wind Will Rove" took me either. "Just curious."

"Harriet's grandson is going to drive me crazy," I told Natalie. I had spent the afternoon with Teyla and Jonah, as I did every Friday, but this time Jonah had dragged us to the low gravity room. They had bounced, and I had watched and laughed along with their unrestrained joy, but I had a shooting pain in my neck from the way my head had followed the arcs of their flight.

Afterward, I'd logged into my class chat to find Nelson had again stirred the others into rebellion. The whole class, except for two I'd describe as timid and one as diligent, had elected not to do the new assignment due Tuesday. They had all followed his lead with a statement "We reject history. The future is in our hands."

"At least they all turned it in early," Nat joked. "But seriously, why are you letting him bother you?"

She stooped to pick up some of the toys scattered across the floor. The kids drew on the table screen with their fingers. Jonah was making a Tyrannosaurus, all body and tail and teeth and feathers. Teyla was still too young for her art to look representational, but she always used space in interesting ways. I leaned in to watch both of them.

"You laugh," I said. "Maybe by the time they're his age now, Nelson will have taken over the entire system. Only the most future-relevant courses. Reject the past. Don't reflect on the human condition. No history, no literature, no dinosaurs."

Jonah frowned. "No dinosaurs?"

"Grandma Rosie's joking, Jonah."

Jonah accepted that. His curly head bent down over the table again.

I continued. "It was one thing when he was a one-boy revolution. What am I supposed to do now that his virus is spreading to his whole class?"

Nat considered for a moment. "I'd work on developing an antidote, then hide it in a faster, stronger virus and inject it into the class. But, um, that's my professional opinion."

"What's the antidote in your analogy? Or the faster, stronger virus?"

Nat smiled, spread her hands. "It wasn't an analogy, sorry. I only know from viruses and toddlers. Sometimes both at once. Now are you going to play for these kids before I try to get them to sleep? They really like the one about the sleepy bumblebee."

She picked Teyla up from her chair, turned it around, and sat down with Teyla in her lap. Jonah kept drawing.

I picked up my fiddle. "What's a bumblebee, Jonah?" He answered without looking up. "A dinosaur."

I sighed and started to play.

Natalie's answer got me thinking. I checked in with Nelson's literature teacher, who confirmed he was doing the same thing in her class as well.

How wrong was he? They learned countries and borders, abstract names, lines drawn and redrawn. The books taught in lit classes captured the human condition, but rendered it through situations utterly foreign to us. To us. To me as much as him.

I had always liked the challenge. Reading about the way things had been in the past made our middle-years condition more acceptable to me. Made beginnings more concrete. Everyone in history lived in middle-years too; no matter when they lived, there was a before and an after, even if a given group or individual might not be around for the latter. I enjoyed tracing back through the changes, seeing what crumbled and what remained.

I enjoyed. Did I pass on my enjoyment? Maybe I'd been thinking too much about why I liked to study history, and not considering why my students found it tedious. It was my job to find a way to make it relevant to them. If they weren't excited, I had failed them.

When I got home from dinner that night, when I picked up my fiddle to play "Wind Will Rove," it was the new, elided version, the one that had escaped me previously. Now I couldn't find the original phrasing again, even with fifty years' muscle memory behind it.

I went to the database to listen to how it actually went, and was relieved when the song came up without trouble. The last variation in the new DB was filed under "Wind Will Rove" but would more accurately have been listed as "Wind Will Roam," and even that one recreated somebody's memory of an interview predating our ship. If this particular song's history hadn't contained all those interviews in which the song's interpreters sang snippets, if Harriet or my grandmother or someone hadn't watched it enough times to memorize it, or hadn't thought it important, we wouldn't have any clue how it went. Those little historic recreations weren't even the songs themselves, but they got their own piece of history, their own stories. Why did they matter? They mattered because somebody had cared about them enough to create them.

I walked into my classroom on Monday, fiddle case over my shoulder, to the nervous giggles of students who knew they had done something brazen and now waited to find out what came of it. Nelson, not giggling, met my gaze with his own, steady and defiant.

"Last week, somebody asked me a question, using the very odd delivery mechanism of my classroom walls." I touched my desk and swiped the graffitied walls blank.

"Today I'm going to tell you that you don't have a choice. You're in this class to learn our broken, damaged history, everything that's left of it. And then to pass it on, probably breaking it even further. And maybe it'll keep twisting until every bit of fact is wrung out of it, but what's left will still be some truth about who we are or who we were. The part most worth remembering."

I put my fiddle case on the desk. Took my time tuning down to DDAD, listening to the whispered undercurrent.

When I liked the tuning, I lifted my bow. "This is a song called 'Wind Will Rove.' I want you to hear what living history means to me."

I played them all. All the known variations, all the ones that weren't lost to time. I rested the fiddle and sang Howie McCabe's faulty snippet of "Windy Grove" from the recreation of his historical interview and Will E. Womack's "Wind Will Roam." I recited the history in between: "Windy Grove" and "Wendigo" and "When I Go." Lifted the fiddle to my chin again and closed my eyes. "Wind Will Rove": three times through in its traditional form, three times through with my own alterations.

"Practice too much and you sound like you're remembering it instead of feeling it," my grandmother used to say. This was a new room to my fiddle; even the old variations felt new within it. My fingers danced light and quick.

I tried to make the song sound like something more than wind. What did any of us know of wind? Nothing but words on a screen. I willed our entire ship into the new song I created. We were the wind. We were the wind and borne by the wind, transmitted. I played a ship traveling through the vacuum. I played life on the ship, footsteps on familiar streets, people, goats, frustration, movement while standing still.

The students sat silent at the end. Only one was an OldTimer, Emily Redhorse, who had been one of the three who actually turned in their assignments; Nelson grew up hearing this music, I know. I was pretty sure the rest had no clue what they heard. One look at Nelson said he'd already formulated a response, so I didn't let him open his mouth.

I settled my fiddle back into its case and left.

There are so many stories about my grandmother. I don't imagine there'll ever be many about me. Maybe one of the kids in this class will tell a story about the day their teacher cracked up. Maybe Emily Redhorse will take a seat in the OldTime one day and light into my tune. Maybe history and story will combine to birth something larger than both, and you, Teyla, you and your brother will take the time to investigate where anecdote deviates from truth. If you wonder which of these stories are true, well, they all are in their way, even if some happened and some didn't.

I've recorded my song variation into the new database, in the "other" section to keep from offending Harriet, for now. I call it "We Will Rove." I think my grandmother would approve. I've included a history, too, starting with "Windy Grove" and "Wind Will Rove," tracing through my grandmother's apocryphal spacewalk and my mother's attempt to find meaning for herself and my daughter's unrecorded song, on the way to my own adaptation. It's all one story, at its core.

I'm working more changes into the song, making it more and more my own. I close my eyes when I play it, picturing a through-line, picturing how one day, long after I'm gone, a door will open. Children will spill from the ship and into the bright sun of a new place, and somebody will lift my old fiddle, my grandmother's fiddle, and will put a new tune to the wind.

Gord Sellar is a Canadian writer currently living in the South Korean countryside with his wife and son, and countless plastic dinosaurs. His work has appeared in many magazines and anthologies since 2007, and in translation in Korean, Italian, Czech, and Chinese. He was a finalist for the John W. Campbell Award for Best New Writer in 2009, and wrote the screenplay for South Korea's first cinematic adaptation of a Lovecraft story, the award-winning "The Music of Jo Hyeja" (2012). He is currently working on an SF novel set in the 1730s.

FOCUS

Gord Sellar

When the news rippled through the classroom in a flurry of smartphone beeps, almost nobody reacted. My Linh knew, though, that she must've done *something* right, and Huong's beaming smile was all the confirmation she needed.

Still, she felt a nagging sense of worry, too. A riot was a riot: unanticipated things happened. Fires, street fights, and eventually a wave of arrests. And then there was her father: she hadn't said a word to him about what they were up to, but dedicated revolutionary that he was, he never missed a good riot. Yet for nearly everyone else in the room, the task of memorizing English vocabulary lists took priority over the events unfolding in Bin Duong City. My Linh sat watching her classmates speed-memorize their way through the boring lists of vocabulary, wondering how many of them had parents working in the factories, and how many would've panicked by now if they weren't high on Focus?

She caught Hoc's eye and noticed Huong nodding toward the exit. A glance at her teacher assured her that he wouldn't stop them leaving. Even on normal days, she didn't have to ask permission to go to the toilet: Mrs. Tran just smiled at her slightly pityingly, not bothering to caution her against skipping class. She was a kindly sort, and vaguely encouraging, but she'd clearly long ago given up on the kids who weren't dosing, even the ones like My Linh who had no choice. "Nobody asked to be born allergic to Focus,"

Mrs. Tran had sometimes said to her, about My Linh and her dad alike, before glancing at Hoc and Huong and saying, "Or immune to it . . ." But that didn't stop her concentrating her teaching efforts on the kids who *were* dosing. They were the ones who were going to succeed, and the kids who couldn't use Focus would never catch up to them anyway.

Out in the hallway, Hoc was grinning like a maniac. "It worked," he half-shouted.

"Of course it did!" My Linh said, almost convinced by her own bravado, though deep down she was worried it'd all backfire and about what might happen if enough arrows pointed in their direction.

"No, I mean it *worked!* Look," he said, holding up his cell phone. The graph on the screen wasn't so much an exponential curve as an almost-vertical line. "That's way *beyond* viral. That's *nuclear.*"

"Let's go," Huong hissed anxiously.

"Yeobo," Yoon-Seok said sweetly into his phone, looking out across the nearly empty dorm managers' cafeteria. "Uh, I think I'm stuck in Binh Duong for tonight. Maybe."

It was a courtesy *maybe:* When riots broke out, there was no uncertainty about his being marooned in the industrial zone for the night. Especially when a power cut had shut down all but the emergency power supply to the factory.

"Are you safe?" was all his wife said, her voice flatter than it should have been: he hadn't said a thing about this to her the night before.

"Yeah, it shouldn't be a problem. We're well-prepared," he said as their baby son squawked hoarsely in the background. That was the understatement of the year, he thought.

"Good," she said, after a moment's hesitation. Their son's voice crescendoed into a shrill howl. "I, uh . . ."

"That's fine, *yeobo,"* he said. "I'll call you later."

"Mmmm," she said and disconnected.

Yoon-Seok glanced at his lunch, but he wasn't hungry. He gestured for an attendant to remove his tray, and the nameless Vietnamese woman who took it thanked him with heavily accented Korean, an inauthentic smile on her face. He half-expected her to frown: people as badly paid as their worker didn't waste food this way, after all, and staff protests had exploded over su waste in the past.

Of *course* she didn't, not with what that woman had flowing through veins. Yoon-Seok knew what it was like to be Focused: he'd dosed hir back in college, secretly, before everyone had started using it. He'd studied through things that had sent other students into the streets in droves. You could tell who was on Focus at the time: they were the only people left in the library, the only people whose priority was grades, and not ousting a corrupt president or opposing the sweatshopification of newly liberated North Korea. When the woman emerged, he found himself looking into her blank eyes, wondering if he'd unsettled his friends back in university the way she did him now. His wife sometimes complained when he had one of his episodes, but he'd come to enjoy the passivity they brought on, the silent . . . well, not contemplation, but just single-minded attentiveness. Sometimes, it was more confusing than peaceful, sure, but that was only occasional.

Without a word to the attendant—she wouldn't care anyway—he walked out into the factory's courtyard, ignoring the automated clank of the building's massive steel locks behind him. He was alone now, the security guards stationed inside the dorms at his insistence, to keep the Focused workers and the Korean management safe. That was how sure he was of his plan, of the facts on which it was founded.

But Yoon-Seok did not feel afraid: he only stared up into the smoke-clotted sky, as the noise of the tumult several streets away washed over him. Despite the reek of burning plastic, the shouts in the distance, he was calm. The gentlest of breezes, almost undetectable, cooled his face as he made his way to the main factory building.

"Together, we're strong!" Tuan repeated, and the crowd marching with him repeated the words in unison. "Together, we're brave!" he shouted, and he knew that if they repeated the words often enough, they *would* be brave.

They would need it: Binh Duong was about to become a war zone: factories burning, exploiters cowed into submission, the people finally rising to frighten those who abused them into good behavior. You could never quite *win* against the factory owners—Tuan had fought through more than enough uprisings to know that—but you could force them toward human decency.

He looked into his group's faces: Binh, the young orphaned woman who'd been fired from her textile factory after ten years' service because she'd missed a week of work taking care of her stricken sister. Thanh, a middle-aged man who'd lost an arm to a laser cutter and then been "retired" with a paltry compensation package. Quy Thi, a elderly woman struggling to support her granddaughter, whose mother had slammed her scooter into a tree and died on the way home from a factory that didn't subsidize the Focus antidote patches, only the on-shift doses.

Everyone had a story, and Tuan knew *every* story mattered.

"Now!" he shouted, and they marched.

"How'd you cut the industrial zones' power supply without knocking it out everywhere else in town?" Huong asked it a little too loudly, her eyes bright with excitement.

But My Linh just grinned and shrugged as she continued to type on the ancient netbook's keyboard: Huong wouldn't understand, even if she did explain. After all, *that* was nothing compared to anonymously springboarding SMS updates across the cloudnet to almost thirty million cheap, pay-as-you go cell phone accounts—the sort of accounts used by the poorest, the likeliest to riot.

But after a few dozen keystrokes, her confidence wilted. She frowned at the netbook's dim little screen.

"What is it?" Hoc blurted, trembling with worry.

"The VPDN," My Linh said. "I dunno why, but it's down." She tapped a few more commands into the thing, frowning as each seemed to fail.

Hoc gasped. "What if they're tracing you back . . ." he hissed, his voice diminishing to a whisper, ". . . to *here?*"

Huong wasn't worried, though: "It's just someone doing *con viec nha*," she quipped. *Housekeeping:* that summed up what most young people thought of the bigwigs up in Hanoi for you: cutting both the transatlantic trunk cables at any sign of a controversy had become typical, after all.

My Linh and Hoc laughed, though, and finally Hoc relaxed with a sigh and sat down. *Finally,* My Linh thought. He'd begun to get on her nerves. And then she was in.

"Got it," she said, sounding very relieved all of a sudden.

"Got what?" Hoc blurted loudly, as Huong rolled her eyes at his recurring panic.

"I'm inside the Communication Ministry's system, and . . ." My Linh stopped, her eyes running over a phrase again as her breath caught in her throat. "I gotta text my dad," she said, her hands trembling as she scrambled for her phone.

There was nothing to do but finish up his preparations and wait for the first mob to arrive, so Yoon-Seok rolled out the last cooler of ice, made sure he had a generous supply of paper cups on the table, and then took his place at the doorway of his uncle's airbag factory. To pass the time, he tried to pick out which of Bin Duong's factories were burning, and which had bribed the right officials for advance warning.

Some part of him had been waiting for this day for years, since his uncle had decided—against his advice—to make mandatory Focus prescriptions official company policy for all workers. Stupid Uncle Min-ho, and his all-important bottom line. Why invest in robotics, however affordable, when you could just dose your workers and save the maintenance costs? Uncle Min-ho hadn't factored in the costs of dealing with an angry throng of locals with nothing to lose. He'd spent five whole days in Vietnam the last five years, and here, he'd spent all five on booze and golf. To Yoon-Seok's objections, all he'd offered was a dismissive shrug and a grin. "It'll be fine," Min-ho had insisted, and that was that.

Still, Yoon-Seok had successfully dealt with such situations before; between his Vietnamese skill—he'd soaked up the vocabulary and grammar in six months, thanks to Focus—and his understanding of Vietnamese culture, he'd quelled several riots the old-fashioned way: respectful lip service, some ice water all around, and good old cooperation. And that had been without the added security prepared today.

The heat troubled him more than his anxiety, what with no air-conditioning inside the darkened factory. The stick-on patch on the inside of his left bicep itched beneath his white shirtsleeve. He did his best to ignore it, for fear of loosening the adhesive if he scratched, and returned to his place beside the massive, blue iron entryway door that stood open to the world. He smiled patiently, a well-practiced, understanding look in his eyes.

The sky-darkening swarm of drones above astonished My Linh as she looked up from the back of Huong's whining scooter. The drones sported the logos of all the local news networks, but also many foreign and online ones, along with lots that were illegally unmarked. Squeezing her knees hard against Huong's hips, she checked her smartphone for a tracker pingback from her dad's phone, but the city's 5G network was completely clogged.

They were overloading the system, she realized with a rueful shake of her head. More *con viec nha,* for all the good it would do. Not everyone on the street was heading to Binh Duong, but surely a number were: young punks, dissidents and malcontents who'd done their years on Focus through high school and uni still wound up penniless, those born early enough to miss out on universal dosing . . . anyone who had a right to a grudge was headed straight for the industrial zone.

My Linh suddenly wished she had an unmarked drone of her own that could track her dad through crowd-pings—the least blockable of all network systems—but Hoc had crashed it months ago and still hadn't worked up the cash to buy a replacement kit yet. She tried to set up a ping through the drones—they were all networked anyway, to prevent aerial crashes—but all she could get back from them was a bird's-eye view of Binh Duong's main thoroughfares, which resembled hopelessly clogged arteries through a haze of dust and black drone-exhaust.

Then a pingback came through. Somehow, her dad's phone had responded to hers despite the chaos and the overload.

"Huong!" she shouted, but when Huong didn't reply right away, My Linh looked up ahead to see what the distraction was. She saw a brutal pile-up of five scooters, dark bodies tangled among the wheels and broken machinery. A cop stood, talking to a young, well-dressed, pale couple beside a sports car with a nasty dent on the left side. The young man had his wallet in his hand, as the cop waved his phone toward a nearby camera mounted on a lightpost.

She stared, disgusted at the scene. All they'd done so far was only a small step. As she and her friends roared past the sordid scene, she frowned. The factories weren't the only thing that needed to be burned right down to the ground . . . .

Just then Hoc pulled up alongside them, driving one-handed as he punched a button on his phone. He'd gotten video of the cop, she realized, and was uploading it now, for the world to discover—and castigate—when the dust settled. It was enough to make My Linh smile a little, as she turned back to her own phone and zoomed the map till she could see where her dad was. "Doobong Autofact," it said.

It wasn't until after she'd squirted the text to the nav screen of Huong's scooter that she recognized the name.

The Korean manager—Tuan couldn't remember his name, though he recognized the man's face, his dull eyes—stood alone at the doorway. That was . . . *brave,* if nothing else.

"Come in," the man said, smiling graciously, waving the mob into the factory with a well-coiffed hand, the nails trim and the fingers clean. It was a soft, feminine hand, to be welcoming a mob armed with baseball bats and sections of pipe and the odd Molotov cocktail. This was the *true* Binh Duong, Tuan thought proudly: their faces were proud, angry—they knew they were angry, that they had a right to their outrage. This pride, this spirit of resistance, was what mattered. And this was what workers dosed on Focus would never, ever do.

When the crowd was inside, the Korean manager gestured toward a seating area already set up. There were paper plates with croissants on them, one on each plastic chair's seat. The mob muttered among themselves, laughing as they mocked the ridiculous gesture. The Korean didn't seem to be bothered by this: He just gestured to the customary table of iced water.

"Ha!" Tuan blurted out, as dramatically as he could, and he declared, "We know Focus is water-soluble!" He said it in Vietnamese, both because he remembered that the Korean spoke enough to understand him, and because he was saying it for the benefit of his fellow dissidents anyway.

"Aren't you thirsty?" the sweating Korean said in passable Vietnamese, as he took a cup from the table and drank the water. "It's so hot today . . ." Tuan realized the man was looking at him, a curious expression on his face. Did the man recognize him? And why did the possibility make him feel *relief*, of all things?

"Chan-mul?" Tuan said. Even all these years later, he still remembered the Korean words for "cold water." His words had the desired effect: The manager seemed surprised, even as he nodded. "What's in it?" he asked, switching to English.

"Nothing," said the Korean manager, his face so guileless Tuan believed him.

"We're not thirsty," Tuan said in Vietnamese, shoving the table aside. "You won't stop us that easily."

Now the man was really staring at Tuan, searching his memories for some hint, and Tuan's earlier relief began to sour. He didn't remember. This man who'd . . . ruined his life, he didn't remember him at all. Tuan raised one foot and kicked over the table, sending the cups tumbling as the jugs shattered, their contents puddling on the floor. Members of Tuan's group started shouting, and a few of them kicked the chairs away, the croissants flying off into the darkness of the factory interior. One of them even struck at the manager with a length of iron pipe, which the Korean blocked with his forearm, yowling in pain.

"I'll tell you what we're really here for," Tuan shouted in English, straining to be heard over the crowd, and only then becoming aware of a strange scent in the air. Then he noticed a soft hissing sound that had begun earlier, but he hadn't consciously registered. He coughed, his throat tightening as all the natural indistinctness of the world around him began to fade and as details began to jump out at him: the droplets of sweat on his skin, the dizzying lightheadedness, the Korean's eyes with their vastly dilated pupils, staring at him in the darkness, and the creaking of a door somewhere in the distance.

It was the entrance to the factory being shut from the outside, he realized, as the interior of the factory was plunged into darkness lit only by the screens of a dozen cell phones. Tuan sniffed the air and realized that it hadn't been the water that'd been dosed: It was the air. There was a gas, an invisible gas. And it wasn't a sleeping gas, or tear gas. With a flicker of panic, and an astonishing clarity of mind, he realized why the sensation was so familiar: The knowledge simply snapped into focus, and Tuan immediately understood, without even the slightest inclination to panic, that the air inside the factory was dosed with Focus.

A drop of sweat trickled down the Korean's forehead as he shook his head, and with a resigned smile, he said, "Oh, I already know . . ."

As they passed the burning tire factory, My Linh gaped at what she and her friends had done. Trucks roared down the streets, loaded with young men and women armed with tools and pipes, cheering like fans at a soccer match. Past them wove hundreds of scooters piloted by angry young men and women, the passengers seated behind the drivers waving banners and flags that decried China, the Free Trade Agreement with America, the government approval of generic Focus for factory use, and three or four other issues besides.

But all of that was normal, or had been normal in past riots. What turned My Linh's stomach was how the army had already shown up. It always took the army a day or two to show up: long enough for a few factories to burn down, for the crowd to vent for a while. Better they attack a few factories than the National Assembly, after all. Yet there were military trucks out already, only a few hours after the beginning of the disturbances. It made no sense at all.

She tried to call her father again but found her phone couldn't even connect to the cellular network at all. Up the street, a group of university students—boys in clean white dress shirts, girls in jeans and blouses—clashed with a small group of soldiers who for some reason were all wearing gas masks. She sniffed the air for any hint of tear gas, but found none, and wondered what the masks were for. Debris—old tires, piles of products, desks and workbenches hauled doors—were all burning, black smoke and a heavy toxic stink filling the drones-choked air. Now, My Linh was suddenly certain that what she'd seen on the government's hidden chat logs was true: this had been planned days before, and high-level people had known about it.

But then why were all the factories burning?

Except they *weren't*, she realized. Only *some* of them were, she realized. They passed a Japanese tire factory wreathed in flames, a cheering crowd of rioters hauling enormous tires out and rolling them, ablaze, into the street. Just a little further down the road, a Singaporean textiles shop sat placid and calm, its windows barred and its front gate locked with massive chains. In front of the burnt-out husk of a European light-bulb factory, a blackened effigy hung from a length of rope strung up over a light pole.

My Linh glanced at Hoc, who was looking up into the drone-choked sky as he kept pace with Huong's scooter. Was there some clue to this mystery up there? My Linh followed his gaze, but found only writhing chaos above, mechanical disorder and the flickering of a dozen lenses, fixed of course on the raging industrial infernos. Somewhere, she heard a police loudspeaker announcement begin, commanding the crowds to go home immediately. She and her friends had barely made it past the trucks and tanks they'd seen on the road into the industrial zone. How could the cops have arrived so soon, unless they'd been waiting since the morning?

Before My Linh had time to consider this any further, Huong shouted, "It's here, right?" back to her, and she realized they *were* finally there: The massive, two-building Korean factory complex looked just like she remembered it, from a couple of visits as a kid. It was as placid as the Singaporean factory had been, the doors closed, though they weren't chained shut. The company sign, in cryptic Korean lettering on the left, and block Roman letters on the right, was the same one My Linh had seen years before: It read DOOBONG AUTOFACT in bright red beside neat lines of Korean lettering.

Every muscle in My Linh's body was tense, and she realized she was holding her breath. Some deeply buried fear arose, impossible to explain beyond the knowledge that this was not how riots were supposed to happen, and some sense that she, and her father, and the whole of Binh Duong—not to mention wherever else riots had broken out—had been terribly, brutally tricked. The fear seemed to be choking her, and she forced herself to inhale as Huong revved the engine and they pulled up the long, empty driveway toward the dark factory.

It wasn't the fire that troubled Yoon-Seok, or the broken table, or the bruises on his forearm: He'd seen mobs do much worse in far less time. It was the way the leader had collapsed and gone into convulsions, frothing at the mouth. Yoon-Seok had seen a man react badly to Focus, once, but it was supposed to be one-in-a-million. Effortlessly, he recalled the statistics he'd looked up at the time: probability dictated that he ought never to see such a reaction again, much less so soon. And yet here lay the mob's leader, his body twisted a chillingly familiar way.

Before he had a chance to think, he shouted in Vietnamese: "Call an ambulance!" Poor though most of the mob was, half of them would have phones. But then Yoon-Seok remembered the phone network was down, and their calls—even repeated with Focused relentlessness—would never get through.

Suddenly, a teenaged girl, a local, appeared out of nowhere, trailed by some friends, all three of them in school uniforms. She ran toward the light, until she saw the convulsing man at Yoon-Seok's feet. She fell to her knees beside him.

"*Ba!*" she screamed, and Yoon-Seok's guts twisted, bile searing the back of his throat, as she turned to face him and, in astonishingly good English, shouted, "What did you do to him?"

"I . . . nothing . . ." Then Yoon-Seok realized, mathematical probability *had* held true. This was *the same man* he'd seen have an allergic reaction a few years back, right there on the floor of Doobong Autofact.

How could he have forgotten him? When the factory-wide Focus policy had come into effect, the worker had come to Yoon-Seok with a sob story about an allergy to Focus, claiming he'd discovered it the day his daughter had almost died getting her first routine dose at school. He'd been a good worker, otherwise, even management material: had he been Korean, the allergy ultimately might not even have mattered.

"But you aren't Korean," he'd said to the man, straightforwardly. It was fact, after all, and if only the man *had* been able to dose on Focus, he would have appreciated the primacy of facts: how simple and pure they are, how crucial to the constitution of the world.

And as the girl ripped open her father's shirt and slapped him on the face, shouting desperately, "Ba! *Ba!*", another fact nagged at Yoon-Seok: however implicitly the plan had been approved, and no matter which officials in Hanoi had quietly provided logistical support for it—the better to be rid of their own troublemaking dissidents—he knew the consequences for nonconsensual dosing of a worker were fatal.

The phone network was out: there was nobody to ask what to do, and Yoon-Seok realized—without caring, with that strange reluctance to move or speak that his wife so often had complained about—what was happening even as his senses sharpened, as the haze and noise and blur of everything drifted into clear, tight focus. The girl, starting to choke. The smudge of dirt on the shoulder of her uniform. Her friends' gasping nearby in the darkness.

The choking sound of the stricken man. The beeping of phones being dialed, fruitlessly, over and over.

One droplet—whether a tear or sweat made no difference to Yoon-Seok—dropped from the girl's chin to her father's cheek. The faint trail it left there was the only thing in the world for Yoon-Seok now.

Linda Nagata is a Nebula and Locus Award–winning writer, best known for her high-tech science fiction, including The Red trilogy, a series of near-future military thrillers. The first book in the trilogy, *The Red: First Light*, was a Nebula and John W. Campbell Memorial Award finalist, and named as a *Publishers Weekly* Best Book of 2015. Her newest novel is the very near-future thriller, *The Last Good Man*. Linda has lived most of her life in Hawaii, where she's been a writer, a mom, a programmer of database-driven websites, and an independent publisher. She lives with her husband in their long-time home on the island of Maui.

THE MARTIAN OBELISK

Linda Nagata

The end of the world required time to accomplish—and time, Susannah reflected, worked at the task with all the leisurely skill of a master torturer, one who could deliver death either quickly or slowly, but always with excruciating pain.

No getting out of it.

But there were still things to do in the long, slow decline; final gestures to make. Susannah Li-Langford had spent seventeen years working on her own offering-for-the-ages, with another six and half years to go before the Martian Obelisk reached completion. Only when the last tile was locked into place in the obelisk's pyramidal cap, would she yield.

Until then, she did what was needed to hold onto her health, which was why, at the age of eighty, she was out walking vigorously along the cliff trail above the encroaching Pacific Ocean, determined to have her daily exercise despite the brisk wind and the freezing mist that ran before it. The mist was only a token moisture, useless to revive the drought-stricken coastal forest, but it made the day cold enough that the fishing platforms at the cliff's edge were deserted, leaving Susannah alone to contemplate the mortality of the human world.

It was not supposed to happen like this. As a child she'd been promised a swift conclusion: duck and cover and nuclear annihilation. And if not annihilation, at least the nihilistic romance of a gun-toting, leather-clad, fight-to-the-death anarchy.

That hadn't happened either.

Things had just gotten worse, and worse still, and people gave up. Not everyone, not all at once—there was no single event marking the beginning of the end—but there was a sense of inevitability about the direction history had taken. Sea levels rose along with average ocean temperatures. Hurricanes devoured coastal cities and consumed low-lying countries. Agriculture faced relentless drought, flood, and temperature extremes. A long run of natural disasters made it all worse—earthquakes, landslides, tsunamis, volcanic eruptions. There had been no major meteor strike yet, but Susannah wouldn't bet against it. Health care faltered as antibiotics became useless against resistant bacteria. Surgery became an art of the past.

Out of the devastation, war and terrorism erupted like metastatic cancers.

We are a brilliant species, Susannah thought. Courageous, creative, generous—as individuals. In larger numbers we fail every time.

There were reactor meltdowns, poisoned water supplies, engineered plagues, and a hundred other, smaller horrors. The Shoal War had seen nuclear weapons used in the South China Sea. But even the most determined ghouls had failed to ignite a sudden, brilliant cataclysm. The master torturer would not be rushed.

Still, the tipping point was long past, the future truncated. Civilization staggered on only in the lucky corners of the world where the infrastructure of a happier age still functioned. Susannah lived in one of those lucky corners, not far from the crumbling remains of Seattle, where she had greenhouse food, a local network, and satellite access all supplied by her patron, Nathaniel Sanchez, who was the money behind the Martian Obelisk.

When the audio loop on her ear beeped a quiet tone, she assumed the alert meant a message from Nate. There was no one else left in her life, nor did she follow the general news, because what was the point?

She tapped the corner of her wrist-link with a finger gloved against the cold, signaling her personal AI to read the message aloud. Its artificial, androgynous voice spoke into her ear:

"Message sender: Martian Obelisk Operations. Message body: Anomaly sighted. All operations automatically halted pending supervisory approval."

Just a few innocuous words, but weighted with a subtext of disaster.

A subtext all too familiar.

For a few seconds, Susannah stood still in the wind and the rushing mist. In the seventeen-year history of the project, construction had been halted only for equipment maintenance, and that, on a tightly regulated schedule.

She raised her wrist-link to her lips. "What anomaly, Alix?" she demanded, addressing the AI. "Can it be identified?"

"It identifies as a homestead vehicle belonging to Red Oasis."

That was absurd. Impossible.

Founded twenty-one years ago, Red Oasis was the first of four Martian colonies, and the most successful. It had outlasted all the others, but the Mars Era had ended nine months ago when Red Oasis succumbed to an outbreak of "contagious asthma"—a made-up name for an affliction evolved on Mars.

Since then there had been only radio silence. The only active elements on the planet were the wind, and the machinery that had not yet broken down, all of it operated by AIs.

"Where is the vehicle?" Susannah asked.

"Seventeen kilometers northwest of the obelisk."

So close!

How was that possible? Red Oasis was over 5,000 kilometers distant. How could an AI have driven so far? And who had given the order?

Homestead vehicles were not made to cover large distances. They were big, slow, and cumbersome—cross-country robotic crawlers designed to haul equipment from the landing site to a colony's permanent location, where construction would commence (and ideally be completed) long before the inhabitants arrived. The vehicles had a top speed of fifteen kilometers per hour, which meant that even with the lightspeed delay, Susannah had time to send a new instruction set to the AIs that inhabited her construction equipment.

Shifting abruptly from stillness to motion, she resumed her vigorous pace—and then she pushed herself to walk just a little faster.

Nathaniel Sanchez was waiting for her, pacing with a hobbling gait on the front porch of her cottage when she returned. His flawless electric car, an anomaly from another age, was parked in the gravel driveway. Nate was eighty-five and rail-thin, but the electric warmth of his climate-controlled coat kept him comfortable even in the biting wind. She waved at him impatiently. "You know it's fine to let yourself in. I was hoping you'd have coffee brewing by now."

He opened the door for her, still a practitioner of the graceful manners instilled in him by his mother eight decades ago—just one of the many things Susannah admired about him. His trustworthiness was another. Though Nate owned every aspect of the Martian Obelisk project—the equipment on

Mars, the satellite accounts, this house where Susannah expected to live out her life—he had always held fast to an early promise never to interfere with her design or her process.

"I haven't been able to talk to anyone associated with Red Oasis," he told her in a voice low and resonant with age. "The support network may have disbanded."

She sat down in the old, armless chair she kept by the door, and pulled off her boots. "Have the rights to Red Oasis gone on the market yet?"

"No." Balancing with one hand against the door, he carefully stepped out of his clogs. "If they had, I would have bought them."

"What about a private transfer?"

He offered a hand to help her up. "I've got people looking into it. We'll find out soon."

In stockinged feet, she padded across the hardwood floor and the hand-made carpets of the living room, but at the door of the Mars room she hesitated, looking back at Nate. Homesteads were robotic vehicles, but they were designed with cabs that could be pressurized for human use, with a life-support system that could sustain two passengers for many days. "Is there any chance some of the colonists at Red Oasis are still alive?" Susannah asked.

Nate reached past her to open the door, a dark scowl on his worn face. "No detectable activity and radio silence for nine months? I don't think so. There's no one in that homestead, Susannah, and there's no good reason for it to visit the obelisk, especially without any notice to us that it was coming. When my people find out who's issuing the orders we'll get it turned around, but in the meantime, do what you have to do to take care of our equipment."

Nate had always taken an interest in the Martian Obelisk, but over the years, as so many of his other aspirations failed, the project had become more personal. He had begun to see it as his own monument and himself as an Ozymandias whose work was doomed to be forgotten, though it would not fall to the desert sands in this lifetime or any other.

"What can I do for you, Susannah?" he had asked, seventeen years ago.

A long-time admirer of her architectural work, he had come to her after the ruin of the Holliday Towers in Los Angeles—her signature project—two soaring glass spires, one eighty-four floors and the other 104, linked by graceful sky bridges. When the Hollywood Quake struck, the buildings had endured the shaking just as they'd been designed to do, keeping their residents safe, while much of the city around them crumbled. But massive fires followed the quake and the towers had not survived that.

"Tell me what you dream of, Susannah. What you would still be willing to work on."

Nathaniel had been born into wealth, and through the first half of his life he'd grown the family fortune. Though he had never been among the wealthiest individuals of the world, he could still indulge extravagant fancies.

The request Susannah made of him had been, literally, outlandish.

"Buy me the rights to the Destiny Colony."

"On Mars?" His tone suggested a suspicion that her request might be a joke.

"On Mars," she assured him.

Destiny had been the last attempt at Mars colonization. The initial robotic mission had been launched and landed, but money ran out and colonists were never sent. The equipment sat on Mars, unused.

Susannah described her vision of the Martian Obelisk: a gleaming, glittering white spire, taking its color from the brilliant white of the fiber tiles she would use to construct it. It would rise from an empty swell of land, growing more slender as it reached into the sparse atmosphere, until it met an engineering limit prescribed by the strength of the fiber tiles, the gravity of the Red Planet, and by the fierce ghost-fingers of Mars' storm winds. Calculations of the erosional force of the Martian wind led her to conclude that the obelisk would still be standing a hundred thousand years hence and likely far longer. It would outlast all buildings on Earth. It would outlast her bloodline, and all bloodlines. It would still be standing long after the last human had gone the way of the passenger pigeon, the right whale, the dire wolf. In time, the restless Earth would swallow up all evidence of human existence, but the Martian Obelisk would remain—a last monument marking the existence of humankind, excepting only a handful of tiny, robotic spacecraft faring, lost and unrecoverable, in the void between stars.

Nate had listened carefully to her explanation of the project, how it could be done, and the time that would be required. None of it fazed him and he'd agreed, without hesitation, to support her.

The rights to the colony's equipment had been in the hands of a holding company that had acquired ownership in bankruptcy court. Nathaniel pointed out that no one was planning to go to Mars again, that no one any longer possessed the wealth or resources to try. Before long, he was able to purchase Destiny Colony for a tiny fraction of the original backers' investment.

When Susannah received the command codes, Destiny's homestead vehicle had not moved from the landing site, its payload had not been unpacked, and construction on its habitat had never begun. Her first directive to the AI in charge of the vehicle was to drive it three hundred kilometers to the site she'd chosen for the obelisk, at the high point of a rising swell of land.

Once there, she'd unloaded the fleet of robotic construction equipment: a mini-dozer, a mini-excavator, a six-limbed beetle cart to transport finished tiles, and a synth—short for synthetic human although the device was no such thing. It was just a stick figure with two legs, two arms, and hands capable of basic manipulation.

The equipment fleet also included a rolling factory that slowly but continuously produced a supply of fiber tiles, compiling them from raw soil and atmospheric elements. While the factory produced an initial supply of tiles, Susannah prepared the foundation of the obelisk, and within a year she began to build.

The Martian Obelisk became her passion, her reason for life after every other reason had been taken from her. Some called it a useless folly. She didn't argue: what meaning could there be in a monument that would never be seen directly by human eyes? Some called it graffiti: *Kilroy was here!* Some called it a tombstone and that was the truth too.

Susannah just called it better-than-nothing.

The Mars room was a circular extension that Nathaniel had ordered built onto the back of the cottage when Susannah was still in the planning stages of the obelisk's construction. When the door was closed, the room became a theater with a 360-degree floor-to-ceiling flex-screen. A high-backed couch at the center rotated, allowing easy viewing of the encircling images captured in high resolution from the construction site.

Visually, being in this room was like being at Destiny, and it did not matter at all that each red-tinted image was a still shot, because on the Red Planet, the dead planet, change came so slowly that a still shot was as good as video.

Until now.

As Susannah entered the room, she glimpsed an anomalous, bright orange spot in a lowland to the northwest. Nathaniel saw it too. He gestured and started to speak but she waved him to silence, taking the time to circle the room, scanning the entire panorama to assess if anything else had changed.

Her gaze passed first across a long slope strewn with a few rocks and scarred with wheel tracks. Brightly colored survey sticks marked the distance: yellow at 250 meters, pink at 500, green for a full kilometer, and bright red for two.

The red stick stood at the foot of a low ridge that nearly hid the tile factory. She could just see an upper corner of its bright-green, block shape. The rest of it was out of sight, busy as always, processing raw ore dug by the excavator from a pit beyond the ridge, and delivered by the mini-dozer. As the factory slowly rolled, it left a trail of tailings, and every few minutes it produced a new fiber tile.

Next in the panorama was a wide swath of empty land, more tire tracks the only sign of human influence all the way out to a hazy pink horizon. And then, opposite the door and appearing no more than twenty meters distant, was Destiny's homestead vehicle. It was the same design as the approaching crawler: a looming cylindrical cargo container resting on dust-filled tracks. At the forward end, the cab, its windows dusty and lightless, its tiny bunkroom never used. Susannah had long ago removed the equipment she wanted, leaving all else in storage. For over sixteen years, the homestead had remained in its current position, untouched except by the elements.

Passing the Destiny homestead, her gaze took in another downward slope of lifeless desert and then, near the end of her circuit, she faced the tower itself.

The Martian Obelisk stood alone at the high point of the surrounding land, a gleaming-white, graceful, four-sided, tapering spire, already 170-meters high, sharing the sky with no other object. The outside walls were smooth and unadorned, but on the inside, a narrow stairway climbed around the core, rising in steep flights to the tower's top, where more fiber tiles were added every day, extending its height. It was a path no human would ever walk, but the beetle cart, with its six legs, ascended every few hours, carrying in its cargo basket a load of fiber tiles. Though she couldn't see the beetle cart, its position was marked as inside the tower, sixty percent of the way up the stairs. The synth waited for it at the top, its headless torso just visible over the rim of the obelisk's open stack, ready to use its supple hands to assemble the next course of tiles.

All this was as expected, as it should be.

Susannah steadied herself with a hand against the high back of the couch as she finally considered the orange splash of color that was the intruding vehicle. "Alix, distance to the Red Oasis homestead?"

The same androgynous voice that inhabited her ear loop spoke now through the room's sound system. "Twelve kilometers."

The homestead had advanced five kilometers in the twenty minutes she'd taken to return to the cottage—though in truth it was really much closer. Earth and Mars were approaching a solar conjunction, when they would be at their greatest separation, on opposite sides of the Sun. With the lightspeed delay, even this new image was nineteen minutes old. So she had only minutes left to act.

Reaching down to brace herself against the armrest of the couch, she sat with slow grace. "Alix, give me a screen."

A sleeve opened in the armrest and an interface emerged, swinging into an angled display in front of her.

The fires that had destroyed the Holliday Towers might have been part of the general inferno sparked by the Hollywood earthquake, but Susannah suspected otherwise. The towers had stood as a symbol of defiance amid the destruction—which might explain why they were brought low. The Martian Obelisk was a symbol too, and it had long been a target both for the media and for some of Destiny's original backers who had wanted the landing left undisturbed, for the use of a future colonization mission that no one could afford to send.

"Start up our homestead," Nate urged her. "It's the only equipment we can afford to risk. If you drive it at an angle into the Red Oasis homestead, you might be able to push it off its tracks."

Susannah frowned, her fingers moving across the screen as she assembled an instruction set. "That's a last resort option, Nate, and I'm not even sure it's possible. There are safety protocols in the AIs' core training modules that might prevent it."

She tapped *send*, launching the new instruction set on its nineteen-minute journey. Then she looked at Nate. "I've ordered the AIs that handle the construction equipment to retreat and evade. We cannot risk damage or loss of control."

He nodded somberly. "Agreed—but the synth and the beetle cart are in the tower."

"They're safe in there, for now. But I'm going to move the homestead—assuming it starts. After seventeen years, it might not."

"Understood."

"The easiest way for someone to shut down our operation is to simply park the Red Oasis homestead at the foot of the obelisk, so that it blocks access to the stairway. If the beetle cart can't get in and out, we're done. So I'm going to park our homestead there first."

He nodded thoughtfully, eyeing the image of the obelisk. "Okay. I understand."

"Our best hope is that you can find out who's instructing the Red Oasis homestead and get them to back off. But if that fails, I'll bring the synth out, and use it to try to take manual control."

"The Red Oasis group could have a synth too."

"Yes."

They might also have explosives—destruction was so much easier than creation—but Susannah did not say this aloud. She did not want Nate to inquire about the explosives that belonged to Destiny. Instead she told him, "There's no way we can know what they're planning. All we can do is wait and see."

He smacked a frustrated fist into his palm. "Nineteen minutes! Nineteen minutes times two before we know what's happened!"

"Maybe the AIs will work it out on their own," she said dryly. And then it was her turn to be overtaken by frustration. "Look at us! Look what we've come to! Invested in a monument no one will ever see. Squabbling over the possession of ruins while the world dies. This is where our hubris has brought us." But that was wrong, so she corrected herself. "*My* hubris."

Nate was an old man with a lifetime of emotions mapped on his well-worn face. In that complex terrain it wasn't always easy to read his current feelings, but she thought she saw hurt there. He looked away, before she could decide. A furtive movement.

"Nate?" she asked in confusion.

"This project matters," he insisted, gazing at the obelisk. "It's art, and it's memory, and it *does* matter."

Of course. But only because it was all they had left.

"Come into the kitchen," she said. "I'll make coffee."

Nate's tablet chimed while they were still sitting at the kitchen table. He took the call, listened to a brief explanation from someone on his staff, and then objected. "That can't be right. No. There's something else going on. Keep at it."

He scowled at the table until Susannah reminded him she was there. "Well?"

"That was Davidson, my chief investigator. He tracked down a Red Oasis shareholder who told him that the rights to the colony's equipment had *not* been traded or sold, that they couldn't be, because they had no value. Not with a failed communications system." His scowl deepened. "They want us to believe they can't even talk to the AIs."

Susannah stared at him. "But if that's true—"

"It's not."

"Meaning you don't want it to be." She got up from the table.

"Susannah—"

"I'm not going to pretend, Nate. If it's not an AI driving that homestead, then it's a colonist, a survivor—and that changes everything."

She returned to the Mars room, where she sat watching the interloper's approach. The wall screen refreshed every four minutes as a new image arrived from the other side of the sun. Each time it did, the bright orange homestead jumped a bit closer. It jumped right past the outermost ring of survey sticks, putting it less than two kilometers from the obelisk—close enough that she could see a faint wake of drifting dust trailing behind it, giving it a sense of motion.

Then, thirty-eight minutes after she'd sent the new instruction set, the Destiny AI returned an acknowledgement.

Her heart beat faster, knowing that whatever was to happen on Mars had already happened. Destiny's construction equipment had retreated and its homestead had started up or had failed to start, had moved into place at the foot of the tower or not. No way to know until time on Earth caught up with time on Mars.

The door opened.

Nate shuffled into the room.

Susannah didn't bother to ask if Davidson had turned up anything. She could see from his grim expression that he expected the worst.

And what was the worst?

A slight smile stole onto her lips as Nate sat beside her on the couch.

The worst case is that someone has lived.

Was it any wonder they were doomed?

Four more minutes.

The image updated.

The 360-degree camera, mounted on a steel pole sunk deep into the rock, showed Destiny profoundly changed. For the first time in seventeen years, Destiny's homestead had moved. It was parked by the tower, just as Susannah had requested. She twisted around, looking for the bright green corner of the factory beyond the distant ridge—but she couldn't see it.

"Everything is as ordered," Susannah said.

The Red Oasis homestead had reached the green survey sticks.

"An AI has to be driving," Nate insisted.

"Time will tell."

Nate shook his head. "Time comes with a nineteen minute gap. Truth is in the radio silence. It's an AI."

Four more minutes of silence.

When the image next refreshed, it showed the two homesteads, nose to nose.

Four minutes.

The panorama looked the same.

Four minutes more.

No change.

Four minutes.

Only the angle of sunlight shifted.

Four minutes.

A figure in an orange pressure suit stood beside the two vehicles, gazing up at the tower.

Before the Martian Obelisk, when Shaun was still alive, two navy officers in dress uniforms had come to the house, and in formal voices explained that the daughter Susannah had birthed and nurtured and shaped with such care was gone, her future collapsed to nothing by a missile strike in the South China Sea.

"We must go on," Shaun ultimately insisted.

And they had, bravely.

Defiantly.

Only a few years later their second child and his young wife had vanished into the chaos brought on by an engineered plague that decimated Hawaii's population, turning it into a state under permanent quarantine. Day after excruciating day as they'd waited for news, Shaun had grown visibly older, hope a dying light, and when it was finally extinguished he had nothing left to keep him moored to life.

Susannah was of a different temper. The cold ferocity of her anger had nailed her into the world. The shape it took was the Martian Obelisk: one last creative act before the world's end.

She knew now the obelisk would never be finished.

"It's a synth," Nate said. "It has to be."

The AI contradicted him. "Text message," it announced.

"Read it," Susannah instructed.

Alix obeyed, reading the message in an emotionless voice. "Message sender: Red Oasis resident Tory Eastman. Message body as transcribed audio: Is anyone out there? Is anyone listening? My name is Tory Eastman.

I'm a refugee from Red Oasis. Nineteen days in transit with my daughter and son, twins, three years old. We are the last survivors."

These words induced in Susannah a rush of fear so potent she had to close her eyes against a dizzying sense of vertigo. There was no emotion in the AI's voice and still she heard in it the anguish of another mother:

"The habitat was damaged during the emergency. I couldn't maintain what was left and I had no communications. So I came here. Five thousand kilometers. I need what's here. I need it all. I need the provisions and I need the equipment and I need the command codes and I need the building materials. I need to build my children a new home. Please. Are you there? Are you an AI? Is anyone left on Earth? Respond. Respond please. Give me the command codes. I will wait."

For many seconds—and many, many swift, fluttering heartbeats—neither Nate nor Susannah spoke. Susannah wanted to speak. She sought for words, and when she couldn't find them, she wondered: am I in shock? Or is it a stroke?

Nate found his voice first: "It's a hoax, aimed at you, Susannah. They know your history. They're playing on your emotions. They're using your grief to wreck this project."

Susannah let out a long breath, and with it, some of the horror that had gripped her. "We humans are amazing," she mused, "in our endless ability to lie to ourselves."

He shook his head. "Susannah, if I thought this was real—"

She held up a hand to stop his objection. "I'm not going to turn over the command codes. Not yet. If you're right and this is a hoax, I can back out. But if it's real, that family has pushed the life support capabilities of their homestead to the limit. They can move into our vehicle—that'll keep them alive for a few days—but they'll need more permanent shelter soon."

"It'll take months to build a habitat."

"*No.* It'll take months to make the tiles to build a habitat—but we already have a huge supply of tiles."

"All of our tiles are tied up in the obelisk."

"Yes."

He looked at her in shock, struck speechless.

"It'll be okay, Nate."

"You're abandoning the project."

"If we can help this family survive, we have to do it—and that will be the project we're remembered for."

"Even if there's no one left to remember?"

She pressed her lips tightly together, contemplating the image of the obelisk. Then she nodded. "Even so."

Knowing the pain of waiting, she sent a message of assurance to Destiny Colony before anything else. Then she instructed the synth and the beetle cart to renew their work, but this time in reverse: the synth would unlink the fiber tiles beginning at the top of the obelisk and the beetle would carry them down.

After an hour—after she'd traded another round of messages with a grateful Tory Eastman and begun to lay out a shelter based on a standard Martian habitat—she got up to stretch her legs and relieve her bladder. It surprised her to find Nate still in the living room. He stood at the front window, staring out at the mist that never brought enough moisture into the forest.

"They'll be alone forever," he said without turning around. "There are no more missions planned. No one else will ever go to Mars."

"I won't tell her that."

He looked at her over his shoulder. "So you are willing to sacrifice the obelisk? It was everything to you yesterday, but today you'll just give it up?"

"She drove a quarter of the way around the planet, Nate. Would you ever have guessed that was possible?"

"No," he said bitterly as he turned back to the window. "No. It should not have been possible."

"There's a lesson for us in that. We assume we can see forward to tomorrow, but we can't. We can't ever really know what's to come—and we can't know what we might do, until we try."

When she came out of the bathroom, Nate was sitting down in the rickety old chair by the door. With his rounded shoulders and his thin white hair, he looked old and very frail. "Susannah—"

"Nate, I don't want to argue—"

"Just *listen*. I didn't want to tell you before because, well, you've already suffered so many shocks and even good news can come too late."

"What are you saying?" she said, irritated with him now, sure that he was trying to undermine her resolve.

"Hawaii's been under quarantine because the virus can be latent for—"

She guessed where this was going. "For years. I know that. But if you're trying to suggest that Tory and her children might still succumb to whatever wiped out Red Oasis—"

"They *might*," he interrupted, sounding bitter. "But that's not what I was going to say."

"Then what?"

"Listen, and I'll tell you. Are you ready to listen?"

"Yes, yes. Go ahead."

"A report came out just a few weeks ago. The latest antivirals worked. The quarantine in Hawaii will continue for several more years, but all indications are the virus is gone. Wiped out. No sign of latent infections in over six months."

Her hands felt numb; she felt barely able to shuffle her feet as she moved to take a seat in an antique armchair. "The virus is gone? How can they know that?"

"Blood tests. And the researchers say that what they've learned can be applied to other contagions. That what happened in Hawaii doesn't ever have to happen again."

Progress? A reprieve against the long decline?

"There's more, Susannah."

The way he said it—his falling tone—it was a warning that set her tired heart pounding.

"You asked me to act as your agent," he reminded her. "You asked me to screen all news, and I've done that."

"Until now."

"Until now," he agreed, looking down, looking frightened by the knowledge he had decided to convey. "I should have told you sooner."

"But you didn't want to risk interrupting work on the obelisk?"

"You said you didn't want to hear anything." He shrugged. "I took you at your word."

"Nate, will you just say it?"

"You have a granddaughter, Susannah."

She replayed these words in her head, once, twice. They didn't make sense.

"DNA tests make it certain," he explained. "She was born six months after her father's death."

"*No.*" Susannah did not dare believe it. It was too dangerous to believe. "They both died. That was confirmed by the survivors. They posted the IDs of all the dead."

"Your daughter-in-law lived long enough to give birth."

Susannah's chest squeezed tight. "I don't understand. Are you saying the child is still alive?"

"Yes."

Anger rose hot, up out of the past. "And how long have you known? How long have you kept this from me?"

"Two months. I'm sorry, but . . ."

But we had our priorities. The tombstone. The Martian folly.

She stared at the floor, too stunned to be happy, or maybe she'd forgotten how. "You should have told me."

"I know."

"And I . . . I shouldn't have walled myself off from the world. I'm sorry."

"There's more," he said cautiously, as if worried how much more she could take.

"What else?" she snapped, suddenly sure this was just another game played by the master torturer, to draw the pain out. "Are you going to tell me that my granddaughter is sickly? Dying? Or that she's a mad woman, perhaps?"

"No," he said meekly. "Nothing like that. She's healthy, and she has a healthy two-year-old daughter." He got up, put an age-marked hand on the door knob. "I've sent you her contact information. If you need an assistant to help you build the habitat, let me know."

He was a friend, and she tried to comfort him. "Nate, I'm sorry. If there was a choice—"

"There isn't. That's the way it's turned out. You will tear down the obelisk, and this woman, Tory Eastman, will live another year, maybe two. Then the equipment will break and she will die and we won't be able to rebuild the tower. We'll pass on, and the rest of the world will follow—"

"We can't know that, Nate. Not for sure."

He shook his head. "This all looks like hope, but it's a trick. It's fate cheating us, forcing us to fold our hand, level our pride, and go out meekly. And there's no choice in it, because it's the right thing to do."

He opened the door. For a few seconds, wind gusted in, until he closed it again. She heard his clogs crossing the porch and a minute later she heard the crunch of tires on the gravel road.

You have a granddaughter. One who grew up without her parents, in a quarantine zone, with no real hope for the future and yet she was healthy, with a daughter already two years old.

And then there was Tory Eastman of Mars, who had left a dying colony and driven an impossible distance past doubt and despair, because she knew you have to do everything you can, until you can't do anymore.

Susannah had forgotten that, somewhere in the dark years.

She sat for a time in the stillness, in a quiet so deep she could hear the beating of her heart.

This all looks like hope.

Indeed it did and she well knew that hope could be a duplicitous gift from the master torturer, one that opened the door to despair.

"But it doesn't have to be that way," she whispered to the empty room. "I'm not done. Not yet."

Gregory Benford is a professor of physics and astronomy at the University of California, Irvine. He is a Woodrow Wilson Fellow, was Visiting Fellow at Cambridge University, and in 1995 received the Lord Prize for contributions to science. In 2007 he won the Asimov Award for science writing. His fiction has won many awards, including the Nebula Award for his novel *Timescape*. He has published forty-two books, mostly novels.

SHADOWS OF ETERNITY

Gregory Benford

> When on some gilded cloud or flower
> My gazing soul would gaze an houre,
> And in those weaker glories spy
> Some shadows of eternity.
>
> —Henry Vaughn, *The Retreate*, 1690

Falling in. She can feel somehow the gossamer sailcraft's long nose-dive into the red star's grav potential, as if her own body were there, plunging arrow-quick, dozens of light years away.

Her pod hummed, using her entire body to convey connections through its induced neural web. Sheets of sensation washed over her skin, bathed in a shower of penetrating responses, all coming from intricate flurries of her nervous system—the burr and tang of temperature, particle plasma flux, spectral flickers, kinesthetic glides and swivels, sharp images of the unending dark, lit by a smoldering dot of a sun.

These merged with her own in-board subsystems, coupled with high-bit-rate feeds the Artilects had already processed and smoothed from the sailcraft's decades of laser-beamed signals back to Earthside.

She went to fast-forward and the sailcraft plunged, its magnetic brakes on full. Down the potential well it flew in star-sprinkled dark. It heard no electromagnetics bearing patterns, from radio through to optical. Yet Earthside knew from a few pixels that one world here held an atmosphere out of equilibrium, clear signs of life that used oxygen and methane. So: life, perhaps minds, but no technology that spoke in waves. This L-dwarf star was of the commonplace majority, perhaps 75% or more of those stars in the disk, fully half of the total stellar mass in the Galaxy.

The craft chose its own path, looping intricately through repeated grav-wraps around three gas giants in the outer system, losing delta-Vs all the while. Now it had lost enough of its interstellar velocity to rummage among the inner worlds—one cold and gaunt, then the prize, long known from Earthside 'scopes: a superEarth.

The sailcraft folded in its mag-web brake and deployed 'scopes as it swanned into a high orbit around the cloudy world, 1.63 Earth masses. Its burgundy star glowered down on cloud decks thick as pancakes in the morning.

Rachel licked her lips. Here was the tasty truth, a world for the unwrapping. Smart and sure, the white metal bird blew itself into full plumage. Its inflatable beryllium sails shone in ruddy daylight, hollow-body banners just tens of nanometers thick, the body swelled by low-pressure hydrogen. These it used to steer into lower orbit, scanning the orbit space for satellites—and finding none.

The overseer Artilect inserted—correlates with the spectral strength of water, with strong water absorption lines as seen in clear-atmosphere planets, with the weakest features suggesting clouds and hazes—and she cut it off.

Now the main show: a self-guided human artifact plunging into a fresh solar system, embodying her: a hairless biped, so noble in reason, so infinite in faculties, heir to all creation—and an animal trapped in a box, really, just lying in a pod and sensing inputs that had flown on wings of electromagnetic song across the light years.

This world she dubbed, to herself, *Windworn*. For such it was. A thick atmosphere ripe with oxygen, smothered in good ol' nitrogen, yet beset with methane, too—clearly a world-air out of chemical balance. Good!—life.

Pearly cloud decks prevented much down-seeing. The Artilect aboard the craft had elected to deploy its one great immersion resource: the balloon.

The smart aero package fell away on its own braking wings and soon enough, slammed through the cottony clouds, its brake shell burning away—and into a realm of thick, filmy air. Blithe spirit, bird thou never wert—blazing through alien skies as a buzzing firework.

The balloon popped into a white teardrop, lighter than this sluggish air and with its heater able to stay buoyant. Ten kilometers below the land opened, solemn dark green and cloud-shrouded.

The first clear glimpse below was of big smooth whitecap ocean waves that crashed like armies against the rearing snow-white mountains guarding the continents. *I should have called it Rawworld,* she thought.

Below the balloon she watched alien vistas unfurl—big broad brown rivers, lakes, crags. The vegetation was gray and black, not green. Just as the astrobio people had said: around small red stars, plants needed to harvest all the ruddy glow. So they evolved to take in all the spectrum, with little to fear from the small slice of ultraviolet, since it was weak.

She watched the land and air carefully as the balloon skated tens of kilometers above, its cameras panning to take it all in. She did a close-up of the data feed, saw small birds flapping below—and roads.

She froze the image. Small dots that might be vehicles. *Yes*—she watched them crawl along. They went to—caves. Entrances to large hills that had slits of windows in their slopes, rank upon rank of them, orderly, horizontal . . . all the way to the summit.

Hills upon hills, marching to the distant horizon. Hills of grassland, hills of rumpled brown rectangular stone, hills with great clefts sharpening their edges. Artificial hills.

Hailstones rattled on the balloon. Microphones recorded long shrills, the trembling of tin in sheets, snapping steel strands. Harsh, brittle rings. Distant bellows, perhaps from the barrel-chested six-footed ambulating creatures far below in their herds of many. Once the hail cleared, the balloon could see things the size of houses burrowing into moist soil, after something. Yawning herbivore throngs looked up at the balloon, showing great rows of rounded molars. Forests, animals, birds—all moved before the surging winds.

The balloon acoustic microphones caught a huge manta ray-like thing conning *Fwap fwap fwap fwap* across the roiling sky, somehow navigating through. She thought, Crazy *thing, looks like it escaped from a cartoon on video,* with its long lazy strokes and manic grin that she saw was a scissor smile sporting long teeth . . . on a bird.

Then—black.

END OF CRAFT REPORT # 3069

a flat statement told her.

An interstellar spacecraft moving at a hundred kilometers per second does not have accidents; accidents have it. The craft turns into a blur of tumbling fragments inside a second.

She let herself drift up from the immersed state—slowly, letting the alien landscapes seep from her mind. It was over. She knew going in that the mission

had snapped off, never heard from again. The balloon, its gossamer thin carbon nanotube and graphene covered in conductive metal skin, the super-light-
weight rectenna—all gone. Something had blocked their transmissions—accident, intervention? No one knew. The mission report ended in a blank wall.

But she had needed to *feel* it. She knew full well this encounter lived
only in thick bricks of data, info-dense and rigid. The lived experience was
real, just turned into 0s and 1s, bringing across light years their stuttering
enlightenments to the SETI Library. Still, it mattered as an abrupt lesson in
how hard interstellar exploration through sailcraft was, and how sudden the
deaths of such adventurers.

When she climbed from the pod she ached all over, stretched, wheezed.
Yet she had done no true exercise, except in her mind.

She was late for her appointment, but she paused to look up through the crystal dome at good ol' Earth, a multicolored crescent marble in the Lunar sky.

All but the last few centuries of human history had played out there.
Throughout that history men and women had filled in the dark unknowns
with imagination. So expeditions crossed oceans and high vacuum until new
lands came into view—in just a few thousand years. Go back that far and
you would see Sumerian ziggurats whose star maps cartooned the sky with
imagined constellations and traced destinies through star-based prognostica-
tions. Someday a robotic follow-up probe might fall again toward the red star
she had just seen, to become the Schliemann of this alien Troy.

That might happen; there were so many stars to reach out and see, and
more candidates by the day. Now she could swim by other strange distant
worlds and feel them, fed by slabs of data—and still sense the great dark
unknowns. Which was her job.

The Prefect raised an eyebrow, pursed his leathery lips. "I gather you are
behind in your summations."

A flat fact. "I am, yes. I have been taking a careful review of some expedition records."

"You are a Trainee, not a Librarian. Nor, if you continue this way, much
hope of becoming one. Best to shape your skills to the essentials."

"I think I can better fathom records if I see the planetary explorations in
direct sensing."

His face soured more, lips turned down, his frown a ladder of creases.
Legendarily, he favored the scowl over the smile. She had to change the
dynamic here.

She stood. "My, you have a window." She had never seen one in a Lunar office.

"I like to have some perspective."

Outside was the sweep of the plaza, pearly in the Earthshine. "A view, yes, I can see—"

"I like some separation from the rest of all this. Also the glass is a constant temptation."

"To . . . what?"

"Throw something through it. Usually a student. Sometimes a Trainee, such as you."

"Ah, I—"

"Fly-in recordings will not reward mere poking around. They have been studied in great detail and can yield nothing more. Especially this red dwarf you just sensed."

"I am not just reviewing—"

"No, you are taking up pod time with full-sense flyby data."

"It was odd, how it suddenly cut off—"

"Many expeditions simply died, yes—accident, equipment failure. Those were the early days, full of verve, over a century ago. Ignore them. I want to see more of your time spent in the *hard* work. Take up third level Messages and work with the Artilects to advance our understanding. Remember, these are not linear languages at Level Three."

"I, I will try."

"And do not use the pods to simply joyride on old explorations." He turned toward the view and she realized her appointment was over. At least she didn't have to exit through the window.

Quick!—a world in a few passing hours. Then to sum it up in the brittle frame of linear sentences, the frail girders of mere flat words:

A ruddy world with lesser grav. One huge sprawl of a continent, plus lesser land mass in the other hemisphere, of humped and dirty rockrimmed mountains. Skies the color of crisp sand. Spiky mountains cut into curiously precise pie slices by iodine rivers that flowed to the continental center, making a vast somber bay of jade waters.

Go closer, lower: giant caterpillars stretched in trees as tall as mountains. The low grav here made for monsters.

Forested slopes in close-up were mushroom trees of violent orange. Huge blue birds with wings like parachutes, bills shaped like Death's sickle, feathers like flapping palm fronds. A plain of plants evoking erect oak leaves. Smaller growths resembling inside-out umbrellas.

Rain turning to snowflakes at high noon on the equator. Rain like drops of blood in the rocky highlands. Mists glowing like white fire in the valleys. Chasms radiating in mountain ranges like fractures in frosted windowpanes. Winding rivers in the fevered tropics, shapely as women's torsos or slim violins. Icecaps featuring swollen growths like blue berets. Storms that solidified like hurled hammerheads across tropical isles. Clouds drifting like pregnant purple cows. Wind-blasted rockwork in curious curved forms, like frozen music. Lurching beasts all angles and ribs, grazing across mustard grasslands.

The sailcraft played out its fat helium balloons, which went roving roving roving until they ran out of lift. These captured close-up the many odd beasts, eyed landscapes for buildings, assayed the sweep of land for betraying rectangles—signs of intelligence, or else of obsessive animals who knew Euclid in their souls.

Grazers aplenty swept by under the balloon's down-looking eyes, plus carnivores, big and furred and fanged. The craft saw big floater insects, too, with steering wings and armor plates and strange inexplicable leggy bits like antennae. These creatures eyed the balloon uneasily, braying roars into the acoustic balloon ears. Some angular beasts gazed upward warily, as if the balloon were a new foe in their air. They bristled, blared and thrust up narrow snouts that ended in the blunt truth of mouths like a pair of pliers. Some, in a narrow canyon lined with goat-like shambling monoliths, shot lances at the balloon eye, which fell far short. Still, perhaps a compliment of sorts.

And again: roads. Towns tucked under ample tree canopies. No electromagnetic emissions beyond the faint and local. Cities under regular humps of hills. Ships dotted the inland sea, white and slender. Yet this advanced society had only a weak signature in the radio, microwaves, and in the other bands, no signals at all.

Then the pod went silent, done. Another failed expedition.

She lingered a while in the quiet. Biting her lip, she wondered if silence was not the true state of the universe, now that the ancestral acoustics of the big bang had faded into scratch-marks in the microwave sky. Silence: far more noble than humanity's squeaks.

This world had been a treat, really. She took planetary records at random, not really knowing what she was seeking. Most worlds in the habitable zone were of a sameness. Solemn planets sleeping in the silence of ice and stone. Seaworlds awash in dark purple waters betraying no life, only its eventual prospect. Baked plains of ancient lava, unblessed by seas or even ponds, a likely match for a collision with a wandering waterworld, should orbital dynamics ever bring one from further out: a Newtonian miracle awaiting. Black volcanic corkscrews spiraling up to the atmospheric roof of planets still in process, getting baked to oblivion. Vast planets of crawling slime. Oceans lapping against barren shores. Plankton mats the size of continents.

To find a mature, thriving biosphere was a blessing. She savored them in the sensory auditorium of her snug pod.

She began to favor the dwarf suns and their narrow habitable zones. Such stars lived long, as old as the galaxy's ten billion years, yet scarcely a fraction along their stable lifespans. So, too, their worlds had millions of millennia to work their slow, gravid marvels. She studied them whenever she could manage the time, outside her own work and research at the Interstellar Library. These labors, she felt, were perhaps foolish but also a proud thing to do, as a fleck of dust condemned to know it is a fleck of dust.

Rachel said to her friend Catkejen, "I'm going crazy. Or maybe I've already arrived."

"Brain-fried with work, maybe," Catkejen said with a sardonic eye-roll, sipping a barely acceptable red wine—but also the only available, fresh from the fragrant farm domes deep underground.

Rachel still wore the single white patch on her collar—"the mark of the least" as they were known. One-patchers were greener than summer grass. Catkejen had two, so was one leg up in the ladder from Trainee to Librarian. Amid the hub and bub of techtalk of the other Trainees she was sporting a fine plum-colored coat with a laced waistcoat in a deftly contrasting shade, crossed diagonally with a red ribbon. With leggings and heater shoes, current Lunar fashion stressed subtle resistance against the creeping cold of their world, despite the ferocious warmth shed by their reactors. Rachel just wore heavy pseud-wool dresses in severe gray, plus close weave black tights—all free downloads and printouts, but yes, dull. Thrifty was not nifty here, but she didn't care. She wanted to escape notice, to tend her own internal gardens.

"I've added to my historical studies of the dwarf stars," Rachel made herself say amid the babble of the open-air restaurant, gazing down on the gray work expanses of the lunar plain below. "Something odd going on there."

"Great era, that was," Catkejen said, distracted by the stellar displays that coursed across their social area ceilings. Rachel thought the images odd, skies of galaxies and erupting stars. The psychers said such spectacles fended off the boxed-in phobias that plagued many Loonies. "Centuries ago, right? First closeups of the neighbors, the 550 'scopes just getting started."

"I'm looking at the old missions, the microwave-beamed sail ships that scoped out the nearbys."

Catkejen eyed a passing guy, maybe looking for an evening elsewhere; some of the higher-ups had their own singleton rooms—great for parties, and of course a romantic perk. Catkejen yawned, a clear come-on signal, but the guy just kept moving. "Yeah, long before we knew what a web of interstellar messaging there was."

Rachel leaned forward to keep Catkejen from diversions. "I'm looking at the 550 lens data, too. Plenty of life-bearing planets around the galaxy's dwarfs, that says. Some with signs of a civilization, too. But most dwarfstar globes are shrouded in clouds, hard to see."

Indeed, Rachel loved roving through the images gathered from coasting telescopes of the great theater in the sky, the worlds of the galaxy itself on display. The sun's focus spot was 550 A.U. out, where gravity gathered starlight into an intense pencil. The many sailship telescopes there fed back distorted images of faraway solar systems, as if seen through a funhouse mirror.

Rachel had learned much by scanning those images. The talent for not dying was distributed undemocratically. Few worlds could dance blithely through a gigayear, or far from their parent star. So many planets—crisp and dry, cloudy and cool, cratered yet with shimmering blue atmospheres—and stars, sometimes in crowded clusters, at times seen close-up and going nova in bright, virulent streamers, or in tight orbits around unseen companions that might be neutron stars or black holes. After a while even exotic alien landscapes became repetitious for her: blue-green mountain ranges scoured by deep gray rivers, placid oceans brimming with green scum, arid tan desert worlds ground down under heavy brooding brown atmospheres. Many ways for life to blossom, or die: ice worlds aplenty beneath starry skies, grasslands with four-footed herds roaming as volcanoes belched red streamers in the distance, oceans with huge beasts wallowing in enormous crashing waves, places hard to identify in the swirling pink mists. *Life adapts, indeed.*

Catkejen rolled her eyes. "Um. That improves your stats?"

"In time, sure. Mostly I just . . . follow my nose."

Catkejen leaned forward too, her ironic wry grin mocking. "Look, your nose should lead you to use the Seekers of Script more. You're behind in code-processing—*way* behind, gal!"

Meaning, of course, *Look, I have two patches already.* The Seekers of Script were supposedly below Trainees, but more experienced in deciphering SETI messages, using brute force methods from cryptology. They assisted Trainees and reported to Librarians. Rachel reported to a Prefect and Catkejen, at a higher level, now answered to the enigmatic Noughts. All this staff layering the SETI Library had amassed through two centuries of calcification.

Rachel dodged the advice. "How's your Nought?"

"Let's say he—uh, it—relishes the cadences of the language."

"Ah! You mean it's an incorrigible windbag." Apparently having no actual sexual organs led to verbal ejaculations instead. Just another gender choice, it seemed.

"Right, downright gushy." Catkejen had changed her hair to tarnished silver but her voice was still of scrap brass. Rachel envied her ability to conform to Library's Byzantine styles. Clothes and skin enhancers were the classic methods of competition and display. Men wore Rapunzel hair down to the shoulder blades at the moment. Women had great tangled thickets of hair in the armpits, often displayed in string-shirts. All this, despite the strange blend of decadent excess and harsh asceticism that prevailed in elite Library culture. To Rachel this was a special puzzle comparable to a labyrinthine SETI message.

"I heard they thinned some Trainees last week," Catkejen whispered, glancing around. "No announcement, just—*poof!*—you notice some are missing."

"Part of the method," Rachel said. They had seen this before. Those Trainees of both sexes, or even none, who had gotten by Earthside by being pert, pretty, perky were soon memories.

The Library had begun as a minor academic offshoot, back when there were few SETI messages and none had been well deciphered. Under rigorous mathematical methods, Artilects, and objective though human minds like the Noughts, it had grown in prestige and influence, into a citadel where there was a five-year wait for a windowless office.

Rachel said, "I hear some Trainees are planning a demonstration against these abrupt firings."

Another of Catkejen's patented eye-rolls. "I mentioned that rumor to my own Prefect. I got one of her rare laughs. She said, "Demonstrations never achieve anything—if they did, we wouldn't allow them.""

"Ah. A word to the wise?"

"Look, my nun-like friend—you've got to get *style* here. Dig into the ramified SETI messages—thousands of 'em, thick as bees—lurking back there in the vaults." Catkejen let her exasperation out in darting phrases. "Learn the pleasure in dispute, in dialectic, in dazzle. Get some freelance dash, peacock strut, daring hypotheses, knockabout synthesis—and get laid."

Rachel felt her face tighten, struggled to manage a smile. "I'm, you know, wrong time of the—"

"Month? Come on, gal!" Eyes flaring, grin spreading, hands shooting out. "When I'm on my period, I just stand in the shower and watch blood run down my legs into the drain and imagine I am a warrior princess who is standing in the aftermath of a battle, where I murdered all my enemies."

At the moment Rachel was mostly about cramp diarrhea. Which meant maybe stay away from the claustrophobic pod and the dwarf stars?

"You don't want to be in the next culling, my friend."

Rachel allowed herself a thin, uncertain smile. "Maybe they keep me on simply to serve as a warning to others."

The Library reception was on the rampart walk above the main plaza. The setting implied antiquity: vaulted and corbelled ceilings, columns sporting reverse flutings and crowned with Corinthian elegance. In a community that spent most of its time in small rooms with faintly oily air, taking advantage of views was essential for social functions. Crescent Earth was just a sliver, a comma, a single eyelash in the star-rich sky.

She looked for the Prefect but he was not in the murmuring crowd. *Probably feasting inside on Muscovy duck with pears and greens balsamico*, she thought, succumbing to the Lunar cliché of fixating on food. The Library hierarchy emerged most visibly in what luxuries one could afford. Rumors proposed fragrant, exotic dishes none had ever seen, but thought they scented in the closed air of the Library. To the nose, there were seemingly few secrets. Whatever a Muscovy duck might be, keeping one a secret seemed impossible. Still, there were ever more rumors about the sealed and secured portions of the Library, where only Prefects or better could venture.

A mecha band played its typical klunketta-klunketta rhythm and she found herself among some other Trainees, buzzing with talk about Earthside matters. She joined the line for the stand-up banquet—in 0.18 g, not a problem. Above, moon birds looking like paint-splattered sparrows banked and swirled. These had plenty of parrot genes, and others swooped in flocks of sharply elongated eagles, and even a huge impossibility she called Moby Hawk.

There was sweet-smelling bread made from an unpronounceable root vegetable, molasses, something called hoppin' john and tart collard greens, plus rich butter from goat's milk. She favored the usual pickup food of crickets, bugs and odd crispy-fried creatures with Byzantine names, and the obligatory pork and chicken. Considering, she pitied the vegetarians; most went back Earthside soon enough.

She wandered, not spotting any friends, and into a circle discussing the deaths in the latest human cold-sleep method.

". . . and they *all* died, within a two year span," a slim woman said mournfully. "I wish they would stop inflicting such torture on us."

Torture? Scan the news at your own risk, she thought.

She was a bit tired of the Lunar sophisticates' habit, their narcissism of borrowed tragedy. It came from viewing from afar—or at least far enough— the perpetual disasters on overcrowded Earth. It struck her as inverted empathy—relate some tragedy from the news and express your sad-eyed care, and soon enough, other people's suffering becomes about you. You convey with raised eyebrow or warped lips that you're owed some measure of the deference and compassion that the victims are.

"They knew the risks going in."

The thin woman frowned. "Well, I'm sure, but—"

"And chose to take them. Too bad it failed, but honestly—how likely is it that we mammals, whose sole hibernators are bears and the like, could take decades of cold sleep?"

"Well, they've been working on this for—what, a century?—and I think the scientists know what they're doing." The woman gave Rachel a sharp look that should have stuck several centimeters out of her back.

"Seems not. They *all* died?"

"Uh, yes. Twenty-five. Some made it for the six years mark, but none past eight."

"How'd they die?"

"The connectomics scientists say their slowed metabolism just stopped. Wouldn't restart."

A light-haired brown man added with a smack of lips, "The report said when they opened the life chests, there was a distinct smell of porcini risotto. Armpits filled with fungus."

A big laugh. This was enough to disband the group before Rachel got in too deep. But something in the issue tickled her mind. Did a century of trying cold-sleep mean it just wasn't possible for complex animals, including aliens?

If so, no visitors, no crewed starships. Even if civilizations arose and persisted, they could only visit other stars robotically. Then all interstellar contacts were the province of artificial intelligences . . . A glimmering of an idea.

Maybe—

"I have noted that you are disobeying," the Prefect said at her elbow.

"Oh! You startled me." Somehow the Prefect's bald head loomed large out here in the open. *Or maybe it just reminds me of how many dead worlds I've seen.*

"You are spending pod time on old reconnaissance. I will have to write a report." Not a flicker of emotion. *Write a report* meant blocking her from becoming a Librarian, maybe forever.

"I have an idea I'm pursuing." Not quite a lie.

A long, slow blink, as if thinking. "I give you three days to stop."

The Prefect turned and walked away with the long lope those born on the moon made in a graceful sway.

At every stage of her life she'd been reasonable, dutiful. But now a vague intuition made her bat away the advice of her friends, and the everyday world of what people said, of tips and tales, theories and tidbits that might add to the Library's already vast stores of alien messages.

The Library had evolved into a factory, producing minds distended out of all proportion—force-fed facts, as unlucky geese are force-fed corn. The succulent foie gras of such minds was then to be dined on by the Library, digesting alien 0s and 1s into a digital aesthete's wisdom. A Librarian's life, like the goose's comfort, was certainly secondary.

Even the Prefect, and that Librarian constriction, she shrugged off; her ascetic trainers Earthside had been Dionysiac compared to him. But she was mature now, nearing fifty and the end of her obedient-student mode.

Instead of worrying, she worked through the latest stellar evolution theories, well buttressed by myriad data links and erudite commentaries. Astronomers loved their data-mountains, indeed.

A star lived very long if it had a tenth of a solar mass and so a tenth of its radius—a pigmy, glowering at its close-clustered children in sullen reds. So a planet in the thin habitable zone of a typical dwarf M star remained in that zone for a hundred billion years. In essence, such stars lasted so long, the length of habitability becomes more of a planetary than a stellar issue. If an intelligent species properly managed its environment, it could persist far longer than any around a Sol-like star, which would grow unstable after about ten billion years, and swell to fill a world's sky, baking it. Any dwarf-star civilization might have begun billions of years before fish crawled up a beach on Earth and learned to breathe the rising oxygen in the air. Such societies had to manage their worlds or die out.

Pondering this, she booked pod time again.

She knew from her Artilect that the Prefect's boss, the Nought Siloh, was checking on her work, so while her period lasted she actually spent time on the message inventory. She made little progress, even with the ever-helpful

Seekers of Script. Picking tiny feelers of meaning from myriad messages—
some seemingly simple, many blizzards of digital chaos—was like trying to
hear a moth in a hurricane.

To the deep translation problem came also that many Messages were
ancient, coding bronzed into memories of dead alien cultures, their beamed
hails simple funeral pyres. Many could be solved by a lost wax method of
digital abstraction, but that often yielded cries of despair in alien tongues.
After a week of work she got a call to report for review.

The Nought named Siloh frowned, apparently its only expression. "Your performance lags. I suppose insights gathered from your inspection of planetary
observations could augment your Message work, yes. But." It stopped, eyeing
her.

Noughts had intricate adjustments to offset their lack of sexual appetites and
apparatus, both physical and mental. They had been developed in the 2330s
to give them a rigorous objectivity in translating the Messages. Somehow this
evolved into the 2400s to mean management of the Library itself.

"I assume your *but* implies that you hold doubts?" She managed a smile
with this but the Nought's frown did not budge.

"I solely wish to remind you that such interests are a diversion," Siloh said,
drawing out vowels, eyes lidded.

"Perhaps not. I have found some . . . curiosities."

"You will find in working with your Artilect—the Transap one, I see,
excellent choice—saying no more than you mean is essential."

"I looked back at a classic case of direct exploration today, Luhman 16.
An old flyby, 6.5 light years out, the nearest L-type dwarf. For a while the
third-closest known star to Sol, after the Centauris and poor lonely Barnard's
star. Point is, it's a binary and both stars had planets—a bonanza, but both
held remnants of shattered cities, billions of years old."

The Nought sniffed. "Of course."

The obvious rebuff made her bear down. It was easier to act herself into a
new way of thinking than to think her way into a new way of acting.

"There's a pattern here. Dead civilizations around dwarf stars."

"The universe is cruel to the unwise. You are ignoring your essential tasks.
Does that seem wise?"

She made herself be systematic.

The dwarf stars were marvels, in their way. She had always been impressed
by their efficiency at packing hydrogen, the stuff of flammable zeppelins,

into such a small space; some were more than twice as dense as lead. The density of Sol was bubblegum by comparison.

Many of their planets were tide-locked, or nearly so. Some had a spin/orbit resonance like Mercury, which rotates three times every two orbits around Sol. Others were split worlds, with a twilight border rich in black and gray forests, with mostly minimal animal life. The best were those that spun lazily in the ruby furnace of their skies.

There were systems whose sun was but a tarnished penny above a world where three moons played at their races. Winds were whips, polishing continents to smooth mausoleums. Such hells of sand gave her itchy flashes as the centuries-old probe explored. She rejected these, and many stony rocks and super-Jovians that circled burning circles in the sky.

There were even worse. Some circles lose enough to their star that atmospheric temperatures exceed the boiling point of water. Clouds of unlikely mixtures of potassium chloride or zinc sulfide, lifted high into the atmosphere, yielding a flat, dull spectrum.

Yet even here brightly glowing plumes reminded her of an underwater scene with turquoise-tinted currents. Strange nebulous strands reached out, echoing starfish, giant beings aloft in an atmosphere that would have crushed a dinosaur. If anything lived there, she did not wish to know of it.

She had two more days to comply with the Prefect's orders. But she couldn't. She kept on mining the recon files, experiencing them whole-body.

In her mind swarmed filmy ideas. She slept restlessly, tossing in sweaty sheets—and alone; no social life seemed worth the lost moments. She skipped meals and snacked on garlic-flavored fried beetles.

Then back in the pod. The Prefect could have cut off her privileges, but no such order came.

Among the dwarf stars Earth had explored, or had seen through the lenses coasting out beyond 550 Astronomical Units, there were some worlds on which fancy sorts of watery membrane learned to think—and made great wet beasts from green crusts and reddish films and fizzing electricity. These were often on warmer, cloudy L-class dwarfs and cooler T-dwarfs, whose atmospheres were clear and sharp. In the solar corona something like manta rays coasted—life on a star. But their client planets were even stranger.

A dawn like a gray colloid. The dwarf's ruddy glow stirred the air like a thick fluid, sending blue streamers through the clotted air, bringing soon enough sharp shafts to bear on black forests below. They already knew, from SETI messages and innumerable probes, both human and alien, some sad truths. A million worlds had brimmed with life but like a puzzle with a sole dreary solution, the show ended soon. Ice or fire snuffed out life's promise.

But on living worlds, there was a plentitude of wonders. There was even oxygen—the slow fuse to the explosion of animal life. On Earth around 635 megayears ago, enough oxygen supported tiny sponges. After 580 million years more, strange creatures as thin as blue crêpes lived on a lightly oxygenated seafloor. Fifty million years later, vertebrate ancestors glided through warm, oxygen-rich seawater much as she had done as a girl.

So dwarf stars with oxygen-rich children had billions of years of advantage over latecomer Earth.

They used their eons, she saw. Probes dropped into the atmospheres of these planets heard distant calls like screechy toots on a rusty trombone, gutbucket growls, sighing cries—from creatures that looked as dull and gray as sluggish rutabagas. Then—goodness gracious, great balls of fire! Odd beings who burst into flame at mating season, apparently after passing on their genes—and leaving the stage in hasty crimson blisters.

Her heart jumped like a mullet, quick and hard, just as she recalled seeing them in the salty warm Gulf bay air where she grew up. *Angels we Have heard on high Sweetly singing o'er The plain,* she thought, as she played back the sounds of distant animals she would never see, beyond mere pixels.

Then the entire vibrant world was gone in a sharp instant.

She staggered a bit, going away from the yawning mouth of the pod. Looking back, it seemed indeed like a giant grin that had swallowed her, and now spat her out, altered. The experience had turned her inside-out, like a pocket no good for holding much anymore.

Somehow the sensorium had been fuller, more invasive this time. Smell carried memory, carried history. She bore now an after-memory of the shimmering redlands she had seen, somehow transmorphed into smells, sounds, and textures in her recollected sum of all she had experienced. The pod made that transition across senses, embedding the past into the sensual present. The pod was an Artilect and so learned her, too, and each new world had held greater impact, from that.

She had seen shattered worlds, those at one with the dull, the indiscriminate dust. Those who could pour no more into the golden vessel of great song, sent across the eons and light years. Their Messages might once have sung of alien Euclids who had looked on beauty bare, and so stitched it into Messages of filmy photons, sent oblivious into the great galaxy's night . . .

Such fools we mortals be . . .

She stopped for a glass of wine and some snack centipedes, delaying the inevitable. A passing friend gazed into her eyes and asked, "Hey, what's biting your bum today?"

Rachel opened her mouth, closed it, and the whole idea she had been seeking came together in that second.

"Shut up," she explained. And went to see the Prefect.

"I'm aware that I'm not the fastest fox in the forest here," she began, after seating. "But I have an idea."

The Prefect brightened. "Ah. Fastest fox—I do appreciate bio analogies, since we live on a dead world." He steepled his hands on the desk and took up an expectant face, eyebrows arched.

She took a deep breath, nostrils flared at the antiseptic air of the Nought's shadowy preserve. "The older dwarf stars with rich biospheres—they're lying low."

"From our probes?"

"Yes—that's why they shot down our observing craft."

"Aha." A salamander stare.

So he wants me to spell it out. "I estimate the rejecting biospheres are several billion years old. They let us approach, even drop balloons, then—wham."

"Indeed. You have done the required statistics?"

"Yes." She let her inboard systems coalesce a shimmering curtain in the air, using the Prefect's office system. The correlation functions appeared in 3D. The Prefect flicked a finger and the minamax hummocks rotated, showing the parameter space—a landscape covering billions of years, thousands of stars.

"Perhaps significant." A frown formed above his one cocked eyebrow. She recalled that the Prefect was the sort who would look out a window at a cloudburst and say, *It seems to be raining*, on the off-chance that somebody was pouring water off the roof.

"They're probably the longest-lived societies in the galaxy, since they're around red stars that hold stable. If they can't do cold-sleep, either—and so can't go interstellar voyaging, like us—they're stuck in their systems. And they're still *afraid*."

The Prefect nodded. "Correct, yes—the cause of the dwarf-star worlds' insularity lies in the far past. An antiquity beyond our knowing, from eras before fish crawled from our seas."

"Whatever could have made them fear *for so long?*"

"We do not know. It is a history . . ." Mixed emotions flitted across his face, as if memory was dancing within view. ". . . for which adjectives are temporarily unavailable."

"We have to be alert!" She got up and paced the office. "These aliens hunkering down around their red and brown stars, they have lasted by being cautious."

A shrug. "That seems obvious."

She had hoped for help, not a blasé, blunt assessment. "So we need to find out more," she said, realizing it was lame.

He leveled a stare. "Intelligence is defined by sufficient detachment from one's own case, to consider it as one of many. A child becomes humanly intelligent the moment it realizes that there are other minds just like its own, working in the same way on the same world available to them. It seems to be the same with societies across the galaxy."

She nodded. "Other worlds, other minds, strange—but they have suffered the same past."

"True. This is not a matter of dry certainties. It is a quest for archeological wisdom."

She whirled, her mouth a grimace, eyes wild. "Whatever they're afraid of it could be, be—*comin' right atchya!*"

He was calm, further confusing her. He gave her a cautious, precise, throat clearing. "I have an allergy to dogma, including my own."

"What's your dogma?"

"Placing the Library on Luna, safely away from the torrents of Earth, was a primary motive. Best to contemplate the stars where one can see them anytime. In other words, take the long view."

She was getting more frustrated by his blithe manner, but resisted raising her voice. "Look, you wanted me to go back to studying decrypting SETI messages, but this, this—I just couldn't give it up."

"Research is not devised, it is distilled."

She let out a loud, barking laugh. "Building logic towers from premises wrung out of thin air, more like it."

"You have got it nearly right."

"Nearly?"

He eyed her narrowly. "We think of the Elizabethan world as one we perceive through our own reductive devising. We think of it as populated by the Queen and Ben Jonson and the Dark Lady and the Bard and a raucous theatre full of groundlings. That's what *we* know, from some texts. But the real Elizabethan world had a lot more people in it than that, and countless more possibilities. Here at the Library, we deal with not a mere handful of centuries. We have received messages sent across thousands of light years, from beacons erected by societies long dead."

"Well, yes—"

"So we need to know more, before deciding anything."

She finally let her anger out. "Nonsense! This is a threat! People need to know." She spread her hands, beseeching him.

"Go and think some more. You are following the right path."

With a wave he dismissed her.

Catkejen came in from a date, all fancied out in a maroon, bioweb Norfolk jacket with fluorescent yellow spirals down the arms, and found Rachel calculating some ideas. "Actual penciling out! Pushing graphite! You should get outside sometime, y'know."

Feeling every inch a pedant, Rachel rose, stretched. "I was backtracking those red stars that had hunkered down."

"You mean the ones that prob'ly knocked out our probes?"

"Yes, plus ones we've seen from the 550 A.U. telescopes, that had ruins on them."

"So you're running backward their orbits around the galaxy?" A disbelieving frown.

"Yes, it's a tough many-body problem—"

"Hey, another example of cross-field confusion. We already have that!"

This was how Rachel learned that astronomers had developed a reverse-history code of extraordinary ability. They had first evolved it to study galactic stellar evolution of spiral arms. Which led to her next audience with the Prefect.

She walked—no, she decided, she *skipped* with schoolgirl joy in the low grav—out of the advanced computational dome, feeling as if she had returned from a great distance.

She blew past the Prefect's office staff and marched straight in on the great man, who was staring at a screen. He looked up, not showing any surprise. "You have more." Not a question.

She flipped on her personal Artilect interface so it projected an image on the office 3D display. "This shows the dwarf stars our probes and the 550 A.U. 'scopes found to be defensive or destroyed. No particular correlation between their locations, notice."

He merely nodded. She had tagged the forty-three cases in bright green. They were scattered through a volume more than a thousand light years on a side—still a mere bubble in the colossal galactic disk. "Now let's run the galaxy backward."

The green dots arced through their long ellipses. The slow spin of the galaxy itself emerged as the bee swarms of stars glided in stately measure. The Sun took a quarter of a billion years to cycle in its slow orbit at about two hundred kilometers a second, taking more than a thousand years to move a light year. Humanity's duration was less than a thousandth of one galactic cycle. From SETI messages marking funeral pyre societies, the Librarians knew that humans were mayflies among sentient cultures, the newest kids on the block.

The Prefect watched the backward-running swarm and raised his eyebrows as the green dots slowly drew nearer each other. "They follow somewhat different orbits, bobbing up and down in the galactic plane, brushing by nearby stars, suffering small tilts in their courses," she said, as though this wasn't obvious. *Was she making too much of this?* She told herself a sharp *no* and went on.

"I can see some, well, clumps of several green specks forming," the Prefect said. "They seem to be . . ." surprise pitched his voice into a tenor note ". . . occasionally passing within a few light years of each other. There! And now . . ." a pause as four dots swooped together ". . . another cluster."

Rachel made herself use her flat, factual voice. "Stats show these were nonrandom, four sigmas out from any bell curve odds."

"They . . . group . . . at different times. How far into the past are we now?"

"Six million years."

He frowned, pursed his lips. "I have never seen this before."

"Astronomers study star dynamics. This is about the hunkered-down planets, or the ones destroyed, orbiting those stars."

The Prefect gave her a sour smile. "So this is another example of the perils of specialization."

"Um, yessir." Let the idea percolate . . . The Prefect bit. "Which means?"

"The endangered worlds were near each other, millions of years ago. Whatever attacked them—killing some societies entirely, scaring others so much they still remember it, guard against it—came at them when they were close to each other."

She paused. Let him figure it out . . .

"Whatever menace does this . . ." The Prefect let his puzzled sentence trail off.

"Wormholes lie somewhere in those intersecting orbits."

The Prefect stiffened. "We know of no wormholes!"

"Right. Absence of evidence is not evidence of absence, as some philosopher said."

A furious head-shake. "But—where could wormholes *come from*? We know they're impossible to build—"

"The Big Bang? We know it was chaotic. Maybe some survived that era. Got trapped into the galaxy when it formed up later. Goes coasting around, just as the stars do."

He blinked, always a good sign. "So when a wormhole mouth gets near a group of stars . . ."

"Something comes through it. Someone—some *thing*—that found a wormhole mouth. Y'know, theory says wormholes aren't simple one-way pipes. They can branch, like subways in space-time. So something comes through, attacks inhabited planets."

The Prefect looked puzzled. Maybe this was coming too fast? Explain, girl. Go technical.

"We—well, I—saw it in the planets around dwarfs, because there are more of them. Better statistics, the pattern shows up."

She let that sink in while the Prefect watched the galaxy grind into its past. More green dots swooped along their blithe paths, nearing each other, coasting on, apart . . . the waltz of eternity, Newton meets Mozart, on and on through thousands of millennia, down through the echoing halls of vast, lost time.

The Prefect was a quick study. His sharp, piercing eyes darted among the bee swarm stars, mouth now compressed, lips white with pressure. "What are the odds that there's one near us?"

This she had not thought about. "Given the number of dwarfs nearby . . . Um. Pretty good."

He smiled, an unusual event. "This is utterly new. When you found the ancient tragedies, I was impressed. If you were wondering, only one in several thousand Trainees catch on to that fact—that secret, I should say."

"Really? And this—the clustering—how often has any Trainee turned that up?"

A quick shake of head. "Never. This is a new discovery."

"Really?" She had thought she would surprise him, get some reward, but . . . *new?*

"No one knows this. Wormholes! Maybe nearby? So—if there's one nearby—where is it?"

This was going too fast for her. "I sure as hell don't know. I'm not an astronomer! I want to be a Librarian."

The Prefect nodded. "So you shall be, in time." He paused, gazing at the slow, sure grind of the galaxy. "We have a saying, we Prefects. "Creativity may be hard to nurture, but it's easy to thwart." You have proven that we do occasionally let talent get through."

She sat silent, not knowing where this was going.

"Also . . . Congratulations."

"What?"

"You have found the unsaid. The essence of research."

"What . . . ?"

"The Library is not a mere decoding society. We must use the full range of exploration, not just the messages. You saw that. You first ferreted out a truth we Prefects do not wish to make known—the deaths of whole worlds, the closing in of others. Your discovery now, the proximity of the stricken worlds—is a gift."

"Gift?"

"Yes. Much we discover needs time to . . . digest. But we become calcified, mere decoders. To become a true Librarian, one must show innate curiosity, persistence, drive."

"I, I just got interested. You leaned on me hard to keep up my studies, not fall behind the others—"

"It is *they* who have fallen behind. We cannot drill creativity into our Trainees. They must display it without being asked."

She gaped at him, not following. "So . . ."

"You are now promoted. You shall not tell your fellow Trainees why. Let them bathe in mystery. Do not say a word of what you have learned."

"But, but—"

For the first time ever, she saw the Prefect smile. "Welcome. I will see to getting you a private office now, as well."

Outside, the night Earth seen through the vast dome was a glowing halo, sunlight forming a thin rainbow circle. She saw his point. Earth was always there, and so were the waiting stars.

And something dark hid in the yawning dark beyond, something even a Nought or a Prefect did not know. Something shadowy in the offing out there in the galaxy, waiting, patient and eternal.

Wormholes? Through which something horrible came? They were out there, hanging like dark doorways between the stars.

It came in a flash she would recall all her life.

Now she knew what she wanted to solve, an arrow to pierce the night beyond and find the doorways. To see across eternity and into the consuming dark above, that awaited all humanity.

Indrapramit Das (aka Indra Das) is an Indian author from Kolkata, West Bengal. His debut novel *The Devourers* (Del Rey / Penguin India) was the winner of the 2016 Lambda Literary Award for Best LGBTQ SF/F/Horror, and shortlisted for the 2015 Crawford Award. His short fiction has been nominated for the Shirley Jackson Award and has appeared in several publications and anthologies, including *Clarkesworld, Tor.com,* and The Year's Best Science Fiction. He is an Octavia E. Butler scholar and a grateful graduate of the Clarion West Writers Workshop, and received his M.F.A. from the University of British Columbia in Vancouver. He has worn many hats, including editor, dog hotel night shift attendant, TV background performer, minor film critic, occasional illustrator, environmental news writer, pretend-patient for med school students, and video game tester.

THE WORLDLESS

Indrapramit Das

Every day NuTay watched the starship from their shack, selling satshine and sweet chai to wayfarers on their way to the stars. NuTay and their kin Satlyt baked an endless supply of clay cups using dirt from the vast plain of the port. NuTay and Satlyt, like all the hawkers in the shanties that surrounded the dirt road, were dunyshar, worldless—cursed to a single brown horizon, if one gently undulated by time to grace their eyes with dun hills. Cursed, also, to witness that starship in the distance, vessel of the night sky, as it set sail on the rippling waves of time and existence itself—so the wayfarers told them—year after year.

The starship. The sky. The dun hills. The port plain. They knew this, and this only.

Sometimes the starship looked like a great temple reaching to the sky. All of NuTay's customers endless pilgrims lining up to enter its hallowed halls and carry them through the cloth that Gods made.

NuTay and Satlyt had never been inside a starship.

If NuTay gave them free chai, the wayfarers would sometimes show viz of other worlds on their armbands, flicking them like so much dijichaff into the air, where they sprouted into glowing spheres, ghost marbles to mimic the air-rich dewdrops that clustered aeon-wise along the fiery filaments of the galaxy. The wayfarers would wave in practiced arkana, and the spheres would twirl and zoom and transform as they grew until their curvature became glimpses of those worlds and their settlements glittering under the myriad suns and moons. NuTay would watch, silent, unable to look away.

Once, Satlyt, brandishing a small metal junk shiv, had asked whether NuTay wanted them to corner a wayfarer in a lonesome corner of the port and rob them of their armband or their data coins. NuTay had slapped Satlyt then, so hard their cheek blushed pink.

NuTay knew Satlyt would never hurt anyone—that all they wanted was to give their maba a way to look at pictures of other worlds without having to barter with wayfarers.

When NuTay touched Satlyt's cheek a moment after striking, the skin was hot with silent anger, and perhaps shame.

Sometimes the starship looked like monolithic shards of black glass glittering in the sun, carefully stacked to look beautiful but terrifying.

Sometimes the starship would change shape, those shards moving slowly to create a different configuration of shapes upon shapes with a tremendous moaning that sounded like a gale moving across the hills and pouring out across the plain. As it folded and re-folded, the starship would no longer look like shards of black glass.

Sometimes, when it moved to reconfigure its shape, the starship would look suddenly delicate despite its size, like black paper origami of a starship dropped onto the plain by the hand of a god.

NuTay had once seen an actual paper starship, left by a wayfarer on one of NuTay's rough-hewn benches. The wayfarer had told them the word for it: origami. The paper had been mauve, not black.

The world that interested NuTay the most, of course, was Earth. The one all the djeens of all the peoples in the galaxy first came from, going from blood to blood to whisper the memory of the first human into all their bodies so they still looked more or less the same no matter which world they were born on.

"NuTay, Earth is so crowded you can't imagine it," one wayfarer had told them, spreading their hands across that brown horizon NuTay was so familiar with. "Just imagine," the wayfarer said. "Peoples were having kin there before there were starships. Before any peoples went to any other star than Sol. This planet, your planet, is a station, nah?"

NuTay then reminded the wayfarer that this was not *their* planet, not really, because it was not a place of peoples but a port for peoples to rest in between their travels across the universe. Dunyshar had no planet, no cultures to imitate, no people.

"Ahch, you know that's the same same," the wayfarer said, but NuTay knew it wasn't, and felt a slight pain in their chest, so familiar. But they knew the wayfarer wouldn't know what this was, and they said nothing and listened as they spoke on. "If this planet is port, then Earth, that is the first city in the universe—Babal, kafeen-walla. Not so nice for you. Feels like not enough atmo for so many peoples if you go there, after this planet with all this air, so much air, so much place."

And NuTay told that wayfarer that they'd heard that Earth had a thousand different worlds on it, because it had a tilt and atmos that painted its lands a thousand different shades of place as it spun around the first Sun.

"Less than a thousand, and not the only world with other worlds on it," the wayfarer said, laughing behind their mask. "But look," the wayfarer raised their arm to spring viz into the air, and there was a picture of a brown horizon, and dun hills. "See? Just like here." NuTay looked at the dun hills, and marveled that this too could be Earth. "Kazak-istan," said the wayfarer, and the placename was a cold drop of rain in NuTay's mind, sending ripples across their skull. It made them feel better about their own dun hills, which caught their eye for all the long days. Just a little bit better.

So it went. Wayfarers would bring pieces of the galaxy, and NuTay would hold the ones of Earth in their memory. It had brown horizon, blue horizon, green horizon, red horizon, gray horizon.

When the starship was about to leave, the entire port plain would come alive with warning, klaxons sounding across the miles of empty dirt and clanging across the corrugated roofs of the shop shanties and tents. NuTay and Satlyt would stop work to watch even if they had customers, because even customers would turn their heads to see.

To watch a starship leave is to witness a hole threaded through reality, and no one can tire of such a vision. Its lights glittering, it would fold and fold its parts until there was a thunderous boom that rolled across the plain, sending glowing cumulus clouds rolling out from under the vessel and across the land.

A flash of light like the clap of an invisible hand, and the clouds would be gone in less than a second to leave a perfect black sphere where the starship had been. If you looked at the sphere, which was only half visible, emerging from the ground a perfect gigantic bubble of nothingness, it would hurt your eyes, because there was *nothing* to see within its curvature. For an intoxicating second there would be hurtling winds ripping dust through the shop shanties, creating a vortex of silken veils over the plain and around the sphere. The shanty roofs would rattle, the horses would clomp in their stables, the wind chimes would sing a shattering song. The very air would vibrate as if it were fragile, humming to the tune of that null-dimensional half-circle embedded in the horizon, a bloated negative sunrise.

In the next moment, the sphere would vanish in a thunderclap of displaced atmos, and there would be only flat land where the starship had once stood.

A few days later, the same sequence would occur in reverse, and the starship would be back, having gone to another world and returned with a new population. When it returned, the steam from its megastructures would create wisps of clouds that hung over the plain for days until they drifted with their shadows into the hills.

Being younger dunyshar, Satlyt worked at the stalls some days, but did harder chores around the port, like cleaning toilets and helping starship crews do basic maintenance work. Every sunrise, NuTay watched Satlyt leave the stall on their dirt bike, space-black hair free to twine across the wind. The droning dirt bike would draw a dusty line across the plain, its destination the necklace of far-off lights extending from where the squatting starship basked in sunrise—the dromes where wayfarers refueled, processed, lived in between worlds. The dirt bikes would send wild horses rumbling in herds across the port plain, a sight that calmed NuTay's weakening bones.

NuTay had worked at the dromes, too, when they were younger and more limber. They'd liked the crowds there, the paradisiacal choirs of announcements that echoed under vaulted ceilings, the squealing of boots on floor leaving tracks to mop up, the harsh and polychrome cast of holofake neon advertising bars, clubs, eateries and shops run by robots, or upscale wayfarer staff that swapped in and out to replace each other with each starship journey, so they didn't have to live on the planet permanently like the dunyshar. Nowadays the dromes were a distant memory. NuTay stayed at the shack, unable to do that much manual labour.

Those that spent their lives on the planet of arrivals and departures could only grow more thin and frail as time washed over the days and nights. The dunyshars' djeens had whispered their flesh into Earth-form, but on a world with a weaker gravity than Earth.

NuTay's chai itself was brewed from leaf grown in a printer tent with a second-hand script for accelerated microclimate—hardware left behind from starships over centuries, nabbed from the junk shops of the port by NuTay for shine and minutes of tactile, since dunyshar were never not lonely and companionship was equal barter, usually (usually) good for friendships.

NuTay would meditate inside the chai-printing tent, which was misty and wet in growing season. Their body caressed by damp green leaves, air fragrant with alien-sweet perfume of plant life not indigenous, with closed eyes NuTay would pretend to be on Earth, the source of chai and peoples and everything. Each time a cycle ended, and the microclimate roasted the leaves to heaps of brown brew-ready shavings, the tent hissed steam like one of NuTay's kettles, and that whistle was a quiet mourning for the death of that tent-world of green. Until next cycle.

The tent had big letters across its fiber on the outside, reading *Darjeeling* in Englis and Nagar script. A placename, a wayfarer had clarified.

When Satlyt was younger, they'd asked NuTay if the dunyshar could just build a giant printer tent the size of the port itself, and grow a huge forest of plants and trees here like on Earth or other worlds. NuTay knew these weren't thoughts for a dunyshar to have, and would go nowhere. But they said they didn't know.

The starshine was easier, brewed from indigenous fungus grown in shit.

Sometimes, as evening fell and the second sun lashed its last threads of light across the dun hills gone blue, or when the starship secreted a mist that wreathed its alloyed spires, the starship looked like a great and distant city. Just like NuTay had seen in viz of other worlds—towers of lights flickering to give darkness a shape, the outline of lives lived.

The starship *was* a city, of course. To take people across the galaxy to other cities that didn't move across time and existence.

There were no cities here, of course, on the planet of arrivals and departures. If you travelled over the horizon, as NuTay had, you would find only more port plains dotted with emptiness and lights and shop shanties and vast circular plains with other starships at their centres. Or great mountain ranges that were actually junkyards of detritus left by centuries of interstellar stops, and dismantled starships in their graveyards, all crawling with scavengers. Some dunyshar dared to live in those dead starships, but they were known to be unstable and dangerous, causing djeens to mutate so kin would be born looking different than humans. If this were true, NuTay had never seen such people, who probably kept to themselves, or died out.

NuTay had heard that if you walked far enough, you could see fields with starships so massive they reached the clouds, hulking across the sky, that these could take you to worlds at the very edge of the galaxy, where you could see the void between this galaxy and the next one—visible as a gemmed spiral instead of a sun.

Once, the wayfarer who'd left the origami starship for NuTay had come back to the stall, months or years later. NuTay hadn't realized until they left, because they'd been wearing goggles and an air-filter. But they left another little paper origami, this time in white paper, of a horse.

Horses were used for low-energy transport and companionship among many of the dunyshar. They had arrived centuries ago as frozen liquid djeens from a starship's biovat, though NuTay was five when they first realized that horses, like humans, weren't *from* the world they lived in. Curiously, the thought brought tears to their eyes when they first found this out.

Sometimes the starship looked like a huge living creature, resting between its journeys, sweating and steaming and groaning through the night.

This it was, in some sense. Deep in its core was residual life left by something that had lived aeons ago on the planet of arrivals and departures: the reason for this junction in space. There was exotech here, found long before NuTay or any dunyshar were born here, ghosts of when this planet *was* a world, mined by the living from other worlds. Dunyshar were not allowed in these places, extraterra ruins where miners, archaeologists, and other pilgrims from across the galaxy gathered. NuTay, like most dunyshar, had little interest in these zones or the ruins of whatever civilization was buried under the dirt of this once-world. Their interest was in the living civilization garlanding the galaxy, the one that was forever just out of their reach.

On their brief travels with Satlyt strapped to their back as a tender-faced baby, NuTay had seen the perimeter of one of these excavation zones from a mile away, floodlights like a white sunrise against the night, flowing over a vast black wall lined with flashing lights. Humming in the ground, and thunder crashing over the flatlands from whatever engines were used to unearth the deep ruins and mine whatever was in them.

NuTay's steed, a sturdy black mare the stablemaster that had bartered her had named Pacho, had been unusually restless even a mile from that zone. NuTay imagined the ghosts of a bygone world seeping from out of those black walls, and trickling into their limbs and lungs and those of their tender child gurgling content against their back.

NuTay rode away as fast as they could. Pacho died a few weeks later, perhaps older than the stablemaster had promised. But NuTay blamed the zone, and rubbed ointment on Satlyt for months after, dreading the morning they'd find their kin dead because of vengeful ghosts from the long dead world that hid beneath this planet's time.

For Satlyt's survival NuTay thanked the stars, especially Sol, that had no ghosts around them.

Satlyt had asked NuTay one day where they'd come from, and whose kin NuTay themself was. NuTay had waited for that day, and had answers for their child, who was ten at the time. They sat by their shack in the evening light, NuTay waving a solar lantern until it lit.

I am a nu-jen dunyashar, Satlyt, they said to their child. This means I have no maba, no parents at all.

Satlyt asked how, eyes wide with existential horror.

Listen. Many . . . djeens were brought here frozen many years ago. I taught you; two humans' djeens whisper together to form a new human. Some humans share their djeens with another human in tiny eggs held in their bellies, and others share it in liquid held between their legs. Two people from some world that I don't know gave their djeens in egg and liquid, so that peoples could bring them here frozen to make new humans to work here, and help give solace to the wayfarers travelling the stars. We are these new humans—the dunyshar. There are many old-jen dunyshar here who have parents, and grandparents, and on and on—the first of their pre-kin were born to surrogates a long time ago. Understand, nah?

Satlyt nodded, perhaps bewildered.

I was nu-jen; the first person my djeens formed here on the planet of arrivals and departures. I was born right there, NuTay stopped here to point at the distant lights of the dromes. In the nursery, where wayfarer surrogates live for nine months growing us, new-jen kin, when there aren't enough people in the ports anymore. They get good barter value for doing this, from the off-world peoples who run these ports.

Who taught you to talk? Who taught you what all you know? asked Satlyt.

The dunyshar, chota kin! They will help their own. All the people in this shanty place, they taught me. The three sibs who raised me through the youngest years and weaned me are all, bless them, dead from time, plain simple. This planet is too light for humans to live too long as Earth and other livable worlds.

Did you sleep with the three sibs so the djeens whispered me into existence?

No, no! No, they were like my parents, I couldn't do that. I slept with another when I grew. Their name was Farweh. Farweh, I say na, your other maba. With them I had you, chota kin.

They are dead, too?

NuTay smiled then, though barely. I don't know, Satlyt. They left, on a starship.

How? They were a wayfarer?

No, they grew up right here, new-jen, same as me. They had long black hair like you, and the red cheeks like you also, the djeens alive and biting at the skin to announce the beauty of the body they make.

Satlyt slapped NuTay's hand and stuck out their tongue.

Oy! Why are you hitting your maba? Fine, you are ugly, the djeens hide away and are ashamed.

Satlyt giggled.

Anyway, such a distracted child. Your other maba, we grew up here together. We had you.

They were here? When I was born?

NuTay pursed their lips. They had promised that their child would have the entire truth.

For a while, hn. But they left. Don't be angry. Farweh wanted to take you. They made a deal with a wayfarer that sold them a spacesuit. They said they could get two more, one emergency suit for babies. Very clever, very canny, Farweh was.

Why?

NuTay took a deep breath. To hold on to a starship. To see eternity beyond the Window, and come out to another world on the other side.

Other maba went away holding on to a starship on the outside?

I see I taught you some sense, chota kin. Yes, it is as dangerous as it sounds. Some people have done it—if they catch you on the other side, they take you away to jail, like in the dromes for murderers and rapists and drunkards. But bigger jail, for other worlds. That is if you survive. Theory, na? Possible. But those who do it, ride the starships on the side, see the other side of time? They never come back. So we can't ask if it worked or no, nah? So I said no. I said I will not take my kin like a piece of luggage while hanging on to the side of a starship. I refused Farweh. I would not take you, or myself, and I demanded Farweh not go. I grabbed their arm and hurt them by mistake, just a little, chota kin, but it was enough for both of us. I let them go, forever.

Farweh . . . maba. Other maba went and never came back.

Shh, chota kin, NuTay stroked a tear away from Satlyt's cheek. You didn't know Farweh, though they are your other maba. I gave them all the tears you can want to honour them. No more.

But you liked Farweh, maba. You grew up with them.

NuTay smiled, almost laughing at the child's sweetness. They held Satlyt before their little face crumpled, letting them cry just a little bit for Farweh, gone to NuTay forever, dead or alive behind the black window of existence.

Many years later, NuTay's kin Satlyt proved themself the kin of Farweh, too, in an echo of old time. They came droning across the plains from the dromes, headlights cutting across the dust while NuTay sipped chai with the other shanty wallahs in the middle of the hawkers' cluster. The starship was gone, out on some other world, so business was slow that evening.

Satlyt thundered onto the dust road in the centre of the shantytown, screeching to a halt, their djeens clearly fired up and steaming from the mouth in the chilly air.

Your kin is huffing, one of the old hawkers grinned with their gums. Best go see to them.

So NuTay took Satlyt indoors to the shack, and asked what was wrong.

Listen, NuTay. Maba. I've seen you, year after year, looking at the wayfarers' pictures of Earth. You pretend when I'm around, but I can see that you want to go there. Go after Farweh.

Go after Farweh? What are you on about, we don't even know whether they went to Earth, or if they're alive, or rotting in some jail on some remote world in the galaxy.

Not for real go after, I mean go, after. Story-type, nah?

Feri tail?

Exact. I know next time the starship comes, it will go to Earth. Know this for fact. I have good tips from the temp staff at the dromes.

What did you barter for this?

Some black market subsidiary exotech from last starship crew, changing hands down at the dromes. Bartered some that came to my hands, bartered some shine, some tactile, what's it matter?

Tactile, keh!

Please, maba. I use protection. You think wayfarers fuck dunysha without protection? They don't want our djeens whispering to theirs, they just want our bodies exotic.

What have you done, chota kin?

Don't worry, maba. I wouldn't barter tactile if I wasn't okay with it. But listen. I did good barter, better than just info. Spacesuit, full function. High compressed oxy capacity. Full-on nine hours. Starship blinks in and out of black bubble, max twenty hours depending on size. The one in our port—medium size, probably ten hours. Plus, camo-field, to blend into the side of the ship. We'll make it. Like Farweh did.

How do you know so much? Where do you get all this tech?

Same way you did, maba. Over years. There are people in the dromes, Satlyt said in excitement. They know things. I talk. I give tactile. I learn. I learn there are worlds, like you did. This? You know this isn't a world. Ghost planet. Fuel station. Port. You know this, we all know this. Farweh had the right idea.

NuTay shook their head. This was it. It was happening again. From the fire of the djeens raging hot in Satlyt's high cheekbones they knew, there was no saying no. Like they'd lost Farweh to time and existence, they would lose Satlyt too. NuTay knew there was no holding Satlyt by the arm to try and stop them, like before—they were too weak for that now.

Even if NuTay had been strong enough, they would never do that again.

It was as if Farweh had disappeared into that black bubble, and caused a ripple of time to lap across the port in a slow wave that had just arrived. An echo in time. The same request, from kin.

What do you say, maba? asked Satlyt, eyes wide like when they were little.

We might die, chota kin.

Then we do. Better than staying here to see your eyes go dead.

Even filtered breathing, the helmet and the suit was hot, so unlike the biting cold air of the planet. NuTay felt like they might shit the suit, but what could one do. There was a diaper inside with bio-absorbent disinfectant padding, or so the wayfarer had said.

They had scaled the starship at night, using a service drone operated by the green-eyed wayfarer who had made the deal with Satlyt, though they had other allies, clearly. Looking at those green Earth-born eyes, and listening to their strange accent but even stranger affection for Satlyt, NuTay realized there might be more here than mere barter greed. This wayfarer felt *bad* for them, wanted to help, which made NuTay feel a bit sick as they clambered into the spacesuit. But the wayfarer also felt something else for Satlyt, who seemed unmoved by this affection, their jaw set tight and face braced to meet the future that was hurtling towards them.

"There'll be zero-g in the sphere once the starship phases into it. Theoretically, if the spacesuits work, you should be fine, there's nothing but vacuum inside the membrane—the edges of the sphere. If your mag-tethers snap, you'll float out towards those edges, which you absolutely do not want. Being inside the bubble is safe in a suit, but if you float out to the edge and touch it, there's no telling what will happen to you. We don't know. You might see the entirety of the universe in one go before dying, but you will die, or no longer be alive in the way we know. Understand? Do not jerk around with the tethers—hold on to each other. Hold on to each other like the kin you are. Stay calm and drift with the ship in the bubble so there's no stress on the tethers. Keep your eyes closed, throughout. Open when you hear the ship's noise again. Do not look at the inside of the bubble, or you might panic and break tether. That's it. Once the ship phases out, things will get tough in a different way, if you're alive. Earth ports are chaos, and there's a chance no one will find you till one of my contacts comes by with a ship-surface drone to get you. There are people on Earth who sympathize with the dunyshar, who want to give them lives. Give you lives. So don't lose hope. There are people who have survived this. I've ushered them to the other side. But if you survive only to have security forces capture you, ask for a refugee lawyer. Got it? *Refugee*. Remember the word. You have been kept here against your will, and you are escaping. Good luck. I'll be inside." The wayfarer paused, breathless. "I wish you could be too. But security is too tight inside. They don't think enough people have the courage to stick to the side of the ship and see the universe naked. And most don't. They don't know, do they."

With that, the wayfarer kissed Satlyt's helmet, and then NuTay's, and wiped each with their gloved hand, before folding themself into the drone and detaching it from the ship. Lightless and silent, they sailed away into the night. NuTay hoped they didn't crash it.

NuTay felt sick, dangling from the ship, even though they were on an incline. Below them, the lights of the launching pad lit a slow mist rising from the bottom of the starship, about four hundred feet down. The skin of the ship was warm and rumbled in a sleeping, breathing rhythm. They switched on the camo-field, which covered them both, though they couldn't see the effects.

Satlyt was frighteningly silent. Chota kin, NuTay whispered to test the range com. Maba, Satlyt whispered back with a sweaty smile.

The starship awoke with the suns. Their uneasy dozing was broken by the light, and by the deeper rumble in the starship's skin. The brown planet of arrivals and departures stretched away from them, in the distance those dun hills. The pale blue sky flecked with thin icy clouds. The port dromes, the dirt roads like pale veins, the shanties glittering under the clear day in the far distance. Their one and only place. Hom, as wayfarers said. A strange word. Those fucking dun hills, thought NuTay.

Bless us Sol and all the stars without ghosts, whispered NuTay. Close your eyes, chota kin.

Remember Farweh, maba, said Satlyt, face wet behind the curved visor. The bottom of the starship exploded into light, and NuTay thought they were doomed, the juddering sending them sliding down the incline. NuTay held Satlyt's gloved hand tight, grip painful, flesh and bone pressed against flesh and bone through the nanoweaves.

I am old, NuTay thought. Let Satlyt live to see Earth.

The light, the sound, was gone.

Satlyt convulsed next to NuTay, who felt every movement of their kin through closed eyes. They embraced, NuTay holding Satlyt tight, a hollow vibration when their visors met. The ship was eerily still under them, no longer warm through the thick suit. Satlyt was making small sounds that coalesced slowly into words. We're alive.

Their breathing harsh in the helmet, the only sound along with the hissing breath of Satlyt into their own mic.

NuTay opened their eyes to see the universe looking back.

Don't look. Don't look. Don't look.

I know you opened your eyes, maba. What did you see?

I don't. Don't look. I saw darkness. Time like a living thing, a . . . a womb, with the light beyond its skin the light from creation, from the beginning of time and the end, so far away, shining through the dark skin. There were veins, of light, and information, pulsing around us. I saw our djeens rippling through those veins in the universe, humanity's djeens. Time is alive, Satlyt. Don't let it see us. Keep your eyes closed.

I will, maba. That is a good story, Satlyt gasped. Remember it, for the refuji lawyer.

Time is alive, and eventually it births all things, just as it ends all things.

When the ship turned warm with fresh thunder, their visors were set aglow, bathing their quivering eyelids with hot red light, the light of blood and djeens. Their spacesuits thumped down on the incline, the tethers umbilical around each other, kin and kin like twins through time entwined, clinging to the skin of a ship haunted by exoghosts.

They held each other tight, and under Sol, knew the light of hom, where the first djeens came from.

Rachael K. Jones grew up in various cities across Europe and North America, picked up (and mostly forgot) six languages, and acquired several degrees in the arts and sciences. Now she writes speculative fiction in Portland, Oregon. Contrary to the rumors, she is probably not a secret android. Rachael is a World Fantasy Award nominee, Tiptree Award honoree, and winner of Writers of the Future. Her fiction has appeared in dozens of venues worldwide, including *Lightspeed, Beneath Ceaseless Skies, Strange Horizons,* and *PodCastle.* Follow her on Twitter @RachaelKJones.

Khaalidah Muhammad-Ali lives in Houston, Texas, with her family. By day she works as a breast oncology nurse. At all other times, she juggles, none too successfully, the multiple other facets of her very busy life. Khaalidah's publications include *Strange Horizons, Fiyah Magazine, Diabolical Plots,* and others. You can hear her narrations at any of the four Escape Artists podcasts, *Far Fetched Fables,* and *Strange Horizons.* As co-editor of *PodCastle* audio magazine, Khaalidah is on a mission to encourage more women and POC to submit fantasy stories. She can be found online at khaalidah.com and on Twitter at @khaalidah.

REGARDING THE ROBOT RACCOONS ATTACHED TO THE HULL OF MY SHIP

Rachael K. Jones and Khaalidah Muhammad-Ali

From: *Alamieyeseigha, Anita*
To: *Alamieyeseigha, Ziza*
Date: *2160-11-11*

Dear Ziza,
You already know what this is about, don't you, dear Sister? The robot raccoons I found clamped along my ship's hull during this cycle's standard maintenance sweep?

Oh, come on. Really? You know I invented that hull sculler tech, right? They've got my corporate logo etched into their beady red eyes so my name flashes on all the walls when their power is low. I admit some of your upgrades were . . . novel. Like the exoshell design—I'll never understand your raccoon obsession. Impractical, but points for style. I hadn't thought you could fit a diamond drill into a model smaller than a Pomeranian's skull, so congrats on that. Not that they made much progress chewing through my double-thick hull, but I'll give credit where credit's due.

Still, it was unsisterly of you, and it's not going to stop me from dropping the terraforming nuke when I get to Mars. Come to grips with reality, sister: you're in the wrong. You always have been, ever since we were girls. Especially since Mumbai accepted my proposal for Martian settlement. *Not yours.*

I'm sending back the robot raccoons in an unmanned probe. *Back*, because yes, I'm still leagues and leagues ahead of you. I only lost a day cleaning up the hull scullers. I've kept the diamond drills. I bet they'll chew right through that Martian rock.

I've also included a dozen white chocolate macadamia nut cookies, because I know it's your birthday tomorrow. Happy birthday!

Now go home.

Love your sister,
Anita

From: *Alamieyeseigha, Ziza*
To: *Alamieyeseigha, Anita*
Date: *2160-11-12*

Dear Anita,

Remember that summer when Father dropped us off at the northern rim of the Poona Crater on Mars? Alone. For two weeks. "This rustic camping trip will be a great learning experience," he said. "My precious daughters will bond."

When I learned that there were no pre-fab facilities and that we were responsible for erecting our own dwelling, sanitation pod, and lab, I started plotting ways to poison our father. You, on the other hand, I am still convinced, were determined to thoroughly enjoy the experience just to spite me.

But Father was a conservationist, and now that I am older, I can appreciate that he was trying to instill that same spirit in us. "Not all life jumps out and bites you in the butt," he used to love to say. And we learned the truth of that when we unearthed a family of as-yet-undiscovered garbatrites in the red dust on one of our sand treks.

We spent hours watching them under high magnification under the STEHM, trying to communicate with them, recording their activities and creating hypotheses about the meanings of their habits. I have to admit, there was a point when I stopped cursing father and started to secretly thank him. And where I sort of, kind of, could maybe see why you weren't so bad after all.

I don't think I'd ever seen you so dedicated to anything before this. You missed meals and stayed up throughout the night trying to communicate with the elder garbatrite. The one you named Benny. Exhausted, you fell asleep at your desk and left the infrared light on too long and effectively fried the poor critter. You cried for days and you even held a formal funeral for Benny, something his fellow garbatrites didn't seem too pleased about.

With that in mind, how could you possibly want to drop a terraforming nuke on a planet you and I both know is already teeming with life? Creating a new habitable world only has merits if it's not already inhabited.

If you won't see reason, then I'll just have to make it impossible for you. The Council for Martian Settlement may have accepted your proposal, but let me remind you that I've never been keen on following the rules.

So, you found the hull scullers, eh? I knew those diamonds would distract you from my real plan. You've always been so . . . materialistic. But hey, someone has to be.

On another note, the cookies were to die for! They were even better than Mother's, but I'll never tell her that. I really appreciate you thinking of me. I have a proposal to make. On our next monthly meal exchange, I'll make your favorite, a big old pot of Anasazi beans and sweet buttered cornbread, if you'll send more of those cookies.

XOXO
Ziza

P.S. My sweet raccoonie-woonies, Bobo and Cow, liked the cookies too. They also send their love.

From: *Alamieyeseigha, Anita*
To: *Alamieyeseigha, Ziza*
Date: *2160-11-15*

Sister:
Come now, Ziza. Let's not make me out to be some kind of villain. Of course I remember that summer. I remember how we licked the condensation inside our lab windows to stay hydrated because Father's Orion Scout childhood

romanticized survival stories. It's the real reason we're such die-hard coffee drinkers nowadays. He ruined the taste of water for us.

And I remember the garbatrites. How could I ever forget? That dusty red boulder we found in the sandstorm provided just enough shelter to pitch our emergency pod while we waited out the squall. Nothing to do but talk with each other, or play with the STEHM. Which meant we chose the STEHM, obviously. It's the closest look I've ever gotten at you, all those disgusting many-legged organisms crawling on your skin and hair, in your saliva, your earwax. You've always had an affinity for vermin.

But I'll be forever grateful you suggested taking samples around the boulder. When we first saw the garbatrites, their tiny little dwellings drilled into rock like mesa cities—that might be the closest I've ever felt to you, each of us taking one eyepiece on the STEHM, our damp cheeks pressed together, our smiles one long continuous arc. When the light brightened or dimmed, they danced in little conga lines. We weren't sure if it was art, or language. Is there really a difference?

There's something I realized when Benny died. The sort of revelation you only have when you're nudging together an atomic coffin beneath an electron microscope with tiny diamond tweezers just three nanometers wide: life is short. Life is painfully short, full of suffering and tragedy and wide, empty spaces. And those rare spots hospitable to life are just boulders tossed into an endless red desert, created by accident or coincidence. The only real good we can do in life is to spread out those boulders, minimize the deserts where we find them. Make a garden from dust. Plant our atomic coffins and let them bloom. Terraform whole planets, so we'll have more than just the blue boulder of Earth.

That's what you never understood, dear sister. It's why when you spent your youth chasing pretty men, I betrothed myself to science, burned my hopes of human love in the furnaces of my ambition. Do you remember when Asante, my poor besotted lab assistant, proposed to me at the Tanzanian Xenobiology Conference? How I laughed! As if any children he could give me would approach the impact my terraforming nuke will make on our species. Never forget, Ziza, that this mission is my life's work, my legacy. You will not stop me.

In other news, I got the Anasazi beans and cornbread, still warm and fresh in their shipping pod. How did you know I had the craving? That was a kindness. I remembered you while making salaat today.

I was less pleased about the virus installed in the shipping pod's warming program. Nice try, but I saw through that in about five seconds. Here's a tip:

next time, beta test it on *all* the shipboard systems I invented, not just the navigation. My sanitation program does more than filter my own crap.

I'm sending you an e-manual on Programming 101, and an ordering catalogue for Anita Enterprises in case you'd like to support the family business.

XOXOXO,
Anita

P.S. Go home.

From: *Alamieyeseigha, Ziza*
To: *Alamieyeseigha, Anita*
Date: *2160-11-28*

Anita,
It's been nearly two weeks since we last spoke, and of course, you know why. When you told me to go home, I knew that you were serious, but I never thought you'd resort to using the health and welfare of our dear mother as bait to get me to turn around and head back to earth.

I'm still trying to figure out how you managed to simulate for video not only our mother's countenance, darkened and marred by some mysterious illness, but her voice, the cadence like smooth stones tumbling in water and her accent. When she pleaded for me to return home, telling me that she was afraid to die alone, of course I turned back.

How much time did it take for you to create those videos, one arriving each day, her looking progressively worse? The worst was that one video with her by the window in her study, Mount Kilimanjaro in the distance. It came on the third day. The sunlight that glinted through her silver hair, like icy filaments, made her look so painfully beautiful, yet it was not enough to erase the shadows beneath her eyes or the sadness in them.

A better question, I suppose, is *"Why?"* Why resort to that when you know how much Mother means to me, especially now that Father is gone? Are you still jealous of our closeness? Do you still believe she loved me most?

Not that you deserve to be, but I'll let you in on a secret. I used to believe Mother loved me more than you as well. One day, I must've been about twelve, in my pathetic need to always be reminded that I was loved and cherished, I asked her why she loved me more than you. I waited a few moments, as she looked skyward, it seemed, for the answer. I was sure she'd say it was because I was more beautiful, more kind, smarter, that I had a more generous spirit, because truth be told, these things are true. But she didn't say that. Mother told me that she did not love me most. Nor did she love you more than me.

Then why do you spend so much more time with me than Anita? Why do you kiss me goodnight and not her? I numbered all the things she did for me and not you. Do you know what she said?

Because you need me more than Anita.

In her way, which was always kind yet honest, Mother was telling me that you were the stronger of the two of us. But now, I wonder. Would a strong person use her sister's weaknesses against her just to win? This was a low blow, Anita.

By now you're probably wondering how I eventually figured out that the videos from Mother were merely a cruel ploy to get me to go back home without a fight. It was the video from Day Eight.

Mother lay in bed, slight as a sliver of grass. When her image popped up on the view screen my heart felt like it was trapped in a vice. She reached out. A tear traveled from the corner of her eye toward the pillow. She coughed, then called out my name. Her voice was so soft, so small and weak.

"Please hurry home, Ziza," she said. "I don't want to die without laying eyes on my favorite girl at least one more time."

Favorite girl? No, Anita. Our mother never would have said that.

You think you're so smart. You think you know everything. Yet, you don't know kindness or humility. You don't even know your own mother.

The decision to dedicate your entire life to science was an error. Life is so much more than entropy, polymerisation, and endothermic reactions. You really can have your coffee and the cream too. You should have married Asante. He would have humanized you. He would have taught you to slow down and enjoy the precious little moments, that together they all add up to a great big life full of disappointments, yes, but also joy and love and mystery. He would have saved you from yourself and cold loneliness.

This is where I remind you that you know nothing about programming that I didn't teach you. Anita Enterprises is the mega-conglomerate it is because of me, your older sister and mentor. If I wanted to shut down every system on your ship, including life support, I could. And believe me, after this latest stunt of yours, I've been giving that idea serious consideration. The fact that I haven't sent a couple of torpedoes your way is a testament to my love for our mother. She'd be angry if I killed you. So, I won't.

See you on Mars.

Ziza
P.S. Don't start none, won't be none.
P.P.S. Bobo and Cow are very displeased with you.

From: *Alamieyeseigha, Anita*
To: *Alamieyeseigha, Ziza*
Date: *2161-01-01*

Ziza,
It's been weeks since I last wrote, but you haven't been far from my thoughts. Far from it.

While I continue toward the planet, I've been passing the time on my escape pod making a list of all the reasons I hate you, numbered and ordered least to greatest. It's a long, long list, forever incomplete. A sister's hate is like the heat death of the universe: infinitely expanding, eternal, the last flame burning in this cold, barren desolation where God abandoned us.

Reason #1,565: I hate the way you eat popcorn with chopsticks to keep your hands clean. Are you too good even for butter smudges?

Reason #480: I hate how you laugh at bad jokes. Puns aren't actually funny, Ziza. Everyone outgrew "why did the chicken cross the road" after elementary school.

Reason #111: Blue eye shadow. Self-explanatory.

Reason #38: "Don't start none, won't be none." *Really?* Better knock that shit off. Like you're not an adult responsible for her own actions.

Reason #16: I hate how Mother named you after herself, like you were the pinnacle of all her hopes, while I was named to placate our pushy grandmother.

Reason #15: I hate how you always laugh at me.

Reason #10: I hate how your favorite animal is the raccoon. You only picked it because it's endangered. You can't resist a lost cause, even if you don't actually want to do anything useful about it.

Reason #9: Seriously, *blue eye shadow.*

Reason #4: That last family dinner we had before Father died, when we took the shuttle out to the Moon to picnic on Mons Agnes while we watched the Perseid meteor shower dancing bright upon Earth's atmosphere like the footsteps of angels. Mother brought her heirloom silver for the occasion; I think we all knew in our hearts it was a special trip. We'd agreed for Father's sake to get along, just for a few hours. He hated how we fought, how we picked at each other like children picking old scabs that won't heal. Do you remember the white curling through his black hair? His cheeks sunk deep by the chemo? He wanted to dish up the jasmine rice and flatbread himself. His hands trembled so badly the peas rolled onto Mother's quilt beneath the picnic pop-up, just skirting the regolith.

We both know I wanted to talk with him about the inheritance. I just wanted my share, my 50/50 split, but Mother was so concerned about poor helpless Ziza, who had run into such tough times after college, chasing after pretty men and idealistic wide-eyed save-the-raccoons causes that she needed a larger cut to keep up her lifestyle. Anita Enterprises cost me everything while all you ever did was chase your girlhood dreams of love and happy endings.

We were having such a great time. Your useless pet raccoons were recharging their solar batteries in your lap. Father told us stories of his childhood, how they didn't even have a family shuttle when he grew up, and you could only sleep rough in wild places like Antarctica's rocky plains. Mother held his hand and kissed him, love shining in her eyes. No matter how sick he got, he was still the dark-skinned 17-year-old godling she'd met on the road to Mount Kilimanjaro in their youth. We even tolerated a few of your puns.

It would not last. I volunteered to scrape the leftovers into the recycler at the service booth down the path. It was so close, I didn't bother to bring a communication device. You deny it, but we both know you followed me. You used the Moon's lower gravity to pile those rocks against the door while I did my chores inside. When I tried to leave, the door wouldn't budge. I could only watch my family from the viewing port, my mother and sister and dying father laughing together, though I couldn't hear them. I screamed and pounded the window, but nobody noticed from the picnic pop-up. No one could hear me through the vacuum of space.

How can I ever forgive you that prank, those precious minutes of our father's health ticking away, and me unable to be there? How can I forgive that lost opportunity, those memories that should have been mine to cherish, to bear me up when I wake at night so desperate to feel his whiskered kiss on my forehead, his voice telling me he's so proud of me, proud of everything I've done?

This is why I hate you, Ziza. This is why I can never stop hating you.

Reason #2: Those diamond drills in your robot raccoons weren't just drills. That cornbread pan wasn't just a pan. You know what, Ziza? In spite of everything else, I only sent you back to Earth with those fake videos to protect you from yourself, and keep you out of harm's way. Because despite this whole list, part of me still loved you, stupid as it sounds. Maybe it's because you're named for Mother. But you tried to dump me into the vacuum of space, Sister Dearest. You tried to murder me in my sleep. You activated the wafer computer in the pan's false bottom, hacked my defenses, and the drills turned my hull into cheese by the time I woke up. If I hadn't mounted the terraforming nuke to the escape pod . . . but I did.

Reason #1: Did you ever love me? Ever, Ziza? I'm not filling this one out yet, because I don't think I've yet hated you as much as a woman can hate her sister. Not yet. But I will.

So I'm going to tell you something else you don't yet know: On the wreck of my shuttle, scraping by on the last of my life support, are a dozen rare raccoon specimens. I was going to release them on Mars after the terraforming ended so they could colonize a safe place far from any predators. My shuttle is set to self-destruct in two days' time. If you leave your current course, you might just have time to save them. Let's find out what you care more about: helpless garbatrites, or near-extinct raccoons.

The shuttle also contains an urn with Father's ashes, wrapped in extra scarves in the top hatch in my quarters. Mother asked me to scatter them on the planet because Father had so many happy memories of camping there with his daughters. I didn't have time to rescue it when I had to abandon ship a few days ago.

I don't have that one on my list yet. Better go add it now.

Hate you always,
Anita

P.S. Why did Ziza fly across the solar system twice? Because she was a *double crosser*. Get it?
P.P.S. Happy New Year, by the way.

From: *Alamieyeseigha, Ziza*
To: *Alamieyeseigha, Anita*
Date: *2161/01/02*

Anita,
By now you've probably realized that regardless of your efforts, your escape pod's trajectory is no longer Mars. You are now on an intercept path with

me. I know that you must be seething, cursing my name, praying for my damnation (you've always been so dramatic), but give me the opportunity to explain.

Your ship was never in danger. The plan was that once you entered in new coordinates to anyplace other than Mars, preferably home, the diamond drills would have set about repairing the holes they'd created in the hull of your ship. Genius ancillary programming, if I do say so myself. All you had to do was turn around. But you, with your flare for the dramatic and unwillingness to give up, even when you know you've lost, decided to jump ship and make the rest of the voyage via the escape pod.

The escape pod. The escape pod with only half the power you'll need to complete the trip to Mars. At the rate you're going you'll be one hundred and three before you even break orbit. If you paid as much attention to the details as you do the drama, you might have remembered that.

Why couldn't all your hot hate keep those poor raccoons warm as your abandoned ship plunges onward toward the cold outer depths of space, too long and too far for either of us to go? I won't be able to save those raccoons, nor Father's ashes, because I will be saving you.

You can thank me later.

Your last message, so thick with evil enmity for your only sibling in the galaxy, reminded me of Tariq, the only man I ever considered staying with for a lifetime. I've tried over the last forty-three years, without an iota of success, to tangle and finally lose my memory of him among the many others. He was brighter than Sirius and sweeter than lugduname, at least to me. I know that long-legged bird wasn't perfect, he chewed with his mouth open and, truth be told, he wasn't very bright but he loved me without reserve.

You didn't like him at first. You called him a "pretty, useless thing," because he didn't have the same knack for business or driving ambition for more, that you did. He was an artist and liked to create beautiful things, to experience the delights of life with all of his senses exposed and ready.

It was through your senses that he finally won you over. So thoughtful was he, that knowing your dislike for him, he still surprised you with your favorite, hot homemade waffles, on your birthday.

When I broke off the engagement with him only a week later, you, who had hated him all along, refused to speak to me for months. You said I'd made the biggest mistake of my life. You called me a fool.

I never told you why I broke off the engagement. And I bet you never knew that even now, there are sleep cycles when instead of sleep, I lay awake imaging how happy I'd be today had I not broken poor Tariq's heart.

I broke off our engagement because of your Reason #1. In answer to your question, I love you more than breath itself, baby sister.

Tariq said to me one day, as we lay beneath the sun in a field of cool holograss, "Any sister who would waste her dying father's final hours arguing over an inheritance is surely too selfish to bear." He took my foot in his hands and kneaded my heel expertly. "I'm willing to tolerate Anita, my love, because of you."

I said nothing to this for a while, mostly because the foot massage was so exquisite that it stole my breath and crossed my eyes. But when he was done, I politely slipped on my shoes, clapped off the holo-vision, and asked him to leave.

"If you love me, you must love my sister too. Anything less is unacceptable," I told him.

So you see, silly sister, you can hate me a million times, but no matter what, I'll still love you, even though you don't deserve it. God, you're such a brat.

Ziza

P.S. Are you seriously pouting about your name? Mother should have named you Shakespeare because you're nothing but drama.

P.P.S. I didn't pile those rocks against the door. That was Bobo and Cow. They were just trying to play hide and seek with you. I guess my sweet raccoonie-woonies won that round.

P.P.P.S. Why did the raccoon cross the solar system? To keep her sister's paw off Mars.

From: *Alamieyeseigha, Anita*
To: *Alamieyeseigha, Ziza*
Date: *2161-01-11*

Dear Ziza,
Greetings from Mars.

Don't worry. Nothing has changed. I have regretfully failed to deploy the terraforming nuke. My mission has failed, for now.

Perhaps even before you read this message, GalactiPol will be taking you into custody. I called them when my escape pod veered off course, when the navigation stopped responding to my counter-hacks. You might have forgotten in your rashness that the Mumbai Council for Martian Development endorsed my plan for terraforming, and that I was their agent. Interfering with my mission meant meddling with the Coalition of Humankind itself.

I didn't call GalactiPol sooner because I wanted to beat you at your own game. So few people in this huge, empty universe can even approach my creativity and intellect. You've always pushed me to the greatest apex of my brilliance. I'm never as inventive as when you're scheming to ruin me. But the thought of losing Father's ashes into the void of space . . . well, it gave me no rest. He doesn't deserve that, not at our hands. I'd hoped you'd fetch the urn, but instead I'm calling an end to our battle of wits.

GalactiPol scooped up my escape pod and listened to my account of your wrongdoings. They have dispatched a salvage vessel to my wreck, and an armed cruiser to arrest you. Unfortunately, I made a fatal mistake: the raccoons. As you well know, I did not have authorization to remove these endangered creatures from Earth.

So they've arrested me too. I've been dropped on Mars for safekeeping while they run the raccoons back to Earth. They've dispatched another cruiser to your coordinates. Soon they will bring you here too, dear Ziza, and for the second time we'll wander the sands together in this desert of red storms, with only wit and curiosity and mutual hatred to keep us alive until someone returns for us.

Did you know part of our old camp is still here? Somehow the shell of our mobile lab held up against the years. Probably because of the garba-trites. Remember we'd left the lab tucked in the shadow of their great stone. Apparently they liked it (perhaps for the way it holds warmth during the cold Martian nights) because they covered it in their tiny homes like a shipwreck bejeweled with coral and barnacles. When I turn on the lights at night, they dance along the seams in swirling shapes, carving microscopic paths through the dust coating, just as frail human biceps have pushed and moved the world until you can see their efforts from space. The Great Wall of China! The glittering glass megascrapers of Nigeria! How floating Melbourne glistens like a blue jewel in the dark, riding the waves forever, its flooded gondola channels sipping the ocean's rise and fall! Our little lab is a world for these tiny creatures. They shout, *We are here. We exist.*

But let's talk about Tariq. Now there's an unhealed wound running to our cores. It's true, Ziza, that you were always the prettiest. I am a plain woman, an experience you can never understand. Your beauty is a passport into people's best nature. Everyone sees in you the face of an angel, and they give you an angel's due. Well, any plain woman knows the converse is true, that we have to prove again and again our worth and goodness to a world that mistakes the grotesque for evil, the ungroomed for lazy, the fat for stupid.

Your Tariq, like all pretty men, suffered from the same assumptions. He was never as good to anyone as he was to you, Ziza Angel-faced. When he didn't ignore me outright, he liked to pick on me for your amusement. He named me Yam Nose and Ogre Teeth, and when I protested, he laughed me off as *too sensitive,* as if I didn't have a right to my dignity. People like him are cruel to girls like me in a thoughtless, automatic way, like they can't imagine us having feelings anymore complex than a dog's. Yes, I detested him. But the day he made me waffles, throwing me one small, quiet kindness, I realized how happy he made you, that you intended to marry him. He'd be around our family a long, long time. I made my peace.

I am sorry you realized so late the flaw in him that was obvious to me from the first. But know, Ziza, that Tariq must accept responsibility for his own character. If you had married him, when you aged and your beauty began to fade, he surely would've turned that same cruelty on you. He may very well have been your soulmate, but take a hard look at your own soul, and ask whether you too mistake your angelic face for more than it is. You are merely human.

So come to Mars, Sister. Come to where this all started that summer our father wanted us to bond, back before we hated the taste of water, before we learned to despise each other in small ways and big. We cannot escape one another. Our hatred has been our brilliance, our secret genius, the harsh red desert that pushed and pinched and goaded us to build towers you can see from the Moon. Imagine what a lifetime of love might have accomplished

Come to Mars, Ziza. Scatter our father's ashes with me. If we cannot make this place bloom with life, at least we can make it a little more dusty.

Anita

From: *Alamieyeseigha, Ziza*
To: *Alamieyeseigha, Anita*
Date: *2161-01-11*

Dearest Anita,
I can see the GalactiPol cruiser from my starboard viewport. Its black and gold stripes practically glow beneath the strobing orange beacon make it look like a psychedelic bumblebee. Most people in my situation, facing

detainment on Mars, endless expensive legal proceedings, possible time in prison, would be locked in the grips of fear and worry. Perhaps even shame. But not me. The one thought stuck in my mind, like a diptera fastened to sticky paper, is how beautiful that cruiser is and how excited I am to begin this second adventure.

It's all about perception.

During that last picnic on the moon, when you were locked in the service booth, Father talked about perception. "Perception is everything. If you can project what you perceive it will become reality. You will believe it. More importantly, whether good or bad, everyone else will believe in your reality as well, and they will believe in you." Not until I read your last letter did I realize how right Father was. And how wrong we have been.

In the mirror I've always seen the imperfect likeness of our mother, not quite as beautiful, not quite as kind, and with but a fraction of her intelligence. I have our father's height and amber-flecked brown eyes, but none of his grace, strength, or athleticism. Yet, somehow you see in me the face of an angel.

In you I see the sharp mind and steady hands of a scientist. A fearless tenacious spirit intent on exploring all possibilities even at great cost, able to articulate your ideas, to change hearts and minds. You have boundless strength, so much so that you have been the central support for Mother and me since Father's death. There is nothing plain about you, little sister, nothing wanting.

How is it that our perceptions have never aligned?

Be right back. GalactiPol is hailing me . . .

From: *Alamieyeseigha, Ziza*
To: *Alamieyeseigha, Anita*
Date: *2161-01-12*

Sorry it has taken me so long to return to this letter, but I had a few calls to make. Officers Gavalia and Ambrose boarded my ship at 2315 and took me into custody. My detainment cell is surprisingly modish, with full amenities including a computer and personal uncensored communication device. I have even been given unrestricted access to their onboard digital library.

According to officer Gavalia, though entry into GalactiPol requires extensive training and a stringent vetting system, they have little opportunity to actually do the type of policing their organization exists to perform. I suppose there just aren't that many galactic criminals to catch these days, besides you and me, that is.

Now where was I? Ah yes. *Perceptions*.

I've been mesmerized by the images you sent of the garbatrite homes, the bright multilayered encrusted structures in every shade of red, orange and pink, lambent lights beneath the gaze of the sun. They expound beauty and ingenuity and life and more than anything, a prescience greater than anything either of us could have conceived.

We've been darting back and forth through this solar system, in an effort to outdo one another, trying our damnedest to affect the change of our choosing, thinking we are so smart and so in control, when in truth, we are no greater than those garbatrites, and perhaps we are even less wise than they.

Perhaps there is a way for us both to have what we wanted, to terraform Mars and to protect the garbatrites. They were always keen to share their world with us and seeing the ingenuity and beauty of their structures, perhaps we can convince them to help us transform the barren surface of Mars into one of cooperative beauty. We can provide the framework for our cities and homes, and they can build upon them, layering their coral-like exoteric structures, creating homes befitting us all, unlike anything in the entire solar system.

I called Tariq shortly after my detainment aboard the GalactiPol cruiser. Before you think me hopeless, let me explain. Besides being happily ensconced in a polyamorous relationship with two of the nicest men and woman I have ever met, he has long since given up on his art (he was never very good anyway) and has been the Chief GalactiPol Officer for several years. I was hoping that there was still enough lingering affection between us that he would agree to assist me in this difficult situation.

Unfortunately, he is unable, as I had hoped, to have the charges against us repealed, but we have been allowed to serve the entirety our sentence on Mars. Together.

Shall we do this, sister? Shall we make our dreams come true?

I envision us making a home from our old pod quarters. Perhaps we can build on an extra room and invite Mother. We can even build a special corral for Bobo and Cow, where they can play happily and where they won't be able to disturb you as you work on your next great experiment. With the help of the garbatrites we can build a greenhouse. We'll grow corn and tomatoes in soil fertilized with the ashes of our father. We will create a real home, a life. And we will relearn one another, our strengths and weakness, our mutual love for each other. One day other Earthers will join us on our red planet and find a world of wonder encased in garbatrite domes. A home.

Can you see it, sister? Good. Now hold that thought in your mind until we are reunited.

With all my love,
Ziza

From: *Alamieyeseigha, Anita*
To: *Alamieyeseigha, Ziza*
Date: *2161-01-13*

Dear Ziza,
Why did the sisters cross the solar system? To get to the other's side.

See you soon,
Anita

Maggie Clark is a Canadian writer and educator currently acclimating to life abroad. Maggie's science fiction stories have appeared in *Analog, Clarkesworld, GigaNotoSaurus,* and *Lightspeed,* as well as Gardner Dozois's *The Year's Best Science Fiction: Thirty-Fourth Annual Collection* and Rich Horton's *The Year's Best Science Fiction & Fantasy: 2017.*

BELLY UP

Maggie Clark

1.

Dirt at dawn. Dirt at dusk.
But while the sun is up
O Mother, have mercy!
Look what grows in us.

—Novuni Proverb

A week after the courts declawed Imbra Tems, the Darwood twins and their cousin Paloma paid him a visit to finish the job. Imbra wasn't hard to track down; he'd returned to his auto shop overlooking Esrin's Gulch, not five klicks from the nearest settlement, and lay under the hot, ticking metal of a ballast tractor when they rolled up in mud-spattered quads. The lesser Darwood, Hurley, pulled so hard on the creeper under Imbra's feet that Imbra hit his head on the exhaust line on his way out, and hardly recognized the trio during his first few seconds under the glare of the red-brown sun. But the meaner Darwood, Tripp, wanted to take things slow, so he gave Imbra time to collect himself; even to look around.

"Well, Dash," said Tripp, using an ancient name, a childhood name for the man lying before him. "How's it feel? They didn't take away how easy you scare, did they? That'd have been some surgery—coward like you, always running at the first sign of trouble."

Hurley snickered, at which point Paloma's continued silence caught Imbra's notice. The tall kid, fifteen at best, had more anger wound up in his wiry frame than the Darwood twins combined. For the Darwoods, Imbra knew this was all domination sport, but in Paloma, Imbra sensed something deeper and more dangerous. He tried to remember the kid's lineage, but the local labor pool had always been built on comers and goers—most itching for just enough work to take them to the elevator, and from the elevator, to the stars. But most never made it, and then things got desperate. People cut corners and other people all the time—too much to recall every bad deal, every civvie who lost a friend or family to one bad bridge project or another. The hardness of life in the valley blurred memories at their edges. The crystal Imbra had been hooked on since childhood didn't help much, either.

"A little, actually." Imbra spoke lightly, a smile fixed on Tripp. "Remember, fear's all about adrenaline. No adrenaline, no fight-or flight. So when they stopped the signal that starts the whole business, they did me a bit of a service. Sure, go on, give me the beating of my life. Can't really stop you, but those mind games won't work, either, so you might as well get started. Maybe in the ribs, though? I still sorta like this face."

Tripp smiled back, but he wasn't pleased. "You were shit before you went into the courts, Dash, and the stink on you's even worse now. Don't go putting on airs."

Imbra shrugged and was about to reply, when a swift boot heel to his stomach drove all the breath and a fair bit of spittle out his mouth. Imbra doubled around the impact site and turned to catch a glimpse of Paloma, already advancing for another stomping, this time to the chest. The kid was pure rage as he moved, the wildness of his kicks and punches a sure sign that he hadn't done much proper fighting, but before Hurley and Tripp could pull Paloma off, Imbra had at least pieced together some of the kid's complaint from the rare word flung between blows. *Mother—Murdered—Lowlife—*

Oh right, thought Imbra, vaguely between strikes. *Her.*

With no heightened blood pressure, no rush of heat in his muscles with the release of fat-cells for future energy, no surge in lung capacity, no loss of hearing or vision to focus his efforts on the immediacy of response, Imbra experienced the beating acutely, his body surprised by each vividly felt blow. At one particularly hard hit, which flung him from the creeper, the back of his head bouncing off the gravel, Imbra wondered if his body would even figure out when it was dying, and if maybe that was what was happening now. But then he heard the Darwood twins—"Easy, settle down, Pal, that's enough"—and the sudden stillness of air and light and shadow all around him gave Imbra pause for breath.

He coughed and spat out a tooth while above him the three men conferred.

"Hey—he dies, and anyone finds out, you'll get the same treatment, understand?"

"But he deserves it."

"Sure, Pal. Sure he does." Tripp clapped a hand hard on Paloma's shoulder. "But you kill him and that's it, see? Keep him around, though, knowing his place, and we've got it made. Dash here'll always be on hand to fix our rides, or pull our freight, or give us that sweet little hovercraft whenever we want it. Besides, putting him in the ground won't bring her back, so what's the point—the waste and the risk of it, you know?"

Paloma's hands curled into fists as he stared down at Imbra. "Some worlds, they put garbage like you into holes in the ground, and they leave you there for years."

Tripp sighed. "Yeah, yeah. And the state pays for it all, and no one gets anything out of it, and everyone's still pissed when the assholes get out with time served. Trust me, Pal, this is better. Social justice with a little on the side for us keepers of the peace—you, Hurl, and me. Right, Dash? You gonna contribute now, for once in your sorry excuse of a life?"

Imbra sat up slowly, arm braced at his ribs; another mouthful of blood hucked to the ground. "Could've just asked, you needed something realigned. That head of yours, maybe."

"Nah. Tripp's a believer in even trades." Hurley bared a grin with wide gaps, teeth lost from too much time in the pits. "Body work for body work."

"Speaking of which—" Tripp tipped his head to the garage. "We're taking Bullet for a spin. Loaner 'til our main rides get spiffed up. You don't mind, do you, Dash?"

Imbra nodded to a shelf through the open door. "Keypass, top drawer. Knock yourselves out. Preferably into a lava flow."

Tripp whistled. "That's not very nice, Dash." Hurley approached Imbra as if to further the point. Imbra eyed Hurley's boots, then the rest of him.

"No, I guess not," said Imbra, meeting Hurley square in the eye. "Not fair to Bullet, going down with the likes of you."

Hurley was smarter than Paloma about his blows, and the ones to Imbra's hip ricocheted through Imbra's bone, sure to leave a deeper ache and more persistent bruising. But Tripp had the hovercraft out soon enough, its silver coat glinting in the midday light, and Hurley was quick to join him up front.

Only Paloma lingered by the ballast tractor, where Imbra had propped up himself against one of its wheels.

"You should be begging for your life," said the kid. "Like she did."

"No—she didn't." Imbra took a ragged breath, the ache in his chest starting to constrict in ways even the declaw couldn't prevent. "I was higher than you'll ever know, but that much is true. I just—I panicked, kid. I already had the goods but I hit her anyway—hard—and I ran. Still, she was strong. Your mum, at the end she just . . ."

Imbra tapered off as Paloma leaned in and took him by his shirt collar and clocked him across the cheekbone. Calmer this time. *Aim's improving, too,* thought Imbra, as the Darwood twins called out "Pal, you coming or what?" and Paloma, dropping his mother's killer and shaking his hand out, stepped over Imbra's body and said, "Yeah, hold up, I'm done." But Imbra, watching the kid not so much as glance back as he stalked off, knew that Paloma would return, and sooner rather than later.

And next time, he'd come alone.

Stev Biggs, the court-appointed adjustment counselor, squinted sideways at the shiner turning Imbra's right cheekbone into a spray of nebula-purples and dusky grey-pinks.

"You oughta be more careful around the tow trucks," said Biggs. "Rough business, walking into a hook and chain like that."

"Comes with the territory." Imbra offered Biggs a cup of roast. "How's the war?"

"Which one." Biggs settled at Imbra's bench and scratched under his wide-brimmed hat, surveying the lay of the garage—graffiti across the walls, tool cases in disarray, more than a little blood spatter on the concrete floor. "Seen plenty of action yourself, it seems."

"Gulch rats. Big ones."

"No kidding." Biggs took a long, loud slurp of brew, eyeing his charge over the mug. "They'll settle eventually, you know. There's not much sport in it, and soon they'll feel ashamed with themselves for doing it at all. That's usually how it goes."

"Or they'll take that shame out on me, too, for making them feel something in the first place. Starting to think we could all do with a declaw, in the valley at least."

Biggs set down his mug. "That kinda attitude, might as well hand everything over to the Allegiance. We need *more* fight, you ask me, if we're going to get through it all."

"That bad?"

"You tell me. General Asarus has the shipyards working all hours, trying to double the fleet by the equinox. Ask me, she's not gonna make deadline, but at least the attempt'll improve foot traffic around these parts—open up the mines, drive recruitment, see more money in bridgeworks again. Might even be good for your business. Who knows."

Imbra's answering snort nudged Biggs into a bit of a smile. "Looks like we didn't take all the fight out of you, did we?"

But that *we* gave Imbra pause, the sudden schism of it. Biggs as old friend. Biggs as brother's keeper. He studied the calluses on Biggs's hands, only a little darker than his own. One creation story going that the sun had scorched their ancestors in a fit of rage. Others saying that the sun loved them so much it tried to get too close, until its children cried out *Mother, you're hurting me!* and the sun, ashamed when she saw what she had done, blushed a livid red-brown forever. Both tales as good as true: all life on Novun a matter of dualities.

"I've heard the stories," said Imbra. "About the ones who walk out of surgery and right off a cliff. Some for what they'd done to deserve the declaw in the first place. Some for what they were afraid everyone else would do, once the law was through."

"But not you."

"No, not me." Imbra's eyes gleamed hard. "Sitting in the courts those last few weeks, while they cleaned all that shit from my system to prep for surgery, I found religion instead."

"I'm afraid to ask which."

Imbra nodded. "Good."

Biggs didn't press. They sat and drank quietly as a long-haul rig rumbled into view, kicking up dust coming past Esrin's Gulch, then slipping into oblivion around the next hill.

"Could always use more men in the shipyards," said Biggs at last.

"Sure. The first place the Allegiance'll target when their fleets arrive."

"You don't know that." Biggs sounded almost chipper. "Could go for the lasers first. Then take out the outer moon defenses. Hop skip and a jump to Novun Prime after that. Seed a solar flare and take off running. You never know what the Allegiance has in mind."

"Or what they want, exactly. The people? The resources?"

"Our guesses get even weirder, up at the courts. There's one woman in archives who thinks—" Biggs seemed about to start on a longer spiel, but one glance at Imbra's ring of bruises gave him pause and softened the sudden heat in his face. "Anyway, all I'm saying is, it'd be quicker, if it happened up in orbit. Down here, with the locals, and your past . . ."

"All life's a risk," said Imbra. "You know that."

"Not everyone gets to pick where they make a last stand, though." Biggs adjusted his hat and stood. "But I guess you're sure you've chosen yours."

The statement grew into a question after Biggs set off, and after Imbra returned to cleaning up the shop. The next run of settlement boys came at dusk, mostly to try to rattle him a little on their way out to some pile-on party in the valley. Paloma wasn't among them.

Paloma came in the night, halfway to dawn—and not, after all, alone. Imbra saw the revolver before the whites of the kid's eyes at the end of the drive.

Imbra watched him awhile, then put the kettle on.

Paloma's hands shook around the firearm as he stepped into the light of the garage, so Imbra moved nice and slow, setting two mugs on a table between them.

"Would've been easier if I'd been in bed, I guess," said Imbra. "Sorry, kid. I'm not sleeping so well these days."

"You think this is a joke? This isn't a joke."

Imbra nodded twice, the second time at the revolver. "That thing registered?"

Paloma hesitated.

"Registered is no good. They'll track you and declaw you. Then you'll end up like me. You think I shouldn't've been done in earlier? All the shit I did for valley mobsters, all the things I did while high—but it took a real slip up, the wrong keypass in the wrong place, for the courts to catch me. You wanna do this, kid, you gotta move in shadows."

Paloma's eyes darted to the implements on hand—the pry tools, the welding rods—even the impact wrenches, if applied with pure blunt force against their target.

"No, too much mess," said Imbra. "You had the right idea with the firearm. You just need an unregistered number. But I know a guy."

"Oh, frigg off," Paloma raised the revolver tensely. "I told you this wasn't a joke."

"And I get that. Only—see it from my end for a sec. You come in, and sure, I'm bigger than you, but if I try to stop you, your adrenaline's gonna kick in more than it already has, while I'm still poking along like this. And for what? Maybe I get the gun from you, maybe it goes off while I try. But a gun's still better than some of the stuff I've got in here. So, yeah, if you go with the gun, it's easier for us both."

"And I already have one. What's it to you if I get caught."

Paloma's brows beaded with perspiration. Imbra held his gaze.

"You're right, kid. I'll be dead. But you're here 'cause I did something rotten. Something I truly regret. You think I wanna go down knowing I've ruined your life twice?"

Paloma snorted, but also watched, finger restless on the trigger, while Imbra took up a thick black marker from the table and scrawled a name and number on a bit of packaging.

"Here," said Imbra. "This is the guy. He's down in the gulch, little outpost away from the road. We can take Bullet, go together. You go in, say I sent you, get the gun. We'll already be in good territory for digging, so then I just fix myself a nice spot, and you shoot me into it. You'll have to do cleanup, but way out there? No one's gonna come looking."

"Like I'm supposed to believe you'll help me kill you."

Imbra shrugged. "Shoot me, then. Right now. Just saying, it's not smart."

"Yeah, you say too much." Paloma raised the revolver again—the one deliberate act in his repertoire. Imbra reached for his mug. Turned it in his hands. Inhaled. At the end of a long sip, his brains still more or less intact, Imbra nodded to the far wall.

"Keypass is back in the top drawer. Ever driven hover before?"

The stretch of road between Imbra's garage and the bottom of the valley was wide enough for Paloma to get a feel for Bullet without too much risk of dropping off a cliff. Auto would kick in regardless, but Imbra had seen novices panic and override, then overcorrect while their hovers were already boosting themselves horizontal, which just led to the whole craft flipping back, and sometimes striking the cliff on its tumble to the ground. Up in orbit, bubble ships avoided the problem by restricting humans to gunner and maintenance duty; on the subcontinent, as with the rest of the system, it was the rare colony that let organics behind any wheel—ground, water, or sky. But Nov's northern continent, with all its geological upheavals and active volcanic sites, remained an uneasy mix of new and old: neural implants and road warriors, space elevators and end-of-the-line towns, tall tales of interstellar combat and local bridges that were always falling down. Courts that knew they weren't up to the task of keeping the peace, but kept swinging dead weight where they could.

Paloma pushed the accelerator hard—too hard for his first time behind the wheel, but Imbra knew this was not the moment to tell the kid to ease up. When they hit the end of the road, at the bottom of the gulch, Imbra pointed to their destination—the only light in the whole stretch of valley desert—and Paloma gave him a withering look before cranking the engine again. Recent flash flooding had left the ground thick with mud, but Bullet surged through at top speed, veering only slightly as Paloma adjusted for the loss in friction. *Not bad.* Imbra glanced at the kid again—a word of praise as toxic as a word of caution, under the circumstances, but still tempting. Before long, they came to a stop outside the little shack.

"Want me to come with you?"

Paloma's eyes narrowed at the quickness of Imbra's words.

"Stay here," said the kid, taking the keypass with him; the revolver tucked into his waistband. Paloma had a harder time in the mud than Bullet, so it took him a few slips to get his bearings and reach the front door. Imbra looked up while he waited—trying, and failing, to triangulate the shipyards above. Imagining General Asarus at the head of her new fleet, pulling off another system-saving maneuver like the one that first made her famous, during the Allegiance standoff at Fort Five. A satellite passed overhead, and then the shot rang out.

Imbra stood by the hovercraft when Biggs eventually emerged, a rifle slung over the adjustment counselor's shoulder.

"Good," said Biggs. "Figured you wouldn't be far off. Someone calls using your name, that's a sign of trouble for sure, but how did you—"

"Eh. He's just a kid. You didn't—"

Biggs cut a hand through the air. "Only spooked him. He's quiet now. Conspiracy to commit murder, though—that'll be something for the courts."

"Even with the circumstances?"

"Especially with them. Even at his age. They'll try him as an adult for targeting a declaw, and do the same to him for sure."

"Counterproposal."

Biggs tipped his hat. "Shoot."

"I go to the shipyards. Kid comes with me."

Even in the low light, Biggs's face cast in shadow, Imbra could see both brows rise.

"He'll come at you again, you know."

"Maybe," said Imbra. "But a kid who goes on a planned, solo hit in this neck of the valley probably doesn't have much of a life worth fighting for."

Biggs considered, then nodded to the door. "And if he says no?"

"Give him his options. You'll see."

Imbra waited while Biggs went back in and talked to the kid. Neither voice got loud enough for Imbra to make out the state of things, but he had plenty to keep himself occupied: The low wind over damp desert underbrush. The suck of mud underfoot. The residual heat of old Bullet, to be left with the garage in Biggs's care by dawn. If he squinted in the dark of night, Imbra could just make out the far ridge of the gulch, where he'd played with Tripp and Hurley and Biggs in another lifetime—a world where every child had been a runner for someone, and Imbra had simply been the fastest, for better and for worse.

In time, Paloma came out glaring, hands tucked under his armpits, cheeks shining with what Imbra allowed might be condensation, while Biggs laid out details for their trip to the space elevator. Imbra tried to feel nearly as much of a rush, a heat inside him like the kid had, and would continue to have, so long as he kept clear of the courts. But in his triumph, Imbra couldn't even rely on a rush of oxytocin—too dangerous, the courts had decided, because of its role in defensive aggression between social groups— so Imbra settled for a nod to both and said nothing when Paloma answered with a gob of spit at his feet.

Imbra waited in the hovercraft while the kid visited his mother's grave, one last time, before the pair was flung up to the stars.

2.

When the lava runs,
You run.
When the water runs,
You swim.

—Novuni Proverb

Imbra had tinnitus within a week in orbit, which helped tune out some of his new supervisor's wilder conspiracy theories, but which also made keeping track of Paloma all the harder. The shipyards—an intricate, sprawling lattice of production modules dedicated to various stages of robotics and manual assembly, testing, and resource management—differed considerably from the large, open factories on Nov's surface. As such, it had never occurred to Imbra that the decibel range in specific space modules, while tolerable to anyone with factory or garage experience, might still be wholly unsuited for long-term auditory health. His supervisor, Miha, liked to say that this was proof they were all being phased out in favor of the machines, but Miha also made no secret of his affiliation with the Path of the Vengeful Sun, so Imbra learned to take the burly man's fatalism as lightly as possible.

"Way I hear General Asarus talking," said Miha on Imbra's second day, "Could be we're all here as decoys, you know? The Allegiance sees that all our manpower's up in orbit, so it ignores the satellites with almost no human presence. But that's where the general gets crafty, see? She has the real weapons waiting on Hav or Isla or one of the other big moons, and she blasts Allegiance to smithereens while they're doing the same to us up here."

"Asarus wouldn't use us like that," another mechanic, Grott, hollered down-corridor. "She's never left a man behind, and she's not starting now. Don't you listen to him, kitten."

Kitten was a term from Nov's subcontinent, where declaws had service roles waiting for them right out of the courts. The south was generally the cleaner, more urban hemisphere, where abuse still happened, but in nicer outfits and living quarters. Imbra hadn't decided if Grott was making some sort of overture, in keeping with one of the major service roles for *kittens* down south, but the northerner kept his distance just in case. The beatings, at least, had ceased upon arrival, leaving only Paloma to watch for in the night.

Miha exhaled loudly at Grott's retort.

"You think that's leaving a man behind? To give everything in service to our people, our solar system—that's why we're here, y'damned southie."

"Hell with that," said Grott—a man of Her Loving Embrace, Imbra surmised from the tattoo on his arm when he floated a drill up-corridor. "I'm here to build things and to fix things. Don't care who I'm building and fixing 'em for, so long as we're all alive at the end of the day. Life's what's worth fighting for—mine, and yours, and even kitten's too."

"Go on, then," said Miha. "Run and hide when Allegiance comes."

"I will," said Grott. "And you all should, too."

Imbra saw more than heard Miha's answering grunt. The ringing in his ears let him turn his thoughts elsewhere as a more heated argument ensued between coworkers: To the long line of bubble ships in need of supercooling assembly before central processors could be installed. To the heady stink of so many bodies in cramped, strangely sterile corridors. To the latest scuttlebutt about how the new kid, Paloma, was already hitting it off with one of the electrical technicians, Ren, a young woman of seventeen. Smart, vivacious, reckless. The kind of girl who'd listen to the kid's sad story and maybe offer herself up as a partner in crime. A better ally for vengeance than Tripp and Hurley, to be sure.

So Imbra slept lightly, if at all—and always, after the first week, with one hand, then the other, cupped to an ear. Testing his hearing. Waiting for some sign of release. Accepting, in the meantime, the incessant hum of shipyard life.

On Imbra's recommendation to Biggs, Paloma had arrived at the shipyards with a ticket to "flight school," an anachronism from when pilot training came first in a ship-officer's education. Mostly, the kid learned how to handle weapons systems on a wide variety of fleet ships, and the ins and outs of basic in-flight maintenance. At first, Paloma was too young for guaranteed field placement and seemed more likely to end up with Ren on ground crew—safer than most for the remainder of the war, with an education and time to reconsider the whole of his young life before heading home.

But then the Allegiance's next fleet arrived four weeks early, at the outskirts of the heliosphere, and took out General Asarus's first line like a hot knife through butter.

Overnight, mechanics throughout the shipyards turned into seasoned strategists. Every spare bulkhead was filled with grids of the solar system, sketched and scratched out and sketched in again to show the strengths and weaknesses of possible attacks in 2D and 3D space. Every active flight officer suddenly be came an expert on AI resistance tactics, too, relentlessly debating programming modifications to allow for riskier, more spontaneous inflight maneuvers. And everyone, it seemed, had plenty of counsel to offer General Asarus, already in-transit to prepare for the next assault, although none would utter those same words of military wisdom to fellow grunts in their sleeping modules first.

"Ah, you wouldn't understand," went one excuse.

"For her ears only!" went another.

Imbra's own ears were still ringing for unrelated reasons, and after listening to his bunkmates worry the subject of Asarus's next moves for well over an hour, he proposed a saying from up north about backseat driving—forgetting, until the words came out, that his audience was mostly from the subcontinent, where nobody drove in the first place, so the analogy fell flat. Next, he tried a Novuni-wide standard about lava and water, which did better—but even then, his fellow mechanics disagreed about where the Allegiance stood on that figurative fight-or-flight scale. Members of Her Loving Embrace clung to the words *lava* and *run* in the ancient saying. Those on the Path, though, remained partial to *swim*, whether the invaders had more in common with cool water or not. Grott asked if Imbra was scared, in trying to get the rest of the men to change the subject, but Imbra shook his head.

"Just tired," he said, turning in his bunk. But his fatigue was no match for the nervous energy of his coworkers, each buoyed by hormonal rushes almost alien to him now.

"The point is, we need to land one good kick in their teeth," said one of the men on the Path, while Imbra tried to sleep. "Something nuclear, right in the heart of it all."

"You volunteering to get close enough for that?" one of the Loving Embracers replied. "You think their AIs would even let you, if you made the attempt?"

"Well, no, but that's why we . . ."

And so minutes turned into hours. By the time his bunkmates finally started sawing in their bunks, Imbra had given up on sleep and lay awake churning over the questions even their most relentless chatter had failed to answer. He could almost visualize the gap in all their proposed strategies: A hole that no mere boast of overt aggression could ever hope to fill. The hole was about the size and shape of a cornered gulch rat down on Nov, once the ragged, prickly thing had dropped to its back—claws up, eyes red, and paws out in something like submission. *Like,* but not quite. That soft grey underbelly always a trap.

By morning shift, footage of the heliosphere disaster from satellites in orbit around Resu played on repeat across mess-hall monitors: a not-so-subtle reminder to get back to work, because the whole damned fleet was counting on them. The first thing Imbra noticed was the speed of the Allegiance ships, tearing into view in diamond formation precisely where they'd do the most damage to Novun Prime defenses, but then slowing quickly enough to do a couple other, brutal sweeps of the region. Within minutes, the only signs of the solar system's outer shielding and ring guard were a few glinting pieces of debris, quickly lost to the dark. The first time the images cycled through, Miha prayed for the dead in one way, and Grott in another, while Imbra studied the grainy images with an attention like reverence. Taking notes. Hearing certain gears fall into place behind the ringing in his ears.

"Huge energy consumption," said Grott. "Coming down from a fraction of the speed of light like that. Not to mention the jerk."

"Possibly no organics on board," Miha agreed. The formation pattern seemed rigid enough to suggest complete autopilot anyway.

"Even then," said Imbra. "You gotta protect the processors."

"Ion shielding," said Grott. "Mini-magneto spheres keep most of the nastiness out."

Imbra whistled. "Even more energy consumption for that set-up, though."

His coworkers nodded, Miha rapping idly at the table as he did. At the far end of the mess, the youngsters showed up in officers' dress—Paloma and Ren among them.

"All getting bubble ships now," said Miha. "Poor bastards."

"Not official yet," said Grott. "The general can still change her mind."

"Why would she? You got a better idea, with the Allegiance already at our doorstep? Should be thanking Mother you're not among them. Someone's gotta prep the fleet."

Imbra looked without looking at Paloma's bench and thought he saw Paloma look without looking back at him, too. Ren, though—Ren stared straight at Imbra, hard as ice, then squeezed Paloma's wrist. Grott, catching the chill of it, winked at Imbra.

"Not to worry, kitten. They can't come for you now. Not with all this going on."

Imbra shook his head. "Not what I'm worried about." The last of the gears turned freely now, though his heart didn't even have the decency to beat wildly at the risk he knew he was entertaining—for himself and one other. He pushed calmly from the table instead. "I'll be in coolant, if you need me. We still keep copper wiring in third-wing storage?"

Miha nodded and waved him off. Imbra hesitated, then took the long way out of the mess—across the room, past the youngsters, elbowing Paloma hard as he floated through. Paloma needed little provocation—arms and legs lashing out, one hand finding Imbra's jumpsuit and the other, as a fist, Imbra's jaw. The other youngsters fell back, making room for ensuing blows, while the older crew proved slow to step in. When two other mechanics eventually did, though, Miha could have sworn that Imbra had Paloma's ear and was whispering something serious enough to give Paloma pause, fist upraised for another blow.

"The hell in Mother's name is he up to," said Miha to Grott.

Grott shrugged. "Kittens, man," he said. "Can't feel much, so you'd be surprised the lengths they go to, to feel anything at all."

Imbra might have agreed, if he'd overheard Grott's comment. As far as lack of feeling went, even the shipyard shifts weighed hard on a body that had no ability to switch into a more vigorous working mode and kept trying to nod off while engaged in high-intensity tasks. That lack of feeling also went some way toward explaining why he kept flexing and clenching his hands on route to the assembly line; he knew his idea was sound, in theory, but he still struggled with why he'd picked the kid to make it a reality. Paloma could easily inform on him, or tell Ren, who'd do the same. And for what reasonable payoff? Imbra had been part of enough precarious ventures to know that chances were slim Paloma would actually show up after shift, let alone put himself in a bubble ship of Imbra's choosing and special design when the fleet deployed.

"Stupid," Imbra muttered, but with the declaw firmly in place, he hadn't even the anger to punch a bulkhead. He let his clenched fist rest at his thigh instead, nails digging into the fabric of his jumpsuit, while he studied the coolant systems and let the steps in his plan turn into mantra, joined only by the constant ringing in his head.

General Asarus debarked from her flagship, the *N.S.S. Ragnara,* during the next day shift. That evening, the whole of the shipyards team received debrief about the Novuni's plan of attack. Some in Imbra's quarters grumbled about the intended scope of the battlefield, but the crankiest mechanics were those working remote weapons' design, which only made sense, since the bulk of Asarus's plan relied on letting the Allegiance fleet get close—very close—and attempting to outmaneuver on familiar ground, with plenty of asteroid debris to use for cover and collision courses. There were too many variables for a human to work out, but with AIs in control of the ships, programmed in the months since Fort Five with the trajectories of tens of thousands of known, minute astral bodies, it almost seemed feasible. Still, the numbers weren't promising; even official holovids made no secret of the fact that the bubble ships, streakers, battle cruisers, and lancers stood outnumbered three to one by the waves of Allegiance ships gathered just past the gas giant Dreya.

No wonder, then, that Grott soon joined the other spiritual objectors on the last shuttle bound for Hav, the planet's largest moon and the Novuni territory best equipped for long-term underground shelter from any invading party.

No wonder, too, that Miha and the others on the Path of the Vengeful Sun took renewed vigor in their work—eagerly priming the fleet as best they could, knowing full well in their aching hearts that the misery of unwanted existence would be at an end soon.

And maybe, Imbra reasoned, why Paloma showed up outside his quarters the night before departure after all. Alone, and unarmed.

"Did you tell anyone?" said Imbra. "Even . . . ?" "She wouldn't let me come, if I did. And she'd be right. Frigg, even leaving her with the others out there, while I go off and do this fool thing—it's a death sentence, isn't it." The question landed as a statement, so Imbra didn't reply at once. He glanced around the otherwise empty module, all his bunkmates busy drinking in the mess, but there was nothing to offer the kid, not even a squeeze-bottle of water. "Most ship's officers are from the south," he said instead. "Nice place. Rich. Automated."

"So, what, this is some sort of weird valley loyalty?"

"No. I'm not even sure if I can do loyalty." Imbra frowned, hands palm up. "No rush of oxytocin, no real bonding, right? At least, I think . . . I don't know. It's all . . ." He cradled his head in his hands, massaging his throbbing temples, hoping to lessen the ringing.

Paloma looked at him with the revulsion that only youth, in all its decisiveness and propensity toward binary thinking, could dredge up. "I don't care," he said heavily.

Imbra raised his gaze and sniffed. Moisture settled strangely, high in the sinuses, in zero-g. "Right, of course. I only meant that—" He took a long breath. "You can drive. Most of these others, especially from the south—they can't. Too used to giving it all up to the AIs. More interested in weapons control than steering, in any case."

Paloma watched his mother's killer steadily. "And that'll save me?"

Imbra had to fight back a desperate laugh, the closest to fear he'd come in weeks.

"O Mother!" he said. "Kid, that might save us all."

Bubble Ship AV04's forward camera caught it first—the sudden tumbling of another bubble ship out of formation, a spray from its port panels indicating some sort of leak. Catastrophic coolant loss to any outside eye, with the ship spinning dead, belly up over and over in the middle of the fray. Meanwhile, AV04 was locked into an engagement course with the Allegiance, its waves of AI ships rising high to the left field of the viewscreen. Other ships started to feel the heat of their enemy's long-range weapons soon after—sides scored until decompression became imminent; comm lines riddled with panicked ship's officers last prayers for themselves and their sun. One little busted bubble ship hurtling so far ahead wasn't much, then, in the scheme of things, with AIs dodging so much debris on both sides.

A streaker ship called the Jalfreda caught the best footage of what happened next—the little bubble ship's tumbling suddenly becoming less predictable, more of an uneven wobble just below the plane of the leisurely advancing Allegiance fleet. To the invading AIs, the little ship surely registered no sign of active onboard processors—not with the coolant gone, and the engines superheating the rest—so it fell into background noise, along with all the other debris still being accounted for on their maps. Then all the Allegiance ships proximate to the little bubble ship went dark—like a ripple, extending outward from Bubble Ship XF32. An EM pulse, knocking out ion shields and disrupting processors in turn.

Those still in the shipyards watched in stunned silence at first—but then that magnetic ripple hit the mechanics, too, in its own way, and with a cry of triumph bodies collided with bodies, detritus flung about the mess. The

EM pulse lessened in intensity as it broadened, so ships at the fringe of the fleet still hurtled forward, unaffected—but with the Allegiance temporarily halved, Novuni fighters stood a better chance. And they took it. Not enough to win, but enough to drag the invaders into a standoff. Then a ceasefire. A broadcast from General Asarus eventually reporting that the Allegiance had promised a rep from one of its time-dilated worlds: a figure of significant corporate authority, who would articulate their demands more clearly than any heard around Novun Prime to date.

"Now," said the general, over vidscreens system-wide three days after first strike. "We negotiate a lasting peace, or we die trying."

In those three days of combat, all aboard the shipyards had alternated between volatile bursts of celebration and anxiety—more drinking, more quarrelling, more breakneck labors over wounded ships back in port. All, that is, except one: Imbra, who slept and work and ate and drank amid the other mechanics' frenzy like a man disembodied, wandering at a remove from creatures so wildly impassioned he almost couldn't believe they were of the same species, let alone tribe. But once the battle was over, Miha clapped Imbra's back just the same, and reassured the northerner that he hadn't missed out on much, not being able to weep as openly for the protracted lease on life that one little ship had brought to all the rest.

Imbra nodded at the gesture but couldn't bring himself to reply, a lump lodged in his throat because the dread still lay within him—deep down, only lacking the right physical response to flourish. He kept replaying footage from the Jalfreda instead: the slow approach of Allegiance, the sudden strike of the EM wave, the darkness, and then, in the midst of it, the slightest movement: the ejection of a lifepod, barely noticeable, from XF32.

Paloma's lifepod resurfaced a week after the ceasefire—a whole week in which his ship's maneuver had been chalked up to General Asarus's craftiness, her unparalleled head for deep strategy beneath all her openness with the fleet about tactics. Only Ren—also alive, if shaken up from her time in the field—suspected otherwise. Within hours of her return to the shipyards, she found Imbra running diagnostics routines and stood at the edge of his work module, her lean frame as tense with anger as Paloma's, on the surface, had been.

"He's alive," said Imbra. "I know he is."

"He'd better be," she said. "Easy enough to toss you out an airlock, if he's not."

Imbra notched a brow. "Lot of hatred from a southerner. You must really love him."

"Don't patronize me," she said. "Declaws don't vote in the south. They don't get a say. They get to shut up and give back to society until their time in the sun is done."

"Does it really matter who contributes, so long as the war comes to an end?"

"Yes," she said and clearly meant it. Imbra's lips twitched, but he held back a smile.

"Credit's all his," he said. "I don't want it. Once he gets back, he'll be a hero. More than he already is. They'll name schools after him, promote him two grades. Salary for life."

Ren didn't look convinced, and Imbra didn't blame her—not even when Paloma returned to the land of the living, haggard and haunted from his time in stasis. Certainly, the celebrations for the Novuni's latest hero were wild enough. His name resounded through the system far and wide enough. And the accolades poured on him were lavish enough, too.

But in the process, in private, Paloma had told someone in command the full story.

Next thing Imbra knew, he was standing before General Asarus herself, on the bridge of the *N.S.S. Ragnara*.

"I could have you thrown to the courts, or straight out an airlock, for what you did," she said. "On your own, without oversight, without permission."

"Yes sir," said Imbra.

"But since it doesn't really change anything in the long run, you might as well live." With that, she pinned bridge crew insignia on his collar and assigned him a bunk on the ship.

3.

> *Even the planet runs in circles.*
> *Mother help the fool*
> *Who thinks in straight lines.*
>
>   —Novuni Proverb

In person, General Asarus remained larger than life, an illusion aided in no small part by a uniform and unwavering gaze that commanded attention, despite the bun crowning her flat-twist hair coming no higher than the shoulders of some of her bridge crew.

Imbra, his own coils a wild tangle more days than not, took with difficulty to the standards of dress and conduct aboard the *N.S.S. Ragnara*. The ways of the valley—Biggs' ease with the law; Tripp and Hurley's excesses on the right side of it—he'd been able to manipulate with only minor physical concessions, while even the shipyards had their share of play, from Grott's teasing to Miha's unhinged banter. But the stringency of life aboard a military vessel had yet to offer any easy evasions. Every day shift at six bells, Imbra stood for inspection—and failed, miserably—and after reprimands and first meal seated himself at eight bells at the back of the war room, reviewing schema after schema littered in the jargon of half a dozen subdisciplines he could barely identify, let alone parse.

"I'm just a valley hick with a knack for machines," he said on the first day, while posing a question about a recurring symbol to the shipmate beside him.

Lieutenant Bastrus answered his question, but not before pinning him with a look that plainly read *well, try harder*.

And Imbra did, though his head felt sluggish for reasons that neither the declaw nor the lingering hearing loss could fully explain. He ran simulations of ambush paths, decoys, and direct, full-frontal assaults across the asteroid field and gas giants, trying to beat an AI in scenarios where the Allegiance had prepped an invading force to overwhelm the system on what civilian news was already triumphantly calling Treaty Day. In every case, Imbra failed, and in every case, he ended the day reporting on his failure to General Asarus herself, her back turned to study the muddy sun through a slice of ship's glass.

"You could get an AI to run these same simulations," he added at the end of his third shift. "Faster, more efficient, probably with better results—sir."

"We have," said Asarus. She steepled her fingers and glanced at Imbra over a shoulder. "And, no, recruit. It's a failure every time. But as I told you in our first conversation, it doesn't matter—none of it—in the long run."

"Sir?"

"They even anticipated you. Did you know that? Not you, specifically, but the trouble you caused. Just as they anticipated—and maybe even constructed—me."

Imbra wore his confusion too plainly to answer.

"The Allegiance," the general explained. "There's been talk that they're shaping the whole contest. That the game was rigged before it began. The well-loved general, the underdog story, the hotshot hero pilot—all of it. Wild theories about their reasons, too, but then, that's what you get when you deal with an ancient people, a people living in time-dilation like nothing we've ever known. Have you heard any of these wild reports?"

Imbra thought of the look on Biggs' face a lifetime ago—the hesitation of a man who knew crazy when he saw it, and who apparently *had* seen it in archives, but who had decided at the last against passing on the disease. "I've heard that the theories get wild, sure."

"But not the theories themselves." Asarus nodded. "Good, I suppose. Some ideas are hard to let go of, once they take root. They eat at your sense of being, your sense of purpose, until there's almost nothing left. You do have a creed, don't you?"

"Of a kind." Imbra noted the general's quick glance at his bare skin—no tattoos to indicate his side on the question of the sun. "Enough to get by."

At the emotion rising then on General Asarus's face, Imbra surprised himself with a sudden tightness, a knot in the muscles below his ribs. He'd almost thought that sort of eagerness behind him, but hers was such a sad, unexpected smile. Another kind of *try harder*.

So he did.

At the beginning of his next shift, Imbra took a different tack, opting to review the ship's onboard archives before taking another run at the simulator. After all, the main trouble with the simulations was temporal: The Allegiance simply had more time on their side. But why? Life on Nov's northern continent hadn't offered the greatest education in system-wide or interstellar history, but Imbra knew that the Allegiance and the Novuni had first met centuries ago, which seemed like plenty of time to stabilize tech trade with such a vast economic power. And sure enough, as the *Ragnara's* records showed, since first contact the Allegiance had indeed offered all the Novuni all manner of trade packages, including one bundle of neurotech responsible for declaw procedures, in exchange for raw and semirefined resources system-wide. There had, however, always been one notable exception to the Allegiance's side of the pot: In every trade brief Imbra came across, any advances related to interstellar travel remained strictly off the table.

Certainly, the Novuni had developed significant EM technologies on their own over the centuries, but they hadn't yet mastered the energy reserves needed for proper long-distance shielding—nor the systems needed to protect human beings through huge shifts in speed at the end of the ride, though the lifepods were getting close. Nor could the Novuni build to such speeds in the first place, although some on Hav were currently tinkering with possibilities involving laser tech. In short, hundreds of years of uneasy partnership on, the Allegiance still largely dictated terms by which anyone around Novun Prime could ever hope to leave the system. And eventually, someone in central gov had objected to this arrangement.

When talks fell apart, though, the Allegiance sent for the fleet surprisingly fast. Imbra remembered hearing tell in the valley of what happened next—how only by dint of General Asarus's quick thinking had a deal been struck at Fort Five to spare lives and return mining operations to their original trade framework—but the accelerated time frame of initial proceedings baffled him as he sifted through official records. General Asarus's peace only held until the miners rebelled, too; after that, the Allegiance took even more exaggerated offense to the Novuni, and its representative left with a declaration of total war.

By shift's end, Imbra could see why so many of his people talked of conspiracy: The point of growing contention between the Novuni and Allegiance could have been predicted from the outset of their dealings, while the Allegiance's split-second decisions, to wage war at the first sign of protest, suggested that someone in the greater galaxy had been waiting for the Novuni to grow restless. Only the reason for such a long-game approach lay out of Imbra's reach when he logged off for the night: If the Allegiance simply wanted the Novun Prime system, why not take it from the outset?

On his next shift, Imbra stared for hours at the speckled panels over his desk and remembered Esrin's Gulch—the heat of it as a child; the threat of magma churning in rivers not so far underfoot, before the dam broke and major bridges fell and the hills and the valleys realigned at great cost to human life. Historians attributed the continent's haphazard geology to the haste of ancient terraformers, but northerners knew better, whatever side of the sun's gospel they preferred: Hazards existed because the Novuni existed; because Mother either reviled or adored them so unbearably much.

As a child, Imbra had always been the fastest over the hot valley stones—Dash, to anyone who knew him—but not because he was the fastest on foot. In a straight sprint over a strip of flat land, he would lose to Tripp and Hurley as often as win, if not more. But give him a path that forked in odd ways, give him land that wouldn't yield, and Imbra had always been quickest to work the trick out.

"You supposed to be working?" Bastrus's voice cut through his daydreams.

"I am working." But Imbra drew himself to a stiff-backed upright position.

"Coulda fooled me."

Imbra nodded to her station—Bastrus rigged up to comms, her own display running simulations of a different magnitude. "Figured out how to evacuate everyone yet?"

Bastrus offered up a grim smile. "Not gonna happen."

"Oh, you're on the Path, too, are you?"

"I dare you to find a Loving Embracer on this ship." She nodded toward the rest of bridge crew. "We all know the futility of the situation. The general doesn't hide anything from us. Still, the real test is dignity at the end. Putting on the best possible show of force."

"Sure, that's one way, I guess." Imbra scratched the side of his face. Bastrus's sidelong glance vaguely resembled amusement.

"Oh, and you've got a better idea."

Imbra shrugged, drumming his hands on the desk. "Just thinking, is all. You know, these AIs in the sims I'm running, they remind me of these twins I used to know. Hurley and Tripp. Loved to win. Always played to win. But if the two ever fought with each other, you knew the outcome from the outset. Tripp always had the upper hand before, so he always won in the end. Just like the AI playing the Allegiance in these sims, against the AI playing our fleets—the Allegiance starts with the upper hand, so it always wins in the end."

"Exactly my point," said Bastrus. "Futile exercise, but one we all endure anyway."

"Except that Tripp never really won against me. Not really. Not when we were young, and not even after I'd been declawed. As a kid, I'd beat him in races over the gulch. As an adult, I took away his satisfaction when he tried to lay into me."

He glanced over the workstation and noted that Bastrus was paying close attention, even if she didn't seem the type to humor him with further questions. Not even a *How*.

"I didn't play to win, see? Can't win against someone who won't accept the stakes."

Bastrus shook her head. "We're not surrendering, if that's what you're thinking. That's not an option. Even if we wanted to, Treaty Day's set for six cycles from now, and already the Allegiance's next wave is just waiting at the edge of the heliosphere. The game they're playing, the way they keep toying with us . . . we're in this until we win or we die."

"I'm not suggesting surrender," said Imbra. "I'm saying—"

But he cut himself off, a deep furrow settling on his brow as more gears turned. The predictability of a clash on Treaty Day, like the predictability of the war itself, cast aspersions on even this brief reprieve from combat, and the rogue EM pulse that first allowed for it. Imbra had simply assumed that AIs registering no AI from a ship in the middle of AI-to-AI combat wouldn't destroy the errant object anyway, but Paloma hadn't even been piloting that well. Just enough to nudge his bubble ship right below the Allegiance's fleet—a fleet that for some reason was advancing toward theirs at a leisurely pace. Had the winning move been, if not anticipated, at the very least permitted by Allegiance from the start?

The thought could not be unthought. Imbra felt a faint chill—the merest echo of a proper fear response—and stood suddenly, gripping his desk at the ensuing wave of nausea.

"Breathe, recruit," said Bastrus. "I'm not catching you if you pass out."

"They could've torn through us in minutes," said Imbra. "But they didn't. They took their time. They waited."

"They sure did." Bastrus's voice was too upbeat. Imbra gave her a hard stare.

"Where's General Asarus?"

"Still in talks, I'd imagine. But you might try the bay."

Bastrus wasn't far off; Imbra found the general in a portside corridor, watching the dull brown glimmer of the sun after flight-crew inspections. *Not praying,* she'd told him after one shift. *Just contemplating how to exist in a universe that operates at such unfathomable magnitudes.*

"I have a plan, sir," he said. "But you're not going to like it."

General Asarus turned slowly, her dark eyes hard enough that his own watered.

"Recruit," she said, "I haven't liked a bit of this from the start."

But she waited for him to go on.

General Asarus chose her own team for Imbra's special assignment, but at Imbra's request she also granted Paloma passage to the flagship to be part of the final send-off. While preparations continued for Treaty Day, and for the evacuation and defense fleet that would be required shortly after, some two dozen willing crewmates were briefed on their impending missions and given the time they needed to grieve. A believer in Her Loving Embrace would have found solace in the idea that life went on, but a crew predominantly set upon the Path of the Vengeful Sun needed to adjust to their new fate: to live longer, much longer, than any of their doomed colleagues left behind.

"Time is not on our side," said General Asarus to her team. "For decades, if not centuries, we've been playing the long game on the Allegiance's terms, and in a few days, it will surely lead to our ruin. We've all seen the size of their ships, the indifference of their agents to genuine calls for peace. What else remains for us, then, but to play the long game, too, the only way the Novuni know how?" She went on to wish her team peace, and prayed with them, and sent them to make final arrangements. Only Imbra she told to hang back.

"Have you been in stasis since the surgery?" When Imbra shook his head, Asarus hummed. "I wonder," she said, "if it will be easier for you. Without all that fear when the body struggles with the stasis fluid, unable to believe what the mind already knows."

"Only one way to find out," said Imbra.

The general watched him closely, as if for signs of visible apprehension. Seeing none, she nodded. "Your friend has arrived, by the way. You can go under any time."

Imbra smiled. "I doubt he'd see himself as a friend."

"Associate, then. But you're sure you wouldn't rather a proper stasis crew?"

"He'll pick it up quickly. He's young, but he's already seen action—and he knows what stasis is like, too."

"That's a benefit, is it?"

"In this case, absolutely."

General Asarus didn't press, so after finalizing other details, Imbra went to confer with his fellow northerner in the docking bay. Paloma looked older, somehow, after weeks of being lauded as a system-wide hero for a set of actions prescribed for him by his mother's killer. He certainly made no attempt to hide his displeasure at seeing Imbra again.

"I could murder you, you know," said the kid. "I could put you under in a way that guarantees you never wake up again."

"I know," said Imbra. "And I'll take that risk. I've owed you that much all along. But if you don't, you're the only one I can count on, to do what I need someone to do."

Paloma's expression remained hostile as Imbra went on, but at least the kid listened, which was all Imbra could hope for. On their way to the lifepods, Imbra was tempted to ask something else—how Ren was; whether Paloma had been back to Nov and visited his mother's grave—but every note of affected camaraderie felt flat and wrong in the back of his throat. Before prepping for immersion, Imbra held out a keypass instead.

"I don't know if you'll ever get back," he said. "But if you do, take this to Biggs. It's a copy, with a holo-note from me. The garage, Bullet, everything—It's yours."

Paloma clicked his teeth, setting the keypass beside the controls. "You can't bribe me that easily." But he paused before adding. "Are you scared yet? Not gonna beg, are you?"

Imbra, lying in the dark womb of the lifepod, shook his head as Paloma started the process, and then the seal came up all around him, and Paloma's last words couldn't be heard through the tiny front window. But Imbra's body, in the end, could not be so easily tricked into calmness. Even with the declaw, he shivered violently as the stasis fluid rose, and his lungs resisted breathing to the bitter end even when fully submerged, and so Imbra went to sleep screaming—and stayed screaming—for what felt like a hundred years.

Ninety-seven years, give or take. His skin felt like twisted bark when the freight crew pulled him from the battered lifepod. At first Imbra could not register his arms and legs, let alone speak, but after days in the infirmary, realizing from the steady beep of machines that his tinnitus had passed, he started to notice larger details outside of himself. The Allegiance insignia, for instance, on the medical officer who so painstakingly coaxed him to health.

"Quite the journey you've been on," said the slender, faintly luminescent being who called itself Yarun. "I guess there's no one we can call?"

Imbra shook his head—a painful, sluggish maneuver. "Where . . . ?"

"On the Ambara. We're a small operation, running supplies to various outposts the cruise ships use for debarks along the way."

Imbra still struggled for basic control over his facial expressions, but his confusion came naturally enough. Yarun hummed understanding, even sympathy.

"Cruise ships," Yarun explained, "for tourists from the Allegiance's central worlds. Those are some wildly rich families, I tell you. Kept in luxury stasis—nothing like your little nightmare, sorry to say—while their ships wander the galaxy, visiting all sorts of attractions. There's one system, I hear, with the most fantastic athletes. Something to do with the density of the world, and its land features, but really—they're a sight to behold. And another world's one big library, an archive of all the galaxy's knowledge. Beautiful promenades."

Imbra swallowed heavily before attempting to speak again. "And—Nov— Novun Prime?"

Creases at the corners of Yarun's eyes suggested incomprehension, but the medical officer pulled up a system file and cried out in triumph. "Ah! Yes, the mausoleum. A solemn little system, that—museums and graveyards almost everywhere, paying tribute to the heroism of those lost in the last Great Allegiance War. Gets a pretty good run of cruise ships passing through. Lots of Allegiance members like to go and wring their hands over that sort of thing. Can't remember what started the whole war—some monstrous affair involving despotic trade agents, I believe. But all so very sad. Never again, you know?" Yarun nodded while scrolling through the file. "Whole fleets wiped out in brutal double-crosses, as well as some of the lunar bases, civilians and all, over ninety years ago. Say, that's not where you're——?"

But when Yarun looked up, Imbra was already touching with amazement the sudden flood of dampness on his cheeks. Yarun offered a gentle smile with its lipless mouth.

"When we scanned you, we saw that you had some sort of neural block. Fascinating monstrosity, stopping the signal for some fairly important hormonal reactions. I know some of the worlds still use these things, but not many. Barbaric, really. So—I know we didn't ask, but we took it out while repairing the rest of the stasis damage. If, if you want it back . . . ?"

"No," said Imbra, choking on the outpouring of his grief. He'd had his suspicions, which was why he had asked Paloma to plot the course for his lifepod differently—to aim it farther than those for the rest of the team, who'd been given flight paths on limited thrusters that would have found their occupants waking maybe ten years later, still in the system and ready to infiltrate any dominant Allegiance force in operation around Novun Prime. A long-term assassination plot, granted, but the Novuni's only real hope of living to fight again.

But the truth of the matter, the cause for the war in the first place, proved even worse than General Asarus had suggested it might be. What sun was theirs, that neither loved nor hated her people, but rather operated with cool indifference towards the Novuni, having raised them up for a slaughter that served the whims of other systems' worlds?

Yarun waited for Imbra to regain some measure of composure.

"We still have to decide what to do with you," it said softly.

"All . . . dead?"

"Your system?" Yarun checked the file. "Well, mostly. But there's a continent on one of the planets, Nov, that was already pretty volatile. Says here that Allegiance didn't bother destroying its settlements, because 'their existence seemed squalid enough'—sorry. Just reading the file. Tough people, though, I imagine, to survive at all out there."

Imbra was silent. At first he humored thoughts of his garage still standing, and Palo ma and Ren having started a family that stretched out over the lost century, and Biggs and Tripp and Hurley having made some sort of decent postwar life for themselves before the valley did them in. But no— the landscape was too fickle, too restless for the sort of feel good story that those who believed in Her Loving Embrace might desire. So he imagined a supervolcano instead, washing the whole mess of the continent's peoples away. But that was too easy, too. A conceit of the Path, restless to be done with an unforgiving world.

Imbra's emotions, left to their own devices, lurched from one extreme to the other for the first time in months—and a century. Still, he knew his own path lay somewhere in the middle of the gospels, or maybe an eternity re moved from both. He remembered the recovery ward in the courts, and how, as the urgent need for more crystal bled from his system, a sudden calmness rose instead: a drug unto itself. The joke had always been on the courts after that day, for the declaw only gave him more of what he wanted—only made it harder, despite his all-too-human inclinations, to remain addicted to anger, fear, and grief.

"You play dead in the valley to survive," said the ancient Novuni man at last. "Dead in your heart, dead in your veins, and eventually, when they catch you doing what everyone does, dead in your brains. But there's another kind of stillness in the Universe, isn't there?"

"Well—yes," said Yarun. "All kinds, I'd imagine."

"Good. Then that's where I'll start."

While Yarun attempted a hesitant reply, involving the possibility of place-ment on a science vessel soon to be passing by, Imbra turned with great effort to the nearest porthole, which revealed a series of stars unknown to him—each with its own peoples, and their own notions of inner peace. He knew then that he couldn't defeat the Allegiance, an empire that went to such lengths to complete itself through domination sport: the complete distortion of other worlds and cultures to suit its idlest wants and needs. Nevertheless, Imbra knew he could at least try to find and name them—all the forms of detachment through which a man might yet go unconquered, though every fiber in his being longed to cry out and give in.

The center of my sky no longer boasts a native sun.

Imbra turned the words over and over in his restless mind, a new sort of Novuni proverb in the making, and set his sights on a day when he might almost believe them, too.

Greg Egan has published more than sixty short stories and thirteen novels. He has won a Hugo Award for his novella "Oceanic" and the John W. Campbell Memorial Award for his novel *Permutation City*. His most recent novel is *Dichronauts*, set in a universe with two time-like dimensions.

UNCANNY VALLEY

Greg Egan

1.

In a pause in the flow of images, it came to him that he'd been dreaming for a fathomless time and that he wished to stop. But when he tried to picture the scene that would greet him upon waking, his mind grabbed the question and ran with it, not so much changing the subject as summoning out of the darkness answers that he was sure had long ago ceased to be correct. He remembered the bunk beds he and his brother had slept in until he was nine, with pieces of broken springs hanging down above him like tiny gray stalactites. The shade of his bedside reading lamp had been ringed with small, diamond-shaped holes; he would place his fingers over them and stare at the red light emerging through his flesh, until the heat from the globe became too much to bear.

Later, in a room of his own, his bed had come with hollow metal posts whose plastic caps were easily removed, allowing him to toss in chewed pencil stubs, pins that had held newly bought school shirts elaborately folded around cardboard packaging, tacks that he'd bent out of shape with misaligned hammer blows while trying to form pictures in zinc on lumps of firewood, pieces of gravel that had made their way into his shoes, dried snot scraped from his handkerchief, and tiny, balled-up scraps of paper, each bearing a four- or five-word account of whatever seemed important at the time, building up a record of his life like a core sample slicing through geological strata, a find for future archaeologists far more exciting than any diary.

But he could also recall a bleary-eyed, low-angle view of clothes strewn on the floor, in a bedsit apartment with no bed as such, just a foldout couch. That felt as remote as his childhood, but something pushed him to keep fleshing out the details of the room. There was a typewriter on a table. He could smell the ribbon, and he saw the box in which it had come, sitting on a shelf in a corner of a stationers, with white letters on a blue background, but the words they spelled out eluded him. He'd always hunted down the fully black ribbons, though most stores had only stocked black-and-red. Who could possibly need to type anything in red?

Wiping his ink-stained fingers on a discarded page after a ribbon change, he knew the whole scene was an anachronism, and he tried to follow that insight up to the surface, like a diver pursuing a glimpse of the distant sun. But something weighed him down, anchoring him to the cold wooden chair in that unheated room, with a stack of blank paper to his right, a pile of finished sheets to his left, a wastebasket under the table. He urgently needed to think about the way the loop in the "e" became solid black sometimes, prompting him to clean all the typebars with an old T-shirt dampened with methylated spirits. If he didn't think about it now, he was afraid that he might never have the chance to think of it again.

2.

Adam decided to go against all the advice he'd received, and attend the old man's funeral.

The old man himself had warned him off. "Why make trouble?" he'd asked, peering at Adam from the hospital bed with that disconcerting vampiric longing that had grown more intense toward the end. "The more you rub their faces in it, the more likely they'll be to come after you."

"I thought you said they couldn't do that."

"All I said was that I'd done my best to stop them. Do you want to keep the inheritance, or do you want to squander it on lawyers? Don't make yourself more of a target than you need to be."

But standing in the shower, reveling in the sensation of the hot water pelting his skin, Adam only grew more resolute. Why shouldn't he dare to show his face? He had nothing to be ashamed of.

The old man had bought a few suits for him a while ago, and left them hanging beside his own clothes. Adam picked one out and placed it on the bed, then paused to run a hand along the worn sleeve of an old, olive-green shirt. He was sure it would fit him, and for a moment he considered wearing it, but then the thought made him uneasy and he chose one of the new ones that had come with the suits.

As he dressed, he gazed at the undisturbed bed, trying to think of a good reason why he still hadn't left the guest room. No one else was coming to claim this one. But he shouldn't get too comfortable here; he might need to sell the house and move into something far more modest.

Adam started booking a car, then realized that he had no idea where the ceremony was being held. He finally found the details at the bottom of the old man's obit, which described it as open to the public. While he stood outside the front door waiting for the car, he tried for the third or fourth time to read the obituary itself, but his eyes kept glazing over. "Morris blah blah blah . . . Morris blah blah, Morris blah . . ."

His phone beeped, then the gate opened and the car pulled into the driveway. He sat in the passenger seat and watched the steering wheel doing its poltergeist act as it negotiated the U-turn. He suspected that whatever victories the lawyers could achieve, he was going to have to pay the "unsupervised driving" surcharge for a while yet.

As the car turned into Sepulveda Boulevard, the view looked strange to him—half familiar, half wrong—but perhaps there'd been some recent reconstruction. He dialed down the tinting, hoping to puncture a lingering sense of being at a remove from everything. The glare from the pavement beneath the cloudless blue sky was merciless, but he kept the windows undimmed.

The venue was some kind of chapel-esque building that probably served as seven different kinds of meeting hall, and in any case was free of conspicuous religious or la-la-land inspirational signage. The old man had left his remains to a medical school, so at least they'd all been spared a trip to Forest Lawn. As Adam stepped away from the car, he spotted one of the nephews, Ryan, walking toward the entrance, accompanied by his wife and adult children. The old man hadn't spent much time with any of them, but he'd gotten hold of recent pictures and showed them to Adam so he wouldn't be caught unaware.

Adam hung back and waited for them to go inside before crossing the forecourt. As he approached the door and caught sight of a large portrait of a decidedly pre-cancerous version of the old man on a stand beside the podium, his courage began to waver. But he steeled himself and continued.

He kept his gaze low as he entered the hall, and chose a spot on the front-most unoccupied bench, far enough in from the aisle that nobody would have to squeeze past him. After a minute or so, an elderly man took the aisle seat; Adam snuck a quick glance at his neighbor, but he did not look familiar. His timing had turned out to be perfect: any later and his entrance might have drawn attention, any earlier and there would have been people milling outside. Whatever happened, no one could accuse him of going out of his way to make a scene.

Ryan mounted the steps to the podium. Adam stared at the back of the bench in front of him; he felt like a child trapped in church, though no one had forced him to be here.

"The last time I saw my uncle," Ryan began, "was almost ten years ago, at the funeral of his husband Carlos. Until then, I always thought it would be Carlos standing up here, delivering this speech, far more aptly and eloquently than I, or anyone else, ever could."

Adam felt a freight train tearing through his chest, but he kept his eyes fixed on a discolored patch of varnish. This had been a bad idea, but he couldn't walk out now.

"My uncle was the youngest child of Robert and Sophie Morris," Ryan continued. "He outlived his brother Steven, his sister Joan, and my mother, Sarah. Though I was never close to him, I'm heartened to see so many of his friends and colleagues here to pay their respects. I watched his shows, of course, but then, didn't everyone? I was wondering if we ought to screen some kind of highlights reel, but then the people in the know told me that there was going to be a tribute at the Emmys, and I decided not to compete with the professional edit-bots."

That line brought some quiet laughter, and Adam felt obliged to look up and smile. No one in this family was any kind of monster, whatever they aspired to do to him. They just had their own particular views of his relationship with the old man—sharpened by the lure of a few million dollars, but they probably would have felt the same regardless.

Ryan kept his contribution short, but when Cynthia Navarro took his place Adam had to turn his face to the pew again. He doubted that she'd recognize him—she'd worked with the old man in the wrong era for that—but the warmth, and grief, in her voice made her anecdotes far harder to shut out than the automated mash-up of database entries and viral misquotes that had formed the obituary. She finished with the time they'd spent all night searching for a way to rescue a location shoot with six hundred extras after Gemma Freeman broke her leg and had to be stretchered out in a chopper.

As she spoke, Adam closed his eyes and pictured the wildly annotated pages of the script strewn across the table, and Cynthia gawping with incredulity at her friend's increasingly desperate remedies.

"But it all worked out well enough," she concluded. "The plot twist that *no viewer saw coming*, that lifted the third season to *a whole new level*, owed its existence to an oil slick from a generator that just happened to be situated between Ms. Freeman's trailer and . . ."

Laughter rose up, cutting her off, and Adam felt compelled once more to raise his eyes. But before the sounds of mirth had faded, his neighbor moved closer and asked in a whisper, "Do you remember me?"

Adam turned, not quite facing the man. "Should I?" He spoke with an east-coast accent that was hard to place, and if it induced a certain sense of déjà vu, so did advertising voice-overs, and random conversations overheard in elevators.

"I don't know," the man replied. His tone was more amused than sarcastic; he meant the words literally. Adam hunted for something polite and noncommittal to say, but the audience was too quiet now for him to speak without being noticed and hushed, and his neighbor was already turning back toward the podium.

Cynthia was followed by a representative of the old man's agents, though everyone who'd known him in the golden age was long gone. There were suits from Warner Bros., Netflix, and HBO, whose stories of the old man were clearly scripted by the same bots that wrote their new shows. As the proceedings became ever more wooden, Adam began suffering from a panic-inducing premonition that Ryan would invite anyone in the hall who wished to speak to step up, and in the awkward silence that followed everyone's eyes would sweep the room and alight on him.

But when Ryan returned to the podium, he just thanked them for coming and wished them safe journeys home.

"No music?" Adam's neighbor asked. "No poetry? I seem to recall something by Dylan Thomas that might have raised a laugh under the circumstances."

"I think he stipulated no music," Adam replied.

"Fair enough. Since *The Big Chill*, anything you could pick with a trace of wit to it would seem like a bad in-joke."

"Excuse me, I have to . . ." People were starting to leave, and Adam wanted to get away before anyone else noticed him.

As he stood, his neighbor took out his phone and flicked his thumb across its surface. Adam's phone pinged softly in acknowledgment. "In case you want to catch up sometime," the man explained cheerfully.

"Thanks," Adam replied, nodding an awkward goodbye, grateful that he didn't seem to be expected to reciprocate.

There was already a small crowd lingering just inside the door, slowing his exit. When he made it out onto the forecourt, he walked straight to the roadside and summoned a car.

"Hey, you! Mr. Sixty Percent!"

Adam turned. A man in his thirties was marching toward him, scowling with such intense displeasure that his pillowy cheeks had turned red. "Can I help you with something?" Adam asked mildly. For all that he'd been dreading a confrontation, now that it was imminent he felt more invigorated than intimidated.

"What the fuck were you doing in there?"

"It was open to the public."

"You're not part of the public!"

Adam finally placed him: He was one of Ryan's sons. He'd seen him from behind as he'd been entering the hall. "Unhappy with the will are you, Gerald?"

Gerald came closer. He was trembling slightly, but Adam couldn't tell if it was from rage or from fear. "Live it up while you can, Sixty. You're going to be out with the trash in no time."

"What's with this 'sixty'?" As far as Adam knew, he'd been bequeathed a hundred percent of the estate, unless Gerald was already accounting for all the legal fees.

"Sixty percent: how much you resemble him."

"Now that's just cruel. I'm assured that by some metrics, it's at least seventy."

Gerald snickered triumphantly, as if that made his case. "I guess he was used to setting the bar low. If you grew up believing that Facebook could give you 'news' and Google could give you 'information,' your expectations for quality control would already be nonexistent."

"I think you're conflating his generation with your father's." Adam was quite sure that the old man had held the Bilge Barons in as much contempt as his great-nephew did. "And seventy percent of something real isn't so bad. Getting a side-load that close to complete is orders of magnitude harder than anything those charlatans ever did."

"Well, give your own scam artists a Nobel Prize, but you'd still need to be senile to think that was good enough."

"He wasn't senile. We spoke together at least a dozen times in the month before he died, and he must have thought he was getting what he'd paid for, because he never chose to pull the plug on me." Adam hadn't even known at the time that that was possible, but in retrospect he was glad no one had told him. It might have made those bedside chats a little tense.

"Because . . . ?" Gerald demanded. When Adam didn't reply immediately, Gerald laughed. "Or is the reason he decided you were worth the trouble part of the thirty percent of his mind that you don't have?"

"It could well be," Adam conceded, trying to make that sound like a perfectly satisfactory outcome. A joke about the studios' bots only achieving ten percent of the same goal and still earning a tidy income got censored halfway to his lips; the last thing he wanted to do was invite the old man's relatives to view him in the same light as that cynical act of shallow mimicry.

"So you don't know *why* he didn't care that you don't know whatever it is that you don't know? Very fucking Kafka."

"I think he would have preferred 'very fucking Heller' . . . but who am I to say?"

"Next week's trash, that's what you are." Gerald stepped back, looking pleased with himself. "Next week's fodder for the wrecking yard."

The car pulled up beside Adam and the door slid open. "Is that your grandma come to take you home?" Gerald taunted him. "Or maybe your retarded cousin?"

"Enjoy the wake," Adam replied. He tapped his skull. "I promise, the old man will be thinking of you."

3.

Adam had a conference call with the lawyers. "How do we stand?" he asked.

"The family's going to contest the will," Gina replied.

"On what grounds?"

"That the trustees, and the beneficiaries of the trust, misled and defrauded Mr. Morris."

"They're saying I misled him somehow?"

"No," Corbin interjected. "US law doesn't recognize you as a person. *You* can't be sued, as such, but other entities you depend on certainly can be."

"Right." Adam had known as much, but in his mind he kept glossing over the elaborate legal constructs that sustained his delusions of autonomy. On a purely practical level, there was money in three accounts that he had no trouble accessing—but then, the same was probably true of any number of stock-trading algorithms, and that didn't make them the masters of their own fate. "So who exactly is accused of fraud?"

"Our firm," Gina replied. "Various officers of the corporations we created to fulfill Mr. Morris's instructions. Loadstone, for making false claims that led to the original purchase of their technology, and for ongoing fraud in relation to the services promised in their maintenance contract."

"I'm very happy with the maintenance contract!" When Adam had complained that one of his earlobes had gone numb, Sandra had come to his home and fixed the problem on the same day he called.

"That's not the point," Corbin said impatiently. Adam was forgetting his place again: Jurisprudentially, his happiness cut no ice.

"So what happens next?"

"The first hearings are still seven months away," Gina explained. "We were expecting this, and we'll have plenty of time to prepare. We'll aim for an early dismissal, of course, but we can't promise anything."

"No." Adam hesitated. "But it's not just the house they could take? The Estonian accounts . . . ?"

Gina said, "Opening those accounts under your digital residency makes some things easier, but it doesn't put the money out of reach of the courts."

"Right."

When they hung up, Adam paced the office. Could it really be so hard to defend the old man's will? He wasn't even sure what disincentives were in place to stop the lawyers from drawing out proceedings like this for as long as they wished. Maybe a director of one of the entities he depended on was both empowered and duty bound to rein them in if they were behaving with conspicuous profligacy? But Adam himself couldn't sack them, or compel them to follow his instructions, just because Estonia had been nice enough to classify him as a person for certain limited purposes.

The old man had believed he was setting him up in style, but all the machinery that was meant to support him just made him feel trapped. What if he gave up the house and walked away? If he cashed in his dollar and euro accounts for some mixture of blockchain currencies before the courts swept in and froze his funds, that might be easier to protect and enjoy without the benefits of a Social Security number, a birth certificate, or a passport. But those currencies were all insanely volatile, and trying to hedge them against each other was like trying to save yourself in a skydiving accident by clutching your own feet.

He couldn't leave the country by any lawful means without deactivating his body so it could be sent as freight. Loadstone had promised to facilitate any trips he wished to make to any of the thirty-nine jurisdictions where he could walk the streets unchaperoned, as proud and free as the pizza bots that had blazed the trail, but the idea of returning to the company's servers, or even being halted and left in limbo for the duration of the flight, filled him with dread.

For now, it seemed that he was stuck in the Valley. All he could do was find a way to make the best of it.

4.

Sitting on two upturned wooden crates in an alley behind the nightclub, they could still hear the pounding bass line of the music escaping through the walls, but at least it was possible to hold a conversation here.

Carlos sounded like the loneliest person Adam had ever met. Did he tell everyone so much, so soon? Adam wanted to believe that he didn't, and that something in his own demeanor had inspired this beautiful man to confide in him.

Carlos had been in the country for twelve years, but he was still struggling to support his sister in El Salvador. She'd raised him after their parents died—his father when he was six months old, his mother when he was five. But now his sister had three children of her own, and the man who'd fathered them was no good to her.

"I love her," he said. "I love her like my own life, I don't want to be rid of her. But the kids are always sick, or something's broken that needs fixing. It never fucking stops."

Adam had no one relying on him, no one expecting him to do anything. His own finances waxed and waned, but at least when the money was scarce no one else suffered, or made him feel that he was letting them down.

"So what do you do to relieve the stress?" he asked.

Carlos smiled sadly. "It used to be smoking, but that got too expensive."

"So you quit?"

"Only the smoking."

As Adam turned toward him, his mind went roaming down the darkness of the alley, impatiently following the glistening thread, unable to shake off the sense of urgency that told him: *Take hold of this now, or it will be lost forever.* He didn't need to linger in their beds for long; just a few samples of that annihilating euphoria were enough to stand in for all the rest. Maybe that was the engine powering everything that followed, but what it dragged along behind it was like a newlyweds' car decorated by a thousand exuberant well-wishers.

He tried grabbing the rattling cans of their fights, running his fingers over the rough texture of all the small annoyances and slights, mutually wounded pride, frustrated good intentions. Then he felt the jagged edge of a lacerating eruption of doubt.

But something had happened that blunted the edge, then folded it in on itself again and again, leaving a seam, a ridge, a scar. Afterward, however hard things became, there was no questioning the foundations. They'd earned each other's trust, and it was unshakeable.

He pushed on into the darkness, trying to understand. Wherever he walked, light would follow, and his task was to make his way down as many side streets as possible before he woke.

This time, though, the darkness remained unbroken. He groped his way forward, unnerved. They'd ended up closer than ever—he knew that with as much certainty as he knew anything. So why did he feel as if he was stumbling blindly through the rooms of Bluebeard's castle, and the last thing he should want to summon was a lamp?

5.

Adam spent three weeks in the old man's home theater, watching every one of the old man's shows, and an episode or two from each of the biggest hits of the last ten years. There could only be one thing more embarrassing than pitching an idea to a studio and discovering that he was offering them a story that they'd already produced for six seasons, and that would be attempting to recycle, not just any old show, but an actual Adam Morris script.

Most of the old man's work felt as familiar as if he'd viewed it a hundred times in the editing suite, but sometimes a whole side plot appeared that seemed to have dropped from the sky. Could the studios have fucked with things afterward, when the old man was too sick and distracted to notice? Adam checked online, but the fan sites that would have trumpeted any such tampering were silent. The only re-cuts had taken place in another medium entirely.

He desperately needed to write a new show. Money aside, how else was he going to pass the time? The old man's few surviving friends had all made it clear before he died that they wanted nothing to do with his side-load. He could try to make the most of his cybernetic rejuvenation; his skin felt exactly like skin, from inside and out, and his ridiculously plausible dildo of a cock wouldn't disappoint anyone if he went looking for ways to use it—but the truth was, he'd inherited the old man's feelings for Carlos far too deeply to brush them aside and pretend that he was twenty again, with no attachments and no baggage. He didn't even know yet if he wanted to forge an identity entirely his own, or to take the other path and seek to become the old man more fully. He couldn't "betray" a lover ten years dead who was, in the end, nothing more to him than a character in someone else's story—whatever he'd felt as he'd dragged the old man's memories into his own virtual skull. But he wasn't going to sell himself that version of things before he was absolutely sure it was the right one.

The only way to know who he was would be to create something new. It didn't even need to be a story that the old man wouldn't have written himself, had he lived a few years longer . . . just so long as it didn't turn out that he'd already written it, pitched it unsuccessfully, and stuck it in a drawer. Adam pictured himself holding a page from each version up to the light together, bringing the words into alignment, trying to decide if the differences were too many, or too few.

6.

"Sixty thousand dollars *in one week?*" Adam was incredulous.

Gina replied calmly, "The billables are all itemized. I can assure you, what we're charging is really quite modest for a case of this complexity."

"The money was his, he could do what he liked with it. End of story."

"That's not what the case law says." Gina was beginning to exhibit micro-fidgets, as if she'd found herself trapped at a family occasion being forced to play a childish video game just to humor a nephew she didn't really like. Whether or not she'd granted Adam personhood in her own mind, he certainly wasn't anyone in a position to give her instructions, and the only reason she'd taken his call must have been some sop to Adam's comfort that the old man had managed to get written into his contract with the firm.

"All right. I'm sorry to have troubled you."

In the silence after he'd hung up, Adam recalled something that Carlos had said to the old man, back in New York one sweltering July, taking him aside in the middle of the haggling over a secondhand air-conditioner they were attempting to buy. "You're a good person, *cariño*, so you don't see it when people are trying to cheat you." Maybe he'd been sincere, or maybe "good" had just been a tactful euphemism for "unworldly," though if the old man really had been so trusting, how had Adam ended up with the opposite trait? Was cynicism some kind of default, wired into the template from which the whole side-loading process had started?

Adam found an auditor with no connections to the old man's lawyers, picking a city at random and then choosing the person with the highest reputation score with whom he could afford a ten-minute consultation. Her name was Lillian Adjani.

"Because these companies have no shareholders," she explained, "there's not that much that needs to be disclosed in their public filings. And I can't just go to them myself and demand to see their financial records. A court could do that, in principle, and you might be able to find a lawyer who'd take your money to try to make that happen. But who would their client be?"

Adam had to admire the way she could meet his gaze with an expression of sympathy, while reminding him that—shorn of the very constructs he was trying to scrutinize—for administrative purposes he didn't actually exist.

"So there's nothing I can do?" Maybe he was starting to confuse his secondhand memories of the real world with all the shows he'd been watching, where people just *followed the money trail*. The police never seemed to need to get the courts involved, and even civilians usually had some supernaturally gifted hacker at their disposal. "We couldn't . . . hire an investigator . . . who could persuade someone to leak . . . ?" Mike Ehrmantraut would have found a way to make it happen in three days flat.

Ms. Adjani regarded him censoriously. "I'm not getting involved in anything illegal. But maybe you have something yourself, already in your possession, that could help you more than you realize."

"Like what?"

"How computer-savvy was your . . . predecessor?"

"He could use a word processor and a web browser. And Skype."

"Do you still have any of his devices?"

Adam laughed. "I don't know what happened to his phone, but I'm talking to you from his laptop right now."

"Okay. Don't get your hopes too high, but if there were files containing financial records or legal documents that he received and then deleted, then unless he went out of his way to erase them securely, they might still be recoverable."

Ms. Adjani sent him a link for a piece of software she trusted to do the job. Adam installed it, then stared numbly at the catalog of eighty-three thousand "intelligible fragments" that had shown up on the drive.

He started playing with the filtering options. When he chose "text," portions of scripts began emerging from the fog—some instantly recognizable, some probably abandoned dead-ends. Adam averted his gaze, afraid of absorbing them into his subconscious if they weren't already buried there. He had to draw a line somewhere.

He found an option called "financial," and when that yielded a blizzard of utility bills, he added all the relevant keywords he could think of.

There were bills from the lawyers, and bills from Loadstone. If Gina was screwing him, she'd been screwing the old man as well, because the hourly rate hadn't changed. Adam was beginning to feel foolish; he was right to be vigilant about his precarious situation, but if he let that devolve into full-blown paranoia he'd just end up kicking all the support structures out from beneath his feet.

Loadstone hadn't been shy with their fees either. Adam hadn't known before just how much his body had cost, but given the generally excellent engineering it was difficult to begrudge the expense. There was an item for the purchase of the template, and then one for every side-loading session, broken down into various components. "Squid operator?" he muttered, bemused. "What the fuck?" But he wasn't going to start convincing himself that they'd blinded the old man with technobabble. He'd paid what he'd paid, and in the hospital he'd given Adam every indication that he'd been happy with the result.

"Targeted occlusions?" Meaning blood clots in the brain? The old man had left him login details allowing him postmortem access to all his medical records; Adam checked, and there had been no clots.

He searched the web for the phrase in the context of side-loading. The pithiest translation he found was: "The selective non-transferal of a pre-scribed class of memories or traits."

Which meant that the old man had held something back, deliberately. Adam was an imperfect copy of him, not just because the technology was imperfect, but because he'd wanted it that way.

"You lying piece of shit." Toward the end, the old man had rambled on about his hope that Adam would outdo his own achievements, but judging from his efforts so far he wasn't even going to come close. Three attempts at new scripts had ended up dead in the water. It wasn't Ryan and his family who'd robbed him of the most valuable part of the inheritance.

Adam sat staring at his hands, contemplating the possibilities for a life worth living without the only skill the old man had ever possessed. He remembered joking to Carlos once that they should both train as doctors and go open a free clinic in San Salvador. "When we're rich." But Adam doubted that his original, let alone the diminished version, was smart enough to learn to do much more than empty bedpans.

He switched off the laptop and walked into the master bedroom. All of the old man's clothes were still there, as if he'd fully expected them to be used again. Adam took off his own clothes and began trying on each item in turn, counting the ones he was sure he recognized. Was he Gerald's Mr. Sixty Percent, or was it more like forty, or thirty? Maybe the pep talks had been a kind of sarcastic joke, with the old man secretly hoping that the final verdict would be that there was only one Adam Morris, and like the studios' laughable "deep-learning" bots, even the best technology in the world couldn't capture his true spark.

He sat on the bed, naked, wondering what it would be like to go out in some wild bacchanalia with a few dozen robot fetishists, fucking his brains out and then dismembering him to take the pieces home as souvenirs. It wouldn't be hard to organize, and he doubted that any part of his corporate infrastructure would be obliged to have him resurrected from Loadstone's daily backups. The old man might have been using him to make some dementedly pretentious artistic point, but he would never have been cruel enough to render suicide impossible.

Adam caught sight of a picture of the two men posing hammily beneath the Hollywood sign, and found himself sobbing dryly with, of all things, grief. What he wanted was Carlos beside him—making this bearable, putting it right. He loved the dead man's dead lover more than he was ever going to love anyone else, but he still couldn't do anything worthwhile that the dead man could have done.

He pictured Carlos with his arms around him. "Sssh, it's not as bad as you think—it never is, *cariño*. We start with what we've got, and just fill in the pieces as we go."

You're really not helping, Adam replied. *Just shut up and fuck me, that's all I've got left.* He lay down on the bed and took his penis in his hand. It had seemed wrong before, but he didn't care now: He didn't owe either of them anything. And Carlos, at least, would probably have taken pity on him, and not begrudged him the unpaid guest appearance.

He closed his eyes and tried to remember the feel of stubble against his thighs, but he wasn't even capable of scripting his own fantasy: Carlos just wanted to talk.

"You've got friends," he insisted. "You've got people looking out for you."

Adam had no idea if he was confabulating freely, or if this was a fragment of a real conversation long past, but context was everything. "Not any more, *cariño*. Either they're dead, or I'm dead to them."

Carlos just stared back at him skeptically, as if he'd made a ludicrously hyperbolic claim.

But that skepticism did have some merit. If he knocked on Cynthia's door she'd probably try to stab him through the heart with a wooden stake, but the amiable stranger who'd sat beside him at the funeral had been far keener to talk than Adam. The fact that he still couldn't place the man no longer seemed like a good reason to avoid him; if he came from the gaps, he must know something about them.

Carlos was gone. Adam sat up, still feeling gutted, but no amount of self-pity was going to improve his situation.

He found his phone, and checked under "Introductions"; he hadn't erased the contact details. The man was named Patrick Auster. Adam called the number.

7.

"You go first," Adam said. "Ask me anything. That's the only fair trade." They were sitting in a booth in an old-style diner named Caesar's, where Auster had suggested they meet. The place wasn't busy, and the adjacent booths were empty, so there was no need to censor themselves or talk in code.

Auster gestured at the generous serving of chocolate cream pie that Adam had begun demolishing. "Can you really taste that?"

"Absolutely."

"And it's the same as before?"

Adam wasn't going to start hedging his answers with quibbles about the ultimate incomparability of qualia and memories. "Exactly the same." He pointed a thumb toward the diners three booths behind him. "I can tell you without peeking that someone's eating bacon. And I think it's apparent that there's nothing wrong with my hearing or vision, even if my memory for faces isn't so good."

"Which leaves . . ."

"Every hair on the bearskin rug," Adam assured him.

Auster hesitated. Adam said, "There's no three-question limit. We can keep going all day if you want to."

"Do you have much to do with the others?" Auster asked.

"The other side-loads? No. I never knew any of them before, so there's no reason for them to be in touch with me now."

Auster was surprised. "I'd have thought you'd all be making common cause. Trying to improve the legal situation."

"We probably should be. But if there's some secret cabal of immortals trying to get re-enfranchised, they haven't invited me into their inner circle yet."

Adam waited as Auster stirred his coffee meditatively. "That's it," he decided.

"Okay. You know, I'm sorry if I was brusque at the funeral," Adam said. "I was trying to keep a low profile; I was worried about how people would react."

"Forget it."

"So you knew me in New York?" Adam wasn't going to use the third person; it would make the conversation far too awkward. Besides, if he'd come here to claim the missing memories as his own, the last thing he wanted to do was distance himself from them.

"Yes."

"Was it business, or were we friends?" All he'd been able to find out online was that Auster had written a couple of independent movies. There was no record of the two of them ever working on the same project; their official Bacon number was three, which put Adam no closer to Auster than he was to Angelina Jolie.

"Both, I hope." Auster hesitated, then angrily recanted the last part. "No, we were friends. Sorry, it's hard not to resent being blanked, even if it's not deliberate."

Adam tried to judge just how deeply the insult had cut him. "Were we lovers?"

Auster almost choked on his coffee. "God, no! I've always been straight, and you were already with Carlos when I met you." He frowned suddenly. "You didn't cheat on him, did you?" He sounded more incredulous than reproving.

"Not as far as I know." During the drive down to Gardena, Adam had wondered if the old man might have been trying to airbrush out his infidelities. That would have been a bizarre form of vanity, or hypocrisy, or some other sin the world didn't have a name for yet, but it would still have been easier to forgive than a deliberate attempt to sabotage his successor.

"We met around two thousand and ten," Auster continued. "When I first approached you about adapting *Sadlands*."

"Okay."

"You do remember *Sadlands*, don't you?"

"My second novel," Adam replied. For a moment nothing more came to him, then he said, "There's an epidemic of suicides spreading across the country, apparently at random, affecting people equally regardless of demographics."

"That sounds like the version a reviewer would write," Auster teased him. "I spent six years, on and off, trying to make it happen."

Adam dredged his mind for any trace of these events that might have merely been submerged for lack of currency, but he found nothing. "So should I be thanking you, or apologizing? Did I give you a hard time about the script?"

"Not at all. I showed you drafts now and then, and if you had a strong opinion you let me know, but you didn't cross any lines."

"The book itself didn't do that well," Adam recalled.

Auster didn't argue. "Even the publishers stopped using the phrase 'slow-burning cult hit,' though I'm sure the studio would have put that in the press release, if it had ever gone ahead."

Adam hesitated. "So, what else was going on?" The old man hadn't published much in that decade; just a few pieces in magazines. His book sales had dried up, and he'd been working odd jobs to make ends meet. But at least back then there'd still been golden opportunities like valet parking. "Did we socialize much? Did I talk about things?"

Auster scrutinized him. "This isn't just smoothing over the business at the funeral, is it? You've lost something that you think might be important, and now you're going all Dashiell Hammett on yourself."

"Yes," Adam admitted.

Auster shrugged. "Okay, why not? That worked out so well in *Angel Heart*." He thought for a while. "When we weren't discussing *Sadlands*, you talked about your money problems, and you talked about Carlos."

"What about Carlos?"

"His money problems."

Adam laughed. "Sorry. I must have been fucking awful company."

Auster said, "I think Carlos was working three or four jobs, all for minimum wage, and you were working two, with a few hours a week set aside for writing. I remember you sold a story to the *New Yorker*, but the celebration was pretty muted, because the whole fee was gone, instantly, to pay off debts."

"*Debts?*" Adam had no memory of it ever being that bad. "Did I try to borrow money from you?"

"You wouldn't have been so stupid; you knew I was almost as skint. Just before we gave up, I got twenty grand in development money to spend a year trying to whip *Sadlands* into something that Sundance or AMC might buy—and believe me, it all went on rent and food."

"So what did *I* get out of that?" Adam asked, mock-jealously.

"Two grand, for the option. If it had gone to a pilot, I think you would have gotten twenty, and double that if the series was picked up." Auster smiled. "That must sound like small change to you now, but at the time it would have been the difference between night and day—especially for Carlos's sister."

"Yeah, she could be a real hard-ass," Adam sighed. Auster's face drained, as if Adam had just maligned a woman that everyone else had judged worthy of beatification. "What did I say?"

"You don't even remember *that*?"

"Remember what?"

"She was dying of cancer! Where did you think the money was going? You and Carlos weren't living in the Ritz, or shooting it up."

"Okay." Adam recalled none of this. He'd known that Adelina had died long before Carlos, but he'd never even tried to summon up the details. "So Carlos and I were working eighty-hour weeks to pay her medical bills . . . and I was bitching and moaning to you about it, as if that might make the magic Hollywood money fall into my lap a little faster?"

"That's putting it harshly," Auster replied. "You needed someone to vent to, and I had enough distance from it that it didn't weigh me down. I could commiserate and walk away."

Adam thought for a while. "Do you know if I ever took it out on Carlos?"

"Not that you told me. Would you have stayed together if you had?"

"I don't know," Adam said numbly. Could this be the whole point of the occlusions? When their relationship was tested, the old man had buckled, and he was so ashamed of himself that he'd tried to erase every trace of the event? Whatever he'd done, Carlos must have forgiven him in the end, but maybe that just made his own weakness more painful to contemplate.

"So I never pulled the pin?" he asked. "I didn't wash my hands of Adelina, and tell Carlos to fuck off and pay for it all himself?"

Auster said, "Not unless you were lying to me to save face. The version I heard was that every spare dollar you had was going to her, up until the day she died. Which is where forty grand might have made all the difference— bought her more time, or even a cure. I never got the medico-logistic details, but both of you took it hard when the Colman thing happened."

Adam moved his half-empty plate aside and asked wearily, "So what was 'the Colman thing'?"

Auster nodded apologetically. "I was getting to that. Sundance had shown a lot of interest in *Sadlands*, but then they heard that some Brit called Nathan Colman had sold a story to Netflix about, well . . . an epidemic of suicides spreading across the country, apparently at random, affecting people equally regardless of demographics."

"And we didn't sue the brazen fuck into penury?"

Auster snorted. "Who's this 'we' with money for lawyers? The production company that held the option did a cost-benefit analysis and decided to cut their losses; twenty-two grand down the toilet, but it wasn't as if they'd been cheated out of the next *Game of Thrones*. All you and I could do was suck it up, and take a few moments of solace whenever a *Sadlands* fan posted an acerbic comment in some obscure chat room."

Adam's visceral sense of outrage was undiminished, but on any sober assessment this outcome was pretty much what he would have expected.

"Of course, my faith in karma was restored, eventually," Auster added enigmatically.

"You've lost me again." The old man's success, once he cut out all the middlemen and plagiarists, must have been balm to his wounds—but Auster's online footprint suggested that his own third act had been less lucrative.

"Before they'd finished shooting the second season, a burglar broke into Colman's house and cracked open his skull with a statuette."

"An Emmy?"

"No, just a BAFTA."

Adam tried hard not to smile. "And once *Sadlands* fell through, did we stay in touch?"

"Not really," Auster replied. "I moved here a long time after you did; I wasted five years trying to get something up on Broadway before I swallowed my pride and settled for playing script doctor. And by then you'd done so well that I was embarrassed to turn up asking you for work."

Adam was genuinely ashamed now. "You should have. I owed it to you."

Auster shook his head. "I wasn't living on the streets. I've done all right here. I can't afford what you've got . . ." He gestured at Adam's imperishable chassis. "But then, I'm not sure I could handle the lacunae."

Adam called for a car. Auster insisted on splitting the bill.

The service cart rattled over and began clearing the table. Auster said, "I'm glad I could help you fill in the blanks, but maybe those answers should have come with a warning."

"*Now* a warning?"

"The Colman thing. Don't let it get to you."

Adam was baffled. "Why would I? I'm not going to sue his family for whatever pittance is still trickling down to them." In fact, he couldn't sue anyone for anything, but it was the thought that counted.

"Okay." Auster was ready to drop it, but now Adam needed to be clear.

"How badly did I take it the first time?"

Auster gestured with one finger, drilling into his temple. "Like a fucking parasitic worm in your brain. He'd stolen your precious novel and murdered your lover's sister. He'd kicked you to the ground when you had nothing, and taken your only hope away."

Adam could understand now why they hadn't stayed in touch. Solidarity in hard times was one thing, but an obsessive grievance like that would soon get old. Auster had taken his own kicks and decided to move on.

"That was more than thirty years ago," Adam replied. "I'm a different person now."

"Aren't we all?"

Auster's ride came first. Adam stood outside the diner and watched him depart: sitting confidently behind the wheel, even if he didn't need to lay a finger on it.

8.

Adam changed his car's destination to downtown Gardena. He disembarked beside a row of fast-food outlets and went looking for a public web kiosk. He'd been fretting about the best way of paying without leaving too obvious a trail, but then he discovered that in this municipality the things were as free as public water fountains.

There was no speck of entertainment industry trivia that the net had failed to immortalize. Colman had moved from London to Los Angeles to shoot the series, and he'd been living just a few miles south of Adam's current home when the break-in happened. But the old man had still been in New York at the time; he hadn't even set foot in California until the following year, as far as Adam recalled. The laptop that he'd started excavating had files on it dating back to the '90s, but they would have been copied from machine to machine; there was no chance that the computer itself was old enough to be carrying deleted emails for flights booked three decades ago, even if the old man had been foolish enough to make his journey so easy to trace.

Adam turned away from the kiosk's chipped projection screen, wondering if any passers-by had been staring over his shoulder. He was losing his grip on reality. The occlusions might easily have been targeted at nothing more than the old man's lingering resentment: If he couldn't let go of what had happened—even after Colman's death, even after his own career had blossomed—he might have wished to spare Adam all that pointless, fermented rage.

That was the simplest explanation. Unless Auster had been holding back, the thought of the old man murdering Colman didn't seem to have crossed his mind, and if the police had come knocking he would surely have mentioned that. If nobody else thought the old man was guilty, who was Adam to start accusing him—on the basis of nothing but the shape and location of one dark pit of missing memories, among the thirty percent of everything that he didn't recall?

He turned to the screen again, trying to think of a more discriminating test of his hypothesis. Though the flow into the side-load itself would have been protected by a massive firewall of privacy laws, Adam doubted that any instructions to the technicians at Loadstone were subject to privilege. Which meant that, even if he found them on the laptop, they were unlikely to be incriminatory. The only way the old man could have phrased a request to forget that he'd bashed Colman's brains out would have been to excise all of the more innocent events that were connected to it in any way, like a cancer surgeon choosing the widest possible sacrificial margin. But he might also have issued the same instructions merely in order to forget as much as possible of that whole bleak decade—when Hollywood had fucked him over, Carlos had been grieving for the woman who raised him, and he'd somehow, just barely, kept it together, long enough to make a new start in the '20s.

Adam logged off the kiosk. Auster had warned him not to become obsessed—and the man was the closest thing to a friend that he had right now. If everyone in the industry really staved in the skulls of everyone who'd crossed them, there'd be no one left to run the place.

He called a car and headed home.

9.

Under protest, at Adam's request, Sandra spread the three sturdy boxes out on the floor, and opened them up to reveal the foam, straps, and recesses within. They reminded Adam of the utility trunks that the old man's crews had used for stowing their gear.

"Don't freak out on me," she pleaded.

"I won't," Adam promised. "I just want a clear picture in my mind of what's about to happen."

"Really? I don't even let my dentist show me his planning videos."

"I trust you to do a better job than any dentist."

"You're too kind." She gestured at the trunks like a proud magician, bowing her head for applause.

Adam said, "Now you have no choice, El Dissecto: You've got to take a picture for me once it's done."

"I hope your Spanish is better than you're making it sound."

"I was aiming for vaudevillian, not voseo." Adam had some memories of the old man being prepared for surgery, but he wasn't sure that it was possible to rid them of survivor's hindsight and understand exactly how afraid he'd been that he might never wake up.

Sandra glanced at her watch. "No more clowning around. You need to undress and lie down on the bed, then repeat the code phrase aloud, four times. I'll wait outside."

Adam didn't care if she saw him naked while he was still conscious, but it might have made her uncomfortable. "Okay." Once she left, he stopped stalling; he removed his clothes quickly, and began the chant.

"Red lentils, yellow lentils. Red lentils, yellow lentils. Red lentils, yellow lentils." He glanced past the row of cases to Sandra's toolbox; he'd seen inside it before, and there were no cleavers, machetes, or chainsaws. Just magnetic screwdrivers that could loosen bolts within him without even penetrating his skin. He lay back and stared at the ceiling. "Red lentils, yellow lentils."

The ceiling stayed white but sprouted new shadows, a ventilation grille, and a light fitting, while the texture of the bedspread beneath his skin went from silken to beaded. Adam turned his head; the same clothes he'd removed were folded neatly beside him. He dressed quickly, walked over to the connecting door between the suites, and knocked.

Sandra opened the door. She'd changed her clothes since he'd last seen her, and she looked exhausted. His watch showed 11:20 p.m. local time, 9:20 back home.

"I just wanted to let you know that I'm still in here," he said, pointing to his skull.

She smiled. "Okay, Adam."

"Thank you for doing this," he added.

"Are you kidding? They're paying me all kinds of allowances and over-time, and it's not even that long a flight. Feel free to come back here as often as you like."

He hesitated. "You didn't take the photo, did you?"

Sandra was unapologetic. "No. It could have gotten me sacked, and not all of the company's rules are stupid."

"Okay. I'll let you sleep. See you in the morning."

"Yeah."

Adam lay awake for an hour before he could bring himself to mutter his code word for the milder form of sleep. If he'd wished, Loadstone could have given him a passable simulation of the whole journey—albeit with a lot of cheating to mask the time it took to shuffle him back and forth between their servers and his body. But the airlines didn't recognize any kind of safe "flight mode" for his kind of machine, even when he was in pieces and locked inside three separate boxes. The way he'd experienced it was the most honest choice: a jump-cut, and thirteen hours lost to the gaps.

In the morning, Sandra had arranged to join an organized tour of the sights of San Salvador. Her employer's insurance company was more concerned about her safety than Adam's, and in any case it would have been awkward for both of them to have her following him around with her toolbox.

"Just keep the license on you," she warned him before she left. "I had to fill out more forms to get it than I would to clear a drone's flight path twice around the world, so if you lose it I'm not coming to rescue you from the scrapyard."

"Who's going to put me there?" Adam spread his arms and stared down at his body. "Are you calling me a Ken doll?" He raised one forearm to his face and examined it critically, but the skin around his elbow wrinkled with perfect verisimilitude.

"No, but you talk like a foreigner, and you don't have a passport. So just . . . stay out of trouble."

"Yes, ma'am."

The old man had only visited the city once, and with Carlos leading him from nightspot to childhood haunt to some cousin's apartment like a ric-ocheting bullet, he'd made no attempt to navigate for himself. But Adam had been disappointed when he'd learned that Beatriz was now living in an entirely different part of town; there'd be no cues along the way, no hooks to bring back other memories of the time.

Colonia Layco was half an hour's drive from the hotel. There were more autonomous cars on the street than Adam remembered, but enough electric scooters interspersed among them to keep the traffic from mimicking L.A.'s spookily synchronized throbbing.

The car dropped him off outside a newish apartment block. Adam entered the antechamber in the lobby and found the intercom.

"Beatriz, this is Adam."

"Welcome! Come on up!"

He pushed through the swing doors and took the stairs, ascending four flights; it wouldn't make him any fitter, but old habits died hard. When Beatriz opened the door of her apartment he was prepared for her to flinch, but she just stepped out and embraced him. Maybe the sight of wealthy Californians looking younger than their age had lost its power to shock anyone before she'd even been born.

She ushered him in, tongue-tied for a moment, perhaps from the need to suppress an urge to ask about his flight, or inquire about his health. She settled, finally, on "How have things been?"

Her English was infinitely better than his Spanish, so Adam didn't even try. "Good," he replied. "I've been taking a break from work, so I thought I owed you a visit." The last time they'd met had been at Carlos's funeral.

She led him into the living room and gestured toward a chair, then fetched a tray of pastries and a pot of coffee. Carlos had never found the courage to come out to Adelina, but Beatriz had known his secret long before her mother died. Adam had no idea what details of the old man's life Carlos might have confided in her, but he'd exhausted all the willing informants who'd known the old man firsthand, and she'd responded so warmly to his emails that he'd had no qualms about attempting to revive their relationship for its own sake.

"How are the kids?" he asked.

Beatriz turned and gestured proudly toward a row of photographs on a bookcase behind her. "That's Pilar at her graduation last year; she started at the hospital six months ago. Rodrigo's in his final year of engineering."

Adam smiled. "Carlos would have been over the moon."

"Of course," Beatriz agreed. "We teased him a lot once he started with the acting, but his heart was always with us. With you, and with us."

Adam scanned the photographs and spotted a thirty-something Carlos in a suit, beside a much younger woman in a wedding dress.

"That's you, isn't it?" He pointed at the picture.

"Yes."

"I'm sorry I didn't make it." He had no memory of Carlos leaving for the wedding, but it must have taken place a year or two before they'd moved to L.A.

Beatriz tutted. "You would have been welcome, Adam, but I knew how tight things were for you back then. We all knew what you'd done for my mother."

Not enough to keep her alive, Adam thought, but that would be a cruel and pointless thing to say. And he hoped that Carlos had spared his sister's children any of the old man's poisonous talk of the windfall they'd missed out on.

Beatriz had her own idea of the wrongs that needed putting right. "Of course, she didn't know, herself. She knew he had a friend who helped him out, but Carlos had to make it sound like you were rich, that you were loaning him the money and it was nothing to you. He should have told her the truth. If she'd thought of you as family, she wouldn't have refused your help."

Adam nodded uncomfortably, unsure just how graciously or otherwise the old man had handed over paycheck after paycheck for a woman who had no idea who he was. "That was a long time ago. I just want to meet your children and hear all your news."

"Ah." Beatriz grimaced apologetically. "I should warn you that Rodrigo's bringing his boyfriend to lunch."

"That's no problem at all." What twenty-year-old engineer wouldn't want to show off the animatronic version of Great Uncle Movie Star's lover to as many people as possible?

When Adam got back to the hotel it was late in the afternoon. He messaged Sandra, who replied that she was in a bar downtown having a great time and he was welcome to join her. Adam declined and lay down on the bed. The meal he'd just shared had been the most normal thing he'd experienced since his embodiment. He'd come within a hair's breadth of convincing himself that there was a place for him here: That he could somehow insert himself into this family and survive on their affection alone, as if this one day's hospitality and good-natured curiosity could be milked forever.

As the glow of borrowed domesticity faded, the tug of the past reasserted itself. He had to keep trying to assemble the pieces, as and when he found them. He took out his laptop and searched through archived social media posts, seeing if he could date Beatriz's wedding. Pictures had a way of getting wildly mislabeled, or grabbed by bots and repurposed at random, so even when he had what looked like independent confirmation from four different guests, he didn't quite trust the result, and he paid a small fee for access to the Salvadorian government's records.

Beatriz had been married on March 4, 2018. Adam didn't need to open the spreadsheet he was using to assemble his timeline for the gaps to know that the surrounding period would be sparsely annotated, save for one entry. Nathan Colman had been bludgeoned to death by an intruder on March 10 of the same year.

Carlos would hardly have flown in for the wedding and left the next day; the family would have expected him to stay for at least a couple of weeks. The old man would have been alone in New York, with no one to observe his comings and goings. He might even have had time to cross the country and return by bus, paying with cash, breaking the trip down into small stages, hitchhiking here and there, obfuscating the bigger picture as much as possible.

The dates proved nothing, of course. If Adam had been a juror in a trial with a case this flimsy, he would have laughed the prosecution out of court. He owed the old man the same standard of evidence.

Then again, in a trial the old man could have stood in the witness box and explained exactly what it was that he'd gone to so much trouble to hide.

The flight to L.A. wasn't until six in the evening, but Sandra was too hungover to leave the hotel, and Adam had made no plans. So they sat in his room watching movies and ordering snacks from the kitchen, while Adam worked up the courage to ask her the question that had kept him awake all night.

"Is there any way you could get me the specifications for my targeted occlusions?" Adam waited for her response before daring to raise the possibility of payment. If the request was insulting in itself, offering a bribe would only compound the offense.

"No," she replied, as unfazed as if he'd wondered aloud whether room service might stretch to shiatsu. "That shit is locked down tight. After last night, it would take me all day to explain homomorphic encryption to you, so you'll just have to take my word for it: Nobody alive can answer that, even if they wanted to."

"But I've recovered bills from his laptop that mention it," Adam protested. "So much for Fort fucking Knox!"

Sandra shook her head. "That means that he was careless—and I should probably get someone in account generation to rethink their line items— but Loadstone would have held his hand very, very tightly when it came to spelling out the details. Unless he wrote it down in his personal diary, the information doesn't exist anymore."

Adam didn't think that she was lying to him. "There are things I need to know," he said simply. "He must have honestly believed that I'd be better off without them—but if he'd lived long enough for me to ask him face to face, I know I could have changed his mind."

Sandra paused the movie. "Very little software is perfect, least of all when it's for something as complex as this. If we fail to collect everything we aim to collect . . ."

"Then you also fail to block everything you aim to block," Adam concluded. "Which was probably mentioned somewhere in the fine print of his contract, but I've been racking my brain for months without finding a single stone that punched a hole in the sieve."

"What if the stones only got through in fragments, but they can still be put together?"

Adam struggled to interpret this. "Are you telling me to take up repressed memory therapy?"

"No, but I could get you a beta copy of Stitcher on the quiet."

"Stitcher?"

"It's a new layer they'll eventually be offering to every client," Sandra explained. "It's in the nature of things, with the current methods, that the side-load will end up with a certain amount of implicit information that's not in an easily accessible form: thousands of tiny glimpses of memories that were never brought across whole, but which could still be described in detail if you pieced together every partial sighting."

"So this software could reassemble the shredded page of a notebook that still holds an impression of what was written on the missing page above?"

Sandra said, "For someone with a digital brain, you're about as last-century as they come."

Adam gave up trying to harmonize their metaphors. "Will it tell me what I want to know?"

"I have no idea," Sandra said bluntly. "Among the fragments bearing implicit information—and there will certainly be thousands of them—it will recognize some unpredictable fraction of their associations, and let you follow the new threads that arise. But I don't know if that will be enough to tell you anything more than the color of the sweater your mother was wearing on your first day of school."

"Okay."

Sandra started the movie again. "You really should have joined me in the bar last night," she said. "I told them I had a friend who could drink any Salvadorian under the table, and they were begging for a chance to bet against you."

"You're a sick woman," Adam chided her. "Maybe next time."

10.

Reassembled back in California, Adam took his time deciding whether to make one last, algorithmic attempt to push through the veil. If the truth was that the old man had been a murderer, what good would come of knowing it? Adam had no intention of "confessing" the crime to the authorities, and taking his chances with whatever legal outcome the courts might eventually disgorge. He was not a person; he could not be prosecuted or sued, but Loadstone could be ordered to erase every copy of his software, and municipal authorities instructed to place his body in a hydraulic compactor beside unroadworthy cars and unskyworthy drones.

But even if he faced no risk of punishment, he doubted that Colman's relatives would be better off knowing that what they'd always imagined was a burglary gone wrong had actually been a premeditated ambush. It should not be for him to judge their best interests, of course, but the fact remained that he'd be the one making the decision, and for all the horror he felt about the act itself and the harm that had been done, his empathy for the survivors pushed him entirely in the direction of silence.

So if he did this, it would be for his benefit alone. For the relief of knowing that the old man had simply been a vain, neurotic self-mythologizer who'd tried to leave behind the director's cut of his life . . . or for the impetus to disown him completely, to torch his legacy in every way he could and set out on a life of his own.

Adam asked Sandra to meet him at Caesar's Diner. He slid a small parcel of cash onto her seat, and she slipped a memory stick into his hand.

"What do I do with this?" he asked.

"Just because you can't see all your ports in the bathroom mirror doesn't mean they're not there." She wrote a sequence of words on a napkin and passed it to Adam; it read like "Jabberwocky" mistranscribed by someone on very bad drugs. "Four times, and that will take the side of your neck off without putting you to sleep."

"Why is that even possible?"

"You have no idea how many Easter eggs you're carrying."

"And then what?"

"Plug it in, and it will do the rest. You won't be paralyzed, you won't lose consciousness. But it will work best if you lie down in the dark and close your eyes. When you're done, just pull it out. Working the skin panel back into place might take a minute or two, but once it clicks it will be a waterproof seal again." She hesitated. "If you can't get it to click, try wiping the edges of both the panel and the aperture with a clean chamois. Please don't put machine oil on anything; it won't help."

"I'll bear that in mind."

Adam stood in the bathroom and recited the incantation from the napkin, half expecting to see some leering apparition take his place in the mirror as the last syllable escaped his lips. But there was just a gentle pop as the panel on his neck flexed and came loose. He caught it before it fell to the floor and placed it on a clean square of paper towel.

It was hard to see inside the opening he'd made, and he wasn't sure he wanted to, but he found the port easily by touch alone. He walked into the bedroom, took the memory stick from the side table, then lay down and dimmed the lights. A part of him felt like an ungrateful son, trespassing on the old man's privacy, but if he'd wanted to take his secrets to the grave then he should have taken all of his other shit with them.

Adam pushed the memory stick into place.

Nothing seemed to have happened, but when he closed his eyes he saw himself kneeling at the edge of the bed in the room down the hall, weeping inconsolably, holding the bedspread to his face. Adam shuddered; it was like being back in the servers, back in the interminable side-loading dream. He followed the thread out into the darkness, for a long time finding nothing but grief, but then he turned and stumbled upon Carlos's funeral, riotous in its celebration, packed with gray-haired friends from New York and a dozen of Carlos's relatives, raucously drowning out the studio executives and sync-flashing the paparazzi.

Adam walked over to the casket and found himself standing beside a hospital bed, clasping just one of those rough, familiar hands in both of his own.

"It's all right," Carlos insisted. There wasn't a trace of fear in his eyes. "All I need is for you to stay strong."

"I'll try."

Adam backed away into the darkness and landed on set. He'd thought it was a risky indulgence to put an amateur in even this tiny part, but Carlos had sworn that he wouldn't take offense if his one and only performance ended up on the cutting room floor. He just wanted a chance to know if it was possible, one way or the other.

Detective Number Two said, "You'll need to come with us, ma'am," then took Gemma Freeman's trembling arm in his hand as he led her away.

In the editing suite, Adam addressed Cynthia bluntly. "Tell me if I'm making a fool of myself."

"You're not," she said. "He's got a real presence. He's not going to do Lear, but if he can hit his marks and learn his lines . . ."

Adam felt a twinge of disquiet, as if they were tempting fate by asking too much. But maybe it was apt. They'd propelled themselves into this orbit together; neither could have gotten here alone.

On the day they arrived, they'd talked a total stranger into breaking through a fence and hiking up Mount Lee with them so they could take each other's photographs beneath the Hollywood sign. Adam could smell the sap from broken foliage on his scratched forearms.

"Remember this guy," Carlos told their accomplice proudly. "He's going to be the next big thing. They already bought his script."

"For a pilot," Adam clarified. "Only for a pilot."

He rose up over the hills, watching day turn to night, waiting for an incriminating flicker of déjà vu to prove that he'd been in this city before. But the memories that came to him were all from the movies: *L.A. Confidential*, *Mulholland Drive*.

He flew east, soaring over city lights and blackened deserts, alighting back in their New York apartment, hunched over his computer, pungent with sweat, trying to block out the sound of Carlos haggling with the woman who'd come to buy their air conditioner. He stared at the screen unhappily, and started removing dialogue, shifting as much as he could into stage directions instead.

She takes his bloodied fist in both hands, shocked and sickened by what he's done, but she understands—

The screen went blank. The laptop should have kept working in the black-out, but the battery had been useless for months. Adam picked up a pen and started writing on a sheet of paper: *She understands that she pushed him into it—unwittingly, but she still shares the blame.*

He stopped and crumpled the sheet into a ball. Flecks of red light streamed across his vision; he felt as if he'd caught himself trying to leap onto a moving train. But what choice did he have? There was no stopping it, no turning it back, no setting it right. He had to find a way to ride it, or it would destroy them.

Carlos called out to Adam to come and help carry the air conditioner down the stairs. Every time they stopped to rest on a darkened landing, the three of them burst out laughing.

When the woman drove away they stood on the street, waiting for a breeze to shift the humid air. Carlos placed a hand on the back of Adam's neck. "Are you going to be all right?"

"We don't need that heap of junk," Adam replied.

Carlos was silent for a while, then he said, "I just wanted to give you some peace."

When he'd taken out the memory stick and closed his wound, Adam went into the old man's room and lay on his bed in the dark. The mattress beneath him felt utterly familiar, and the gray outlines of the room seemed exactly as they ought to be, as if he'd lain here a thousand times. This was the bed he'd been struggling to wake in from the start.

What they'd done, they'd done for each other. He didn't have to excuse it to acknowledge that. To turn Carlos in, to offer him up to death row, would have been unthinkable—and the fact that the law would have found the old man blameless if he'd done so only left Adam less willing to condemn him. At least he'd shown enough courage to put himself at risk if the truth ever came out.

He gazed into the shadows of the room, unable to decide if he was merely an empathetic onlooker, judging the old man with compassion—or the old man himself, repeating his own long-rehearsed defense.

How close was he to crossing the line?

Maybe he had enough, now, to write from the same dark place as the old man—and in time to outdo him, making all his fanciful ambitions come true.

But only by becoming what the old man had never wanted him to be. Only by rolling the same boulder to the giddy peak of impunity, then watching it slide down into the depths of remorse, over and over again, with no hope of ever breaking free.

11.

Adam waited for the crew from the thrift store to come and collect the boxes in which he'd packed the old man's belongings. When they'd gone, he locked up the house, and left the key in the combination safe attached to the door.

Gina had been livid when he'd talked to Ryan directly and shamed him into taking the deal: The family could have the house, but the bulk of the old man's money would go to a hospital in San Salvador. What remained would be just enough to keep Adam viable: paying his maintenance contract, renewing his license to walk in public, and stuffing unearned stipends into the pockets of the figureheads of the shell companies whose sole reason to exist was to own him.

He strode toward the gate, wheeling a single suitcase. Away from the shelter of the old man's tomb, he'd have no identity of his own to protect him, but he'd hardly be the first undocumented person who'd tried to make it in this country.

When the old man's life had disintegrated, he'd found a way to turn the shards into stories that meant something to people like him. But Adam's life was broken in a different way, and the world would take time to catch up. Maybe in twenty years, maybe in a hundred, when enough of them had joined him in the Valley, he'd have something to say that they'd be ready to hear.

Kelly Robson's book *Gods, Monsters and the Lucky Peach* is newly out from
Tor.com Publishing. Her short fiction has appeared in *Clarkesworld, Tor.com,
Asimov's Science Fiction,* and multiple year's best anthologies. In 2017, she was
a finalist for the 2017 John W. Campbell Award for Best New Writer. Her
novella "Waters of Versailles" won the 2016 Aurora Award and was a finalist
for both the Nebula and World Fantasy Awards. She lives in Toronto with her
wife, fellow SF writer A.M. Dellamonica.

WE WHO LIVE IN THE HEART

Kelly Robson

Ricci slipped in and out of consciousness as we carried her to the ante-
rior sinus and strapped her into her hammock. Her eyelids drooped
but she kept forcing them wide. After we finished tucking her in, she
pulled a handheld media appliance out of her pocket and called her friend
Jane.

"You're late," Jane said. The speakers flattened her voice slightly. "Are you
okay?"

Ricci was too groggy to speak. She poked her hand through the hammock's electrostatic membrane and panned the appliance around the sinus.
Eddy and Chara both waved as the lens passed over them, but Jane was only
interested in one thing.

"Show me your face, Ricci. Talk to me. What's it like in there?"

Ricci coughed, clearing her throat. "I dunno. It's weird. I can't really
think." Her voice slurred from the anesthetic.

I could have answered Jane, if she'd asked me. The first thing newbies
notice is how strange it smells. Human olfaction is primal; scents color our
perceptions even when they're too faint to describe. Down belowground, the
population crush makes it impossible to get away from human funk. Out
here, it's the opposite, with no scents our brains recognize. That's why most
of us fill our habs with stinky things—pheromone misters, scented fabrics,
ablative aromatic gels.

Eventually, Ricci would get around to customizing the scentscape in her big new hab, but right then she was too busy trying to stay awake. Apparently she'd promised Jane she'd check in as soon as she arrived, and not just a quick ping. She was definitely hurting but the call was duty.

"There's people. They're taking care of me." Ricci gazed blearily at our orang. "I was carried in by a porter bot. It's orange and furry. Long arms."

"I don't care about the bot. Tell me about you."

"I'm fine, but my ears aren't working right. It's too noisy."

We live with a constant circulatory thrum, gassy gurgles and fizzes, whumps, snaps, pops, and booms. Sound waves pulse through every surface, a deep hum you feel in your bones.

Jane took a deep breath, let it out with a whoosh. "Okay. Go to sleep. Call me when you wake up, okay?"

Ricci's head lolled back, then she jerked herself awake.

"You should have come with me."

Jane laughed. "I can't leave my clients. And anyway, I'd be bored."

Ricci squeezed her eyes shut, blinked a few times, then forced them wide.

"No you wouldn't. There's seven other people here, and they're all nuts. You'd already be trying to fix them."

Vula snorted and stalked out of the sinus, her long black braids slapping her back. The rest of us just smiled and shook our heads. You can't hold people responsible for what they say when they're half-unconscious. And anyway, it's true—we're not your standard moles. We don't want to be.

Only a mole would think we'd be bored out here. We have to take care of every necessity of life personally—nobody's going to do it for us. Tapping water is one example. Equipment testing and maintenance is another. Someone has to manage the hygiene and maintenance bots. And we all share responsibility for health and safety. Making sure we can breathe is high on everyone's our priority list, so we don't leave it up to chance. Finally, there's atmospheric and geographical data gathering. Mama's got to pay the bills. We're a sovereign sociopolitical entity, population: eight, and we negotiate our own service contracts for everything.

But other than that, sure, we have all the free time in the world. Otherwise what's the point? We came out here to get some breathing room—mental and physical. Unlike the moles, we've got plenty of both.

Have you ever seen a tulip? It's a flowering plant. No nutritional value, short bloom. Down belowground, they're grown in decorative troughs for special occasions—ambassadorial visits, arts festivals, sporting events, that sort of thing.

Anyway. Take a tulip flower and stick an ovoid bladder where the stem was and you've got the idea. Except big. Really big. And the petals move. Some of us call it Mama. I just call it home.

The outer skin is a transparent, flexible organic membrane. You can see right through to the central organ systems. The surrounding bladders and sinuses provide structure and protection. Balloons inside a bigger balloon, filled with helium and hydrogen. The whole organism ripples with iridescence.

We live in the helium-filled sinuses. If you get close enough, you can see us moving around inside. We're the dark spots.

While Ricci slept, I called everyone to the rumpus room for a quick status check. All seven of us lounged in the netting, enjoying the free flowing oxygen/hydrogen mix, goggles and breathers dangling around our necks.

I led the discussion, as usual. Nobody else can ever be bothered.

"Thoughts?" I asked.

"Ricci seems okay," said Eddy. "And I like what's-her-name. The mole on the comm."

"Jane. Yeah, pretty smile," said Bouche. "Ricci's fine. Right Vula?"

Vula frowned and crossed her arms. She'd hooked into the netting right next to the hatch and looked about ready to stomp out.

"I guess," she said. "Rude, though."

"She was just trying to be funny," said Treasure. "I can never predict who'll stick and who'll bounce. I thought Chara would claw her way back down belowground. Right through the skin and nosedive home."

Chara grinned. "I still might."

We laughed, but the camaraderie felt forced. Vula had everyone on edge.

"We'll all keep an eye on Ricci until she settles in," Eleanora said. "Are we good here? I need to get back to training. I got a chess tournament, you know."

"You always have a tournament." I surveyed the faces around me, but it didn't look like anyone wanted to chat.

"As long as nobody hogs the uplink, I never have any problems," said Bouche. "Who's training Ricci?"

"Who do you think?" I said. We have a rule. Whoever scared off the last one has to train the replacement.

We all looked at Vula.

"Shit," she said. "I hate training newbies."

"Stop running them off then," said Chara. "Be nice."

Vula scowled, fierce frown lines scoring her forehead. "I've got important work to do."

No use arguing with Vula. She was deep in a creative tangle, and had been for a while.

"I'll do it," I said. "We better train Ricci right if we want her to stick."

When Ricci woke up, I helped her out of the hammock and showed her how to operate the hygiene station. As soon as she'd hosed off the funk, she called Jane on her appliance.

"Take off your breather for a moment," Jane said. "Goggles too. I need to see your face."

Ricci wedged her fingernails under the seal and pried off her breather. She lifted her goggles. When she grinned, deep dimples appeared on each cheek.

Jane squinted at her through the screen. She nodded, and Ricci replaced the breather. It attached to her skin with a slurp.

"How do I look?" Ricci asked. "Normal enough for you?"

"What's the failure rate on that thing?"

"Low," Ricci said.

Point two three percent. Which *is* low unless you're talking about death. Then it's high. But we have spares galore. Safety nests here, there, and everywhere. I could have chimed in with the info but Jane didn't want to hear from me. I stayed well back and let Ricci handle her friend.

"Has anyone ever studied the long-term effects of living in a helium atmosphere?" Jane asked. "It can't be healthy."

"Eyes are a problem." Ricci tapped a finger on a goggle lens. "Corneas need oxygen so that's why we wear these. The hammocks are filled with air, so we basically bathe in oxygen while we're sleeping. But you're right. Without that the skin begins to slough."

Jane made a face. "Ugh."

"There's air in the common area, too—they call it the rumpus room. That's where they keep the fab and extruder. I'm supposed to be there now. I have to eat and then do an orientation session. Health, safety, all that good stuff."

"Don't forget to take some time to get to know your hab-mates, okay?"

"I met them when I got here."

"One of them is Vula, the artist, right? The sculptor. She's got to be interesting."

Ricci shrugged. "She looked grumpy."

I was impressed. Pretty perceptive for someone who'd been half-drowned in anesthetic.

"What's scheduled after training?"

"Nothing. That's the whole point of coming here, right?"

"I wondered if you remembered." A smile broke over Jane's face, star-bright even when glimpsed on a small screen at a distance. "You need rest and recreation."

"Relaxation and reading," Ricci added.

"Maybe you'll take up a hobby."

"Oh, I will," said Ricci. "Count on it."

Yes, I was spying on Ricci. We all were. She seemed like a good egg, but with no recourse to on-the-spot conflict intervention, we play it safe with newbies until they settle in. Anyone who doesn't like it can pull down a temporary privacy veil to shield themselves from the bugs, but most don't bother. Ricci didn't.

Plus we needed a distraction.

Whether it's half a million moles in a hole down belowground or eight of us floating around in the atmosphere, every hab goes through ups and downs. We'd been down for a while. Some of it was due to Vula's growly mood, the worst one we'd seen for a while, but really, we just needed a shake-up. Whether we realized it or not, we were all looking to Ricci to deliver us from ourselves.

During orientation, Ricci and I had company. Bouche and Eddy claimed they needed a refresher and tagged along for the whole thing. Chara, Treasure, and Eleanora joined us halfway through. Even Vula popped out of her hab for a few moments, and actually made an effort to look friendly.

With all the all the chatter and distraction, I wasn't confident Ricci's orientation had stuck, so I shadowed her on her first maintenance rotation. The workflow is fully documented, every detail supported by nested step-by-steps and supervised by dedicated project management bugs that help take human error out of the equation. But I figured she deserved a little extra attention.

Life support is our first priority, always. We clear the air printers, run live tests on the carbon dioxide digesters, and ground-truth the readings on every single sensor. It's a tedious process, but not even Vula complains. She likes to breathe as much as any of us.

Ricci was sharp. Interested. Not just in the systems that keep us alive, but in the whole organism, its biology, behavior, and habitat. She was even interested in the clouds around and the icy, slushy landscape below. She wanted to know about the weather patterns, wind, atmospheric layers—everything. I answered as best I could, but I was out of the conversational habit.

That, and something about the line of her jaw had me tongue-tied.

"Am I asking too many questions, Doc?" she asked as we stumped back to the rumpus room after checking the last hammock.

"Let's keep to the life-and-death stuff for now," I said.

Water harvesting is the next priority. To get it, we have to rise to the aqua-pause. There bright sunlight condenses moisture on the skin and collects in the dorsal runnels, where we tap it for storage.

Access to the main inflation gland is just under the rumpus room. Ricci squeezed through the elasticized access valve. The electrostatic membrane pulled her hair into spikes that waved at the PM bots circling her head. I stayed outside and watched her smear hormone ointment on the marbled surface of the gland. Sinuses creaked as bladders began to expand. As we walked through the maze of branching sinuses, I showed her how to brace against the roll and use the momentum to pull herself through the narrow access slots. Once we got to the ring-shaped fore cavity, we hooked our limbs into the netting and waited.

Rainbows rippled across the expanded bladder surfaces. We were nearly spherical, petals furled, and the wind rolled us like an untethered balloon. The motion makes some newbies sick, and they have to dial up anti-nauseant. Not Ricci. She looked around with anticipation, as if she were expecting to see something amazing rise over the vast horizon.

"Do you ever run into other whales?" she asked.

"I don't much care for that term," I said. It came out gruffer than I intended.

A dimple appeared at the edge of her breather. "Have you been out here long, Doc?"

"Yes. Ask me an important question."

"Okay." She waved her hand at the water kegs nested at the bottom of the netting, collapsed into a pile of honeycomb folds. "Why don't you carry more water?"

"That's a good question. You don't need me to tell you though. You can figure it out. Flip through your dash."

The dimple got deeper. Behind her darkened goggles, her eyelids flickered as she reviewed her dashboards. Naturally it took a little while; our setup was new to her. I rested my chin on my forearms and waited.

She surfaced quicker than I expected.

"Mass budget, right? Water is heavy."

"Yes. The mass dashboard also tracks our inertia. If we get too heavy, we can't maneuver. And heavy things are dangerous. Everything's tethered and braced, and we have safety nets. But if something got loose, it could punch through a bladder wall. Even through the skin, easy."

Ricci looked impressed. "I won't tell Jane about that."

We popped into the aquapause. The sun was about twenty degrees above the horizon. Its clear orange light glanced across the thick violet carpet of helium clouds below. Overhead, the indigo sky rippled with stars.

Bit of a shock for a mole. I let Ricci ogle the stars for a while. Water ran off the skin, a rushing, cascading sound like one of the big fountains down belowground. I cleared my throat. Ricci startled, eyes wide behind her goggles, then she climbed out of the netting and flipped the valve on the overhead tap. Silver water dribbled through the hose and into the battery of kegs, slowing the expanding pleated walls.

Ricci didn't always fill the quiet spaces with needless chatter. I liked that. We worked in silence until the kegs were nearly full, and when she began to question me again, I welcomed it.

"Eddy said you were one of the first out here," Ricci said. "You figured out how to make this all work."

I answered with a grunt, and then cursed myself. If I scared her away Vula would never let me forget it.

"That's right. Me and a few others."

"You took a big risk."

"Moving into the atmosphere was inevitable," I said. "Humans are opportunistic organisms. If there's a viable habitat, we'll colonize it."

"Takes a lot of imagination to see this as viable."

"Maybe. Or maybe desperation. It's not perfect but it's better than down belowground. Down there, you can't move without stepping on someone. Every breath is measured and every minute is optimized for resource resilience. That might be viable, but it's not human."

"I'm not arguing." Ricci's voice pitched low, thick with emotion as she gazed at the stars in that deep sky. "I love it here."

Yeah, she wasn't a mole anymore. She was one of us already.

One by one, the kegs filled and began flexing through their purification routine. We called in the crablike water bots and ran them through a sterilization cycle.

Water work done, the next task was spot-checking the equipment nests. I let Ricci take the lead, stayed well back as she jounced through the cavities and sinuses. She was enthusiastic, confident. Motivated, even. Most newbies stay hunkered in their hammocks for a lot longer than her.

We circled back to the rumpus room, inventoried the nutritional feedstock, and began running tests on the hygiene bots. I settled into the netting and watched Ricci pull a crispy snack out of the extruder.

"You must know all the other crews. The ones who live in the . . ." Ricci struggled to frame the concept without offending me.

"You can call them whales if you want. I don't like it, but I've never managed to find a better word."

She passed me a bulb of cold caffeine.

"How often do you talk to the people who live in the other whales, Doc?"

"We don't have anything to do with them. Not anymore."

"How come?"

"The whole reason we came out here is so we don't have to put up with anyone else's crap."

"You never see the other whales at all? Not even at a distance?"

I drained the bulb. "These organisms don't have any social behavior."

"But you must have to talk to them sometimes, don't you? Share info or troubleshoot?"

I collapsed the bulb in my fist and threw it to a hygiene bot.

"You lonely already?"

Ricci tossed her head back and laughed, a full belly guffaw. "Come on, Doc. You have to admit that's weird."

She was relentless. "Go ahead and make friends with the others if you want," I growled. "Just don't believe everything they say. They've got their own ways of doing things, and so do we."

We checked the internal data repeaters and then spent the rest of the shift calibrating and testing the sensor array—all the infrastructure that traps the data we sell to the atmospheric monitoring firms. I kept my mouth shut. Ricci maintained an aggressive cheerfulness even though I was about as responsive as a bot. But my glacier-like chilliness—more than ten years in the making—couldn't resist her. My hermit heart was already starting to thaw.

If I'd been the one calling Jane every day, I would have told her the light is weird out here. We stay within the optimal thermal range, near the equator where the winds are comparatively warm and the solar radiation helps keep the temperature in our habitat relatively viable. That means we're always in daylight, running a race against nightfall, which is good for Mama but not so good for us. Humans evolved to exist in a day-night cycle and something goes haywire in our brains when we mess with that. So our goggles simulate our chosen ratio of light and dark.

Me, I like to alternate fifty-fifty but I'll fool with the mix every so often just to shake things up. Vula likes the night so she keeps things dimmer than most. Everyone's different. That's what the moles don't realize, how different some of us are.

"I did a little digging, and what I found out scared me," Jane said the next time Ricci checked in. "Turns out there's huge gaps in atmospheric research. The only area that's really well monitored is the equator, and only around the beanstalk. Everywhere else, analysis is done by hobbyists who donate a few billable hours here and there."

Ricci nodded. "That's what Doc said."

Hearing my name perked me right up. I slapped down two of my open streams and gave their feed my whole attention.

"Nobody really knows that much about the organism you're living inside. Even less about the climate out there, and nearly nothing about the geography, not in detail. I never would have supported this decision if I'd realized how . . ." Jane's pretty face contorted as she searched for the word. "How *willy-nilly* the whole situation is. It's not safe. I can't believe it's even allowed."

"Allowed? Who can stop us? People go where they want."

"Not if it's dangerous. You can't just walk into a sewage treatment facility or air purification plant. It's unethical to allow people to endanger themselves."

Ricci snorted, fouling the valves on her breather and forcing her to take a big gulp of helium through her mouth.

"Not all of us want to be safe, Jane." The helium made her voice squeaky.

Jane's expression darkened. "Don't mock me. I'm worried about you."

"I know. I'm sorry," Ricci squeaked. She exhaled to clear her lungs and took a deep slow breath through her nose. Her voice dropped to its normal register. "Listen, I've only been here a few days."

"Six," Jane said.

"If I see anything dangerous, you'll be the first to know. Until then, don't worry. I'm fine. Better than fine. I'm even sleeping. A lot."

That was a lie. The air budget showed Ricci hadn't seen much of the inside of her hammock. But I wasn't worried. Exhaustion would catch up with her eventually.

"There's something else," Jane said. "I've been asking around about your hab-mates."

"Vula's okay. It's just that lately none of her work has turned out the way she wants. You know artists. Their professional standards are always unreachable. Set themselves up to fail."

"It's not about Vula, it's Doc."

Ricci bounced in her netting. "Oh yeah? Tell me. Because I can't get a wink out of that one. Totally impervious."

I maximized the feed to fill my entire visual field. In the tiny screen in Ricci's hand, Jane's dark hair trailed strands across her face and into her mouth. She pushed them back with an impatient flick of her fingers. She was in an atrium, somewhere with stiff air circulation. I could just make out seven decks of catwalk arching behind her, swarming with pedestrians.

"Pull down a veil," Jane said. "You might have lurkers."

"I do," Ricci answered. "Four at least. I'm the most entertaining thing inside Mama for quite a while. It doesn't bother me. Let them lurk."

But Jane insisted, so Ricci pulled down a privacy veil and the bug feed winked out.

I told myself whatever Jane had found out didn't matter. It would bear no relation to reality. That's how gossip works—especially gossip about ancient history. But even so, a little hole opened up under my breastbone, and it ached.

Only six days and I already cared what Ricci thought. I wanted her to like me. So I set about trying to give her a reason.

A few days later, we drifted into a massive storm system. Ricci's first big one. I didn't want her to miss it, so I bounced aft and hallooed to her at a polite distance from her hab. She was lounging in her netting, deep in multiple streams, twisting a lock of her short brown hair around her finger.

She looked happy enough to see me. No wariness behind her gaze, no chill.

We settled in to watch the light show. It was an eye-catcher. Bolts zagged to the peaks of the ice towers below, setting the fog alight with expanding patches of emerald green and acid magenta.

Two big bolts forked overhead with a mighty *whump*. Ricci didn't even jump.

"What was that?" she asked.

I was going to stay silently mysterious, but then remembered I was trying to be friendly.

"That," I said, "was lunch."

A dark splotch began to coalesce at the spot where the two bolts had caressed each other, a green and violet pastel haze in the thin milky fog. We banked slowly, bladders groaning, massive sinus walls clicking as we changed shape to ride the wind currents up, up, and then the massive body flexed just enough to reveal two petals reaching into the coalescing bacteria bloom.

Ricci launched herself out of the netting and clung to the side of her hab, trying to get a better view of the feeding behavior. When the bloom dissipated, she turned to me.

"That's all it does, this whale? Just search for food?"

"Eat, drink, and see the sights," I said. "What else does anyone need from life?"

Good company, I thought, but I didn't say it.

The light show went on for hours. Ricci was fascinated from start to finish. Me, I didn't see it. I spent the whole storm watching the light illuminate her face.

What else does anyone need from life? That was me trying to be romantic. Clumsy. Also inaccurate.

When we first moved out here, my old friends and I thought our habs would eventually become self-contained. Experience killed that illusion pretty quick. We're almost as dependent on the planetary civil apparatus as anyone.

Without feedstock, for example, we'd either starve or suffocate—not sure which would happen first. It has a lot of mass, so we can't stockpile much.

Then there's power. Funding it is a challenge when you're supplying eight people as opposed to eight million. No economy of scale in a hab this size. It's not the power feed itself that's the problem, but the infrastructure. We're always on the move, so the feed has to follow us around and provide multiple points of redundancy. Our ambient power supply costs base market value plus a massive buy-back on the research and development.

Data has to follow us around too, but we don't bother with redundancy. It's not critical. You'd think it was more important than air, though, if you saw us when the data goes down. Shrieking. Curses. Bouche just about catatonic (she's a total media junkie). Eleanora wall-eyed with panic especially if she's in the middle of a tournament (chess is her drug of choice). Vula, Eddy, and me in any state from suave to suicidal depending on what we're doing when the metaphorical umbilical gets yanked out of our guts.

Treasure and Chara are the only ones who don't freak out. Usually they're too busy boning each other.

Without data, we couldn't stay here, either. If we only had each other to talk to, it'd be a constant drama cycle, but we're all plugged into the hab cultures down belowground. We've got hobbies to groom, projects to tend, performances to cheer, games to play, friends to visit.

Finally, as an independent political entity, we need brokers and bankers to handle our economic transactions and lawyers to vet our contracts. We all need the occasional look-in from medtechs and physical therapists. And when we need a new crew member, we contract a recruiter.

"You look tired," Jane said the next time Ricci called. "I thought you said you were sleeping."

Ricci hung upside down in her netting. She'd made friends with the orang. It squatted in front of her, holding the appliance while she chatted with Jane.

"I've been digging through some old work." She dangled her arms, hooked her fingers in the floor grid, and stretched. "I came up with a new approach to my first dissertation."

Jane gaped. Her mouth worked like she was blowing bubbles.

"I know," Ricci added. "I'll never change, right?"

"Don't you try that with me." Jane's eyes narrowed. "You have a choice—"

Ricci raised her hands in mock surrender. "Okay. Take it easy."

"—you can keep working on getting better, or you can go back to your old habits."

"It's not your fault, Jane. You're a great therapist."

"This isn't about me, you idiot," Jane yelled. "It's about you."

"I tried, Jane." Ricci's voice was soft, ardent. "I really tried. So hard."

"I know you did." Jane sucked in a deep breath. "Don't throw away all your progress."

They went on and on like that. I didn't listen, just checked in now and then to see if they were still at it. I knew Ricci's story. I'd read the report from the recruiter. The privacy seal had timed out but I remembered the details.

Right out of the crèche she'd dived into an elite chemical engineering program, the kind every over-fond crèche manager wants for their favorite little geniuses. Sound good, doesn't it? Isn't that where you'd want to put your little Omi or Occam, little Carey or Karim? But what crèche managers don't realize—because their world is full of guided discovery opportunities and subconscious learning stimuli—is that high-prestige programs are grinders. Go ahead, dump a crèche-full of young brilliants inside. Some of them won't come out whole.

I know; I went through one myself.

When Ricci crashed out of the chem program within spitting distance of an advanced degree, she bounced to protein engineering. She did a lot of good work there before she cracked. Then she moved into pharmaceutical modeling. A few more years of impressive productivity before it all went up in smoke. By that time she wasn't young anymore. The damage had accumulated. Her endocrinologist suggested intensive peer counseling might stop the carnage, so in stepped Jane, who applied her pretty smile, her patience, and all her active listening skills to try to gently guide Ricci along a course of life that didn't include cooking her brain until it scrambled.

At the end of that long conversation through the appliance, Ricci agreed to put her old work under lockdown so she could concentrate on the here-and-now. Which meant all her attention was focused on us.

Ricci got into my notes. I don't keep them locked down; anyone can access them. Free and open distribution of data is a primary force behind the success of the human species, after all. Don't we all learn that in the crèche?

Making data available doesn't guarantee anyone will look at it, and if they do, chances are they won't understand it. Ricci tried. She didn't just skim through, she really studied. Shift after shift, she played with the numbers and gamed my simulation models. Maybe she slept. Maybe not.

I figured Ricci would come looking for me if she got stumped, so I de-hermited, banged around in the rumpus room, put myself to work on random little maintenance tasks.

When Ricci found me, I was in the caudal stump dealing with the accumulated waste pellets. Yes, that's exactly what it sounds like: half-kilogram plugs of dry solid waste covered in wax and transferred from the lavs by the hygiene bots. Liquid waste is easy. We vaporize it, shunt it into the gas exchange bladder, and flush it through gill-like permeable membranes. Solid waste, well, just like anyone we'd rather forget about it as long as possible. We rack the pellets until there's about two hundred, then we jettison them.

Ricci pushed up her goggles and scrubbed knuckles over her red-rimmed eyes.

"Why don't you automate this process like you do for liquids?" Ricci asked as she helped me position the rack over the valve.

"No room for non-essential equipment in the mass budget," I said.

I dilated the interior shutter and the first pellet clicked through. A faint pink blush formed around the valve's perimeter, only visible because I'd dialed up the contrast on my goggles to watch for signs of stress. A little hormone ointment took care of it—not too much or we'd get a band of inflexible scar tissue, and then I'd have to cut out the valve and move it to another location. That's a long, tricky process and it's not fun.

"There's only two bands of tissue strong enough to support a valve." I bent down and stroked the creamy striated tissue at my feet. "This is number two, and really, it barely holds. We have to treat it gently."

"Why risk it, then? Take it out and just use the main valve."

A sarcastic comment bubbled up—*have you never heard of a safety exit?*—but I gazed into her big brown eyes and it faded into the clouds.

"We need two valves in case of emergencies," I mumbled.

Ricci and I watched the pellets plunge through the sky. When they hit the ice slush, the concussive wave kicked up a trail of vapor blooms, concentric rings lit with pinpoints of electricity, so far below each flash just a spark in a violet sea.

A flock of jellies fled from the concussion, flat shells strobing with reflected light, trains of ribbon-like tentacles flapping behind.

Ricci looked worried. "Did we hit any of them?"

I shook my head. "No, they can move fast."

After we'd finished dumping waste, Ricci said, "Say, Doc, why don't you show me the main valve again?"

I puffed up a little at that. I'm proud of the valves. Always tinkering, always innovating, always making them a little better. Without the valves, we wouldn't be here.

Far forward, just before the peduncle isthmus, a wide band of filaments connects the petals to the bladder superstructure. The isthmus skin is thick with connective tissue, and provides enough structural integrity to support a valve big enough to accommodate a cargo pod.

"We pulled you in here." I patted the collar of the shutter housing. "Whoever prepared the pod had put you in a pink body bag. Don't know why it was such a ridiculous color. When Vula saw it, she said, 'It's a girl!'."

I laughed. Ricci winced.

"That joke makes sense, old style," I explained.

"No, I get it. Birth metaphor. I'm not a crechie, Doc."

"I know. We wouldn't have picked you if you were."

"Why did you pick me?"

I grumbled something. Truth is, when I ask our recruiter to find us a new hab-mate, the percentage of viable applications approaches zero. We look for a specific psychological profile. The two most important success factors are low self-censoring and high focus. People who say what they think are never going to ambush you with long-fermented resentments, and obsessive people don't get bored. They know how to make their own fun.

Ricci tapped her fingernail on a shutter blade.

"Your notes aren't complete, Doc." She stared up at me, unblinking. No hint of a dimple. "Why are you hoarding information?"

"I'm not."

"Yes, you are. There's nothing about reproduction."

"That's because I don't know very much about it."

"The other whale crews do. And they're worried about it. You must know something, but you're not sharing. Why?"

I glared at her. "I'm an amateur independent researcher. My methods aren't rigorous. It would be wrong to share shaky theories."

"The whale crews had a collective research agreement once. You wrote it."

She fired the document at me with a flick of her finger. I slapped it down and flushed it from my buffer.

"That agreement expired. We didn't renew."

"That's a lie. You dissolved it and left to find your own whale."

I aimed my finger at the bridge of her goggles and jabbed the air. "Yes, I ran away. So did you."

She smiled. "I left a network of habs with a quarter billion people who can all do just fine without me. You ran from a few hundred who need you."

Running away is something I'm good at. I bounced out of there double-time. Ricci didn't call after me. I wouldn't have answered if she had.

The next time she talked to Jane, Ricci didn't mention me. I guess I didn't rate high enough on her list of problems. I didn't really listen to the details as they chatted. I just liked having their voices in my head while I tinkered with my biosynthesis simulations.

Halfway through their session, Vula pinged me.

You can quit spying, she said. None of us are worried about Ricci anymore.

I agreed, and shut down the feed.

Ricci's been asking about you, by the way, Vula added. Your history with the other whales.

Tell her everything.

You sure?

I've been spying on her for days. It's only fair.

Better she heard the story from Vula than me. I still can't talk about it without overheating, and they tell me I'm scary when I'm angry.

Down belowground the air is thick with rules written and unwritten, the slowly decaying husks of thirty thousand years of human history dragged behind us from Earth, and the most important of these is cooperation for mutual benefit. Humans being human, that's only possible in conditions of resource abundance—not just actual numerical abundance, but more importantly, the *perception* of abundance. When humans are confident there's enough to go around, life is easy and we all get along, right?

Ha.

Cooperation makes life possible, but never easy. Humans are hard to wrangle. Tell them to do one thing and they'll do the opposite more often than not. One thing we all agree on is that everyone wants a better life. Only problem is, nobody can agree what that means.

So we have an array of habs offering a wide variety of socio-cultural options. If you don't like what your hab offers, you can leave and find one that does. If there isn't one, you can try to find others who want the same things as you and start your own. Often, just knowing options are available keeps people happy.

Not everyone, though.

Down belowground, I simply hated knowing my every breath was counted, every kilojoule measured, every moment of service consumption or contribution accounted for in the transparent economy, every move modeled by human capital managers and adjusted by resource optimization analysts. I got obsessed with the numbers in my debt dashboard; even though it was well into the black all I wanted to do was drive it up as high and as fast as I could, so nobody would ever be able to say I hadn't done my part.

Most people never think about their debt. They drop a veil over the dash and live long, happy, ignorant lives, never caring about their billable rate and never knowing whether or not they siphoned off the efforts of others. But for some of us, that debt counter becomes an obsession.

An obsession and ultimately an albatross, chained around our necks.

I dreamed about an independent habitat with abundant space and unlimited horizons. And I wasn't the only one. When we looked, there it was, floating around the atmosphere.

Was it dangerous? Sure. But a few firms provide services to risk takers and they're always eager for new clients. The crews that shuttle ice climbers to the poles delivered us to the skin of a very large whale. I made the first cut myself.

Solving the problems of life was exhilarating—air, food, water, warmth. We were explorers, just like the mountain climbers of old, ascending the highest peaks wearing nothing but animal hides. Like the first humans. Revolutionary.

Our success attracted others, and our population grew. We colonized new whales and once we got settled, our problems became more mundane. I have a little patience for administrative details, but the burden soon became agonizing. Unending meetings to chew over our collective agreements, measuring and accounting and debits and credits and assigning value to everyone's time. This was exactly what we'd escaped. Little more than one year in the clouds, and we were reinventing all the old problems from scratch.

Nobody needs that.

I stood right in the middle of the rumpus room inside the creature I'd cut into with my own hands and gave an impassioned speech about the nature of freedom and independence, and reminded them all of the reasons we'd left. If they wanted their value micro-accounted, they could go right back down belowground.

I thought it was a good speech, but apparently not. When it came to a vote, I was the only one blocking consensus.

I believe—hand-to-heart—if they'd only listened to me and did what I said everything would have been fine and everyone would have been happy.

But some people can never really be happy unless they're making other people miserable. They claimed I was trying to use my seniority, skills, and experience as a lever to exert political force. I'd become a menace. And when they told me I had to submit to psychological management, I left.

Turned out we'd brought the albatross along with us, after all.

When Jane pinged me a few days later, I was doing the same thing as millions down belowground—watching a newly-arrived arts delegation process down the beanstalk and marveling at their dramatic clothing and prosthetics.

I pinged her back right away. Even though I knew she would probably needle me about my past, I didn't hesitate. I missed having Ricci and Jane in my head, and life was a bit lonely without them. Also, I was eager to meet her. I wasn't the only one; the whole crew was burning with curiosity about Ricci's pretty friend.

When Jane's fake melted into reality, she was dressed in a shiny black party gown. Long dark hair pouffed over her shoulders, held off her face with little spider clips that gathered the locks into tufts. Her chair was a spider model too, with eight delicate ruby and onyx legs that cradled her torso.

"Hi, Doc," she said. "It's nice to meet you, finally. I'm a friend of Ricci's. I think you know that, though."

A friend. Not a therapist, peer counselor, or emotional health consultant. That was odd. And then it dawned on me: Jane had been donating her time ever since Ricci joined us. She probably wanted to formalize her contract, start racking up the billable hours.

When I glanced through her metadata, and my heart began to hammer. Jane's rate was sky high.

"We can't float your rate," I blurted. "Not now. Maybe eventually. But we'd have to find another revenue stream."

Jane's head jerked back and her gaze narrowed.

"That's not why I pinged you," she said. "I don't care about staying billable—I never did. All I want to do is help people."

I released a silent sigh of relief. "What can I do for you?"

"Nothing. I just wanted to say hi and ask how Ricci's getting along."

"Ricci's fine. Nothing to worry about." I always get gruff around beautiful women.

She brightened. "She's fitting in with you all?"

"Yeah. One of the crew. She's great. I love her." I bit my lip and quickly added, "I mean we all like her. Even Vula, and she's picky."

I blushed. Badly. Jane noticed, and a gentle smile touched the corners of her mouth. But she was a kind soul and changed the subject.

"I've been wondering something, Doc. Do you mind if I ask a personal question?"

I scrubbed my hands over my face in embarrassment and nodded.

She wheeled her chair a bit closer and tilted toward me. "Do you know what gave you the idea to move to the surface? I mean originally, before you'd ever started looking into the possibility."

"Have you read Zane Grey's *Riders of the Purple Sage*?" I asked. "You must have."

"No." She looked confused, like I was changing the subject.

"You should. Here."

I tossed her a multi-bookmark compilation. Back down belowground, I'd given them out like candy at a crèche party. She could puzzle through the diction of the ancient original or read it in any number of translations, listen to a variety of audio versions and dramatic readings, or watch any of the hundreds of entertainment docs it had inspired. I'd seen them all.

"This is really old. Why did you think I'd know it?" She flipped to the summary. "Oh, I see. One of the characters is named is Jane."

"Read it. It explains everything."

"I will. But maybe you could tell me what to look for?" Her smile made me forget all about my embarrassment.

"It's about what humans need to be happy. Sure, we evolved to live in complex interdependent social groups, but before that, we were nomads, pursuing resource opportunities in an open, sparsely populated landscape. That means for some people, solitude and independence are primary values."

She nodded, and I could see she was trying hard to understand.

"Down belowground, when I was figuring all this out, I tried working with a therapist. When I told him this, he said, 'We also evolved to suffer and die from violence, disease, and famine. Do you miss that, too?'"

Jane laughed. "I hope you fired him. So one book inspired all this?"

"It's not just a book. It's a way of life. The freedom to explore wide open spaces, to come together with like-minded others and form loose knit communities based on mutual aid, and to know that every morning you'll wake up looking at an endless horizon."

"These horizons aren't big enough?" She waved at the surrounding virtual space, a default grid with dappled patterns, as if a directional light source were shining through gently fluttering leaves.

"For some, maybe. For me, pretending isn't enough."

"I'll read it. It sounds very . . ." She pursed her lips, looking for the right word. "Romantic."

I started to blush again, so I made an excuse and dropped the connection before I made a fool of myself. Then I drifted down to the rumpus room and stripped off my goggles and breather.

"Whoa," Bouche said. "Doc, what's wrong?"

Eleanora turned from the extruder to look at me, then fumbled her caffeine bulb and squirted liquid across her cheek.

"Wow." She wiped the liquid up with her sleeve. "I've never seen you look dreamy before. What happened?"

I'm in love, I thought.

"Jane pinged me," I said instead.

Bouche called the whole crew. They came at a run. Even Vula.

In a small hab, any crumb of gossip can become legendary. I made them beg for the story, then drew it out as long as I could.

"Can you ask her to ping me?" Eddy asked Ricci when I was done.

"I would chat with her for more than a couple minutes, unlike Doc," said Treasure.

Chara grinned lasciviously. "Can I lurk?"

The whole crew in one room, awake and actually talking to each other was something Ricci hadn't seen before, much less all of us howling with laughter and gossiping about her friend. She looked profoundly unsettled. Vula bounced over to the extruder, filled a bulb with her favorite social lubricant, and tossed it to Ricci.

"Tell us everything about Jane," Chara said. Treasure waggled her tongue.

"It's not like that." Ricci frowned. "She's a friend."

"Good," they chorused, and collapsed back onto the netting, giggling.

"I've been meaning to ask—why do you use that hand-held thing to talk to her, anyway?" Chara said. "I've never even seen one of those before."

Ricci shook her head.

"Come on, Ricci. There's no privacy here," Vula said. "You know that. Don't go stiff on us."

Ricci joined us in the netting before answering. When she picked a spot beside me, my pulse fluttered in my throat.

"Jane's a peer counselor." She squeezed a sip from the bulb and grimaced at the taste. "The hand-held screen is one of her strategies. Having it around reminds me to keep working on my goals."

"Why do you need peer counseling?" asked Chara.

"Because I . . ." Ricci looked from face to face, big brown eyes serious. Everyone quieted down. "I was unhappy. Listen, I've been talking with some people from the other whale crews. They've been having problems for a while now, and it's getting worse."

She fired a stack of bookmarks into the middle of the room. Everyone began riffling through them, except me.

"That's too bad," I said.

"Don't you want to know what's going on, Doc?" asked Chara.

I folded my arms and scowled in the general direction of the extruder.

"No," I said flatly. "I don't give a shit about them."

"Well, you better," Vula said. "Because if it's happening to them, it could happen to us. Look."

She fired a feed from a remote sensing drone into the middle of the room. A group of whales had gathered a hundred meters above a slushy depression between a pair of high ridges. They weren't feeding, just drifting around aimlessly, dangerously close to each other. When they got close to each other, they unfurled their petals and brushed them along each other's skin.

As we watched, two whales collided. Their bladders bubbled out like a crechie's squeeze toy until it looked like they would burst. Seeing the two massive creatures collide like that was so upsetting, I actually reached into the feed and tried to push them apart. Embarrassing.

"Come on Doc, tell us what's happening," said Vula.

"I don't know." I tucked my hands into my armpits as if I was cold.

"We should go help," said Eddy. "At least we could assist with the evac if they need to bail."

I shook my head. "It could be dangerous."

Everyone laughed at that. People who aren't comfortable with risk don't roam the atmosphere.

"It might be a disease," I added, "We should stay as far away as we can. We don't want to catch it."

Treasure pulled a face at me. "You're getting old."

I grabbed my breather and goggles and bounded toward the hatch.

"Come on Doc, take a guess," Ricci said.

"More observation would be required before I'd be comfortable advancing a theory," I said stiffly. "I can only offer conjecture."

"Go ahead, conjecture away," said Vula.

I took a moment to collect myself, and then turned and addressed the crew with professorial gravity.

"It's possible the other crews haven't been maintaining the interventions that ensure their whales don't move into reproductive maturity."

"You're saying the whales are horny?" said Bouche.

"They look horny," said Treasure.

"They're fascinated with each other," said Vula.

Vula had put her finger on exactly the thing that was bothering me. Whales don't congregate. They don't interact socially. They certainly don't mate.

"I'd guess the applicable pseudoneural tissue has regenerated, perhaps incompletely, and their behavior is confused."

Ricci gestured at the feed, where three whales collided, dragging their petals across each other's bulging skin. "This isn't going to happen to us?"

"No, I said. "Definitely not. Don't worry. Unlike the others, I've been keeping on top of the situation."

"But how can you be sure?" And then realization dawned over Ricci's face. "You knew this was going to happen, didn't you?"

"Not exactly."

She launched herself from the netting and bounced toward me. "Why didn't you share the information? Keeping it secret is just cruel."

I backed toward the hatch. "It's not my responsibility to save the others from their stupid mistakes."

"We need to tell them how to fix it. Maybe they can save themselves."

"Tell them whatever you want." I excavated my private notes from lockdown, and fired them into the middle of the room. "I think their best option would be to abandon their whales and find new ones."

"That would take months," Vula said. "Nineteen whales. More than two hundred people."

"Then they should start now." I turned to leave.

"Wait." Ricci looked around at the crew. "We have to go help. Right?"

I gripped the edge of the hatch. The electrostatic membrane licked at my fingertips.

"Yeah, I want to go," Bouche said. "I'd be surprised if you didn't, Doc."

"I want to go," said Treasure.

"Me too," Chara chimed in. Eddy and Eleanora both nodded.

Vula pulled down her goggles and launched herself out of the netting. "Whales fucking? What are we waiting for? I'll start fabbing some media drones."

With all seven of them eager for adventure, our quiet, comfortable little world didn't stand a chance.

We're not the only humans on the surface. Not quite. Near the south pole a gang of religious hermits live in a deep ice cave, making alcohol the old way using yeast-based fermentation. It's no better than the extruded version, but some of the habs take pity on them so the hermits can fund their power and feedstock.

Every so often one of the hermits gives up and calls for evac. When that happens, the bored crew of a cargo ship zips down to rescue them. Those same ships bring us supplies and new crew. They also shuttle adventurers and researchers around the planet, but mostly they sit idle, tethered halfway up the beanstalk.

The ships are beautiful—sleek, fast, and elegant. As for us, when we need to change our position, it's not quite so efficient. Or fast.

When Ricci found me in the rumpus room, I'd already fabbed my gloves and face mask, and I was watching the last few centimeters of a thick pair of protective coveralls chug through the output.

"I told the other crews you'd be happy to take a look at the regenerated tissue and recommend a solution, but they refused," she said. "They don't like you, do they?"

I yanked the coveralls out of the extruder.

"No, and I don't like them either." I stalked to the hatch.

"Can I tag along, Doc?" she asked.

"You're lucky I don't pack you into a body bag and tag you for evac."

"I'm really sorry, Doc. I should have asked you before offering your help. When I get an idea in my head, tend to just run with it."

She was all smiles and dimples, with her goggles on her forehead pushing her hair up in spikes and her breather swinging around her neck. A person who looks like that can get away with anything.

"This is your idea," I said. "Only fair you get your hands dirty."

I fabbed her a set of protective clothing and we helped each other suit up. We took a quick detour to slather appetite suppressant gel on the appropriate hormonal bundle, and then waddled up the long dorsal sinus, arms out for balance. The sinus walls clicked and the long cavity bent around us, but soon the appetite suppressant took hold and we were nearly stationary, dozing gently in the clouds.

On either side towered the main float bladders—clear multi-chambered organs rippling with rainbows across their honeycomb-patterned surfaces. Feeder organs pulsed between the bladder walls. The feeders are dark pink at the base, but the color fades as they branch into sprawling networks of tubules reaching through the skin, grasping hydrogen and channeling it into the bladders.

At the head of the dorsal sinus, a tall, slot-shaped orifice give us access to the neuronal cavity. I shrugged my equipment bag off my shoulder, showed Ricci how to secure her face mask over her breather, and climbed in.

With the masks on, to talk we had to ping each other. I was still a bit angry so no chit-chat, business only. I handed her the laser scalpel.

Cut right here. I sliced the blade of my gloved hand vertically down the milky surface of the protective tissue. *See these scars?* I pointed at the gray metallic stripes on either side of the imaginary line I'd drawn. *Stay away from them. Just cut straight in between.*

Ricci backed away a few steps. I don't think I'm qualified to do this.

You've been qualified to draw a line since you were a crechie. When she began to protest again, I cut her off. *This was your idea, remember?*

Her hands shook, but the line was straight enough. The pouch deflated, draping over the skeleton of the carbon fiber struts I'd installed way back in the beginning. I pulled Ricci inside and closed the incision behind us with squirts of temporary adhesive. The wound wept drops of fluid that rapidly boiled off, leaving a sticky pink sap-like crust across the iridescent interior surface.

Is this the whale's brain? Ricci asked.

I ignored the question. Ricci knew it was the brain—she'd been studying my notes, after all. She was just trying to smooth my feathers by giving me a chance to show my expertise.

Not every brain looks like a brain. Yours and mine look like they should be floating in the primordial ocean depths—that's where we came from, after all. The organ in front of us came from the clouds—a tower of spun glass floss threaded through and through with wispy, feather-like strands that branched and re-branched into iridescent fractals. My mobility control leads were made of copper nanofiber embedded in color-coded silicon filaments: red, green, blue, yellow, purple, orange, and black—a ragged, dull rainbow piercing the delicate depths of an alien brain.

Ricci repeated her question.

Don't ask dumb questions, Ricci.

She put her hands up in a gesture of surrender and backed away. Not far— no room inside the pouch to shuffle back more than one step.

The best I can say is it's brain-like. I snapped the leads into my fist-sized control interface. The neurons are neuron-like. Is it the whole brain? Is the entire seat of cognition here? I can't tell because there's not much cognition to measure. Maybe more than a bacterium, but far less than an insect.

How do you measure cognition? Ricci asked.

Controlled experiments, but how do you run experiments on animals this large? All I can tell you is that most people who study these creatures lose interest fast. But here's a better measure: After more than ten years, a whale has never surprised me.

Before today, you mean.

Maneuvering takes a little practice. We use a thumb-operated clicker to fire tiny electrical impulses through the leads and achieve a vague form of directional control. Yes, it's a basic system. We could replace it with something more elegant but it operates even if we lose power. The control it provides isn't exactly roll, pitch, and yaw, but it's effective enough. The margin for error is large. There's not much to hit.

Navigation is easy, too. Satellites ping our position a thousand times a second and the data can be accessed in several different navigational aids, all available in our dashboards.

But though it's all fairly easy, it's not quick. My anger didn't last long. Not in such close quarters, especially just a few hours after realizing I was in love with her. It was hardly a romantic scene, both of us swathed head-to-toe in protective clothing, passing a navigation controller back and forth as we waggled slowly toward our destination.

In between bouts of navigation, I began telling Ricci everything I knew about the organ in front of us: A brain dump about brains, inside a brain. Ha.

She was interested; I was flattered by her interest. Age-old story. I treated her to all my theories, prejudices, and opinions, not just about regenerating pseudoneuronal tissue and my methods for culling it, but the entire scientific research apparatus down belowground, the social dynamics of hab I grew up in, and the philosophical underpinnings of the research exploration proposal we used to float our first forays out here.

Thank goodness Ricci was wearing a mask. She was probably yawning so wide I could have checked her tonsils.

Here. I handed her the control box. *You drive the rest of the way.*

We were aiming for the equator, where the strong, steady winds have carved a smooth canyon bisecting the ice right down to the planet's iron core. When we need to travel a long distance, riding that wind is the fastest route.

Ricci clicked a directional adjustment, and our heading swung a few degrees back toward the equator.

What does the whale perceive when we do this? Ricci waggled the thumb of her glove above the joystick. When it changes direction, are we luring it or scaring it away?

Served me right for telling her not to ask simple questions.

I don't really know, I admitted.

Maybe it makes them think other whales are around. What if they want to be together, just like people, but before now they didn't know how. Maybe you've been teaching them.

My eyebrows climbed. I'd never considered how we might be influencing whale behavior, aside from the changes we make for our own benefit.

That's an interesting theory, Ricci. Definitely worth looking into.

Wouldn't it be terrible to be always alone?

I'd always considered myself a loner. But in that moment, I honestly couldn't remember why.

Once we're in the equatorial stream, we ride the wind until we get into the right general area. Then we wipe off the appetite suppressant, and hunger sends us straight into the arms of the nearest electrical storm.

The urge to feed is a powerful motivator for most organisms. Mama chases all the algae she can find, and gobbles it double-time. For us on the inside, it's like an old-style history doc. Everyone stays strapped in their hammocks and rides out the weather as we pitch around on the high seas.

I always enjoy the feeding frenzy; it gets the blood flowing.

I'd just settled to enjoy the wild ride when Ricci pinged me.

Two crews tried surgical interventions on the regenerated tissue. Let me know what you think, okay? Maybe now we can convince them to let you help.

The message was accompanied by bookmarks to live feeds from the supply ships. The first feed showed a whale wedging itself backward into a crevasse, its petals waving back and forth as it wiggled deeper into the canyon-like crack in the ice.

The other feed showed a whale scraping its main valve along a serrated ridge of ice. Its oval body stretched and flexed, its bladders bulged. Its petals curled inward, then snapped into rigid extension as the force of its body crashed down on the ice's knife edge.

Inside both whales, tiny specks bounced through the sinuses. I could only imagine what the crew was doing—what I would do in that situation. If they wanted to live, they had to leave. Fast.

A chill slipped under my skin. My fault. If those whales died, if those crews died, I was to blame. Me alone. Not the two crews. They were obviously desperate enough to try anything. I should have contacted them myself, and offered whatever false apologies would get them to accept my help.

But chances are it wouldn't have changed the outcome, except they would have had me to blame. Another entry in my list of crimes.

Frost spread across my flesh and raised goosebumps. I tugged on my hammock's buckles to make sure they were secure against the constant pitching and heaving, dialed up the temperature, and snuggled deeper into my quilt. I fired up my simulation model and wandered through towering mountains of pseudoneural tissue, pondering the problem, delving deeper and deeper through chains of crystallized tissue until they danced behind my eyelids. Swirling, stacking, combining, and recombining . . .

I was nearly asleep when I heard Ricci's voice.

"Hey, Doc, can we talk?"

I thought I was dreaming. But no, she was right outside my hammock, gripping the tethers and getting knocked off her feet with every jolt and flex. Her goggled and masked face was lit by a mad flurry of light from the bolts coruscating in every direction just beyond the skin.

"Are you nuts?" I yanked open the hammock seal. "Get in here."

She plunged through the electrostatic barrier and rolled to the far side of my bed. When she came up, her hair stood on end with static electricity.

"Whoa." She swiped off her goggles and breather, stuffed them in one of the hammock pouches, then flattened the dark nimbus of her hair with her palms and grinned. "It's wild out there."

I pulled my quilt up to my chin and scowled. "That was stupid."

"Yeah, I know but you didn't ping me back. This is an important situation, right? Life or death."

I sighed. "If you want to rescue people, there are vocations for that."

"Don't we have a duty to help people when we can?"

"Some people don't want to be helped. They just want to be left alone."

"Like you?"

"Nothing you're doing is helping me, Ricci."

"Okay, okay. But if we can figure out a way to help, that's good too. Better than good. Everyone wins."

Lying there in my hammock, facing Ricci sprawled at the opposite end and taking up more than half of the space, I finally figured out what kind of person she was.

"You're a meddler, Ricci. A busybody. You were wasted in the sciences. You should have studied social dynamics and targeted a career in one-on-one social work."

She laughed.

"Listen." I held out my hand, palm up. She took it right away, didn't hesitate. Her hand was warm. Almost feverish. "If you want to stay in the crew, you have to relax. Okay? We can't have emergencies every week. None of us are here for that."

She squeezed my hand and nodded.

"A little excitement is fine, once in a while," I continued. "Obviously this is an extraordinary situation. But if you keep looking for adventure, we'll shunt you back to Jane without a second thought."

She twisted the grip into a handshake and gave me two formal pumps. Then she reached for the hammock seal. She would have climbed out into the maelstrom if I hadn't stopped her.

"You can't do that," I yelled. "No wandering around when we're in a feeding frenzy. You'll get killed. Kill us too, if you go through the wrong bladder wall."

She smiled then, like she didn't believe me, like it was just some excuse to keep her in my hammock. And when she settled back down, it wasn't at the opposite end. She snuggled in right beside me, companionable as anything, or even more.

"Don't you get lonely, Doc?" she asked.

"Sometimes," I admitted. "Not much."

Our hammocks are roomy, but Ricci didn't give me much space, and though the tethers absorb movement, we were still jostling against each other.

"Because you don't need anybody or anything." Her voice in my ear, soft as a caress.

"Something like that."

"Maybe, eventually, you'll change your mind about that."

What happened next wasn't my idea. I was long out of practice, but Ricci had my full and enthusiastic cooperation.

Down belowground, I was a surgeon, and a good one. My specialty was splicing neurons in the lateral geniculate nucleus. My skills were in high demand. So high, in fact, that I had a massive support team.

I'm not talking about a part-time admin or social facilitator. Anyone can have those. I had an entire cadre of people fully dedicated to making sure that if I spent most of my time working and sleeping, what little time remained would be optimized to support physical, emotional, and intellectual health. All my needs were plotted and graphed. People had meetings to argue, for example, over what type of sex best maintained my healthiest emotional state, and once that was decided, they'd argue over the best way to offer that opportunity to me.

That's just an example. I'm only guessing. They kept the administrative muddle under veil. Day-to-day, I only had contact with a few of my staff, and usually I was too busy with my own work to think about theirs. But for a lot of people, I was a billable-hours bonanza.

But despite all their hard work, despite the hedonics modeling, best-practice scenarios, and time-tested decision trees, I burned out.

It wasn't their fault. It was mine. I was, and remain, only human.

I could have just reduced my surgery time. I could have switched to teaching or coaching other surgeons. But no. Some people approach life like it's an all-or-nothing game. That's me. I couldn't be all, so I decided to become nothing.

Until Ricci came along, that is.

When the storm ended, the two of us had to face a gauntlet of salacious grins and saucy comments. I didn't blush, or at least not much. Ricci had put the spark of life in a part of me that had been dark for far too long. I was proud to have her in my crew, in my hammock, in my life.

The whole hab gave us a hard time. The joke that gave them the biggest fits, and made even Vula cling helplessly to the rumpus room netting as she convulsed with laughter, involved the two of us calling for evac and setting up a crèche in the most socially conservative hab down belowground. Something about imagining us in swathed in religious habits and swarming with crechies tweaked everyone's funny bones.

Ricci weathered the ridicule better than me. I left to fill the water kegs, and by the time I returned, the hilarity had worn itself out.

The eight of us lounged in the rumpus room, the netting gently swaying to and fro as we drifted in the bright directional light of the aquapause. Water spilled off the skin and threw dappled shadows across the room. Vula had launched the media drones and we'd all settled down to watch the feeds.

More than once I caught myself brainlessly staring at Ricci, but I kept my goggles on so nobody noticed. I hope.

Two hundred kilometers to the northwest and far below us, the seventeen remaining whales congregated in the swirling winds above a dome-shaped mesa that calved monstrous sheets of ice down its massive flanks. A dark electrical storm massed on the horizon, with all its promise of rich concentrations of algae, but the whales didn't move toward it, just kept circulating and converging, plucking at each other's skin.

Three hundred kilometers west lay the abandoned corpses of two whales, their deflated bladders draped over warped sinus skeletons half-buried in slush.

Our media drones got there too late to trap the whales' death throes, and I was glad. But Vula and Bouche trapped great visuals of the rescue, showing the valiant supply ship crews swooping in to pluck brightly colored body bags out of the air. Maybe the crews put a little more of a spin on their maneuvering than they needed to, but who could blame them? They rarely got a job worth bragging about.

One of Bouche's media broker friends put the rescue feeds out to market. They started getting good play right away. Bouche fired the media licensing statement into the middle of the room. The numbers glowed green and flickered as they climbed.

"Look at these fees," she said. "This will underwrite our power consumption for a couple years."

"That's great, Bouchie," I murmured, and flicked the statement out of my visual field.

Night was coming, and it presented a hard deadline. If the whales didn't move before dark, they'd all die.

Ricci moved closer to me in the netting and rested her cheek on my shoulder. I turned my head and touched my lips to her temple, just for a moment. I was deep in my brain simulation, working on the problem. But I kept an eye on the feeds. When the whales collided, I held my breath. As the bladders stretched and budged, I cringed, certain they'd reach their elastic limit and we would see a whale pop, its massive sinuses rupture, its skin tear away and its body plunge to splatter on the icy surface below. But they didn't. They bounced off each other in slow motion and resumed their aimless circulation.

Hours passed. Eddy got up, extruded a meal, and passed the containers around the netting. Chara and Treasure slipped out of the room. Vula was only half-present—she was working in her studio, sculpting maquettes of popped bladders and painfully twisted corpses.

Eddy yawned. "How long can these whales live without feeding?"

I forced a stream of breath through my lips, fluttering the fringe of my bangs. "I don't know. Indefinitely, maybe, if the crews can figure out a way to provide nutrition internally."

"If they keep their whales fed, maybe they'll just keep stumbling around, crashing into each other." Vula's voice was slurred, her eyes unfocused as she juggled multiple streams.

"I'm more worried about nightfall, actually," I said.

Ever since we'd dragged ourselves out of my hammock, Ricci had been trying to pry information from emergency response up the beanstalk, from the supply ship crews who were circling the site, and from the whale crews. They were getting increasingly frantic as time clicked by, and keeping us informed wasn't high on their list of priorities.

I rested my palm on the inside of Ricci's knee. "Are the other crews talking to you yet?"

She sat up straight and gave me a pained smile. "A little. I wasn't getting anywhere, but Jane's been giving me some tips."

That woke everyone up. Even Vula snapped right out of her creative fugue.

"Is Jane helping us?" Chara asked, and when Ricci nodded she demanded, "Why are you keeping her to yourself?"

Ricci shrugged. "Jane doesn't know anything about whales."

"If she's been helping you maybe she can help us too," said Eddy.

"Yeah, come on Ricci, stop hogging Jane." Bouche raked her fingers through her hair, sculpting it into artful tufts. "I want to know what she thinks of all this."

"All right," Ricci said. "I'll ask her."

A few moments later she fired Jane's feed into the room and adjusted the perspective so her friend seemed to be sitting in the middle of the room. She wore a baggy black tunic and trousers, and her hair was gathered into a ponytail that draped over the back of her chair. The pinnas of her ears were perforated in a delicate lace pattern.

Treasure and Chara came barreling down the access sinus and plunged through the hatch. They hopped over to their usual spot in the netting and settled in. Jane waved at them.

"We're making you an honorary crew member," Eddy told Jane. "Ricci has to share you with us. We all get equal Jane time."

"I didn't agree to that," said Ricci.

"Fight over me later, when everyone's safe." Jane said. "I don't understand why the other crews are delaying evacuation. Who would risk dying when they can just leave?"

Everyone laughed.

"This cadre self-selects for extremists." Eddy rotated her finger over her head, encompassing all of us in the gesture. "People like us would rather die than back down."

"I guess you're not alone in that," said Jane. "Every hab has plenty of stubborn people."

"But unlike them, we built everything we have," I said. "That makes it much harder to give up."

"Looks like someone finally made a decision, though." Ricci maximized the main feed. Jane wheeled around to join us at the netting.

Glowing dots tracked tiny specks across the wide mesa, pursued by flashing trails of locational data. Vula's media drones zoomed in, showing a succession of brightly colored, hard-shell body bags shunting though the main valves. Sleet built up along their edges, quickly hardening to a solid coating of ice.

"Quitters," Treasure murmured under her breath.

Jane looked shocked.

"If you think you know what you'd do in their place, you're wrong," I said. "Nobody knows."

"I'd stay," Treasure said. "I'll never leave Mama."

Chara grinned. "Me too. We'll die together if we had to."

Bouche pointed at the two of them. "If we ever have to evac, you two are going last."

Jane's expression of shock widened, then she gathered herself into a detached and professional calm.

Ricci squeezed my hand. "The supply ships want to shuttle some of the evacuees to us instead of taking them all the way to the beanstalk. How many can we carry?"

I checked the mass budget and made a few quick calculations. "About twenty. More if we dump mass." I raised my voice. "Let's pitch and ditch everything we can. If it's not enough we can think about culling a little water and feedstock. Is everyone okay with that?"

To my surprise, nobody argued. I'd rarely seen the crew move so fast, but with Jane around everyone wanted to look like a hero.

Life has rarely felt as sunny as it did that day.

Watching the others abandon their whales was deeply satisfying. It's not often in life you can count your victories, but each of those candy-colored, human-sized pods was a score for me and a big, glaring zero for my old, unlamented colleagues. I'd outlasted them.

Not only that, but I had a new lover, a mostly-harmonious crew of friends, and the freedom to go anywhere and do anything I liked, as long as it could be done from within the creature I called home.

But mostly, I loved having an important job to do.

I checked our location to make sure we were far enough away that if the other whales began to drift, they wouldn't wander into the debris stream. Then we paired into work teams, pulled redundant equipment, ferried it to the main valve, and jettisoned it.

I kept a tight eye on the mass budget, watched for tissue stress around the valve, and made strict calls on what to chuck and what to keep.

Hygiene and maintenance bots were sacrosanct. Toilets and hygiene stations, too. Safety equipment, netting, hammocks—all essential. But each of us had fifty kilos of personal effects. I ditched mine first. Clothes, jewelry, mementos, a few pieces of art—some of it real artisan work but not worth a human life. Vula tossed a dozen little sculptures, all gifts from friends and admirers. Eddy was glad to have an excuse to throw out the guitar she'd never learned to play. Treasure had a box of ancient hand-painted dinnerware inherited from her crèche; absolutely irreplaceable, but they went too. Chara threw out her devotional shrine. It was gold and took up most of her mass allowance, but we could fab another.

We even tossed the orang bot. We all liked the furry thing, but it was heavy. Bouche stripped out its proprietary motor modules and tossed the shell. We'd fab another, eventually.

If we'd had time for second thoughts, maybe the decisions would have been more difficult. Or maybe not. People were watching, and we knew it. Having an audience helped us cooperate.

It wasn't just Jane we were trying to impress. Bouche's media output was gathering a lot of followers. We weren't just trapping the drama anymore, we were part of the story.

Bouche monitored our followship, both the raw access stats and the digested analysis from the PR firm she'd engaged to boost the feed's profile. When the first supply ship backed up to our valve and we began pulling body bags inside, Bouche whooped. Our numbers had just gone atmospheric.

We were a clown show, though. Eight of us crowded in the isthmus sinus, shuttling body bags, everyone bouncing around madly and getting in each other's way. Jane helped sort us out by monitoring the overhead cameras and doing crowd control. Me, I tried not to be an obstruction while making load-balancing decisions. Though we'd never taken on so much weight at once, I didn't anticipate any problems. But I only looked at strict mathematical tolerances. I'm not an engineer; I didn't consider the knock-on effects of the sudden mass shift.

In the end, we took on thirty-eight body bags. We were still distributing them throughout the sinuses when Ricci reported the rescue was over.

That's it. The cargo ships have forty-five body bags. They're making the run to the beanstalk now.

Is that all? If the ships are full, we could prune some feedstock.

Everyone else is staying. They're still betting their whales will move.

When the last body bag was secured so it wouldn't pitch through a bladder, I might have noticed we were drifting toward the mesa. But I was too busy making sure the new cargo was secure and accounted for.

I pinged each unit, loaded their signatures into the maintenance dashboard, mapped their locations, checked the data in the mass budget, created a new dashboard for monitoring the new cargo's power consumption, consumables, and useful life. Finally, I cross-checked our manifest against the records the supply ships had given us.

That was when I realized we were carrying two members of my original crew.

When Ricci found me, I was pacing the dorsal sinus, up and down, arguing with myself. Mostly silently.

"If you're having some kind of emotional crisis, I'm sure Jane would love to help," she said.

I spun on my heel and stomped away, bouncing off the walls.

She yelled after me. "Not me though. I don't actually care about your emotional problems."

I bounced off a wall once more and stopped, both hands gripping its clear ridged surface.

"No?" I asked. "Why don't you care?"

"Because I'm too self-involved."

I laughed. Ricci reached out and ruffled her fingers through the short hair on the back of my neck. Her touch sent an electric jolt through my nerves.

"Maybe that's why we get along so well," she said softly. "We're a lot alike."

Kissing while wearing goggles and a breather is awkward and unsatisfying. I pulled her close and pressed my palms to the soft pad of flesh at the base of her spine. I held her until she got restless, then she took my hand and led me to the rumpus room.

Bouche lounged in the netting, eyes closed.

"Bouchie is giving a media interview," Ricci whispered. "An agent is booking her appearances and negotiating fees. If we get enough, we can upgrade the extruder and subscribe to a new recipe bank."

I pulled a bulb out of the extruder. "She'll be hero of the hab."

"You could wake them up, you know."

"Wake up who?" I asked, and took a deep swig of sweet caffeine.

"Your old buddies. In the body bags. Wake them up. Have it out."

I managed to swallow without choking. "No, I don't think so."

"Maybe they'll apologize."

I laughed, a little too hard, a little too long, and only stopped when Ricci began to look offended.

"We can't wake them," I said. "Where would they sleep until we got to the beanstalk?"

"They can have my hammock." She sidled close. "I'll bunk with you."

We kissed then, and properly. Thoroughly. Until I met Ricci, I'd been a shrunken bladder; nobody knew my possible dimensions. Ricci filled me up. I expanded, large enough to contain whole universes.

"No. They're old news." I kissed her again and ran my finger along the edge of her jaw. "It was another life. They don't matter anymore."

Strange thing was, saying those words made it true. All I cared about was Ricci, and all I could see was the glowing possibility of a future together, rising over a broad horizon.

Twilight began to move over us. We only had a little time to spare before we recalled the media drones, wiped off the appetite suppressant, and left the other crews to freeze in the dark.

We gathered in the rumpus room, all watching the same feed. Whales circulated above the mesa. Slanting sunlight cast deep orange reflections across their skins, their windward surfaces creamy with blowing snow. Inside, dark spots bounced around the sinuses. If I held my breath, I could almost hear their words, follow their arguments. When I bit my lip, I tasted their tears.

"More than a hundred people," Jane said. "I still don't understand why they'd decide to commit suicide. A few maybe, but not so many."

"Some will evac before it's too late." Vula shrugged. "And as for the rest, it's their own decision. I can't say I would do anything different. And I hope I never find out."

I shivered. "Agreed."

"It doesn't make sense," Jane said. "Someone must be exercising duress."

"Nobody forces anyone to do anything out here, any more than they do down belowground," said Treasure.

"Yeah," said Chara. "We're not crechies, Jane. We do what we want."

Jane sputtered, trying to apologize.

"It's okay," Eddy told her. "We're all upset. None of us really understand."

"The whales still might move," said Bouche. "They can spend a little time in the dark, right Doc?"

I set a timer with a generous margin for error and fired it into the middle of the room. "Eight minutes, then we have to leave. The other whales will have a little more than thirty minutes before they freeze at full dark. Then their bladders burst."

Chara and Treasure pulled themselves out of the netting.

"We're not watching this," Chara said. "If you want to hang overhead and root for them to evac, go ahead."

We all waved goodnight. The two of them stumped away to their hammock, and silence settled over the rumpus room. Just the whoosh and murmur of the bladders, and the faint skiff of wind over the skin. A few early stars winked through the clouds. They seemed compassionate, somehow. Understanding. Looking at those bright pinpoints, I understood how on ancient Earth, people might use the stars to conjure gods.

I put my arm around Ricci's shoulders and drew her close. She let me hold her for two minutes, no more, and then she pulled away.

"I can't watch this either," she said. "I have to do something."

"I know." I drew her hand back just for a moment and planted a kiss on the palm. "It's hard."

Vula nodded, and Jane, too. Eddy and Bouche both got up and hugged her. Eleanora kept her head down, hiding her tears. The electrostatic membrane crackled as Ricci left.

"Do you know some of the people down there, Doc?" asked Jane.

"Not anymore," I said. "Not for a long time."

We fell quiet again, watching the numbers on the countdown. Ricci had left her shadow beside me. I felt her cold absence; something missing that should be whole. I could have spied on her, see where she'd gone, but no. She deserved her privacy.

The first little quake shuddering through the sinuses told me exactly where she was.

I checked our location, blinked, and then checked it again. We were right over the mesa, above the other whales, all seventeen of them. Wind, bad luck, or instinct had had brought us there—but did it matter? Ricci—her location mattered. She was in the caudal stump, with the waste pellets, and the secondary valve.

No. Ricci, no. I slapped my breather on and launched myself out of the rumpus room, running aft as fast as I could. *Don't do that. Stop.*

I lost my footing and bounced hard. *You might hit them. You might . . .*

Kill them.

When I got to the caudal stump, Ricci was just clicking the last pellet through the valve. If we'd dumped them during the pitch and ditch, none of it would have happened. But dry waste is light. We'd accumulated ten pellets, only five kilograms, so I hadn't bothered with them.

But a half-kilo pellet falling from a height can do a lot of damage.

I fired the feed into the middle of the sinus. One whale was thrashing on the slushy mesa surface, half-obscured by the concussive debris. Two more were falling, twisting in agony, their bladders tattered and flapping. Another three would have escaped damage, but they circulated into the path of the oncoming pellets, each one burst in turn, as if a giant hand had reached down and squeezed the life out of them.

Ricci was in my arms, then. Both of us quaking, falling to our knees. Holding each other and squeezing hard, as if we could break each other's bones with the force of our own mistakes.

Six whales. Twenty-two people. All dead.

The other eleven whales scattered. One fled east and plunged through the twilight band into night. Its skin and bladders froze and burst, and its sinus skeleton shattered on the jagged ice. Its crew had been one of the most stubborn—none had evacuated. They all died. Ten people.

In total, thirty-two died because Ricci made an unwise decision.

The remaining ten whales re-congregated over a slushy depression near the beanstalk. Ricci had bought the surviving crews a few more hours, so they tried a solution along the lines Ricci had discovered. Ice climbers use drones with controlled explosive capabilities to stabilize their climbing routes. They tried a test; it worked—the whales fled again, but in the wrong direction and re-congregated close to the leading edge of night.

In the end, the others evacuated. All seventy got in their body bags and called for evac.

By strict accounting, Ricci's actions led to a positive outcome. I remind her of that whenever I can. She says it doesn't matter—we don't play math games with human lives. Dead is dead, and nothing will change that.

And she's right, because the moment she dumped those pellets, Ricci became the most notorious murderer our planet has ever known.

The other habs insist we hand her over to a conflict resolution panel. They've sent negotiators, diplomats—they've even sent Jane—but we won't give her up. To them, that proves we're dangerous. Criminals. Outlaws.

But we live in the heart of the matter, and we see it a little differently.

Ricci did nothing wrong. It was a desperate situation and she made a desperate call. Any one of us might have done the same thing, if we'd been smart enough to think of it.

We're a solid band of outlaws, now. Vula, Treasure, Chara, Eddy, Bouche, Eleanora, Ricci, and me. We refuse to play nice with the other habs. They could cut off our feedstock, power, and data, but we're betting they won't. If they did, our blood would be on their hands.

So none of us are going anywhere. Why would we leave? The whole planet is ours, with unlimited horizons.

A.C. Wise's short fiction has appeared in *Clarkesworld, Tor.com*, and *The Year's Best Dark Fantasy and Horror 2017*, among other places. She has two collections published with Lethe Press, and her debut novella, *Catfish Lullaby*, was published by Broken Eye Books in early 2018. She's been a finalist for the Lambda Literary Award, and a winner of the Sunburst Award for Excellence in Canadian Literature of the Fantastic. In addition to her fiction, she contributes a monthly review column to *Apex Magazine*. Find her online at www. acwise.net.

A CATALOGUE OF SUNLIGHT AT THE END OF THE WORLD

A.C. Wise

June 21, 2232—Svalbard

The twenty-first of June, the Summer Solstice, the longest day and the shortest night. That means less here at the top of the world where, in this season, we have sunlight twenty-four hours a day. But it seemed like an appropriate day to start this project nonetheless.

In just over a week, the generation ship *Arber* will depart on its journey. The docking clamps will release, and it will go sailing off into space to find the future of humanity. This is my parting gift, a catalogue of sunlight from the world left behind.

Of course the sun will still be there, getting farther away as they travel, but it won't be the same. The people on that ship—*those* ships, leaving from all points above the globe—will never again see sunlight the way it looks here and now. They won't see the sky bruise purple and hushed gold or the violent shades of lavender, rose, and flame as the sun creeps toward the horizon. They'll never see the way this sun sparkles off water in a fast-moving brook or dapples the ground beneath a canopy of leaves. It won't pry its way through their blinds in the morning, or slip under doors and through all the cracks sealed up against its intrusion. They won't know the persistence of it, the sheer amount of it. They'll only know its loss.

Maybe the *Arber*'s children, or their children's children will see starlight on the dust of some distant world, watch it pool in the craters of their first new footsteps and call it the sun. But not the ones leaving. The ones who grew up under its light. This is my gift to them. A little something to take with them into the cold and the dark.

Today, the light is pure. There isn't a cloud in the sky to cut it, no breeze to stir it off our skins. All the shadows are sharp-edged. There's so much of it, it's easy to forget it's there. Ubiquitous sun. It gets over everything and under everything and inside it. Today, the light of the sun has almost no color at all, but if you squint just right, you can prism it, see the rainbow fractures flaring away from it. That is the sun here today, children. The sun you're leaving behind. There has never been another just like it, and there never will be again.

There. That part is for the future. This part is for the present and the past. For you and me, Mila.

Kathe came to see me today and asked me one more time to go with them. *There's room*, she said. *You could stay with me, Linde, Ivan, and the kids until we figure things out.* She didn't mention Thomas.

Kathe has pull. It comes with being Head of Resource Management, Northern Division. She could make it happen, our girl. That's what she does, after all. She manages resources. If she says there's room for me, then there's room. She could probably get me the nicest berth on the ship, if I asked.

Space travel is for the young, I told her. It's no place for an old man like me. Besides, this is my home. I like it here. This is where I belong.

But your children, she said. *Your grandchildren.*

Her eyes. It's hard to look at them sometimes. They remind me so much of you. I think she knew she'd already lost the fight.

What's the point of space? It's just another place to be without you. I have my kettle here. I have my woolen socks and my favorite mug. I have a library full of books and music. I've even adopted a cat. Or it's adopted me. A little grey kitten I've named Predator X. They won't have cats in space. They'll have genetic material, of course, but it's hard to cuddle a test tube on a cold winter's night and be comforted by its purr.

May 23, 2171—Prince Edward Island

To hell with separating past and future. This is my catalogue, and I'll tell it how I choose and to who I choose, and I choose you, Mila.

Obviously May 23, 2171 isn't today's date, and I'm not on Prince Edward Island. It's when and where we were married. The sunlight on that day deserves to be memorialized.

It was golden in the way sunlight never is outside of photographs and memories. It caught in your hair, turning those fly-away strands you could never get to behave—even on that day—into individual threads of crystal. It was sunlight in its ideal form, its most romantic form. They say it's lucky to have rain on your wedding day, but I think that's just something to make people feel better when their bouquets and tuxedoes and cakes and dozen white doves are all soggy and miserable.

We were married on the beach, on the dunes, with the waves in the background and wild sea grass running everywhere around us. Those dunes are gone now. In another few years, the whole island will be gone, lost to rising sea levels like New Orleans and Florida, London and Venice. So many cities swallowed whole. But back then, it was beautiful.

Lupines and red sand—those stick out in my mind. You insisted on traveling back to your family's home because your grandmother wasn't well enough to travel, and you wanted her to give you away. I didn't have any people of my own left, so one place was as good as another to me. You were all the family I wanted and needed back then. Now that my life is coming full circle, I'm finding that's true once again.

The day I proposed to you was the day I stole the Gibraltar Campion from the seed vault. *Silene tomentosa,* your favorite flower. The first time I saw you, you were looking at a 3-D projection of it, part of the vault's new finding aid. I didn't know it at the time, but that was your program. You were also the one who got rare and endangered flowers added to the vault along with staple crops. You said beautiful things should be saved as well as useful ones, and besides bees and pollination and flowers—even rare and temperamental ones—are part of our ecosystem, too.

On the day we met, you were looking at the Gibraltar Campion from every angle, studying it with a scientist's eye. I don't think you knew anyone was watching you. Then, for just a moment, your expression changed; you weren't looking at the flower like a scientist anymore. You frowned and reached out like you wanted to brush your finger along the pale silk of its petal.

Had you ever seen one in person? I imagined how many years you'd spent studying it and how you'd launched a whole program to protect it and other flowers like it. But had you ever held its thin stem between your fingers or breathed it in to see if it had a scent? That unguarded moment of fascination and longing—that's the moment I fell in love.

It was hell getting the Campion to grow. I sweated over it in secret, afraid of giving it too much water, not enough. But I did get it to grow. That was always my gift. Can't cook worth a damn. Never had a scrap of musical talent or enough coordination to play sports. Green thumbs, though. I have those like nobody's business. It's why I was hired on at the Global Seed Vault in the first place. It's what led me to you, so I can't complain.

Smuggling my Gibraltar Campion into Canada without getting caught— that was a special hell all of its own. Then I presented you with the bouquet—the sad, single-flower bouquet I was so proud of—right before you walked down the aisle of sand and sea grass, and you almost called the wedding off right then and there.

What the hell were you thinking? you said. Do you have any idea how rare the Gibraltar Campion is? They brought it back from the dead. It was nearly extinct. What the hell do you think the vault is for anyway?

Storing up flowers so no one ever sees them? A vault full of potential, but never the reality?

Of course I didn't say that aloud. I wouldn't dare.

Some things are meant to be enjoyed, is what I did say, and I tried to charm you with a smile. Sometimes you have to appreciate what you have while you have it, instead of holding on to it for someday. You just have to live and let go and stop worrying about the future.

You called me selfish and a dozen other more unsavory names. You almost shoved me into the water. God, I was young and stupid back then. But somehow, I convinced you to marry me anyway.

You stayed mad at me through the whole ceremony. You refused to hold the Campion, so I held it, and you glared at me the whole time you said your vows. At the end though, you smiled a little, too. Then you cried; we both cried, and you told me if I ever did anything that stupid again you would throw my body into a bottomless crevasse where it would never be found. When we kissed, it tasted like salt, and we crushed the Campion between us, and we laughed so hard we started crying all over again.

I miss you, Mila. Every goddamn day.

June 23, 2232—Svalbard

There was a big party down on the beach today. A goodbye for everybody leaving and everyone staying behind. We lit a huge bonfire, which seems strange in the middle of the day, but when the sun never goes down, what else can you do?

This is what the sun looked like five days before everyone went away. Weak, like tea or good scotch watered down a thousand times. Like if you took a glass and kept adding ice to it every time you took a sip, trying to stretch that last bit of alcohol just a little farther. Sunlight, divided infinitely and spread thin, the faintest hint of peat and smoke on the tongue.

It was mostly overcast, but every now and then something would break loose in the great patchwork of grey and a beam of light would come shooting through. It might pin the stones on the shore or a little boy's hair as he ran toward the water. It might catch a mother and daughter in a tender moment of goodbye or fall on the waves and break over and over again. Sunlight is like that, fickle and faithless. It shines on us all.

Listen to me getting melancholy. Then again, it is the end of the world.

Everyone was there. We probably only made up a handful, compared to other celebrations around the world, but this was ours. We roasted fish on wooden spits. There were marshmallows and tofu hotdogs. Someone made a spicy curry with goat meat; someone else made a giant pot of borscht. There were real English popovers. There was even an attempt at poutine. You would have loved it.

A kitchen party. That's what it reminded me of. Not that I'd ever been to one, but from your descriptions—everyone getting together, each person bringing food and something to drink and an instrument. Your grandmother used to throw them, just like the old days, you said. The whole house would be open to anyone who wanted to join in, music spilling out of every door and window all night long.

The party on the beach was like that, music and dancing, and all of it just seemed to roll on and on. Kathe was there with Linde and Ivan and the kids. Thomas was there, too, with Leena and their kids. Honestly, I'm surprised they never left Svalbard, Thomas especially. We chose this life, but Thomas and Kathe were born into it. Maybe they stayed because they'd already put down roots here or maybe because we have the illusion of safety up here at the top of the world, while wildfires and earthquakes, mudslides caused by deforestation and rising tide lines ravage the globe.

Whatever the reason, I'm glad they stayed; I got to see my grandchildren. On the day of the party, they all ran around on the shore together, chasing the black-legged kittiwakes and the long-tailed skua. Even Dani, who's almost thirteen now, too old for playing and entering that awkward stage of being caught between everything.

Kathe came to talk to me when things quieted down and the mood turned somber. We all looked up and remembered the space elevator was still going non-stop, bringing people and supplies up to the station and then to the *Arber*, all those eager and heartbroken people, ready to start their future.

What will you do when we're all gone, Dad? Kathe asked. We sat side by side, looking out at the ocean.

We'll get by, I told her. There will just be less of us. The Andersens are staying, and the Guptas. Raj is already planning a rotating dinner party. Everyone will take a turn hosting, and we'll keep each other company. Besides, things aren't too bad here, not like it is further south, and we still have the elevator and the station if things do get bad. In the meantime, I'll have my garden, and I have Predator X. Helen Holbrook is going to teach me how to make cheese if I help her milk her goats.

I tried to make it sound cheerful, like it would be a continuation of the party on the beach, but smaller. Kathe didn't look like she believed me. In truth, I knew there would be lonely days, but there would be days I relished my solitude, too. When you get to be my age, you surprise yourself by how often you're content to just sit and think.

We sat quietly for a bit then. It reminded me of when Kathe was little, before Thomas was born. In fact, it was when you were pregnant with Thomas. While you napped in the afternoons, I would bring Kathe to the beach to collect stones and look for fossils. She never shared our love of growing things, that one, though she was curious as hell. It was all about stillness with Kathe, the frozen remnants of the past. Funny, then, that she's the one going up into the stars, not me.

And Thomas, well . . . Maybe I should have tried harder to understand him and the things he loved, but with Kathe it was so much easier. She wore her heart on her sleeve, while Thomas was so closed and serious. He was never a little boy, not really. It was more like he was born a grown-up, and he was just waiting for his body to catch up with his mind.

We'll still talk, I told Kathe after a while, as long as the ship is in communication range. And after that, we'll have the ansible. Besides, it's not like I'll be alone, if you're worried about me.

I do worry, she said. That's a daughter's job.

When did you get old enough for that to be true? I asked, and that made her smile at last. It was good to see. Besides, I said, it's not like the world is really ending. Just changing, that's all.

I know, but there are some things I don't want to change, Kathe said, and right then she wasn't Head of Resource Management, Northern Division, she was just our little girl again, and it nearly broke my heart. You've been there for me my whole life, me and Tom both, and I don't know what I'll do without you.

I squeezed her hand, and we both blinked against more than just smoke from the bonfire.

You'll be fine, kiddo.

I was searching for something else to say, something inspirational and comforting, but Thomas came over and nudged the tip of Kathe's boot with his toe.

Can I talk to Dad for a minute? he said. Alone.

I can't remember the last time I heard Thomas call me *Dad*. I didn't think I would ever hear it again.

Kathe looked surprised, but she gave Thomas her spot and gave us our privacy.

I know Kathe has tried to talk you into taking a place on the ship about a hundred times. Thomas kept his hands in his pockets while he talked, his gaze on the horizon. I'm not going to rehash all that. I just wanted to let you know she's not the only one. I know we haven't always seen eye to eye, but you're my father.

I opened my mouth to say something or maybe just take a breath in surprise, but Thomas held up his hand to stop me.

Just let me finish. He looked down and didn't raise his head again.

When Mom died, it was the hardest thing I'd ever had to watch. I know, and Thomas held his hand up again, even though he didn't look at me. *I'm not here to open old wounds. I just wanted to say it was hard, but you were there for Mom, every day. Kathe and I were there, too. She had her family all around her. She didn't have to go through any of it alone. When your time comes, I just thought . . . I always thought we'd be there for you.*

He looked up finally. His eyes aren't like yours, or Kathe's. They're more like my mother's. I didn't know what to say to him, Mila. I've never known. He touched my shoulder, let his hand rest for a moment, then walked away.

I've been thinking about it since leaving the beach. Thomas deserves an explanation. And Kathe. Maybe you deserve an explanation, too.

We spent our lives building the future, saving all those plants and flowers in the vault, not to mention our own future with Kathe and Thomas. Now that the future's here, I'm terrified. Thomas was right, watching you die was the hardest thing I've ever had to do. I don't want that for our children, and I don't want that for myself.

Maybe a bit of it is selfish. A man gets to a certain age, and he wants to live his life on his own terms. I think I understand the choices you made now a little better than I used to. When the end comes, when my end comes, I want to go quick and painless, not hooked up to machines. I'll choose the time and place of my death, when I'm ready, and I want it to be here on Earth with you.

In space, even death will be different. Kathe explained it to me. There's a morgue on the generation ship that is also a chapel and a burial chamber and a cryo-storage unit. Aboard the *Arber*, people will have the option of being ejected into space, being recycled—protein and calcium and other vital elements broken down and reused in a variety of ways—or being stored until their remains can be buried on the same alien world where our new crops will grow. That's what death looks like in the next great age of humanity.

I understand that Thomas and Kathe want to be with me at the end, but this is the point where our roads diverge. You and me, we did what we could to build the future, Mila, but it isn't *for* us. Why should Kathe and Thomas bring grief with them among the stars when they can carry memories instead? I want them to remember me as I am now, not the way I might be one day down the road.

It's like we said all those years ago—sometimes you just have to live in the moment and enjoy what you have now, not hold on for one day and what's to come. I want to enjoy what's here while I can. We were the last generation who could have turned the tide. By the time Kathe and Thomas came along, it was too late to undo the mess we'd made. Climate change had already passed the tipping point, and whatever measures we put in place from then on out could only slow things down, not reverse them.

Perhaps it sounds egotistical, but I feel I owe it to the Earth to stay with her as long as I can. No one, not even a planet, should have to die alone.

August 16, 2200—Colorado

I'm going to cheat and talk about starlight, instead of the sun. Then again, the sun is a star, even if we usually don't think of it that way. The stars on this particular day are important to remember; it's the day we started saying goodbye.

We were vacationing in Buena Vista, staying at a resort built up around a hot spring. We went skinny-dipping in the springs on our last night, and even though it was high season, we had the place entirely to ourselves. You leaned back against the pool's edge, and said, *Well, I'm dying.* Just like that.

You'd been losing weight for a while, but I wanted to pretend it was just your appetite slowing down now that we were both past middle age. You'd already considered all your options, you told me, talked to all the doctors. You'd tried everything there was to try—radiation pills, alternative therapy, even the more aggressive forms of chemo like they had in the old days. Those weeks you told me you were visiting your sister? You were really puking your guts out, suffering, but you didn't want me to worry until you were really sure there was something to worry about.

The only thing left to try was gene therapy, and that was a bridge too far. It's fine for babies, you said, fetuses in the womb who don't know any better, but I know who I am and I wouldn't feel like myself anymore if I let them scrub me clean. It's my own body's cells betraying me. Maybe I just have to live with that. Besides, why go through all that trouble and expense when at my age, there's only a five percent chance of success? I want to enjoy as much of the time I have left as I can, not spend it hooked up to machines.

Then you reached into the backpack you'd carried out to the hot springs with us and pulled out a small terra cotta pot holding a Gibraltar Campion. It might have been from the very same seed batch as the one I grew for you all those years ago. Yours was barely a seedling though, growing crooked like it wouldn't survive a strong wind.

I never did have your knack for it, you said. You held out the pot to me and smiled that lopsided smile of yours. Sometimes you just have to live for the moment, right? Appreciate what you have and not worry about the future.

Damn you for throwing my words back at me. How dare you give up? How dare you throw everything away when we still had so much living to do? But I could only stare at you and the Campion.

You let a full minute of silence go by before you asked me if I was okay. If *I* was okay when you were the one dying. What could I say? All my words dried up in that moment. You took my hand. We sat in the hot spring, your fingers in mine under the water, and tears ran down my face. Later, we made love, and I was crying then, too. I think I cried more that night than I did at your funeral.

The sky was utterly clear. There's nothing like a skyscraper for miles in Buena Vista and next to no light pollution. On a night as clear as the one on which you told me you were dying, the sky was a bowl of blue so dark it passed into black and came out the other side.

That blue-dark bowl closed over the mountains, sealing us in, but everywhere we looked, there was light. I want to say the stars were bright, and they were, but they were so bright and there were so many of them, they looked fuzzy.

The stars between the stars were visible, and somehow it was different than looking at them from the top of the world, even though there isn't much light pollution in Svalbard either. The stars seemed farther away. They seemed alive, like the whole of the dark was crawling with silver. I could almost see the arm of the Milky Way unfurling around us. It was enough to make me dizzy. Or maybe that was the hot water from the spring. Or the thought of letting you go.

Right before we fell asleep that night, you lay spooned against my back. I held your hands, your arms pulled all the way around me. I thought if I held on tight enough, maybe you wouldn't go. You leaned forward and whispered in my ear, *Take care of my flower for me, when I'm gone.*

I still have the damn thing, Mila. Or at least its descendant. It's sitting on my windowsill. Predator X hasn't knocked it over yet, not for lack of trying. I want that flower to be the last thing I see in this world. When I'm too old and frail to walk around anymore, I'll keep it by my bedside. It's a little piece of you, so when I die, I won't be doing it alone.

June 24, 2232—Svalbard

Linde and Ivan are taking the kids to get settled on the ship today. Kathe will join them just before launch. Thomas and Leena are already on board.

Before Linde and Ivan boarded, Ivan asked me if I was sure I hadn't changed my mind. I never expected him to be the one. I had to bite my tongue to keep from asking if Kathe had put him up to it, but there was genuine regret in his eyes. Linde shook my hand, firm and strong as always. Ivan hugged me. I couldn't ask for better children-in-law.

Sometimes I think of the dangers Kathe, Linde, Ivan, and even Thomas will face up there. What would you think of me, letting our children, their spouses, our grandchildren go off into the dark alone? Kathe, Linde, Ivan, Thomas, and Leena will likely never see an alien world, let alone set foot on one. It'll be their children, their children's children who will colonize the stars. If they make it that far.

I think of all the things that could go wrong—a critical failure in the engines; explosive decompression blowing them all out into space; a plague; failure of the ship-board crops and death by slow starvation. Those possibilities are next to none. Kathe gave me the figures, something like a 0.001% chance. Me being on board certainly wouldn't tip the balance one way or another. Still, it's a parent's job to worry.

This is what the sun looked like on the day my grandchildren climbed aboard the space elevator and we all said goodbye.

The ocean was a sullen color, like pewter, but with a shine. Maybe tarnished silver would be a better comparison, the surface dull but with a brightness hidden underneath. The sun had a pinkish tint to it. Pink is normally a warm color, but this pink was cold. Like the inside of a shell fresh out of the sea or a thin sliver of pickled ginger. Like skin, when all the warmth of blood and a beating heart has gone out of it and it's just a container, no longer full.

There were clouds, a very few of them, scattered across the sky. The kittiwakes and skua glided on the wing, and every now and then one of them would let out a cry.

Ella, that's Kathe and Linde and Ivan's youngest, cried when she hugged me. She put her arms around my waist, and pressed her face into my stomach. I think she's too young to really understand the nature of this goodbye, but she could read the mood. Ryan, he's the middle child, promised to video call every day as long as they were in range. Dani, the eldest, didn't seem to know what to say. They shook my hand like Linde had, very formal, and that was the end.

I watched the elevator as far as I could. After a while the sun shifted to a white-yellow, cold, pure. The color of goodbye.

June 26, 2176—Luang Prabang

There's nothing particularly special about this day, no reason it deserves to be memorialized, but life isn't all about the big moments. In fact, life is mostly what happens in-between, and the sun shines on those days, too. That's what this catalogue is intended to capture, after all.

I remember the day because it's the day I stopped thinking about the future as an abstract. For as long as we'd known each other, we'd been working toward *the future*, cataloging and protecting and gathering seeds in the vault at Svalbard. But that future was a nebulous concept. It was for someone else, not us. That day, I started thinking about the future as a personal concept, like maybe one day we'd have a family, and they would make everything we were trying to do to make the world a better place—even in small ways—worthwhile.

We were about 60 miles outside of Luang Prabang on that day, hiking. I don't remember the names of all the villages we passed through, but we started at the temple at Mt. Phoushi, overlooking the Mekong River.

We were there to pick up three new and heartier strains of *Oryza sativa*—rice, in layman's terms. They could have been shipped to the vault, but you convinced the director to let us act as couriers. We changed each other over the years, Mila. When we first met, you would quote rules and regulations and procedure for hours on end. I like to think I taught you to appreciate the spirit of the law, as much as the letter of it. It's like the way my concept of the future changed. I'd like to think I helped you see that we weren't just protecting plants as a nebulous concept; we were protecting living things you could touch and hold in your hand and appreciate for more than just their potential.

And you taught me to see a wider world. Before I met you, I never thought much beyond the present moment. You expanded everything. I loved you more than I loved myself, and that made my world so much larger than it had ever been before. You taught me that the future is worth protecting, even the parts I won't live to see. You taught me to have hope.

We did some touristy things in Luang Prabang—the temple, the Royal Palace, the Night Market—but it's the hike I remember the most. Our guides took us in a boat across the Nam Xuang. I think there were about ten of us, total. Tourism was on the decline already in those days. We hiked for maybe five or six hours, past rice paddies and through jungles. We stopped in a little village where we watched children play soccer.

And that was where it hit me, the idea of having a personal stake in the future. We hadn't even talked about kids yet, but I found myself wondering what our family would be like. Not if we would have one; it suddenly seemed like a given. We were so in love, how could that love help but spill over and spread outward and keep on multiplying itself?

I wondered if our kids would be happy. If they'd play soccer, running around with pure, unfettered joy. I wondered if they would grow up to have kids of their own.

When Kathe was born, I worried about so many things. I wanted to do everything to protect her. You were the one who finally got me to relax, to let go a little. She would be her own person; we'd given her everything she needed to get a good start in life. And you were right, Mila. We raised some good kids. Or, really, they grew into good people, and we managed to not fuck it up by getting in their way.

After that first village, we hiked to another village where all the houses were on stilts, and they gave us strong rice wine to sample. At our last stop, the villagers had set out a dinner to share with the hikers and our guides on a long wooden table in a barn. Before we ate, we watched the sun go down. It was less a sunset and more a sense of the light being swallowed by the mist, diffusing and turning the sky the color of a new peach, sliced thin and still holding the warmth of the day—sweet and melting and bright on the tongue.

What I remember most is the way the light caught in a curl of your hair, just before the sun vanished. It reminded me of our wedding day, except instead of flyaway strands, the hair stuck in the sweat on the back of your neck. It was like you'd found a way to braid the sunlight and make it a part of you.

I know that sounds incredibly sappy, but it's true. Or, at least, I've built it into truth over the years. That's what people left alone with their thoughts and their grey kittens named after prehistoric animals do. They invent narratives to make sense of their lives and to fix the pattern of those lives more firmly in their minds. Even if that isn't the way the sunlight looked on that particular day, that is how I choose to remember it. That is the image I'm sending out among the stars.

June 30, 2232—Svalbard

Today was the last day, or the first day, depending on how you look at it. The *Arber* has officially set sail, or whatever word one uses for the departure of a ship the size of a city without masts or cloth or anything resembling a sail.

This is the first day of the new age of humanity.

Our children's children's children, will they even be human anymore? Born in space, living all those years on a ship under sunlamps and breathing recycled air. Will they still call themselves human when they land on a new world and make it their own?

I don't have any answers. How can I speak to the big questions of life when the small ones still elude me? How do you love someone and let them go? How can someone be a stranger and still be your own flesh and blood? How can you feel closer to someone who isn't even on Earth any more than you ever did when they were right there beside you?

Indulge me for a moment, Mila. I know you always hoped my relationship with Thomas would be more like my relationship with Kathe. The truth is, there was always a rift between us. Maybe we both sensed it, and so we kept our distance. Or maybe it was just a failure on both of our parts to try.

When you died, the rift widened, and everything came crashing down. Thomas blamed me. He told me in no uncertain terms that I should have *forced* you to undergo gene therapy. As if your body, and the decisions you made regarding it, were any business of mine. I told him over and over again it wasn't what you wanted. You'd considered and discarded that option.

There were days I agreed with him though, and that hurt the most. I lashed out at him, when I really wanted to lash out at you. At the end, when you were delirious, I couldn't help thinking—could I have done more? *Could I have forced you?* In the end, I respected your wishes. In the end, I sat by and watched you die.

I know, there are no guarantees that the gene therapy would have worked. It might have led to more suffering. But I can't help wondering . . . You dedicated your life to the vault and to Svalbard, to cheating nature by finding stronger, heartier crops to withstand droughts and monsoons. You were determined to do everything you could to give them more than a fair and fighting chance to survive. Why wouldn't you take that road yourself?

I didn't understand at the time. I think I'm closer to understanding now. At my age, death is no longer a nebulous concept far away. I've thought about it and what I do and do not want it to be. I don't want to be hooked up to machines on a space ship fighting for a few more hours or months or years. I don't want to be stuck in a cold-freeze drawer just so my distant descendants can put flowers on my grave under an alien sun. It's *my* death; I want to own it. Death is the last thing we do as human beings, so I'm damned well going to do it on my own terms.

Does that make sense, Mila? That I can blame you and hate that you left me and still send our children off into space and insist on staying behind? I suppose we're all a bundle of contradictions in the end. Maybe that's what ultimately what makes us human. No matter what other changes or adaptations occur, that will survive.

Kathe came and sat on the porch with me before boarding the last elevator to the station. We sipped strong black coffee. She held my hand. We didn't speak. In the end, at *the* end, we sat and watched the skua and the kittiwakes. We watched the sun play on the water. Then she kissed my cheek and that was goodbye.

I watched the sky for a long time after she left. I imagined if I shaded my eyes just right, I would be able to see something as the *Arber* set sail. I would know, or feel it deep in my bones. But there wasn't anything to see.

No, that isn't quite true. There was the sun. On the last day, on the first day, the sun was bright and clean and it threw a halo around itself, a celebration or one last goodbye, although it was only those who were staying behind who would ever see. The light on the last day of the world was every color the sun could be, all the colors it won't be in space.

I read once that every person who sees a halo around the sun or the moon sees their own individual halo. Even two people standing right next to each other wouldn't see exactly the same thing. The light breaks through different atmospheric crystals for each of them, no two beams fracturing in quite the same way. Every halo is unique.

I suppose that's all there is. I'm sending this out into the stars to travel to new worlds, so new generations will be able to look back to know how the sun looked on a particular day back where their parents' parents' parents came from. So they'll know how the sun looked to one specific person as it bounced off the water or rested against the skin of someone he loved or slipped beneath the rim of the world.

Now, I'm going to make myself another cup of coffee and sit out on the porch a little while longer. Maybe I can even coax Predator X onto my lap. I may be alone, but I'm not lonely. I have everything I need. You're buried here, and from the moment I met you, I've never known how to be anywhere else but with you. The future is out there among the stars, but I'm where I belong. I'm home.

Karin Lowachee was born in South America, grew up in Canada, and worked in the Arctic. Her first novel, *Warchild*, won the 2001 Warner Aspect First Novel Contest. Her third novel, *Cagebird*, won the Prix Aurora Award in 2006 for Best Long-Form Work in English and the Spectrum Award also that year. Her books have been translated into French, Hebrew, and Japanese, and her short stories have appeared in anthologies edited by Nalo Hopkinson, John Joseph Adams, Jonathan Strahan, and Ann VanderMeer. Her fantasy novel, *The Gaslight Dogs*, was published through Orbit Books USA.

MERIDIAN

Karin Lowachee

They all tried to save me.

"I think this one's still alive."
"Tag him."

In that space between life and death, you make a decision whether to wake up. Maybe that's when time ceases to matter. I felt older than four years old and too young to remember. My world was telling me not to remember how the strange crew and its dead-eyed captain came to our far-away colony and nothing was the same again.

I might've fought, giving them a reason to shoot me.

Or maybe there was no reason at all.

A long time later, after I was better, I heard them. Other people. Not the same bad crew. Speaking outside the door of the medical room where they kept me. It was a family ship, and they talked about dropping me at the nearest station, but—

"He'll just cycle through the system, and how will that help?"

"Well, what do you wanna do with him?"

"Maybe we can just keep him here."

"We don't even know his name. He won't talk to us. In the system, they'd be able to find out. They'd have the colony manifest. DNA records."

DNA. In school, they ran a test for fun to find out where on Earth I was from and what kind of people I belonged to, people who had lived long ago on a far-away planet. East Asian: 61%. Spanish European: 22%. Anglo-Saxon: 17%. I coloured a map of Earth, highlighting the places those people had come from and took it home to show my parents and brothers. We had things in common that spoke of our heritage: dark eyes that tilted at the corners; dark hair.

"I don't want to give him to the system," this woman said.

"Now we're kidnappers?" said the man.

"We weren't the ones who attacked his colony."

"No, we just swept in like those pirates right after."

"You're being ridiculous. We legitimately found him. Only him. Look at him. It was the *pirates* who did it. You want to hand him over to EHHRO?"

"He might still have family outside of the Meridia colony. We don't have the right."

"Where's EarthHub now? What're their human rights organizations doing when their colonies are being attacked?"

"Look—we'll hand him over. If no other family speaks up, we'll apply to foster him. Eventually adopt him if it comes to that. They'll want to get him out of their hands so it shouldn't be too hard. That way no authorities will get on our ass."

"Your name's Paris, do you remember?"

I remembered. But a part of me didn't want to.

This new lady at the station said my last name was Azarcon. They'd gotten my DNA and matched it to the records. Paris Azarcon. I remembered my two older brothers. It hurt right where I'd been shot. Right through my body.

Mama and Daddy. They were shot first. In their heads.

So much screaming.

My brother, Cairo, stood in front of me, trying to protect me, but it didn't make a difference.

"Paris?"

I didn't want to remember anymore. I ran to a corner.

Days like this. Back and forth. Do you remember anything else? They all wanted me to remember until I screamed at them to stop it.

Then they said they were going to send me away from the station. That someone wanted me. It didn't matter. I didn't care anymore.

"Your name's Paris, and this family is going to take you to their ship to live. They found you and they care about you. We'll check in a little later, okay? But you can go with them now."

"How old are you now?"
     I held up my hand, fingers spread.
     "Five years old. That's good. Do you know your name?"
     "Paris."
     "How about your last name?"
     I didn't want to say it.
     These people weren't my family, even though they said they were now.
     I thought of the map of Earth that I'd coloured. A planet I'd never been to. It was nothing like Meridia and its rocky ground, where Daddy and Mama and my oldest brother, Bern, worked at the mines.
     "It's going to be Rahamon," the lady said. She called herself Captain Kahta. "That's your last name," she said. "Look here on this ID tag. You always wear this around your neck, okay? Paris Rahamon. The newest crew member of *Chateaumargot.*"

Everything was muddy in my mind for a long time. I only knew what the captain and her mister said about how they'd caught a signal from a moon. They found me shot in the back outside my home, but I was still breathing. When they said those things, it was like they were telling me a story from a slate, one that someone else made up, except I didn't have pictures to go with it. Maybe there was a drawn image of what my colony looked like, but I didn't see it, couldn't remember, and nobody let me look it up. The captain and her mister took me to a station and got me help. After a while, when I was fixed, they came back to get me and the station let me go. They said I had a new life now and it was good. Nobody would make me go back to the other life anymore.
     I didn't want to talk about my real family anyway.
     I didn't want to talk about the things I remembered before they were all gone. Everything was going to fade. For a while, after first waking up, I barely remembered anything. Then it started to come back and that was worse.
     Back and forth. Remembering and forgetting. Remembering.

They wanted me to like *Chateaumargot.* They bought me toys and clothes, and at first I didn't have to work. Their teenaged daughter looked after me when the captain or her mister weren't around. Sanja played with me and took me around the ship to show me the garden and the games and the gym. Captain Kahta saw me when she finished work, and Mister Chandar cooked for me or showed me how to build models of ships and stations, though he said I would have to grow older before I did other stuff. He probably meant *work*.

For a few months aboard the ship, life was like that and I forgot most days after they passed. Captain Kahta said that was okay. They seemed happy having me, even though I didn't talk much and hardly ever felt like playing games with them. They stopped trying to force me to play games when I took their toys and threw them against the wall. For a few days all I did was break the things they gave me, so then they gave up.

On my first birthday with them, I hit Sanja in the eye and she screamed. I didn't mean to give her a black eye but she'd forced me to sit and do math. I hated math. It was frustrating and she kept pushing. I told her she wasn't my mom so she needed to stop. She said Captain Kahta wanted me to learn math, and I said Captain Kahta wasn't my mom either. Sanja got this look in her eyes like she was mad even though it was true, and she put the slate back in front of me and told me to stop being a brat and do my work. So I punched her face.

Mister Chandar locked me in my cabin alone. My stomach was growly by the time Captain Kahta came in. She sat on my bed next to me.

"Paris, why did you hit Sanja?"

I stared at my hands.

"Paris?"

"I don't know."

"I think you do. Sanja says you don't want to do the math work."

I shrugged. What did it matter?

"Paris. Look at me."

I looked at Captain Kahta. Her dark eyes looked sad. For me. The dot on her forehead seemed to judge me. The people on the station had looked like that too, from what I remembered. I wished they would stop.

"Paris, you can't go around hitting your sister."

"She's not my sister!"

Captain Kahta leaned back as if I'd hit her in the face too.

"She's not my sister and you're not my mom!"

"Okay, okay."

"I don't care about math!"

"Paris, sit down."

I started to run around the cabin. She couldn't stop me. Not until she grabbed me around the waist and held me down on the bed. I kicked and screamed at her. Mister Chandar came in and held me down too. They said things to each other, but I wasn't listening. Sanja came in with an injet and pressed it to my arm.

Everything slowed down. Even me.

The ship was big. Tall, cold corridors, all white and grey. There were lots of adults but some kids too, older than Sanja or younger, like me. Every sixth day a vid screened in rec and we got extra treats than what was usually available from the galley. Sometimes I stayed and watched the vid, but sometimes they bored me and I snuck out in the dark.

I wandered around the ship when I wasn't supposed to, but I didn't like being minded all the time. Sanja handed me off to the other older kids sometimes and none of them liked it when I acted up. Sometimes I didn't mean to act up, but everything grew frustrating. All of these rules about where I wasn't supposed to go, and checkups in medical, and toys I was supposed to be interested in, and food I was supposed to eat. These faces weren't the faces from my storybook memory. When I had nightmares, nobody came to save me.

Sometimes I remembered riding on the back of a four wheeler, holding an older boy around the waist. He'd tell me, "Don't fall off, Puppy!" My brother Cairo. But I couldn't remember his face anymore.

I had a lot of nightmares. The lady on the station said to record them when I woke up and send them to her, but I didn't like to put words to them, so most of the time I didn't. Mister Chandar or Captain Kahta was supposed to talk to me about them and help me record them, but after the first six months they stopped. I guessed they got busy. The ship travelled a lot and I didn't check in all the time with the lady on the station. I didn't ask Captain Kahta about it. If I didn't need to do these things anymore, then maybe that meant I was okay. Or they didn't care. I didn't think they had to care since they weren't my family.

My brothers Cairo and Bern. And Mama and Daddy. Now every time I thought the word "family," I also thought of the word "dead."

I turned seven on *Chateaumargot*. Captain Kahta and Mister Chandar threw a party. All the kids came, even the ones who called me weird and talked behind my back. Sanja tried to put a cardboard hat on my head. I knocked it away. After that, nobody was happy. They weren't happy with me and the ice cream melted all over my cake. I felt a little bad so I was nice for the rest of the party and even hugged Captain Kahta afterward so she would smile. She hugged me back real tight.

"Are you happy, Paris?"

I didn't really know what she meant by being happy, like maybe if I liked my cake and the presents. The games and new clothes.

"Yeah. Everything's good."

She touched my hair and smiled, like she knew I was lying.

The other kids on *Chateaumargot* didn't stay nice. But neither did I. I got into fights a lot until every week Mister Chandar locked me in my quarters. I sent some of the kids to medical and sometimes I went to medical. Bruises and cuts and a couple black eyes shared amongst us. Then one shift when we'd docked at a station, Captain Kahta came to get me after breakfast and took me by the hand. She walked me to my quarters and told me to pack some of my favourite things. My clothes and whatever toys I liked.

"Why?"

"I'll help you, honey."

"Help me with what?"

She cried and held me, so I couldn't do anything but stand there and let her be. Everything felt dark and silent, like someone had covered my ears and eyes.

She and Mister Chandar took me off the ship, and we went down the dock to another ship's airlock. That ship let us inside the airlock but not quite inside the ship. We met another woman. She introduced herself as Madame Leung. She was shorter than Captain Kahta and had dark eyes like me. Madame Leung took me by the shoulders and smiled.

"You look just like your picture, Paris."

What picture? Captain Kahta crouched down in front of me and told me to go and live with Madame Leung now.

"Why? Why?"

Captain Kahta's eyes were shining, and she just shook her head. "You'll be better here with Madame Leung," was all she said. Then she straightened up, and they said things to each other in a language that I didn't know. Mister Chandar squeezed my shoulder and then they left the airlock.

They left me on this new ship and I couldn't do anything about it.

So I screamed.

Madame Leung dragged me to quarters inside her ship. Another woman joined her to wrangle me. They locked me in, and through the intercom she said, "I'll come back when you're done."

That was it. No matter how much noise I made, nobody came.

Madame Leung told me everything. Captain Kahta and Mister Chandar didn't feel they could provide me with the best, they didn't know how to handle me, and they feared for the other children on board because of the fights I got into.

The idea of saving me wasn't as good as the reality.

"You're getting worse," Madame Leung said. "That won't happen here."

Captain Kahta wouldn't take me back to the station from long ago, and the lady who had given me away in the first place didn't ask.

"We're busy ships!" said Madame Leung. "Who wants to go all the way back to a station to deal with that shit?"

It was easier, out here in deep space, to hand me to another family ship like Madame Leung's. Her ship, *Dragon Empress,* transported medical drugs to far-flung stations and colonies in need. But Madame Leung and her crew weren't a part of EarthHub's humanitarian organizations.

"We're not pirates," she said. "I don't attack places and murder people. We just provide a service."

"Why do you want me?"

She crouched down in front of me. I was sitting on the bunk. The quarters were smaller than what I'd had on *Chateaumargot.* The lights were narrow pricks in the ceiling, like sunrays through bullet holes.

"I like kids, Paris. Kids grow up to be good soldiers. Like my boys. I have a lot of boys here as it is, they know their work. You'll do great with them, you'll see."

Madame Leung said they were going to get my records purged. It would be easy since so many records of so many kids were all over the place, and with the right amount of money, people did anything you wanted. That way nobody would come looking for me.

Nobody was left to come looking for me anyway. When Madame Leung smiled at me, it was like she knew it too.

As far as Madame Leung was concerned, I was a Dragon. No longer a Rahamon, and definitely not an Azarcon. She never asked about my actual family or where I came from. I doubt she would've cared if Captain Kahta had offered the information. Captain Kahta, who trunked me off as someone else's responsibility, likely hadn't explained much about my origins.

I was physically healthy and mentally able to handle complex tasks. Madame Leung made me one of her boys and that was that. One in a crew of four hundred men and boys who followed her lead. The drug queen of the Dragons, the *Dragon Empress*. Deep space depended on her, she said, to cure it of its ills.

She didn't mean the war or the aliens or the pirates. If you couldn't change anything, you could at least anesthetize.

I dreamed of my family. My parents' faces, their presence, blurred out from my memory like a vid not quite calibrated right. But my brothers, my protectors, they remained vivid.

I didn't believe in guardian angels because seeing them only in my mind's eye was more like hell.

Over the years under Madame Leung's tutelage and the hammering of her "boys" to make me into her version of a good soldier, one who kept his mouth shut and evaded authorities on station, the memories trickled back. Like the first bits of dust that were the only evidence of an exploded star, the further I went into deep space with the *Empress*, the closer I came to my own past.

Maybe it was because of these adopted "brothers," foisted on me, equipped with powers of loving persecution. Unlike the kids on *Chateaumargot*, Madame Leung's gang accepted me with a rough sort of respect. The lady herself handpicked me, and though they didn't spare me when she disciplined my rebellious nature, they offered security and freedom at the same time.

I carried a gun. I learned the trade of drug trafficking, of clandestine meetings on stations and in half-forgotten refugee colonies. Some of our clients were even EarthHub soldiers, more wary-eyed than we were but equally invested in the market. Some used our pharmaceuticals for their intended purposes, others didn't. As long as they paid us, it was none of our business.

Adolescence passed in a haze of tattoos, training, and tradecraft. The colourful ink emblazoned on my arms and back were needle tapped in the ancient way, not with a gun. I marked my years by the images that flowered across my skin: a tiger, an Earth mountainscape, a constellation of stars, and of course, the elaborate golden dragon winding its way down my spine. Sometimes, at the height of my pain, when I lay across the *horishi*'s table, I heard my brothers' voices, their ghosts whispered back in those moments.

Pain begat pain. What was the antidote for it? I'd been closest to Cairo. My oldest brother Bern held a more distant place, a peripheral shadow in the shape of our father. He'd fought back too, and the laser bolt slammed between his eyes.

Cairo's voice surfaced with each needle puncturing into the shallow points beneath my skin.

He said, "*Run*, Puppy!"

His nickname for me. Because I was the baby.

Once, in the middle of the tattooing, I shoved at the pain. At the *horishi*. Blood scored across my skin, ruining the line she'd been drawing. I made her start on a new image. I'd seen it in the ship's educational files while voraciously reading about an ancient civilization from a country I'd never seen.

I told her to ink an Egyptian ankh over my heart, and she didn't ask.

Age was a meaningless thing in space, especially on a ship. Maybe I was some form of adult, chronologically in my twenties. But to look in the mirror was a different story altogether, with pictures that didn't match up. Still a teenager to outside eyes. My own face reminded me of the ones who swam back to me in the dark, in sleep, in blissed out moments with occasional drugs in my system. We all took part, never to excess, but skating that line was a part of this world.

My third world. One was my heart, the second was my armour, and the third was my artillery. Two of those things protected the other.

I hung out with a boy named Soochan. He was a little more gentle than the other boys, probably because he was addicted to sweet leaf. He tended to smile, even when shit was going down around him, a beatific expression like a saint in the throes of religious epiphany. Once when a buyer tried to shaft us, Soochan was almost sorry. He made her face the wall of the station tunnel where we'd been doing the deal; his voice was so soft. "Just close your eyes, baby, and this won't hurt a bit." He whipped her once with his gun and kicked her a few times, then stole what he could off her body—an old platinum ring, her data dots. "Madame Leung don't like stiffers," he said. Still smiling.

On this ride between deals, the ship's drives hummed like a hive of bees all around us. Soochan sprawled on my bunk, blowing smoke rings to the ceiling between slurred rambles. I tried to read, but the words upended and crawled over one another like roaches running from the light. Nothing made sense. Maybe it was the drugs, but the nightmares had been plentiful lately, taking my concentration into the dark.

In the middle of Soochan's words, he said, ". . . Azarcon . . ."

My lulled focus sharpened like a shiv. From my seat on the deck with my legs outstretched, slate in hand, I said, "What?"

"What?" he echoed back, the corner of his mouth tilting upward as if giving coordinates to his eyes. Clouded by smoke and whatever wandering thoughts he let off the leash.

"You said something. A name."

"Uh—"

"Azarcon?" My name. My first world. Of course, he didn't know.

"Don't you read? Your head's in that slate so damn much." His hand flit, making the smoke from his sweet leaf cigret carve the air. "Captain Cairo Azarcon. EarthHub's latest bulldog of deep space."

I thought I was done collecting worlds. I thought Madame Leung had tied me to hers for the rest of my living days, one of her soldiers, one of her boys, all of the security and sanctimonious criminality of a group of people with no loyalty but to their own. Who needed more?

But this fourth world crashed into me and sheered to the side the next moment, casting me against my own armour.

"Captain Cairo Azarcon," I said, like an invocation of the devil.

My brother lived.

When Captain Kahta had found me, had there been no others? Hadn't she seen Cairo? Or had the pirates who had taken our colony also taken the one member of my family who'd lived and left nothing but the dead and thought-dead for the *Chateaumargot* to find.

There was nobody to ask.

I went on a treasure hunt around the Send. I excavated and saved every possible mention, note, and passing criticism lobbed toward my resurrected older brother. I became an Azarconologist, twice divorced from the name but like any spouse rendered obsolete by a new mate, I looked back with judgment. On myself if not on the one who'd left me.

I wanted to judge. I found shoddy pictures of a handsome man attached to reports of bravery and ruthless alien strit killing. He tended to avoid cams, so the only people who had a clear picture of him also had access to his military records or his daily life. But there was enough to see a resemblance. Dark eyes and dark hair. Tall. The kind of carriage in the spine that would rarely bend for anybody. He was the young scourge of aliens everywhere. He made his name as a fighter pilot but now commanded the spacecarrier *Macedon*. Specific corners of the Send said he was one to watch, like they were talking about a celebrity. The deep space war made military heroes.

My corner of the galaxy didn't bow down to heroes. I didn't care about the war.

He was a new father. Captain Cairo Azarcon was married and had a son.

I was an uncle.

What did blood mean?

I wanted to hate him. Didn't he look for me? Couldn't he have found me? In the entire galaxy, why didn't his honed military skills somehow raze the stars for his little brother? Who told him I was dead, and why did he believe them? Why didn't he refuse to stop looking until he had tangible proof of my death?

Neither of us were children now, and maybe, with so many years behind him, my brother also preferred to forget.

At Basquenal Rimstation 19, I met a woman at the bar and shacked up with her in a private den. After sex, she told me she was an investigative journalist and she'd been looking into my ship. She said this while smoking a cigret in my face. I was uniformly unsurprised. For some reason, when you had sex with a stranger, anything they said just seemed to go along.

"You think my ship's a pirate? Because it isn't. It's not interesting enough to be a pirate."

"No," she said. She'd only told me her first name: Mabel. Her hair was long and silver but her face was young. Maybe from suspended aging treatments, so there was no telling her real age. Not that it mattered. "No," she repeated. "Not a pirate, but they do recruit in unconventional ways."

"Yeah?" I took the cigret from her and dragged. I could tell she was trying to read my eyes, but I'd been told enough times that I was "stoic," that my stare walled people off and forced them to lay siege. So I watched her building a siege tower word by word.

"I found a node on the Send. Where the children are traded."

She squinted at me as if this was supposed to mean something. When she didn't get anything, she pressed on.

"They disguise it, of course. It looks like a parenting node where people are just talking about their kids. Getting advice. Arranging meetups at various stations. But there're codewords. Pictures and codewords. These people know what to look for and how to ask for it."

"Why are you telling me this? You want me to spy for your story?"

"No—but Paris, your name was there." She glanced at my tags.

"My name Paris? Lots of kids are named Paris." But my stomach began to form an ice rock, deep in the centre.

"Isn't your last name Rahamon?"

I hadn't told her that. It wasn't something you told to someone you just shacked with. And maybe she could read my eyes after all.

My last name wasn't Rahamon. I was reminded every time I heard it.

She said, "I recognized your first name and your face. Your picture had been posted. You were a little boy but the resemblance is obvious." She climbed off the bed and went to her clothes, which were strewn on the floor in our haste to get together. Her body was flawless in a way that probably spoke of enhancements, but I hadn't really noticed in the act. Now, as she leaned down to fish something out of her jacket pocket, I just wanted to get away.

But I couldn't seem to move from the bed. This room. Or out of my own skin. She returned, sliding back beside me with a slate in her hand. She brushed at it, and soon lines of text and an image popped up.

A photo of me. As a child. I knew my own face like you did a vague stranger. Difficult to place but not forgotten.

I looked away before I allowed myself to read the words beside the image. The cigret burned between my fingers, so I pulled on it some more.

"Bright, enthusiastic, inquisitive boy," she read. It was obvious that she was reading from the text, not making up the words. "Energetic and requires a lot of attention and compassion. He's had a rough history, but he's sweet and capable of loving. A family without any other children would do well."

"Stop."

"They write these posts like they're advertising for pet swaps."

"I said stop it."

I climbed off the bed, flicked the cigret into the trash, and grabbed my clothes. "I was legitimately adopted. I don't know what the hell you're looking at."

"Adopted by the *Dragon Empress?*"

No. And we both knew it.

I didn't reply. Once I got my boots on, I grabbed my gun off the table and left her in the den.

All of my worlds were colliding.

Mabel found me at the bar, four drinks deep. Soochan was there, drunk and high too. "Heeey Mama," he kept saying. Several of my other brothers from the *Empress* danced haphazardly to the music funneling in the centre of the floor.

"Paris," Mabel said, glancing at Soochan.

"Heeey Mama. Heeey Parchisi, she want your comm code?"

We ignored him. I wondered what either of them would do if they knew my real origin.

What should I be doing?

Everywhere I went now, I thought of my brother. Swapping drugs for cred or weapons, it was Cairo. Drinking myself into a stupor, it was Cairo. Fucking a woman, it was Cairo.

The ankh on my chest that I saw every day. What had possessed me to wear that reminder? My body was now a walking séance ritual, begging the ghosts to follow. To answer back, letter by letter, yes or no. I invited them now to shake my seating and short-circuit my tech. To stand behind me in the dark when I wandered the corners of the ship.

My brother was a ghost. The kind who made marks on the living.

"Please," Mabel said. "We need to talk."

How many kids were outside the system, like me? How many had been put into the system only to be torn out like a splinter? Children that couldn't be handled so they were hijacked. Especially refugee kids, Mabel said. Good ships with good intentions found themselves over their heads and no longer wanted to deal with the kids.

It wasn't a bad life, I heard myself telling her, the two of us in a corner booth while the music kept winding up and falling down and everyone around us moved like mannequins of broken robotics.

"Do you remember when you were taken?" she asked.

Do you remember? That question refused to pick another path. It hunted me everywhere.

"What're you going to do," I said. "Put me back? That ship has flown— literally."

"I could find out if you have any family—"

"I don't." It came out of my mouth like every answer I'd given to anyone who asked. No family but the Dragon. No ship but the *Dragon*. No place but the Dragons. Deep space was our home. Mabel took it as stated and I carried on. "The captain of the *Chateaumargot* had checked. Or the case worker that I had—whoever. Social Services. I don't even remember the name of the first station they'd put me at. They purged the records anyway."

Mabel frowned. "The station?"

"Yeah."

"Why?"

I gave her a flat stare then let her track my gaze to Soochan, still sitting at the bar mouthing off to the air.

"We're not pirates but we're not saints."

What if, I thought. What if I gave this journalist my real world name?

Soochan suddenly appeared at my shoulder, leaning over the table. "Leh we go, Parchisi."

"Be there in a second." I pushed his hand away as it coursed through my hair. Big brother, except he wasn't. He wandered off to hook up with our other brothers, now headed off the dance floor.

I had this information locked inside my chest. If I let it out, what other explosion would it cause? Would that birth yet another world, one that I couldn't predict or control? Another situation I couldn't defend myself against?

No one could know.

To Mabel: "Can you do me a favour?"

Her eyebrows arched.

"Whatever you need for your story, I'll tell you. As a source. No names, on your word."

She nodded. "Anonymous. I promise."

"Because you know what I'll do if you break our deal."

She'd seen the gun. More importantly she'd seen the ink on my body and read the affiliation well enough.

"What's your question?" she said.

"Find out *Macedon*'s next port of call." I did, in the end, slip her my comm code. "And let me know ASAP."

Somehow she came through. The message on my system said simply: *Austro Station*. And gave a date.

It wasn't difficult to go to Austro Station, despite what we did for a living. Austro was a main hub even for us, with its rampant underdeck activity and illicit commerce. I didn't have to mention a thing to Madame Leung, beyond the usual conversation about scoring big there. We bought and sold drugs at Austro for the rich elite in the higher modules because exploitation was the true ecosystem of the galaxy.

The *Dragon Empress* docked at the station a day after *Macedon*. To the galaxy outside, we were basic trade merchants in harmless cargo like transsteel and mechanical goods. It was a different story for the boys Madame Leung sent off in other directions on deck. I was one of that crew.

Now I *had* to conjure my brother's face—in the delicate balance of stalking the dock where the carriers were moored, not going too close, but hovering outside the broad doors to catch every person that flowed back and forth. Casing the airlock directly was impossible in such a restricted area. Instead, I disappeared from my Dragon brothers in the hopes of seeing another. Hiding myself behind garish kiosks and aromatic food stalls. I felt like a pervert, but maybe that was fitting. A perverse turn in my life. As if the universe agreed, it made me wait and gave me ample opportunity to get the fuck out of there.

Of course I didn't.

I wanted to see him. I recognized his walk before anything else. In all the years, that detail hadn't changed. He was taller, and he tried to hide beneath a hoodie and civilian clothes, passing through the concourse toward the carrier docks. But I knew those shoulders and the gait of someone who knew where he was going. He didn't cover up out of fear, but from stealth.

I moved with him, slipping along the edges of the crowd between his path and mine. It took me a minute to notice the child.

A little boy. Maybe four or five, but who could tell? They held hands. The boy carried a stuffed bear wearing soft armour, its furry ears dragging on the deck.

I was that age once. Cairo held my hand like that.

It's me, I wanted to shout. As if those two words could make up for a decade or more as some humans reckoned time.

Come back.

It happened all at once; the little boy said something and Cairo leaned down to pick him up in his arms, barely breaking stride. Smaller arms went around broad shoulders. The bear dropped to the deck in their wake and Cairo kept walking, oblivious.

I saw the boy open his mouth to protest and then I was there. The crowd was no longer a wall. I hadn't made the conscious decision, but I found myself holding the stuffed toy, reaching to touch Cairo's arm.

He turned before I could tap him, sensing proximity maybe. Or his son's distress. The little boy twisted in his arms to keep his own eyes on the toy, reaching toward it. Toward me.

"He dropped this," I heard myself say.

My brother wasn't the only one covered up. My hood was pulled low, long sleeves covered all of my ink. Maybe he saw my mouth move but that was it. I stared somewhere at his chest and below. At the blue boots his son wore, dangling at his side.

The bear left my outstretched hands, plucked to safety.

"What do you say, Ryan?" A deep voice. But I knew that accent.

Meridian. Like mine. What it had been three worlds ago.

"Thank you," a small voice said.

"Welcome."

"Thank you," my brother said.

I just nodded.

They turned to go. He wasn't going to waste time on a stranger.

I looked up as they moved further into the concourse crowd, still headed toward the carriers. Cairo didn't turn around, but his son was looking over his shoulder, holding the armoured bear in his arms.

The boy had blue eyes. Not like mine. Not like his father's. Big, searching blue eyes that stared at me as if he knew. Ryan, Cairo had said. My nephew.

I didn't follow them. They walked away and I stayed where I was, the ghost they left behind.

Now all I do is remember.

My fourth world is the clearest. Sun bright and comet swift, all I can do is chase it. Maybe one day I'll be able to enter in again. Like it's a room left open for me. Like a voice offering a greeting, something as simple as hello. Maybe next time I'll look up and stare him straight in the eyes, dark eyes like mine, with just enough tilt at the corners to speak of our common ancestry. His son's gaze was a start, but it was only the edge of the solar system. There's more.

Soochan found me sitting on the deck outside of the carrier docks. He twitched, all nervous.

"Them Marines gonna sweep you away from their stoop, you can't stay here. Come back to the *Empress*."

He didn't ask why I was sitting there. Maybe he thought I was high.

I'm waiting for them to come back, I wanted to say. But of course I didn't. It wasn't the truth anyway. What would I say in that moment if they had?

I'm your brother, take me with you? Take my DNA and test it against yours. Check how far back we're connected. Tell me where you've been all this time, when time slipped so easily between the stars. What war are you fighting? Will you fight mine for a while?

Save me just this once.

Come back, my brother. Come back, Cairo. You're tattooed on my skin, beneath my heart, inside my blood. I tried to forget you, but nothing worked.

I want you to hear me say our family name. I'll only say it to you. No one else would understand what it means.

You were my first world.

Kathleen Ann Goonan is a writer, speaker, and recovering academic. She has published seven widely translated novels, including the first novel of her Nanotech Quartet, *Queen City Jazz* (a NYT Notable Book) in 1994 and *In War Times* (Tor, 2007), winner of the John W. Campbell Memorial Award and the American Library Association's Best Novel of the Year. Her novels have been shortlisted for the Clarke, BSFA, and Nebula Awards. She has published over fifty short works in markets such as *Discover Magazine, Asimov's, Omni, Appalachian Heritage, F&SF,* and many anthologies. Her latest academic publication was in *Sisters of Tomorrow* (edited by Lisa Yaszek and Patrick B. Sharpe, Wesleyan, 2016). She is working on two novels and a screenplay. She is a member of the Advisory Board of the School of Literature, Media, and Communication at Georgia Tech and is a member of X Prize's Lifeboat Foundation.

THE TALE OF THE ALCUBIERRE HORSE

Kathleen Ann Goonan

> Here stands a house all built of thought,
> And full to overflowing
> Of treasures and of precious things,
> Of secrets for my knowing.
> —Olive Beaupré Miller, *The Latch Key*

There is a theory that consciousness arises through self-organizing mass. This takes ages. Think of the thousands of years the oldest bristlecone pine grew, nearly five thousand, and it could grow older, if it had a chance, though it no longer has that chance. Except here. And maybe somewhere, but that is a mighty thin maybe.

Nevertheless, think of all the systems that went into growing that tree, all that time. What kind of entity can possibly understand time that long, except that bristlecone pine? And then, think of all the time we have been riding this horse. Who could understand that?

If anyone could, they would seem like magical creatures to us. That's why this is a fairy tale.

Time is a Kelvin–Helmholtz function. You know, like the clouds in Van Gogh's Starry Night. We surf the waves, the whorl, the crush of energies that cause time, that cause us. You may disagree with it, but that's our present theory. It seems that our particular neighborhood of time, which created us, is the only weather in which consciousness can survive. We are the products of a very fragile environment.

We are the magic beans Jill climbs the beanstalk to find.

We are life.

Pele, two days older than one hundred and five, waits in crowded Galaxies Bar on *Moku*, the Entertainment, Amusement and, much less importantly, R&D Exoplanetary Exploration Ship. Robotic and print construction commenced in 2030, when Pele was forty, during one of the rare confluences of available capital and passionate interest in space.

Pele's hands are folded in her lap in an attitude of calm, but she simmers, despite the faint scent of gardenia, the low tones of a flowing music specifically designed to generate a state of relaxed attention, and the zen landscaping. A tube of green tea floats unopened near her shoulder, its tether clipped to the table. Dr. Zi, Chief Safety Engineer, is late for this meeting, one that Pele requested and that the ship's scheduling algorithm arranged.

Lights are always low in Galaxies, unlike other bars on *Moku* designed for dancing or the roar of a hundred unheard conversations. As usual, it's two-thirds populated by tourists and crew. The Velcro floor is scattered with zabutons and low, gently glowing cylinders that serve as tables. A row of portholes affords a spectacular view of Mars rising as *Moku* slowly spins.

"Sorry I'm late, Dr. Hsu." Zi, in full quasi-military Chief Safety Engineer regalia, billed hat and all, drops onto a zabuton. Peering over his shoulder, he unbuttons his shirt pocket, removes his ever-present salad tube, takes a pull, and slips it back into his pocket, which he buttons.

Pele says, "I want to discuss last week's report, in which I raise serious issues. You didn't respond."

Zi is busy scanning the room. "Ah! There she is. Eleven o'clock." He waves, showing most of his teeth in a camera-ready smile that beams from his well-tanned, rugged face.

Stormy, a raven-haired reality star, threads her way around seated groups of people toward them, encased in a retro space suit that emphasizes her long legs and shapes her breasts into pointy weapons. The camera drones trailing her blink like synchronous fireflies, as required by law.

Pele shakes her head emphatically in Stormy's direction, uninterested in being dragged into the kind of propaganda puff pieces with which Zi is building his celebrity.

Stormy pivots as quickly as the Velcro on the two contact points of her very high heels allows and heads off at a right angle, trolling for the perfect feel-good space chat.

Zi frowns. "You just blew a perfect opportunity to communicate with the public."

"I communicate very well with the public, except when you bump my podcast, like you did yesterday." Pele, temporary liaison between the many factions on board, sees new fault lines daily, foresees minor disasters and deflects them before they emerge, furnishes solutions, and shares concerns in forceful, direct language with those on the ship and on Earth who need to know. She also drops a weekly public podcast, working hard to present this information gracefully, so as to avoid being characterized as an alarmist crank by the all-powerful entertainment industry.

"You need to re-slant it."

"I said exactly what I meant to say. The issues I raised concerning the Gifted Child Congress are urgent. There have been thirty-seven of these children on board for six weeks now, and I've sent you five related Concern Communiqués—each with two red exclamation points—thus far. Should I try using more?"

"So say something nice for a change. Your campaign against them failed."

"Just because everyone, including their parents, were snowed regarding the very real health risks—"

"We are completely protected by nanotech shielding."

"No meaningful sample for that conclusion, despite all the glossy advertising, but here they are, so we can gather information for more meaningful studies for the rest of their lives—and ours. However, my present concerns are about something different."

"I've read your CC's. They contain weird assertions. Rumors, in fact, that don't rise to the level of requiring a CC. Yes—these children are not normal—that's their strength! They're the superstars of the future. This is the third Congress in the past ten years. Wildly successful. Great publicity. They're bringing in billions of dollars. Flip your concerns, for Christ's sake. Valentina actually had a paper accepted by *Space Life Journal*, one she completed while here. She is amazing—ten years old! Grew up on the Argentinian pampas, on an estancia. Home-schooled. Discovered by a competition she entered. I was planning to steer the interview you just blew off in that direction."

Pele knows Valentina as Bean, as do the other children. "Valentina *is* amazing." She does not ask if Zi has read Valentina's startling paper. She does not want to embarrass him. "They all are amazing. That's part of my concern."

"Why concern? We need to talk them up."

"I talk about my job, which is to be a crank, if that's what you want to call it. An honest, vocal crank, and I am worried. Doesn't it matter at all that *Moku* is a disaster waiting to happen? In so many ways?"

"We've got backups galore."

Sometimes Pele cannot believe that he is a many-degreed engineer. But too ambitious; a young fifty-something on the make. So many luminaries have springboarded out of *Moku* that it's regarded as a pipeline to fame.

On the instant, Pele decides to have him removed. He is smart enough to understand that he is ignoring key issues not just at his own peril, but at the peril of others. He has put his own path to celebrity above his larger responsibilities, and has just definitively underlined his reckless stance.

She knows exactly who has bought his complacency. It is easy for her to make her face unreadable, but perhaps her doing so right now is the tell he's been looking for. Even now, after a lifetime of effort to gain fluency in the language of emotion-filled faces, she has not completely mastered the human tap-dance of mask and reveal that normal children easily absorb, despite her neuroplasticity infusions and cognitive therapies.

She does not wish to be normal. But aspects of normality would often be helpful.

Zi leans forward, sets both hands on the table, and links his fingers. His big smile makes jolly-looking crinkle lines at the corners of his eyes. She is sure he knows just how jolly they are. His voice warm and hearty, he says, "Hey, isn't children's literature one of your areas of expertise?"

This is a new tack. "Seventy years ago, it was. I'm not at all up-to-date, and wasn't then. Just books, written before 1965. But yes, it was a passion." Indeed, one of her rickety bridges to life. "And?"

"I recall a video of you speaking at an international conference after you received your first doctorate. You were a very passionate and effective communicator about how the brains of children on the autistic spectrum can be physically changed through engagement with literature. All the more impressive because—"

She smiles; nods. "I'm Asperger's. As are most of our visiting children. Part of my international cachet, I might add." Two can play at his game.

"Um, yes. Of course. We're all open books here, no pun intended. I'm just thinking you might help organize our vast children's library. It's a terrible jumble—all those files shot up here willy-nilly from all over the world. You can link these kids to it—"

Pele leans forward, laces together her own fingers, lights up her own wide, brown face with a warm, face-crinkling smile. "Great idea. That task might serve to distract me from effectively executing my responsibilities. Or maybe I should write another paper that bridges two fields of physics, and create a new field. The first was a hit. I won a small prize."

She does not usually talk this way. She was brought up to be modest, but he has vastly overplayed his hand. Her small stature, her long, shimmering white hair, and even, still, the fact that she is a woman, have often caused others to underestimate her. She was here long before him, and will be here long after he is gone. But she still can't tell whether he understands that he has picked the wrong foe.

He straightens his back. "You can't fight money, even if you do have Nobel authority. *Moku* runs on the entertainment and tourist industries."

"I agree. And technological, scientific, and academic research is the dog. Setting a timetable for actual travel to an exoplanet seems to be our least concern. In the two years since you arrived, you or your proxies have generated many irrelevant but effective roadblocks and dismantled several long-running initiatives. Not many people have examined your record thus far, but a close scrutiny reveals a definite pattern."

He juts his head forward and stares at her with open hostility. "You're out of your—do you really?—" He raises both hands in a questioning attitude, drops them to his side, and laughs. "Wow. It doesn't matter, then, that there is *no place to go?*"

"There are many places we could go. Potentially, an infinite number of habitable planets. We're finding a new one, literally, every day."

"Yes, but *we* cannot get there."

Pele decides to take advantage of this teachable moment. Perhaps she can awaken him to *Moku*'s true wonder. "We are approaching an age in which we might be able to mesh our growing understanding of quantum processes with new technologies, a time in which the specific needs of a particular possibility might generate a new paradigm regarding our ability to move through space and time. In that reality, it could seem only instants until all habitable planets are populated."

He nods. "You are talking, of course, about your particular pet, the theoretical Alcubierre drive. Powered by the equally theoretical Casimir vacuum." His eyes gleam with true humor, for a moment. "Wouldn't that be something! But just a pipe dream."

She says, "We've made a lot of advances since you took your one required theoretical physics course thirty years ago. I'd love to set aside time to talk to you about how much we've learned since then. You are right about one thing—*Moku* has been vital to forwarding our ability to learn more about so many subjects. It is a scientific wonderland. And, in fact, I will hand off this job next month and return to my own research. Sometimes it's useful to give that part of my brain time to process information on its own. That's how it works for me. Call this just another stint in the patent office." She grins at him with fierce, friendly energy; she knows her eyes are twinkling. "I think that we're on the verge of some very, very big changes. Things that will truly change humanity."

He shakes his head. "There's no appetite for that."

"Of course not. We have a fabulous playground here. It's like when Walt Disney died and his Experimental Prototype City of Tomorrow morphed from a serious attempt at living the dream of the future to one of the most successful amusement parks of all time."

He stares blankly. He has no idea what she's talking about.

No surprise. She says, "Not everyone shares your view."

She refers to her fellow research scientists and astronauts, to their wild romance with space, to how hard they work, on the other side of this Mobius strip, in the humming hive of *Moku*, and its environments of rain forest, high sierra, deep sea, and other ecosystems vital to life to realize these dreams.

It is her dream, too.

That is why she is trying to fill her present post to the best of her ability. All of her fellow shipboard dreamers, in their long lives, have followed many passions, done much good work, earned many, many degrees. Each takes turns doing the necessary administrative work of keeping the dream alive. An outsider would only botch things. Their core group has logged much more space time than is strictly allowable, on ISS, Tranquility, Mars. They are hungry for space and all that it means.

Dr. Zi is not one of them. Zi and figureheads like him come, increase their ratings, and go.

She clears her throat. "It is your sworn duty, as Chief Safety Engineer, to ensure the safety of this ship." She almost says *Unless you have a conflict of interest*, but because she is trying hard, and because she has simmered down, she does not.

She presses on. "Sure, the Mars tragedy has been smoothed away after only four years. All the reports are buried by interminable committees while celebrities take up everyone's short attention span with their gaudy pairings and unpairings. Money can manipulate anything." She does not say *Including you*, but decides he could not hear that even if she shouted it to his face.

"I fail to see your point."

"It's been a while. Let's review. Seven lovely young reality stars, men and women without a shred of technical background, set out in a rover as a publicity lark and drive over a cliff. Live feed killed before it gets to Earth; no backups. Easy. The world mourns for a while, but without visuals, pretty soon it's like it never happened.

"Here on *Moku*, we have seventy-two entertainment workers—publicity crews, trainers, scripters, and assorted interesting many-gendered, well-known celebs who have gone through a few drills but who have been lulled into thinking that we are not hanging in space in a complex system that at this instant is undergoing massive, continuous updates and repairs. A hundred and twelve tourists. Fifty-seven parents. Their children. I'm not talking about the crew, the academics, the research scientists, all of whom have at least four doctorates, know the risks, and are emergency-ready. The civilians do not know the risks. It is your *job* to care. To protect them. And there is a matter of the highest urgency that—"

"Dr. Hsu, I resent these implications." A ping sounds. He stands. "Time for me to lead a tour through the Nanotech VR Lab."

She also stands, and says, working her device, "If you could possibly inspect the lab, while you are there, in regard to these three issues . . . I mean if you have *time* . . . in fact . . . I've sent this to all Level 5 personnel."

He roars, "You will *not* go over my head!"

"I'll share to the same contacts my full, updated report within the hour. I expect you to read it and to respond."

He fumbles with another shot of salad—vodka-infused? she wonders—and makes his way through the crowded bar, another of Pele's safety nightmares. As is the *Moku* Gift Shop, the Full Immersion Module (Experience Surfing the Rings of Saturn!) and the Hotel.

A parent who has been hovering nearby takes Dr. Zi's place. Ann is Ghanaian, a lovely, warm woman, wearing a dress of bold African colors, proud that her strange, heartbreaking baby has grown to be not only functional, but wondrous. As are all the parents.

"Dr. Hsu, it is *so* good to finally have a chance to actually *talk* with you." She takes both of Pele's hands in hers and squeezes. Pele squeezes back as Ann continues talking. "Thank you for the wonderful things you have done for Kevin. You are such a role model. You were our beacon on this long, long journey. If you could do it, so could Kevin. You know how it is—a roller coaster. The realization that your child is . . . *different*. The diagnosis—the *work*—" Tears stand in her dark eyes.

"I do know," says Pele, because first, she knew it from the inside. Though this is a common conversation for her, she gives each her full, deep attention. "It does get easier. I promise. You have done all the right things. Every day, there are breakthroughs."

Ann blinks, and her tears overflow. She dashes them away, and a smile lights her lovely face. "What you're doing here—it's just incredible. I never dreamed that Kevin would be *communicating* with so many other people—all of the international children who were on the first Gifted Expeditions! They are all so brilliant—and so many are Asperger's spectrum. My husband and I can't make head nor tail of what they do, and we are both professors. It's all so technical, and in their own codes, but apparently they work in shifts, twenty-four seven—"

This is like a deep gong sounding. The puzzle Pele was trying to discuss with Zi snaps into a single, frightening picture.

Pele keeps her voice low and calm, her eyes steady on Ann's eyes. "Ann, this is very important. I need to see this information. I—"

Something on the far side of the bar catches Pele's eyes. Her fiancée, Gustavo, threads his way through small groups of parents gathering for Marsrise. Just the sight of him has the power to change her into a different person, which she welcomes. She is happy, relaxed, made new. She is still in love, after two years.

She waves; he changes course toward her, his movements uncharacteristically urgent.

Gustavo is warm, sweet, humble, and kind, his twin fields astrobiology and artificial life. She has not been married for two decades, when her second partner regendered, as Pele had always thought probable. Twelve great-grandchildren thrive all over the world, and she follows their rich lives with avid interest. He has a similar family.

Gustavo drops onto an empty zabuton next to Pele. He smiles, but his grave expression crystallizes Pele's apprehensions, assembling inchoate murmurings she has caught edge of—and voiced—in a final, definitive snap of realization.

He glances at Ann, nods in greeting, and takes a deep breath. Pele knows he is making his voice sound normal with great effort. "Can you spare a moment for a conference in the Venus Room?"

Code for serious emergency.

The hair on Pele's arms rises.

All crew members are ready to fully assume many roles on the ship, according to situation and scenario, and are well-qualified for each.

He is calling her to one of hers. And he must remain here.

He grabs her hand, squeezes it with tremendous warmth. Turns his face for a brief kiss, an embrace she returns, giving herself to it completely, suddenly knowing it might be their last.

She rises, gives Ann and Gustavo a brief Buddhist nod, hands pressed together, and in that action prays for all sentient beings. Since her childhood, this prayer has been vast, and, as she followed her devotions, her definition of the scope has grown daily.

"Excuse me, please." As she passes murmuring groups of people she feels resigned, sad, but also infinitely lightened, pulled by glowing, roiling galaxies, by the romance she first felt upon the midnight sea between Tonga and Hawai'i, when she was twelve, the stars so close she could almost grab them by the fistful, when time seemed like a miraculous toy, something she could put her mind to and learn, a story to which she might give voice.

She has always been that child. As she approaches the lock, she cannot help breaking into a run, eager as all those children. All her sensible, deep fears cannot hold her back. She turns at the last movement and becomes a mudra. Signs to Gustavo:

Aloha

He signs back. She sees tears on his face, feels them on hers.

She spins abruptly; enters the real world.

Fairy tales are as good a way as any to say these things. They lived in cities as they had in dark forests. They live in space and they live in time, however strange it has become.

This is the foot of the wave function hitting bottom. This is the flying foam of the wave flickering off, blending with, becoming another kind of time, dynamic, compelling.

This is a girl walking downhill on the flank of a mountain overlooking Pearl Harbor, bare feet on hot white concrete, immersed in plumeriascented eversummer, flipping a small, white, smooth stone into the air, leaning forward, catching it, and thinking: if *this* flip, and *this* flip, and *this* flip could be described by mathematics, that is a thing I would like to learn.

She is the princess, waking.

She is the one who wakes time.

There is a console immediately inside Pele's portal, amongst the wires, tubes, and pipes of a functioning spacecraft, positioned on one of the long arms that lead to the fifty acre central atrium. Opening several screens at once, she sees that her fears are correct.

Someone has begun the launch. In fact, four days earlier. No one knew; she doesn't know why they know now. A shadow program.

Yes, they are brilliant.

Ninety minutes left until the nukes, behind the shield, move them from their perch. The entertainment and other modules are not designed to stand the thrust, a situation she opposed from their inception. After that—well, Zi is partly right. Who knows what might happen? She has always fought for reconfiguring the ship to support a different drive, but it remains theoretical, so she had little support. Still, many possibilities are embedded in *Moku*. Solar sails; many models of generation ships to which the ship can mechanically reconfigure. And other possibilities, awaiting the kind of nanotech enlivenment that has not yet been born.

Pele says, "Override launch progression," her voice empowered to enact the procedure, as are the voices of a few colleagues.

"Cancelled," says a child's voice above her right ear.

Within minutes, she realizes that she is powerless to stop the launch. If she cannot stop it, no one can; her colleagues have equal abilities.

"Invoking emergency plan seven," she says. Seven will detach the external modules of hotels, gift shops, restaurants, and bars, after evacuating civilians, whom she sees are being extracted from the virtual environments, the ecosystems, the build-your-own-exoplanet immersion attraction. They will head back to Earth, safe. She sees that, luckily, a third of the civilians are in their hotel rooms, probably sleeping.

A face appears; it is her colleague Selena, brushing a wisp of brown hair away from her eyes. "Pele. We're all on L3, 7."

Blue dots on a map. "Together? In a breakaway?" Breakaways are, essentially, modules to be jettisoned in an emergency. She finds the yellow dots, the children. "Why are the children all on the bridge?" But she knows why.

"You don't understand," says Selena. "We all need to talk. In person. Now. Hurry."

She does understand. She does hurry.

Pele enters the breakaway breathless, and sees her friends, her colleagues, her fellow dreamers, surrounded by screens on which blink schematics, warnings, plans, arguing.

She has known all of them for a very long time. They have labored together, here and in their various universities, think-tanks, and labs, over the past fifty years, as technologies changed and changed and changed again, holding to the same vision, generating theoretical and actual drives, ship design, exoplanet possibilities, and iterations of *Moku* in model and, slowly, in reality. Most have rotated onto *Moku* for a total of at least five years, with breaks, and something is always new when each arrives. They are only a handful compared to all their colleagues on Earth, the Moon, Mars, and various space communities. They have never been together in this particular configuration, which changes monthly as some rotate out and others in, but have known each other from meetings and through their work for longer than most humans have lived. They number thirty-two.

She knows that they, like she, feel as if *Moku* is their own body.

"Pele is here," says Selena, and they all turn.

Pele says, "Earth should know, by now. We'll have radio backup."

Bijo, usually laboring in his beloved rain forest, which will never be ready, shakes his head, bowed like a slender, heavy-headed blossom after a downpour. "We are completely isolated. The children have blocked all communication."

The face of Ta'a'aeva, a glowing, bulky Polynesian girl, her short, black kinky hair shaved in a zigzag, her face patterned by a fierce, asymmetrical tattoo, appears on a screen. "We see you are all there. I am the spokesperson for the Intergalactic Federation of Gifted Children." Her deep, melodious voice rings through the compartment.

"We were all GC's," says Quinn, his thatch of dark hair falling across his face, hands on his hips, facing the screen. "Now we're Gifted Adults. Not quite as shiny as we were brought up to think we were. Knocked on our asses a few times. As far as I can tell, what really makes us gifted is getting back up again after that happens, every time. Living to be adults, which we have done. As adults, it's up to us to decide what to do so that you can live to be this old."

"This isn't a joke. You have no choice," says Ta'a'aeva, her voice calm. "We are leaving for Object Shining Leaf. You are all coming with us."

"Object Shining Leaf? The only place we're going is back to Earth," Quinn says, with finality.

Ta'a'aeva says, "The civilians are being returned to Earth. All of you are staying with us."

"May I please speak with Bean?" says Pele.

"Bean is busy."

But then Bean's shy, olive-colored face appears on another screen. She and Pele look at one another for a moment. Bean blinks, and swallows.

Quinn says, loudly, "Look here," but Pele shushes him with a hand.

"Bean, what's happening?"

Ta'a'aeva says, "I'll tell you," but Bean speaks, in a whispery, uninflected voice, and slowly. "We have recoded the ship. All of the children who have been here before, too. All of us have worked on it for years. Some of us since we were little. I didn't even know what this was, really, when I started. They gave me things to do. Every problem was like a new toy or a new puzzle. It was fun." She closes her eyes and nods as if to some internal rhythm. Her screen goes dark.

Ta'a'aeva says, "Half of us want to kick you off the ship. Me included. We don't need any bosses. We want to get adults out of the picture. You live too long and hog up all the air. You can't think in new ways. You have a vested interest in maintaining the status quo."

"That's not true!" says Quinn, hotly.

Ta'a'aeva ignores him. "Some of the insecures think we might need you eventually."

"Like now," says Mi, a swarm robotics specialist. "My respectful advice is that you call this off."

"Not possible. We initiated the launch sequence for the Orion drive before we even arrived. The nukes are armed. No one noticed, right? Think about that."

"But why?"

Ta'a'aeva wrinkles her nose in disdain. "*Moku* was completed thirty years ago. She could have left then. But, mysteriously, the launch is always delayed. Brave, willing crews spend years in training limbo, all wasted."

"Not at all true!" objects Petr, a German who studies communication. "Their training yields crucial information."

Ta'a'aeva makes a moue of anger, which her tattoos intensify. "*Moku* has been turned into a money-making boondoggle. An amusement park. A research facility. A vacation destination. We are moving humanity's dream forward. Now. You won't find a way out." She disappears.

No way out? These words give Pele a fleeting, subconscious jolt.

"She's a brilliant engineer," says Victor. "We'd better believe her. She modeled something very like this in one of her past projects. If anyone can do it, she can. I personally approved her. I'm sorry I didn't realize—"

"That her dreams were real?" Selena smiles, closes her eyes, and resumes her habitual tuneless humming. "I'm leaving. I have great-greats." Selena, a mathematician, most often appears to be doing nothing. She walks a lot, taking swings through all the environments with a small backpack and hiking sticks. She lobbied vigorously for a High Sierra environment, and got it, manifesting a little-used gift for politics, though perhaps all simply went as one of her sociological models predicted.

Quinn says, "My vote is for staying, getting this under control, and stopping the launch. It is our responsibility to the world, and we have a moral responsibility to keep the children from the consequences of their unreason."

"Nicely put," says Prajan, tall as a corn stalk and as thin. He has slung himself against a wall, head bent over his device. He looks up, his eyes questioning; challenging. "So do you have a plan? Because the more I dig, the more I find that they trapped us here."

His mobile face shifts to immense amusement, and then his startling, uproarious laugh is magnified by the metal walls. "Heads in jars! That's what we'll be. Sparkling in a row, nutrient juice shot through with starlight, like in all those old, crumbling pulp magazines and sci-fi movies!" Wrapping his arms around himself, he bends over. "AHHAAhahaha." Tears trickle from the corners of his eyes, and he flicks them away with the forefingers of both hands. "Who says dreams can't come true? And usually at the most goddamned inconvenient time." He stuffs his device in his pocket, gazes downward, and continues to erupt in weak chuckles.

Wilhelm, a steady middle-aged physician, sighs, his brown, usually merry eyes sad. "I'm with Selena. I've got to get back home. I'm sure most of us are in the same boat. Ta'a'aeva is right. Space travel is not my dream. Using an off-planet environment to generate new therapies, new interventions, for all of us on Earth and Mars, is. And let's be honest. All of us, or our companies, have profited, and Jane is not the only attorney in our midst with the responsibility of making sure that their employer's contracts are honored, whether they be government, academic, or private industry, well past our own long lifetimes. Frankly, I've never even considered that they might at some point expire."

Quinn says, "They're just too damned smart. Their parents paid for genetic and neuroplasticity enhancements. AI nannies. They're probably not even human anymore."

"They are," says Pele firmly, "as much as any of us are." Silence.

By the way all of them shift their eyes from side to side, Pele sees they are all thinking things they dare not say.

Pele is finding it hard to focus.

Before the Hsus, during the nameless time, some kind hand floated Pele on her back, at night, in warm, protected waters, where she could watch the stars. Ala Moana, perhaps.

They know she was born in Honolulu, but there is a gap from that time until she was, literally, captured in an alley by social workers, restrained, drugged, confined, despaired over, until one day she found herself at the top of a mountain.

Petr squints, working his device. After a moment, he looks up.

"I've closed all of our outside communications with an emergency override, but they'll break through quickly. Let's talk."

She didn't know it was the top of a mountain; she did not use words, but the pictures were new, bright, powerful. There was distant blue, stretching forever, far below. Gigantic white big-porched house. Children of all sizes, staring at her.

Walter Hsu, an astrophysicist, and Sunny Hsu, a renowned child therapist, had quite a collection of children—five foster-children and three of their own—at the end of the road on Aiea Heights, along with transient young nannies sparkling with laughter, refugee chefs of all nationalities, visiting international experts on every imaginable subject, screenwriters and crackpots, and a crowd of helpers, all part of the tribe.

Behind the house, tropical forest, a park, to the peak of the mountain. On the other side, miles away, a steep drop to the Kona side of Oahu. Huge mango tree dropping fruit the kids had to shovel into the gully once a week. Their neighbor's manicured Japanese garden at the far side of their house site, complete with a grumpy old Japanese gardener shaking his fist when they trespassed. A treehouse. The crumbling remnants of a sacred Hawaiian stone platform, a *heiau*, far down in the forest, the older children's secret.

But for now, there are just Pele's snapshots. Blue. Green. Wind on her skin. Faces, faces, faces. Teeth and eyes.

"Give her room, kids," says Sunny.

Briskly, Theresa, silent till now, sets forth a plan for containing and jettisoning the children back to Earth, a split-second manipulation of partitions, robots, and gas.

Here are two stories. Pele does not remember them. Yet, within her, they fight.

This is the first story:

Pele makes a dash for the trees, but the man grabs her by the waist. His face, when he hunkers down, is big and smiling. "My name is Walter. He takes her hand. "Let's take a look around." For some reason, she walks with him.

No one else can touch her.

She won't let them comb her hair. She shrieks and runs away.

Walter cuts it off swiftly; gently. She feels her head in wonder. Stares at them. Darts into the forest.

Weeks later, perhaps. Months. How would she know? Pele screams, flings a chair across the room, laughs. Kicks over a tall vase, which shatters.

"Whoops," says Sunny, rushing into the living room, carrying an empty black garbage bag. "Should have put that up." She grabs Pele and drops into a chair, holding Pele tightly in her lap.

Pele is a storm of sharp elbows, wriggling on the crinkly, slippery bag. She straightens, bends, twists, fights with all her might, grunting and crying in rage. She has to escape! She will! She is stronger and faster than everyone! She always gets away!

"That's okay," says Sunny from behind her. "You can fight me." Sunny's long, black hair brushes the side of Pele's face. Pele tries to grab it, but Sunny deftly uses her left arm to hold down both of Pele's arms, her right hand to push back her hair.

As she writhes, Pele feels Sunny's strong, skinny arms around her. She bounces on Sunny's hard, bony thighs. When she kicks with her heels, Sunny leans down, pins her legs. "That's okay. I won't let you hurt me. You can fight with me."

The other children gather round, watching from a safe distance. Sunny yells, "Get away, you kids! This is our time. Pele's and mine." They scatter.

Pele turns her head to bite; a firm, flat hand presses her chin, keeps it forward. "I can't let you hurt me."

Pele spits; drool runs down her face. She shrieks. "Faugh!"

Sunny says, insistently, her voice low and firm, "What do you want?"

Pele bears down and pees. Surely this woman will let her go!

"I have a plastic bag on my lap, Pele. Pee all you want."

Pele erupts into a frenzy, but is gently, firmly, held.

"What do you want?" Sunny says. "Tell me. *Tell* me!"

It bursts from her. "Let me go!"

"Ah! All right!" The arms release. She springs free!

Pele faces Sunny, scowling. Sunny smiles at her, gently. "You see? Talking does things. I am listening."

She opens her arms. Crying, Pele rushes into them, and nestles in a warm embrace. "Let go," she demands.

Sunny's arms open.

She still doesn't talk. But she knows she can, if necessary. And that someone is listening.

This is the second story:

The whole family is at Oahu's Pali overlook, behind a low stone wall. The parking lot is full; people mill around, exclaiming, buffeted by the wind.

The drop below is steep; breathtaking.

Pele likes it up here. She likes it a lot. She shrieks like the wind. "Whoooo. Eeeeeeaaaah!" She runs to the side, spies a faint trail, leaps over the stone wall. Runs faster. Get away!

Get away!

The side goes down, straight down. The wind pushes at her. She trips on a root, starts to fall.

A strong arm grabs her. "Pele!"

Walter leans against a tree behind them, holding her so tightly that it hurts. He is shaking. He is crying.

"Please, Pele. Please. Don't ever do that again."

Pele listens to Theresa's plan.

Selena interrupts. "This has a fifty percent chance of succeeding. Actually . . . I'm tuned into their chatter . . . closer to forty, though it does fluctuate." She closes her eyes in that dreamy way of hers, a slight smile on her face. "No . . . now sixty-two point five three seven . . ."

Pele says, "No. Absolutely not. We are responsible for the children. Some of them will die."

"It serves them—" begins Quinn, then realizes what he's saying. They are all getting heated; they are on the verge of panic.

"We have two thousand, three hundred and thirty-two seconds to decide," says Selena.

Quinn says, "Well, Pele, it seems that you're in charge, and that you're on their side. Instead of the punishment they deserve for jeopardizing the one thing that's unified our planet, and into which we have poured immense treasure, they'll just leave and die, and so will we, as their prisoners. *Moku* is still here because it is, truly, perpetually unfinished. Technology is always changing. But the chief reason is that the voyage is impossible to survive in any meaningful way."

Ala Moana, press-worthy hullaballoo, picnicking families, hula dancers, the mayor of Honolulu, slack-key guitar, the smell of roasting pig. All are gathered for the ceremonial setting forth of *Moe'uhane*, a fifty-foot traditionally built double-hulled canoe, to Tahiti. Tall, triangular sails, filled with wind that keeps the anchor line taut, blaze red in the noonday sun.

It is called Wayfaring, the Polynesian way of sailing over vast distances, targeting an island of a few square miles using complex techniques that draw on memory, wave patterns, star navigation. As birds cross the sea in their thousand-mile journeys, so do they sail.

Walter is a friend of Bob, who will guide *Moe'uhane* on its long trip using only traditional star navigation. The Hsu tribe is right up front on bamboo mats when Bob begins his star chant. His deep voice rises.

"Hoku lei'i . . ."

Pele, a brown, skinny five-year-old in a faded red bathing suit, one long black braid undone, steps forward into his circle, opens her mouth and joins the chant, in Hawaiian, completely unselfconscious. Her singing voice, unlike her harsh, flat speaking voice, is sweet and high.

She *knows* this ancient chant—the directions for finding not just one island, but many, thousands of miles across the trackless sea.

Walter and Sunny share a look. This comes from a different part of the brain than speech. Laid in early, during the mystery years.

Another way in. Another way out.

When twelve, Pele crews on a star-navigation trip to Samoa on the *Moe'uhane* with her father, other scientists and adventurers, and Bob.

Waves rush beneath them with a show, rhythmic *whoosh*. The canoe rises and falls, its lashed joints creaking, its tall sails filled with salt wind. Pele, drenched with spray, stands braced on the forward platform, holding tight to the kaula ihu, the forestay line, with one hand. Thus immersed in immense, intensely black night, Pele answers with her voice. Pulsing stars move chant from deepest memories to her chest. She is a living tone, vibrating with ancient mindmap, with *voyage; mission: huaka'i*; a parade through time and space, which she now leads as pathfinder. She is a still point in deep infinity whose slow, reeling movement finds voice in song, lapped, increasingly for Pele, by mathematics.

As she chants, Bob gently shapes and teaches. But he has also learned from her. Whoever taught her, and then abandoned her, for whatever reason, was a master navigator.

"Look—there," he says, when they pause. "Iwakeli'i. Cassiopeia."

Walter points. "Tau Ceti. Might have livable planets."

Pele stretches on tiptoe, links one arm around the ihu, opens her hands wide, pulls stars to her chest, looks at Walter and asks, "How?"

There are fourteen emergency protocols regarding kidnapping, hostages— their situation—that they can put into play via a private sign language they all know.

But someone has to make the call. Everyone looks at Pele.

The wordless place of pictures that Pele has concealed so well through all the tests, all her life, once she knew it might come back to bite her, rears up like a tidal wave that's touched bottom in its travel over fathoms of water.

There is holding.

There is letting go.

She does both.

"All of you are leaving. I will stay, with them. *Au i ke kai me he manu ala!*" With that, holding them with the energy born of their own surprise, like the throw of a jujitsu master, she steps back, closes the portal, and launches them.

To cross the sea like a bird.

Like released seed pods, the modules, expelled, move rapidly from the *Moku*, their manual control overridden by programming the children created. The slice of Mars grows. Pele releases her held breath when her information panel notes ignition of their maneuvering rockets, which will increase their speed.

"Hsu!" Zi's contorted face is on her monitor. "There will be repercussions." The sound of wild screaming floods into the comm channel, drowning out Zi's voice. He switches to another channel. She can still hear dull thuds.

Quinn, in their breakaway, appears. "Pele!"

She says, "Is everyone safe?"

Selena's voice breaks in. "I would not have predicted this success."

Quinn's black eyes hold more than rage. Terror, or just the rapid analytics required to deal with the unfolding situation? He barks, "Success? Broken bones. Abrasions. One death thus far. Sure to be more." Pele hears a great commotion on the other screen; recognizes Ann and other parents as they crowd round the fish-eye lens. "Come back," shouts Ann. "Return Kevin right now!"

Jane, the lawyer, yells, "You have committed piracy. Kidnapping. Treason. Child abuse. Manslaughter."

Pele orders, "All craft move away with maximum speed. I have no control. The nukes, activated by the GCC, will detonate in seconds. They are contained, but—"

A tall, young boy is next to her. He touches her elbow. "Dr. Hsu. I am Eliott. Chimerist." The wailing, frantic parents arrayed before him quiet. To them, Eliott says, "We apologize for injuries. We did our best to create a plan that would minimize them. We are all well. We have not been kidnapped. The reverse, perhaps. We have sent you our story. Listen to it. Do not blame our colleagues on Earth. You cannot blame us, of course. We are children. Communications are now blocked until we choose to re-open them."

To Pele, he says "Hurry."

In Nucleus, the op center of *Moku*, Pele sees thirty-seven children—short, tall, round, thin, each from a different country and culture, monitoring and managing the ship, a cohesive crew with their own Esperanto, which Pele took care to learn. Many, like Ta'a'aeva, are not Aspies; she knows that she has focused on those who are because of her own history.

Pele makes a rapid tour, gives a few suggestions, which are seriously considered and often executed. She could be in any of the many ships, private and government-backed, that she has had the privilege to serve on over the past fifty years.

Bean, ten, is the youngest. Ta'a'aeva's on-board fourteenth birthday drew a record-making number of viewers just last week, and she is oldest. Most have at least one college degree. Pele has interacted with all of them, and henceforth—but there is no way to understand this enormity—neither she nor they will ever know any other humans.

"Don't worry," says Eliott. "We have done this, virtually, a million times. We know all the contingencies."

"And my decision?"

"Scenario 174."

She knows she could ask any of them and they would know that number, all the others, and what each would have entailed, just as she knew what Venus Room meant.

The ship announces, "Crew, prepare for nuclear ignition."

Pele steps into the nearest empty booth on the wall of the circular space, which cocoons her, leaving her face free. For a wild, silly second, Pele is reminded of nothing so much as being strapped into a tilt-a-whirl at the state fair, waiting to be spun through the air, held to the wall by the force of gravity.

She can hear their conversation in her headphones, and sees a good number of their faces. Only a few look appropriately grave. Some grin. She hears a wild, shrieking laugh, and some self-congratulatory talk of victory, as if this is a virtual game they have won. Perhaps it is.

How can they imagine the horrors Pele foresees? They are so terribly young. They have had no chance to learn about life, and now they never will. The freedom of Earth, the freedom of choosing another road, and another, and another. The delight of communicating with and learning from a rich, diverse population. The road they face is hard, narrow, and probably impossible. Doubt, anger, and regret rage through her; she struggles against the restraints, her chest a dark, sad weight. She has saved them only for an impossible task.

She always blacks out at five g's, but until then, she desperately thinks, plans, wonders, *What can I do to help them survive?*

Pele is six. She sits crosslegged on a large, cool rock across from her brother Jack. Their knees almost touch. The waterfall, which the kids often visit, is small, but makes a pleasing sound as it rushes over rocks. The tumble of fresh water washes the air. Small dark fish hang in the shadows. Fallen red lehua blossoms drift on the surface.

Jack is fifteen, one of the Hsus's three natural children. Dapples of light brighten his straight, black, shoulder-length hair as wind shifts the forest canopy above them and blows it across his face. He is the only one of the children she has anything to do with. The others just seem like a lot of noise.

"Okay. Let's try again. Look at my face. Can you tell how I feel?"

She stares intently at Jack's teeth, sorting the long call of the i'iwi, the amakihi's chatter, the sweet song of the apanane.

"No, Pele. My eyes. Raise your chin. Look."

She does. He draws his eyebrows together, glares at her. "Tell me—what am I feeling?"

She shrugs.

He thrusts his face forward, retaining the ferocious look, and says, "I am angry! Now I will make you feel angry. Pele, you are stupid!"

She leaps to her feet and lunges down at him, fists forward. He catches her wrists, one in each of his hands. "That is anger, Pele. You feel angry. I feel the same way. I am angry that you tried to hit me! Tell me what my face looks like! My mouth! My eyebrows! My wrinkles!"

As he holds her wrists in mid-air, it dawns on her. "I can tell how you feel by looking at your face?"

He lets go and nods. She drops back onto the rock and rests her chin in her hands. The water is dark green, then clear and sparkling where the sun hits it.

He says, "Now you look worried. You're thinking. What are you thinking?"

She says forcefully, "I am wondering why you are bothering me. I am thinking that this is too much work."

"It's work for me too. But I like to work with you. You're my sister, and I want to help you."

"I don't need help."

He says, very gently, "Please look at my face for just a minute."

She does, reluctantly. "You are looking right at me. Into my eyes."

"Tell me how my face looks."

"Your eyes are open very wide. Your look is strong. It almost hurts me.

It makes me feel . . ."

He nods encouragingly. "Feel what?"

"I don't know. Is there a word?"

"I am trying to tell you with this look that I care about you."

She wonders how she can memorize a look, and how Jack's look would seem on someone else's face. It all seems quite impossible. "Why?"

"My older brother lived here when I was little. He was our parents' biological child too. He could never look at me. I loved him. He's a grownup now. His name is Edmond Hsu. He's a mathematician, eh? You can see his work online. He started college when he was twelve and lives on the mainland now. I was always sad that he would never look at me. Mom told me that I shouldn't be sad, that he didn't know what we were feeling and thinking."

"So?"

"I think that you can know, Pele." He smiles.

She looks back at the pool. "Then what do I feel now?" She knows that she feels vaguely out-of-sorts. She is not sure what any of this means.

"Grumpy." He jumps up. "Come on. Bet I can beat you back to the trail-head!"

She gets up more slowly and stands, hands on her hips, nodding. "Grumpy."

Another day, he hands her a wet rag while she is in the back yard throwing rotten mangoes at a big tree in the gully and watching them smash. "Wash your hands. I know you can read. Try reading this."

"No!" She throws *The Wizard of Oz* on the ground as he walks away.

Irritated that this does not bother him, she picks it up, wipes mango goo from the cover, and reads aloud to the gully in a shouting voice: "When Dorothy, who was an orphan, first came to her, Aunt Em had been so startled by the child's laughter that she would scream and press her hand upon her heart whenever Dorothy's merry voice reached her ears; and she still looked at the little girl with wonder that she could find anything to laugh at."

She turns and faces the house, where Jack might still be listening. She hopes he is. "So? I am an orphan. I scream a lot. AIEEEE! And sometimes I hate it when people laugh!"

The trees swish in the wind, and the palms make rain-pattering sounds beneath the blue sky.

She does nothing for three days except read *The Wizard of Oz*. When she is finished, she marches into Jack's room, where he is studying, and smacks it down on his desk.

"I am very angry with you," she shouts.

"Why?"

"Because this made me sad and afraid and worried."

"Anything else?"

"I was happy and sad at the same time when Dorothy got back home. I hated it!" "Why?"

"I just did!"

Jack smiles as she stomps from the room. Next, he gives her a curious old volume, *My Bookhouse: Through Fairy Halls*. It is a hefty book, bound in black leather, with vivid pictures that seem like music, because of the way they move in Pele's mind. It smells funny. The pages are dry. "Take care of it," he says.

Pele is walking on a treadmill. A girl stands next to her, watching.

"Are you Bean?"

"That's the first time you remembered."

"I told you a story."

The girl looks straight at Pele. Her eyes are hazel with flecks of gold. "A girl lived in the mountains of Tibet. She was trying to escape from the Chinese and broke her leg and nearly starved to death." Bean purses her lips, looking confused. "You said I couldn't give her any powers, and I couldn't earn any weapons, so I couldn't help her. Things just happened and then it was over and nobody won, but she did get out and became a hero. You said it would change my brain. I tried to measure that, but I couldn't. I think I need more stories to do that, or I have to figure out a new way of measuring."

"Usually when I was your age I liked a story if it made me cry."

Bean flashes her a startled look. "You liked to cry?"

Pele smiles. "It is kind of strange, isn't it?"

Bean frowns. "I will tell you my story. It is about a horse. I don't know if you would like it. It doesn't have an ending."

"I think I know your story. But there are many ways to tell every story. Tell it to me again. I'm sure that it will make me cry."

As Pele strides back into trance, into dream, Bean wonders why tears flow from beneath Pele's closed eyelids.

"Pele!"

Ta'a'aeva stands in front of her. Bean leans close, against her left arm. They are all gathered, all looking at her.

Ta'a'aeva speaks. "We need your help. It is almost completed, we think. But you are the one who can do it. We are glad you have come. But be here! Please wake up!"

Obviously, a dream.

Pele, in her own little house, a chicken coop in a row of chicken coops long ago completely sanitized, used, and abandoned by various Hsu children.

Hers has weather-smoothed streaks of white paint, abundant sun that lies on the floor in a slant, a shelf where hens once roosted crowded with a row of old books. Large, castoff cushions on the floor.

She is seven.

Her brothers and sisters rush down the gully, a crescendoing cavalcade of pounding feet. They surround her house, yelling. Rocks bounce off the side. Diane peers in the window, howls with laughter. "She's reading those silly fairy tales again!"

"Yeah, she likes those old books. I loaned her my screen and found it in the trash can!"

They leap around the chicken coop, yelling, singing, beating on it with sticks, making it shake when they try to push it over.

Pele, lying on her stomach, barely hears them. She is in worlds of ogres, fairies, magic boots, menehunies, stupid children, endless journeys, flying carpets, talking animals, and powerful goddesses like her namesake, a dangerous woman whose actions are unpredictable and thrilling, who created the Hawaiian Islands with her volcanoes. They are more real than people, and certainly much more interesting.

She does not even notice when the clatter recedes. Rain patters on big-leaved trees, sun speeds across the floor, she smells sweetly rotting mangoes mixed in the brisk, whipping breeze, and reads.

Sunny's sideways head and shoulders darken the coop's small door. "It's getting dark. Come inside."

Pele, her head propped on her elbows, is reading about a giant. "No."

Sunny smiles, sets a water bottle, a package of dried squid, and a book light inside, then leaves.

When Pele wakes the next morning in her own bed, she has a memory of being carried through the night, and the stars. Next to her on the bed is *Through Fairy Halls*, her favorite of the Bookhouse volumes. She opens it and starts to read. Grimm, Anderson, the Blue and Green and Red books follow, and then folk and fairy tales from around the world. Wise and wily rabbits, lions, crickets and tortoises argue, beguile, win, lose. And Fairyland itself?

Oh, there is music and dancing in Fairyland. No yesterday, and no tomorrow. Pipes call. Trumpets sound. The low are made high, and the high are surprised and chagrined.

There is a dangerous edge to Fairyland, which Pele enjoys. One flirts with it to one's own peril.

And part of her now, the living dreaming part, knows that she has crossed the border. Nightingales, clear springs, great rose-trees whose rich scents confound the senses. The large made small; the small, large, and one's own self made true.

And Time a leafy, sun-dappled orchard.

Gray horse, crunch of sweet, crisp fruit, swish of long silver tail.

Long ago. Ever-now.

She is Gulliver, pounded by tiny fists.

"Please, please, wake up! We need your help! We can't do it alone! Please, please, wake up!"

She opens her eyes. Bean is there. "You have been asleep for a long, long time, Pele." Her eyes are grave.

"This is too slow," says Kevin, shaking her arm. "We're only transiting Venus. We'll never get to Shining Leaf."

Ignoring trumpet fanfares, Pele calculates, considering Orion's acceleration, that she has been asleep for three months.

Ta'a'aeva says, "We can't make the drive work. You know how. Tell us! Tell us, and we'll engineer it. You know that we can."

Pele says, "Get me out of this." As they unstrap her cocoon, she looks at a nearby screen. "I've been exercising three hours a day on the bike? Really?"

"You weren't awake," says Eliott. "You were in a trance."

"Indeed," she says, taking in the compressed graphic of her brainwaves for the past few months, noting the sharp spikes that she knows linger in her mind like haunting, exotic music, calling her to return.

It takes all her will to remain where she is, on *Moku*, where she has committed a powerful, monstrous act. She sees the resolve of the children arrayed around her and knows that she cannot gain control of the ship. She knows that they would have done this without her help.

She tries to believe that they are better off with her here. She must make that true.

She also sees, scrolling, continuous, messages from Earth. With a touch, she speeds them up, goes backwards, absorbs them like a blow, for it is all her fault.

And Gustavo. She searches wildly, finds a tiny line of news—

"No!" She raises her hands to cover her face, and sobs, slumping back into the cocoon, curling up so that no one, no one, can see her.

She does not re-emerge for another spell. But now, her dreams are new. She is working.

Bean sees Pele first.

She is standing just outside Nucleus, where diagrams, equations, charts, and virtual models of FTL drives litter the air in transparent, three-dimensional overlays. She has been watching, listening to the hum of intense concentration, several intertwining musics that tangle and leap within her long-quiet mind, and getting ready to turn and re-enter her cocoon.

The displays rainbow Bean's slight body as she approaches Pele, her stare a powerful command. She takes Pele's hand and, as the others gather, leads her to an array of cushions. Pele settles on one, back straight, legs crossed, and says, direct from her hard-won beginner's mind, "You don't really need me. Are you ready to tell us, Bean?"

First, Bean's eyes widen as she tilts her head at Pele.

Pele nods. "I know."

Bean frowns and clenches her fists. "I've been trying. It's closed in. Like a hard nut. I can't tell it. No one understands."

"Try another way."

Bean takes a deep breath, then shakes her head and makes her long hair swirl round her face. She stretches her long legs out in front of her, grasps the soles of her feet with her hands, tucks her head in, and silences.

"Bean, who is in this story?" asks Pele.

She asks three times. Finally Bean says, her head still down, her voice muffled, "It is a story about a horse." She walks her hands up her calves, singing more than speaking, bends both knees to the right, and kneels, her spine ramrod straight, hands moving as in a hula, shaping the story in space. "Sometimes the story seems short, and sometimes I know that it is actually very, very long. "On the pampas, I ride Alcubierre, my silver mare, all day through the wheat. It parts and lets us through." Her hands speak in swift, darting signs now: her own language, Pele knows, which they must learn.

Another way in. Another way out.

"It makes a swishing sound, like wind, and then the sounds are a music that might keep me there forever. They are . . . enchanting."

Pele hears what Bean hears; it assails her even now, calling her.

But she cannot, will not, succumb.

Bean's eyelids are half-closed. She speaks as if in a trance. "Alcubierre *pulls* the mountain closer when she gallops. She and I—we do not move. We remain the same, and in the same place. The wheat is *time*. Flowing and parting around me.

"I thought of this story for a whole year. I worked on it in my head when I rode. I see us from above. Alcubierre's tail flows out behind her, white, blending and waving with the golden wheat. It is long . . . long . . . long . . ." She lowers her head as if in apology and whispers, "But still. The story is not in words."

"Ah," says Pele, grateful when Bean stops speaking, and the imperative music fades. She has tried to wake before. It may be still a dream.

But she does not think so. "Show us."

The showing unfolds. It is complex, and long, as Pele knew it would be, and wakes her fully. All of them struggle to understand, to master various parts of it, to use theory to imagine this drive, to picture the concept of the space that it would use.

Xia, Chief Nanotechnologist, prepares to infuse the ship with her work and the work of a million materials engineers, biomedical engineers, environmental scientists—a synthesis of every science and engineering discipline—generated from a century of research and application.

They gather for a ceremony. Xia's black eyes are serious and steady when she speaks. "We will be enabled, today, through *enlivenment,* which is how we describe this coming change, to manipulate the matter of our ship at the atomic level. The rules we hereby embed within the ship are the final arbiter of what is and is not permissible, and the laws of physics govern what is possible. Among other benefits, we will all enjoy perfect health from now on."

Nucleus fills with huge, idealized atoms, strings of splitting and reconnecting DNA, and long sections of text. One section glows next to Pele, and she rapidly scans it, aghast.

Grinning, Xia shouts, "And we will all have tremendous fun!" Everyone except Pele whoops and cheers.

"Should we discuss it and vote?" asks Pele. They all look at her with amazement. "I've seen this before. It's a plan for—it *is*, I gather, a universal assembler—"

"There's nothing to vote on," Xia explains, her voice as gentle as if speaking to a small child. She holds a sheaf of small, square envelopes in one hand. "This was always part of the plan. All of us have contributed to it, in one way or another. We all know everything there is to know about it."

The fields of nanotechnology, a discipline drawing on all scientific disciplines, have blown far past Drexler's early visions. Pele has sat on international committees that debated the use of various iterations of nanotechnology. Some were approved, and some, which embodied the possibility of change so rapid and radical that the results could not be predicted, were left unused, and locked away.

Pele understands, and now knows that they understand as well, that this particular iteration is the ability to change matter swiftly, from the bottom up, to grow rather than to machine. This chameleon-like ability, this new plasticity, will include themselves—their minds, their bodies—as well as their surroundings. Everything. Within what limits? The limits of physics have not been fully explored. Not by a long shot. Things will change, evolve, and Pele doesn't know what, or how. Neither do they.

Alicia gives everyone an envelope. Pele opens hers and pulls out a round, paperish object.

"Why does this look like a communion wafer?" she asks.

"A what?" ask several children.

"The circle was my idea," says Bean. "It's . . . simple. It doesn't have any religion in it."

"I wanted water balloons that we could explode and scatter the replicators around," says Ta'a'aeva, scowling. "Nobody listens to me."

"Do we eat it?" asks Pele.

"You can," says Xia, but, imitating the children, Pele presses hers to the side of the ship, where, warmed by her hand, it is rapidly absorbed.

A brief, dazzling light rushes through the walls of Nucleus. The children break into wild dance, laughing, and spinning through the air.

O brave new world, thinks Pele, that has such people in't! She recalls her child-self, almost flying off the sheer cliff, and wants to grab them, and hold them back.

But it is far too late for that.

She soars and spins with the rest of them. Laughs. Forgets.

Is brave, again. For now.

The enlivenment, as the nanotech changes move through the ship, transforming its matter to a medium that they can easily manipulate, is slow at first, but increases in speed exponentially.

It makes their work much easier, and their environment becomes more dense, as if full of worlds it had been waiting to manifest.

Despite her fears, it is good, as far as she can tell. A rich and joyous thing.

The children, she realizes, do know more than she does.

For instance: Pele, strolling through the city, enters a musty used bookstore. It draws her in, past piles and towering shelves of books, farther and farther, until she realizes that she is in the children's library that Zi mentioned. Each title strikes her heart. Some make her cry. All open worlds in her mind, worlds she thought long-gone; worlds that submerge her, change, and release her.

With wonder, she pulls out an old, tattered, black book. On its cover is an illustration of a girl and boy unlatching an arched, stout, wooden door set in a stone wall. *The Latch Key.* Opening it, she first reads the frontis poem, written by Olive Beaupré Miller:

> Its windows look out far and wide
> From each of all its stories.
> I'll take the key and enter in;
> For me are all its glories.

When Pele looks up, after reading for hours, the store is gone; the street, likewise, has vanished. She sets the book aside, perches on a rock, stares at the stars, and remembers Gustavo, her children, his children, and her descendants, for a long, sweet time.

She hears those children shout to one another as they hide-and-seek in Earth's long, green summer evenings, sees them splash in their nightly bath and then their faces in soft lamplight, eyelids closing, as she reads to them these old, strong tales.

Perhaps, she thinks, that is the most good I have ever done.

She uses their new technology to create a tiny, whitewashed cottage that hangs in rain forest on a steep volcanic mountain. Far below, lush tongues of green, fringed with shining, black volcanic sand, invade the sea, which deepens to *kane*, the deep, blue shade of distance. Tatami mats cover the wide-plank koa floor. The trade wind rattles the hanging photos of Sunny, Walter, and all the kids against the wall. A bookshelf manifests any books she wants, including an old, well-worn copy of *Through Fairy Halls*, with its luminous cover plate of a girl and boy rushing ahead of a diaphanous winged fairy.

Pele sits on her front porch in a rocking chair, paging through the large, heavy book thoughtfully, as the growing drive undergoes troubleshooting and the songs of long-extinct finches wind through her thoughts. She hikes down an ever-manifesting ridge, rappels down a cliff to a tiny beach where she tests herself in treacherous currents, and flings herself, naked, on olivine sand, falling asleep to the roar of the surf. And wakes to space, ablaze with the stars she long planned to grasp.

Her soul rests a brief time, all she allows.

Then, while the children work, Pele turns to what needs to be done. She absorbs the threats, the messages, the stages of grief from Earth. It is hard. She can only do a bit of this task at a time, but she battles through it. She is the only adult here. It is her responsibility.

She wants badly to invent Sunny to have someone to talk to, and though she could, it would only be herself, so she does not. She is afraid to think about why she slept so long. She both knows and does not know, and both are useless to try to understand.

She knows her purchase on this new reality is tenuous. The part of her that loosed them is not rational, and she has fought it all her life.

But there is something she must do now that is more important than anything else she has ever done. That task holds her sternly *here*, on *Moku*, with its precious cargo of life.

Moku holds the world genome. They will start species, including humans, growing when they get close. To somewhere. After an unimaginable piece of time, when it is likely that none of them will be here, or that they will be so different that one could spend a million years just imagining the possibilities. What *Moku* will nurture, and why, will be based on immense data about the planet. A complex task, the vindication of what she has enabled, awaits.

Pele wonders, what will these new humans, these mammals who absorb culture, know? Who and what will teach them? When they forage among the wilderness of what the ship holds, who will they become? What culture will they construct?

It is her task to help them answer this question.

When she calls the children together, they protest. "We are working," says Ta'a'aeva, standing with her arms crossed as thirty-seven children gather in Nucleus.

"You haven't spoken to your parents since we left. You need to do that. Now."

Kevin sucks in his lips and clenches his hands, as he always does in times of stress, to keep them from trembling.

Ta'a'aeva's face hardens.

Alicia, who is thirteen, curses, rips a cushion from the floor, and floats it as hard as she can in Pele's general direction. "I told my mother I was leaving and that I'm never coming back!"

Bean bursts into tears and pushes herself down the tunnel to her berth.

"I hear all of you," says Pele. "Your feelings are mixed up, and hard to live with. How do you think they feel?"

"I'm tired of always trying to think about what other people are feeling," declares Xavier. "It's too hard."

"It's the hardest thing to do," says Pele.

When rent by a meteor, the ship heals. This is not magic. This is science.

Pele, Nedda, Bean, and Takay are sitting on the porch of her cottage, reading books.

As if in a dream, or a myopic haze, Pele sees sky and sea shatter, revealing an assault of blinding stars, and hears a huge rush, as on a beach where massive waves tower and break, and then they are enclosed by a thick, opaque membrane.

Pele is surprised when they all stand and begin to sing, each in a different language, in different tunes and meters, and that it sounds so beautiful. Time seems more slow, and although together they all speak their ever evolving Esperanto, they sing songs from their own earliest childhoods. Pele's mouth opens; her own song comes out, rich and deep from her chest, from her toes, from the far spaces of memory: the Wayfaring chant. From star to star to star. Like a bird transverses the sea. Maybe, indeed, she moves them with this chant. It seems so.

As they sing, life encloses not-life with a net that then thickens, expelling not-life with energy captured from the meteor. Not death—a lucky catch! The net extracts minerals, oxygen, carbon dioxide.

The scrim of matter opaques. They are made whole; enclosed.

They have new stuff to play with, to sustain them. The ship uses the meteor to grow more space, add more air, water the lettuce, grow the infant bristlecone pines in High Sierra.

To regrow the shattered cottage, and chairs, where they sit rocking, turning pages slowly, as a standing wave edges the blue Pacific far below, and plumeria sweeten the air.

They have communicated with one another by this time. The children and their parents.

Their parents had not remembered how strong the force of growing is. They had not remembered how they fought to leave home.

They wanted some kind of magic to protect their children, but all their love could not invent it. The children had torn themselves away, but that is what children do.

Before all this, the parents had worked very hard, even before the children were conceived, because this was The Future, and there was a lot that they could do. These parents wanted their children to be the very smartest, the very best, the most successful. They particularly did not want their children to turn out like the children of their relatives or their friends, who always did a terrible job, and in whose children the ways in which they had gone wrong were so obvious. They would do better.

When the children became teenagers, their sweet child faces changed, and their behaviors were not encouraging. Even though the parents had been teenagers and were sure that they would understand their own, a dark magic veil had grown between them.

I think that this is the first mention of magic in this fairy tale, but I'm not sure. Don't be too hard on us for not knowing exactly when this happened. A lot of fairy tales don't even realize that's what they are, much less come right out and admit it.

Anyway, once the kids were teenagers, the parents lost control. And yes, they were afraid, because they remembered how stupid they had been, and they had tried with all their might to deflect or change this stupid energy, and because it was The Future and they knew more about brains and human development, they thought they had it licked.

But no. They were still the same old humans in important ways.

The children didn't know that they were acting like robots and that they would miss their parents. They didn't know that just growing up creates this energy, and that there was nothing they could do about it. So all of the humans on Earth were pouring out their love, which was helpless to do anything now.

If the children had known how sad their parents would be, they would never have done it. At this point they are beginning to understand, but still do not learn how deep sadness can be. Not yet. Perhaps no one reaches the end of it, and, to survive, must simply choose another path, one with more useful stories. But, as you may know, that is another part of this story.

Worse than all that, the children finally realized that they had stolen something that their parents had worked hard for, *Moku*. The ship, and all of space and time, wasn't meant just for the children. It was meant for everyone in The Future, and for all the people in the world to benefit from. The people of Earth didn't realize this when they were building it. They thought they were making something they could let go of.

It didn't turn out that way.

It was all heartrendingly sad.

Finally, they had to let go.

The parents, the children. The children, Earth.

The people on Earth take a long time to decide how to say goodbye. They form committees, consider proposals, argue violently or with subtle skill, make deals, publish editorials, write learned papers.

It is taking longer and longer for Earth and *Moku* to communicate.

Finally, one day when it is almost too late, at a signal no one recalls initiating, they gather in cathedrals and squares and sing. They sing from flotillas of boats tethered together while they drink rum beneath fiery, poignant sunsets. They sing from observatories to the deep night sky, and as night flips swiftly to day in Bogota.

They sing from self-driving vehicles. Old people stop their tennis games to sing. Children sing in schools; there are still schools, only much better ones. Tech advisors, stock manipulators, and people who still do not have clean water but who do have a device sing. They sing from bars, from the Moon, and from every point in space where humans live.

When the song arrives at the ship, as they are passing Neptune's orbit, they piece it together and gather, standing, and listen, looking back from whence they came, those tiny dots of life holding all they have ever known. Seas, mountains, the three remaining tigers. The deep time and lucky chance that caused life. Winds that flatten vast fields of wheat with great, caressing hands, like the hands that once caressed them with such love and care.

This is what they hear:

> Sleep, my child, and peace attend thee,
> All through the night
> Guardian angels God will send thee,
> All through the night
> Soft the drowsy hours are creeping
> Hill and vale in slumber steeping
> I my loving vigil keeping
> All through the night.

The children, and Pele, hold hands and cry, knowing what they have lost.

Pele knows that, for the children, it is the first step. It changes their brains. She does not know how she will get past it.

Perhaps, she thinks later, alone and staring at the place she thought she always wanted to be, she never will.

> And now within the old gray tower
> We've climbed the winding stair,
> And look out over all the earth

From topmost window there.

Far stretches all the world away,
And naught shuts out the sky,
As knights and maids and all of life
Go marching, marching by.
                    —Olive Beaupré Miller, *From the Tower Window*

Finally, as they pass out of the solar system, it is time. They must get moving. They must set forth. They must transform.

And they do need her; they did bring her for a reason. She has lived this project, this drive, for decades, every detail of it. Bean's work has brought it to life, but there is no way to know how it will manifest, if they will survive, and, if they do, how it will change them. That part of it is greater than that which one can imagine.

All is in readiness. She is awake. The fulcrum is here. She has the lever to move it.

The minds, the dreams, of the children are the weight. They offer her thoughts, ideas, visions, insights, like flowers, which she gathers, and they all spark together, pointing toward fruition, the shift that will carry life forward.

This is humanity's main chance. She knows, but cannot think about, how important that is.

She prepares to play a vast chord, the way her piano teacher taught her, knowing it all first, in the instant before her spread fingers descend to the cool, hard, certain keys, back straight, elbows wide, with all she is contained within that force.

Pele plays.

This is the chord that sounds.

They are a creature of the deep sea, of interstellar space.

They are a thought, and thought is matter.

The ship, the matter, is like a film above, a fluid, a lens on the surface of their sky, the division between fluid and gas.

They coalesce: they rise.

Arrayed around Pele at that moment is a human orchestra, potential symphonies, jazz rhapsodies, new musics for which new brains to hear must be invented. On new planets, they may whirl and dance, skipping through the universe like stones, breaking through the surface tension of the strange fugue of time in which they are embedded, and sink back into life.

"Oh," she says, "oh." She bends over, weeping.

First comes Bean, whose willowy arms surround but barely touch her. Then Ta'a'aeva's rough embrace, her strong, gasping voice. Javail's tall blond head bending down to touch hers, and then they are all in a huddle, embracing tightly, crying, swaying, and, finally, laughing as they break.

"We will find the place we need," says Javail, his ever-adolescent voice breaking as he speaks, yet, as always, he sounds eminently reasonable. "As you can see, we have all the time in the world."

"We may need more," observes Pele, her voice harsh, and they break into applause that sounds, to Pele, like surf sounding at Kaena Point.

That is the last they see of her for a very long time.

There is music and frolic in the special time of Fairyland. No yesterday, and no tomorrow. Pipes call. Trumpets sound.

Nightingales, clear springs, the great rose-trees.

Magic. Some good, some bad, but uncaring of humans, rather like space.

Alcubierre eats Casimir Vacuums for breakfast, rips them out of a field with her big yellow teeth and chomps on them. The edges of the vacuums stick out of the sides of her mouth like gold straw and tiny blue flowers and move up and down as she chomps and snorts.

They are one speck of pollen on a single stamen of one small blue flower that bobs up and down in her mouth.

The Librarian carries a wooden clock.

It is chiefly oak. Framed by an oaken octagon a bit smaller than the main octagonal structure that holds the clock's mechanics and chimes, the face is protected by a glass door ten inches in diameter that one can open with a small latch. The hours are Roman numerals, painted on a cream-colored metal face. In black, swirling copperplate, a single word: *Excelsior*.

It has a smaller glass door, below, that one can open to start the pendulum swinging.

The Librarian carries it cradled in her left arm, like a baby. Therefore, it does not tick, for the pendulum drops against the back of its compartment.

The hands of the clock are silver, their deliciously narrow, elongated arrows a final flourish, pointing at the hour, the minute, and the infinite in-betweens.

A key rattles inside its small, latched drawer at the bottom of the pendulum when she walks, and the three square holes in the face's clock emit faint light. Sometimes she unlatches the drawer, opens it, and examines the key closely, with a look of wonder on her face. Then she returns it to its drawer and re-latches the tiny brass hook.

Every so often, she opens the door of the clock's face, tilts her head, smiles, and moves first the long arrow to a place that seems random, and then the small hand. She beams at the clock, shuts the door, and goes about her business. She never inserts the key. She never winds the clock.

If she has to do something requiring the use of her left hand, she sets the clock carefully in a safe place and immediately retrieves it when done. She straps it in beside her when she sleeps.

This seems a burdensome practice, but it gives her pleasure. Laying bets regarding various aspects of what she does with the clock have become popular.

It gives us something to do.

In one of the vacuums—there are many—I grew this voice that says *we*. I don't know how, though I am trying to tell you.

I might have grown it when I was Nancy Drew, in her blue roadster, driving through dark space, past planets. One . . . two . . . three . . . ten thousand . . . it took a long time. Then there were white farmhouses just off a dusty dirt road, hidden behind summer trees, their big heads tossing in the hot wind as if they had something haughty to say.

Inside one house with open windows a planet mobile rotated in the breeze. A girl with long black braids, lying on a double wedding ring quilt made by her grandmother, pointed to them and said, "Strike Hypatia off the list. And Dulcinea, too." They disappeared from the mobile, and others appeared.

I sped into the brain of the little girl and it was all myth, science, clockwork, precise, wires, pulses, blood, AI, luminous, expanding, nova, pressure, big bang, dust, and me, driving past on country lane in a blue roadster, hair streaming violently far, far, far out behind me, pushed by my own speed, seeing white snowball bushes in the front yard, and a cherry tree, and a woman gathering billowing white sheets from a clothesline, and a girl inside analyzing planetary composition.

You can see why I can't tell you exactly how it happened.

Pele looks like Pele, except that her eyes are different. She won't look at anyone. She does smile a lot. She calls herself The Librarian and says she would like to help us.

This is when the clock shows up. You know about that already.

We can't really blame her for acting this way. She had many areas of expertise when we stole the *Moku*, like all the other adults on the ship, but she was uniquely special, so we stole her too.

She knew how to make our horse.

She thinks that she chose to help us by staying with us and saved all the other adults by sending them back to Earth. She thinks she is our savior.

We let her think that because whenever she realizes that we have control, she acts in ways that are not helpful to us.

For instance, when the prince arrives to kiss her (and is the prince us, and what we did? it seems possible) she pushes him down, kicks him in the side three times (once or twice is not enough, while four or more is overdoing it), and strides off down a long, winding road, over hill and dale, hands in her pockets, whistling, looking at everything with a keen and watchful eye.

She walks through rain, hail, sleet, and snow, singing about it, all bundled up, sometimes an old woman, sometimes a young maiden, and then through summer meadows that climb the flanks of mountains, her clock in a bag that she throws over her shoulder. She wears loose, purple linen pants with large pockets, which she fills with things that seem useless.

She sees beautiful, glowing stones by the side of the path—one gray, one gold, and one rainbowed with layers of minerals. She picks them up and examines each, a large smile on her face. She puts them in her right-hand pants pocket.

To us they look like dull old rocks, but then somehow, like magic, we see them through her eyes, and know what they are. The stones and the power of stones are stories. She is gathering all the stories everyone has ever told, and *our* stories, and keeping them safe in her pocket until we know how to tell them. There are so many stories in that pocket that you would think her pants would fall down, but though the stories are endless, and the stones are all different, they do not, for the stones are magic stones; the pants magic pants.

Only if we sit around a fire that lights our faces and dances to the dark treetops whenever one of us throws on branches scavenged from the woods, throwing sparks into the night, does she consent to pull out a stone and tell us a story. We have to beg and yell at her. She says that only then are our brains receptive, when we are parched of stories.

She says this is a way to go back to the beginning, to break down our brains to a place we had bypassed in our speed to understand, and that was during the time that we were supposed to look at other faces and wonder what they were thinking. We were supposed to learn to understand when they were sad, when they were happy, and when they had feelings that were more complex, like a flavor or scent or a sound that comes out of the deep dark forest that is a sweet, mysterious music that calls you to come. She says this is the beginning of love.

When she talks like that, when she tells us stories, her voice is rich and deep, her face fluid, when often it is flat, like some of ours.

Her stories change our brains. We can even measure where and how much. It's something to do.

Her eyes get very wide, or narrow to slits. Her mouth assumes strange shapes. Sometimes she opens it wide and screams, reaches to the sky and grabs at it, her hands open, then grasps as she suddenly! in an instant! catches something and pulls it to her chest, and bows her head over it, and her long white hair veils her mysterious face, pale in the moonlight, silent as one of her stones, and we cry without knowing why, feeling helpless and at the same time knowing that she will help.

It is the age of stories. We suck them down like nectar.

We search for our new home. We move like a sea creature through the dark, generating our own electricity. Fluid, ever-changing, Ship translucent or solid-seeming, as we wish.

We grow no older. Why? Biological processes continue; of course. We live. We do the things we need to do, but our horse is wise, and knows much more than we.

Pele is still there, though they don't know it. Or they do, sometimes. She fears a foray through some other kind of spacetime weather in which they will all age to telomerase endgame and die in what seems minutes. Who knows.

The instant that divides life and death. We must learn to skip it.

Periods of waking like cards constantly shuffled, the deck and game continually changing—the rules, the faces, the very basis of the numbers and what they mean.

"This one is too cold," says Isho, who is Goldilocks. "And this one is too hot."

"And none is just right, and none will ever be," screams Ta'a'aeva, who is always the biggest bear. She storms away from the cottage. Isho and Kevin, the middle-sized bear, drop into tiny green chairs, sobbing.

"That's not how it goes!" says Alouette, kneeling and holding Isho and Kevin in a skinny-armed embrace. "You know the story. Happy ending, and all that."

"No," says Kevin, his voice wild. "No! None of them are right. None of them ever will be right! There is no place for us in any universe except Earth.

And it is gone!" He flings himself at Pele and tries to hit her in a flurry of punches. "My mother is gone! My father is gone! My sisters and brothers are gone! All these stories are lies!"

Pele holds him back for a moment, and just at the right time, she lets him collapse against her. She grabs him, holds him, rocks him back and forth. "I know, Kevin. Except this is not the end of the story. It's not the end at all."

Kevin fights free and runs.

Pele drops to the tiny stairs of the cottage and drops her head to her hands. It no longer matters whether she did the right thing or the wrong thing. Those words have no meaning. Here they are.

Ta'a'aeva returns from wherever she went, and stands next to Pele. "Sit up straight." Pele feels the girl's sure fingers dance against her scalp, hears the swift *thush thush* of braiding. "We are Wayfaring. We need to watch the sky, the birds, the waves. Kevin," she shouts. "Check out the signature of the star we found yesterday."

Kevin's sullen voice, muffled by tears, issues from the forest. "There is no signature. There is no star." A rock bounces off the side of the cottage. "Liar."

Pele hears Ta'a'aeva's low chuckle. "Yesterday we grew new eyes. I just found out. Go and see. It's true."

Kevin hurries away.

Xia, the big organdy bow on her dress untied and trailing behind her, says, "Pele, none of us believe in these stories, you know. They're all a bunch of hooey. An artificial organization that gathers reality together like a bouquet of flowers, just picking the prettiest ones and ignoring everything that has turned brown already. And that organized bouquet still dies the next day and gets thrown in the trash. We pretend to make you happy."

"That's quite wonderful of you," Pele says. "I appreciate it." She does not point out that in another of their *flashes*, their realities, their lives—whatever you might call it, when they wake, and wake again, resume their lives like nodes of blinking light in the depths of the deepest sea, none of them would have even understood that Pele could be happy or sad, and if they had, it would not have mattered to them.

Her clock is on the wall of the tiny bedroom upstairs. We wonder if she knows it.

Kevin is right.

We might have missed the news. It might have failed to penetrate to where we were. It would have been better if we had never known. Instead, it is a scream of deepest sorrow that runs through the ship, penetrates to our very core.

We are now, evermore, and henceforth alone.

The Earth, and all its life, is gone.

There was a nuclear war. All their painstaking and careful safeguards could not hold against a handful of people who did not care for life.

Unknowable *flashes*, garbled pictures, sick-making nightmares, and mornings of waking in our own beds as the sweet birds sing. There is no way to measure that time.

We wonder if the Librarian's clock has anything to do with this. But she will not say.

Ta'a'aeva keeps telling Pele that she had no choice, that they had sussed her out from the beginning. Pele knows that isn't true. They had no idea why she did it. They didn't know because neither did she. It is a big fat tragic mystery.

She makes that mystery into a vase that she keeps on her kitchen window. She fills the vase with starlight as the memory-threads holding her to Earth stretch, and finally snap, leaving her weightless.

She needs weight to live.

We read the stars, their signatures and histories, and calculate the planets they may have spawned. There are gas giants, dead rocks too cold or too dark for what we might call life, and some don't spin, but some of them have water and it is toward them that we navigate until we are close enough for searing disappointment.

During our navigation, we turn into ourselves again. We remember that our personalities are formed by the languages of genes, not stories, but that our actions can be influenced by the stories we learn. It's actually very scary. When we are lucky enough to grow up with stories of love, and not meanness and hate, then we can love. Love makes us happy. Stories of hate teach us only how to be victorious and to hurt others. What is most scary is how many ways we can hurt each other without even knowing that we have, or how hard it is to learn to act in ways that do not hurt others the next time. That is because there is never a same next time, so something has to be constant and at the same time fluid inside of you in the place that acts. Sometimes it is easy to think that there isn't anything anyone can do about this. Sometimes sadness teaches lessons that lead to more sadness, but sometimes it can lead to changed behavior. Sometimes happiness cannot figure out how to give itself to others. Sometimes joy can only be lived, a lucky chance that one takes, a risk that says damn the consequences. But sometimes the consequences can lead to all kinds of bad places. One must keep air inside a bladder and shoot back to the sun.

Not everyone knows how to do this.

Not everyone has a bladder, air, a sea, or a sun.

We are lucky.

We wake from another coldsleep. Sometimes we are in cocoons; other times, in coffins and kissed to consciousness by the prince-of-allgood-dreams; sometimes we pass the time as equations or as prime numbers: one unique majestic mountain peak after another. That's infinity. That's real fun. And, of course, it takes a very long time. Or so it seems.

We incorporate ourselves and grow ourselves and enhance ourselves with the genes of other species. We invent new species. We discard them, and sometimes they discard us. Then we bloom again, but different, somewhat. Still, we keep the memory of Life, rich Life, towards which we long with all our hearts. And the palette of a planet which we will change. Which will change us.

Life.

We fire the forest, stand back from the searing heat, retreat behind a clear panel and watch the blaze.

Though they live longer than anything else, bristlecone pines eventually need fire for regenesis. On Earth, lightning performed that function.

Yes, it has been that long. And longer.

Alcubierre has no colors, or more colors than we can know. She is immense; invisible.

Some of us grow new senses that we use to pat Alcubierre on her withers, even though it looks as if we are making the bed or splitting firewood or watching ants have wars. These are things no one has to do any longer, but some of us think it is helpful to believe they are doing them, so we make work for ourselves and say it keeps us sane.

Alcubierre is so huge that we will never see the beginning or end of her. In fact, the only way to think about her is with other kinds of symbols, not words.

That accounts for how the story keeps changing. Who we are and how we tell it.

We look at Pele's vase. "What is that?" asks Xia.

Pele says, "It is sadness too strong to bear. But it is something I need to feel. If we cannot understand how our actions impact others, we will bring nothing to the place we are going."

Kevin frowns. "That makes no sense at all."

It does to me.

The Librarian has been in the library for a very, very long time. Through two coldsleeps at least. Now she sits, smiling at the clock.

Amelia, who has been lying on her back, thinking, jumps up, smiling. "I have an idea!"

She gently lifts the clock from the Librarian's hands.

The Librarian stands, stiffly. She moves her arms forward a few inches but no farther. She stares at the clock, her mouth slightly open, distress in her eyes.

Amelia opens the little door holding the rattling key, and then the door to the face that contains the keyholes.

"That won't work," says Ta'a'aeva.

"We must keep trying," says Amelia. She winds, winds, winds each mechanism. "Hold this," she says, handing the key to Jaques. She opens the door for the pendulum, and sets it ticking.

Then she takes the clock and presses it to the wall. It adheres, becoming a part of the ship, and something of the ship flows into it.

The Librarian gasps. "No!" She runs to the clock and tries to wrestle it from the wall. As she yanks on it she wails, "No! No! No!" But she does allow Amelia to gently move her aside.

"Look," says Amelia.

The Librarian has changed to Pele, Pele of the mobile face, the warm, beautiful brown eyes.

"Thank you," she says.

Sometimes Pele prepares for the invasion.

Invisibly, in particles, they scout the terrain of Terra Nova, Planet X. It breaks down in this way:

1. It is empty, ready for us, with no life, but able to accept life, or with life that will not interfere with ours, or
2. They are ready for us, or something like us. The branches:
   1. Annihilation
   2. Rejection

3. Acceptance/modification
4. Surrender

Of these four, Pele fancies most number three. Except: what are they save identity?

Yet identity undergoes constant modification.

This is a special kind of hell. She decides to enjoy a thousand amazing sunsets to refresh herself.

Pele wonders how to say what is happening. "Time passes?" "Spacetime moves?" "We *flash,* and *flash* again, in long instants, out of darkness, and into light?"

They play, and play again, in endless iterations.

The running of the ship, the thought-ship? Inflections wash through it each moment, Earth-based inflections of thought wrought from the hard thrash of human dreams, human longing. So they are all dancing-ship stories. That's all they are: stories. Pele's unique slice of older-time gives her wry perspective. She can be outside the story. She stubbornly refuses to surrender. It-is-not-real, she thinks, seeing them all at play, leaping from bloody mayhem to the estranging magic of *Through Fairy Halls,* and, often, lying spent and weeping on a riverbank after being swept up in the billions of dark stories that comprise their heritage.

It takes all her strength and more, drawn from a rich stew of inspiring works, to pull them back from self-annihilation. For what choice is there, they collectively feel, after being soaked in the deep evil that humans do, but to remove themselves from the picture?

Whether or not they are right, she hurls tales of goodness, blazing thunderbolts, into their minds. They wake bright-faced, with a jolt, ready for the new day. She doesn't exactly dust her hands in self-satisfaction, but she does try not to wonder too hard if she's done the right thing. Who is she to shield them from grief; from sorrow, from deep reflection, or from growth?

She just tries to keep them from hurting one another, and from hurting them or herself. What else can she do?

She tries to be older and wiser. She absorbs old movies; re-views *Casablanca* as a lesson about how one bestows grace through artful lies concocted on the run, new tales to make things go right. These are lessons she missed while on Earth. She spoke from stalwart truth, never mind what pain it caused. How can one make these calculations, though, when in the midst of chaos, which is where she lives, in a constantly re-invented throng of young entities who cannot understand literatures truly until they have gained in wisdom? And who cannot gain wisdom except through sorrow, which she does not wish to thrust upon them? Sorrow generally bestows cynicism, and she is back in the same old revolution, lifted up and down until they die except

They cannot die.

We are scattered into particles. We are a speeding cloud, intent.

It is a word at last, the word that's been there all along, our Kansas home:

Courage! With a Brooklyn accent.

Whatever, wherever, that is.

"Courage," we shout. Our brave chests expand, our heads a single thought, shooting for we know not what, re-organized by new information every instant, but shooting forward, now, at last, to Planet.

We will find ways to infuse any matter we find. We will organize and blend, we will crush and release.

For we are the mighty, the awful, the terrifying power of life itself. We are infinitely tiny, infinitely large.

Our words describe the states that we create; the states create us, and a bond sings through it all.

Courage!

We crash onto every wave-hushed shore, every cold rocky outpost, every object that will hold us, with equal, eager, organizing force, programs of life, and flower, for a brief instant of stability, everywhere at once, a wide delight of life itself. We pass the instant of death, the deep drag of dread and sadness, the roiling, drowning crush of force upon force. We rush up the beaches, we drift to the high peaks, we burrow, nest, burst, and sing.

And leave ourselves, that dream of us, behind, and continue.

An instant from far here to far there, like the instant dividing life from death, but skipping that, as it must be skipped.

This is the story of how a bunch of kids kidnapped a physicist who was also a librarian so that they could get to a new planet, one far outside of our solar system. It sounds like a fairy tale because it might be.

It is really very simple.

We cross a roaring creek on a rickety bridge, fishing pole on our shoulder, in a deep mountain chasm, heading home in an evening of cold, settling mist, alone.

Yet heading somewhere.

A tentative confidence sparkles, a stand of tiny pink Galax that Pele does not pick. She hikes upward through an early spring forest of re-awakened earth, its moist smell of leaf-loam and the rush of the new-born creek fed by high snowmelt a cool, moist blessing, as is the fact of day, where trees hide most of the sky and those tempting, empty stars. She comes across it again and again in her solitary hikes, and each time kneels and contemplates it with renewed, deep, solitary wonder: it and her. A different life, with a different story, but a story nonetheless.

Life, in all that lifelessness.

After a thousand such *flash*-lives filled with wonder, bursting into time, she returns to here, knows it to be real, and for the first time, Pele does not recoil.

Why did she do it? Why did she let them go?

Was it hubris—wanting to see if her science project would really work?

Was it a heroic act, a Noah for the arc?

Blind, rushing ignorance?

This is our house.

This is our bed.

These are our chairs.

"We have left Oz in a magic balloon," says Targa, lying on his back with his hands laced behind his neck. "We made the fire, like the professor. So who is the Wicked Witch of the West who will punish us for trying to get to our new home?"

"Pele," yells Oscar.

"No!" several chorus. Ki says, "Pele is Glinda!"

"Pele is the sleeping princess,"

"She's awake." "Not really."

"And so are we all munchkins?" asks Juno indignantly. "Or flying monkeys?"

"I'm a flying monkey," says Targa, flipping over and pushing off, soaring with arms extended.

"And do we have hearts?"

"I am working on mine," says Bean, splaying two long-fingered hands across her chest. "I am working very, very hard."

Pele, hunched near-fetal in her berth, hears voices. She always does, but these wake her, for some reason. She opens one eye and sees that they have furnished her with a crystal ball with which to watch the proceedings. She allows herself a brief, tiny smile, uncurls, stretches, and leans forward on her elbows. "Wicked witch," she votes aloud, her long-unused vocal chords pushing it out as a rusty whisper.

They all look at the monitor, wave and cheer. "Pele! Pele! Pele!"

She tests the most important word: "Courage!"

"Courage," they yell back. "Courage!"

How long can longing last? Is English really so sparse?

Pele finds the German word *sehnsucht*. Sounds like a sneeze. And that C.S. Lewis said it is "That unnamable something, desire for which pierces us like a rapier at the smell of bonfire, the sound of wild ducks flying overhead, the title of *The Well at the World's End*, the opening lines of "Kubla Khan," the morning cobwebs in late summer, or the noise of falling waves, carrying the freight of longing's complexity, modified by underlying stratum of utopias particular to each individual."

But English has its strengths, for longing indeed is . . . long. Endless, in fact. Until what she imagines will be that eyeblink, sudden as their previous transition to the inescapable longing of perpetual now.

Presently, that is Pele's name for this planet.

Sehnsucht. "Zeenzucht," Pele says, and saying it changes her brain. Or something. Maybe.

Despite all we know and all we have learned about Shining Leaf, as Ta'a'aeva insists we call this planet, there is much that remains unknown.

Shining Leaf is just a blip. Another *flash*, a nanosecond opening that, taking, we risk all.

We have seeded other planets with our clones. As far as we know, they all died. We all died. But here we are. Still.

We are, at last, restless. In fact, we are able to realize that we are mad.

That we are ready to choose.

Pele never votes. "I voted once," she says, and we say, "Yes, and we are glad that you did."

She makes us promise something. And, at last, we do.

We cannot even talk about the painful changes that swept through us when we disengaged the drive. How it looked, felt. The precise analytics, biological and physical. How long it took in mundane time. The unspinning. Realizing the door of us, each unique. *Moku* could tell that story, and those in the future will want to know.

Having lived it is enough for us.

Moku was our home. It sustained us in our search, kept us alive, taught us much, but kept us in a state of fear and hesitation. We wanted to grow up badly enough to die if it did not work. Like Pinocchio, we wanted to be real.

We saw our main chance, and we took it.

And so became human again.

How can you tell the choice between good and evil when that choice is hard upon you? How do you recognize it? Is there a way to measure the road not taken? Why would that matter?

We have learned much about taking risk. We could not help moving into this.

From the Giant's abode in the sky, Jack stole the harp that plays by itself.

The ship is that: we stole it.

From the Giant's abode in the sky, Jack stole the goose that lays the golden egg.

Perhaps that is us.

Will we live happily ever after?

Time will tell.

When a horse wins a race, she is heaped with flowers. She snorts and prances and feels proud.

Our horse, on which we placed all bets, won.

So many suns, so many planets that did not suit. You know that tale. Some, seeded by us with life, might now be flourishing, but we will never know.

It is not luck that brought us here, to this perfect planet, with its perfect star.

It was courage.

Beneath this glorious, intense blue-violet sky, buffeted by sea-wind, I know, ineluctably, that I am *here*, on this loud coast. Crashing waves suck rattling, tumbling stones back into the shorebreak, nicking my bare feet and calves with delicious sharp pings. Sunset-tinged clouds billow like great swans on the horizon. I pull in breaths of sweet salt air, keeping an eye on my great-granddaughter, playing tag with rushing foam.

Shining Leaf is no game, no illusion, no manufactured reality, and it is no fairy tale. I spin round and see the gully-ridden cliff behind me rise, thick with massive virgin trees, relatives of red alder, bigleaf maple, Sitka spruce—trees that relish deep morning fog. They ascend in tiers of wind-tossed greens to the long grasslands above.

The pampas stretch for fifty miles to snow-peaked mountains, where just below the tree line buffeting winds twist and gnarl the bristlecone pines. Across the plains gallop herds of savannah animals, for our biosystems found homes here as well, and have flourished. And when I ride my real horse there, she actually moves, and we do reach the plane trees.

Sometimes, after opening my bedroll and making tea, a human speck amid a sea of high, sweet-smelling grasses where the sound of the rushing wind combing and flattening the grass is equally sweet, I gaze at the stars among which I lived for I do not know how long and am infused, suddenly, by a sense of deep and utter strangeness, illuminated by that . . . *flash* we all felt—or were—on *Moku*.

It seems just a second, but I cannot be sure how long it lasts, that *flash* during which I am transformed; illuminated. It could be eons. It could be Planck time, the tiniest bit of time we can measure. But when I am there, and perhaps always, I am like a pebble of pure consciousness, tossed into the most lucid medium imaginable, where my ripples intersect with and are changed by other patterns, and this goes on forever.

It is then that I know that I am not as I was, and it is then that I long to be back among the stars, and to never touch land again.

But here, I invent new languages to map the house of thought I build. My thoughts were useful once; they may be useful again. Or not.

I could tell you how our chimerists, biophysicists, engineers, artists, and mathematicians generated experimental interim environments to test and refine our interaction with this new planet as we explored it virtually, hungering to land and climb its towering young mountains and sail its vast seas. We studied its weather patterns, developed plans for symbiosis, testing and re-testing, accelerating path after path, answering question after question, for we had time, and we had to be satisfied. But that is all in our library; you can experience it there. We grew, changed, exploded into larger life, real life, using *Moku*'s vast genetic library and modeling algorithms to make decisions about populating Shining Leaf with ourselves and other fauna, learning from stories of failures on Earth, merging with what was here. The very last step, the most serious, was deciding where best to settle, and how.

We chose well. We changed, very slightly, to adapt to Shining Leaf, to its particular chemistries, its atmosphere, and its wilder seas, which Ta'a'aeva's tribe explores with zest, though *Moku* mapped its every fractal coast, her motto being "the map is not the territory." We grew defenses against that which would have killed us, larger and different lungs to inhale and use a slightly different atmosphere. Alcubierre gave us time to do that.

We live in towns and villages scattered around the planet, and have plans for golden cities, both far and near, which now assemble. We have new sciences, new technologies, communications networks that run on new symbioses, and the sure knowledge that we are still changing, because life is change, and because change is life.

I have young Bean's heart and mind, yet my grown mind is different, a human/spacetime hybrid, and my hard-grown soul my own.

Is a soul courage? Is it philosophical depth? Is it simple immortality? Is it the being that runs through us, animates us, the foundation of all love and hope and deep satisfaction in the art of living, in community, in life itself?

Here, we and our children chart their own courses; they are pioneers, seekers, builders, dreamers. One son is an artist: one daughter, an engineer. My many descendants flourish.

The wind, evening-strong, blows back my hair. I lean down and pluck up a cool, gleaming golden stone from the tumble, hold its water-honed, near-translucent thinness up to our new star and think of all the time this one stone holds and might reveal, from when it exploded into being until now, after being crushed and washed and tumbled and honed into this beauty that I, also a part of the same story, can see, hold, taste, and smell.

I give it to my great-granddaughter, who is four, to play with and she flips it in the air and laughs. Her eyes are hazel, like my father's.

I think of the librarian, who died long, long ago, and know for a certainty, which has not always been the case, that she was real, and that this is not a fairy tale, but something we have done.

We named our star for her: Pele.

She helped me grow a soul.

And that makes everything worth it.

> Here's a heigh and a ho! for the purpose strong,
> And the bold stout hearts that roam,
> And sail the Seven Seas of Life
> To bring such treasures home!
> —Olive Beaupré Miller, *The Treasure Chest*

—With everlasting thanks to Irma Gwendolyn Knott
Poems herein by Olive Beaupré Miller, *My Bookhouse*,
The Bookhouse for Children Publishers, Chicago, Illinois, 1920

Yoon Ha Lee's debut *Ninefox Gambit* won the Locus Award for Best First Novel and was a finalist for the Hugo, Nebula, and Clarke Awards. His short fiction has appeared in *Tor.com, Clarkesworld, Lightspeed, Beneath Ceaseless Skies, The Magazine of Fantasy and Science Fiction*, and other venues. He lives in Louisiana with his family and cat, and has not yet been eaten by gators.

EXTRACURRICULAR ACTIVITIES

Yoon Ha Lee

When Shuos Jedao walked into his temporary quarters on Station Muru 5 and spotted the box, he assumed someone was attempting to assassinate him. It had happened before. Considering his first career, there was even a certain justice to it.

He ducked back around the doorway, although even with his reflexes, he would have been too late if it'd been a proper bomb. The air currents in the room would have wafted his biochemical signature to the box and caused it to trigger. Or someone could have set up the bomb to go off as soon as the door opened, regardless of who stepped in. Or something even less sophisticated.

Jedao retreated back down the hallway and waited one minute. Two. Nothing.

It could just be a package, he thought—paperwork that he had forgotten?—but old habits died hard.

He entered again and approached the desk, light-footed. The box, made of eye-searing green plastic, stood out against the bland earth tones of the walls and desk. It measured approximately half a meter in all directions. Its nearest face prominently displayed the gold seal that indicated that station security had cleared it. He didn't trust it for a moment. Spoofing a seal wasn't that difficult. He'd done it himself.

He inspected the box's other visible sides without touching it, then spotted a letter pouch affixed to one side and froze. He recognized the handwriting. The address was written in spidery high language, while the name of the recipient—one Garach Jedao Shkan—was written both in the high language and his birth tongue, Shparoi, for good measure.

Oh, Mom, Jedao thought. No one else called him by that name anymore, not even the rest of his family. More important, how had his mother gotten his address? He'd just received his transfer orders last week, and he hadn't written home about it because his mission was classified. He had no idea what his new general wanted him to do; she would tell him tomorrow morning when he reported in.

Jedao opened the box, which released a puff of cold air. Inside rested a tub labeled KEEP REFRIGERATED in both the high language and Shparoi. The tub itself contained a pale, waxy-looking solid substance. *Is this what I think it is?*

Time for the letter:

> *Hello, Jedao!*
> *Congratulations on your promotion. I hope you enjoy your new command moth and that it has a more pronounceable name than the last one.*

One: What promotion? Did she know something he didn't? (Scratch that question. She always knew something he didn't.) Two: Trust his mother to rate warmoths not by their armaments or the efficacy of their stardrives but by their *names*. Then again, she'd made no secret that she'd hoped he'd wind up a musician like his sire. It had not helped when he pointed out that when he attempted to sing in academy, his fellow cadets had threatened to dump grapefruit soup over his head.

> *Since I expect your eating options will be dismal, I have sent you goose fat rendered from the great-great-great-etc.-grandgosling of your pet goose when you were a child. (She was delicious, by the way.) Let me know if you run out and I'll send more.*
>
> *Love,*
> *Mom*

So the tub contained goose fat, after all. Jedao had never figured out why his mother sent food items when her idea of cooking was to gussy up instant noodles with an egg and some chopped green onions. All the cooking Jedao knew, he had learned either from his older brother or, on occasion, those of his mother's research assistants who took pity on her kids.

What am I supposed to do with this? he wondered. As a cadet he could have based a prank around it. But as a warmoth commander he had standards to uphold.

More importantly, how could he compose a suitably filial letter of appreciation without, foxes forbid, encouraging her to escalate? (Baked goods: fine. Goose fat: less fine.) Especially when she wasn't supposed to know he was here in the first place? Some people's families sent them care packages of useful things, like liquor, pornography, or really nice cosmetics. Just his luck.

At least the mission gave him an excuse to delay writing back until his location was unclassified, even if she knew it anyway.

Jedao had heard a number of rumors about his new commanding officer, Brigadier General Kel Essier. Some of them, like the ones about her junior wife's lovers, were none of his business. Others, like Essier's taste in plum wine, weren't relevant, but could come in handy if he needed to scare up a bribe someday. What had really caught his notice was her service record. She had fewer decorations than anyone else who'd served at her rank for a comparable period of time.

Either Essier was a political appointee—the Kel military denied the practice, but everyone knew better—or she was sitting on a cache of classified medals. Jedao had a number of those himself. (Did his mother know about those too?) Although Station Muru 5 was a secondary military base, Jedao had his suspicions about any "secondary" base that had a general in residence, even temporarily. That, or Essier was disgraced and Kel Command couldn't think of anywhere else to dump her.

Jedao had a standard method for dealing with new commanders, which was to research them as if he planned to assassinate them. Needless to say, he never expressed it in those terms to his comrades.

He'd come up with two promising ways to get rid of Essier. First, she collected meditation foci made of staggeringly luxurious materials. One of her officers had let slip that her latest obsession was antique lacquerware. Planting a bomb or toxin in a collector-grade item wouldn't be risky so much as *expensive*. He'd spent a couple hours last night brainstorming ways to steal one, just for the hell of it; lucky that he didn't have to follow through.

The other method took advantage of the poorly planned location of the firing range on this level relative to the general's office, and involved shooting her through several walls and a door with a high-powered rifle and burrower ammunition. Jedao hated burrower ammunition, not because it didn't work but because it did. He had a lot of ugly scars on his torso from the time a burrower had almost killed him. That being said, he also believed in using the appropriate tool for the job.

No one had upgraded Muru 5 for the past few decades. Its computer grid ran on outdated hardware, making it easy for him to pull copies of all the maps he pleased. He'd also hacked into the security cameras long enough to check the layout of the general's office. The setup made him despair of the architects who had designed the whole wretched thing. On top of that, Essier had set up her desk so a visitor would see it framed beautifully by the doorway, with her chair perfectly centered. Great for impressing visitors, less great for making yourself a difficult target. Then again, attending to Essier's safety wasn't his job.

Jedao showed up at Essier's office seven minutes before the appointed time. "Whiskey?" said her aide.

If only, Jedao thought; he recognized it as one he couldn't afford. "No, thank you," he said with the appropriate amount of regret. He didn't trust special treatment.

"Your loss," said the aide. After another two minutes, she checked her slate. "Go on in. The general is waiting for you."

As Jedao had predicted, General Essier sat dead center behind her desk, framed by the doorway and two statuettes on either side of the desk, gilded ash-hawks carved from onyx. Essier had dark skin and close-shaven hair, and the height and fine-spun bones of someone who had grown up in low gravity. The black-and-gold Kel uniform suited her. Her gloved hands rested on the desk in perfect symmetry. Jedao bet she looked great in propaganda videos.

Jedao saluted, fist to shoulder. "Commander Shuos Jedao reporting as ordered, sir."

"Have a seat," Essier said. He did. "You're wondering why you don't have a warmoth assignment yet."

"The thought had crossed my mind, yes."

Essier smiled. The smile was like the rest of her: beautiful and calculated and not a little deadly. "I have good news and bad news for you, Commander. The good news is that you're due a promotion."

Jedao's first reaction was not gratitude or pride, but *How did my mother—?* Fortunately, a lifetime of *How did my mother—?* enabled him to keep his expression smooth and instead say, "And the bad news?"

"Is it true what they say about your battle record?"

This always came up. "You have my profile."

"You're good at winning."

"I wasn't under the impression that the Kel military found this objectionable, sir."

"Quite right," she said. "The situation is this. I have a mission in mind for you, but it will take advantage of your unique background."

"Unique background" was a euphemism for *We don't have many commanders who can double as emergency special forces.* Most Kel with training in special ops stayed in the infantry instead of seeking command in the space forces. Jedao made an inquiring noise.

"Perform well, and you'll be given the fangmoth *Sieve of Glass*, which heads my third tactical group."

A bribe, albeit one that might cause trouble. Essier had six tactical groups. A newly minted group tactical commander being assigned third instead of sixth? Had she had a problem with her former third-position commander?

"My former third took early retirement," Essier said in answer to his unspoken question. "They were caught with a small collection of trophies."

"Let me guess," Jedao said. "Trophies taken from heretics."

"Just so. Third tactical is badly shaken. Fourth has excellent rapport with her group and I don't want to promote her out of it. But it's an opportunity for you."

"And the mission?"

Essier leaned back. "You attended Shuos Academy with Shuos Meng."

"I did," Jedao said. They'd gone by Zhei Meng as a cadet. "We've been in touch on and off." Meng had joined a marriage some years back. Jedao had commissioned a painting of five foxes, one for each person in the marriage, and sent it along with his best wishes. Meng wrote regularly about their kids—they couldn't be made to shut up about them—and Jedao sent gifts on cue, everything from hand-bound volumes of Kel jokes to fancy gardening tools. (At least they'd been sold to him as gardening tools. They looked suspiciously like they could double for heavy-duty surgical work.) "Why, what has Meng been up to?"

"Under the name Ahun Gerav, they've been in command of the merchanter *Moonsweet Blossom*."

Jedao cocked an eyebrow at Essier. "That's not a Shuos vessel." It did, however, sound like an Andan one. The Andan faction liked naming their trademoths after flowers. "By 'merchanter' do you mean 'spy'?"

"Yes," Essier said with charming directness. "Twenty-six days ago, one of the *Blossom*'s crew sent a code red to Shuos Intelligence. This is all she was able to tell us."

Essier retrieved a slate from within the desk and tilted it to show him a video. She needn't have bothered with the visuals; the combination of poor lighting, camera jitter, and static made them impossible to interpret. The audio was little better: ". . . *Blossom*, code red to Overwatch . . . Gerav's in . . ." Frustratingly, the static made the next few words unintelligible. "Du Station. You'd better—" The report of a gun, then another, then silence.

"Your task is to investigate the situation at Du Station in the Gwa Reality, and see if the crew and any of the intelligence they've gathered can be recovered. The Shuos heptarch suggested that you would be an ideal candidate for the mission. Kel Command was amenable."

I just bet, Jedao thought. He had once worked directly under his heptarch, and while he'd been one of her better assassins, he didn't miss those days. "Is this the only incident with the Gwa Reality that has taken place recently, or are there others?"

"The Gwa-an are approaching one of their regularly scheduled regime upheavals," Essier said. "According to the diplomats, there's a good chance that the next elected government will be less amenable to heptarchate interests. We want to go in, uncover what happened, and get out before things turn topsy-turvy."

"All right," Jedao said, "so taking a warmoth in would be inflammatory. What resources will I have instead?"

"Well, that's the bad news," Essier said, entirely too cheerfully. "Tell me, Commander, have you ever wanted to own a merchant troop?"

The troop consisted of eight trademoths, named *Carp 1* to *Carp 4*, then *Carp 7* to *Carp 10*. They occupied one of the station's docking bays. Someone had painted each vessel with distended carp-figures in orange and white. It did not improve their appearance.

The usual commander of the troop introduced herself as Churioi Haval, not her real name. She was portly, had a squint, and wore gaudy gilt jewelry, all excellent ways to convince people that she was an ordinary merchant and not, say, Kel special ops. It hadn't escaped his attention that she frowned ever so slightly when she spotted his sidearm, a Patterner 52, which wasn't standard Kel issue. "You're not bringing that, are you?" she said.

"No, I'd hate to lose it on the other side of the border," Jedao said. "Besides, I don't have a plausible explanation for why a boring communications tech is running around with a Shuos handgun."

"I could always hold on to it for you."

Jedao wondered if he'd ever get the Patterner back if he took her up on the offer. It hadn't come cheap. "That's kind of you, but I'll have the station store it for me. By the way, what happened to *Carp 5* and *6*?"

"Beats me," Haval said. "Before my time. The Gwa-an authorities have never hassled us about it. They're already used to, paraphrase, 'odd heptarchate numerological superstitions.'" She eyed Jedao critically, which made her look squintier. "Begging your pardon, but do you *have* undercover experience?"

What a refreshing question. Everyone knew the Shuos for their spies, saboteurs, and assassins, even though the analysts, administrators, and cryptologists did most of the real work. (One of his instructors had explained that "You will spend hours in front of a terminal developing posture problems" was far less effective at recruiting potential cadets than "Join the Shuos for an exciting future as a secret agent, assuming your classmates don't kill you before you graduate.") Most people who met Jedao assumed he'd killed an improbable number of people as Shuos infantry. Never mind that he'd been responsible for far more deaths since joining the regular military.

"You'd be surprised at the things I know how to do," Jedao said.

"Well, I hope you're good with cover identities," Haval said. "No offense, but you have a distinctive name."

That was a tactful way of saying that the Kel didn't tolerate many Shuos line officers; most Shuos seconded to the Kel worked in Intelligence. Jedao had a reputation for, as one of his former aides had put it, being expendable enough to send into no-win situations but too stubborn to die. Jedao smiled at Haval and said, "I have a good memory."

The rest of his crew also had civilian cover names. A tall, muscular man strolled up to them. Jedao surreptitiously admired him. The gold-mesh tattoo over the right side of his face contrasted handsomely with his dark skin. Too bad he was almost certainly Kel and therefore off-limits.

"This is Rhi Teshet," Haval said. "When he isn't watching horrible melodramas—"

"You have no sense of culture," Teshet said.

"—he's the lieutenant colonel in charge of our infantry."

Damn. Definitely Kel, then, and in his chain of command, at that. "A pleasure, Colonel," Jedao said.

Teshet's returning smile was slow and wicked and completely unprofessional. "Get out of the habit of using ranks," he said. "Just Teshet, please. I hear you like whiskey?"

Off-limits, Jedao reminded himself, despite the quickening of his pulse. Best to be direct. "I'd rather not get you in trouble."

Haval was looking to the side with a where-have-I-seen-this-dance-before expression. Teshet laughed. "The fastest way to get us caught is to behave like you have the Kel code of conduct tattooed across your forehead. Whereas *no one* will suspect you of being a hotshot commander if you're sleeping with one of your crew."

"I don't fuck people deadlier than I am, sorry," Jedao said demurely.

"Wrong answer," Haval said, still not looking at either of them. "Now he's going to think of you as a challenge."

"Also, I know your reputation," Teshet said to Jedao. "Your kill count has got to be higher than mine by an order of magnitude."

Jedao ignored that. "How often do you make trade runs into the Gwa Reality?"

"Two or three times a year," Haval said. "The majority of the runs are to maintain the fiction. The question is, do you have a plan?"

He didn't blame her for her skepticism. "Tell me again how much cargo space we have."

Haval told him.

"We sometimes take approved cultural goods," Teshet said, "in a data storage format negotiated during the Second Treaty of—"

"Don't bore him," Haval said. "The 'trade' is our job. He's just here for the explode-y bits."

"No, I'm interested," Jedao said. "The Second Treaty of Mwe Enh, am I right?"

Haval blinked. "You have remarkably good pronunciation. Most people can't manage the tones. Do you speak Tlen Gwa?"

"Regrettably not. I'm only fluent in four languages, and that's not one of them." Of the four, Shparoi was only spoken on his birth planet, making it useless for career purposes.

"If you have some Shuos notion of sneaking in a virus amid all the lectures on flower-arranging and the dueling tournament videos and the plays, forget it," Teshet said. "Their operating systems are so different from ours that you'd have better luck getting a magpie and a turnip to have a baby."

"Oh, not at all," Jedao said. "How odd would it look if you brought in a shipment of goose fat?"

Haval's mouth opened, closed.

Teshet said, "Excuse me?"

"Not literally goose fat," Jedao conceded. "I don't have enough for that and I don't imagine the novelty would enable you to run a sufficient profit. I assume you have to at least appear to be trying to make a profit."

"They like real profits even better," Haval said.

Diverted, Teshet said, "You have goose fat? Whatever for?"

"Long story," Jedao said. "But instead of goose fat, I'd like to run some of that variable-coefficient lubricant."

Haval rubbed her chin. "I don't think you could get approval to trade the formula or the associated manufacturing processes."

"Not that," Jedao said. "Actual canisters of lubricant. Is there someone in the Gwa Reality on the way to our luckless Shuos friend who might be willing to pay for it?"

Haval and Teshet exchanged baffled glances. Jedao could tell what they were thinking: *Are we the victims of some weird bet our commander has going on the side?* "There's no need to get creative," Haval said in a commendably diplomatic voice. "Cultural goods are quite reliable."

You think this *is creativity*, Jedao thought. "It's not that. Two battles ago, my fangmoth was almost blown in two because our antimissile defenses glitched. If we hadn't used the lubricant as a stopgap sealant, we wouldn't have made it." That much was even true. "If you can't offload all of it, I'll find another use for it."

"You do know you can't cook with lubricant?" Teshet said. "Although I wonder if it's good for—"

Haval stomped on his toe. "You already have plenty of the medically approved stuff," she said crushingly, "no need to risk getting your private parts cemented into place."

"Hey," Teshet said, "you never know when you'll need to improvise."

Jedao was getting the impression that Essier had not assigned him the best of her undercover teams. Certainly they were the least disciplined Kel he'd run into in a while, but he supposed long periods undercover had made them more casual about regulations. No matter, he'd been dealt worse hands. "I've let you know what I want done, and I've already checked that the station has enough lubricant to supply us. Make it happen."

"If you insist," Haval said. "Meanwhile, don't forget to get your immunizations."

"Will do," Jedao said, and strode off to Medical.

Jedao spent the first part of the voyage alternately learning basic Tlen Gwa, memorizing his cover identity, and studying up on the Gwa Reality. The Tlen Gwa course suffered some oddities. He couldn't see the use of some of the vocabulary items, like the one for "navel." But he couldn't manage to *un*learn it, either, so there it was, taking up space in his brain.

As for the cover identity, he'd had better ones, but he supposed the Kel could only do so much on short notice. He was now Arioi Sren, one of Haval's distant cousins by marriage. He had three spouses, with whom he had quarreled recently over a point of interior decoration. "I don't know anything about interior decoration," Jedao had said, to which Haval retorted, "That's probably what caused the argument."

The documents had included loving photographs of the home in question, an apartment in a dome city floating in the upper reaches of a very pretty gas giant. Jedao had memorized the details before destroying them. While he couldn't say how well the decor coordinated, he was good at layouts and kill zones. In any case, Sren was on "vacation" to escape the squabbling. Teshet had suggested that a guilt-inducing affair would round out the cover identity. Jedao said he'd think about it.

Jedao was using spray-on temporary skin, plus a high-collared shirt, to conceal multiple scars, including the wide one at the base of his neck. The temporary skin itched, which couldn't be helped. He hoped no one would strip-search him, but in case someone did, he didn't want to have to explain his old gunshot wounds. Teshet had also suggested that he stop shaving—the Kel disliked beards—but Jedao could only deal with so much itching.

The hardest part was not the daily skinseal regimen, but getting used to wearing civilian clothes. The Kel uniform included gloves, and Jedao felt exposed going around with naked hands. But keeping his gloves would have been a dead giveaway, so he'd just have to live with it.

The Gwa-an fascinated him most of all. Heptarchate diplomats called their realm the Gwa Reality. Linguists differed on just what the word rendered as "Reality" meant. The majority agreed that it referred to the Gwa-an belief that all dreams took place in the same noosphere, connecting the dreamers, and that even inanimate objects dreamed.

Gwa-an protocols permitted traders to dock at designated stations. Haval quizzed Jedao endlessly on the relevant etiquette. Most of it consisted of keeping his mouth shut and letting Haval talk, which suited him fine. While the Gwa-an provided interpreters, Haval said cultural differences were the real problem. "Above all," she added, "if anyone challenges you to a duel, don't. Just don't. Look blank and plead ignorance."

"Duel?" Jedao said, interested.

"I knew we were going to have to have this conversation," Haval said glumly. "They don't use swords, so get that idea out of your head."

"I didn't bring my dueling sword anyway, and Sren wouldn't know how," Jedao said. "Guns?"

"Oh no," she said. "They use *pathogens*. Designer pathogens. Besides the fact that their duels can go on for years, I've never heard that you had a clue about genetic engineering."

"No," Jedao said, "that would be my mother." Maybe next time he could suggest to Essier that his mother be sent in his place. His mother would adore the chance to talk shop. Of course, then he'd be out of a job. "Besides, I'd rather avoid bringing a plague back home."

"They *claim* they have an excellent safety record."

Of course they would. "How fast can they culture the things?"

"That was one of the things we were trying to gather data on."

"If they're good at diseasing up humans, they may be just as good at manufacturing critters that like to eat synthetics."

"While true of their tech base in general," Haval said, "they won't have top-grade labs at Du Station."

"Good to know," Jedao said.

Jedao and Teshet also went over the intelligence on Du Station. "It's nice that you're taking a personal interest," Teshet said, "but if you think we're taking the place by storm, you've been watching too many dramas."

"If Kel special forces aren't up for it," Jedao said, very dryly, "you could always send me. One of me won't do much good, though."

"Don't be absurd," Teshet said. "Essier would have my head if you got hurt. How many people *have* you assassinated?"

"Classified," Jedao said.

Teshet gave a can't-blame-me-for-trying shrug. "Not to say I wouldn't love to see you in action, but it isn't your job to run around doing the boring infantry work. How do you mean to get the crew out? Assuming they survived, which is a big if."

Jedao tapped his slate and brought up the schematics for one of their cargo shuttles. "Five per trader," he said musingly.

"Du Station won't let us land the shuttles however we please."

"Did I say anything about landing them?" Before Teshet could say anything further, Jedao added, "You might have to cross the hard way, with suits and webcord. How often have your people drilled that?"

"We've done plenty of extravehicular," Teshet said, "but we're going to need *some* form of cover."

"I'm aware of that," Jedao said. He brought up a calculator and did some figures. "That will do nicely."

"Sren?"

Jedao grinned at Teshet. "I want those shuttles emptied out, everything but propulsion and navigation. Get rid of suits, seats, all of it."

"Even life support?"

"Everything. And it'll have to be done in the next seventeen days, so the Gwa-an can't catch us at it."

"What do we do with the innards?"

"Dump them. I'll take full responsibility."

Teshet's eyes crinkled. "I knew I was going to like you."

Uh-oh, Jedao thought, but he kept that to himself.

"What are *you* going to be doing?" Teshet asked.

"Going over the dossiers before we have to wipe them," Jedao said. Meng's in particular. He'd believed in Meng's fundamental competence even back in academy, before they'd learned confidence in themselves. What had gone wrong?

Jedao had first met Shuos Meng (Zhei Meng, then) during an exercise at Shuos Academy. The instructor had assigned them to work together. Meng was chubby and had a vine-and-compass tattoo on the back of their left hand, identifying them as coming from a merchanter lineage.

That day, the class of twenty-nine cadets met not in the usual classroom but a windowless space with a metal table in the front and rows of two-person desks with benches that looked like they'd been scrubbed clean of graffiti multiple times. ("Wars come and go, but graffiti is forever," as one of Jedao's lovers liked to say.) Besides the door leading out into the hall, there were two other doors, neither of which had a sign indicating where they led. Tangles of pipes led up the walls and storage bins were piled beside them. Jedao had the impression that the room had been pressed into service at short notice.

Jedao and Meng sat at their assigned seats and hurriedly whispered introductions to each other while the instructor read off the rest of the pairs.

"Zhei Meng," Jedao's partner said. "I should warn you I barely passed the weapons qualifications. But I'm good with languages." Then a quick grin: "And hacking. I figured you'd make a good partner."

"Garach Jedao," he said. "I can handle guns." Understatement; he was third in the class in Weapons. And if Meng had, as they implied, shuffled the assignments, that meant they were one of the better hackers. "Why did you join up?"

"I want to have kids," Meng said.

"Come again?"

"I want to marry into a rich lineage," Meng said. "That means making myself more respectable. When the recruiters showed up, I said what the hell."

The instructor smiled coolly at the two of them, and they shut up. She said, "If you're here, it's because you've indicated an interest in fieldwork. Like you, we want to find out if it's something you have any aptitude for, and if not, what better use we can make of your skills." *You'd better have* some *skills* went unsaid. "You may expect to be dropped off in the woods or some such nonsense. We don't try to weed out first-years quite that early. No; this initial exercise will take place right here."

The instructor's smile widened. "There's a photobomb in this room. It won't cause any permanent damage, but if you don't disarm it, you're all going to be walking around wearing ridiculous dark lenses for a week. At least one cadet knows where the bomb is. If they keep its location a secret from the rest of you, they win. Of course, they'll also go around with ridiculous dark lenses, but you can't have everything. On the other hand, if someone can persuade that person to give up the secret, everyone wins. So to speak."

The rows of cadets stared at her. Jedao leaned back in his chair and considered the situation. Like several others in the class, he had a riflery exam in three days and preferred to take it with undamaged vision.

"You have four hours," the instructor said. "There's one restroom." She pointed to one of the doors. "I expect it to be in impeccable condition at the end of the four hours." She put her slate down on the table at the head of the room. "Call me with this if you figure it out. Good luck." With that, she walked out. The door whooshed shut behind her.

"We're screwed," Meng said. "Just because I'm in the top twenty on the leaderboard in *Elite Thundersnake 900* doesn't mean I could disarm real bombs if you yanked out my toenails."

"Don't give people ideas," Jedao said. Meng didn't appear to find the joke funny. "This is about people, not explosives."

Two pairs of cadets had gotten up and were beginning a search of the room. A few were talking to each other in hushed, tense voices. Still others were looking around at their fellows with hard, suspicious eyes.

Meng said in Shparoi, "Do *you* know where the bomb is?"

Jedao blinked. He hadn't expected anyone at the Academy to know his birth tongue. Of course, by speaking in an obscure low language, Meng was drawing attention to them. Jedao shook his head.

Meng looked around, hands bunching the fabric of their pants. "What do you recommend we do?"

In the high language, Jedao said, "You can do whatever you want." He retrieved a deck of jeng-zai cards—he always had one in his pocket—and shuffled it. "Do you play?"

"You realize we're being graded on this, right? Hell, they've got cameras on us. They're watching the whole thing."

"Exactly," Jedao said. "I don't see any point in panicking."

"You're out of your mind," Meng said. They stood up, met the other cadets' appraising stares, then sat down again. "Too bad hacking the instructor's slate won't get us anywhere. I doubt she left the answer key in an unencrypted file on it."

Jedao gave Meng a quizzical look, wondering if there was anything more behind the remark—but no, Meng had put their chin in their hands and was brooding. *If only you knew*, Jedao thought, and dealt out a game of solitaire. It was going to be a very dull game, because he had stacked the deck, but he needed to focus on the people around him, not the game. The cards were just to give his hands something to do. He had considered taking up crochet, but thanks to an incident earlier in the term, crochet hooks, knitting needles, and fountain pens were no longer permitted in class. While this was a stupid restriction, considering that most of the cadets were learning unarmed combat, he wasn't responsible for the administration's foibles.

"Jedao," Meng said, "maybe you've got high enough marks that you can blow off this exercise, but—"

Since *I'm not blowing it off* was unlikely to be believed, Jedao flipped over a card—three of Doors, just as he'd arranged—and smiled at Meng. So Meng had had their pick of partners and had chosen him? Well, he might as well do something to justify the other cadet's faith in him. After all, despite their earlier remark, weapons weren't the only things that Jedao was good at. "Do me a favor and we can get this sorted," he said. "You want to win? I'll show you winning."

Now Jedao was attracting some of the hostile stares as well. Good. It took the heat off Meng, who didn't seem to have a great tolerance for pressure. *Stay out of wet work*, he thought; but they could have that chat later. Or one of the instructors would.

Meng fidgeted; caught themselves. "Yeah?"

"Get me the slate."

"You mean the instructor's slate? You can't possibly have figured it out already. Unless—" Meng's eyes narrowed.

"Less thinking, more acting," Jedao said, and got up to retrieve the slate himself.

A pair of cadets, a girl and a boy, blocked his way. "You know something," said the girl. "Spill." Jedao knew them from Analysis; the two were often paired there, too. The girl's name was Noe Irin. The boy had five names and went by Veller. Jedao wondered if Veller wanted to join a faction so he could trim things down to a nice, compact, two-part name. Shuos Veller: much less of a mouthful. Then again, Jedao had a three-part name, also unusual, if less unwieldy, so he shouldn't criticize.

"Just a hunch," Jedao said.

Irin bared her teeth. "He *always* says it's a hunch," she said to no one in particular. "I *hate* that."

"It was only twice," Jedao said, which didn't help his case. He backed away from the instructor's desk and sat down, careful not to jostle the solitaire spread. "Take the slate apart. The photobomb's there."

Irin's lip curled. "If this is one of your fucking clever *tricks*, Jay—"

Meng blinked at the nickname. "You two sleeping together, Jedao?" they asked, sotto voce.

Not sotto enough. "*No*," Jedao and Irin said at the same time.

Veller ignored the byplay and went straight for the tablet, which he bent to without touching it. Jedao respected that. Veller had the physique of a tiger-wrestler (now *there* was someone he wouldn't mind being caught in bed with), a broad face, and a habitually bland, dreamy expression. Jedao wasn't fooled. Veller was almost as smart as Irin, had already been tracked into bomb disposal, and was less prone to flights of temper.

"Is there a tool closet in here?" Veller said. "I need a screwdriver."

"You don't carry your own anymore?" Jedao said.

"I told him he should," Irin said, "but he said they were too similar to knitting needles. As if anyone in their right mind would knit with a pair of screwdrivers."

"I think he meant that they're stabby things that can be driven into people's eyes," Jedao said.

"I didn't ask for your opinion, Jay."

Jedao put his hands up in a conciliatory gesture and shut his mouth. He liked Irin and didn't want to antagonize her any more than necessary. The last time they'd been paired together, they'd done quite well. She would come around; she just needed time to work through the implications of what the instructor had said. She was one of those people who preferred to think about things without being interrupted.

One of the other cadets wordlessly handed Veller a set of screwdrivers. Veller mumbled his thanks and got to work. The class watched, breathless.

"There," Veller said at last. "See that there, all hooked in? Don't know what the timer is, but there it is."

"I find it very suspicious that you forfeited your chance to show up everyone else in this exercise," Irin said to Jedao. "Is there anyone else who knew?"

"Irin," Jedao said, "I don't think the instructor told *anyone* where she'd left the photobomb. She just stuck it in the slate because that was the last place we'd look. The test was meant to reveal which of us would backstab the others, but honestly, that's so counterproductive. I say we disarm the damn thing and skip to the end."

Irin's eyes crossed and her lips moved as she recited the instructor's words under her breath. That was another thing Jedao liked about her. Irin had a *great* memory. Admittedly, that made it difficult to cheat her at cards, as he'd found out the hard way. He'd spent three hours doing her kitchen duties for her the one time he'd tried. He *liked* people who could beat him at cards. "It's possible," she said grudgingly after she'd reviewed the assignment's instructions.

"Disarmed," Veller said shortly after that. He pulled out the photobomb and left it on the desk, then set about reassembling the slate.

Jedao glanced over at Meng. For a moment, his partner's expression had no anxiety in it, but a raptor's intent focus. Interesting: What were they watching for?

"I hope I get a quiet posting at a desk somewhere," Meng said.

"Then why'd you join up?" Irin said.

Jedao put his hand over Meng's, even though he was sure that they had just lied. "Don't mind her," he said. "You'll do fine."

Meng nodded and smiled up at him.

Why do I have the feeling that I'm not remotely the most dangerous person in the room? Jedao thought. But he returned Meng's smile, all the same. It never hurt to have allies.

A Gwa patrol ship greeted them as they neared Du Station. Haval had assured Jedao that this was standard practice and obligingly matched velocities.

Jedao listened in on Haval speaking with the Gwa authority, who spoke flawless high language. "They don't call it 'high language,' of course," Haval had explained to Jedao earlier. "They call it 'mongrel language.'" Jedao had expressed that he didn't care what they called it.

Haval didn't trust Jedao to keep his mouth shut, so she'd stashed him in the business office with Teshet to keep an eye on him. Teshet had brought a wooden box that opened up to reveal an astonishing collection of jewelry. Jedao watched out of the corner of his eye as Teshet made himself comfortable in the largest chair, dumped the box's contents on the desk, and began sorting it according to criteria known only to him.

Jedao was watching videos of the command center and the communications channel, and tried to concentrate on reading the authority's body
language, made difficult by her heavy zigzag cosmetics and the layers of
robes that cloaked her figure. Meanwhile, Teshet put earrings, bracelets, and
mysterious hooked and jeweled items in piles, and alternated helpful glosses
of Gwa-an gestures with borderline insubordinate, not to say lewd, suggestions for things he could do with Jedao. Jedao was grateful that his ability to
blush, like his ability to be tickled, had been burned out of him in Academy.
*Note to self: Suggest to General Essier that Teshet is wasted in special ops. Maybe
reassign him to Recreation?*

Jedao mentioned this to Teshet while Haval was discussing the cargo manifest with the authority. Teshet lowered his lashes and looked sideways at
Jedao. "You don't think I'm good at my job?" he asked.

"You have an excellent record," Jedao said.

Teshet sighed, and his face became serious. "You're used to regular Kel, I see."
Jedao waited.

"I end up in a lot of situations where if people get the notion that I'm a Kel
officer, I may end up locked up and tortured. While that could be fun in its
own right, it makes career advancement difficult."

"You could get a medal out of it."

"Oh, is *that* how you got promoted so—"

Jedao held up his hand, and Teshet stopped. On the monitor, Haval was
saying, in a greasy voice, "I'm glad to hear of your interest, madam. We
would have been happy to start hauling the lubricant earlier, except we had
to persuade our people that—"

The authority's face grew even more imperturbable. "You had to figure out
whom to bribe."

"We understand there are fees—"

Jedao listened to Haval negotiating her bribe to the authority with half an
ear. "Don't tell me all that jewelry's genuine?"

"The gems are mostly synthetics," Teshet said. He held up a long earring
with a rose quartz at the end. "No, this won't do. I bought it for myself, but
you're too light-skinned for it to look good on you."

"I'm wearing jewelry?"

"Unless you brought your own—scratch that, I bet everything you own is
in red and gold."

"Yes." Red and gold were the Shuos faction colors.

Teshet tossed the rose quartz earring aside and selected a vivid emerald ear
stud. "This will look nice on you."

"I don't get a say?"

"How much do you know about merchanter fashion trends out in this march?"

Jedao conceded the point.

The private line crackled to life. "You two still in there?" said Haval's voice.

"Yes, what's the issue?" Teshet said.

"They're boarding us to check for contraband. You haven't messed with the drugs cabinet, have you?"

Teshet made an affronted sound. "You thought I was going to get Sren high?"

"I don't make assumptions when it comes to you, Teshet. Get the hell out of there."

Teshet thrust the emerald ear stud and two bracelets at Jedao. "Put those on," he said. "If anyone asks you where the third bracelet is, say you had to pawn it to make good on a gambling debt."

Under other circumstances, Jedao would have found this offensive—he was *good* at gambling—but presumably Sren had different talents. As he put on the earring, he said, "What do I need to know about these drugs?"

Teshet was stuffing the rest of the jewelry back in the box. "Don't look at me like that. They're illegal both in the heptarchate and the Gwa Reality, but people run them anyway. They make useful cover. The Gwa-an search us for contraband, they find the contraband, they confiscate the contraband, we pay them a bribe to keep quiet about it, they go away happy."

Impatient with Jedao fumbling with the clasp of the second bracelet, Teshet fastened it for him, then turned Jedao's hand over and studied the scar at the base of his palm. "You should have skinsealed that one too, but never mind."

"I'm bad at peeling vegetables?" Jedao suggested. Close enough to "knife fight," right? And much easier to explain away than bullet scars.

"Are you two *done*?" Haval's voice demanded.

"We're coming, we're coming," Teshet said.

Jedao took up his post in the command center. Teshet himself disappeared in the direction of the airlock. Jedao wasn't aware that anything had gone wrong until Haval returned to the command center, flanked by two personages in bright orange space suits. Both personages wielded guns of a type Jedao had never seen before, which made him irrationally happy. While most of his collection was at home with his mother, he relished adding new items. Teshet was nowhere in sight.

Haval's pilot spoke before the intruders had a chance to say anything. "Commander, what's going on?"

The broader of the two personages spoke in Tlen Gwa, then kicked Haval in the shin. "Guess what," Haval said with a macabre grin. "Those aren't the real authorities we ran into. They're pirates."

Oh, for the love of fox and hound, Jedao thought. In truth, he wasn't surprised, just resigned. He never trusted it when an operation went too smoothly.

The broader personage spoke again. Haval sighed deeply, then said, "Hand over all weapons or they start shooting."

Where's Teshet? Jedao wondered. As if in answer, he heard a gunshot, then the ricochet. More gunshots. He was sure at least one of the shooters was Teshet or one of Teshet's operatives: They carried Stinger 40s and he recognized the characteristic whine of the reports.

Presumably Teshet was occupied, which left matters here up to him. Some of Haval's crew went armed. Jedao did not—they had agreed that Sren wouldn't know how to use a gun—but that didn't mean he wasn't dangerous. While the other members of the crew set down their guns, Jedao flung himself at the narrower personage's feet.

The pirates did not like this. But Jedao had always been blessed, or perhaps cursed, with extraordinarily quick reflexes. He dropped his weight on one arm and leg and kicked the narrow pirate's feet from under them with the other leg. The narrow pirate discharged their gun. The bullet passed over Jedao and banged into one of the status displays, causing it to spark and sputter out. Haval yelped.

Jedao had already sprung back to his feet—damn the twinge in his knees, he should have that looked into—and twisted the gun out of the narrow pirate's grip. The narrow pirate had the stunned expression that Jedao was used to seeing on people who did not deal with professionals very often. He shot them, but thanks to their loose-limbed flailing, the first bullet took them in the shoulder. The second one made an ugly hole in their forehead, and they dropped.

The broad pirate had more presence of mind, but chose the wrong target. Jedao smashed her wrist aside with the knife-edge of his hand just as she fired at Haval five times in rapid succession. Her hands trembled visibly. Four of the shots went wide. Haval had had the sense to duck, but Jedao smelled blood and suspected she'd been hit. Hopefully nowhere fatal.

Jedao shot the broad pirate in the side of the head just as she pivoted to target him next. Her pistol clattered to the floor as she dropped. By reflex he flung himself to the side in case it discharged, but it didn't.

Once he had assured himself that both pirates were dead, he knelt at Haval's side and checked the wound. She had been very lucky. The single bullet had gone through her side, missing the major organs. She started shouting at him for going up unarmed against people with guns.

"I'm getting the medical kit," Jedao said, too loudly, to get her to shut up. His hands were utterly steady as he opened the cabinet containing the medical kit and brought it back to Haval, who at least had the good sense not to try to stand up.

Haval scowled, but accepted the painkiller tabs he handed her. She held still while he cut away her shirt and inspected the entry and exit wounds. At least the bullet wasn't a burrower, or she wouldn't have a lung anymore. He got to work with the sterilizer.

By the time Teshet and two other soldiers entered the command center, Jedao had sterilized and sealed the wounds. Teshet crossed the threshold with rapid strides. When Haval's head came up, Teshet signed sharply for her to be quiet. Curious, Jedao also kept silent.

Teshet drew his combat knife, then knelt next to the larger corpse. With a deft stroke, he cut into the pirate's neck, then yanked out a device and its wires. Blood dripped down and obscured the metal. He repeated the operation for the other corpse, then crushed both devices under his heel. "All right," he said. "It should be safe to talk now."

Jedao raised his eyebrows, inviting explanation.

"Not pirates," Teshet said. "Those were Gwa-an special ops."

Hmm. "Then odds are they were waiting for someone to show up to rescue the *Moonsweet Blossom*," Jedao said.

"I don't disagree." Teshet glanced at Haval, then back at the corpses. "That wasn't you, was it?"

Haval's eyes were glazed, a side effect of the painkiller, but she wasn't entirely out of it. "Idiot here risked his life. We could have handled it."

"I wasn't the one in danger," Jedao said, remembering the pirates' guns pointed at her. Haval might not be particularly respectful, as subordinates went, cover identity or not, but she *was* his subordinate, and he was responsible for her. To Teshet: "Your people?"

"Two down," Teshet said grimly, and gave him the names. "They died bravely."

"I'm sorry," Jedao said; two more names to add to the long litany of those he'd lost. He was thinking about how to proceed, though. "The real Gwa-an patrols won't be likely to know about this. It's how I'd run the op—the fewer people who are aware of the truth, the better. I bet *their* orders are to take in any surviving 'pirates' for processing, and then the authorities will release and debrief the operatives from there. What do you normally do in case of actual pirates?"

"Report the incident," Haval said. Her voice sounded thready. "Formal complaint if we're feeling particularly annoying."

"All right." Jedao calmly began taking off the jewelry and his clothes. "That one's about my size," he said, nodding at the smaller of the two corpses. The suit would be tight across the shoulders, but that couldn't be helped. "Congratulations, not two but three of your crew died heroically, but you captured a pirate in the process."

Teshet made a wistful sound. "That temporary skin stuff obscures your musculature, you know." But he helpfully began stripping the indicated corpse, then grabbed wipes to get rid of the blood on the suit.

"I'll make it up to you some other time," Jedao said recklessly. "Haval, make that formal complaint and demand that you want your captive tried appropriately. Since the nearest station is Du, that'll get me inserted so I can investigate."

"You're just lucky some of the Gwa-an are as sallow as you are," Haval said as Jedao changed clothes.

"I will be disappointed in you if you don't have restraints," Jedao said to Teshet.

Teshet's eyes lit.

Jedao rummaged in the medical kit until he found the eye drops he was looking for. They were meant to counteract tear gas, but they had a side effect of pupil dilation, which was what interested him. It would help him feign concussion.

"We're running short on time, so listen closely," Jedao said. "Turn me over to the Gwa-an. Don't worry about me; I can handle myself."

"Je—Sren, I don't care how much you've studied the station's schematics, you'll be outnumbered thousands to one *on foreign territory.*"

"Sometime over drinks I'll tell you about the time I infiltrated a ring-city where I didn't speak any of the local languages," Jedao said. "Turn me in. I'll locate the crew, spring them, and signal when I'm ready. You won't be able to mistake it."

Haval's brow creased. Jedao kept speaking. "After you've done that, load all the shuttles full of lubricant canisters. Program the lubricant to go from zero-coefficient flow to harden completely in response to the radio signal. You're going to put the shuttles on autopilot. When you see my signal, launch the shuttles' contents toward the station's turret levels. That should gum them up and buy us cover."

"*All* our shuttles?" Haval said faintly.

"Haval," Jedao said, "stop thinking about profit margins and repeat my orders back to me."

She did.

"Splendid," Jedao said. "Don't disappoint me."

The Gwa-an took Jedao into custody without comment. Jedao feigned concussion, saving him from having to sound coherent in a language he barely spoke. The Gwa-an official responsible for him looked concerned, which was considerate of him. Jedao hoped to avoid killing him or the guard. Only one guard, thankfully; they assumed he was too injured to be a threat.

The first thing Jedao noticed about the Gwa-an shuttle was how roomy it was, with wastefully widely spaced seats. He hadn't noticed that the Gwa-an were, on average, that much larger than the heptarchate's citizens. (Not that this said much. Both nations contained a staggering variety of ethnic groups and their associated phenotypes. Jedao himself was on the short side of average for a heptarchate manform.) At least being "concussed" meant he didn't have to figure out how the hell the safety restraints worked, because while he could figure it out with enough fumbling, it would look damned suspicious that he didn't already know. Instead, the official strapped him in while saying things in a soothing voice. The guard limited themselves to a scowl.

Instead of the smell of disinfectant that Jedao associated with shuttles, the Gwa-an shuttle was pervaded by a light, almost effervescent fragrance. He hoped it wasn't intoxicating. Or rather, part of him hoped it was, because he didn't often have good excuses to screw around with new and exciting recreational drugs, but it would impede his effectiveness. Maybe all Gwa-an disinfectants smelled this good? He should steal the formula. Voidmoth crews everywhere would thank him.

Even more unnervingly, the shuttle played music on the way to the station. At least, while it didn't resemble any music he'd heard before, it had a recognizable beat and some sort of flute in it. From the others' reactions, this was normal and possibly even boring. Too bad he was about as musical as a pair of boots.

The shuttle docked smoothly. Jedao affected not to know what was going on and allowed the official to chirp at him. Eventually a stretcher arrived and they put him on it. They emerged into the lights of the shuttle bay. Jedao's temples twinged with the beginning of a headache. At least it meant the eye drops were still doing their job.

The journey to Du Station's version of Medical took forever. Jedao was especially eager to escape based on what he'd learned of Gwa-an medical therapies, which involved too many genetically engineered critters for his comfort. (He had read up on the topic after Haval told him about the dueling.) He did consider that he could make his mother happy by stealing some pretty little microbes for her, but with his luck they'd turn his testicles inside out.

When the medic took him into an examination room, Jedao whipped up and felled her with a blow to the side of the neck. The guard was slow to react. Jedao grasped their throat and grappled with them, waiting the interminable seconds until they slumped, unconscious. He had a bad moment when he heard footsteps passing by. Luckily, the guard's wheeze didn't attract attention. Jedao wasn't modest about his combat skills, but they wouldn't save him if he was sufficiently outnumbered.

Too bad he couldn't steal the guard's uniform, but it wouldn't fit him. So it would have to be the medic's clothes. Good: the medic's clothes were robes instead of something more form-fitting. Bad: even though the garments would fit him, more or less, they were in the style for women.

I will just have to improvise, Jedao thought. At least he'd kept up the habit of shaving, and the Gwa-an appeared to permit a variety of haircuts in all genders, so his short hair and bangs wouldn't be too much of a problem. As long as he moved quickly and didn't get stopped for conversation—

Jedao changed, then slipped out and took a few moments to observe how people walked and interacted so he could fit in more easily. The Gwa-an were terrible about eye contact and, interestingly for station-dwellers, preferred to keep each other at a distance. He could work with that.

His eyes still ached, since Du Station had abominably bright lighting, but he'd just have to prevent people from looking too closely at him. It helped that he had dark brown eyes to begin with, so the dilated pupils wouldn't be obvious from a distance. He was walking briskly toward the lifts when he heard a raised voice. He kept walking. The voice called again, more insistently.

Damn. He turned around, hoping that someone hadn't recognized his outfit from behind. A woman in extravagant layers of green, lilac, and pink spoke to him in strident tones. Jedao approached her rapidly, wincing at her voice, and hooked her into an embrace. Maybe he could take advantage of this yet.

"You're not—" she began to say.

"I'm too busy," he said over her, guessing at how best to deploy the Tlen Gwa phrases he knew. "I'll see you for tea at thirteen. I like your coat."

The woman's face turned an ugly mottled red. "You like my *what*?" At least he thought he'd said "coat." She stepped back from him, pulling what looked like a small perfume bottle from among her layers of clothes.

He tensed, not wanting to fight her in full view of passersby. She spritzed him with a moist vapor, then smiled coolly at him before spinning on her heel and walking away.

Shit. Just how fast-acting were Gwa-an duels, anyway? He missed the sensible kind with swords; his chances would have been much better. He hoped the symptoms wouldn't be disabling, but then, the woman couldn't possibly have had a chance to tailor the infectious agent to his system, and maybe the immunizations would keep him from falling over sick until he had found Meng and their crew.

How had he offended her, anyway? Had he gotten the word for "coat" wrong? Now that he thought about it, the word for "coat" differed from the word for "navel" only by its tones, and—hells and foxes, he'd messed up the tone sandhi, hadn't he? He kept walking, hoping that she'd be content with getting him sick and wouldn't call security on him.

At last he made it to the lifts. While stealing the medic's uniform had also involved stealing their keycard, he preferred not to use it. Rather, he'd swapped the medic's keycard for the loud woman's. She had carried hers on a braided lanyard with a clip. It would do nicely if he had to garrote anyone in a hurry. The garrote wasn't one of his specialties, but as his girlfriend the first year of Shuos Academy had always been telling him, it paid to keep your options open.

At least the lift's controls were less perilous than figuring out how to correctly pronounce items of clothing. Jedao had by no means achieved reading fluency in Tlen Gwa, but the language had a wonderfully tidy writing system, with symbols representing syllables and odd little curlicue diacritics that changed what vowel you used. He had also theoretically memorized the numbers from 1 to 9,999. Fortunately, Du Station had fewer than 9,999 levels.

Two of the other people on the lift stared openly at Jedao. He fussed with his hair on the grounds that it would look like ordinary embarrassment and not *Hello! I am a cross-dressing enemy agent, pleased to make your acquaintance.* Come to that, Gwa-an women's clothes were comfortable, and all the layers meant that he could, in principle, hide useful items like garrotes in them. He wondered if he could keep them as a souvenir. Start a fashion back home. He bet his mother would approve.

Intelligence had given him a good idea of where Meng and their crew might be held. At least, Jedao hoped that Du Station's higher-ups hadn't faked him out by stowing them in the lower-security cells as opposed to the top-security ones. He was betting a lot on the guess that the Gwa-an were still in the process of interrogating the group rather than executing them out of hand.

The layout wasn't the hard part, but Jedao reflected on the mysteries of the Gwa Reality's penal code. For example, prostitution was a major offense. They didn't even fine the offenders, but sent them to remedial counseling, which surely *cost* the state money. In the heptarchate, they did the sensible thing by enforcing licenses for health and safety reasons and taxing the whole enterprise. On the other hand, the Gwa-an had a refreshingly casual attitude toward heresy. They believed that public debate about Poetics (their version of Doctrine) strengthened the polity. If you put forth that idea anywhere in the heptarchate, you could expect to get arrested.

So it was that Jedao headed for the cellblocks where one might find unlucky prostitutes and not the ones where overly enthusiastic heretics might be locked up overnight to cool off. He kept attracting horrified looks and wondered if he'd done something offensive with his hair. Was it wrong to part it on the left, and if so, why hadn't Haval warned him? How many ways could you get hair wrong anyway?

The Gwa-an also had peculiarly humanitarian ideas about the surroundings that offenders should be kept in. Level 37, where he expected to find Meng, abounded with fountains. Not cursory fountains, but glorious cascading arches of silvery water interspersed with elongated humanoid statues in various uncomfortable-looking poses. Teshet had mentioned that this had to do with Gwa-an notions of ritual purity.

While "security" was one of the words that Jedao had memorized, he did not read Tlen Gwa especially quickly, which made figuring out the signs a chore. At least the Gwa-an believed in signs, a boon to foreign infiltrators everywhere. Fortunately, the Gwa-an hadn't made a secret of the Security office's location, even if getting to it was complicated by the fact that the fountains had been rearranged since the last available intel and he preferred not to show up soaking wet. The fountains themselves formed a labyrinth and, upon inspection, it appeared that different portions could be turned on or off to change the labyrinth's twisty little passages.

Unfortunately, the water's splashing also made it difficult to hear people coming, and he had decided that creeping about would not only slow him down, but make him look more conspicuous, especially with the issue of his hair (or whatever it was that made people stare at him with such affront). He rounded a corner and almost crashed into a sentinel, recognizable by Security's spear-and-shield badge.

In retrospect, a simple collision might have worked out better. Instead,

Jedao dropped immediately into a fighting stance, and the sentinel's eyes narrowed. *Dammit*, Jedao thought, exasperated with himself. *This is why my handlers preferred me doing the sniper bits rather than the infiltration bits.* Since he'd blown the opportunity to bluff his way past the sentinel, he swept the man's feet from under him and knocked him out. After the man was unconscious, Jedao stashed him behind one of the statues, taking care so the spray from the fountains wouldn't interfere too much with his breathing. He had the distinct impression that "dead body" was much worse from a ritual purity standpoint than "merely unconscious," if he had to negotiate with someone later.

He ran into no other sentinels on the way to the office, but as it so happened, a sentinel was leaving just as he got there. Jedao put on an expression he had learned from the scariest battlefield medic of his acquaintance back when he'd been a lowly infantry captain and marched straight up to Security. He didn't need to be convincing for long, he just needed a moment's hesitation.

By the time the sentinel figured out that the "medic" was anything but, Jedao had taken her gun and broken both her arms. "I want to talk to your leader," he said, another of those useful canned phrases.

The sentinel left off swearing (he was sure it was swearing) and repeated the word for "leader" in an incredulous voice.

Whoops. Was he missing some connotational nuance? He tried the word for "superior officer," to which the response was even more incredulous. *Hey Mom*, Jedao thought, *you know how you always said I should join the diplomatic corps on account of my always talking my way out of trouble as a kid? Were you ever wrong. I am the worst diplomat ever.* Admittedly, maybe starting off by breaking the woman's arms was where he'd gone wrong, but the sentinel didn't sound upset about *that*. The Gwa-an were very confusing people.

After a crescendo of agitation (hers) and desperate rummaging about for people nouns (his), it emerged that the term he wanted was the one for "head priest." Which was something the language lessons ought to have noted. He planned on dropping in on whoever had written the course and having a spirited talk with them.

Just as well that the word for "why" was more straightforward. The sentinel wanted to know why he wanted to talk to the head priest. He wanted to know why someone who'd had both her arms broken was more concerned with propriety (his best guess) than alerting the rest of the station that they had an intruder. He had other matters to attend to, though. Too bad he couldn't recruit her for her sangfroid, but that was outside his purview.

What convinced the sentinel to comply, in the end, was not the threat of more violence, which he imagined would have been futile. Instead, he mentioned that he'd left one of her comrades unconscious amid the fountains and the man would need medical care. He liked the woman's concern for her fellow sentinel.

Jedao and the sentinel walked together to the head priest's office. The head priest came out. She had an extremely elaborate coiffure, held in place by multiple hairpins featuring elongated figures like the statues. She froze when Jedao pointed the gun at her, then said several phrases in what sounded like different languages.

"Mongrel language," Jedao said in Tlen Gwa, remembering what Haval had told him.

"What do you want?" the high priest said in awkward but comprehensible high language.

Jedao explained that he was here for Ahun Gerav, in case the priest only knew Meng by their cover name. "Release them and their crew, and this can end with minimal bloodshed."

The priest wheezed. Jedao wondered if she was allergic to assassins. He'd never heard of such a thing, but he wasn't under any illusions that he knew everything about Gwa-an immune systems. Then he realized she was laughing.

"Feel free to share," Jedao said, very pleasantly. The sentinel was sweating.

The priest stopped laughing. "You're too late," she said. "You're too late by thirteen years."

Jedao did the math: eight years since he and Meng had graduated from Shuos Academy. Of course, the two of them had attended for the usual five years. "They've been a double agent since they were a cadet?"

The priest's smile was just this side of smug.

Jedao knocked the sentinel unconscious and let her spill to the floor. The priest's smile didn't falter, which made him think less of her. Didn't she care about her subordinate? If nothing else, he'd had a few concussions in his time (real ones), and they were no joke.

"The crew," Jedao said.

"Gerav attempted to persuade them to turn coat as well," the priest said. "When they were less than amenable, well—" She shrugged. "We had no further use for them."

"I will not forgive this," Jedao said. "Take me to Gerav."

She shrugged. "Unfortunate for them," she said. "But to be frank, I don't value their life over my own."

"How very pragmatic of you," Jedao said.

She shut up and led the way.

Du Station had provided Meng with a luxurious suite by heptarchate standards. The head priest bowed with an ironic smile as she opened the door for
Jedao. He shoved her in and scanned the room.

The first thing he noticed was the overwhelming smell of—what *was* that
smell? Jedao had thought he had reasonably cosmopolitan tastes, but the
platters with their stacks of thin-sliced meat drowned in rich gravies and
sauces almost made him gag. Who needed that much meat in their diet? The
suite's occupant seemed to agree, judging by how little the meat had been
touched. And why wasn't the meat cut into decently small pieces so as to
make for easy eating? The bowls of succulent fruit were either for show or the
suite's occupant disliked fruit, too. The flatbreads, on the other hand, had
been torn into. One, not entirely eaten, rested on a meat platter and was dissolving into the gravy. Several different-sized bottles were partly empty, and
once he adjusted to all the meat, he could also detect the sweet reek of wine.

Most fascinatingly, instead of chopsticks and spoons, the various plates
and platters sported two-tined forks (Haval had explained to him about
forks) and knives. Maybe this was how they trained assassins. Jedao liked
knives, although not as much as he liked guns. He wondered if he could
persuade the Kel to import the custom. It would make for some lively high
tables.

Meng glided out, resplendent in brocade Gwa-an robes, then gaped. Jedao
wasn't making any attempt to hide his gun.

"Foxfucking hounds," Meng slurred as they sat down heavily, "*you*. Is that
really you, Jedao?"

"You know each other?" the priest said.

Jedao ignored her question, although he kept her in his peripheral vision
in case he needed to kill her or knock her out. "You graduated from Shuos
Academy with high marks," Jedao said. "You even married rich the way you
always talked about. Four beautiful kids. Why, Meng? Was it nothing more
than a story?"

Meng reached for a fork. Jedao's trigger finger shifted. Meng withdrew
their hand.

"The Gwa-an paid stupendously well," Meng said quietly. "It mattered a
lot more, once. Of course, hiding the money was getting harder and harder.
What good is money if you can't spend it? And the Shuos were about to catch
on anyway. So I had to run."

"And your crew?"

Meng's mouth twisted, but they met Jedao's eyes steadfastly. "I didn't want things to end the way they did."

"Cold comfort to their families."

"It's done now," Meng said, resigned. They looked at the largest platter of meat with sudden loathing. Jedao tensed, wondering if it was going to be flung at him, but all Meng did was shove it away from them. Some gravy slopped over the side.

Jedao smiled sardonically. "If you come home, you might at least get a decent bowl of rice instead of this weird bread stuff."

"Jedao, if I come home they'll *torture me for high treason*, unless our heptarch's policies have changed drastically. You can't stop me from killing myself."

"Rather than going home?" Jedao shrugged. Meng probably did have a suicide fail-safe, although if they were serious they'd have used it already. He couldn't imagine the Gwa-an would have neglected to provide them with one if the Shuos hadn't.

Still, he wasn't done. "If you do something so crass, I'm going to visit each one of your children *personally*. I'm going to take them out to a nice dinner with actual food that you eat with actual chopsticks and spoons. And I'm going to explain to them in exquisite detail how their Shuos parent is a traitor."

Meng bit their lip.

More softly, Jedao said, "When did the happy family stop being a cover story and start being real?"

"I don't know," Meng said, wretched. "I can't—do you know how my spouses would look at me if they found out that I'd been lying to them all this time? I wasn't even particularly interested in other people's kids when this all began. But watching them grow up—" They fell silent.

"I have to bring you back," Jedao said. He remembered the staticky voice of the unnamed woman playing in Essier's office, Meng's *crew*, who'd tried and failed to get a warning out. She and her comrades deserved justice. But he also remembered all the gifts he'd sent to Meng's children over the years, the occasional awkwardly written thank-you note. It wasn't as if any good would be achieved by telling them the awful truth. "But I can pull a few strings. Make sure your family never finds out."

Meng hesitated for a long moment. Then they nodded. "It's fair. Better than fair."

To the priest, Jedao said, "You'd better take us to the *Moonsweet Blossom*, assuming you haven't disassembled it already."

The priest's mouth twisted. "You're in luck," she said.

Du Station had ensconced the *Moonsweet Blossom* in a bay on Level 62. The Gwa-an passed gawped at them. The priest sailed past without giving any explanations. Jedao wondered whether the issue was his hair or some other inexplicable Gwa-an cultural foible.

"I hope you can pilot while drunk," Jedao said to Meng.

Meng drew themselves up to their full height. "I didn't drink *that* much."

Jedao had his doubts, but he would take his chances. "Get in."

The priest's sudden tension alerted him that she was about to try something. Jedao shoved Meng toward the trademoth, then grabbed the priest in an arm. What was the point of putting a priest in charge of security if the priest couldn't *fight*?

Jedao said to her, "You're going to instruct your underlings to get the hell out of our way and open the airlock so we can leave."

"And why would I do that?" the priest said.

He reached up and snatched out half her hairpins. Too bad he didn't have a third hand; his grip on the gun was precarious enough as it was. She growled, which he interpreted as *Fuck you and all your little foxes.* "I could get creative," Jedao said.

"I was warned that the heptarchate was full of barbarians," the priest said.

At least the incomprehensible Gwa-an fixation on hairstyles meant that he didn't have to resort to more disagreeable threats, like shooting her subordinates in front of her. Given her reaction when he had knocked out the sentinel, he wasn't convinced that would faze her anyway. He adjusted his grip on her and forced her to the floor.

"Give the order," he said. "If you don't play any tricks, you'll even get the hairpins back without my shoving them through your eardrums." They were very nice hairpins, despite the creepiness of the elongated humanoid figures, and he bet they were real gold.

Since he had her facing the floor, the priest couldn't glare at him. The frustration in her voice was unmistakable, however. "As you require." She started speaking in Tlen Gwa.

The workers in the area hurried to comply. Jedao had familiarized himself with the control systems of the airlock and was satisfied they weren't doing anything underhanded. "Thank you," he said, to which the priest hissed something venomous. He flung the hairpins away and let her go. She cried out at the sound of their clattering and scrambled after them with a devotion he reserved for weapons. Perhaps, to a Gwa-an priest, they were equivalent.

One of the workers, braver or more foolish than the others, reached for her own gun. Jedao shot her in the hand on the way up the hatch to the *Moonsweet Blossom*. It bought him enough time to get the rest of the way up the ramp and slam the hatch shut after him. Surely Meng couldn't accuse him of showing off if they hadn't seen the feat of marksmanship; and he hoped the worker would appreciate that he could just as easily have put a hole in her head.

The telltale rumble of the *Blossom*'s maneuver drive assured him that Meng, at least, was following directions. This boded well for Meng's health. Jedao hurried forward, wondering how many more rounds the Gwa-an handgun contained, and started webbing himself into the gunner's seat.

"You wouldn't consider putting that thing away, would you?" Meng said. "It's hard for me to think when I'm ready to piss myself."

"If you think *I'm* the scariest person in your future, Meng, you haven't been paying attention."

"One, I don't think you know yourself very well, and two, I liked you much better when we were on the same side."

"I'm going to let you meditate on that second bit some other time. In the meantime, let's get out of here."

Meng swallowed. "They'll shoot us down the moment we get clear of the doors, you know."

"Just *go*, Meng. I've got friends. Or did you think I teleported onto this station?"

"At this point I wouldn't put anything past you. Okay, you're webbed in, I'm webbed in, here goes nothing."

The maneuver drive grumbled as the *Moonsweet Blossom* blasted its way out of the bay. No one attempted to close the first set of doors on them. Jedao wondered if the priest was still scrabbling after her hairpins, or if it had to do with the more pragmatic desire to avoid costly repairs to the station.

The *Moonsweet Blossom* had few armaments, mostly intended for dealing with high-velocity debris, which was more of a danger than pirates if one kept to the better-policed trade routes. They wouldn't do any good against Du Station's defenses. As *signals*, on the other hand—

Using the lasers, Jedao flashed HERE WE COME in the merchanter signal code. With any luck, Haval was paying attention.

At this point, several things happened.

Haval kicked Teshet in the shin to get him to stop watching a mildly pornographic and not-very-well-acted drama about a famous courtesan from 192 years ago. ("It's historical so it's educational!" he protested. "One, we've got our signal, and two, I wish you would take care of your *urgent needs* in your own quarters," Haval said.)

Carp 1 through *Carp 4* and *7* through *10* launched all their shuttles. Said shuttles were, as Jedao had instructed, full of variable-coefficient lubricant programmed to its liquid form. The shuttles flew toward Du Station, then opened their holds and burned their retro thrusters for all they were worth. The lubricant, carried forward by momentum, continued toward Du Station's turret levels.

Du Station recognized an attack when it saw one. However, its defenses consisted of a combination of high-powered lasers, which could only vaporize small portions of the lubricant and were useless for altering the momentum of quantities of the stuff, and railguns, whose projectiles punched through the mass without much effect. Once the lubricant had clogged up the defensive emplacements, *Carp 1* transmitted an encrypted radio signal with the command that caused the lubricant to harden in place.

The *Moonsweet Blossom* linked up with Haval's merchant troop. At this point, the *Blossom* only contained two people, trivial compared to the amount of mass it had been designed to haul. The merchant troop, of course, had just divested itself of its cargo. The nine heptarchate vessels proceeded to hightail it out of there at highly non-freighter accelerations.

Jedao and Meng swept the *Moonsweet Blossom* for bugs and other unwelcome devices, an exhausting but necessary task. Then, at what Jedao judged to be a safe distance from Du Station, he ordered Meng to slave it to *Carp 1*.

The *Carp 1* and *Moonsweet Blossom* matched velocities, and Jedao and Meng made the crossing to the former. There was a bad moment when Jedao thought Meng was going to unhook their tether and drift off into the smothering dark rather than face their fate. But whatever temptations were running through their head, Meng resisted them.

Haval and Teshet greeted them on the *Carp 1*. After Jedao and Meng had shed the suits and checked them for needed repairs, Haval ushered them all into the business office. "I didn't expect you to spring the trademoth as well as our Shuos friend," Haval said.

Meng wouldn't meet her eyes.

"What about the rest of the crew?" Teshet said.

"They didn't make it," Jedao said, and sneezed. He explained about Meng's extracurricular activities over the past thirteen years. Then he sneezed again.

Haval grumbled under her breath. "Whatever the hell you did on Du, Sren, did it involve duels?"

"'Sren'?" Meng said.

"You don't think I came into the Gwa Reality under my own"—sneeze—"name, did you?" Jedao said. "Anyway, there might have been an incident . . ."

Meng groaned. "Just how good is your Tlen Gwa?"

"Sort of not, apparently," Jedao said. "I *really* need to have a word with whoever wrote the Tlen Gwa course. I thought I was all right with languages at the basic phrase level, but was the proofreader asleep the day they approved it?"

Meng had the grace to look embarrassed. "I may have hacked it."

"You what?"

"If I'd realized *you'd* be using it, I wouldn't have bothered. Botching the language doesn't seem to have slowed you down any."

Wordlessly, Teshet handed Jedao a handkerchief. Jedao promptly sneezed into it. Maybe he'd be able to give his mother a gift of a petri dish with a lovely culture of Gwa-an germs, after all. He'd have to ask the medic about it later.

Teshet then produced a set of restraints from his pockets and gestured at Meng. Meng sighed deeply and submitted to being trussed up.

"Don't look so disappointed," Teshet said into Jedao's ear. "I've another set just for you." Then he and Meng marched off to the brig.

Haval cleared her throat. "Off to the medic with you," she said to Jedao. "We'd better figure out why your vaccinations aren't working and if everyone's going to need to be quarantined."

"Not arguing," Jedao said meekly.

Some days later, Jedao was rewatching one of Teshet's pornography dramas while in bed. At least, he thought it was pornography. The costuming made it difficult to tell, and the dialogue had made *more* sense when he was still running a fever.

The medic had kept him in isolation until they declared him no longer contagious. Whether due to this precaution or pure luck, no one else came down with the duel disease. They'd given him a clean bill of health this morning, but Haval had insisted that he rest a little longer.

The door opened. Jedao looked up in surprise.

Teshet entered with a fresh supply of handkerchiefs. "Well, Jedao, we'll reenter heptarchate space in two days, high calendar. Any particular orders you want me to relay to Haval?" He obligingly handed over a slate so Jedao could look over Haval's painstaking, not to say excruciatingly detailed, reports on their current status.

"Haval's doing a fine job," Jedao said, glad that his voice no longer came out as a croak. "I won't get in her way." He returned the slate to Teshet.

"Sounds good." Teshet turned his back and departed. Jedao admired the view, wishing in spite of himself that the other man would linger.

Teshet returned half an hour later with two clear vials full of unidentified substances. "First or second?" he said, holding them up to the light one by one.

"I'm sorry," Jedao said, "first or second what?"

"You look like you need cheering up," Teshet said hopefully. "You want on top? You want me on top? I'm flexible."

Jedao blinked, trying to parse this. "On top of wh—" *Oh.* "What's *in* those vials?"

"You have your choice of variable-coefficient lubricant or goose fat," Teshet said. "Assuming you were telling the truth when you said it was goose fat. And don't yell at Haval for letting me into your refrigerator; I did it all on my own. I admit, I can't tell the difference. As Haval will attest, I'm a *dreadful* cook, so I didn't want to fry up some scallion pancakes just to taste the goose fat."

Jedao's mouth went dry, which had less to do with Teshet's eccentric choice of lubricants than the fact that he had sat down on the edge of Jedao's bed. "You don't have anything more, ah, conventional?" He realized that was a mistake as soon as the words left his mouth; he'd essentially accepted Teshet's proposition.

For the first time, Jedao glimpsed uncertainty in Teshet's eyes. "We don't have a lot of time before we're back in heptarchate space and you have to go back to being a commander and I have to go back to being responsible," he said softly. "Or as responsible as I ever get, anyway. Want to make the most of it? Because I get the impression that you don't allow yourself much of a personal life."

"Use the goose fat," Jedao said, because as much as he liked Teshet, he did not relish the thought of being *cemented* to Teshet: It would distract Teshet from continuing to analyze his psyche, and, yes, the man was damnably attractive. What the hell, with any luck his mother was never, ever, *ever* hearing of this. (He could imagine the conversation now: "Garach Jedao Shkan, are you meaning to tell me you finally found a nice young man and you're *still* not planning on settling down and providing me extra grandchildren?" And then she would send him *more goose fat.*)

Teshet brightened. "You won't regret this," he purred, and proceeded to help Jedao undress.

Aliette de Bodard lives and works in Paris. She is the author of the critically acclaimed Obsidian and Blood trilogy of Aztec noir fantasies, as well as numerous short stories which have garnered her two Nebula Awards, a Locus Award, and two British Science Fiction Association Awards. Her space opera books include *The Tea Master and the Detective*, a murder mystery set on a space station in a Vietnamese Galactic empire, inspired by the characters of Sherlock Holmes and Dr. Watson. Recent works include the Dominion of the Fallen series, set in a turn-of-the-century Paris devastated by a magical war, which comprises *The House of Shattered Wings* (Roc/Gollancz, 2015 British Science Fiction Association Award, Locus Award finalist), and its standalone sequel *The House of Binding Thorns* (Ace, Gollancz).

IN EVERLASTING WISDOM

Aliette de Bodard

The path to enlightenment is through obedience to wisdom, and who is wiser than the Everlasting Emperor?

It's the words that keep Ai Thi going, day after day—the ceaseless flow of wisdom from the appeaser within her, reminders that the Everlasting Emperor loves her and her sacrifice—that she's doing her duty, day after day, making sure that nothing discordant or dissident can mar the harmony that keeps the Empire together.

Her daily rounds take her through the Inner Rings of Vermillion Crab Station: she sits on the train, head lolled back against the window, thinking of nothing in particular as the appeaser does their work, sending the Everlasting Emperor's words into passengers' subconscious minds. Ai Thi sees the words take root: the tension leaves the air, the tautness of people's worries and anger drains out of them, and they relax, faces slack, eyes closed, all thoughts in perfect harmony. The appeaser shifts and twists within Ai Thi, a familiar rhythm of little bubbles in her gut, almost as if she were pregnant with her daughter Dieu Kiem again.

The worst enemy is the enemy within, because it could wear the face of your brother or mother.

Loyalty to the Everlasting Emperor should be stronger than the worship offered to ancestors, or the respect afforded to parents.

The words aren't meant for Ai Thi: they go through her like running water, from the appeaser to her to the passengers on the train. She's the bridge—the appeaser is lodged within her, but they're an alien being and need Ai Thi and her fellow harmonisers to speak the proper language, to teach them the proper words.

Ai Thi knows all the words. Once, they were the only thing that kept her going.

It is the duty of children to die for their parents, and the duty of all subjects to give their life for the Everlasting Emperor—though he never asks for more than what is necessary, and reasonably borne.

Ai Thi has only confused, jumbled memories of her implantation—a white, sterilised room that smells of disinfectant; the smooth voice of doctors and nurses, telling her to lie down on the operating table, that everything will be fine. She woke up with her voice scraped raw, as if she'd screamed for hours; with memories of struggling against restraints—but when she looked at her wrists and ankles, there was no trace of anything, not a single abrasion. And, later, alone in her room, a single, horrifying recollection: asking about pain-killers and the doctors shaking their heads, telling her she had to endure it all without help, because analgesics were poison to the appeaser's metabolism.

Her roommate Lan says that they do give drugs—something to make the harmonisers forget the pain, the hours spent raving and twisting and scream-ing while the appeasers burrow into their guts.

It's all absurd, of course. It must be false impressions brought on by the drugs and the procedure, for why would the Everlasting Emperor take such bad care of those that serve him?

Ai Thi remembers waking up at night after the implantation, shivering and shaking with a terrible hunger—she was alone in the darkness, small and insignificant, and she could call for help but she didn't matter—the doctors had gone home and no one would come, no one remembered she was there. Around her, the shadows of the room seemed to twist and come alive—if she turned and looked away, they would swallow her whole, crush her until noth-ing was left. She reached for the rice cakes on the table—and they slid into her stomach, as thin and as tasteless as paper, doing nothing to assuage the hunger. Empty, she was empty, and nothing would ever fill that hole within her . . .

Not her hunger. Not her loneliness. The appeaser's. Cut off from the communion of their own kind, they so desperately needed contact to live, so desperately craved warmth and love.

You're not alone, Ai Thi whispered. You are a subject of the Everlasting Emperor, and he loves you as a father loves his children.

You're not alone.

Night after night, telling them the words from her training, the ones endlessly welling up out of her, like blood out of a wound. The Everlasting Emperor was human once, but he transcended that condition. He knows all our weaknesses, and he watches over us all. He asks only for respect and obedience in return for endless love.

You—we are part of something so much greater than ourselves: an Empire that has always been, that will always be as timeless as the Heavens. Through us—through the work of hundreds, of thousands like us, it will endure into this generation, and into the next.

Night after night, until the words became part of the appeaser—burrowed into them as they had burrowed within Ai Thi's guts—until they ceaselessly spoke in her sleep, giving her back her own words with unwavering strength.

Beware what you read. The Quynh Federation reaches everywhere, to disseminate their lies: you cannot trust news that hasn't been vetted.

Ai Thi gets down at her usual station: White Crane Monastery, close to the barracks. She has one last quadrant to go through on her rounds, Eggshell Celadon, making sure that the families there understand the cost of war fought beyond the Empire's boundaries, and the necessity of the war effort.

As she turns into a corridor decorated with a splash of stars, she hears the footsteps behind her. A menial, going to work—a kitchen hand, like Ai Thi used to be before she volunteered—or a sweeper, supervising bots as they clean the quadrant. But at the next corridor—one that holds the machinery of the station rather than cramped family compartments—the footsteps are still here.

She turns, briefly, catching a glimpse of hempen clothes, torn sleeves, and the glint of metal. From the appeaser, a vague guess that whoever it is is determined: the appeaser can't read human thoughts, can't interpret them, or the harmonisers' and enforcers' work would be that much simpler. What they know from human behaviour, they learned from Ai Thi.

Captain Giang's advice to her trainees: always choose the ground for a confrontation, rather than having choice forced on you.

Ai Thi stops, at the middle of the corridor—no nooks or crannies, no alcoves where her pursuer can hide. Within her the appeaser is silent and still, trying to find the proper words of the Everlasting Emperor for the circumstances, gathering strength for a psychic onslaught.

She's expected a group of dissidents—Sergeant Bac said they were getting bolder in the daily briefing—but it's just one person.

A woman in shapeless bot-milled clothes, bottom of the range—face gaunt, eyes sunken deep, lips so thin they look like the slash of a knife. Her hands rests inside her sleeves, fingers bunched. She has a knife or a gun. "Harmoniser," the woman whispers. "How can you—how can you—"

Ai Thi spreads her hands, to show that she is unarmed; though it isn't true. The appeaser is her best and surest weapon, but only used at the proper time. "I serve the Everlasting Emperor."

The woman doesn't answer. She merely quickens her pace. Her hand swings out, and it's a gun that she holds, the barrel glinting in the station's light, running towards Ai Thi and struggling to aim.

No time.

Ai Thi picks one saying, one piece of wisdom, from all the ones swarming in her mind. The Everlasting Emperor loves all his subjects like children, and it is the duty of children to bow down to their parents.

Bow down.

And she lets the appeaser hurl it like a thrown stone, straight into the woman's thoughts. No subtlety, not the usual quiet influence, the background to everyone's daily lives—just a noise that overwhelms everything like a scream.

Bow down.

The woman falters, even as her gun locks into place: there's a sound like thunder—Ai Thi throws herself to the side, momentarily deafened—comes up for breath, finding herself still alive, the appeaser within her driving her on.

Bow down.

She reaches the woman, twists a wrist that has gone limp. The gun clatters to the ground. That's the only sound in the growing silence—that, and the woman's ragged breath. The appeaser within Ai Thi relaxes, slightly. She can feel their disapproval, their fear. Cutting it too close. She could have died. *They* could have died.

Ai Thi lifts the woman to her feet, effortlessly. "You shouldn't have done this," she says. "Who sent you?"

She hasn't expected an answer—the woman's mind should still be filled with the single message the appeaser used to drown all cognitive function—but the thin, pale lips part. "I sent myself. You—you starve us, and expect us to smile."

"We all sacrifice things. It's the price to pay for safety," Ai Thi says, automatically, and then takes another look at the woman. All skin and bones—Ai Thi is strong from training, but the woman hardly weighs anything, and her cheeks are far gaunter than even those of menials— and, as she looks into the woman's eyes, she sees nothing but raw, naked desperation, an expression she knows all too well.

Who sent you?

I sent myself.

Two years ago, an eternity ago, Ai Thi looked at that same gaze in the mirror, working herself down to the bone for not enough money, not enough food, going to bed hungry every night and listening to Dieu Kiem's hacking cough, and knowing that no doctor would tend to the poor and desperate. She made a choice, then: she volunteered for implantation, knowing she might not survive it—volunteered to serve the Everlasting Emperor in spite of her doubts. But, if she hadn't made that choice—if she'd let fear and frustration and hunger whittle her down to red-hot rage—

This might have been her, with a gun.

Ai Thi is meant to call for the enforcers, to turn the woman over to them for questioning, so that they can track down and break the dissident cell or foreign agency that sent her. That would be the loyal, righteous thing to do. But . . .

But she's been here. She knows there's no cell—merely the end of a road; a last, desperate gesture that, if it doesn't succeed, will at least end everything.

Ai Thi walks back to the barracks with the woman over her shoulder—by then she's all spent, and lies in Ai Thi's grip like wrung cloth. Ai Thi lays her down in an alcove before the entrance, a little out of sight. "Wait here," she says.

By the time Ai Thi comes back, she half expects the woman to be gone. But she's still there, waiting—she sits on the floor with her legs drawn against her, huddling as though it might make her smaller.

"Here," Ai Thi says. She grabbed what she could from the refectory— couldn't dally, or she'd be noticed: two small rice cakes, and a handful of cotton fish.

The woman looks at her, warily; snatches all three things out of her hand.

"Go gently, or you'll just vomit it." Ai Thi crouches, watching her. The appeaser within her is quiet. Curious. "It's not poisoned."

The woman's laugh is short, and unamused. "I didn't think it was." She nibbles, cautiously, at the rice cakes; eating half of one before she slips the rest inside her sleeves.

"What's your name?"

A hesitation, then: "Hien Hoa. You'd find out, anyway."

"I don't have supernatural powers," Ai Thi says, mildly.

"No, but you have the powers of the state." Hoa stops, then; afraid she's gone too far.

Ai Thi shakes her head. "I'm not going to turn you in. I'd have done it already, if I was."

"Why—"

Ai Thi shrugs, though she doesn't quite know what to say. "Everyone deserves a second chance, I guess." She rises, ignoring the twinges of pain in her muscles. "Stay out of trouble, will you? I'd hate to see someone else bring you in."

Straying from the Everlasting Emperor's path is a grievous misconduct, but every misconduct can be atoned for—every fault can be forgiven, if the proper amends are made, the proper re-education achieved.

To Sergeant Bac, at her debriefing in the squad room, Ai Thi says nothing of Hoa. She heads next to Captain Giang's office, for her weekly interview.

The captain sits behind her desk, staring at the aggregated reports of her company, nodding, from time to time, at something that pleases or bothers her. On the desk before her is a simple *am* and *duong* logo, a half-black, half-white circle curved in the shape of an appeaser: the emblem of the harmonisers. "I see your last check-up was three months ago," she says.

Ai Thi nods.

"You're well, I trust?" Captain Giang says—only half a question. "No stomach pains. No headaches that won't go away. No blood in your urine."

The danger symptoms—the ones Ai Thi could recite by heart—a sign that the delicate symbiosis that links her and the appeaser is out of kilter, and that they could both die. "I . . . I don't think so," Ai Thi says.

Giang looks at her, for a while. "You don't look like yourself," she says, frowning.

She knows. No. There is no way she can know. Ai Thi draws a deep, ragged breath. "There's much unease," she says, finally, a half-truth. "People are . . . taut. Like a string about to snap." And there is only so much slack the harmonisers can pick up, only so much wisdom they can dispense to people whose only thoughts and worries are what they'll be eating come tomorrow.

"I see. Why do you think that is?"

Gaunt eyes, and Hoa's thin, bruised lips, and the careful way she's hoarded the food; for giving to someone else. Ai Thi says, finally, "May I speak freely?"

"Always." Giang frowns. "This isn't a jail or a re-education camp. We trust your loyalty."

Of course they do, and of course they can. Ai Thi would never do anything against the Everlasting Emperor: he keeps the fabric of society together. "The war effort against the Quynh Federation is costly. Food is more and more expensive, and this creates . . . anger. Jealousy. They think the soldiers favoured." And the harmonisers, and the enforcers, and the scholars that keep the machinery of the Empire going.

Giang doesn't speak, for a while. Her broad face is emotionless. "They would," she says. "But the soldiers pay dearly for that food. People on the station aren't at risk of losing limbs or pieces of their mind, or being tortured for information on the Empire." Ai Thi can feel, distantly, Giang's own appeaser, a thin thread at the back of her mind, whispering about love and need and duty, all the sayings she already knows by heart.

She says, "I know this."

"And they don't?" Giang sighs. "I'm not questioning your conclusions, private. But as you know, the war isn't going well. The Everlasting Emperor is going to announce an increase of the war effort."

"You said the soldiers paid for the food because they were at greater risk. But we—" Ai Thi says.

Giang raises an eyebrow. "Are we not?" Her gaze is sardonic, and Ai Thi remembers Hoa's gun going off, the thunder filling her ears. "We'll be the first against the wall, if things do break down." It sounds like a warning, though Ai Thi isn't sure who she means it for.

Perhaps us, the appeaser whispers, but they barely sound worried. Only about Hoa, which surprises Ai Thi; but of course they would know all about hunger and need.

"There's much unrest," Giang says. "I don't want you to patrol in pairs—you cover less ground—but it might become necessary. Private Khanh was attacked by a group of three dissidents masquerading as beggars, and only barely escaped."

"Is he—" Ai Thi asks, but Giang shook her head.

"He's fine. We didn't manage to catch them, though." Giang sounds annoyed. "Cinnabar Mansions Quadrant reported two riots in as many weeks. As you said, people are wound taut."

"But we'll be fine," Ai Thi says, before she can think.

"Of course we will. The Empire has weathered wars and fire and riots long before we were both born," Giang says. She makes a gesture with her hands. "Dismissed, private. Enjoy your rest."

It's only after Ai Thi has left the office, halfway to her room and the light comedy vid she was looking forward to, that she realises that the warm feeling of utter certainty within her is from Giang's appeaser.

The foundations of the Everlasting Empire: the censors, rooting out disinformation from vids and newscasts. The scholars, making the laws everyone must abide by. The harmonisers and enforcers, keeping the fabric of the Empire clear of dissidence. And the soldiers, defending the borders against enemy incursions.

"There's someone at the gates asking after you, lil sis," Lan says. She laughs, throwing her head back in a gesture so familiar it's barely annoying anymore. "A menial. From your old life?"

Lan comes from the Inner Rings, the wealthiest Station inhabitants. She caused some scandal at an examination, and her family gave her the choice of enlisting with the harmonisers, or with the soldiers on the front. She's Ai Thi's roommate, and she means well, but sometimes her assumptions about people grate. To wit: Ai Thi didn't keep contact with anyone from her old workplaces—such attachments aren't encouraged, in any case.

It can't be Second Aunt, because Ai Thi is currently in communication with home, and spoke to her not a minute past. "Can you ask them to wait?" Ai Thi says. Her time for outside calls is almost up, in any case. She turns back to Dieu Kiem. "Sorry. Duty calling."

Her daughter makes a grimace in her field of vision. She's a ghostly overlay in Ai Thi's implants, a tall and willowy girl who seems to have shot up three heads since Ai Thi was last given a permission home. "Captain Giang." She looks as though she's about to laugh. "Fine, but can you tell Great Aunt I want the network key?"

Ai Thi purses her lips. "She told me you hacked it and had every wall display copies of Huong Trang's poems. The more explicit ones."

"As practise," Dieu Kiem snorts. "Too easy."

She's growing up too fast, too strong. Ai Thi wants to tell her to be careful, but there's nothing illegal or reprehensible in what she's doing—just harmless pranks, the kind even the Everlasting Emperor would smile upon. But where does dissidence start?

She has no answer. She logs off in spite of Dieu Kiem's complaints, promising her that she'll have a word with Second Aunt—wondering, once again, how time passes, how little she sees of her own daughter.

Sacrifices aren't necessary, but they are all the more valued when they do occur.

The appeaser within her is . . . sad? There's a peculiar tautness in her mind, as if the entire world were about to come apart. She understands that they're sad, too, grieving for time lost.

"Thank you," she says, aloud, shaking her head. "But it's nothing we can't survive."

Warmth from within her; a sated need. The appeaser curls back to their usual, watchful self, chewing on sayings and wisdom they might need for their next patrol.

Outside the gates, Hoa is waiting for her. Ai Thi fights off the urge to pinch herself. "I didn't think—"

"That I'd come back?" Hoa is still gaunt and pale, but there's a light in her eyes that wasn't there before. Ai Thi is afraid to ask where it comes from, but Hoa merely shakes her head. "I found a second job." She grins, waving a basket towards Ai Thi. "And I owe you a meal."

They walk towards a nearby white space in silence. Ai Thi reaches out, deftly shaping a small corner of it into a lush green space, like the jungles in the stories of her childhood. Hoa sits down at the foot of a huge fig tree, setting down the basket between ghostly roots—Ai Thi hasn't reshaped reality, merely added a layer of illusion that they share across their implants.

Inside the basket are four puffed-up dough pieces, and grilled maize. Hoa hands them out, grimacing. "I wasn't sure if—" she pauses, embarrassed—"if you ate more."

Ai Thi guesses the unsaid words. "Because of the appeaser? A little, but not much." It's not like being pregnant. The appeaser is small, and will never grow within her: they have already had their children, the next generation of appeasers raised in tanks for implantation in the next generation of trainees.

They eat the first fried dough piece in silence, not quite sure what to say to each other. Ai Thi doesn't know why Hoa came back. She says, finally, "I saw you take the rice cakes. You have a family?"

Hoa looks at her for a while. "I thought you knew everything."

Ai Thi laughs. "I wish. But no. I'm not the Census Office."

"A toddler," Hoa says. "Three years old."

"Mine is older," Ai Thi says, with a sigh. "Thirteen years old and all opinions." She's not sure why she says, "I almost never see her. Duty."

Hoa laughs, a little sadly. It doesn't sound strained or forced, though the atmosphere is still tense. "You're different."

"From other harmonisers?" Ai Thi shrugs, and finally speaks the truth. "I was where you are, once. Working in a restaurant in the daytime, and cleaning the corridors at night. Starving myself to feed my child."

Hoa is staring at her. "That's why you became a harmoniser? For money?" There is . . . an edge to her voice, a hint of disapproval that's not meant to exist. Captain Giang is right. The fabric of society is fraying.

"Because I had nowhere else to go," Ai Thi says, simply. "Because . . . because I listened to the voice of the Everlasting Emperor, and he gave me a second chance."

"You've never seen him," Hoa says. A question, a challenge.

"Once," Ai Thi says. She doesn't need to close her eyes to remember. She was standing at the back of the harmonisers' ranks, and even from there she felt the radiance of his presence, wave after wave of warmth filling her, the world wavering and bending until it was all she could do not to fall on her knees. "He was everything they say he was, and more."

Hoa is silent, for a while. "Faith," she says, and her voice is full of wonder. "I thought—" she shakes her head. "I suppose it takes a lot, to get implanted. May I—" Her hand reaches out, resting close to Ai Thi's torso.

Ai Thi nods. Hoa's fingers rest on her gut, pressing down, lightly. The appeaser gurgles within her—kicks towards Hoa, who withdraws as if burnt. The appeaser's disappointment burns in Ai Thi like acid, spreading outwards through the only channel they know how to use.

Before the Everlasting Emperor, all citizens are weighed equally: the only thing that matters is their loyalty.

Hoa takes one, two steps backwards, her face twisting as the full blast of emotions hits her. "What—"

"They're hurt," Ai Thi says. "Because you think they're less than human."

Hoa opens her mouth. She's going to say that of course they're not human, that they're just an alien parasite, and all the insults Ai Thi has had hurled at her by dissidents. Ai Thi cuts her off before she can speak, "They're lonely. Always lonely. That's the price they pay for service to the Everlasting Emperor."

Hoa closes her mouth. Her face goes through contortions. "I'm sorry." And she kneels, hand held out, making it clear that it's not to Ai Thi she's apologising.

Warmth spreading through Ai Thi—the appeaser. They like her.

Hoa reaches out, holds out a piece of dough again. "Hungry?" she asks.

Ai Thi eats it. It feels sweeter than honey as it slides down her throat, the appeaser's approval a small sun within her, spreading to all her limbs—an odd, unsettling, but welcome feeling.

At length, Hoa speaks, again. "So they're starving you, too."

Ai Thi shakes her head. "I don't understand—"

"Of love and kin and warmth." Hoa's voice is sad. "Hollowing you out, and leaving nothing but words."

Ai Thi wants to say something about wisdom, about the Everlasting Emperor, about necessary sacrifices, but the words seem to shrivel in her mouth. Hoa's burning eyes hold her—the same desperate need she saw in them, back when she almost arrested her, except that it's . . . pity?

"I'm sorry. You shouldn't be doing this to yourself," Hoa says again, and it *is* pity. Compassion. She doesn't understand, she doesn't see how much the Everlasting Emperor keeps Ai Thi going, doesn't understand how much the words mean, how they keep the world together—except that Dieu Kiem is growing up without her, and all that Ai Thi can remember is the appeaser's desperate, lonely hunger, a bottomless well that nothing can ever fill . . .

She's up, and running away from the park before she can think, heedless to Hoa's calls. She only stops when she gets to her room, breathing hard and feeling as though the air she inhales never reaches her burning lungs.

The Everlasting Emperor has always been, and will always be. The Empire is as long-lasting as the stars in the heavens. As long as the bonds between mother and daughter, between brother and brother endure, then it, too, shall.

There's a noise outside like the roar of the sea. Ai Thi wakes up, and the sound swells to fill her entire universe. "Mother? Mother?"

Dieu Kiem, through her implants. "Child. How did you—"

Her daughter's voice is tight, on the verge of panic. "Hacked your coms. That's not the point. Mother, you need to move. They say there are riots all over the station. "

What—how? Ai Thi fumbles, trying to find something solid—she rubs a hand on her guts, feeling the reassuring mass of the appeaser within her. "Child? Child?"

Dieu Kiem's voice comes in fast, words jumbled together. "The Everlasting Emperor ordered the closure of half the granaries across all quadrants. An enforcer shot someone, and then—"

"Closure. Why? For the war effort?" Ai Thi asks, but there's no answer. Nothing but silence on the coms now, but the roar is still there, and she knows it's that of a crowd massed at the gates. She could call up the outside cameras on her implants, but there's no point.

It's night in the barracks. Lan is on patrol—should be, if she wasn't caught in the riots. Ai Thi has known for a while that things are taut, but for riots to be this widespread, this fast? Things are bad. Very bad. Ai Thi hits the general alert on the network. She heads to the squad room first, but it's deserted and silent—and shifts course, to get to Giang's office.

She finds the Captain putting on her jacket, straightening her official rank patch on her chest, the eyes of the tiger shining in the dim light. "Captain—"

"I know." Giang's voice is curt.

Mankind is but one step away from lawlessness. Only the word of Heaven and of the Everlasting Emperor keeps us from becoming monsters to one another.

Barely contained panic within Ai Thi—Giang's appeaser, not hers—hers is silent and watchful, but not surprised.

"We have to hold," Captain Giang says. "We need to re-establish harmony and order." She shakes her head. Again that feeling of rising panic within Ai Thi, the edge of something so strong Giang can barely contain it.

"Captain—"

Giang is halfway to the door already. "There's no time, private. Come."

Something is wrong. Not the riot, not the crowd, not what seems like a station-wide panic. Captain Giang wouldn't lose her head over that. And she's not currently broadcasting emotions at Ai Thi. Whatever causes that panic is so strong that it's simply spilling outwards, like the hurt of Ai Thi's appeaser when Hoa wouldn't touch them.

And why hasn't she mentioned reinforcements? "Captain," Ai Thi says, again. "We'll hold, but what about Plum Blossom Company?"

Giang turns then. For a moment, her composure breaks, and the face she shows to Ai Thi is the white, ashen one of a corpse, a bewildered, lost and hungry ghost. "The dissidents have overwhelmed the Palace of Heaven and Earth, private. The Everlasting Emperor is dead."

Dead.

No.

The roar in Ai Thi's ears isn't the sound of the crowd—it's a long, desperate scream that scrapes her throat raw, and she can't tell if it's coming from her or the appeaser.

"How can he—" she starts, stops, unable to voice the enormity of it. "How—"

Giang has pulled herself together again. "I don't know," she says. "But that's not what matters. There are no reinforcements coming, private."

Outside, on Ai Thi's implants, the crowd has trampled the two harmonisers guarding the gates. A press of people is battering at the gates, and it's only a matter of time until the fragile metal gives way.

Dead.

The Empire is as long lasting as the stars in the heavens, as the bonds of filial duty between parents and children.

The Empire . . .

They'll die, holding the barracks. Die trying to impose harmony on a crowd that's too large and too big for them to control.

"Captain, we can't—"

"I know we can't hold." Giang is at the door: she doesn't turn around anymore. Ai Thi calls up the inside of the gates on her implants, sees another press: Kim Cuc and Tuyet and Vu and half the harmonisers in the barracks in a loose formation that mixes all squads under the orders of Sergeant Bac and Sergeant Hong, sending wave after wave of appeaser thoughts towards the crowd, trying to calm them down. It's like throwing stones and hoping to stop the ocean.

Giang says, "We swore an oath to the Emperor, private. Loyalty unto death."

Giang's appeaser: warmth and contentment within Ai Thi, the satisfaction of duty done to the bitter end. *It is the duty of all subjects to give their life . . .*

Within Ai Thi, her appeaser stirs—brings up, not the Everlasting Emperor's voice, but Hoa's compassion-filled gaze, Hoa's voice, a rock against which the other appeaser's thoughts shatter.

You shouldn't be doing this to yourself.

"It's not . . ." Ai Thi says. She's surprised at how steady her voice sounds.

"I beg your pardon?" Giang stops then.

"It's not our duty," Ai Thi says. "That's not how that saying ends, Captain."

He never asks for more than what is necessary, and reasonably borne.

The Everlasting Emperor is dead. There is nothing that says they have to die, too.

Ai Thi's appeaser has fallen silent, knowing exactly what she wants. She feels the thoughts from Giang's appeaser, dancing on the edge of her mind—duty, loyalty, death, a trembling wall she can barely hold at bay for long.

Giang moves back into her office, comes to stand before her. "This isn't a discussion, private. It's an order."

Necessary. Reasonably borne. Ai Thi uncoils, then—even as, within her, the appeaser moves—a psychic onslaught centred around a single, pinpoint thought. Giang grunts, goes down on one knee, eyes rolling up in her face, and Ai Thi's hand strikes her jugular, taking her down.

Ai Thi stands, breathing hard, over Giang's unconscious body—for a moment, at a loss at what she's done, what she should do—but there is only one thing that she can do, after all. The rioters will come for their families next, and neither Second Aunt nor Dieu Kiem have had any training in combat or eluding pursuers. There's a risk she'll lead the crowd straight to them, but it's offset by what she and the appeaser can bring them. She can help. She has to.

Ai Thi thinks of the other harmonisers, lined against the doors and waiting for them to cave in. She heads towards the squad room. Within her, rising emptiness, a howling need—how will they survive, with the Everlasting Emperor dead—what does wisdom mean, anymore, if its incarnation is no more—nothing, there is nothing left . . .

In the squad room, there's only Lan, bloodied and out of breath, who smiles grimly at her. "It's a war zone out there. Fortunately they haven't found the back door yet, but I don't know how long we can hold."

Ai Thi's voice comes from very far away—a stranger's, utterly emotionless—because the alternative would be an endless scream. "The Everlasting Emperor is dead. Captain Giang . . . says to run. To scatter back to our families. There's no point in holding. We've already lost."

They've lost everything. They—

For a long, agonisingly long moment, Lan stares at her—as if she knew, as if she could read straight into Ai Thi's mind. She smiles again, almost with fondness. "Families. Of course."

Her hand rests, lightly, on Ai Thi's shoulder, squeezes once, twice. "I'll tell them, though not everyone will listen. But you run, lil sis."

And then she's gone, and it's just Ai Thi, walking through empty corridors towards the back of the barracks, the roar of the crowd receding into meaninglessness.

It's not too late. She can go out of the barracks—go back the way Lan came from—go get her aunt and daughter before the rioters find new targets—she can run, as fiercely, as far away as she can—to the heart of the Quynh Federation if need be. They can make a new life, one that's no longer in service to the Everlasting Emperor.

They can—

The Emperor is dead, and nothing will ever be right again—the appeaser reaching, again and again, for words, remembering that they mean nothing now.

"Ssh," Ai Thi says, aloud, to the appeaser. "It'll be all right. It's nothing we can't survive." And, slowly, gently, sings the lullabies she used to sing to Dieu Kiem when she was a child—again and again as they both run from the shadow of the barracks—again and again until the songs fill the hollow, wordless silence within her.

Finbarr O'Reilly is an Irish speculative fiction writer who likes to explore how broken technologies or unearthly events affect intimate locales. Why would you want to write about alien battleships invading New York when you can imagine little green men asking for directions from a short-tempered undertaker in Carrigtohill, County Cork? Finbarr has worked as a journalist for almost 20 years, most of those as a sub-editor (copyeditor) in newspapers such as the *Irish Times, Irish Examiner,* and *Daily Telegraph.* He currently works as the production editor of a magazine for car dealers. He believes it is testament to his powers of imagination that he has never purchased an automobile and doesn't drive. Like many Irish writers, Finbarr lives in self-imposed exile. He currently resides with his wife and two children in a small town in Lincolnshire, UK, too far from the sound of gulls and the smell of saltwater. He tweets at @finoreilly.

THE LAST BOAT-BUILDER IN BALLYVOLOON

Finbarr O'Reilly

"There are of a certainty mightier creatures, and
the lake hides what neither net nor fine can take."
—William Butler Yeats, *The Celtic Twilight*

The first time I met Más, he was sitting on the quayside in Ballyvoloon, carving a nightmare from a piece of linden. Next to him on the granite blocks that capped the seawall lay a man's weatherproof jacket and hat, in electric pink. The words "petro-safe" were pin-striped across them in broad white letters, as if a spell that would protect him from the mechanical monster he whittled.

Short of smoking a pipe, Más looked every inch a nineteenth-century whaler. Veined cheeks burned and burnished by sun and wind to a deep cherry gloss, thick gray hair matted and flattened from his souwester and whiskers stiff enough with salt to resist the autumnal breeze blowing in from the harbor mouth.

I had arrived in Ballyvoloon early on a Friday morning. My pilot would not fly till Monday, so I spent the weekend walking the town. Its two main streets, or "beaches" as the locals called them, ran east and west of a concrete, T-shaped pier.

It was near the bottom of the "T" that Más set out his pitch every day, facing the water, but sheltered by thousands of tonnes of rock and concrete.

Ballyvoloon was a town best approached from the sea. The faded postcards on sale along the beachfront showed it from that rare perspective. Snapped from the soaring pleasure decks of ocean-going liners long scrapped or sunk, ribbons of harlequin houses rose from coruscant waters, split by the immense neo-Gothic cathedral that crowns the town. Nowadays, the fret-sawn fascias of pastel shopfronts shed lazy flakes of paint into the broad streets and squares below. It has faded, but there is grandeur there still.

Between the town's rambling railway station and my hotel, I had passed a dozen or more artists, their wares tied to the railings of the waterside promenade, or propped on large boards secured to lampposts, but none dressed like Más. Nor did any carve like him.

"That looks realistic," I said, my heart pounding, as he snicked delicate curls of blond wood from the block with a thick-spined blade.

"There's not much point sugarcoating them," he said, his voice starting as a matter-of-fact drawl, but ending in the singsong accent of the locals.

"How long have you been a sculptor?" I asked.

"I'm not a sculptor. This is just something to occupy the hands."

"The devil's playthings, eh?"

He stopped carving and looked up at me through muddy green eyes.

"Something like that."

Más lowered the squid he was working on and cast around in the pocket of his jacket. He removed three of the monsters, perfectly carved, but in different sizes and woods, one stained black and polished. The colors seemed to give each one slightly different intents, but none was reassuring.

Other artists carved or drew or painted the squid, but they had smoothed out the lines, removed the barbs, the beaks, gave the things doe-eyes and even smiles and made them suitable to sit atop a child's bedclothes or a living room bookshelf.

Más did the opposite. He made the horrific more horrifying. He made warm, once-living wood look like the doubly dead, glossy plastic of the squids. These were not the creatures we had released, but their more deadly and cunning offspring.

I hid my excitement as well as I could.

"Sixty for one or one hundred for a pair," he said.

Más let the moment stretch until the sheer discomfort of it drove me to buy.

His mood brightened and he immediately began packing up his belongings. I had clearly overpaid and he could afford to call it a day.

"See you so," he said, cheerfully and sauntered off into the town.

Once I was back at the hotel, I unwrapped the parcel and inspected the sculptures, to confirm my suspicions.

The other artists may have outsold Más's squid six or seven times, but he was the only of them who had seen a real one.

> "Twelve years after the squid were introduced, the west coast of Europe endured a number of strange phenomena. Firstly, the local gull population bloomed. The government and the squids' manufacturer at the time said it was a sign of fish stocks returning to normal, that it was evidence the squid were successful in their mission.
>
> "Local crab numbers also exploded, to the point that water inlets at a couple of coastal power stations were blocked. The company linked this to the increased gull activity, increasing the amount of food falling to the seafloor."
>
> —Hawes, J., *How We Lost the Atlantic, p32*

The first flight was late in the afternoon, a couple of hours before sunset. This would give me the best chance of spotting things in the water, as it was still bright enough to see and anything poking above the surface would cast a longer shadow.

The pilot, a taciturn, bearded fellow in his sixties called Perrott, flicked switches and toggles as he went through what passed for a safety briefing.

"If we ditch, it will take about fifteen minutes for the helo to reach us from the airport. The suits will at least make that wait comfortable, assuming, you know . . ."

We both wore survival suits of neon-pink non-petro, covering everything but hands and heads. His was molded to his frame and visibly worn on the elbows and the seat of his pants. Mine squeaked when I walked and still smelled of tart, oleophobic soy.

"Yes. I know," I said, as reassuringly as I could manage.

As he tapped dials and entered numbers on a clipboard, I thought of my first flight over water.

My sea training was in Wales, where an ancient, ex-RNLI helicopter dropped me about half a mile from shore. It was maybe twenty-five feet to the water, but the fall was enough to knock the breath out of me. The crew made sure I was still kicking and moved back over land. The idea was to get me to panic, I suppose. They needn't have worried. The helicopter was away for a total of eight minutes and if my heart could have climbed my gullet to escape my chest, it would have.

After they pulled me back up, I asked the winchman how I had done.

"No worse than most," he shouted.

He took a flashbang grenade from a box under the seat, pulled the pin, and dropped it out the open door. He counted down from four on his fingers. Over the roar of the rotors, I heard neither splash nor detonation. The winchman made sure I was harnessed, then pointed out the door and down.

A couple of miles away, I could see three or four squid making for a spot directly beneath us, all of them moving so fast they left a wake.

He gave me a torturer's grin.

"Better than some."

> "We seen them first, the slicks. That's what they looked like in the pictures, like some tanker or bulker had washed her tanks. But as we got close we could see it was miles and miles of chopped up fish. And the smell! That's what the locals still call that summer—the big stink.
>
> "When we got back we found out the squid had become more . . . hungry, I suppose, and instead of pulling the bits of plastic out of the water, they started pulling 'em out of the fish. Sure we had been eating that fish for years and it never did us any harm."
>
> —Trevor Cunniffe, trawlerman, in an interview
> for *Turn Your Back to the Waves*, an RTÉ radio documentary
> marking fifty years since the squids' introduction

After two days of fruitless flights, I was grounded by fog. Late in the afternoon, I went to a pub. I sat at the long side of the L-shaped bar, inhaling the fug of old beer and new urinal cakes.

The signage, painted in gold leaf on the large windows, had faded and peeled, so I asked a patron what the place was called. "Tom's" was the only reply, offering no clue if this was the original name of the pub or the latest owner.

Between the bottles shelved on the large mirror behind the bar, I saw the figure of a man in a candy-striped pink jacket through the rippled privacy glass of the door. It opened and Más walked in. He gently closed it behind him and moved to a spot at the end of the bar. He kept his head down, but couldn't escape recognizing some regulars and nodded a salute to them.

Emboldened by alcohol, I raised my drink.

"How is the water today?" I asked.

The barmaid gave me a look as if to ask what I was doing engaging a local sot, but I smiled at her for long enough that she wandered off, reassured or just bored at my insincerity.

"About the same," said Más. "Visibility's not very good."

"No," I said. "That's why I'm in here. No flights today."

"Are you off home then," Más asked.

I interpreted the question as an invitation and walked over to take the stool next to him.

"Not quite," I said. "Will you have a drink?"

"I will," he said. "So, what has you in town?"

At first, Más didn't seem too bothered when I explained who I worked for, or at least he didn't ask the usual questions or put forward the usual conspiracy theories about the squid.

"A job's a job, I suppose."

His eyes wrinkled, amused at a joke hidden to me. "So do ye all have jobs in England, then?"

Ireland had been on universal income for the better part of two decades. It was hard to see how people like Más would have survived otherwise.

"No, not by a long chalk. The only reason I got this one is I wasn't afraid to cross the sea in a plane."

"More fool you."

"You have to die of something, I told them. And it was quite exciting, in the end."

As the light faded, the mid-afternoon drinkers gave way to a younger, louder crowd, but Más and I still sat, talking.

I described the huge reservoir near where I lived in Rutland, where people could still swim and sail and fish, and how everyone worried that the squid would somehow reach it, denying us access, like Superior or the Caspian.

He asked me what on Earth would make me leave such a place.

"I wanted to see the world. I needed a job," I said.

He laughed. "Those used to be the reasons people joined the Navy."

Perrott's plane was old, but well serviced. It started first time and once we finished our climb, the engine settled into a bagpipe-like drone.

We crossed the last headland and the cheerful baize below, veined in drystone walls, gave way to gray waves, maned in white.

He radioed the Cork tower to tell them we were now over open water and that the rescue team was on formal standby.

He adjusted the trim of the plane to a point where he was happy to let the thing fly itself and joined me in scanning the waters below.

It was less than half an hour, until his pilot's eye spotted it. Perrott took the controls again and banked to give me a better view. I let the video camera run, while I used the zoom lens to snap any identifying features.

From the size of the blurred shape rippling just beneath the surface, I could tell it was old, seventh or eighth generation, perhaps, but I really wanted a more detailed look.

I told Perrott I would like to make another pass.

"If only we had a bomb, eh?" he said. Sooner or later, everyone suggests it.

"We tried that," I said.

"Oh yeah?"

Perrott had signed a non-disclosure agreement before the flight. It didn't matter what I told him. Most of it was already on the Internet, in any case.

"Yes. First they bombed an oil platform in the Gulf of Mexico and opened up its wellhead. Miles from shore, so any oil that escaped would be eaten by the squid or burned in the fire."

Hundreds of thousands of the things had come, enough that you could see the black stain spread on satellite images. I had only watched the video. I couldn't imagine how chilling it had been to observe it happen live.

"Then the Americans dropped three of the biggest non-nukes they've got on them."

"It didn't work, then?"

"No. Any squid more than a dozen feet or so below the surface were protected by the water. We vaporized maybe half of them. After that they stayed deep, mostly."

I didn't tell Perrott about the Mississippi and how the squid had retaliated. Let him read that on the Internet too.

"Well, they may be mindless, but they're not stupid," he said.

We flew on until the light failed, but, as if it had heard him, the beast did not reappear.

> "It would be wrong to think of the squid as a failure of technology. The technology worked, from the plastic filtration, to the self-replication and algorithmic learning.
>
> "Also do not forget that they succeeded in their original purpose— they did clean up the waters and they did save fish stocks from extinction.
>
> "The failure, if you can truly call it that, is ours. We failed to see that life, even created life, will never behave exactly as we intend.

"The failure was not in the squids' technology, or in their execution. It was in our imagination."

—From the inaugural address of Ireland's last president,
Francis Robinson

A basket of chips and fried 'goujons' of catfish had appeared in front of us, gratis. I dived in, sucking sea salt and smoky, charred fish skin from my fingertips. Más looked over the bar into the middle distance.

"Don't tell me you don't like fish," I said. "That would be too funny."

"That's not real fish."

Más had progressed to whiskey and a bitter humor sharpened his tongue.

"It tastes pretty real," I said. I had heard all the scare stories about fish farming.

He held up a calloused hand, as if an orator or bard about to recite. The other was clenched, to punctuate his thoughts.

"Why is it, do you think, that we are trying to replicate the things we used to have?

"Like, if most people can still eat 'fish,' or swim in caged bloody lidos, or if cargo comes by airship or whatever, then the more normal it becomes. And it shouldn't be bloody normal. It's not normal."

The barmaid rolled her eyes. Clearly, she had heard the rant before.

I told him I agreed with the swimming bit inasmuch as I wouldn't personally miss it terribly if I could never do it again, but that farmed fish didn't bother me and that I thought most people never considered where their goods came from, even before the squid.

Disappointment, whether at me or the world, wilted in his face before he let the whiskey soften him again. His shoulders lowered, his hands relaxed and the melody of his voice reasserted itself.

"When I was a boy, my father once told me a story about trying to grow trees in space."

I coughed mid-chew and struggled to dislodge a crumb of batter from my throat. With tears in my eyes, I waved him on. I don't know why, but it amused me to hear an old salt like Más talk about orbital horticulture.

"Well, these guys on Spacelab or wherever, they tried growing them in perfect conditions, perfect nutrients, perfect light, even artificial gravity. They would all shoot straight up, then keel over and die. Every tree seed they planted—pine, ash, oak, cypress—they all died. Nobody could figure out what was wrong. Everything a plant could need was provided, perfectly measured. These were the best cared for plants in the world."

"In the solar system," I ribbed him.

"Right. In the solar system. Except for one thing. Do you know what was missing?

"No. Tell me."

"A breeze. Trees develop the strength, the woody cells, to support their weight by resisting the blow of the wind. Without it, they falter and sicken."

I didn't really get his point and told him so.

"You can't sharpen a blade without friction. You can't strengthen a man, or a civilization, without struggle. Airships and swimming pools and virtual bloody sailing. It's all bollocks. We should be hauling these things out of the water, like they said we would."

He gestured through the window of the bar to the gray bulk of the cathedral looming in the fog.

"There was a reason Jesus was a fisherman," said Más, as if a closing statement.

I didn't know what to say to that.

The barmaid leaned over the bar to clear the empty baskets.

"Jesus was a carpenter, Más," she said.

"Six sea scouts, aged eleven to fourteen, had left the fishing town of Castletown-berehaven in a rigid inflatable boat, what they call a 'rib.' Their scout leader was at the helm, an experienced local woman named De Paor.

"The plan was to take the boys and girls out around nearby Bere Island to spot seals and maybe porpoises.

"About an hour into the journey, contact was lost. The boat was never found, but most of the bodies washed up a day or so later, naked and covered in long ragged welts. Initial theories said they must have been chewed up by a propeller on a passing ship, but there was nothing big enough near the coast.

"Post-mortem examinations clinched it. The state pathologist pulled dozens of small plastic barbs from each child. They were quickly identified as belonging to the squid.

"A later investigation concluded that the fault lay with a cheap brand of sunscreen one of the children had brought and shared with her shipmates. A Chinese knock-off of a French brand, it contained old stocks of petro-derived nanoparticles. Just as the squid had pulped tonnes of fish to get at the plastic in their flesh in year twelve, they had tried to remove all traces of the petro from the children."

—Jennings, Margaret, *When The World Stopped Shrinking*, p34

Más's house was beyond the western end of the town, past a small turning circle for cars. A path continued to a rocky beach, but was used only by courting couples, dog walkers, or drinking youngsters. A wooden gate led off the beach, where a small house sat behind a quarter-acre of lawn and an old boathouse.

Síle, the barmaid, had told me where he lived. Más usually gave up carving at about four, she said, had a few drinks in a few places and was usually home about six.

I started for the main house, when I heard a noise. A low murmur, like a talk radio station heard through a wall. It was coming from the boathouse.

I made my way across the lawn. Almost unconsciously I was walking crablike on the balls of my feet, with my arms outstretched for balance. The boathouse was in bad shape. Green paint had blistered on the ship-lapped planks and lichen or moss had crept halfway up the transom windows above the large double doors.

The fabric of the place was so weathered I didn't have to open them. Planks had shrunk and split at various intervals, leaving me half a dozen spyholes to the interior. I quietly pressed my eye to one and peered inside.

Under the light of a single work lamp, I could see Más standing at a bench, his back to me, and wearing a T-shirt and jeans. Without the souwester, he looked more like an ageing rock star than a fisherman and more like twice my age than the three times I had assumed.

Beyond him lay several bulky piles, perhaps of wood, covered by tarpaulin and shrouded in shadow.

A flagstone floor ran all the way to the other wall, where there lay a dark square of calm water—a man-made inlet of dressed stone, from which rose the cold smell of the sea. A winch was bolted to the floor opposite a rusty iron gate that blocked the water from the estuary. Smaller, secondary doors above protected the interior from the worst of the elements.

As he worked, Más whistled.

I recognized enough of the tune to know it was old, but its name escaped me. It felt as manipulative as most traditional music—as Más whistled the chorus, it sounded like a happy tune, but I knew there would be words to accompany it and odds were, they would tell of tragedy.

Más began to wind down, cleaning tools with oil-free cloths. I had told myself this was not spying, this was interest, or concern. But suddenly, I became embarrassed. I silently padded back across his lawn. I would call on him another night.

As I stepped back onto the path between two overgrown rhododendron bushes, my foot collided with a rusty old garden lantern with a musical crash.

I just had enough presence of mind to turn again so I was facing the house, trying to look like I had just arrived.

It was in time for Más to see me as he emerged from the boathouse to investigate. I waved as nonchalantly as I could.

He leaned back inside the door and must have flicked a switch, as his garden was suddenly bathed in light from a ring of security floods under the eaves of his house.

I waved again as he re-emerged, confident that he could at least see me this time.

"Oh it's you," he said.

"Hi. Yes, the barmaid, Síle, gave me your address. I hope you don't mind.

"Well, come in so. I have no tea, I'm afraid. I may have some chicory."

I raised the bottle in my hand and gave it a wiggle.

> "In the early days after their 'revolution,' the squid featured in one scare story after another. They would evolve legs and stalk the landscape like Wells's Martians, they would form a super-intelligence capable of controlling the world's nuclear arsenal, or they would start harvesting the phytoplankton that provide most of the world's breathable oxygen.
>
> "In the end, they did what biological organisms do—they found their own equilibrium. Any reactions of theirs since are no more a sign of 'intelligence' than a dog defending its front yard."
> —Edward Mission, *The Spectator's Big Book of Science*

Perrott banked the plane again. It was the first flight during which I had felt ill. The day was squally and overcast, the sky lidded with a leaden dome of cloud.

The squid breached the water, rolling its "tentacles" behind it. There was no reason for the maneuver, according to the original designers, which made it look even more biological. But even from this altitude, I could see the patterns of old plastic the thing had used to build and periodically repair itself.

"He's a big one," said Perrott, who was clearly enjoying himself.

The beast dived again. Just as it sank out of sight in the dying light, I counted eight much smaller shadows behind it. Each breached the surface of the water and rolled their tentacles, just as their colossal "parent" had.

"Shit."

These were sleeker machines, of a green so deep it may as well have been black. There was no wasted musculature, no protrusions to drag in the water as they slipped by. These things would never reach the size of the squid that had manufactured them, but that didn't matter. They were fast and there were more of them.

"Problem?" said Perrott.

"Yes. Somebody isn't playing by the rules."

"I had a friend. Val. Killed himself."

Más had had a lot to drink, mostly the whiskey I had brought, but also a homemade spirit, which smelled faintly methylated. His face sagged under the influence of alcohol, but his voice became brighter and clearer with each drink. The stove roared with heat, the light from its soot-stained window washing the kitchen in sepia.

I wasn't sure if he was given to maudlin statements of fact such as this when drunk, or whether this was an opening statement, so I said "I'm sorry to hear that. When did that happen?"

"A while back."

I was still adrift—I didn't know if it was a long time ago and he had healed, or recently and his emotions were strictly battened down. Before I could ask another qualifying question, he continued.

"When we were teenagers, a couple of years after the squid were introduced, Val and I went fishing from the pier one October when the mackerel were in."

"By God, they were fun to catch. Val had an old fiberglass rod that belonged to his dad, or his granddad. The cork on the handle was perished, the guides were brown with rust, but as long as you used a non-petro line, the squid didn't bother you in those days. We caught a lot of fish that year.

"So as we pulled them out, I would unhook them and launch them back into the tide. They were contaminated with all sorts of stuff, heavy metals, plastic, even carbon fiber from the boat hulls. After I had done this once or twice, Val asked me why. I said 'well you can't eat them, so why not let them go.' And Val said 'fuck them, they're only fish.'

"After that, every fish he caught, every one, he would brain and chop up there on the pier and leave for the gulls to eat. He was my friend, but he was cruel.

"The trouble with the squid is they think about us the way Val thought about fish. We're not food, we're not sport. I'm not sure they know what we are. I'm not sure they care."

For a moment, sobriety surfaced. Más looked forlorn. I dreaded the words that would come next. I had become quite good at predicting his laments and tirades.

"We don't fight for it, for the territory, or for the people we lost. For the love of God, these things ate children, and we just accept it. We should be out there every bloody day, hunting these things."

I told him I understood the desire to hurt them, that many had tried, but it just didn't work like that. That most people preferred to pretend they just weren't there, like fairy-tale villagers skirting the wood where the big bad wolf lived.

"But why," he demanded.

"Well they are 'protected' now, for starters," I said. "They fight back. But I suppose the main reason is it's easier than the reality."

"Easier," he scoffed.

He raised his glass, to let me know it was my turn to speak. But I didn't know how to comfort him. So I let him comfort me.

"Your family owned trawlers, right? What's it like? To go out on the ocean?"

Drunk, in the heat of his kitchen, I closed my eyes and listened.

> "The raincoat suicides were a foreseeable event inasmuch as such events happen after many profound and well-publicised changes to people's understanding of the world around them. The Wall Street Crash, Brexit, the release of the Facebook Files. It is a form of end-of-days-ism that we have seen emerge again and again, from military coups to doomsday cults.
>
> "Most of the people who took their own lives had previously displayed signs of moderate to severe mental illness. That the locations of more than two hundred of the deaths were confined to areas with high sea cliffs, such as Dover in England or the Cliffs of Moher in Co Clare, adds fuel to the notion that these were tabloid-inspired suicides, sadly, but predictably, adopted by already unwell people."
>
> —Jarlath Kelleher, The Kraken sleeps: reporting of suicide as 'sacrifice' in British and Irish media (Undergraduate thesis, Dublin Institute of Technology)

He pulled the tarpaulin off with a flourish. The green-black boat sat upside down on two sawhorses, like an orca, stiff with rigor mortis, beached on pointed rocks.

It was a naomhóg. In the west, I found out later, it was called a currach, but this far south, people called it a naomhóg. Depending on who you asked, it meant 'little saint' or 'young saint,' as if the namers were asking God and the sea to spare it.

It was made of a flexible skin, stretched tightly over a blond wooden frame. I dropped to the floor to look inside, still unable to talk. I knew nothing about boat-building in those days, but the inside looked like pure craftsmanship.

It was almost the most rudimentary of constructed vessels and in place of oars it had long spars of unfeathered wood. But where a normal naomhóg was finished with hide or canvas and waterproofed with pitch, Más's boat was hulled in what looked like glossy green-black plastic stretched over its ribs and stapled in place on the inside of the gunwale.

I ran my hand along the hull. The skin, which looked constantly wet, was bone-dry and my fingers squeaked. They left no fingerprints. I knew instantly what it was, but I wished I didn't.

"Will you come with me? I'd like to show you my harbor. We might even catch something."

He was so proud, of his vessel, of his hometown. I couldn't say anything else.

"I will," I lied. "Tomorrow, if the fog lifts."

"I remember the harbour before the squid. The water teemed with movement. Ships steamed up the channel to the container ports upriver, somehow avoiding the small launches, in a complicated dance against outgoing or incoming tides, taking people to and from work at the steel-works on the nearest of the islands. Under the guidance of a harbour-master sitting in his wasp-striped control tower, warships slipped sleekly from the naval base to hunt drug smugglers or Icelandic trawlers. An occasional yacht tied up at the floating pontoon of a small waterside restaurant. In summer, children dared each other to 'tombstone' from the highest point of the piers.

"When I returned to the island, it might as well have been sur-rounded by tarmac, like a derelict theme park. Nobody even looked to the sea. It was easier that way."

—Elaine Theroux, *The Great Island*

It was bright outside when I left Más's house. He had more friends, or at least acquaintances, than I had thought. None outwardly seemed to blame me for what had happened. Many expressed surprise he had made it that far.

Más himself had been less forgiving. After I turned him in, the local police superintendent let me talk to him. Más told me he hated me, called me a "fucking English turncoat." He spat in my face.

I told him he didn't understand. That he had been lucky until now. Lucky he hadn't been killed. That they hadn't retaliated.

I wanted to tell him we were working on things to kill them, to infect them, to turn them on each other. I wanted to tell him to wait until the harbor mouth was closed, that the nets were in place, that he could soon take to the water off Ballyvoloon every day. That I would go with him.

But I couldn't and none of it would have mattered anyway.

I had betrayed him. And I found I could live with it.

Between Más's house and Ballyvoloon is a harbor-side walkway known simply as 'the water's edge.' The pavement widens dramatically in two places to support the immense red-brick piers of footbridges that connect the old Admiralty homes, on the other side of the railway line, to the sea. I climbed the wrought iron steps to the peak and surveyed the harbor, my arms resting on the mossy capstones of the wall. The sun was rising over the eastern headland, bright and cold.

I took the phone from my pocket and watched the coroner's video.

It was mostly from one angle, from a camera I had often passed high atop an antique lamppost preserved in the middle of the main street. The quality was good, no sound, but the colors of Ballyvoloon were gloriously recreated in bright sunshine. The camera looked east, past the pier and along the beach to the old town hall, now a Chinese takeaway.

There, just visible over the roof of the taxi stand office, sat Más on his rock, whittling and chipping at a piece of wood. The email from the coroner said he had sat there all morning, but she must have supposed that I didn't need to watch all of that.

At 4pm, his usual knocking-off time, he stood, stretched his back in such an exaggerated way I thought I could hear the cracks of his vertebrae, and packed his things into a large, waterproof sail bag. Carrying his pink-and-white jacket over one arm, he walked toward the camera, hailing anyone he met with a wave, but no conversation.

However, rather than cross the beach for the bar at Tom's, he turned left down the patched concrete of the pier.

At that time of day it was deserted. The last of the stalls had packed up, the tourists had made for their trains or their buses.

The angle switched to another camera, on the back of the old general post office, perhaps. It showed Más standing with his toes perfectly aligned to the edge of the concrete pier's "T." After a few minutes, he removed several things from his pockets, folded his jacket, and placed it on the concrete.

He opened the bag and withdrew a banana-yellow set of antique, old-petro waterproofs. He stepped into the thick, rubbery trousers before donning the heavy jacket and securing its buttons and hooks.

He walked to the top of the rotten steps, looked up at the cathedral and made a sign of the cross. Then he descended the steps, sinking from view.

There was nothing for more than a minute, but the video kept running, the pattern of wavelets kept approaching the shore, birds kept wheeling in the sky.

In a series of small surges, the prow of the naomhóg emerged from under the pier, then Más's head, his face towards the town, then the rest of his body and the boat.

I had to hand it to him. He could have launched his vessel at dead of night from the little boathouse where he had built the others, but he chose the part of town most visible to the cameras, at a time when few people would be around to stop or report him.

With each pull on the oars, he sculled effortlessly through the gentlest of swells, his teeth bared in joy.

His yellow oilskins shone in contrast against the dark greens of his boat and the surrounding water as he made for the mouth of his harbor and the open sea beyond.

> "Yet fish there be, that neither hook, nor line, nor snare, nor net, nor engine can make thine."
>
> —John Bunyan, *The Pilgrim's Progress*

Robert Reed is the author of nearly three hundred published stories and novels. His most successful properties are wrapped around a giant star ship dubbed the Great Ship, and its mysterious cargo—an entire world named Marrow. "The Speed of Belief" is set in that universe, as is his next novel, *The Dragons of Marrow*. A short movie has been made from Reed's novella "Truth." Called *Prisoner X*, it is available for purchase from all the usual streaming venues. Reed lives in Lincoln, Nebraska.

THE SPEED OF BELIEF

Robert Reed

1.

Water dreamed of flowing downhill, and despite their bluster and brains, humans were nothing but fancy water.

That robust, endlessly useful lesson came early. Rococo was growing up on a colony world undergoing the final stages of terraforming. Man-brewed storms were transforming the barren highlands, and knowing where the new rivers would rise, the boy would find high ridges where he could watch the churning, muck-infused flows. Majestic violence was a reliable pleasure, and he adored the painful rich stink of alien rock being torn apart. But most of all, Rococo loved his own wild panic, and standing where everybody could see him, he couldn't help but dance along with the trembling world.

Strangers warned the boy to be smart and step back. Friends knew that he was quite smart, and so they begged him to be more careful, please. But Rococo's parents didn't trust his brains or his common sense, and that's why they simply banned their son from wandering the wastelands alone. But of course rules were nothing but treaties, and every treaty was just words wrapped around flaws. A charming lad could always convince some old fool to go with him, and then through one clever trick or another, he would slip away to do just what he wanted.

Then one day a mountainside collapsed. Rococo was prancing joyously, and then with no warning, rock and flood swallowed him. Rancid salty mud killed the body in every little way. Oxygen metabolisms shut down. His bioceramic brain retreated inside itself. Limbs were torn off, his chest was gored, and the shattered head was finally buried under a young river delta. Blind and helpless, that remarkable mind had little choice but to consider its own nature. And that's when Rococo began to appreciate how he was being carried through life by some very simple urges. Curiosity, for instance. That was a drug forcing him to find out what would happen next. He also had an instinctive love for mayhem, his senses coming alive only when the world turned wild. And there was always satisfaction in doing what nobody else would try, which was evidence that smug pride was the most useless, marvelous force in the Universe.

Modern humans had engineered minds wrapped inside ageless, nearly immortal flesh. But their flesh was still mostly water. Water was a sanctuary for the ancient emotions. Love and lust, status and revenge. Those were the simple dictates in every person's actions. Furthermore, emotion had a pathological need to string the Universe into a personal narrative. Every person lived within a story. That tale was adaptable and selfish, and it worked best if it served the soul's needs. No matter how small, every journey demanded purpose. Just rising from the chair and crossing the room involved planning and a successful arrival. But where the average person was happy with small successes, Rococo wanted more. That's what he decided sixty thousand years ago. Robots and family dogs were yanking his corpse out of the river mud, and his parents were weeping over and screaming at the mummified face, and AI doctors preparing to heal him completely. But the boy inside witnessed none of that drama. He was a calm soul reveling in his mighty ambitions, an epiphany born inside a temporary grave. And now he understood that he would risk anything for just the thin chance of being part of history.

"People don't dream," Rococo began, as a joke and not as a joke. He felt as if he believed every word, declaring, "It's our water that dreams, and that's what makes us simple. Solvents are uncomplicated and transparent. Water or liquid methane, sulfuric acid or supercritical carbon dioxide. Every species is compelled by the fantasies of its broth."

Pausing, he tried to gauge his audience's reaction.

Silent indifference held sway.

"And nobody is better suited than me when it comes to deciphering what an organism believes," he continued. "Knowing the beast across the table: That's what makes the premier diplomat. Which isn't my only skill, no. But it's a talent, and I'm not an animal that keeps quiet about his talents. Particularly when I'm walking beside the Ship's most famous exobiologist."

These were old boasts, but Rococo had never made them sound so ludicrously grand. He wanted to push the issue this morning. Eight days after their vault landed in the high country, and seven days into a desperate march across this lovely, half-dead wilderness, he was hungry for energy. Rococo wanted to kindle scorn or mocking laughter and maybe an exchange of insults. Big emotions would give everyone enough fire to keep them distracted. The question was: How would Mere react to his inspired nonsense about dreams?

Two more steps, and then the tiny woman stopped walking. Staring at the horizon, not at him, she said nothing. A native bug landed on her head and then flew away again, and she said nothing. They had a destination and a timetable, but it was more important to make everyone wait. Then, as if addressing the horizon, she said, "Water doesn't dream, and only an idiot would think so."

Diplomats could smile on command—either a human grin or some disarming, alien-inspired expression. But Rococo never lost sight of ultimate destinations. Whatever happened, he wanted to become Mere's lover, and at this point in the negotiations, smiles would diminish his odds. Frictions were essential, and that's why he bristled. "Don't try to insult me," he warned. "I've destroyed worlds because someone insulted me."

Not true, although he had seen a few worlds die.

Mere finally looked at him. "Have I ever told you?" she asked. "You're a silly, pretentious man, and you have no deep understanding of any creature besides your ridiculous, self-important self."

A good swing. He granted her that much.

"But simple ideas are pushing us," he maintained. "They shove us across worlds and through the aeons. You've seen it, Mere. More than anyone, you've experienced what ideas do to the tiny soul. Yet you still won't concede the truth. That I know something useful. Because you're stale and stubborn and full of pride. The ancient, wondrous Mere."

The woman's gaze returned to the horizon. Rugged, ice-clad mountains rose into the dusty sky. A valley was resting at the mountains' feet, and all of that ground should have been the darkest blue-black. But the valley was mostly gray, the air stinking of cinders more than life, and knowing the tragic reasons why, a weaker soul might have sat down and quit.

But there weren't any weaklings in this group.

Mere had a starved slip of a body that never grew tired, and she had big lovely eyes that looked human and looked alien, managing the trick inside the same glance. The ageless lady had endured the most spectacular life: Raised by extinct, deeply peculiar aliens, she carried a unique outlook toward

the Universe. And later, having survived the long, unlikely voyage to the
Great Ship, she became the captains' favorite instrument to investigate the
most alien worlds.

Rococo also had considerable experience with every sort of creatures. He
was the Ship's first diplomat, after all. And like a lot of observers, he held the
opinion that despite being human, Mere was a species of One.

They didn't have time to stand, yet the woman stood. For another precious minute, nobody moved. Then Mere finally turned, looking at Rococo
when she said, "Water doesn't dream, you idiot. It's the salt."

"The salt?"

"Water's the container. Ions passing across borders. That's where our simple lives come from. We're walking, talking salt."

Ah. She was teasing him.

Rococo's laugh was honest, but he cut it short for effect.

Then the captivating woman turned to the third person in their ranks.
"Amund, what do you think? Is it water that dreams, or is it salt?"

Amund wasn't immortal. A luddy by birth and by outlook, he rarely
showed any patience for these long debates.

Until now.

The man turned serious. Hands opened and then closed, forming fists.
The aging face turned harsh, but the eyes were soft. "You've got your shit
backward," the luddy stated. "There's just one dream. Water and salt, people
and rivers. And all of us obey the dream."

There was no bioceramic brain inside him, just water and salt, and Amund
had come here for one exceptionally awful reason. Except the reason had
gone missing, and regardless of what happened to his ancient companions,
he was certain to die without fulfilling his purpose.

Three people traveling across a half-dead world.

How could anything so simple become so complicated?

Wildfires had remade the land. Combustive wildfires, not nuclear blasts. At
least not here. But the dense native air was heavily oxygenated, and the bedrock had been scorched clean of its forests and soil. Which made the walking
easier, yes. Just another two days, plus the usual delays for Amund's fatigue,
and they finally reached the valley and the river. Only it wasn't the river they
would have hoped for. Spring water and melted snow fell into a body that
made no noise beyond bubbles chewing at pitched rock. The waterscape was
thinly populated, every swimming creature ready to eat its neighbors. But
of course the water knew how to move, and that was another stroke of luck.

To return home, Rococo needed to reach this river's end. He dropped the pack that was carrying their survival kit, and wading in up to his waist, he pulled off his shirt and extended the sleeves, setting the garment on its back.

"Do us the favor, friend," he said. "Learn to float."

Living clothes were popular with a few sentients—commensal skins and engineered organics, plus slaves worn for one brutal tradition or another. This shirt wasn't alive, but the fabric carried a tiny mind and many useful talents, including a genius for rebuilding itself into useful and unuseful forms. Gathering dissolved minerals and little breaths of air, the garment expanded and inflated itself, and the man stood over it, offering suggestions and then his approving silence.

Rococo's home world was massive and bathed in UV light, and that environment had dictated his carefully tailored frame: The long body and short powerful limbs, plus a chest harkening back to an age when power was carried as muscle and big ribs wrapped around the mortal heart. Projecting a sense of youth, his bare skin was brilliantly black in the day's glare. That handsome face never needed adjustment, an elegant ooid wrapped around widely spaced, deeply purple eyes. His teeth were gold and the gray hair never grew past the point where the nubs were barely felt, and he had a smart voice that could shout until the sky rang, or the voice might say very little and say it softly and everybody heard the words just the same.

Mere wasn't even a third his size, yet she enjoyed her own power. The black hair was thick and grown long, and her body was as tough as hyperfiber, or at least seemed to be. This woman had outlived her homeworld, and serving the Great Ship, she had traveled alone to the most bizarre realms, risking her life many times. It was easy to believe that no other human, alive or lost to history, was as wondrously peculiar as her, or a tenth as lucky, or a millionth as blessed.

Mere knelt where the river was swiftest, toes to the water, her hands coaxing her shirt to change its form.

Rococo had no choice. Her breasts wanted to be seen, and he watched them until he could feel them under his hands. His imagination did the caressing, and enjoying this one immortal pleasure, he smiled.

Then he noticed the luddy staring at her too.

Funny. A man could admire any lady, knowing that he might never touch her. And despite pride and his own high opinions of himself, that same man could accept celibacy all the way home to the Great Ship.

But this was too much of a stare. Amund wasn't just giving a polite, appreciative glance. No, the mortal was very serious about his lust. A butcher carving his way to the bone. That's what he looked like. Not a vicious stare, or cold, but definitely immune to humor or other distractions. To Amund, nothing in the Universe mattered as much as a creature older than hundreds of generations of luddies.

"Amund," said Rococo.

Nothing changed. The voice that couldn't be ignored was being ignored.

Again, louder this time, the diplomat said, "Amund."

A name old beyond old.

The thin, sunburnt face turned slowly, grudgingly looking at his competitor's face. A brain with more water than thought needed time to frame its response. Giving him no time, Rococo said, "Just as we planned. Wet your shirt and we start floating downstream before sunset."

Saying nothing, Amund kicked off a pair of freshly grown boots and stepped past the bare-chested Mere, clambering down a steeply cut bank, frigid water quickly to his chest, to his chin. Then a pained voice yelled, "Hey, shirt."

He said, "Make me a boat or drown me. You decide which."

2.

Amund was little more than a boy when the captain came to his home. But that boy had a finished body, and being healthy as well as crafty-smart, he had several young women already helping plan out his promising life.

His future seemed to be locked inside one kind of wonderful, and Amund thought that he understood what his story would be. But then Washen strode into the Highland of Little Sins. That was a remarkable occasion on its own merit. Captains never visited the sanctuary, certainly not a captain as powerful and famous as this entity. Knowing voices claimed that she was one of the Master Captain's favorites, and Washen brought a famous history as well as that very famous face. Amund knew the face well enough to recognize it from the high ledge. That's where the children were told to gather while the important adults stood below, forming a neat half-circle around an immortal machine carrying a lady's face and a god's invincible powers.

Every Highland citizen was human. That was the law. Humans were archaic animals, noble and true, while every captain was a contraption full of mechanical parts and magic. And without question, Washen was a striking machine. Tall and graceful as a willow, not only did she look more human than Amund would have guessed, but nothing about her voice or manners seemed artificial. The local hour was twilight. With darkness spreading, the visitor bent low before the important residents. She had mastered their local language, presumably for this single occasion. With passion, Washen spoke about the honor of breathing holy air and apologized for the pollution that she had brought to them. But important matters had been pressed into her hands. She warned her audience that duty sometimes gave her little time to act. And while she was asking for an enormous favor, the captain promised to deliver ample compensation as well as the hope that this insult, horrible as it was, could be forgotten by future generations.

Amund didn't want to be impressed, but he was. This captain had mastered certain customs, and how many minutes did that take her?

"But she's not a 'her,' " he muttered under his breath.

"What's that?"

"What you see down there," he said. "That's nothing but machines wrapped inside machines."

Where stone turned to air, he was lying on his stomach, his favorite girl beside him. She was a beauty by every measure, though less creative than some. Perhaps a little simple, and very definitely conservative. Yet Amund's lover was charmed by that woman-faced creation, and that's probably why she didn't appreciate his tone, slipping out of his grasp and then crawling out of his reach.

Abandoned, Amund had little choice but to watch the drama below.

"This beautiful realm is your home, and your home lives inside my ship, and the Great Ship lives within the Galaxy," Washen said. "As I stand here, one distant world is actively begging. It wants permission from the Master Captain to come onboard. Which is wonderful news. Captains are sworn to many jobs. But after we ensure the safety of our passengers and the safety of this vessel, our primary task is to welcome every guest that we can carry. For a reasonable fee, we make them comfortable, and we allow them to build homes among us, and we promise to carry them safely through this glorious wheel of stars."

The Highland was a cavern furnished with jungles and jungle birds and artful crisscrossing waterfalls. It was also rich with blindfolds and stubborn indifference to everything beyond these wet green walls. Amund's neighbors looked as if they absorbed the machine's prattle without complaint. Didn't they understand? Washen was stripping the situation down to its simplest, most appealing core. Amund saw the trick. This was what he would do, if his chore was to explain stars to idiots or language to dogs. And that's why he was offended. Dressed in charm, offering up some carefully crafted words, this outrageous entity had mastered a dog's vocabulary.

" 'Where-the-rivers-live,' " said the machine.

"What is that?" Amund's lover asked. "What's that mean?"

The boy didn't know. And judging by faces, nobody else understood. A muddled, confused rumble filled the cavern, and Washen responded by taking a step backward before repeating that very peculiar phrase.

"'Where-the-rivers-live.'" She said, "That's our best translation of the world's name. A large terran planet. There's a dense atmosphere, minimal seasons. More ocean than land, but every continent has a spine of young mountains. The natives possess a vibrant, relatively advanced toolkit of technologies. In that, nothing is unique. Except for the fact that the population is a little under one thousand individuals, and each citizen is a living, sentient river."

Washen said, "River," and the cavern was suddenly flooded with illusions. Sculpted light was focused on every open eye, and sounds were driven into the ears and teased the vestibular systems. Suddenly Amund felt like a bird. Towering white clouds stood in an otherwise azure sky, and below him, the exuberant vegetation was every shade of blue. What looked like a dark blue river was pinned to the valley floor. Save for those colors, that could be any earthly jungle. But when he dropped low over the river, the water ceased to be water. The quivering dark surface was more gelatin than fluid. Capable of motion in any direction, this river was pushing upstream, and it was far larger than the trickles flowing through the Highlands or even the Earth's famous rivers. Flexible trunks that weren't trees lined the nearest shoreline, a canopy of arms or tentacles pushing toward the sky. Except those weren't arms and they weren't tentacles. Amund was reminded of sea anemones. That's what these were. Gigantic terrestrial anemones. And against every expectation, the boy was thinking how interesting and how pretty everything was.

Curiosity was an indulgence at best, a hazard at the worst. The Highlands couldn't have survived two generations if its citizens chased every sweet question. But long history and his culture didn't matter. All at once, Amund was intensely, selfishly curious.

The captain's voice returned.

"The Great Ship is a beggar too," Washen said. "Our hull is covered with telescopes that beg the Milky Way for light and radio noise. My ship never stops studying local planets and the distant ones too. And between the telescopes are enough antennae to shout at those worlds, begging to be heard and to be answered by any mind with the means and the desire.

"What you're seeing here is a fresh transmission. Where-the-rivers-live sent these images along with explanatory texts and certain diplomatic overtures.

This world is six billion years old and clever. Commensalism is the norm. Unrelated species have woven themselves into unified bodies. The native genetics have found a very stable point where there's no boundary between the forest and the river. What you see is one creature, and, as it happens, this entity controls the central watershed of the wettest continent. Rather like our Amazon does. Except this river is longer than the Amazon, and it extends far beyond the continent. Which is another marvel, and if you want to see where the living water flows, don't close your eyes for more than a moment."

Amund clamped his eyes shut.

A foolish, incurious reflex, and he didn't know why he did it. Perhaps the eyes were thinking for him. Opening them again, he discovered that the spell had been broken, the living river was lost, and he had nothing to see but his lover staring at nothing, her gaze spellbound, shameful. Everyone but Amund was happily trapped inside that other world. And nobody else understood. That machine-infused captain had one goal for her day, and she knew just what to say to them and just what to show to them.

The boy had suffered enough. Slip home, close his door, and pretend to sleep or eat or accomplish any other human task. That's what he was planning to do. Except his legs had a different opinion. Instead of taking him home, they found the quickest stairs, carrying him toward the captain and her fine voice and that very pretty face—the polished face of a beautiful marble statue dedicated to some ancient, unreachable deity.

Washen's voice continued to sing out.

"Serving as a captain, I've been fortunate enough to meet multitudes," she boasted. "Species from very strange worlds, and species from worlds unnervingly similar to the Earth. And every point between. But this realm, Where-the-rivers-live, is like nothing else. It's fresh and it's wondrous, and on the basis of novelty alone, I would invite a trickle of any river into the Great Ship. I would build a habitat where their nature and beauty could thrive. And if the creature didn't have the resources to afford passage? I'd pay its way. That's how interesting these creatures are to me.

"But there isn't any need for charity. Where-the-rivers-live happens to be the only inhabited world inside a solar system rich with potential. This transmission came with an offer. In exchange for passage on the Great Ship and certain new technologies, the living rivers will grant us full possession of two hot planets and two cold moons. Four worlds, each of which can be terraformed, and any one of which can become a home for humans."

She said the local word for "humans." That was a critical detail. Or she was careless, which seemed very unlikely. By then, Amund had reached the cavern floor. Elders and the high faithful were crowded around the captain. A few of them had stopped watching the show, but they continued to stare at their guest, mindlessly smiling and nodding. Most of the audience remained lost in the astonishments. But of course nothing they saw had to be real. Everything was a lie. That possibility ambushed Amund, frightening him and making him angrier than ever. Which was rather pleasant. The boy enjoyed being enraged by the one-sided nature of this mess. An immortal machine had marched into their little cave to tell them a ridiculous story, forcing them to watch invented lights and invented sounds, and this was such an easy trick for a god, making stupid little humans believe in any preposterous world.

But why would Washen lie?

To embarrass Amund's people, obviously.

That paranoid idea was exactly what he needed. Rage gave him courage, and courage gave him the power to say anything or do anything.

"Safety for the passengers," said Washen. "That's every captain's first duty. After that, we care for the Great Ship, and then, we welcome new passengers onboard. But there's a fourth duty waiting. Humanity used to be a minor species. We were late to the business of star travel, but then we found the Great Ship. In the tens of thousands of years since, this beggar of a starship has left multitudes in its wake. New worlds by the thousands, all claimed by our people. Immortals like myself, and humans like you. And those colonists, your brethren and mine, will rule the galaxy for the next ten billion years."

With that, she paused.

The invisible spectacle must have finished. Eyes were blinking, faces smiling or frowning, and many people shyly looked at their neighbors, trying to gauge what this magician's trick had done to their tiny souls.

That's when the great captain was rudely interrupted.

"So what the shit do you want from us?"

Amund shouted those caustic words.

Turning, Washen looked at nobody but the rude boy.

He instantly regretted his action, but in the next moment he was angry all over again. For his doubts, for her invasion. But mostly because he was a stupid little bit of humanity. Amund existed only because the captain machines allowed him to live inside what was little more than a tiny drawer. Washen's kindness was what kept all of them alive. Unless it was her utter indifference to their little existences, and when the time came, she would throw them out, replacing them with richer, more interesting tenants.

That's what passed through one young head.

Washen's thoughts were a mystery, then and always. What kinds of elaborate calculations was she making, transforming this complex, ever-shifting event into the best action? But of course the mathematics were easy. After all, she was one of the finest machines ever fabricated, standing before a tribe of primitives, all of them easily swayed and just as easily forgotten.

"So what the shit do you want from us?"

For a long breath, nothing happened. Except that Amund kept finding reasons to grow angrier.

"The Great Ship," the captain began.

Another pause.

"And our hands," said Washen, holding her hands towards the basalt sky. "Ships and hands have limits. We're passing through the Galaxy, and yes, we're aiming for the most fascinating portions of the Milky Way. But our speed and course are inflexible. Most solar systems remain out of reach. In reality, there's only a narrow cylinder of space that our shuttles can reach, and then they have to return to us again.

"Where-the-rivers-live is very close to that cylinder's edge. Velocities are law. Time is short. And wise as these rivers seem to be, they don't have their own starships. They might build some workable craft soon. Even a tiny river has astonishing talents, and working together with a world's full resources . . . well, they could possibly launch a starship or two in the next few years. But there isn't time to wait and hope. If we want the rivers to live with us, we have to make our own round trip. And to achieve that, there is a plan. The plan is underway already. This morning, a special streakship was launched. That ship was pre-built and then mothballed for a day like this. It's massive and full of fuel and exceedingly well protected from the dangers of deep space. But there is no crew. Shaped nukes and war-grade lasers are accelerating it to a healthy fraction of light speed. It's exactly the kind of vessel that can race out to an alien world, landing under the guidance of AI pilots, and then wait for its passengers to board."

Washen was ageless. Except when she paused, as she did then, she looked like a woman who had endured a long, difficult day.

Two breaths and she spoke again.

"The living rivers have explained themselves. And that includes some inflexible ideas about ceremony and symbol and the value of life. Which they cherish, by the way. More than most species, the sanctity of organism is held in the highest regard. Perhaps because they are so few, and by any measure, they are so very old."

The captain took a long step forward, studying the ignorant young fellow who seemed to have forgotten how to talk.

"Their largest river claims to be older than earthly vertebrates, older than our sponges," she said. "So we're battling some instinctive, unyielding ideas. There are also the horrible limitations of time and our room to maneuver. We spotted their world years ago, studied them and built an offer of friendship. Two Venus-class worlds, two icebound moons. That was our initial offer. Which is a fair price, a modest price, considering the technologies we'll share and the places that we will take them. And the rivers have agreed with us. They'll give us everything we want. Four substantial worlds, with space for hundreds of trillions of good people. When you talk about mortals. If you can imagine millions of generations of humans living beneath this orange sun."

Washen took another step forward, standing that much closer to Amund.

He wanted to run.

His feet preferred to hold their ground.

"One icy moon will be warmed and then bathed in a delicious atmosphere," the captain promised. "Then it will be given to you, the humans, and you and your trillions of children will live out their lives on this spectacular new realm."

Except there wasn't any joy in the machine's words or her face. She was a grim, all-knowing god, talking to tiny entities who couldn't appreciate the shitty choices that she had to walk through.

"Four worlds would be an enormous gain for our species," she said. "But it requires one quick mission that culminates with a brief, brief ceremony."

"Which is what?" Amund meant to shout, but his words emerged as a guttural whisper.

Did she hear him?

"What ceremony?" asked twenty other voices.

"This is a very ancient dance," Washen explained, "One creature must symbolically merge with another. Two unrelated rivers must join. And to accomplish that, the rivers demand that we offer a single mortal. 'A piece of your river,' they call it. Which means that they're demanding a human sacrifice."

Amund was ready to feel surprised, yet he wasn't. He anticipated being enraged, but nothing like anger offered its help. One life? Not only did that seem reasonable, it was such a tiny gesture, and he was instantly thinking about the people that he grew up with. Idiots who wouldn't be missed, at least after a few happy years.

"Two officers will accompany our offering," Washen continued.

It was the first and only time someone used that word.

"Offering."

She said, "My finest exobiologist and my best diplomat are going. The goal is to change the terms of this agreement. Surrender an arm or kidney, or give away a beating heart that we can replace without fuss. But I can't guarantee survival for anyone. This will be a long sprint through deep space, and shit happens. Yes, it does. But if this mission does reach Where-the-rivers-live, and if any deal is struck, then more starships will be dispatched. Slower, much larger and safer vessels will drop away from the Great Ship, make some complicated dances with other stars, and after a few centuries, your descendants will set down on your new home."

She paused, and most of the audience imagined Paradise.

"I won't make your choices," she said. "And I wish I could explain more and answer every question. You must have endless questions. But there's a timetable at work. Moments matter. The second streakship has to carry passengers, which means that it can't accelerate as quickly. And it has to launch within two hours and seventeen minutes, or it doesn't leave. Which might be the best solution. That could be argued.

Do nothing, let this opportunity pass, and consider ourselves fortunate, even if we aren't."

On the one hand, Amund was listening carefully. Yet he was also thinking about nothing. An empty place waited inside his skull, black and ready. Ready for what? Then it arrived. The obvious, unavoidable idea. Hundreds, perhaps thousands of luddite communities were scattered across the Great Ship. "Luddies." That's what the machines called humans. Luddite was an ancient word that was never charitable, never endearing. And if time was critical, then dozens of captains must be standing inside those enclaves. Right now, each persuasive machine was making her best plea to the silly luddies. One tiny, awful sacrifice. That's all that was needed, and the gods were playing a very cruel game.

Infuriated, the boy felt justified as he marched straight toward an entity who couldn't have looked taller or more formidable. His plan was to smack Washen and get killed for it. Which almost certainly wouldn't happen. What harm could he do to any captain? But no, that promise of violence made him brave, and the courage lasted until she smiled at him, revealing what on any face looked like grave, sorrowful pain.

A step short, he paused.

His little world fell silent, every eye fixed on the empty air between the two of them.

And that's when Amund finally realized what was obvious. That he wasn't angry at captains or distant alien rivers. Not then, not ever. The emotions lived inside him, and they couldn't be anywhere else. Self-doubt and self-loathing had eaten away too much. He was a frail incurious idiot, suddenly looking back at the elders and up at the woman that he had slept with and probably would have had children with.

"Except I won't sleep with her again," he was thinking.

Why was he thinking that?

Standing at the center of the only world he knew, Amund was utterly helpless, trying and failing to see where any silly idea came from.

3.

Exobiologists didn't take worlds as lovers, and no mission deserved to be confused for an elaborate, high-stakes courtship. Missions were missions. That was the blunt, clean, simple, and inescapable truth. Civilians, ignorant captains, and even a few of Mere's colleagues insisted on confusing the exploration of new realms with sex. But sex was simple. Lust wanted to be kindled again and again, and that's why it was so very easy to lose one object of affection and find another. For Mere, an impressive sequence of temporary husbands had proven the fallibility of love. She had had alien ex-husbands and the rare human, plus hundreds of intense brief passions. Well-schooled in every aspect of coupling, Mere enjoyed herself well enough, thank you. But walking gracefully across the face of a new world was something else entirely—an undertaking so much larger and richer and far more rewarding than any fireball infatuation.

In love, there was a rough sense of equality. Two souls in harmony, and so on and on. But even the ugliest little world was far greater than any soul. There were missions where Mere's footsteps and her shadows were never noticed. And even if her presence was experienced by the natives, what did that mean? Very little. No world ever dreamed about Mere's touch or the heat of her breath, and even if ten billion citizens knew Mere's face, it didn't mean that one of them ever woke up expecting her beside him in bed.

Missions were asymmetric, and because of that, they were infinitely beautiful. Standing where no human had stood was so much richer than copulating with a beast or high officer. Romance meant choice, but Mere never had choices with worlds. She went where she was needed and did what she did very well, and for as long as necessary, too. Had she ever studied a realm that didn't deserve to be admired, if not outright worshipped? Once, perhaps twice, but no more than that. Love held the promise of disappointment, even out and out treachery. But the sane mind couldn't be disappointed by worlds, much less blame them for their failures. Creative, experienced eyes could see the momentums that defined a planet, and Mere understood first-hand how the great momentums refused to be changed. Orbits and seasons were decided by suns that cared nothing about their children. Likewise, the world's inhabitants carried their biological limits as well as a compelling, often poorly understood history, and enduring cultures were entitled to their grudges, plus the occasional out and out war.

But individuals weren't worlds. Individuals didn't have excuses, and that was certainly one reason why Mere's marriages rarely lasted longer than a decade or two.

No individual deserved any excuse.

That's what the little woman believed, and she held herself to the same maxim. Her job was to be as a one-souled invader. She might be disguised, swimming unnoticed among the schooling aliens. Or to suit some dramatic need, she rode thunder and fire into a world capital, little arms raised as she introduced herself as a small, peculiar god. Each mission had its first goal and its second and the rest. Each was a mess of calculation and improbability. The hardest, best, and most often memorable missions were those where Mere and only Mere decided who would ride on board the Great Ship. Did she make mistakes? Too many, yes. The Ship's history wore a few blunders. And because Mere was ageless and strong in so many ways, the woman could spend centuries considering her personal grief about each blundering step.

She despised evil, but true evil was scarce in the Universe, and once identified, it usually proved frail. Broken thinking and self-made idiots were common hazards, but they weren't the most dangerous enemy. The inability to feel responsibility: That was what terrified Mere. It was the capacity of too many colleagues to misstep horribly and then retreat back to safety, nothing learned, not so much as a wisp of grief inside their happy minds. And worse than that, there were people with famous biographies and tremendous powers who didn't deserve to throw their boasts at others.

Rococo.

Mere's opinion was Mere's. Few shared her disgust for the diplomat. Even reasonable, compassionate Washen disagreed with her tiny, alien-born exo-biologist.

Of course it helped that Rococo began his service to the Great Ship long before Mere arrived. Also, the man's work had transformed alien worlds into good friends, and partly because of his considerable record, humanity was spread across a twenty thousand light-year journey. And Rococo was instrumental in some famous missions and critical moments where the impossible was accomplished. For instance, he willingly joined the bal'tin on a breeding/slaughter mat, legs properly crossed while ten thousand entities coupled and died around him. That was a nightmare ready to test even the most flexible-minded entity. Yet Rococo managed to sit where no other diplomat would sit, offering the best words while enduring the foulest odors. And now the bal'tin were devoted allies, and their metal-rich comets were home to millions of human settlers.

Mere understood the diplomat's mission. A proud, vainglorious creature like Rococo could accomplish miracles.

But she also happened to be the first scout to meet with the bal'tin. Before any diplomat arrived, she lived in their ranks for years, secretly and then openly. As the first face of the Great Ship, she instructed her new friends about her origins and the ancient laws of the Galaxy, preparing the way for the researchers and diplomats bearing down inside that much larger second wave. And in every report, Mere was blunt. The bal'tin were blessed with unusual minds. Left alone, they would likely avoid the disasters that often killed species and worlds. War wouldn't be an issue. They loved death too much to waste it on useless slaughter. They also didn't have careless hands that too often led to ecological disasters or vicious AIs. No future was set in hyperfiber, but the bal'tin were on a tangent that might lead them across thousands of light-years, and as a consequence, the Milky Way would be a much, much richer place.

But the scout was only a scout, and she was replaced by a fellow with huge reservoirs of charm and confidence. Rococo sat on the same ritual mats that Mere had experienced. He had to suffer the most bizarre behaviors known to exobiologists, and to his credit, he endured longer than Mere had. And the outcome was a deal that left humanity with a considerable portion of that solar system's resources. Comets weren't often laced with iron and uranium; bal'tin comets were a prospector's dream. The natives would have flourished once they reached their Oort, but one exceptional diplomat impressed them too well, and now the odds had changed, the bal'tin far less likely to mount any assaults on galactic history.

"There's no translation for their name," she mentioned.

They were several years into the present mission. Their streakship was still accelerating, obliterating fuel until that point where they would flip and then fire the engines again, convincing the Universe to slow down around them.

"But the concept behind the name is simple enough," Rococo said. "The Universe is a spectacularly narrow line, and that line is drawn between spawn and oblivion. The bal'tin are celebrating that line. That's what I kept telling myself. And that's why it was critical to sit there calmly, farting preplanned farts, and if they wanted to play with my genitals, I let them."

"I know the mats," she reminded him. "And I know how to fart, too."

Rococo had a fine smile when he wanted. But not then. "So, Mere. What is your difficulty about me?"

"You took more than you should have," she said.

He laughed. Without his usual decorum, Rococo acted as if she was an idiot and pitiable because of her silly mind.

Amund was sitting nearby. He had little choice. Their ship's mass had been stripped away at every turn, increasing their range but limiting space. Amund only had his tiny quarters and this slightly larger common room, and they were accelerating to the brink of what a mortal body could tolerate. Simple motion was a struggle for the young man. More than not, he would spend years on his back, and with nothing to watch but two ancients acting like petty bureaucrats.

But not that day. That day, the man interrupted them. A sharp little voice said, "I have an opinion, if you want to hear it."

"I do," Rococo said.

"By all means," said Mere.

Their companion was a stubborn, frustrating puzzle. Whatever they called themselves, humans or luddies, the mortals were usually courageous believers in the temporary nature of life, and most importantly, they were endowed with the sacred duty of passing out of existence, making way for others. Yet Amund didn't seem to be that sort of animal. Surrendering his life for a cause? No, he was missing the noble heart, and more importantly, the self-congratulatory flair. And there was no trace of the natural explorer either. They were traveling to a realm as alien as any, yet day after day, he asked nothing. Read nothing. Even went so far as to ignore the latest broadcasts from the rivers. Even his conviction for his faith failed to convince. He was an authentic human sharing a tiny volume with machines that pretended to be human, yet he couldn't muster the proper disgust. Particularly when he stared at Mere, which was often and always with a keen intensity. In other words, Amund was exactly the wrong kind of fellow to willingly sacrifice anything so precious as his own life.

"I have an opinion, if you want to hear it."

"I do."

"By all means."

He smiled, in a fashion. "First of all, I don't give a shit about those left-behind aliens. The bal'tin."

Rococo smiled, and Mere smiled.

Their companion glanced at the diplomat. Then he twisted his neck and stared at Mere. Whatever he wanted to say was ready. That much was obvious. Perhaps he wrote the words months ago, biding his time for the perfect moment.

"Just so I'm certain," Amund said. "You two have never worked with each other. Not in any direct fashion. Is that right?"

They never had, no. And they wouldn't have collaborated here, except both were available when the rivers shouted at the Great Ship, and a mission built on high stakes and inflexible parameters had to use the very best people.

"Well, that answers one mystery," the mortal decided, lifting his body from the cushions, apparently for no reason but to shrug his shoulders at them.

"What does that explain?" Mere asked.

"We're going to visit some peculiar beasts," Amund said. "As soon as we get there, the two of you are going to do your dances and give speeches, trying every kind of magic. And when the job's done, you'll declare the winner."

That earned a long pause from his audience.

"That's all that this loud stupid endless dance of yours is trying to decide," Amund said. "Who is the goddamn best."

4.

Five days of floating and then water stopped being water. The cold river thickened and grew blue, but still not blue enough and not nearly thick enough. This was good news or bad. The immortals offered conflicting opinions along with evidence that always seemed starved. Which was the inevitable problem. Orbiting war machines had hammered their little streakship. Nothing but their crash vault survived the landing. Sensors and other fancy tools would have been invaluable, if only they could have been salvaged. What they possessed was one heavy backpack with a survival kit onboard. The fist-sized reactor was powering a Remora-built factory, food and pure water delivered without fail. The kit also supplied lights in the darkness, and for one of their ranks, medical help. Everything else was done by the smart fabrics. Clothes and boots, boats and shelter. Honestly, if the immortals were a little less brilliant and a little more shrewd, they would never leave their homes. Shirts and trousers could march into the unknown Universe. Ruled by some very strong underwear, of course. With gloves and boots ready for the really hard shit.

"You're laughing," Rococo said.

"I am," Amund agreed.

Mere was kneeling below them, studying the boundary between normal water and what was alive. The living rivers were built from protein weaves, concentrated salts, and dissolved metals, giving the bodies their characteristic density, the irresistible mass. That's why the wild river flowed over the blue flesh, and the flesh drank what it wanted for the next few hundred meters, which was the point where the wild water was swallowed up and gone.

Amund and Rococo stood on higher ground, accompanied by a knee-high forest of blue-gray toadstools that weren't toadstools. Little winged beasts were resting nearby. They resembled bats but perched like birds. Not alien so much as wrong. This ecosystem was simple, weedy, and inefficient, but the living river was close. Its blue body was viscous and warmer than the surroundings, promising that it had recovered from the firestorms. The immortals were assuming that the river was conscious. Which was a good sign, Mere claimed. Rococo claimed. But that didn't mean that this was the same river that spoke to the Great Ship, promising planets and moons. In some fashion or another, that creature was a casualty of a very peculiar war.

A long while passed, and then Mere finally stood, gesturing to her colleague.

"Wish us luck," Rococo said.

"I'm stupid," Amund said. "But I'm not superstitious."

Laughing at that, Rococo set down the pack and walked down to join Mere. The two of them spoke for a moment and then walked together without walking together, working their way downstream.

Amund tried to lift the pack and kit with one hand and couldn't. He barely succeeded with both hands and his back. This world had too much gravity, which was another reason to feel endlessly tired. After age, that is. The pack was hyperfiber mesh doctored to look like old canvas. Amund made a request, triggering small motions inside, and he reached beneath the top flap, his hand closing around an edible flask filled with a flavored water. Then he drank the chilled sweetness before eating the exterior like an apple.

The immortals continued their hike, and Amund tried to think about anything besides them. The antirad patch riding his neck began to itch. He scratched at the irritation. Machines didn't care about radiation, certainly not at these background levels. But without the patch, Amund would die in a matter of months. And without the filters moored inside his windpipe and lungs, the over-oxygenated air would poison him in minutes. This was a landscape populated with survivors, and that included one extremely fortunate human.

Another laugh, and without the help of mood enhancers or alcohol.

What a day!

A final piece of honest ground allowed the two machines to stand beside the gelatinous blue. That's when a historic conversation commenced, or there was no conversation. Either way, they spoke to the river and nothing happened. Mere and Rococo offered words, and nothing changed, and nobody should be surprised. The captains had taught this world the Ship's common language, but that was before the carnage. That was before most or all of the original river boiled away. This new creature might be as ignorant as a baby. They might have to start from the beginning, teaching the baby how to talk and what to think about them. And superstitious or not, it was hard to ignore the luck required to reach the return ship and reach it with time to spare.

That first streakship was Amund's home for too many years. He never liked it and always dreamed about escaping from it. Yet there were moments, baffling frustrating moments, when he caught himself grieving for that frail machine.

"Salvation." That was their nickname for the return ship. Standing like a mechanical hill, like a castle of superior hyperfibers and fusion engines, *Salvation* had landed years ago. It set down on a small coastal island. The onboard AIs were always awake, busily sending out promises that the machinery was healthy, fueled and eager to help. But those giant engines were configured to launch directly into space, not rise slowly and then conveniently set down beside them. Half of the continent needed to be crossed. There was no other way. And without a wild river to ride, this living river had to help. Otherwise the walk would take months or years to complete, and long before that was done, the Great Ship would be unreachable.

And Amund would most likely be dead too. A thousand obvious causes offered themselves. Accidental falls, self-inflicted wounds. Cancers born from myriad decaying atoms. Or inevitable age. But not Mere and not Rococo. Even marooned on this broken world, their modern guts would learn to digest the native organics, and the fallout would cause nothing more than odd, beautiful blemishes. Standing together or apart, the immortals would be able to watch the stars slowly shuffle positions in the night sky. Three hundred thousand years later, the Great Ship would come back around, and those two machines might still be standing here. Except for little changes wrought by the experience, they would be the same machines. And blessed with perfect memories, they would have the power to see Amund's face and hear his voice, remembering every word that he shared as well as his bitter little laugh. In that fashion, the human would be kept alive long after his time.

The sun moved today, and the machines didn't move. What was human about them looked bent-shouldered and worried.

"We're screwed," Amund muttered.

Then came a slight pressure. The patch on his neck was being touched by a finger, but not his finger. And with the pressure came heat, not scorching but distinct and out-of-place.

A voice was behind the finger.

"You," it said.

Not a man's voice, not a child's. Female, perhaps.

"What about me?" he asked.

"A pure river."

Amund began to turn, but several warm fingers grabbed hold, fixing his head where it was.

"Who's a pure river?" he asked.

"You are."

The voice was close, and she sounded scared. Except nothing about the voice could be trusted. A vast strange and utterly gigantic creature was projecting noise for the same reasons that anything spoke to anything. To be understood, and hopefully, to manipulate her audience.

"You are the pure river," the alien said. "You are the undiluted true river that came from the stars to join us."

A few words, and one man's life shifted.

"That's how I look to you?" asked Amund.

"How you look, how you are," she reported. Then a long blue digit appeared beside his head, jointless and rigid and very thin. What wasn't a real finger was pointing at Mere and Rococo. "Machines," she said.

"My companions?"

"You call them 'machines.' "

"So. You've been watching us, have you?"

"Since your arrival," she warned.

This surviving trickle of a river had an unsuspected reach. Studying them through the flying bugs, perhaps? Amund smiled at the news, feeling nervous and alive. "What do you think about those two machines?" he asked.

"They terrify us."

That deserved a good laugh. But Amund stifled the reaction. "Why are you scared?"

"They attacked us."

"Did they?"

"Yes."

"But how did they attack you?" he wanted to know.

Silence.

Holding a hand to the sun, the pure river cut the glare in his eyes. "What weapons did they use?"

"Poison," she said.

"I don't understand."

"Poisonous beliefs," she said.

Amund nodded politely, understanding nothing.

The blue digit was retracted.

"Those dangerous machines down there," Amund said. "They're hoping to reach that second starship. Which leads to the question: Are you going to help them?"

"No."

"No?"

"They are dangerous, and I won't help them."

Amund lowered his hand, sunlight burning his eyes. "Believe it or not, you sound like the pure little rivers I grew up with."

"How do I sound?"

"Like a cowardly little puddle of piss," Amund said.

The giant river said nothing.

"Those monsters don't scare me," he added. And after that, Amund felt as if he could take his time, sitting quietly while deciding what he wanted most, and then finding the very best way to make it all come true.

                              5.

Bold action or bolder inaction. Those were possibilities, but only once. Only at the beginning and for a ludicrously narrow moment. Ignorance was the chief problem, but there was also a reflexive sense of duty, and at least in Rococo's case, thousands of years of hubris stirring him to action. Those living rivers were a grand mystery, and mysteries always generated curiosity. The actual voyage promised to be a routine haul across empty, well-mapped space inside a proven machine. The diplomat had survived wilder dashes through space. It was the target world that was unique, barely studied, and unlike anything else. But at least they had the long voyage to prepare. In that light, the plan felt reasonable. Where-the-rivers-live promised to maintain its high-density broadcasts. The Great Ship would continue studying their target and send updates. Even better, Rococo and Mere were the best two for this work. And the third member of the crew was free to offer odd insights as well as his skeptical silence—qualities that Rococo appreciated more and more as the journey unfolded.

The midway point was reached without incident. Telescopic data from home remained enthusiastic, but of course those were old images growing even staler when they traveled back up to the streakship. The direct alien transmissions were a few years old but younger with every breath, and they offered updates about every subject: Industrial growth and half-finished star drives, plus some exceptionally precise measurements about the world's general enthusiasm.

"Bullshit."

Amund refused to be confident.

"Pictures and noise," the luddy warned. "Those aliens shape the data however they want."

Naturally, every broadcast was a staged event. That was true when humans threw shadow puppets up on their cave walls, and it was certainly true about the rivers as well.

"This could all be a con job," Amund said.

Rococo didn't believe that. There was no great deception. AIs analyzed the feeds, proven algorithms raking the data for lies and signs of madness and any other flaws. Because every lie carried telltale flaws. But this was a long-closed society opening up to a greater world. The evidence said nothing else. Inspired by the Great Ship, those ancient rivers had decided to reach into space. To help their prospects, they were giving away four of their worlds, but that left plenty of other cold moons and comets for them to claim and then transform.

They were two years out, and nothing had changed. Nothing was wrong. Not a sign, not a rumor. But in mid-broadcast, the largest river stopped transmitting, and within minutes the rest of that world had fallen silent. A full day passed without words. Mere was working with the shipboard telescopes, trying to boost their sensitivity high enough to get a good glimpse of what was happening. But before she finished, the voices returned. Except they weren't voices. The scarce and weak and urgent transmission showed them nothing but wordless imagery. Every river had been struck by fusion weapons. The aliens were boiled on the land and shredded under the ocean. The diplomatic mission was dead, every agreement lost. And Rococo realized that years ago, facing a choice, the bold, brave, and exceptionally wise decision would have been to do anything but go on this fool mission.

"I should have strangled my curiosity."

He said that to himself and the others. Obviously, telescopes and automated probes could have done the necessary research, and today the three of them would be sitting safe inside the Great Ship, watching a distant world burn itself to a cinder.

But of course this was where they were. Trapped inside a streakship whose engines were punching at the Universe. There were zero choices. They were on a collision course with disaster, nowhere else to fly. Mere and Rococo continued studying the rare broadcasts. Preferring to ignore awful news, Amund remained inside his cabin for days at a time, appearing only to hear a few specifics. And even though he had little experience with aliens, and very steep barriers to learning, the man did try to make sense of what was happening.

"It's greed," he declared. "The rivers got selfish, and some of them went to war with the others."

Rococo and Mere shared a glance.

Reading faces, Amund said, "Unless I'm wrong. And I know you're not shy about telling me that."

"It's not war," Rococo said.

"What then? Did two big rivers get into a brawl?"

The luddy had made another obvious, very human mistake. "War" and "brawl" were two good human words, and deceptive. Rococo had the same problem. He couldn't reliably explain the situation, and that's why he smiled at the exobiologist, saying, "Tell our friend his mistake."

"Oh, I was wrong, too," she offered.

It was sickening, this abundance of ignorance.

"If I'd studied those first transmissions more thoroughly," Mere began. "Or better, if I'd taken the trouble to model the rivers' biology. I could have seen the problem. If I'd made all the right assumptions, which I probably wouldn't have done. But let's pretend I did."

When Mere spoke, Amund stared at her. Even when the topic was too new and too complicated, the mortal appeared to be intrigued by whatever she had to offer. And when Mere wasn't speaking, the man would watch her face and watch her hands, waiting for that inevitable moment when those odd, oversized eyes glanced at poor idiot him.

And with the same sturdy resolve, Amund kept ignoring Rococo. The most obvious drama in the Universe was the luddy's hatred for the other male onboard this one-lady ship.

"This isn't war, and this isn't a grudge match," Mere was saying. "The blast patterns. The transmission patterns. And both of you, pay close attention. Look at the flow in these videos."

Rococo focused on the images, but he wasn't sure what he should be seeing. He and that other fellow were on the same footing, both spellbound by the tiny woman who was explaining how thoughts and planning crept their way through each of these great rivers.

"The speed of belief," she said.

Thousands of years old, and Rococo had never heard that expression.

"What the hell is that?" Amund asked for both of them.

"The speed of belief," she repeated. "One river acts like a single organism. It moves and speaks as if it's unified. Which is very reasonable. We know its thoughts are quick. Chemoelectrical speeds, hundreds of kilometers in a second. The largest river can react to any outside stimulation and every interior need. Resources pulled from the crust. Reserves tapped for projects deemed suitable. Like its desire to build starships. The rivers claimed that they didn't see the need before us. They barely had enough curiosity to build giant eyes and watch the Universe. And what did they see out here? Tiny creatures gathered around lesser stars or riding inside ridiculous little spaceships. And a lot of empty cold space too.

"But then the rivers saw us. They saw the Great Ship. Here was the first genuine marvel. A billion years old, and the organisms had finally found their superior. And because of that, they made promises to do everything possible to gain passage on our grand home."

She paused, returning Amund's gaze.

Did he understand any of this?

The man was sitting up, which was unusual. But this was an important, sit-upworthy moment. That body would never adapt to the high gees, yet he never complained about aches or the occasional cracked bone. Rococo held some uncharitable opinions about Amund, but despite being doubtful and sullen, the man never quit proving that he was also an exceptionally tough mortal.

"What does that mean?" the luddy asked. " 'The speed of belief?' "

Mere glanced at her colleague. "Would you like to explain?"

"You'll manage so much better," Rococo said instantly. The portrait of gracious confidence, he had no interest in trying to convince the others that he knew what he was saying.

Mere nodded and thankfully continued.

"Belief isn't thought," she said. "And belief isn't a reflex either. What we believe is woven into our nature, and regardless of how we act and what we say, we can never kill the voice that says, 'This is what should be, and the rest of it is wrong.'

"And the principle of belief . . . well, that can be far, far more important inside giant creatures. Vast minds have to work around their size and sluggish reflexes. That's why convictions are something held everywhere at once. Every million tons of neurological matter is infused with complex expectations and stubborn faiths. The river has one mind, yes. But not a mind we would recognize. Spread yourself across thousands of kilometers. Trillions of tons of stubborn water. That's what I think we're watching here. At some level, the rivers decided to embrace this new existence, building industries and reactors and tremendous new machines. Except nothing was decided. One belief had the power, and that power was wielded right up until the contrary belief decided enough was the hell enough."

Rococo stopped her. Lifting a hand, he said, "Wait. That last transmission, the one that got cut out in the middle."

Mere nodded, smiling grimly.

"The largest river was sending us some very detailed plans," he said. "Plans for the conquest of its solar system, including construction of a hundred billion kilometer long river that would spiral out from the sun. A living river thriving inside cultured diamond and fusion light."

"That might have been the trigger," Mere admitted. "A fantasy of dream and high physics, and it was too much. Too crazy, too wild. Too dangerous. There's no being certain here, but sure, that's why the conservative beliefs had enough and panicked. One daydream, and that's what nearly killed this world."

Amund was relatively young, not particularly gray, and carrying those boyish eyes. But his voice had always been older than his appearance, more lucid, and far more thoughtful than Rococo might have expected.

Speaking plainly and slowly, Amund said, "This giant mess. What we're flying toward. You're claiming it's because some voice or voices told a story nobody else liked?"

Mere said, "I don't know."

Then, "But I believe that's possible, yes."

There was a joke here, but nobody laughed. Glancing at Rococo, Mere's expression grew even more serious than before. Something new had to be shared, perhaps something that she just discovered.

"What else?" Amund asked.

"What else?" Rococo echoed.

"There's another belief at work here," she warned. "I can see it in the last few broadcasts. The rivers that are alive now . . . they don't just simply hate the deal made with us. They're acting like they don't want to allow us to come close. Maybe we're contaminants. Or we're a disease. Perhaps we're even monsters."

"But you are all those things," Amund said. "Didn't you know?"

The immortals tried to laugh, and the luddy grinned while saying nothing else.

Closing her eyes, Mere examined the latest data.

Rococo couldn't shake that crippling premonition of being doomed.

"Their world's mangled," she reported. "But there's enough organization and industry left to throw new satellites into orbit. Right now, my best look is showing me a single pusher stardrive powered by hundred-megaton charges. It's orbiting close to the sun. Judging by its orbit and its focus, I'd guess that it's watching a specific piece of the sky. The piece of sky that we'll fall out of. And it could be used to intercept intruders. Which is nobody except for us."

Their engines surged or Rococo was suddenly weaker. Either way, he felt his legs folding, delivering him to the cabin's floor.

"Any more splendid news?" Amund asked.

"Actually there is good," she said. "The rivers tried to attack our other streakship. I don't know how many bombs were launched. But what's the difference between a comet approaching at half-light speed and a fusion charge bearing down at a few thousand kilometers per hour? The difference is that bombs are easier to stop. Lasers tore them apart. Only a few detonated, and those at a distance, and the streakship's armor is too high-grade and proud to shatter."

She paused long enough to sigh.

"Our salvation ship claims to be ready to launch, and that's what I would make it do now. I'd launch it now and have it meet us and save us. If I could get the orbital motions to agree. But the motions don't work and never will. The one blessing we have is that if we survive the megatons, and if we live to reach the surface, and if we happen to be in walking distance too . . . well, then we have a viable way home."

One of them was destined to die soon, regardless of events. And he was the one who insisted on laughing.

"Belief," Amund said.

"That's what this is about?" Amund asked.

"Stubborn, stubborn, slow to change, and far too big to see the need," he said. Then he shook his head, saying, "Shit, that sounds like you and me. And particularly, both of you."

6.

The rivers' pre-catastrophe broadcasts used the Ship's language, and that's what the two of them spoke now. Most of the day was invested in vain efforts at conversation. The creature didn't respond but there was no end of noise, moving water and the slurping of slow gelatins mixed with the chirpy whine of little creatures lurking along the shoreline. Sometimes Mere would hear what sounded like a spoken word. Or Rococo. Except no, that was imagination at play. Only one of them heard the voice, not the other. Fear and fatigue were on display, and despair, the desperate mind inventing a soft "hello" just to feed itself that momentary dash of hope.

Preset strategies were followed, but without any sense of being heard, Rococo eventually abandoned that original script. A wink to Mere, and he launched into a peculiar story about the roaring majesty of a newborn river, and how a boy stood too close and was swallowed, drowning without dying and then left lost inside a wasteland of mud.

Mere found herself listening, and then listening carefully. But just as she became intrigued by the buried head and the thoughts trapped within its mind, the story was interrupted.

A clipped, clumsy sentence was offered.

"I hear you," said the river.

"Are you listening?" They'd asked that hours ago. Was this the river's response, and what did its timing mean? Mere had no way to answer either question. She'd never conversed directly with any river. Was the alien innately slow? Maybe those words had to be drawn from memories stored hundreds of kilometers from here. Or maybe rivers were patient, or this river was being cautious. Unless it had taken this much time to build a working mouth. Or the river wanted to ignore them entirely, and this phrase had leaked free, like a small social blunder.

"I hear you," came out from that blue-gray surface.

A rather human, entirely feminine voice.

Rococo quit sharing his secrets.

Then the river said, "I hear you and understand every word, and you say you need me."

"We need you," Mere agreed.

"You need to be somewhere else," said the river.

Rococo said, "Yes."

"On your great ship," said the river. "But you need to cross me and stand inside your little ship. Yes yes yes?"

"Yes" was an excellent word for most situations.

Mere said, "Yes."

There was a pause, almost too brief to notice. Then the voice declared, "I will carry you."

It was Mere's experience that the Universe was built from questions. And every question, particularly the richest few, triggered a cascade of possible answers. But she refused to push any hypothesis ahead of the others. In her work, guesses were hazards. Every insight invited belief, and nothing was more dangerous than revelation. The exobiologist never stopped fighting the impulse to frame what she was seeing. Believing the bare minimum. That was a wise strategy, and that's why she couldn't accept the river's good words or its sudden promise to help.

Whatever the situation, it was time to call to Amund.

The mortal hadn't moved for hours. Sitting on the high ground, he nodded down at her while pulling a hand across his mouth, as if pushing his jaw closed. Then he stood, one arm and then both arms helping him lift the backpack and kit, and as he walked down the brief hill, Mere noticed what was different about Amund. The local gravity was intense, and the man had to be tired, but she thought that she saw the beginnings of a swagger riding on those short, careful steps.

The river had fallen silent. Sacks of salty water gathered on its surface, proteins inside the sacks weaving structures that quickly linked with their neighbors. Then the water was yanked away from the sacks, with a shrill keening screech, leaving behind a peculiar and mostly dry object that looked like a boat and smelled exactly like fresh meat.

Mere didn't believe any good news, but Rococo was a portrait of enthusiasm. Looking back at the mortal, he shouted, "We have a yacht now."

Amund was smiling and then he wasn't.

Winking at Mere, Rococo said, "Every world looks better when you don't have to walk it. Don't you agree?"

The gift was no yacht. The object resembled ancient pontoon boats, except unlike any vessel cobbled out of animal hides or spun boron, this boat would never float. Certainly not like two bottles riding on a current. The river was semi-solid and denser than water, the darkest blue flesh marbled with little white threads and spinning red wheels of light. To her bare palm, the creature was warm enough to be pleasant and a little stubborn when shoved. A person could walk across its surface, but only for as long as the river cooperated. On a whim, it could liquefy. That's what the old videos showed. Whenever it wished, the river could engulf the pontoons and platform and then everybody on board. That grim prospect had to be in Rococo's mind too. Yet the man didn't hesitate to walk across the blueness and climb on board, practically running from one end to the other. Following warily, Mere found a wood-like platform edged with simple low rails. There were three cabins, each with a flat roof and its own walls, and one door that could be swung closed. And there was a fourth room with nothing inside but a toilet. The biggest shock was how planned everything was, functional and unadorned yet entirely useable, perhaps even comfortable.

What should the two of them offer in response? Praises and thanks, perhaps. With few hard threats against anyone who might try to set a trap. Rococo and Mere shared glances, trying to guess each other's mind.

Amund had reached the shoreline.

And the blue flesh rippled, pontoons rising up on newborn ridges. This must be how they would move. What wasn't a river would carry them on its wiggling skin, and what wasn't a river valley would pass on both sides. Mere didn't want to make guesses, much less fall for wrong speculations, but a sudden confidence shook away some of her doubts.

She looked at Amund again.

The mortal seemed to prefer the shore.

Like muscle, like people, a living river preferred to find easy routes. That's why their distributions resembled earthly rivers. Born in the sea, lazy flesh was pushed wherever the climbing was easiest, which meant following existing drainages. Living tissues absorbed rain and glacial melt as well as the minerals and every organic treat. Each creature fed on an extraordinary range of energy sources. Sunlight and wild insects were food. Infrared radiation from the ground was food. But the most coveted meals were from beneath the ocean floor and the high mountains. Piezoelectric and geothermal. That's what delivered true, trustworthy power.

To Mere, this was a wonderland. Regardless of what life brought, death tomorrow or in another ten million years, she might never experience an entity so strangely remarkable as this.

That sounded like belief, didn't it?

She laughed to herself.

Rococo noticed, and for one reason or many, he laughed with her.

Then both looked at the shoreline, at Amund.

Was he going to balk at the ride? No. His hesitations ended with a few long steps across the river. Then he was standing beside them, saying nothing, letting the pack and kit fall to the deck, but breathing hard while staring at Mere.

Something was different, was wrong.

Possibilities offered themselves. Mere accepted none of them, but her intention was to flat-out ask their companion about his mood.

Except there wasn't time for questions.

Looking past both of them, Amund called out, "I'm ready."

The boat that wasn't a boat shivered.

"And I want this to be a quick trip," Amund commanded.

Suddenly the boat rose even higher, and they were streaking downstream.

Laughing, Rococo sounded like a nervous boy.

Mere felt warm and afraid.

Meanwhile the man in charge seemed to relish their reactions, stepping between them as a smile came and then faded again, a slight embarrassment offered with the hard words, "For the moment, both of you are under my protection."

What was this?

And the man in charge said, "Madam, I want you to know. I'm looking forward to sleeping with you."

7.

Leaving his homeworld, bound for duty aboard the Great Ship, the youngster envisioned his life as a sequence of long leaps through darkness, with spectacles and wonders waiting at the end.

That was a self-absorbed notion, and deserved. The Great Ship commanded respect as well as envy, and it was in the best interest of every world to enthrall the Ship's diplomats. As the ultimate tourist, Rococo was sure to be afforded every comfort, every grace. Standing on the windswept lip of an endless canyon, walking the sacred glen past the sacred desert, or, if the mood struck, riding what wasn't a whale into the depths of a frigid methane sea: Those were memorable events from his first thousand years.

But spectacle rises only so high. Even an intensely curious mind grows numb to vistas and symphonies and all of those rich, sweet stinks. And every grand majesty eventually becomes nothing but another good day.

Yet this living river . . .

The beast was like nothing else.

And their journey to the coast?

Without the high stakes, this voyage would have been momentous. But the perils were close and impossible to forget. Amund, for instance. The man was dying. Age was murdering him, and the omnipresent radiation, and the capricious will of an alien had elevated him to a high, utterly ridiculous station. But for how long? Meanwhile the two immortals were stripped of every resource, nothing to aid them but considerable experience and the fact that one of them had survived worse disasters than this. Which was Mere. Rococo had never experienced any mission this harrowing. But why would he? Diplomats weren't explorers. The captains didn't toss his kind into shit-storms. And in particular, they wouldn't risk Rococo, one of their best. Not for an adventure with less than 2 percent chance of survival. Which was his estimate, weighing what he knew and what his guts said.

"Two percent," he mentioned to Mere.

She stared at the living river and the swiftly passing shoreline. Having outlived at least one world, he assumed she would generate a more optimistic number. But no, she surprised him.

With confidence, she said, "I don't know."

"It's an estimate," he allowed.

Then she warned him, "Guesses are just another danger." And on that cryptic note, she turned away, walking into the cabin that she was sharing with the dying man.

Rococo remained on the bow of what wasn't a boat. Boats were buoyant, but there was nothing to float on here. What wasn't a river carried them where it wished, and it was wishing them toward the ocean, usually at speeds that drove strong winds into his face. Everything in sight was one creature, a wonder of salt-infused gel and migrating impulses, bioelectric currents and free oxygen, plus reflexes and crosspurposed desires and whatever memories happened to have survived the recent nightmare. Unless every memory had endured, which was possible. Who knew? A field team and labs and AI savants running free. That's what they needed, and that was impossible. This river was safe from study, and a man riding the swift nonboat couldn't understand what he was seeing, much less appreciate what he couldn't see, and that was another reason why Rococo found himself spellbound.

The beast had grown wider and presumably much deeper over the last few days. More than three kilometers across, the blue-black gelatin appeared slick and dark and exceptionally nonreflective. Water always invited the sky, but this wasn't water. They rode on a ribbon of meat and reflex and furious power. And where true rivers were flat, this creature made itself tall, flexing into a ridge that carried tiny people and their tiny prison where it wanted, as quickly or as slowly as it wished. Now, for instance. Rococo felt the sudden change of direction. What wasn't a current swept him close to what wasn't a shoreline, and he stared at a scraggly false forest of sessile bodies waving long tendrils at him or at the sky. Maybe they were feeding on airborne plankton, or perhaps this was something else entirely. Watching the forest dance, he realized that the tip of each tendril was cracking like a whip. Bits of tissue were torn loose, and the bits rose high and then fell until wings sprouted and those new bodies flew away, dissolving into the thick alien sky.

Had he seen this before? Inside the videos sent by the original river, did Rococo ever observe this talent?

No.

A skill unleashed during the rebuilding phase? Rococo suspected Mere would feel just as ignorant as he did. No, there was a person to ask, but he was inside his cabin with his lover. This world didn't bother speaking to diplomats or exobiologists. Only Amund was given that honor, and only on the river's schedule. "Next time the two of you chat," Rococo should say. "Ask about the tendrils sprouting wings. Would you please?"

He smiled out of habit and held tight to the railing. The river had yanked itself as high as ever, Rococo perched at the edge of what looked like a wet purple cliff, and that's when the sessile forest vanished. Busy life was instantly replaced with what looked like a dead city. Blockish shapes resembled buildings, and there were signs of fire that must have burned hotter as they continued downstream, the black outlines of foundations sketched on the blasted ground, and then long reaches of filthy irradiated glass. Cities were human inventions, and of course this world never had cities. But a facility must have stood here, a sprawling factory where the previous river refined metals and wove the antennae that spoke to the Great Ship, and maybe the bones of those early starships. Maybe this was an intentional side trip, one man shown the devastation wrought by some very bad thoughts. Or maybe this was all chance. Either way, the blast zone impressed him. Rococo estimated distances and the megatons, both of which were substantial. And then the glass vanished, the river spreading into a gelatinous purple lake inside a crater, and Rococo couldn't stop thinking about what a nuclear device would do to his tiny, perpetually scared mind.

Suddenly that 2 percent chance of survival felt wildly optimistic. He suffered that revelation and then embraced it. Freedom always came when the odds were at their worst. There was no getting off this world. The new river didn't trust them, and maimed as it was, it had enough power to demand whatever it believed was best, and that included ignoring the two creatures that could transform its future in the most amazing ways.

Holding his breath, Rococo listened to his thoughts.

Far out on the lake, the beast was pulling itself into what looked like a mountain, and then it lifted the prison and prisoners until they were at the summit, hundreds of meters above the land. That's when they stopped, and a great voice rose from below, shaking the world as it called out, "Amund."

A few moments passed before the naked man appeared, obviously interrupted from pleasures that didn't appreciate interruptions.

Rococo continued to hold his breath, his body tingling, alternate metabolisms waking as the last of his oxygen was spent.

Still naked, Amund hurried down the blue slope, and where nobody else could hear him, he paused, speaking a few words while waving his hands.

Mere emerged, wearing clothes and a watchful, unreadable expression.

Rococo breathed again.

The sugar inside his flesh began to burn, the tingling becoming a general warmth, and once again, his thoughts shifted. He wanted to speak to Mere. Honestly and unheard. But that meant using a tongue that the creature beneath them couldn't understand.

More breathing, more thinking.

The luddy continued to wave his hands, chatting happily with one of the largest creatures in the galaxy.

Rococo cleared his throat. "I'm thinking of that bal'tin proverb."

The bal'tin were familiar to both of them, and that included a language that this world couldn't have heard.

Mere stared at him.

Rococo offered a brief statement that sounded like music.

Straightening her back, the woman smiled and then let the smile fall away. This hadn't been a long meeting. Amund was already returning to the prison, marching uphill because his great friend wouldn't think of making the journey easy for aging legs. How much radiation was punching up from the lake floor? Probably quite a lot. The entire world was saturated with fallout, and Amund was halfway dead, and even if the cancers didn't kill him, it was only a matter of decades before he was finished.

With those bleak thoughts swirling, Rococo offered another bal'tin proverb. "Doom and eggs, doom and eggs," he sang. "Our souls are the boxes that carry forth the doom and the eggs."

As he spoke, he realized that he was crying.

When did the tears start?

Rococo had never earned a warm smile from Mere. Until now. The tiny woman looked at him, offering a sigh while showing him such a delicious smile. She cared. She felt for him and for both of them. Perhaps she even thought about holding his hand. And there weren't enough sensors in the Universe to measure the pleasure that smile delivered to one old and very doomed diplomat.

8.

Some voices wanted Amund frozen. The streakship was being fueled and provisioned, and he had minutes to prepare for a quick trip to the Ship's port, and after that, a sudden introduction to his fellow crewmembers. But friends and strangers had to approach him before he left the Highlands. Using confident voices, they advised him to step inside a cold bottle. None of them had any firsthand experience with spaceflight, much less alien desires, but they promised that his life would be spared at the end of this adventure, and did he want to waste his youth living inside a streakship? His ex-lover was particularly adamant. The voyage was sure to be dull, and he really should freeze himself for both journeys, out and back again. But she didn't go so far as promising to wait for him, ludicrous as that would be. Instead she offered a fetching look, saying, "I'll have a daughter or two by then, and I know they'll be eager to meet the most famous human ever born in the Highlands."

Those were the last human words spoken to Amund's face.

When he reached the Port Alpha, a few low-ranking machines took the trouble to offer the same advice. Deep space was full of obstacles. One shard of comet could slip past his streakship's defenses, and the impact would slow their trajectory by several hundred meters a second. And when that happened, the liquid bodies inside would continue forward at several hundred meters every second. Thrown against the walls, Amund would be turned into dead goo. Nobody wanted that. "Sleep through the journey out, enjoy a fine adventure on the target world, and then you're free of this ridiculous obligation," they told him. "Another good sleep, get swaddled in kinetic buffers, and who's bigger than you when you come home?"

And all those pretty girls waiting, no doubt.

Amund listened to every word, but what he heard were the selfish fears:

These machines didn't want their human wasted, and they certainly didn't want to lose the four new worlds that his tiny death was going to buy.

Washen never mentioned cold bottles, and perhaps she didn't know what her officers were suggesting. Her last moments with Amund were spent introducing the two-person crew, then with warm touches, reiterating her boundless appreciation for what one noble man was doing.

Rococo never brought up the topic of freezing anyone. What mattered was boasting about his infinite skills as a diplomat and how he would face down the rivers. "Saving a young man's life," he said.

Except he didn't say, "Saving a graying, half-spent man's life." Did he?

In a day jammed with the unforeseen, the greatest surprise was Mere. So tiny next to the captains and diplomats and everyone else. So plainly, ridiculously different. Amund didn't think of her as pretty, yet he couldn't stop staring at the little face that looked starved because it was starved. This body and those enormous bottomless eyes were born on a crippled starship. Amund heard that story. With a rush of words, Rococo told how she crashed on an alien world where she was tormented like a demon and worshipped like a god. Mere was human only in the most glancing fashion . . . but wait, she wasn't human. Amund forgot what was obvious. This was another immortal machine who couldn't be trusted. Those wrong eyes were full of sympathy, or she was pretending to care. Either way, she offered very few words. No talk about cold bottles or her thanks for his sacrifice or even the particulars of the mission. She just took hold of him, her hand hot and his hand suddenly feeling cold. Mere gripped him just enough to prove her unnatural strength, and then she smiled in the saddest fashion, confessing, "I like very little about this mission. Just so you understand."

Mere wasn't beautiful, but gods didn't have to wear beauty. It was enough that they were powerful, ageless entities deserving adoration and long stares, and any mortal would be stupid not to be thrilled to live in their shadows.

The low-ranking machines were the ones that argued for the cold bottle. Those would-be deities were scrambling for anything that smelled like power. "We're going to save you," they promised. As if they had any role in future events. "A kidney, a hand. You give the rivers a gift, and they let the rest of you return home again. You won't be half a year older, and then you're the young hero leading your people to the new world."

How simple/stupid did they think he was?

"No bottles," he told them emphatically, and just once. The entities had perfect recall, after all. Let them remember the words and his blatant scorn. "I'm going to live a few years, and then I'll die one way or another," he said.

"But you're not fooling me into hope. Because there isn't any hope. And that's the same for all of you. Machines don't run forever, no matter how much you try to fool yourselves."

The voyage proved even more grueling than expected. Regardless of pain-killers and cushions, the hard acceleration made Amund ache, and each new day was desperate to repeat every day that came before. The ship's mess could generate any food, but he usually ate the same reliable meals. He knew where he would lie down and what he would think about when he let his mind wander, and for those early months, Amund thought about ex-lovers and the cavern that had seemed so tiny until he came to live here.

Those left-behind people were obviously thinking about him. Good wishes kept arriving, and there were some elaborate, intimate messages buried among the clichés. Responding to everybody was tedious, and he gave up that chore soon enough. But a few people received his thanks along with observations about a dreary life inside a machine-infested closet, and sure enough, that honesty helped diminish the inflow until a week might pass without noise from home.

One of the later messages was memorable. A girl who Amund had never met sent him a long video of herself. She resembled Mere, undersized and big-eyed. But she was also a child through and through, and a youngster's enthusiasm was on display. Grinning, she told him that she had studied the river's video very closely, the same video shown to everybody in the Highland. She realized that Amund saw only a few moments before he ran downstairs to volunteer. "Everybody knows your story," she said. But the rest of the video was far, far more impressive. "Don't you think so?" Of course the living rivers weren't rivers. They were more like trees, and the bulk of every tree was hidden underground. The dense, supersalted gel didn't stop at the ocean. The aliens reached across the continental shelves after rising from the depths, and they glowed as they moved, feeding on volcanic seams and microbes and sunlight brought from above. That was the spectacle worth seeing. Not the ordinary business on land, but on the ocean floor. That was what she would see, if she could. And she only hoped that Amund had time and the oppor-tunity to experience that very wonderful paradise for himself.

Amund had never bothered to watch the full video. Inspired by the enthu-siasm, he took the challenge and felt impressed, but not as awed as his new friend sounded. No, she was what impressed him. "You seem like such a bright, excited person," he told her in his reply. "My advice? Get the fuck out of that cavern. Go out and live anywhere else that will take you."

That message went home, and after that, nobody called to him.

Which was perhaps what Amund wanted all along.

It was impossible to guess what his companions would talk about on any day, or even inside a single minute. Topics varied widely, crazily, often shifting in mid-sentence. But Amund knew that he wouldn't understand much, and the subjects' importance would evade him. Yet that ridiculous noise became a reliable joy in a small, painful life. Two gods shooting the shit, and sometimes, now and again, offering up words that fascinated the human in their midst.

Those gods weren't having sex. But Rococo's lust was aimed at Mere's blatant indifference, and his frustration was another reliable joy.

Maybe all that would change when they reached the rivers. An entire world as their playground and out of sight of the doomed man, the gods would take their pleasures by any and all means. Imagining sex with Mere. That was another trusted pleasure. She was a wise god who didn't want Rococo, and of course she didn't have desires for a mortal beast like Amund. Mere had lived happily among aliens. She even married a few of them. This female deity seemed capable of any perversion, which meant that she was saving herself for the rivers. Her next husband was a ten thousand kilometer ribbon, and how could anything as small and ordinary as Rococo feel reason to be optimistic? But freed from hope, Amund could spin endless fantasies about the god-machine.

Not a terrible fate, all in all.

Then the rivers started to murder each other. An entire world was burning, and that's when Amund honestly contemplated the cold bottle. Suspend his life, and with him unaware, they would land beside the first streakship. That vessel was safe enough, protected by hyperfiber and aggressive banks of defensive lasers—two features missing from their minimal ship. Frozen, Amund would endure one kind of dreamless nonexistence, and if he woke again, they would be approaching the Great Ship, most of his life left to be lived.

Except he never mentioned the bottle.

And the others didn't offer.

The following times were interesting and awful. Morning began with breakfast and premonitions of disaster. A comet shard was about to strike their thin, low-mass hull. Amund knew it, and later, he was equally sure that a nuclear weapon would meet them. The sense of doom gave each moment its spark, and every minute crossed felt like victory. And the human was surprisingly fond of this new life, fear churning emotions while his thoughts kept bending in fresh, peculiar ways. He didn't waste neurons dwelling on bottles or his left-behind life. It was an endless, secret joy to stretch out on the padded mattress, watching gods struggle with events beyond their control, maybe beyond their understanding.

One hundred million kilometers out, Mere looked at him and then looked away, telling the wall, "Bottle time."

Bombs and the need to make hard maneuvers left no choice. Amund had to be frozen and wrapped in protective garb, then loaded with the rest of the essentials inside the crash vault. He was one kind of dead when the ship suffered a string of attacks, and then the vault was on the ground and the hyperfiber door was blown clear. The defrosting took hours, his last breath still inside the soft pink lungs. Alien air was allowed past preset filters, and a wardrobe of smart clothing swaddled him, helping lift his temperature to happy human norms.

A fiercely hot hand touched his forehead. A mother's gesture, and Amund recoiled.

Mere said his name.

"Who?" he asked.

The vast eyes blinked, startled.

"Who are you?" he asked.

But he couldn't fool the tiny god. She laughed, warming him with her gentle pleasure. Then with a minimum of sentences and a few hopeful nods of her head, she explained what had to be done if they were going to survive.

"Wait," Amund interrupted.

She stopped talking.

"The old deal is shit, isn't it?"

"And there's no good reason to slaughter you," she teased.

Rococo was standing close but not standing with them. The man obviously wanted to add his genius to the conversation, but he managed to keep his machine tongue quiet.

"If we go home," Amund said to Mere.

"If," she agreed.

"I want to ride inside the bottle."

"With the rest of your days ahead," Rococo interjected.

The man was unlikable. But Amund nodded as if those were the wisest words ever spoken, and then he did what he had never done before. One of his cold hands reached out, touching smooth hot skin and the very sharp cheekbones of a face that couldn't be more amazing.

"That's not why," he told Mere.

"No?" she asked.

"No," he confessed. "I just want the chance to stop thinking about you."

9.

"I'm looking forward to sleeping with you."

Those words were buried inside the noise about protecting them. But having said them, Amund didn't repeat himself, not even in the most tangential, cursory fashion. That first night, after their kit provided dinner, the three of them sat on the open deck. Nobody spoke. The only noise was the groaning and creaking of the giant beneath them. Amund never mentioned sleeping arrangements. Mere watched the tired face and the man's bent posture, noticing how the left hand rubbed the right elbow. That joint was giving him trouble. Arthritis, perhaps. The backpack was heavy, yet he had carried it down to the river. The kit could synthesize any substance, and that's why she opened the pack and verbally walked it through a menu of archaic compounds. Pink tabs of salicylic acid and sugar were delivered, and Mere studied the mortal once again. A creature of water and passion, and so far removed from simple.

The medicine remained inside her tiny hand.

Standing, Mere said nothing. From the corner of an eye, she saw Rococo watching her slow walk. Maybe Amund watched her, too. She didn't look back at the man. She was done trying to decipher him.

The sun was nearly set when she entered the cabin that Amund had already chosen. His boots were waiting inside the door, self-cleaned and new heels generated for the next hike. The room was dark and felt small and smelled a little like blood agar. She left the door open. A woven bed was waiting in the back corner, the mattress pulpy and soft and just a little damp, and it would be awful sleeping. Mere wondered if she could ask their protector to speak to the river, give the creature a little helpful instruction about making people comfortable.

Entering the cabin, Amund was greeted by soft laughter.

To the blackness, he said, "Hello."

"Here," she answered.

He closed the door, and that was all he did for the time being. Standing opposite her, Amund was breathing loudly enough to be heard over the creaking river. The lack of windows did nothing to isolate them. Every motion beneath them was felt, the twitches and shivers and the rising sensation as they were carried aloft, accelerating downstream. Mere shivered out of fatigue and fear, and then she laughed once again, louder this time.

"What's funny?" Amund asked.

He still stood beside the closed door. Two thin lines of starlight managed to slip past. Mere's eyes had totally adapted, but mortals had lousy night vision. And Amund wasn't young anymore.

"You and the river," she said. "The two of you were having a conversation on the hillside."

Her companion shifted his weight from one leg to the other.

"While we were being useless, you and it were achieving important diplomatic overtures."

"She."

"Okay. She."

Amund took one blind step forward.

"I have something for you," Mere said.

The river shuddered and creaked, but the larger sound was a deep breath being taken and then held.

"Medicine," she said. "For your elbow."

"Is that what you did in the kit?"

"Yes."

Amund didn't speak.

"What did you think I was doing?"

"Making poison," he said. "Or some kind of madness pill. You know. So you can enslave my will and all."

Interesting, paranoid ideas.

"I wish I'd thought of that," she said.

Amund broke out laughing, but not for long and not hard. Then he crossed the room until his feet blindly hit hers.

"Sorry," he said.

"For what part of this?"

The man sat beside Mere, but a good deal of the bed was between them. "She and I talked, sure. She told me what she thinks about you. And Rococo. She was ready to kill both of you, just as soon as she thought of the best way."

"But you stopped her."

He didn't respond.

"You saved us."

He sighed. "Apparently so."

"Hold out your hand," Mere said.

Amund reached for the voice, and she grabbed his hand with her empty hand. His skin was cool and damp, rather like the bed was cool and damp. But she suspected that Amund would make a far more comfortable mattress.

Mere held three of his fingers inside her five.

He pulled back until he felt pressure, and then he relaxed.

"If I say, 'No,' to sex," she said.

He said, "Well."

He said nothing.

"Open your mouth," she said.

His face was in profile, and in that very poor light Mere saw the mouth obey her command, his entire body alert and blind and very hopeful.

She dropped two pills onto the tongue.

"Sweet," he said.

"You're right, it's poison," she said. "And it takes only forty years to work."

Then Amund was laughing and not quietly. He laughed until he sobbed, and Mere wasn't certain when she began to chuckle at some of this or all of this.

Sitting like that, they stayed awake half the night, gradually moving closer on the unappealing mattress, and Mere kept hold of those three fingers while both of them pulled reasons to laugh out of nothing at all.

10.

Amund was making love to one god when a second god called to him. He didn't dress or bother to let his erection die. A happy fleck of naked water, he hurried off to speak with the river. This would be a pivotal conversation. He had that sense from the beginning, and the human felt a little omniscient when his premonition came true. Among her many promises, the river claimed that they would reach the coast tomorrow, around midday, and the waiting streakship wasn't far beyond the horizon. Great news was heaped on top of great news. Amund practiced what he would say first and next and last. Returning to the nonboat, the human was wishing that smiles could be infinite. How enormous would his face and mouth have to be to capture this transcendent joy? Then he noticed the two gods standing behind the railing. They watched him, and Amund let his finite face drop for a moment, watching his bare feet crossing the blue flesh. Then he looked up again. Mere and Rococo were standing close to one another, perhaps a little closer than before. Amund was still in an exceptionally good mood, and Mere was smiling too. But at Rococo, and not just politely smiling.

Humans, genuine mortal humans, were less than brilliant. But even ordinary middle-aged men had the innate genius to find the meaning in faces.

Amund looked at those faces. Tenderness and acceptance and a new chain of possibilities were on display, and he saw the future. Those two machines were going to sleep together. Suddenly the highest, frothiest portions of Amund's joy were being shaved away. That was what the revelation did to him. Amund was jubilant and then he wasn't. He was the pinnacle of history for untold billions, and then without losing that gift, he became another lover for a woman who might have a thousand husbands before her life and soul were obliterated on some alien world.

Amund didn't know what to do next. He felt as if he was watching himself finish the walk, one hand grabbing the railing and his body climbing onboard with as much grace as possible, each piece of him acting of its own accord. He was responsible for nothing, including what he said to the others. "A pleasant day," his voice allowed. But not Amund. Amund was a ghost trapped behind the flesh and behind the words, as surprised as anyone when he entered the toilet room and closed the door, one hand and then the other slowly rubbing the face that still couldn't put an end to the endless smile.

Three minutes, and he stepped back into the sun.

Rococo was standing at the bow. The nonboat was moving again, sliding down a long slope fast enough that the machine had to tilt a little bit forward, leaning against the wind. But Mere had disappeared. Amund looked in her cabin first, but she wasn't there. What if she was waiting inside Rococo's cabin? That's what Amund saw, in his mind. She was lying on Rococo's bed, waiting for a god, which was exactly what she deserved. Amund waited for jealousy to take hold. He was hoping for ugly emotions, something to give the next moments even more importance. But even when he was convinced that Mere had abandoned him, he couldn't find any useful anger or need for vengeance.

To himself, he muttered, "What makes a god?"

Power, vast and deadly but also capable of great accomplishments.

Amund pushed open the door of his cabin. Mere had returned to bed, and she was naked again. What had been her clothes had formed blankets across the damp, fleshy mattress. She smiled at Amund and sat up a little more, starting to speak and then thinking better of it. What did she notice in his face? Probably more than he would ever tease out of her face.

"Four gods," he said.

She blinked. "What's that?"

"Sorry. Nothing." Amund offered the apology. But he meant it. Four gods were present, but it just so happened that one of the deities had only a few hours remaining, and then he would be nothing but a mortal man again.

The nonboat twisted slightly, and sunlight fell through the open and over the naked woman. So scrawny, so odd. She was a stick with tiny breasts and the wrong eyes, and Amund wondered why he had ever cared so much about sex with that creature. Then in the next instant, he wanted to throw himself on top of her and take her until he was exhausted. Which was what he should do, he told himself. Because this could well be the last time for this sort of fun.

"Come outside," he heard himself saying.

Mere tilted her head, those eyes gaining a slightly different perspective.

Then he added, "I have news," and still naked, he walked to the bow, claiming a patch of the deck where he was close to Rococo.

How much did he hate this man?

Not nearly enough, he decided.

But that didn't mean there weren't good reasons for what was going to happen. That's why Amund didn't wait for Mere to dress and join them. He looked at a face that never changed, and feeling a smile building, he told the face and the machine behind it, "There's a new agreement. In place of that old, lost treaty of yours. That's what I've been doing these last days."

The surprise seemed genuine, suspicions tagging along behind.

"A new agreement," the diplomat repeated.

"But not for four worlds," Amund said. "I convinced the river to agree to give us full rights to both hot worlds and the original two ice moons, plus twelve other moons. And one gas giant. Which is pretty useless in the short term. But maybe someday. And also, I've won the right for the colonists to bid on this system's Oort, if someday they ever want to do that."

Rococo opened his mouth.

One word emerged.

"Good," he said.

"It is," Amund agreed.

Mere was clothed and emerging from the cabin.

Amund continued. "And by colonists, I mean humans. Mortals. Nothing but. This solar system is and will always be a sanctuary for luddies, whether they're human or big ribbons of living gel."

Rococo said, "Oh." Then his natural poise took charge, and he said, "Goddamn impressive, sir."

"Sir," he said.

Mere was close but the wind was blowing, and what could she hear?

Amund leaned against the man, his mouth next to Rococo's ear. And that was when he said, "Oh, and the river still needs its sacrifice. And she left it up to me to choose which one of us gets the honor."

11.

Rococo was friendly with three former luddies, a fourth was an out-and-out enemy, and there was a fifth luddy who he met while she was still a child. Apparently he made an impression, because two decades later, having decided to leave the faith, she asked this important immortal to accompany her to a facility that did nothing but transform her kind into his kind.

"I want to live and live and live," she claimed, holding her companion's knee. "But can I confess what scares me?"

"That you'll grow bored," Rococo said.

She was startled until she stepped outside herself. Then she laughed, admitting, "That's the cliché, I suppose. Lives always become tiresome, and ten thousand years leaves a girl empty and dull."

"That's what some people want to believe," he said. "But then again, luddies need every reason to think themselves right. No matter how much of a lie that reason happens to be."

"So you don't feel bored."

Rococo winked at her, and with a happy voice said, "They won't tell you. The luddies who want to keep you small. But that thing you call boredom? It doesn't exist. Not for my kind. Monotony and apathy are symptoms of a weak mind, not a condition that afflicts those with too much time. For us, life is furiously rich. With our memories and our big eye for detail, it's very difficult to keep us from being enthusiastically involved in every facet of the day. Every breath and good thought and the little pains too. Which are almost never large pains, by the way. Every circumstance is another fascinating element inside a grand parade that doesn't need to stop for any reason short of death."

His friend went through the necessary surgeries and rebirth, and unlike a few patients, she quickly adapted to her new state. And fifty years later, while Rococo was leading a distant mission, he received news that his friend died in a tragic accident involving plasmas and AI errors.

The two of them were never lovers. Yet the woman was first in his thoughts that evening, and she stayed with Rococo throughout the sleepless night. Long stretches of conversation came to mind, word for word, and there were intervals where memory was far larger than the present. Once again, Rococo was sharing a drink with a perpetually young lady who was throwing her new cognitive skills at new languages and exotic faiths, all while touring exotic corners of the Great Ship. She was also making friends and then throwing the same friends aside when they proved to be the wrong sorts for a girl who was preparing for the next million years.

"A million years," she said.

Night had reached its middle, and Rococo sat on the deck, in the open. Sometimes he looked at stars, sometimes down at his empty hands. But all he saw was a girl who was so thrilled, standing on the edge of Forever, and all she was asking from the Universe was a brief million years.

Three times, Mere came to him in the night. The first two visits proved nothing but that the man didn't want to speak to her, regardless of what she said. But that didn't stop her from explaining that Amund was a shit. He was a shit who should have told them what was happening, even if the river forbad any warnings. "He could have used the Highland language to keep us ready. I learned enough words to follow the topic. If he had thought about doing that, which he would have. If the shit had ever bothered to try."

Shrugs didn't capture Rococo's indifference.

Silently gazing at the back of his hands. That's what convinced her to walk away. Twice.

Somewhat more effective was the third visit. With the sun rising behind them, Mere sat on the deck, legs crossed, near enough to Rococo that they might bump knees. With a careful quick voice, she said, "Of course it's possible that everything is a lie."

He looked at her, looked away. "About a sacrifice."

She nodded.

"And he's the one who decides who."

This time, Mere glanced at her own hands. Waiting him out, apparently.

Finally, Rococo said, "I believe the man."

"Why?"

"Because I don't know him," he explained.

Face and mouth both asked, "What do you mean?"

"I mean that if I did know the man, then I'd be able to yank the fabrications from the truth. For instance, if I'd slept with the fellow. Then I'd have a perspective. Then maybe I wouldn't feel as if I'm guessing about everything."

"Everything," she repeated. "Including this alleged agreement," he said. "We don't know if this world has offered worlds to us, much less tossing us most of the solar system. And how can we be sure that luddies are the only organisms that are welcome here? We have no details. We have nothing but words and posturing from a creature that you don't know either. Do you, Mere?"

"Not particularly well," she said.

The sun was suddenly bright and wonderfully warm, baking into his flesh. "All right," Rococo said. Then after a long pause, he added, "I'm going through the morning as a doomed man. All right? That's how I want to approach my last day, even if it isn't today. All right."

When they reached the ocean, the river had built itself into a towering blue-black wave. Five hundred meters above the surface of any normal river, they were being shoved forward so fast that the air blasted past them. But Rococo remained outside. Stress or habit was at play, or maybe the absence of imagination that comes with the gallows. The man could do nothing but watch the ocean retreating before the gelatin wall and before him. What wasn't calmness had come into him, or maybe this quiet had always been present, in secret. Being someone who was always loud or ready to become loud, he didn't know the tricks about lasting silence. But he was trying to learn. How much time remained? Don't calculate that. The best trick was to do nothing but sit and watch everything at once, committing nothing to memory because nothing was more useless now than fresh remembrances. Not for Rococo, not anymore. Just sit still and merge with each breath and the glorious sight of saltwater fleeing from a giant that was bearing him faster and faster toward their destination.

There.

The streakship was waiting exactly where it was expected, where it promised. Thick legs straddled an island that had sunk into the waves, just from its terrific mass. Where the destroyed streakship had been minimal hyperfiber and maximum vacuum, this beast was a marvel of deep armor and utter indifference to its surroundings. It was a bright gray cone that could have hidden happily inside a mountain range. It was a machine that would welcome them and protect them, and if the resident AIs were tweaked just so, the ship would fall in love with each of them, probably forever.

"What if Amund was lying?"

Rococo said it to the wind or himself, or maybe no one. Maybe the wind was talking to him, or the river had marshaled the words, perfectly mimicking how Rococo sounded to himself.

Either way, the hope was offered, and an instant later, it died.

Amund never explicitly said, "I'll have you killed." Because that was such an obvious answer. But what if the river and this world didn't think that Rococo was enough of a sacrifice? If these entities didn't approve of immortals, maybe Mere was on the platter, too. Which meant that Amund could step alone into the streakship, and being the only surviving member of this awful mission, he would easily take charge.

These ideas needed time to bake, except there was no time.

Rococo saw quite a lot, but most of his focus was on the gray cone trying to stand above the onslaught of flesh and vengeful rage.

When he stood, he stood quickly, putting his back to the wind. The pack and kit were secured to the deck's middle. Rococo claimed both and entered his cabin, opened the pack and gave instructions. Was this request too detailed, too odd? Was he wasting valuable time? But no, Remoras had built the kit, and Remoras designed wondrous machines. A sculpture of pure carbon—the narrow diamond blade and an elaborate, bone-shaped graphite hilt not meant to fit any human hand, but useful enough for a man about to commit murder.

The streakship was minutes away, and the towering wave decided to slow itself, beginning a steady, graceful collapse.

Rococo stepped inside Amund's cabin. Sitting on the mattress, legs too stiff to be crossed, the mortal body was wearing comfortable clothes without boots. For a moment, nothing happened. The man looked as if he might rise any moment, or he might close his eyes and nap. But then the bal'tin ceremonial knife caught the sunlight, flashing like a beacon, and Amund responded with a sudden sound. A laugh, or perhaps something else. It could have been a sob, a muddled word, or maybe just some miserable noise escaping on its own.

Rococo managed two steps before his legs quit working, before both hands failed him and the weapon struck the floor.

Softly, one of them said, "Do what you want."

Whose voice was that? Rococo wasn't certain, and he didn't care. What mattered was that he had done nothing wrong. He was bringing his colleague a fancy memento, and no crimes were being attempted, nothing was behind him but an open door and sunshine.

Except Rococo had said, "Do what you want."

"Thanks for the advice," the other man said. "I'll try to do just that."

Retreat began with a small step, then a pause. Embarrassment took hold, forcing Rococo to drop his eyes.

Amund pulled in his legs and rose, both arms helping fight gravity. Then he stepped close, saying, "You're the great diplomat. And so smart, too. If I believed half of what you've told me, I'd have no choice but to consider you one of the most brilliant creatures ever born from circuits and salt."

Rococo looked up, finding hard eyes and a broad grin that quickly turned into an ugly, disgusted expression.

"You're the genius," Amund said. "So of course you realized the truth. Probably long ago."

"What truth?"

"Well, that the rivers, and I mean all of the rivers, have been playing a spectacular game with us."

"Game?" Rococo muttered.

"Or don't you see it?" Laughter bubbled out of him, but the man's expression remained cold, furious. "When the rivers first learned about you, millions of tiny immortal machines riding inside one giant machine, they were afraid. Disasters were looming. Maybe like never before, they spoke to one another. They asked what they could do to save themselves. And after consideration and hard debate, they decided to send you promises. Four worlds offered, and three of those worlds were dedicated to the machines. Except they never wanted you on their shoreline. That's why they demanded someone like me. One pure river. And after a lot of hard, invisible preparations, they staged a terrible war between stubborn beliefs."

"Staged," Rococo echoed.

"Be honest," Amund said. "Bad as this damage looks, how many rivers were killed? Zero. That's how many. Each creature is diminished, yes. But still enormous compared to little us. And then they attacked our ship, stripping our resources to a desperate minimum. But of course that should have bothered a genius like you. Against tremendous odds, you survived. So did I. We lived because that was the plan, and then the river spoke to me. Which was the main reason why I was invited in the first place. To negotiate."

Rococo had no voice.

"The rivers were hoping I'd settle for four worlds, the same as you did. But I saw the game and held out for quite a lot more. Which is why I have to thank you. Half of my life listening to you chatter about how great you were at your job, and I learned a few things. Stupid as I am, I still managed a treaty guaranteeing that these aliens will be surrounded by billions of pure rivers but very few machines."

Rococo couldn't remember his last breath. Through clenched teeth, he asked, "And I'll be the sacrifice?"

"No, I am," Amund said instantly, without regrets. "I always have been. Aren't you paying attention?" Then he stepped close and bent just low enough to grab up the knife, holding it sideways on two flattened hands while adding, "You're not the great diplomat. They pulled a con on you. From the start and without you suspecting. And here I am, the dreamy piece of water that saw what you couldn't even imagine."

The knife weighed nothing, and the flesh offered no resistance when the tip went inside the man's stomach and out again.

Amund collapsed, letting out a long scream.

A tiny portion of the sunlight was blocked when Mere ran inside, grabbing Rococo's hands. "What are you doing, why would you?" she was asking. "How does this help anything anyone anywhere . . . ?"

She was carving up her own fingers, trying to yank the diamond blade free of his grip. But Rococo wouldn't let go. Feeling nothing and hearing nothing, his mind was focused only on the idea that if he was very good, and very lucky, only a million years would have to pass before this woman would willingly touch him again.

12.

Three weeks after the streakship launched, bound for the Great Ship, the AI doctors pronounced Amund well enough to travel. His stitches hadn't healed completely, and the scar tissue would never vanish. But those problems were bearable, and at least his guts were back where they belonged.

Besides, there was too much to do.

Amund was always the sacrifice. The one lie that he told was that he had any choice in this matter. But there wasn't going to be a staged event full of fake religious noise. The culmination of change and age and his own willing-ness to continue: That was why he would die. His flesh had nowhere to go but to join with the rivers, and these creatures were older and far more patient than any captain or clerk wandering long among the stars.

Along with the AI doctors, Mere had left behind portions of the streak-ship's machine shop and enough raw material to build a fleet of reasonably mindless devices. And following his instructions, a submarine was built and ready.

The river still listened to him, but it wasn't talking back anymore. Which was understandable. Honestly, what more could be said at this point?

Amund stepped inside the submarine and asked to be moved. No engines were necessary. The ship supplied breath and clear windows and spotlights. But those lights weren't needed. That was obvious soon after the river pulled him under the surf. The blue flesh of the land was replaced by glowing white flesh that lit the water and Amund's face and his great wide smile. The entire day was spent crossing the continental shelf, and then the edge came and the river set him where he could see the spectacle. A great current was crawling its way out of the depths. A waterfall flowing backward, milky and brilliant and vast. The world was shaking as the river pulled its reserves out of the abyssal plain: The first surge of an invasion that would rebuild the planet in less time than it would take this one man to die of old age.

How many people were able to watch a new world made?

Everybody could, of course.

But at the end of the day, how many ever took notice?

Madeline Ashby is a science fiction writer and futurist living in Toronto. Her most recent novel, *Company Town,* was a CBC Books Canada Reads finalist, and winner of the Copper Cylinder Award. She is also the author of the Machine Dynasty series. She has written science fiction prototypes for Intel Labs, the Institute for the Future, SciFutures, Nesta, Data & Society, the Atlantic Council, and others. You can find her at madelineashby.com.

DEATH ON MARS

Madeline Ashby

"Is he still on schedule?"

Donna's hand spidered across the tactical array. She pinched and threw a map into Khalidah's lenses. Marshall's tug glowed there, spiralling ever closer to its target. Khalidah caught herself missing baseball. She squashed the sentiment immediately. It wasn't really the sport she missed, she reminded herself. She just missed her fantasy league. Phobos was much too far away to get a real game going; the lag was simply too long for her bets to cover any meaningful spread. She could run a model, of course, and had even filled one halfway during the trip out. It wasn't the same.

Besides, it was more helpful to participate in hobbies she could share with the others. The counselors had been very clear on that subject. She was better off participating in Game Night, and the monthly book club they maintained with the Girl Scouts and Guides of North America.

"He's on time," Donna said. "Stop worrying."

"I'm not worried," Khalidah said. And she wasn't. Not really. Not about when he would arrive.

Donna pushed away from the terminal. She looked older than she had when they'd landed. They'd all aged, of course—the trip out and the lack of real produce hadn't exactly done any of them any favors—but Donna seemed to have changed more dramatically than Khalidah or Brooklyn or Song. She'd cut most of her hair off, and now the silver that once sparkled along her roots was the only color left. The exo-suit hung loose on her. She hadn't been eating. Everyone hated the latest rotation of rations. Who on Earth—literally, who?—thought that testing the nutritional merits of a traditional Buddhist macrobiotic diet in space was a good idea? What sadistic special-interest group had funded that particular line of research?

"It will be fine," Donna said. "*We* will be fine."

"I just don't want things to change."

"Things always change," Donna said. "God is change. Right, Octavia?"

The station spoke: "Right, Donna."

Khalidah folded her arms. "So do we have to add an Arthur, just for him? Or a Robert? Or an Isaac? Or a Philip?"

The station switched its persona to Alice B. Sheldon. Its icon spun like a coin in the upper right of Khalidah's vision. "We already have a James," the station said. The icon winked.

"Khalidah, look at me," Donna said. Khalidah de-focused from the In-Vision array and met the gaze of her mission manager. "It won't be easy," the older woman said. "But nothing out here is. We already have plenty of data about our particular group. You think there won't be sudden changes to group dynamics, down there?"

She pointed. And there it was: red and rusty, the color of old blood. Mars.

His name was Cody Marshall. He was Florida born and bred, white, with white-blond hair and a tendency toward rosacea. He held a PhD in computer science from Mudd. He'd done one internship in Syria, building drone-supported mesh nets, and another in Alert, Nunavut. He'd coordinated the emergency repair of an oil pipeline there using a combination of declassified Russian submersibles and American cable-monitoring drones. He'd managed the project almost single-handedly after the team lead at Alert killed himself.

Now here he was on Phobos, sent to debug the bore-hole driller on Mars. A recent solar storm had completely fried the drill's comms systems; Donna insisted it needed a complete overhaul, and two heads were better than one. Marshall couldn't do the job from home—they'd lose days reprogramming the things on the fly, and the drill bits were in sensitive places. One false move and months of work might collapse around billions of dollars of research, crushing it deep into the red dirt. He needed to be close. After all, he'd written much of the code himself.

This was his first flight.

"I didn't want to be an astronaut," he'd told them over the lag, when they first met. "I got into this because I loved robots. That's all. I had no idea this is where I would wind up. But I'm really grateful to be here. I know it's a change."

"If you make a toilet seat joke, we'll delete your porn," Song said, now. When they all laughed, she looked around at the crowd. "What's funny? I'm serious. I didn't come all the way out here to play out a sitcom."

Marshall snapped his fingers. "That reminds me." He rifled through one of the many pouches he'd lugged on board. "Your mom sent this along with me." He coasted a vial through the air at her. Inside, a small crystal glinted. "That's your brother's wedding. And your new nephew's baptism. Speaking of sitcoms. She told me some stories to tell you. She didn't want to record them—"

"She's very nervous about recording anything."

"—so she told me to tell them to you."

Song rolled her eyes. "Are they about Uncle Chan-wook?"

Marshall's pale eyebrows lifted high on his pink forehead. "How'd you guess?"

Again, the room erupted in laughter. Brooklyn laughed the loudest. She was a natural flirt. Her parents had named her after a borough they'd visited only once. In high school, she had self-published a series of homoerotic detective novels set in ancient Greece. The profits financed med school. After that, she hit Parsons for an unconventional residency. She'd worked on the team that designed the exo-suits they now wore. She had already coordinated Marshall's fitting over the lag. It fit him well. At least, Brooklyn seemed pleased. She was smiling so wide that Khalidah could see the single cavity she'd sustained in all her years of eschewing most refined sugars.

Khalidah rather suspected that Brooklyn had secretly advocated for the macrobiotic study. Chugging a blue algae smoothie every morning seemed like her kind of thing. Khalidah had never asked about it. It was better not to know.

But wasn't that the larger point of this particular experiment? To see if they could all get along? To see if women—with their lower caloric needs, their lesser weight, their quite literally cheaper labor, in more ways than one—could get the job done on Phobos? Sure, they were there on a planetary protection mission to gather the last remaining soil samples before the first human-oriented missions showed up, thereby ensuring the "chain of evidence" for future DNA experimentation. But they all knew—didn't they—what this was really about. How the media talked about them. How the internet talked about them. Early on, before departure, Khalidah had seen the memes.

For Brooklyn, Marshall had a single chime. Brooklyn's mother had sent it to "clear the energy" of the station. During the Cold Lake training mission, she'd sent a Tibetan singing bowl.

For Khalidah, he had all 4,860 games of last year's regular season. "It's lossless," he said. "All 30 teams. Even the crappy ones. One of our guys down at Kennedy, he has a brother-in-law in Orlando, works at ESPN. They got in touch with your dad, and, well . . ."

"Thank you," Khalidah said.

"Yeah. Sure." Marshall cleared his throat. He rocked on his toes, pitched a little too far forward, and wheeled his arms briefly to recover his balance. If possible, he turned even pinker, so the color of his face now matched the color of his ears. "So. Here you go. I don't know what else is on there, but, um . . . there it is. Enjoy."

"Thank you." Khalidah lifted the vial of media from his hand. Her crystal was darker than Song's. Denser. It had been etched more often. She stuffed it in the right breast pocket of her suit. If for some reason her heart cut out and the suit had to give her a jolt, the crystal would be safe.

"And for you, Donna. Here's what we talked about. They gave you double, just in case."

Donna's hand was already out. It shook a little as Marshall placed a small bottle in it. The label was easy to see. Easy to read. Big purple letters branded on the stark white sticker. Lethezine. The death drug. The colony of nanomachines that quietly took over the brain, shutting off major functions silently and painlessly. The best, most dignified death possible. The kind you had to ask the government for personally, complete with letters of recommendation from people with advanced degrees that could be revoked if they lied, like it was a grant application or admission to a very prestigious community. Which in fact it was.

"What is that?" Brooklyn asked.

It was a stupid question. Everyone knew exactly what it was. She was just bringing it out into the open. They'd been briefed on that. On making the implicit become explicit. On voicing what had gone unasked. Speaking the unspeakable. It was, in fact, part of the training. There were certain things you were supposed to suppress. And other things that you couldn't let fester. They had drilled on it, over and over, at Cold Lake and in Mongolia and again and again during role-plays with the station interface.

"Why do you have that?" Brooklyn continued, when Donna didn't answer. "Why would he give that to you?"

Donna pocketed the bottle before she opened her mouth to speak. When she did, she lifted her gaze and stared at each of them in turn. She smiled tightly. For the first time, Khalidah realized the older woman's grimace was not borne of impatience, but rather simple animal pain. "It's because I'm dying," she said.

She said it like it was a commonplace event. Like, "Oh, it's because I'm painting the kitchen," or "It's because I took the dog for a walk."

In her lenses, Khalidah saw the entire group's auras begin to flare. The auras were nothing mystical, nothing more than ambient indicators of what the sensors in the suits were detecting: heart rate, blood pressure, temperature, odd little twitches of muscle fibers. She watched them move from baseline green to bruise purple—the color of tension, of frustration. Only Song remained calm: her aura its customary frosty mint green, the same shade once worn by astronauts' wives at the advent of the Space Race.

"You *knew*?" she managed to say, just as Marshall said, "You didn't *tell* them?"

Khalidah whirled to stare at him. His mouth hung open. He squinted at Donna, then glanced around the group. "Wait," he said. "Wait. Let's just take a minute. I . . ." He swallowed. "I need a minute. You . . ." He spun in place and pointed at Donna. "This was a shitty thing to do. I mean, really, truly, deeply, profoundly not cool. Lying to your team isn't cool. Setting me up to fail isn't cool."

"I have a brain tumor," Donna said blandly. "I'm not necessarily in my right mind."

"Donna," Song said quietly.

Oh, God. Donna was dying. She was dying and she hadn't told them and minty-green Song had known about it the whole damn time.

"You knew," Khalidah managed to say.

"Of course she knew," Donna said. "She's our doctor."

Donna was dying. Donna would be dead, soon. Donna had lied to all of them.

"It's inoperable," Donna added, as though talking about a bad seam in her suit and not her grey matter. "And in any case, I wouldn't want to operate on it. I still have a few good months here—"

"A few *months*?" Brooklyn was crying. The tears beaded away from her face and she batted at them, as though breaking them into smaller pieces would somehow dismantle the grief and its cause. "You have *months*? That's it?"

"More or less." Donna shrugged. "I could make it longer, with chemo, or nano. But we don't have those kinds of therapies here. Even if we did, and the tumor did shrink, Song isn't a brain surgeon, and the lag is too slow for

Dr. Spyder to do something that delicate." She jerked a thumb at the surgical assistant in its cubby. "And there's the fact that I don't want to leave."

There was an awful silence filled only by the sounds of the station: the water recycler, the rasp of air in the vents, an unanswered alert chiming on and off, off and on. It was the sound the drill made when it encountered issues of structural integrity and wanted a directive on how to proceed. If they didn't answer it in five more minutes, the chime would increase in rate and volume. If they didn't answer it after another five minutes, the drill itself would relay a message via the rovers to tell mission control they were being bad parents.

And none of that mattered now. At least, Khalidah could not make it matter, in her head. She could not pull the alert into the "urgent" section of her mind. Because Donna was dying, Donna would be dead soon, Donna was in all likelihood going to kill herself right here on the station and what would they do—

Donna snapped her fingers and opened the alert. She pushed it over to tactical array where they could all see it. "Marshall, go and take a look."

Marshall seemed glad of any excuse to leave the conversation. He drifted over to the array and started pulling apart the alert with his fingers. His suit was still so new that his every swipe and pinch and pull worked on the first try. His fingers hadn't worn down yet. Not like theirs. Not like Donna's.

"Can you do that?" Khalidah asked Donna. When Donna didn't answer, she focused on Song. "Can she do that?"

Song's face closed. She was in full physician mode now. Gone was the cheerful woman with the round face who joked about porn. Had the person they'd become friends with ever truly been real? Was she always this cold, underneath? Was it being so far away from Earth that made it so easy for her to lie to them? "It's her body, Khal. She doesn't have any obligation to force it to suffer."

Khalidah tried to catch Donna's eye. "You flew with the Air Force. You flew over Syria and Sudan. You—"

"Yes, and whatever I was exposed to there probably had a hand in this," Donna muttered. "The buildings, you know. They released all kinds of nasty stuff. Like first responder syndrome, but worse." She pinched her nose. It was the only sign she ever registered of a headache. "But it's done, now, Khalidah. I've made my decision."

"But—"

"We all knew this might be a one-way trip," Song added.

"Don't patronize me, Song," Khalidah snapped.

"Then grow up," Song sighed. "Donna put this in her living will ages ago. Long before she even had her first flight. She was preapproved for Lethezine, thanks to her family's cancer history. There was always a chance that she would get cancer on this trip, given the radiation exposure. But her physicians decided it was an acceptable risk, and she chose to come here in full awareness of that risk."

"I'm right here, you know," Donna said. "I'm not dead yet."

"You could still retire," Khalidah heard herself say. "You could go private. Join a board of trustees somewhere, or something like that. They'd cover a subscription, maybe they could get you implants—"

"I don't *want* implants, Khal, I want to die *here*—"

"I brought some implants," Marshall said, without turning around. He slid one last number into place, then wiped away the display. Now he turned. He took a deep breath, as though he'd rehearsed this speech the whole trip over. Which he probably had. Belatedly, Khalidah noticed the length of his hair and fingernails. God, he'd done the whole trip alone. The station couldn't bear more than one extra; as it was, he'd needed to bring extra scrubbers and promise to spend most of the time in his own hab docked to theirs.

"I brought implants," he continued. "They're prototypes. No surgery necessary. Houston insisted. They wanted to give you one last chance to change your mind."

"I'm not going to change my mind," Donna said. "I want to die here."

"Please stop saying that." Brooklyn wiped her eyes. "Please just stop saying that."

"But it's the truth," Donna said, in her maddening why-isn't-everyone-as-objective-about-this-as-I-am way. "My whole life, I've wanted to go to Mars. And now I'm within sight of it. I'm not going to leave just because there's a lesion on my brain. Not when I just got here." She huffed. "Besides. I'd be no good to any of you on chemo. I'd be sick."

"You *are* sick," Khalidah snapped.

"Not that sick." Song lifted her gaze from her nails and gestured at the rest of them. "None of you noticed, did you? Both of you thought she was fine."

"Yeah, no thanks to you."

"Don't take that tone with me. She's my patient. I'd respect your right to confidentiality the same way I respected hers."

"You put the mission at risk," Khalidah said.

"Oh my God, Khal, stop talking like *them*." Brooklyn's voice was still thick with tears. "You're not mission control. This has nothing to do with the *mission*."

"It has *everything* to do with the mission!" Khalidah rounded on Donna. "How could you do this? How could you not tell us? This entire experiment hinges on social cohesion. That's why we're here. We're here to prove . . ."

Now the silence had changed into something wholly other. It was much heavier now. Much more accusatory. Donna folded her arms.

"What are we here to prove, Khalidah?"

Khalidah shut her eyes. She would be professional. She would not cry. She would not get angry. At least, no angrier than she already was. She would not focus on Donna's betrayal, and her deceit, and the fact that she had the audacity to pull this bullshit so soon after . . . Khalidah took a deep breath.

She would put it aside. *Humans are containers of emotion.* She made herself see the words in the visualizing interface they had for moments like this. *When someone else's emotions spill out, it's because their container is full.* She focused on her breathing. She pictured the color of her aura changing in the others' lenses. She imagined pushing the color from purple to green, healing it slowly, as though it were the evidence of a terrible wound.

"I'm fine," she said. "I'm fine. I'm sorry."

"That's good," Donna said. "Because we're not here to *prove* any one particular thing or another. We're here to run experiments, gather the last Martian samples before the crewed missions begin, and observe the drills as they dig out the colony. That's all we're here to do. You may feel pressure to do something else, due to the nature of this team, but that's not why we're here. The work comes first. The policy comes later."

The *Morrígu* was divided into three pods: Badb, Macha, and Nemain. No one referred to them that way, of course—only Marshall had the big idea to actually try stumbling through ancient Gaelic with his good ol' boy accent. He gave up after two weeks. Nonetheless, he still referred to his unit as the *Corvus*.

"Nice of them to stick with the crow theme," he said.

"Ravens are omens of death," Donna said, and just like that, Game Night was over. That was fine with Khalidah. Low-gravity games never had the degree of complexity she liked; they had magnetic game boards, but they weren't entirely the same. And without cards or tokens they couldn't really visualize the game in front of them, and basically played permutations of *Werewolf* or *Mafia* until they learned each other's tells.

Not that all that experience had helped her read Donna and Song's dishonesty. Even after all their time spent together, in training, on the flight, on the station, there was the capacity for betrayal. Even now, she did not truly know them.

Not yet, Khalidah often repeated to herself, as the days stretched on. *Not yet.* Not for the first time, she wished for a return to 24-hour days. Once upon a time, they had seemed so long. She had yearned for afternoons to end, for lectures to cease, for shifts to close. Now she understood that days on Earth were beautifully, mercifully short.

Sometimes Khalidah caught Donna watching her silently, when she didn't think Khalidah would notice. When Khalidah met her eyes, Donna would try to smile. It was more a crinkling of the eyes than anything else. It was hard to tell if she was in pain, or unhappy, or both. The brain had no nerve endings of its own, no pain receptors. The headaches that Donna felt were not the tissue's response to her tumor, but rather a warning sign about a crowded nerve, an endless alarm that rang down through her spinal column and caused nausea and throbbing at odd hours. Or so she said.

Khalidah's first email was to her own psychiatrist on Earth, through her personal private channel. It was likely the very same type of channel Donna had used to carry on her deception. *Can a member of crew just hide any medical condition they want?* she wrote.

Your confidentiality and privacy are paramount, Dr. Hassan wrote back from Detroit. You have sacrificed a great deal of privacy to go on this mission. You live in close quarters, quite literally right on top of each other. So the private channels you have left are considered sacrosanct. Communications between any participant and her doctor must remain private until the patient chooses to disclose.

This was not the answer Khalidah had wanted to hear.

Imagine if it were you who had a secret, Dr. Hassan continued, as though having anticipated Khalidah's feelings on the matter. *If you were experiencing the occasional suicidal ideation, for example, would you want your whole crew to know, or would you wait for the ideations to pass?*

It was a valid counterargument. Mental health was a major concern on long-haul missions. Adequate care required stringent privacy. But Donna's cancer wasn't a passing thought about how much easier it would be to be dead. She was actually dying. And she hadn't told them.

Now, after all that silence on the matter, the cancer seemed to be all anyone could talk about.

"I've almost trained the pain to live on Martian time," Donna said, one morning. "Most patients feel pain in the morning, but they feel it on an Earth schedule, with full sunlight."

Khalidah could not bring herself to smile back, not yet. Doing so felt like admitting defeat.

"She won't die any slower just because you're mad at her," Brooklyn said, as they conducted seal checks on the suits.

"Leave me alone," Khalidah said. Brooklyn just shrugged and got on with the checklist. A moment later, she asked for a flashlight. Khalidah handed it to her without a word.

"Have you watched any of the games your dad sent?" Marshall asked, the next day.

"Please don't bring him up," Khalidah said.

Five weeks later, the vomiting started. It was an intriguing low-gravity problem—barf bags were standard, but carrying them around wasn't. And Donna couldn't just commandeer the shop-vac for her own personal use. In the end, Marshall made her a little butterfly net, of sorts, with an iris at one end. It was like a very old-fashioned nebulizer for inhaling asthma medication. Only it worked in the other direction.

Not coincidentally, Marshall had brought with him an entire liquid diet intended specifically for cancer patients. Donna switched, and things got better.

"I'll stick around long enough to get the last samples from Hellas," she said, sipping a pouch of what appeared to be either a strawberry milkshake or an anti-nausea tonic. She coughed. The cough turned into a gag that she needed to suppress. She clenched a fist and then unclenched it, to master it. "I want my John Hancock on those damn things."

"Don't you want to see the landing?" Marshall asked. "You know, hand over the keys, see their faces when they see the ant farm in person for the first time?"

"What, and watch them fuck up all our hard work?"

They all laughed. All of them but Khalidah. How could they just act like everything was normal? Did the crew of the Ganesha mission even know that Donna was sick? Would the team have to explain it? How would that conversation even happen? ("Welcome to Mars. Sorry, but we're in the middle of a funeral. Anyway, try not to get your microbes everywhere.")

Then the seizures started. They weren't violent. More like gentle panic attacks. "My arm doesn't feel like my arm anymore," Donna said, as she continued to man her console with one hand. "No visual changes, though. Just localized disassociation."

"That's a great band name," Marshall said.

Morrígu tried to help, in her own way. The station gently reminded Khalidah of all the things that she already knew: that she was distracted, that she wasn't sleeping, that she would lie awake listening for the slightest tremor in Donna's breathing, and that sometimes Brooklyn would reach up from her cubby and squeeze Khalidah's ankle because she was listening too. The station made herself available in the form of the alters, often pinging Khalidah when her gaze failed to track properly across a display, or when her blood pressure spiked, or when she couldn't sleep. Ursula, most often, but then Octavia. *God is Change*, the station reminded her. *The only lasting truth is Change.*

And Khalidah knew that to be true. She did. She simply drew no comfort from it. Too many things had changed already. Donna was dying. Donna, who had calmly helped her slide the rods into the sleeves as they pitched tents in Alberta one dark night while the wolves howled and the thermometer dropped to 30 below. Donna, who had said, "Of course you can do it. That's not the question," when Khalidah reached between the cots during isolation week and asked Donna if the older woman thought she was really tough enough to do the job. Donna, without whom Khalidah might have quit at any time.

"You watch any of those games yet?" Marshall asked, when he caught her staring down at the blood-dark surface of the planet. Rusted, old. Not like the wine-dark samples that Song drained from Donna each week.

Khalidah only shook her head. Baseball seemed so stupid now.

"Your dad, he really wanted to get those to you before I left," Marshall reminded her.

Khalidah took a deep, luxuriant breath. "I told you not to mention him, Marshall. I asked you nicely. Are you going to respect those boundaries, or are we going to have a problem?"

Marshall said nothing, at first. Instead he drifted in place, holding the nearest grip to keep himself tethered. He hadn't learned how to tuck himself in yet, how to twist and wring himself so that he passed through without touching anyone else. Everything about his presence there still felt wrong.

"We don't have to be friends," he said, in measured tones. He pointed down into Storage. "But the others, they're your friends. Or they thought they were. Until now."

"They lied to me."

"Oh, come on. You think it wasn't tough for Song to go through that? You think she enjoyed it, not telling you? Jesus Christ, Khalidah. Maybe you haven't noticed, but a lot of us made a lot of sacrifices to get this far."

"Oh, I'm sure it was *so* difficult for you, finding out you'd get to go to Mars—"

"—Phobos."

"—Phobos, without anything like the training we had to endure, just so you could pilot your finicky fucking drill God knows where—"

"Hey, now, I happen to like my finicky fucking drill very fucking much," Marshall said. He blinked. Then covered his face with his hands. He'd filed his nails down and buzzed his hair in solidarity with Donna. His entire skull was flushed the color of a new spring geranium. "That . . . didn't come out right."

Khalidah hung in place. She drew her knees up to her chest and floated. It had been a long time since she'd experienced secondhand embarrassment. Something about sharing such a tiny space with the others for so long ground it out of a person. But she was embarrassed for Marshall now. Not as embarrassed as he was, thank goodness. But embarrassed.

"They sent me *alone*, you know," he said, finally, through the splay of his fingers. He scrubbed at the bare stubble of his skull. "*Alone*. Do you even know what that means? You know all those desert island questions in job interviews? When they ask you what books you'd bring, if you were stranded in the middle of nowhere? Well, I *read* all of those. *War and Peace*. *Being and Nothingness*. Do you have any idea how good I am at solitaire, by now?"

"You can't be good at solitaire, it's—"

"But I did it, because they said it was the best chance for giving Donna extra time. If they'd sent two of us, you'd all have to go home a hell of a lot faster. You wouldn't be here when *Ganesha* arrives. So I did it. I got here. Alone. I did the whole trip by myself. So you and Donna and the whole crew could have more time."

Khalidah swallowed hard. "Are you finished?"

"Yes. I'm finished." He pushed himself off the wall, then bounced away and twisted back to face her. "No. I'm not. I think you're being a total hypocrite, and I think it's undermining whatever social value the *Morrígu* experiment was meant to have."

Khalidah felt her eyebrows crawl up to touch the edges of her veil. "Excuse me?"

"Yeah. You heard me. You're being a hypocrite." He lowered his voice. "Do your friends even know your dad died? Did you tell them that he was dying, when you left? Because I was told not to mention it, and that sure as hell sounds like a secret to me."

Khalidah closed her eyes. The only place to go, in a space this small, was inward. There was no escape, otherwise. She waited until that soft darkness had settled around her and then asked, "Why are you doing this?"

"Because you're *not* alone, out here. You *have* friends. Friends you've known and worked with for years, in one way or another. So what if Donna jerked you around? She jerked me around too, and you don't see me acting like a brat about it. Or Brooklyn. Or Song. Meanwhile you've been keeping this massive life-changing event from them this whole time."

Now Khalidah's eyes opened. She had no need for that comforting blanket of darkness now. "My father dying is not a massive life-changing event," she snapped. "You think you know all my secrets? You don't know shit, Marshall. Because if you did, you'd know that I haven't spoken to that bastard in 10 years."

As though trying to extract some final usefulness from their former mistress, the drills decided to fail before the Banshee units returned with their samples, and before *Ganesha* arrived with the re-up and the Mars crew. Which meant that when *Ganesha* landed, the crew would have to live in half-dug habs.

"It's the goddamn perchlorate," Donna whispered. She had trouble swallowing now, and it meant her voice was constantly raw. "I told them we should have gone with the Japanese bit. It drilled the Shinkansen, I said. Too expensive, they said. Now the damn thing's rusted all to shit."

Which was exactly the case. The worm dried up suddenly, freezing in place—a "Bertha Bork," like the huge drill that stalled under Seattle during an ill-fated transit project. They'd rehearsed this particular error. First they ordered all the rovers away in case of a sinkhole, and then started running satellites over the sink. And the drill himself told them what was wrong. The blades were corroded. After five years of work, too much of the red dirt had snuck down into the drill's workings. It would need to be dug out and cleaned before it could continue. Or it would need to be replaced entirely.

The replacement prototype was already built. It had just completed its first test run in the side of a flattened mountain in West Virginia. It was strong and light and better articulated than the worm. But the final model was supposed to come over with *Ganesha*. And in the meantime, the hab network still needed major excavation.

"What's the risk if we send one of the rovers to try to uncover it?" Song asked. "We've got one in the cage; it wrapped up its mission ages ago. Wouldn't be too hard to reconfigure."

"Phobos rovers might be too light," Marshall said. "But the real problem is the crashberry; it'll take three days to inflate and another week to energize. And that's a week we're not drilling."

"We could tell *Ganesha* to slow down," Khalidah said.

"They're ballistic capture," Marshall said. "If they slow down now, they lose serious momentum."

"They'd pick it up on arrival, though."

"Yeah . . ." Marshall sucked his teeth. "But they're carrying a big load. They could jackknife once they hit the well, if they don't maintain a steady speed." He scrubbed at the thin dusting of blonde across his scalp. "But we have to tell them about this, either way. Wouldn't be right, not updating them."

Khalidah snorted. The others ignored her.

"Can we redirect the Banshees?" Brooklyn asked. "Whiskey and Tango are the closest. We could have them dump their samples, set a pin, tell them to dig out the worm, and then come back."

Khalidah shook her head. "They're already full. They're on their way to the mail drop. If we redeployed them now, they wouldn't be in position when *Ganesha* arrives. Besides, they're carrying Hellas—we can't afford to compromise them."

"Those samples are locked up like Fort Knox," Brooklyn said. "What, are you worried that the crew of *Ganesha* will open them up by mistake? Because that's pretty much guaranteed not to happen."

"No, but—"

"There's a storm in between Whiskey and the worm," Marshall said. He pointed at an undulating pattern of lines on the screen between two blinking dots. "If we send Whiskey now, we might lose her forever. And the samples. And we still wouldn't be any further with the drill. Fuck."

He pushed away from the console, knuckling his eyes. Khalidah watched the planet. In the plate glass, she caught Donna watching her. Her friend was much thinner now. They'd had to turn off her suit, because it no longer fit snugly enough to read her heartbeat. Her breath came in rasps. She coughed often. Last month, Song speculated that the cancer had spread to her lungs; Donna claimed not to care very much. Khalidah heard the older woman sigh slow and deep. And she knew, before Donna even opened her mouth, what she was about to suggest.

"There's always the *Corvus*," Donna said.

"No," Khalidah said. "Absolutely not."

But Donna wasn't even looking at her. She was looking at Marshall. "How much fuel did they really send, Marshall? You got here awfully fast."

Marshall licked his lips. "Between what I have left over and what *Ganesha* is leaving behind for you midway, there's enough to send you home."

"Which means *Corvus* has just enough to send me *down*, and give me thrust to come back."

"Even if that were true, you could still have a seizure while doing the job," Song said.

"Then I'll take my anti-seizure medication before I leave," Donna said.

"The gravity would demolish you, with the state you're in," Marshall said. "It should be me. I should go. I know *Corvus* better, and my bone density is—"

"That's very gallant of you, Mr. Marshall, but I outrank you," Donna reminded him. "Yes, I tire easily. Yes, it's hard for me to breathe. But I'm stronger than I would be if I were on chemo. And the suit can both give me some lift and push a good air mix for me. Right, Brooklyn?"

Brooklyn beamed. "Yes, ma'am."

"And Marshall, if any of those things do occur, I need you up here to remote-pilot *Corvus* from topside and get the samples back here." She gestured at the map. "If you tell Tango to meet me, I can take her samples and put them on *Corvus*. Then I get in Tango's cargo compartment and drive her around the storm, to the worm. I dig out the drill, and you restart it from up here. When I come back, you have the samples, and *Ganesha* has another guestroom." She grinned. The smile made her face into a skull. "Easy peasy," Donna said.

"You know you're making history, right?" Marshall asked, as they performed the final checks on *Corvus*. "First human on Mars, and all that. You're stealing *Ganesha's* thunder."

Donna coughed. "Don't jinx it, Marshall."

"How are your hands?"

Donna held them up. Slowly, she crunched her thickly gloved digits into fists. "They're okay."

"That's good. Go slow. The Banshees take a light touch."

"I know that, Marshall."

He pinked. "I know you know. But I'm just reminding you. Now, I'll get you down there, smooth as silk, and when it's time to come home you just let us know, okay?"

Donna's head tilted. She did that when she was about to ask an important question. For a moment it reminded Khalidah so much of the woman she'd been and the woman they'd lost that she forgot to breathe. "Is it home now, for you?"

Marshall's blush deepened. He really did turn the most unfortunate shade of sunburned red. "I guess so," he said. "Brooklyn, it's your turn."

Brooklyn breezed in and, flipping herself to hang upside down, performed the final checks on Donna's suit. "You've got eight hours," she said. "Sorry it couldn't be more. Tango is already on her way, and she'll be there to meet you when you land."

"What's Tango's charge like?"

"She's sprinting to meet you, so she'll be half-empty by the time she hits the rendezvous point," Marshall said. "But there's a set of auxiliary batteries in the cargo area. You'd have to move them to get into the cockpit anyhow."

Donna nodded. The reality of what was about to happen was settling on them. How odd, Khalidah thought, to be weightless and yet to feel the gravity of Donna's mission tugging at the pit of her stomach. The first human on Mars. The first woman. The first cancer patient. She had read a metaphor of illness as another country, how patients became citizens of it, that place beyond the promise of life, and now she thought of Donna there on the blood-red sands, representing them. Not just a human, but a defiantly mortal one, one for whom all the life-extension dreams and schemes would never bear fruit. All the members of the *Ganesha* crew had augmentations to make their life on Mars more productive and less painful. Future colonists would doubtless have similar lifehacks. Donna was the only visitor who would ever set an unadulterated foot on that soil.

"I'll be watching your vitals the whole time," Song said. "If I don't like what I see, I'll tell Marshall to take control of Tango and bring you back."

Donna cracked a smile. "Is that for my benefit, or the machine's?"

"Both," Song said. "We can't have you passing out and crashing millions of dollars' worth of machine learning and robotics."

And then, too soon, the final checks were finished, and it was time for Donna to go. The others drifted to the other side of the airlock, and Brooklyn ran the final diagnostic of the detachment systems. Khalidah's hands twitched at her veil. She had no idea what to say. *Why did you lie to us? Did you really think that would make this easier? What were you so afraid of?*

Donna regarded her from the interior of her suit. She looked so small inside it. Khalidah thought of her fragile body shaking inside its soft volumes, her thin neck and her bare skull juddering like a bad piece of video.

"I want—"

"Don't," Donna said. "Don't, Khal. Not now."

For the first time in a long time, Khalidah peeped at Donna's aura through the additional layer in her lenses' vision. It was deep blue, like a very wide and cold stretch of the sea. It was a color she had never seen on Donna. When she looked at her own pattern, it was much the same shade.

Marshall chose this moment to poke his head in. "It's time."

Donna reached over to the airlock button. "I have to go now, Khalidah."

Before Khalidah could say anything, Marshall had tugged her backward. The door rolled shut. For a moment she watched Donna through the small bright circle of glass. Then Donna's helmet snapped shut and she wore a halo within a halo, like a bull's-eye.

The landing was as Marshall promised: smooth as silk. With *Corvus* he was in his element. He and the vessel knew each other well. They'd moved as much of *Corvus*'s cargo as they could into temporary storage outside the hab; the reduced weight would give Donna the extra boost on the trip back that she might need.

Donna herself rode out the landing better than any of them expected. She took her time unburdening herself of her restraints, and they heard her breathing heavily, trying to choke back the nausea that now dominated her daily life. But eventually she lurched free of the unit, tuned up the jets on her suit, jiggered her air mix, and began the unlocking procedure to open *Corvus*. They watched her gloved hands hovering over the final lock.

"I hope you're not expecting some cheesy bullshit about giant leaps for womankind," Donna said, panting audibly. She sounded sheepish. For Donna, that meant she was nervous. "I didn't really have time to prepare any remarks. I have a job to do."

Brooklyn wiped her eyes and covered her mouth. Marshall passed her a tissue, and took one for himself.

"You've wanted this since you were a little girl, Donna," Song said. "Go out there and get it."

Together they watched the lock spin open, and Donna eased herself out. There was Tango, ready and waiting. And there was Mars, or at least their little corner of it, raw and open and red like a wound.

"I wish I could smell it," Donna said. "I wish I could taste the air. It feels strange to be here and yet not be here at the same time. You can stand here all you want and never really touch it."

"You can look at the samples when you bring them back," Brooklyn managed to say.

Donna said nothing, only silently made her way to Tango and moved the samples back to *Corvus*. Then she began the procedure to get Tango into manual. Her feed cut out a couple of times, but only briefly; they hadn't thought to test the signal on the cameras themselves. Her audio was fine, though, and Marshall talked her through when she had questions. In the end it ran like any other remote repair. Even the dig went well; clearing the dirt from the drill and restarting it from the control panel was a lot simpler than any of them had expected.

Halfway back to *Corvus*, Tango slowly rolled to a stop.

"Donna, check your batteries," Marshall suggested.

There was no answer. Only Donna's slow, wet breathing.

"Donna, copy?"

Nothing. They looked at Song; Song pulled up Donna's vitals. "No changes in her eye movements or alpha pattern," Song whispered. "She's not having a seizure. Donna. Donna! Do you need help?"

"No," Donna said, finally. "I came here to do a job, and now I'm finished with it. I'm done."

Something in Khalidah's stomach turned to ice. "Don't do this," she whispered, as Marshall began to say "No, no, no," over and over. He started bashing things on the console, running every override he could.

"No, you don't, you crazy old broad," he muttered. "I can get Tango to drive you back, you know!"

"Not if I've ripped out the receiver," Donna said. She sounded exhausted. "I think I'll just stay here, thank you. *Ganesha* can deal with me when they come. You don't have to do it. You'd have had to freeze me, anyway, and vibrate me down to crystal, like cat litter, and—"

"Fuck. You."

It was the first full complete sentence that Khalidah had spoken to her in months. So she repeated it.

"Fuck you. Fuck you for lying to us. Again. Fuck you for this selfish fucking bullshit. Oh, you think you're being so romantic, dying on Mars. Well fuck you. We came here to prove we could live, not . . ." Her lips were hot. Her eyes were hot. It was getting harder to breathe. "Not whatever the fuck it is you think you're doing."

Nothing.

"Donna, please don't," Brooklyn whispered in her most wheedling tone. "Please don't leave us. We need you." She sounded like a child. Then again, Khalidah wasn't sure she herself sounded any better. Somehow this loss contained within it all the other losses she'd ever experienced: her mother, her father, the slow pull away from the Earth and into the shared unknown.

"This is a bad idea," Marshall said, his voice calm and steady. "If you want to take the Lethezine, take the Lethezine. But you don't know how it works—what if it doesn't go like you think it will, and you're alone and in pain down there? Why don't you come back up, and if something goes wrong, we'll be there to help?"

Silence. Was she deliberating? Could they change her mind? Khalidah strained to hear the sound of Tango starting back up again. They flicked nervous, tearful glances at each other.

"Are you just going to quit?" Khalidah asked, when the silence stretched too long. "Are you just going to run away, like this? Now that it's hard?"

"You have no idea how hard this is, Khal, and you've never once thought to ask."

It stung. Khalidah let the pain transform itself into anger. Anger, she decided, was the only way out of this problem. "I thought you didn't *want* me to ask, given how you never *told* us anything until it was too late."

"It's not my fault I'm dying!"

"But it's your fault you didn't tell us! We would have—"

"You would have convinced me to go home." Donna chuckled. It became a cough. The cough lasted too long. "Because you love me, and you want me to live. And I love you, so I would have done it." She had another little coughing jag. "But the trouble with *home* is that there's nothing to go back to. I've thrown my whole life into this. I've had to pass on things—real things—to get to this place. But now that I'm here, I know it was worth it. And that's how I want to end it. I don't want to die alone in a hospital surrounded by people who don't understand what's out here, or why we do this."

Khalidah forced her voice to remain firm. "And so you want to die alone, down there, surrounded by nothing at all?"

"I'm not alone, Khal. You're with me. You're all with me, all the time."

Brooklyn broke down. She pushed herself into one corner. Khalidah reached up, and held her ankle, tethering her into the group. She squeezed her eyes shut and felt tears bud away. Song's beautiful ponytail drifted across her face. Arms curled around Khalidah's body. Khalidah curled her arms around the others. They were a Gordian knot, hovering far above Donna, a problem she could not solve and could only avoid.

"That's right, Donna," Marshall said. "We're here. We're right here."

"I'm sorry," Donna said. "I'm sorry I lied. I didn't want to. But I just . . . I wanted to stay, more than I wanted to tell you."

"I'm sorry, too," Khalidah said. "I . . ." She wiped at her face. Her throat hurt. "I *miss* you. Already."

"I miss you, too. I miss all of you." Donna sniffed hard. "But this is where we're supposed to be. Because this is where we are at our best."

They were quiet for a while. There was nothing to do but weep. Khalidah thought she might weep forever. The pain was a real thing—she had forgotten that it hurt to cry. She had forgotten the raw throat and pounding head that came with full-body grief. She had forgotten, since her mother, how physically taxing it could be.

"Are you ready, now?" Song asked, finally. She wiped her eyes and swallowed. "Donna? Are you ready to take the dose?"

The silence went on a long time. But still, they kept asking, "Are you ready? Are you ready?"

Rich Larson was born in Galmi, Niger, has studied in Rhode Island and worked in southern Spain, and now lives in Ottawa, Canada. His short fiction appears in numerous Year's Best anthologies and has been translated into Chinese, Vietnamese, Polish, Czech, French, and Italian. He was the most prolific author of short science fiction in 2015, 2016, and possibly 2017 as well. His debut novel, *Annex*, comes out in July 2018, and his debut collection, *Tomorrow Factory*, follows in October 2018. Find more at richwlarson.tumblr.com.

AN EVENING WITH SEVERYN GRIMES

Rich Larson

"Do you have to wear the Fawkes in here?" Girasol asked, sliding into the orthochair. Its worn wings crinkled, leaking silicon, as it adjusted to her shape. The plastic stuck cold to her shoulder blades, and she shivered.

"No." Pierce made no move to pull off the smirking mask. "It makes you nervous," he explained, groping around in the guts of his open Adidas trackbag, his tattooed hand emerging with the hypnotic. "That's a good enough reason to wear it."

Girasol didn't argue, just tipped her dark head back, positioning herself over the circular hole they'd punched through the headrest. Beneath it, a bird's nest of circuitry, mismatched wiring, blinking blue nodes. And in the center of the nest: the neural jack, gleaming wet with disinfectant jelly.

She let the slick white port at the top of her spine snick open.

"No cheap sleep this time," Pierce said, flicking his nail against the inky vial. "Get ready for a deep slice, Sleeping Beauty. Prince Charming's got your shit. Highest-grade Dozr a man can steal." He plugged it into a battered needler, motioned for her arm. "I get a kiss or what?"

Girasol proffered her bruised wrist. Let him hunt around collapsed veins while she said, coldly, "Don't even think about touching me when I'm under."

Pierce chuckled, slapping her flesh, coaxing a pale blue worm to stand out in her white skin. "Or what?"

Girasol's head burst as the hypnotic went in, flooding her capillaries, working over her neurotransmitters. "Or I'll cut your fucking balls off."

The Fawkes' grin loomed silent over her; a brief fear stabbed through the descending drug. Then he laughed again, barking and sharp, and Girasol knew she had not forgotten how to speak to men like Pierce. She tasted copper in her mouth as the Dozr settled.

"Just remember who got you out of Correctional," Pierce said. "And that if you screw this up, you'd be better off back in the freeze. Sweet dreams."

The mask receded, and Girasol's eyes drifted up the wall, following the cabling that crept like vines from the equipment under her skull, all the way through a crack gouged in the ceiling, and from there to whatever line Pierce's cronies had managed to splice. The smartpaint splashed across the grimy stucco displayed months of preparation: shifting sat-maps, decrypted dossiers, and a thousand flickering image loops of one beautiful young man with silver hair.

Girasol lowered the chair. Her toes spasmed, kinking against each other as the thrumming neural jack touched the edge of her port. The Dozr kept her breathing even. A bone-deep rasp, a meaty click, and she was synched, simulated REM brainwave flowing through a current of code, flying through wire, up and out of the shantytown apartment, flitting like a shade into Chicago's dark cityscape.

Severyn Grimes felt none of the old heat in his chest when the first round finished with a shattered nose and a shower of blood, and he realized something: the puppet shows didn't do it for him anymore.

The fighters below were massive, as always, pumped full of HGH and Taurus and various combat chemicals, sculpted by a lifetime in gravity gyms. The fight, as always, wouldn't end until their bodies were mangled heaps of broken bone and snapped tendon. Then the technicians would come and pull the digital storage cones from the slick white ports at the tops of their spines, so the puppeteers could return to their own bodies, and the puppets, if they were lucky, woke up in meat repair with a paycheck and no permanent paralysis.

It seemed almost wasteful. Severyn stroked the back of his neck, where silver hair was shorn fashionably around his own storage cone. Beneath him, the fighters hurtled from their corners, grappled, broke, and collided again. He felt nothing. Severyn's adrenaline only ever seemed to spike in boardrooms now. Primate aggression through power broking.

"I'm growing tired of this shit," he said, and his bodyguard carved a clear exit through the baying crowd. Follow-cams drifted in his direction, foregoing the match for a celebspotting opportunity: the second-wealthiest bio-businessman in Chicago, 146 years old but plugged into a beautiful young body that played well on cam. The god-like Severyn Grimes slumming at a puppet show, readying for a night of downtown debauchery? The paparazzi feed practically wrote itself.

A follow-cam drifted too close; Severyn raised one finger, and his bodyguard swatted it out of the air on the way out the door.

Girasol jolted, spiraled down to the floor. She'd drifted too close, too entranced by the geometry of his cheekbones, his slate gray eyes and full lips, his swimmer's build swathed in Armani and his graceful hands with Nokia implants glowing just under the skin. A long ways away, she was dimly aware of her body in the orthochair in the decrepit apartment. She scrawled a message across the smartpaint:

HE'S LEAVING EARLY. ARE YOUR PEOPLE READY?

"They're, shit, they're on their way. Stall him." Pierce's voice was distant, an insect hum, but she could detect the sound of nerves fraying.

Girasol jumped to another follow-cam, triggering a fizz of sparks as she seized its motor circuits. The image came in upside down: Mr. Grimes clambering into the limo, the bodyguard scanning the street. Springy red hair and a brutish face suggested Neanderthal gene-mixing. Him, they would have to get rid of.

The limousine door glided shut. From six blocks away, Girasol triggered the crude mp4 file she'd prepared—sometimes the old tricks worked best—and wormed inside the vehicle's CPU on a sine wave of sound.

Severyn vaguely recognized the song breezing through the car's sponge speakers, but outdated protest rap was a significant deviation from his usual tastes.

"Music off."

The backseat was sealed in silence. The car took an uncharacteristically long time calculating their route before finally jetting into traffic. Severyn leaned back to watch the dark street slide past his window, lit by lime green neon and the jittering ghosts of holograms. A moment later he turned to his bodyguard, who had the Loop's traffic reports scrolling across his retinas.

"Does blood excite you, Finch?"

Finch blinked, clearing his eyes back to a watery blue. "Not particularly, Mr. Grimes. Comes with the job."

"I thought having reloaded testosterone would make the world . . . Visceral again." Severyn grabbed at his testicles with a wry smile. "Maybe an old mind overwrites a young body in more ways than the technicians suspect. Maybe mortality is escapable, but old age inevitable."

"Maybe so," Finch echoed, sounding slightly uncomfortable. First-lifers often found it unsettling to be reminded they were sitting beside a man who had bought off Death itself. "Feel I'm getting old myself, sometimes."

"Maybe you'd like to turn in early," Severyn offered.

Finch shook his head. "Always up for a jaunt, Mr. Grimes. Just so long as the whorehouses are vetted."

Severyn laughed, and in that moment the limo lurched sideways and jolted to a halt. His face mashed to the cold glass of the window, bare millimeters away from an autocab that darted gracefully around them and back into its traffic algorithm. Finch straightened him out with one titanic hand.

"What the fuck was that?" Severyn asked calmly, unrumpling his tie.

"Car says there's something in the exhaust port," Finch said, retinas replaced by schematic tracery. "Not an explosive. Could just be debris."

"Do check."

"Won't be a minute, Mr. Grimes."

Finch pulled a pair of wire-veined gloves from a side compartment and opened the door, ushering in a chilly undertow, then disappeared around the rear end of the limousine. Severyn leaned back to wait, flicking alternately through merger details and airbrushed brothel advertisements in the air above his lap.

"Good evening, Mr. Grimes," the car burbled. "You've been hacked."

Severyn's nostrils flared. "I don't pay you for your sense of humor, Finch."

"I'm not joking, parasite."

Severyn froze. There was a beat of silence, then he reached for the door handle. It might as well have been stone. He pushed his palm against the sunroof and received a static charge for his trouble.

"Override," he said. "Severyn Grimes. Open doors." No response. Severyn felt his heartbeat quicken, felt a prickle of sweat on his palms. He slowly let go of the handle. "Who am I speaking to?"

"Take a look through the back window. Maybe you can figure it out."

Severyn spun, peering through the dark glass. Finch was hunched over the exhaust port, only a slice of red hair in sight. The limousine was projecting a yellow hazard banner, cleaving traffic, but as Severyn watched an unmarked van careened to a halt behind them. Masked men spilled out. Severyn thumped his fist into the glass of the window, but it was soundproof; he sent a warning spike to his security, but the car was shielded against adbombs, and theoretically against electronic intrusion, and now it was walling off his cell signal.

All he could do was watch. Finch straightened up, halfway through peeling off one smartglove when the first black-market Taser sparked electric blue. He jerked, convulsed, but still somehow managed to pull the handgun from his jacket. Severyn's fist clenched. Then the second Taser went off, painting Finch a crackling halo. The handgun dropped.

The masked men bull-rushed Finch as he crumpled, sweeping him up under the arms, and Severyn saw the wide leering smiles under their hoods: Guy Fawkes. The mask had been commandeered by various terroractivist groups over the past half-century, but Severyn knew it was the Priesthood's clearest calling card. For the first time in a long time, he felt a cold corkscrew in his stomach. He tried to put his finger on the sensation.

"He has a husband." Severyn's throat felt tight. "Two children."

"He still will," the voice replied. "He's only a wage-slave. Not a blasphemer."

Finch was a heavy man and his knees scraped along the tarmac as the Priests hauled him toward the van's sliding door. His head lolled to his chest, but Severyn saw his blue eyes were slitted open. His body tensed, then—

Finch jerked the first Priest off-balance and came up with the subcutaneous blade flashing out of his forearm, carving the man open from the hip to ribcage. Blood foamed and spat and Severyn felt what he'd missed at the puppet show, a burning flare in his chest. Finch twisted away from the other Priest's arm, eyes roving, glancing off the black glass that divided them, and then a third Taser hit him. Finch fell with his jaws spasming; a Priest's heavy boot swung into him as he toppled.

The flare died inside Severyn's pericardium. The limousine started to move.

"He should not have done that," the voice grated, as the bleeding Priest and then Finch and then the other Priests disappeared from sight. Severyn watched through the back window for a moment longer. Faced forward.

"I'll compensate for any medical costs incurred by my employee's actions," he said. "I won't tolerate any sort of retribution to his person."

"Still talking like you've got cards. And don't pretend like you care. He's an ant to you. We all are."

Severyn assessed. The voice was synthesized, distorted, but something in the cadence made him think female speaker. Uncommon, for a Priest. He gambled.

"What is your name, madam?"

"I'm a man, Parasite."

Only a split second of hesitation before the answer, but it was more than enough to confirm his guess. Severyn had staked astronomical shares on such pauses, pauses that couldn't be passed off as lag in the modern day. Signs of unsettledness. Vulnerability. It made his skin thrum. He imagined himself in a boardroom.

"No need for pretenses," Severyn said. "I merely hoped to establish a more personable base for negotiation."

"Fuck you." A warble of static. Maybe a laugh. "Fuck you. There's not going to be any negotiation. This isn't a funding op. We just caught one of the biggest parasites on the planet. The Priesthood's going to make you an example. Hook you to an autosurgeon and let it vivisect you on live feed. Burn what's left of you to ash. No negotiations."

Severyn felt the icy churn in his stomach again. Fear. He realized he'd almost missed it.

Girasol was dreaming many things at once. Even as she spoke to her captive in realtime, she perched in the limousine's electronic shielding, shooting down message after desperate message he addressed to his security detail, his bank, his associates. It took her nearly a minute to realize the messages were copypasta. Grimes was trying to trigger an overuse failsafe in his implants, generate an error message that could sneak through to Nokia.

Such a clever bastard. Girasol dipped into his implants and shut them down, leaving him half-blind and stranded in realtime. She felt a sympathetic lurch as he froze, gray eyes clearing, clipped neatly away from his data flow. If only it was that easy to reach in and drag him out of that pristine white storage cone.

"There aren't many female Priests," Grimes said, as if he hadn't noticed the severance. "I seem to recall their creed hates the birth control biochip almost as much as they hate neural puppeteering." He flashed a beatific smile that made Girasol ache. "So much love for one sort of parasite, so much ichor for the other."

"I saw the light," Girasol said curtly, even though she knew she should have stopped talking the instant he started analyzing, prying, trying to break her down.

"My body is, of course, a volunteer." Grimes draped his lean arms along the backseat. "But the Priesthood does have so many interesting ideas about what individuals should and should not do with their own flesh and bone."

"Volunteers are as bad as the parasites themselves," Girasol recited from one of Pierce's Adderall-fueled rants. "Selling their souls to a digital demon. The tainted can't enter the kingdom of heaven."

"Don't tell me a hacker riding sound waves still believes in souls." "You lost yours the second you uploaded to a storage cone."

Grimes replied with another carefully constructed probe, but Girasol's interest diverted from their conversation as Pierce's voice swelled from far away. He was shouting. Someone else was in the room. She crosschecked the limo's route against a staticky avalanche of police scanners, then dragged herself back to the orthochair, forcing her eyes open.

Through the blur of code, she saw Pierce's injured crony, the one who'd been sliced belly to sternum, being helped through the doorway. His midsection was swathed in bacterial film, but the blood that hadn't been coagulated and eaten away left a dripping carmine trail on the linoleum.

"You don't bring him *here*," Pierce grated. "You lobo, if someone saw you—"

"I'm not going to take him to a damn hospital." The man pulled off his Fawkes, revealing a pale and sweat-slick face. "I think it's, like, shallow. Didn't get any organs. But he's bleeding bad, need more cling film—"

"Where's the caveman?" Pierce snapped. "The bodyguard, where is he?"

The man waved a blood-soaked arm towards the doorway. "In the parcade. Don't worry, we put a clamp on him and locked the van." His companion moaned and he swore. "Now where's the aid kit? Come on, Pierce, he's going to, shit, he's going to bleed out. Those stairs nearly did him in."

Pierce stalked to the wall and snatched the dented white case from its hook. He caught sight of Girasol's gummy eyes half-open. "How close are you to the warehouse?" he demanded.

"You know how the Loop gets on weekends," Girasol said, feeling her tongue move inside her mouth like a phantom limb. "Fifteen. Twenty."

Pierce nodded. Chewed his lips. Agitated. "Need another shot?" "Yeah."

Girasol monitored the limo at the hazy edge of her mind as Pierce handed off the aid kit and prepped another dose of hypnotic. She thought of how soon it would be her blood on the floor, once he realized what she was doing. She thought of slate gray eyes as she watched the oily black Dozr mix with her blood, and when Pierce hit the plunger, she closed her own and plunged with it.

Severyn was methodically peeling back flooring, ruining his manicured nails, humming protest rap, when the voice came back.

"Don't bother. You won't get to the brake line that way."

He paused, staring at the miniscule tear he'd made. He climbed slowly back onto the seat and palmed open the chiller. "I was beginning to think you'd left me," he said, retrieving a glass flute.

"Still here, Parasite. Keeping you company in your final moments."

"Parasite," Severyn echoed as he poured. "You know, if it weren't for people like you, puppeteering might have never developed. Religious zealots are the ones who axed cloning, after all. Just think. If not for that, we might have been uploading to fresh blank bodies instead of those desperate enough to sell themselves whole."

He looked at his amber reflection in the flute, studying the beautiful young face he'd worn for nearly two years. He knew the disembodied hacker was seeing it too, and it was an advantage, no matter how she might try to suppress it. Humans loved beauty and underestimated youth. It was one reason Severyn used young bodies instead of the thickset middle-aged Clooneys favored by most CEOs.

"And now it's too late to go back," Severyn said, swirling his drink. "Growing a clone is expensive. Finding a volunteer is cheap." He sipped and held the stinging Macallan in his mouth.

Silence for a beat.

"You have no idea what kind of person I am."

Severyn felt his hook sink in. He swallowed his drink. "I do," he replied. "I've been thinking about it quite fucking hard, what with my impending evisceration. You're no Priest. Your familiarity with my security systems and reticence to kill my bodyguard makes me think you're an employee, former or current."

"People like you assume everyone's working for them."

"Whether you are or not, you've done enough research to know I can easily triple whatever the Priesthood is paying for your services."

"There's not going to be any negotiation. You're a dead man."

Severyn nodded, studying his drink, then slopped it out across the upholstery and smashed the f lute against the window. The crystal crunched. Severyn shook the now-jagged stem, sending small crumbs to the floor. It gleamed scalpel-sharp. Running his thumb along it raised hairs on the nape of his neck.

"What are you doing?" the voice blared.

"My hand slipped," Severyn said. "Old age." A fat droplet of blood swelled on his thumb, and he wiped it away. He wasn't one to mishandle his bodies or rent zombies for recreational suicide in drowning tanks, freefalls. No, Severyn's drive to survive had always been too strong for him to experiment with death. As he brought the edge to his throat he realized that killing himself would not be easy.

"That won't save you." Another static laugh, but this one forced. "We'll upload your storage cone to an artificial body within the day. Throw you into a pleasure doll with the sensitivity cranked to maximum. Imagine how much fun they'd have with that."

The near-panic was clarion clear, even through a synthesizer. Intuition pounded at Severyn's temples. The song was still in there, too.

"You played yourself in on a music file," Severyn said. "I searched it before you shut off my implants. 'Decapitate the state/wipe the slate/create.' Banal, but so very catchy, wasn't it? Swan song of the Anticorp Movement."

"I liked the beat."

"Several of my employees became embroiled in those protests. They were caught trying to coordinate a viral strike on my bank." Severyn pushed the point into the smooth flesh of his throat. "Nearly five years ago, now. I believe the chief conspirator was sentenced to twenty years in cryogenic storage."

"Stop it. Put that down."

"You must have wanted me to guess," Severyn continued, worming the glass gently, like a corkscrew. He felt a warm trickle down his neck. "Why keep talking, otherwise? You wanted me to know who got me in the end. This is your revenge."

"Do you even remember my name?" The voice was warped, but not by static. "And *put that down.*"

The command came so fierce and raw that Severyn's hand hesitated without his meaning to. He slowly set the stem in his lap. "Or you kept talking," he said, "because you missed hearing his voice."

"Fucking parasite." The hacker's voice was tired and suddenly brittle. "First you steal twenty years of my life and then you steal my son."

"Girasol Fletcher." There it was. Severyn leaned back, releasing a long breath. "He came to me, you know." He racked his digital memory for another name, the name of his body before it was his body. "Blake came to me."

"Bullshit. You always wanted him. Had a feed of his swim meets like a pedophile."

"I helped him. Possibly even saved him."

"You made him a puppet."

Severyn balled a wipe and dabbed at the blood on Blake's slender neck. "You left him with nothing," he said. "The money drained off to pay for your cryo. And Blake fell off, too. He was a full addict when he came to me. Hypnotics. Spending all his time in virtual dreamland. You'd know about that." He paused, but the barb drew no response. "It couldn't have been for sex fantasies. I imagine he got anything he wanted in realtime. I think maybe he was dreaming his family whole again."

Silence. Severyn felt a dim guilt, but he pushed through. Survival.

"He was desperate when he found me," Severyn continued. "I told him I wanted his body. Fifteen-year contract, insured for all organic damage. It's been keeping your cryo paid off, and when the contract's up he'll be comfortable for the rest of his life."

"Don't. Act." A stream of static. "Like you did him a favor."

Severyn didn't reply for a moment. He looked at the window, but the glass was still black, opaqued. "I'm not being driven to an execution, am I?"

Girasol wound the limousine through the grimy labyrinth of the industrial district, guiding it past the agreed-upon warehouse where a half-dozen Priests were awaiting the delivery of Severyn Grimes, Chicago's most notorious parasite. Using the car's external camera, she saw the lookout's confused face emerging from behind his mask.

On the internal camera, she couldn't stop looking into Blake's eyes, hoping they would be his own again soon.

"There's a hydrofoil waiting on the docks," she said through the limousine speakers. "I hired a technician to extract you. Paid him extra to drop your storage cone in the harbor."

"The Priesthood wasn't open to negotiations concerning the body."

Far away, Girasol felt the men clustered around her, watching her prone body like predatory birds. She could almost smell the fast-food grease and sharp chemical sweat. "No," she said dully. "Volunteers are as bad as the parasites themselves. Blake sold his soul to a digital demon. To you."

"When they find out you betrayed their interests?"

Girasol considered. "Pierce will rape me," she said. "Maybe some of the others, too. Then they'll pull some amateur knife-and-pliers interrogation shit, thinking it's some kind of conspiracy. And then they may. Or may not. Kill me." Her voice was steady until the penultimate word. She calculated distance to the pier. It was worth it. It was worth it. Blake would be free, and Grimes would be gone.

"You could skype in CPD."

Girasol had already considered. "No. With what I pulled to get out of the freeze, if they find me I'm back in permanently."

"Skype them in to wherever my bodyguard is being held."

He was insistent about the caveman. Almost as if he gave a shit. Girasol felt a small slink of self-doubt before she remembered Grimes had amassed his wealth by manipulating emotions. He'd been a puppeteer long before he uploaded. Still trying to pull her strings.

"I would," Girasol said. "But he's here with me."

Grimes paused, frowning. Girasol zoomed. She'd missed Blake's face so much, the immaculate bones of it, the wide brow and curved lips. She could still remember him chubby and always laughing.

"Can you contact him without the Priests finding out?" Grimes asked.

Girasol fluttered back to the apartment. She was guillotining texts and voice-calls as they poured in from the warehouse, keeping Pierce in the dark for as long as possible, but one of them would slip through before long. She triangulated on the locked van using the parcade security cams. "Maybe," she said.

"If you can get him free, he might be able to help you. I have a non-duress passcode. I could give it to you." Grimes tongued the edges of his bright white teeth. "In exchange, you call off the extraction."

"Thought you might try to make a deal."

"It is what I do." Grimes's lips thinned. "You lack long-term perspective, Ms. Fletcher. Common enough among first-lifers. The notion of sacrificing yourself to free your progeny must seem exceptionally noble and very fucking romantic to you. But if the Priesthood does murder you, Blake wakes up with nobody. Nothing. Again."

"Not nothing," Girasol said reflexively.

"The money you were paid for this job?" Grimes suggested. "He'll have to go into hiding for as long as my disappearance is under investigation. The sort of people who can help him lay low are the sort of people who'll have him back on Sandman or Dozr before the month is out. He might even decide to go puppet again."

Girasol's fury boiled over, and she nearly lost her hold on the steering column. "He made a mistake. Once. He would never agree to that again."

"Even if you get off with broken bones, you'll be a wanted fugitive as soon as Correctional try to thaw you for a physical and find whatever suckerfish the Priests convinced to take your pod." Grimes flattened his hands on his knees. "What I'm proposing is that you cancel the extraction. My bodyguard helps you escape. We meet up to renegotiate terms. I could have your charges dropped, you know. I could even rewrite Blake's contract."

"You really don't want to die, do you?" Girasol's suspicion battled her fear, her fear of Pierce and his pliers and his grinning mask. "You're digital. You saying you don't have a backup of your personality waiting in the wings?"

She checked the limo's external cams and swore. A carload of Priests from the warehouse was barreling up the road behind them, guns already poking through the windows. She reached for the in-built speed limits and deleted them.

"I do," Grimes conceded, bracing himself as the limo accelerated. "But he's not me, is he?"

Girasol resolved. She bounced back to the apartment, where the Priests were growing agitated. Pierce was shaking her arm, even though he should have known better than to shake someone on a deep slice, asking her how close she was to the warehouse. She flashed TWO MINUTES across the smartpaint. Then she found the electronic signature of the clamp that was keeping Grimes's bodyguard paralyzed inside the van. She hoped he hadn't suffered any long-term nerve damage. Hoped he would still move like quicksilver with that bioblade of his.

"Fair enough," Girasol said, stretching herself thin, reaching into the empty parcade. "All right. Tell me the passcode and I'll break him out."

Finch was focused on breathing slowly and ignoring the blooming damp spot where piss had soaked through his trousers. The police-issue clamp they'd stuck to his shoulder made most other activities impossible. Finch had experience with the spidery devices. They were designed to react to any arousal in the central nervous system by sending a paralyzing jolt through the would-be agitator's muscles. More struggle, more jolt. More panic, more jolt.

The only thing to do with a clamp was relax and not get upset about anything. Finch used the downtime to reflect on his situation. Mr. Grimes had fallen victim to a planned ambush, that much was obvious. Electronic intrusion, supposedly impossible, must have been behind the limo's exhaust port diagnostic.

And now Mr. Grimes was being driven to an unknown location, while Finch was lying on the floor of a van with donair wrappers and rumpled anti-puppetry tracts for company. A decade ago, he might have been paranoid enough to think he was a target himself. Religious extremists had not taken kindly to Neanderthal gene mixing at first, but they also had a significant demographic overlap with people overjoyed to see pale-faced and blue-eyed athletes dominating the NFL and NBA again.

Even the flailing Bulls front office had managed to sign that half-thally power forward from Duke. Finch couldn't remember his name. Cletus something. Sometimes Finch wished he'd kept going with football, but his fiancé had cared more about intact gray matter than money. Of course, he hadn't been thrilled when Finch chose security as an alternative source of income, but . . .

In a distant corner of his mind, Finch felt the clamp loosening. He kept breathing steadily, kept his heartbeat slow, kept thinking about anything but the clamp loosening. Cletus Rivas. That was the kid's name. He'd pulled down twenty-six rebounds in the match-up against Arizona. Finch brought his hand slowly, slowly up toward his shoulder. Just to scratch. Just because he was itchy. Closer. Closer.

His fingers were millimeters from the clamp's burnished surface when the van's radio blared to life. His hand jerked; the clamp jolted. Finch tried to curse through his lockjaw and came up with mostly spit. So close.

"Listen up," came a voice from the speaker.

Finch had no alternative.

"I can turn off the clamp and unlock the van, but I need you to help me in exchange," the voice said. "I'm in apartment 401, sitting in an orthochair, deep sliced. There are three men in the room. The one you cut up, the one who Tasered you, and one more. They've still got the Tasers, and the last one has a handgun in an Adidas bag. I don't know where your gun is."

Finch felt the clamp fall away and went limp all over. His muscles ached deep like he'd done four hours in the weight room on methamphetamine—a bad idea, he knew from experience. He reached to massage his shoulder with one trembling hand.

"Grimes told me a non-duress passcode to give you," the voice continued. "So you'd know to trust me. It's Atticus."

Finch had almost forgotten that passcode. He'd wikied to find out why it made Mr. Grimes smirk but lost interest halfway through a text on Roman emperors.

"You have to hurry. They might kill me soon."

Hurrying did not sound like something Finch could do. He took three tries to push himself upright on gelatin arms. "Is Mr. Grimes safe?" he asked thickly, tongue sore and swollen from him biting it.

"He's on a leisurely drive to a waiting ferry. He'll be just fine. If you help me."

Finch crawled forward, taking a moment to drive one kneecap into the inactive clamp for a satisfying crunch, then hoisted himself between the two front seats and palmed the glove compartment. His Mulcher was waiting inside, still assembled, still loaded. He was dealing with some real fucking amateurs. The handgun molded to his grip, licking his thumb for DNA confirmation like a friendly cat. He was so glad to find it intact he nearly licked it back.

"Please. Hurry."

"Apartment 401, three targets, one incapacitated, three weapons, one lethal," Finch recited. He tested his wobbling legs as the van door slid open. Crossing the dusty floor of the parcade looked like crossing the Gobi desert.

"One other thing. You'll have to take the stairs. Elevator's out."

Finch was hardly even surprised. He stuck the Mulcher in his waistband and started to hobble.

Half the city away, Severyn wished, for the first time, that he'd had his cars equipped with seatbelts instead of only impact foam. Trying to stay seated while the limousine slewed corners and caromed down alleyways was impossible. He was thrown from one side to the other with every jolting turn. His kidnapper had finally cleared the windows and he saw, in familiar flashes, grimy red Southside brick and corrugated steel. The decades hadn't changed it much, except now the blue-green blooms of graffiti were animated.

"Pier's just up ahead. I told my guy there's been a change of plans." Girasol's voice was strained to breaking. Too many places at once, Severyn suspected.

"How long before the ones you're with know what's going on?" he asked, bracing himself against the back window to peer at their pursuers. One Priest was driving manually, and wildly. He was hunched over the steering wheel, trying to conflate what he'd learned in virtual racing sims with reality. His partner in the passenger's seat was hanging out the window with some sort of recoilless rifle, trying to aim.

"A few minutes, max."

A dull crack spiderwebbed the glass a micrometer from Severyn's left eyeball. He snapped his head back as a full barrage followed—smashing like a hailstorm into the reinforced window. By the time they burst from the final alley, aligned for a dead sprint toward the hazard-sign-decorated pier, the limousine's rear was riddled with bullet holes. Up ahead, Severyn could make out the shape of a hydrofoil sliding out into the oil-slick water. The technician had lost his nerve.

"He's pulling away," Severyn snapped, ducking instinctively as another round raked across the back of the car with a sound of crunching metal.

"Told him to. You're going to have to swim for it."

Severyn's stomach churned. "I don't swim."

"You don't swim? You were All-State."

"Blake was." Severyn pried off his Armani loafers, peeled off his jacket, as the limousine rattled over the metal crosshatch of the pier. "I never learned."

"Just trust the muscle memory." Girasol's voice was taut and pleading. "He knows what to do. Just let him. Let his body."

They skidded to a halt at the lip of the pier. Severyn put his hand on the door and found it blinking blue, unlocked at last.

"If you can tell him things." She sounded ragged now. Exhausted. "Tell him I love him. If you can."

Severyn considered lying for a moment. A final push to solidify his position. "It doesn't work that way," he said instead, and hauled the door open as the Priests screeched to a stop behind him. He vaulted out of the limo, assaulted by unconditioned air, night wind, the smell of brine and oiled machinery.

Severyn sucked his lungs full and ran full-bore, feeling a hurricane of adrenaline that no puppet show or whorehouse could have coaxed from his glands. His bare feet pounded the cold pier, shouts came from behind him, and then he hurled himself into the grimy water. An ancient panic shot through him as ice flooded his ears, his eyes, his nose. He felt his muscles seize. He remembered, in a swath of old memory code, that he'd nearly drowned in Michigan once.

Then nerve pathways that he'd never carved for himself fired, and he found himself cutting up to the surface. His head broke the water; he twisted and saw the gaggle of Priests at the edge of the water, Fawkes masks grinning at him even as they cursed and reloaded the rifle. Severyn grinned back, then pulled away with muscles moving in perfect synch, cupped hands biting the water with every stroke.

The slap of his body on the icy surface, the tug of his breath, the water in his ears—alive, alive, alive. The whine of a bullet never came. Severyn slopped over the side of the hydrofoil a moment later. Spread-eagled on the slick deck, chest working like a bellows, he started to laugh.

"That was some dramatic shit," came a voice from above him.

Severyn squinted up and saw the technician, a twitchy-looking man with gray whiskers and extra neural ports in his shaved skull. There was a tranq gun in his hand.

"There's been a change of plans," Severyn coughed. "Regarding the extraction."

The technician nodded, leveling the tranq. "Girasol told me you'd say that. Said you're a world-class bullshit artist. I'd expect no less from Severyn fucking Grimes."

Severyn's mouth fished open and shut. Then he started to laugh again, a long gurgling laugh, until the tranq stamped through his wet skin and sent him to sleep.

Girasol saw hot white sparks when they ripped her out of the orthochair and realized it was sheer luck they hadn't shut off her brain stem. You didn't tear someone out of a deep slice. Not after two hits of high-grade Dozr. She hoped, dimly, that she wasn't going to go blind in a few days' time.

"You bitch." Pierce's breath was scalding her face. He must have taken off his mask. "You *bitch*. Why? Why would you do that?"

Girasol found it hard to piece the words together. She was still out of body, still imagining a swerving limousine and marauding cell signals and electric sheets of code. Her hand blurred into view, and she saw her veins were taut and navy blue. She'd stretched herself thinner than she'd ever done before, but she hadn't managed to stop the skype from the end of the pier. And now Pierce knew what had happened.

"Why did you help him get away?"

The question came with a knee pushed into her chest, under her ribs. Girasol thought she felt her lungs collapse in on themselves. Her head was coming clear. She'd been a god only moments ago, gliding through circuitry and sound waves, but now she was small, and drained, and crushed against the stained linoleum flooring.

"I'm going to cut your eyeballs out," Pierce was deciding. "I'm going to do them slow. You traitor. You puppet."

Girasol remembered her last flash from the limousine's external cams: Blake diving into the dirty harbor with perfect form, even if Grimes didn't know it. She was sure he'd make it to the hydrofoil. It was barely a hundred meters. She held onto the novocaine thought as Pierce's knife snicked and locked.

"What did he promise you? Money?"

"Fuck off," Girasol choked.

Pierce was straddling her now, the weight of him bruising her pelvis. She felt his hands scrabbling at her zipper. The knife tracing along her thigh. An old panic kicked at her.

"Oh," she said. "You want that kiss now?"

His backhand smashed across her face, and she tasted copper. Girasol closed her eyes tight. She thought of the hydrofoil slicing through the bay. The technician leaning over Blake's prone body with his instruments, pulling the parasite up and away, reawakening a brain two years dormant. She'd left him messages. Hundreds of them. Just in case.

"Did he promise to fuck you?" Pierce snarled, finally sliding her pants down her bony hips. "Was that it?"

The door chimed. Pierce froze, and in her peripheral Girasol could see the other Priests' heads turning toward the entryway. Nobody ever used the chime. Girasol wondered how Grimes's bodyguard could possibly be so stupid, then noticed that a neat row of splintery holes had appeared all across the breadth of the door.

Pierce put his hand up to his head, where a bullet had clipped the top of his scalp, carving a furrow of matted hair and stringy flesh. It came away bright red. He stared down at Girasol, angry, confused, and the next slug blew his skull open like a shattering vase.

Girasol watched numbly as the bodyguard let himself inside. His fiery hair was slick with sweat and his face was drawn pale, but he moved around the room with practiced efficiency, putting two more bullets into each of the injured Priests before collapsing to the floor himself. He tucked his hands under his head and exhaled.

"One hundred and twelve," he said. "I counted."

Girasol wriggled out from under Pierce and vomited. Wiped her mouth. "Repairman's in tomorrow." She stared down at the intact side of Pierce's face.

"Where's Mr. Grimes?"

"Nearly docking by now. But he's not in a body." Girasol pushed damp hair out of her face. "He's been extracted. His storage cone is safe. Sealed. That was our deal."

The bodyguard was studying her intently, red brows knitted. "Let's get going, then." He picked his handgun up off the floor. "Gray eyes," he remarked. "Those contacts?"

"Yeah," Girasol said. "Contacts." She leaned over to give Pierce a bloody peck on the cheek, then got shakily to her feet and led the way out the door.

Severyn Grimes woke up feeling rested. His last memory was laughing on the deck of a getaway boat, but the soft cocoon of sheets made him suspect he'd since been moved. Something else had changed, too. His proprioception was sending an avalanche of small error reports. Limbs no longer the correct length. New body proportions. By the feel of it, he was in something artificial.

"Mr. Grimes?"

"Finch." Severyn tried to grimace at the tinny sound of his voice, but the facial myomers were relatively fixed. "The *mise á jour,* please."

Finch's craggy features loomed above him, blank and professional as ever. "Girasol Fletcher had you extracted from her son's body. After we met her technician, I transported your storage cone here to Lumen Technohospital for diagnostics. Your personality and memories came through completely intact and they stowed you in an interim avatar to speak with your lawyers. Of which there's a horde, sir. Waiting in the lobby."

"Police involvement?" Severyn asked, trying for a lower register.

"There are a few Priests in custody, sir," Finch said. "Girasol Fletcher and her son are long gone. CPD requested access to the enzyme trackers in Blake's body. It looks like she hasn't found a way to shut them off yet. Could triangulate and maybe find them if it happens in the next few hours."

Severyn blinked, and his eyelashes scraped his cheeks. He tried to frown. "What the fuck am I wearing, Finch?"

"The order was put in for a standard male android." Finch shrugged. "But there was an electronic error."

"Pleasure doll?" Severyn guessed. Electronic error seemed unlikely.

His bodyguard nodded stonily. "You can be uploaded in a fresh volunteer within twenty-four hours," he said. "They've done up a list of candidates. I can link it."

Severyn shook his head. "Don't bother," he said. "I think I want something clone-grown. See my own face in the mirror again."

"And the trackers?"

Severyn thought of Blake and Girasol tearing across the map, heading somewhere sun-drenched where their money could stretch and their faces couldn't be plucked off the news feeds. She would do small-time hackwork. Maybe he would start to swim again.

"Shut them off from our end," Severyn said. "I want a bit of a challenge when I hunt that bitch down and have her uploaded to a waste disposal."

"Will do, Mr. Grimes."

But Finch left with a ghost of a smile on his face, and Severyn suspected his employee knew he was lying.

Peter Watts (www.rifters.com) is a former marine biologist who clings to some shred of scientific rigor by appending technical bibliographies onto his novels. His debut novel (*Starfish*) was a *New York Times* Notable Book, while his fourth (*Blindsight*)—a rumination on the utility of consciousness which has become a required text in undergraduate courses ranging from philosophy to neuroscience—was a finalist for numerous North American genre awards and winner of numerous awards overseas. His shorter work has won the Shirley Jackson and a Hugo Awards.

ZEROS

Peter Watts

Asante goes out screaming. Hell is an echo chamber, full of shouts and seawater and clanking metal. Monstrous shadows move along the bulkheads; meshes of green light writhe on every surface. The Sāḥilites rise from the moon pool like creatures from some bright lagoon, firing as they emerge; Rashida's middle explodes in dark mist and her top half topples onto the deck. Kito's still dragging himself toward the speargun on the drying rack—as though some antique fish-sticker could ever fend off these monsters with their guns and their pneumatics and their little cartridges that bury themselves deep in your flesh before showing you what five hundred unleashed atmospheres do to your insides.

It's more than Asante's got. All he's got is his fists.

He uses them. Launches himself at the nearest Sāḥilite as she lines up Kito in her sights, swings wildly as the deck groans and drops and cants sideways. Seawater breaches the lip of the moon pool, cascades across the plating. Asante flails at the intruder on his way down. Her shot goes wide. A spiderweb blooms across the viewport; a thin gout of water erupts from its center even as the glass tries to heal itself from the edges in.

The last thing Asante sees is the desert hammer icon on the Sāḥilite's diveskin before she blows him away.

Five Years

Running water. Metal against metal. Clanks and gurgles, lowered voices, the close claustrophobic echo of machines in the middle distance.

Asante opens his eyes.

He's still in the wet room; its ceiling blurs and clicks into focus, plates and struts and Kito's stupid graffiti (*All Tautologies Are Tautologies*) scratched into the paint. Green light still wriggles dimly across the biosteel, but the murderous energy's been bled out of it.

He tries to turn his head, and can't. He barely feels his own body—as though it were made of ectoplasm, some merest echo of solid flesh fading into nonexistence somewhere around the waist.

An insect's head on a human body looms over him. It speaks with two voices: English, and an overlapping echo in Twi: "Easy, soldier. Relax."

A woman's voice, and a chip one.

Not Sāḥilite. But armed. Dangerous.

Not a soldier he wants to say, wants to *shout*. It's never a good thing to be mistaken for any sort of combatant along the west coast. But he can't even whisper. He can't feel his tongue.

Asante realizes that he isn't breathing.

The Insect woman (a diveskin, he sees now: her mandibles an electrolysis rig, her compound eyes a pair of defraction goggles) retrieves a tactical scroll from beyond his field of view and unrolls it a half-meter from his face. She mutters an incantation and it flares softly to life, renders a stacked pair of keyboards: English on top, Twi beneath.

"Don't try to talk," she says in both tongues. "Just look at the letters."

He focuses on the N: it brightens. O. T. The membrane offers up predictive spelling, speeds the transition from sacc' to script:

NOT SOLDIER FISH FARMER

"Sorry." She retires the translator; the Twi keys flicker and disappear. "Figure of speech. What's your name?"

KODJO ASANTE

She pushes the defractors onto her forehead, unlatches the mandibles. They fall away and dangle to one side. She's white underneath.

IS KITO

"I'm sorry, no. Everyone's dead."

Everyone else, he thinks, and imagines Kito mocking him one last time for insufferable pedantry.

"Got him." Man's voice, from across the compartment. "Kodjo Asante,

Takoradi. Twenty-eight, bog-standard aqua—wait; combat experience. Two years with GAF."

Asante's eyes dart frantically across the keyboard: ONLY FARMER NOT

"No worries, mate." She lays down a reassuring hand; he can only assume it comes to rest somewhere on his body. "Everyone's seen combat hereabouts, right? You're sitting on the only reliable protein stock in three hundred klicks. Stands to reason you're gonna have to defend it now and again."

"Still." A shoulder patch comes into view as she turns toward the other voice: WestHem Alliance. "We could put him on the list."

"If you're gonna do it, do it fast. Surface contact about two thousand meters out, closing."

She turns back to Asante. "Here's the thing. We didn't get here in time. We're not supposed to be here at all, but our CO got wind of Sally's plans and took a little humanitarian initiative, I guess you could say. We showed up in time to scare 'em off and light 'em up, but you were all dead by then."

I WASN'T

"Yeah, Kodjo, you too. All dead."

YOU BROUGHT ME BA

"No."

BUT

"We gave your brain a jump start, that's all. You know how you can make a leg twitch when you pass a current through it? You know what *galvanic* means, Kodjo?"

"He's got a Ph.D. in molecular marine ecology," says her unseen colleague. "I'm guessing yes."

"You can barely feel anything, am I right? Body like a ghost? We didn't reboot the rest of you. You're just getting residual sensations from nerves that don't know they're dead yet. You're a brain in a box, Kodjo. You're running on empty.

"But here's the thing: you don't *have* to be."

"Hurry it up, Cat. We got ten minutes, tops."

She glances over her shoulder, back again. "We got a rig on the *Levi Morgan*, patch you up and keep you on ice until we get home. And we got a rig *there* that'll work goddamn miracles, make you better'n new. But it ain't cheap, Kodjo. Pretty much breaks the bank every time we do it."

DON'T HAVE MONEY

"Don't want *money*. We want you to work for us. Five-year tour, maybe less depending on how the tech works out. Then you go on your way, nice fat bank balance, whole second chance. Easy gig, believe me. You're just a passenger in your own body for the hard stuff. Even boot camp's mostly autonomic. Real accelerated program."

NOT WESTHEM

"You're not Hegemon either, not any more. You're not much of anything but rotting meat hooked up to a pair of jumper cables. I'm offering you salvation, mate. You can be Born Again."

"Wrap it the fuck *up*, Cat. They're almost on top of us."

"'Course if you're not interested, I can just pull the plug. Leave you the way we found you."

NO PLEASE YES

"Yes what, Kodjo? Yes pull the plug? Yes leave you behind? You need to be specific about this. We're negotiating a contract here."

YES BORN AGAIN YES 5 YEAR TOUR

He wonders at this shiver of hesitation, this voice whispering *maybe dead is better*. Perhaps it's because he *is* dead; maybe all those suffocating endocrine glands just aren't up to the task of flooding his brain with the warranted elixir of fear and desperation and *survival at any cost*. Maybe being dead means never having to give a shit.

He does, though. He may be dead but his glands aren't, not yet. He didn't say no.

He wonders if anyone ever has.

"Glory Hallelujah!" Cat proclaims, reaching offstage for some unseen control. And just before everything goes black:

"Welcome to the Zombie Corps."

Savior Machine

That's not what they call it, though.

"Be clear about one thing. There's no good reason why any operation should ever put boots in the battlefield."

They call it *ZeroS*. Strangely, the Z does not stand for *Zombie*.

"There's no good reason why any competent campaign should involve a battlefield in the first place. That's what economic engineering and Cloud Control are for."

The S doesn't even stand for *Squad*.

"If they fail, that's what drones and bots and TAI are for."

Zero Sum. Or as NCOIC Silano puts it, *A pun, right? Cogito ergo*. Better than *The Spaz Brigade*, which was Garin's suggestion.

Asante's in Tactical Orientation, listening to an artificial instructor that he'd almost accept as human but for the fact that it doesn't sound bored to death.

"There's only one reason you'll ever find yourselves called on deck, and that's if everyone has fucked up so completely at conflict resolution that there's nothing left in the zone but a raging shitstorm."

Asante's also running up the side of a mountain. It's a beautiful route, twenty klicks of rocks and pines and mossy deadfall. There might be more green growing things on this one slope than in the whole spreading desert of northern Africa. He wishes he could see it.

"Your very presence means the mission has already failed; your job is to salvage what you can from the wreckage."

He can't see it, though. He can't see much of anything. Asante's been blind since Reveille.

"Fortunately for you, economics and Cloud Control and tactical AI fail quite a lot."

The blindness isn't total. He still sees light, vague shapes in constant motion. It's like watching the world through wax paper. The eyes *jiggle* when you're a Passenger. Of course the eyes always jiggle, endlessly hopping from one momentary focus to the next—*saccades*, they're called—but your brain usually edits out those motions, splices the clear bits together in post to serve up an illusion of continuity.

Not up here, though. Up here the sacc rate goes through the roof and nothing gets lost. Total data acquisition. To Asante it's all blizzard and blur, but that's okay. There's something in here with him that can see just fine: his arms and legs are moving, after all, and Kodjo Asante isn't moving them.

His other senses work fine; he feels the roughness of the rope against his palms as he climbs the wall, smells the earth and pine needles bedding the trail. Still tastes a faint hint of copper from that bite on the inside of his cheek a couple klicks back. He hears with utmost clarity the voice on his audio link. His inner zombie sucks all that back too, but eardrums don't saccade. Tactile nerves don't hop around under the flesh. Just the eyes: that's how you tell. That and the fact that your whole body's been possessed by Alien Hand Syndrome.

He calls it his Evil Twin. It's a name first bestowed by his Dad, after catching eight-year-old Kodjo sleepwalking for the third time in a week. Asante made the mistake of mentioning that once to the squad over breakfast. He's still trying to live it down.

Now he tries for the hell of it, wills himself to *stop* for just an instant. ET runs and leaps and crawls as it has for the past two hours, unnervingly autonomous. That's the retrosplenial bypass they burned into his neocortex a month ago, a little dropgate to decouple *mind* from *self*. Just one of the mods they've etched into him with neural lace and nanotube mesh and good old-fashioned zap'n'tap. Midbrain tweaks to customize ancient prey-stalking routines. An orbitofrontal damper to ensure behavioral compliance (*can't have your better half deciding to keep the keys when you want them back*, as Maddox puts it).

His scalp itches with fresh scars. His head moves with a disquieting inertia, as if weighed down by a kilogram of lead and not a few bits of arsenide and carbon. He doesn't understand a tenth of it. Hasn't quite come to grips with life after death. But dear God, how *wonderful* it is to be so strong. He feels like this body could take on a whole platoon single-handed.

Sometimes he can feel this way for five or ten whole minutes before remembering the names of other corpses who never got in on the deal.

Without warning ET dances to one side, brings its arms up and suddenly Asante can *see*.

Just for a millisecond, a small clear break in a sea of fog: a Lockheed Pit Bull cresting the granite outcropping to his left, legs spread, muzzle spinning to bear. In the next instant Asante's blind again, recoil vibrating along his arm like a small earthquake. His body hasn't even broken stride.

"Ah. Target acquisition," the instructor remarks. "Enjoy the view." It takes this opportunity to summarize the basics—target lock's the only time when the eyes focus on a single point long enough for passengers to look out—before segueing into a spiel on line-of-sight networking.

Asante isn't sure what the others are hearing. Tiwana, the only other raw recruit, is probably enduring the same 101 monologue. Kalmus might have moved up to field trauma by now. Garin's on an engineering track. Maddox has told Asante that he'll probably end up in bioweapons, given his background.

It takes nineteen months to train a field-ready specialist. ZeroS do it in seven.

Asante's legs have stopped moving. On all sides he hears the sound of heavy breathing. Lieutenant Metzinger's voice tickles the space between his ears: "Passengers, you may enter the cockpit."

The switch is buried in the visual cortex and tied to the power of imagination. They call it a *mandala*. Each recruit chooses their own and keeps it secret; no chance of a master key for some wily foe to drop onto a billboard in the heat of battle. Not even the techs know the patterns, the implants were conditioned on double-blind trial-and-error. *Something personal*, they said. *Something unique, easy to visualize.*

Asante's mandala is a sequence of four words in sans serif font. He summons it now—

ALL TAUTOLOGIES
ARE TAUTOLOGIES

—and the world clicks back into sudden, jarring focus. He stumbles, though he wasn't moving.

Right on cue, his left hand starts twitching.

They're halfway up the mountain, in a sloping sunny meadow. There are *flowers* here. Insects. Everything smells alive. Silano raises trembling arms to the sky. Kalmus flumps on the grass, recovering from exertions barely felt when better halves were in control, exertions that have left them weak and wasted despite twice-normal mito counts and AMPK agonists and a dozen other tweaks to put them in the upper tail of the upper tail. Acosta drops beside her, grinning at the sunshine. Garin kicks at a punky log and an actual goddamn *snake* slithers into the grass, a ribbon of yellow and black with a flickering tongue.

Tiwana's at Asante's shoulder, as scarred and bald as he is. "Beautiful, eh?" Her right eye's a little off-kilter; Asante resists the impulse to stare by focusing on the bridge of her nose.

"Not beautiful enough to make up for two hours with a hood over my head." That's Saks, indulging in some pointless bitching. "Would it kill them to give us a video feed?"

"Or even just put us to sleep," Kalmus grumbles. They both know it's not that simple. The brain's a tangle of wires looping from basement to attic and back again; turn off the lights in the living room and your furnace might stop working. Even pay-per-view's a nonstarter. In theory, there's no reason why they couldn't bypass those jiggling eyes entirely—pipe a camera feed directly to the cortex—but their brains are already so stuffed with implants that there isn't enough real estate left over for nonessentials.

That's what Maddox says, anyway.

"I don't really give a shit," Acosta's saying. The tic at the corner of his mouth makes his grin a twitchy, disconcerting thing. "I'd put up with twice the offline time if there was always a view like this at the end of it." Acosta lives for any scrap of nature he can find; his native Guatemala lost most of its canopy to firestorm carousels back in '42.

"So what's in it for you?" Tiwana asks.

It takes a moment for Asante to realize the question's for him. "Excuse me?"

"Acosta's nature-boy. Kalmus thinks she's gonna strike it rich when they declassify the tech." This is news to Asante. "Why'd *you* sign up?"

He doesn't quite know how to answer. Judging by his own experience, ZeroS is not something you *sign up* for. ZeroS is something that finds you.

It's an odd question, a private question. It brings up things he'd rather not dwell upon.

It brings up things he already dwells on too much.

"Ah—"

Thankfully, Maddox chooses that moment to radio up from Côté: "Okay, everybody. Symptom check. Silano."

The Corporal looks at his forearms. "Pretty good. Less jumpy than normal."

"Kalmus."

"I've got, ah, ah . . ." She stammers, struggles, finally spits in frustration. "*Fuck.*"

"I'll just put down the usual aphasia," Maddox says. "Garin."

"Vision flickers every five, ten minutes."

"That's an improvement."

"Gets better when I exercise. Better blood flow, maybe."

"Interesting," Maddox says. "Tiwan—"

"*I see you God I see you!*"

Saks is on the ground, writhing. His eyes roll in their sockets. His fingers claw handfuls of earth. "*I see!*" he cries, and lapses into gibberish. His head thrashes. Spittle flies from his mouth. Tiwana and Silano move in but the audio link crackles with the voice of God, "Stand away! Everyone stand back *now!*" and everyone obeys because God speaks with the voice of Lieutenant David Metzinger and you do not want to fuck with *him*. God's breath is blowing down from Heaven, from the rotors of a medical chopper beating the air with impossible silence even though they all see it now, they all see it, there's no need for stealth mode there never was it's always there, just out of sight, just in case.

Saks has stopped gibbering. His face is a rictus, his spine a drawn bow. The chopper lands, its *whup whup whup* barely audible even ten meters away. It vomits medics and a stretcher and glossy black easter-egg drones with jointed insect legs folded to their bellies. The ZeroS step back; the medics close in and block the view.

Metzinger again: "Okay, meat sacks. Everyone into the back seat. Return to Côté."

Silano turns away, eyes already jiggling in their sockets. Tiwana and Kalmus go over a moment later. Garin slaps Asante's back on the way out— "Gotta go, man. Happens, you know?"—and vanishes into his own head.

The chopper lifts Saks into the heavens.

"Private Asante! *Now!*"

He stands alone in the clearing, summons his mandala, falls into blindness. His body turns. His legs move. Something begins to run him downhill. The artificial instructor, always sensitive to context, begins a lecture about dealing with loss on the battlefield.

It's all for the best, he knows. It's safest to be a passenger at times like this. All these glitches, these—side-effects: they never manifest in zombie mode.

Which makes perfect sense. That being where they put all the money.

Station To Station

Sometimes he still wakes in the middle of the night, shocked back to consciousness by the renewed knowledge that he still exists—as if his death was some near-miss that didn't really sink in until days or weeks afterward, leaving him weak in the knees and gasping for breath. He catches himself calling his mandala, a fight/flight reaction to threat stimuli long-since expired. He stares at the ceiling, forces calm onto panic, takes comfort from the breathing of his fellow recruits. Tries not think about Kito and Rashida. Tries not to think at all.

Sometimes he finds himself in the Commons, alone but for the inevitable drone hovering just around the corner, ready to raise alarms and inject drugs should he suffer some delayed and violent reaction to any of a hundred recent mods. He watches the world through one of CFB Côté's crippled terminals (they can surf, but never send). He slips through wires and fiberop, bounces off geosynchronous relays all the way back to Ghana: satcams down on the dizzying Escher arcology of the Cape Universitas hubs, piggybacks on drones wending through Makola's East, marvels anew at the giant gengineered snails—big as a centrifuge, some of them—that first ignited his passion for biology when he was six. He haunts familiar streets where the kenkey and fish always tasted better when the Chinese printed them, even though the recipes must have been copied from the locals. The glorious chaos of the street drummers during Adai.

He never seeks out friends or family. He doesn't know if it's because he's not ready, or because he has already moved past them. He only knows not to awaken things that have barely gone to sleep.

Zero Sum. A new life. Also a kind of game used, more often than not, to justify armed conflict.

Also *Null Existence.* If your tastes run to the Latin.

They loom over a drowning subdivision long-abandoned to the rising waters of Galveston Bay: cathedral-sized storage tanks streaked with rust and ruin, twelve-story filtration towers, masses of twisting pipe big enough to walk through.

Garin sidles up beside him. "Looks like a crab raped an octopus."

"Your boys seem twitchy," the Sheriff says. (Asante clenches his fist to control the tremor.) "They hopped on something?"

Metzinger ignores the question. "Have they made any demands?"

"Usual. Stop the rationing or they blow it up." The Sheriff shakes his head, moves to mop his brow, nearly punches himself in the face when his decrepit Bombardier exoskeleton fratzes and overcompensates. "Everything's gone to shit since the Edwards dried up."

"They respond to a water shortage by blowing up a desalination facility?"

The Sheriff snorts. "Folks always make sense where you come from, Lieutenant?"

They reviewed the plant specs down to the rivets on the way here. Or at least their zombies did, utterly silent, borrowed eyes flickering across video feeds and backgrounders that Asante probably wouldn't have grasped even if he *had* been able to see them. All Asante knows—by way of the impoverished briefings Metzinger doles out to those back in Tourist Class—is that the facility was bought from Qatar back when paint still peeled and metal still rusted, when digging viscous fossils from the ground left you rich enough to buy the planet. And that it's falling into disrepair, now that none of those things are true anymore.

Pretty much a microcosm of the whole TExit experience, he reflects.

"They planned it out," the Sheriff admits. "Packed a shitload of capacitors in there with 'em, hooked 'em to jennies, banked 'em in all the right places. We send in quads, EMP just drops 'em." He glances back over his shoulder, to where—if you squint hard enough—a heat-shimmer rising from the asphalt might almost assume the outline of a resting Chinook transport. "Probably risky using exos, unless they're hardened."

"We won't be using exos."

"Far as we can tell some of 'em are dug in by the condensers, others right next to the heat exchangers. We try to microwave 'em out, all the pipes explode. Might as well blow the place ourselves."

"Firepower?"

"You name it. Sig Saurs, Heckler-Kochs, Maesushis. I think one of 'em has a Skorp. All kinetic, far as we know. Nothing you could fry."

"Got anything on legs?"

"They've got a Wolfhound in there. 46-G."

"I meant you," Metzinger says.

The Sheriff winces. "Nearest's three hours away. Gimped leg." And at Metzinger's look: "BoDyn pulled out a few years back. We've been having trouble getting replacement parts."

"What about local law enforcement? You can't be the only—"

"Half of them *are* law enforcement. How'd you think they got the Wolfhound?" The Sheriff lowers his voice, although there aren't any other patriots within earshot. "Son, you don't think we'd have invited you in if we'd had any other choice? I mean Jayzuz, we've got enough trouble maintaining lawnorder as it is. If word ever got out we had to bring in outside help over a goddamn *domestic dispute . . .*"

"Don't sweat it. We don't wear name tags." Metzinger turns to Silano. "Take it away, Sergeant-Major."

Silano addresses the troops as Metzinger disappears into the cloaked Chinook: "Say your goodbyes, everybody. Autopilots in thirty."

Asante sighs to himself. Those poor bastards don't stand a chance. He can't even bring himself to blame them: driven by desperation, hunger, the lack of any other options. Like the Sāḥilites who murdered *him*, back at the end of another life: damned, ultimately, by the sin of being born into a wasteland that could no longer feed them.

Silano raises one hand. *"Mark."*

Asante calls forth his mandala. The world goes to gray. His bad hand calms and steadies on the forestalk of his weapon.

This is going to be ugly.

He's glad he won't be around to see it.

Heroes

He does afterward, of course. They all do, as soon as they get back to Côté. They're still learning. The world is their classroom.

"Back in the Cenozoic all anybody cared about was *reflexes*." Second-Lieutenant Oliver Maddox—sorcerer's apprentice to the rarely-seen Major Emma Rossiter, of the Holy Order of Neuroengineering—speaks with the excitement of a nine-year-old at his own birthday party. "Double-tap, dash, down, crawl, observe fire—all that stuff your body learns to do without thinking when someone yells *Contact*. The whole program was originally just about speeding up those macros. They never really appreciated that the subconscious mind *thinks* as well as reacts. It *analyzes*. I was telling them that years ago but they never really got it until now."

Asante has never met *Them*. They never write, They never call. They certainly never visit. Presumably They sign a lot of checks.

"Here, though, we have a *perfect* example of the tactical genius of the zombie mind."

Their BUDs recorded everything. Maddox has put it all together post-mortem, a greatest-hits mix with remote thermal and PEA and a smattering of extraporential algorithms to fill in the gaps. Now he sets up the game board—walls, floors, industrial viscera all magically translucent—and initializes the people inside.

"So you've got eighteen heavily-armed hostiles dug in at all the right choke points." Homunculi glow red at critical junctures. "You've got a jamming field in effect, so you can't share telemetry unless you're line-of-sight. You've got an EMP-hardened robot programmed to attack anything so much as squeaks, deafened along the whole spectrum so even if we *had* the backdoor codes it wouldn't hear them." The Wolfhound icon is especially glossy: probably lifted from BoDyn's promotional archive. "And you've got some crazy fucker with a deadman switch that'll send the whole place sky-high the moment his heart stops—or even if he just thinks you're getting too close to the flag. You don't even know about that going in.

"And yet."

Maddox starts the clock. Inside the labyrinth, icons begin to dance in fast-forward.

"Garin's first up, and he completely blows it. Not only does he barely graze the target—probably doesn't even draw blood—*but he leaves his silencer disengaged*. Way to go, Garin. You failed to neutralize your target, and now the whole building knows where you are."

Asante remembers that gunshot echoing through the facility. He remembers his stomach dropping away.

"Now here comes one of Bubba's buddies around the corner and—Garin misses *again!* Nick to the shoulder this time. And here comes the real bad-ass of the bunch, that Wolfhound's been homing in on Garin's shots and that motherfucker is armed and hot and . . ."

The 46-G rounds the corner. It does not target Garin; it lights up the *insurgents*. Bubba and his buddy collapse into little red piles of pixel dust.

"They did *not* see that coming!" Maddox exults. "Fragged by their own robot! How do you suppose *that* happened?"

Asante frowns.

"So two baddies down, Garin's already up the ladder and onto this catwalk before the robot gets a bead on him but Tiwana's at the other end, way across the building, and they go LOS for about half a second"—a bright thread flickers between their respective icons—"before Tiwana drops back down to ground level and starts picking off Bubbas over by the countercurrent assembly. And *she* turns out to be just as shitty a shot as Garin, and just as sloppy with her silencer."

Gunfire everywhere, from everyone. Asante remembers being blind and shitting bricks, wondering what kind of *aboa* would make such an idiot mistake until the Rann-Seti came up in his own hands, until he felt the recoil and heard the sound of his own shot echoing like a 130-decibel bullseye on his back. He wondered, at the time, how and why someone had sabotaged everyone's silencers like that.

Maddox is still deep in the play. "The bad guys have heard the commotion and are starting to reposition. By now Asante and Silano have picked up the shitty-shot bug and the BoDyn's still running around tearing up the guys on its own side. All this opens a hole that Kalmus breezes through—anyone want to guess the odds she'd just happen to be so perfectly positioned?—which buys her a clean shot at the guy with the deadman switch. Who she drops with a perfect cervical shot. Completely paralyzes the poor bastard *but* leaves his heart beating strong and steady. Here we see Kalmus checking him over and disabling his now-useless doomsday machine.

"This all took less than five minutes, people. I mean, it was eighteen from In to Out but you're basically mopping up after five. And just before the credits roll, Kalmus strolls up to the wolfhound calm as you please and *pets* the fucker. Puts him right to sleep. Galveston PD gets their robot back without a scratch. Five minutes. Fucking magic."

"So, um." Garin looks around. "How'd we do it?"

"Show 'em, Kally."

Kalmus holds up a cuff-link. "Apparently I took this off deadman guy."

"Dog whistles, Ars and Kays." Maddox grins. "50KHz, inaudible to pilot or passenger. You don't put your robot into rabid mode without some way of telling friend from foe, right? Wear one of these pins, Wolfie doesn't look at you twice. *Lose* that pin and it rips your throat out in a fucking instant.

"Your better halves could've gone for clean, quiet kills that would've left the remaining forces still dug-in, still fortified, and not going anywhere. But one of the things that fortified them was BoDyn's baddest battlebot. So your better halves didn't go for clean quiet kills. They went for noise and panic. They shot the dog whistles, drew in the dog, let it attack its own masters. Other side changes position in response. You *herded* the robot, and the robot herded the insurgents right into your crosshairs. It was precision out of chaos, and it's even more impressive because you had no comms except for the occasional optical sync when you happened to be LOS. Gotta be the messiest, spottiest network you could imagine, and if I hadn't seen it myself I'd say it was impossible. But somehow you zombies kept updated on each other's sitreps. Each one knew what it had to do to achieve an optimal outcome assuming all the others did likewise, and the group strategy just kind of—*emerged*. Nobody giving orders. Nobody saying a goddamn word."

Asante sees it now, as the replay loops and restarts. There's a kind of beauty to it; the movement of nodes, the intermittent web of laser light flickering between them, the smooth coalescence of signal from noise. It's more than a dance, more than teamwork. It's more like a . . . a distributed organism. Like the digits of a hand, moving together.

"Mind you, this is not what we say if anyone asks," Maddox adds. "What we say is that every scenario in which the Galveston plant went down predicted a tipping point across the whole Post-TExit landscape. We point to 95% odds of wide-spread rioting and social unrest on WestHem's very doorstep—a fate which ZeroS has, nice and quietly, prevented. Not bad for your first field deployment."

Tiwana raises a hand. "Who would ask, exactly?"

It's a good question. In the thirteen months since Asante joined Zero Sum, no outsider has ever appeared on the grounds of CFB Côté. Which isn't especially surprising, given that—according to the public records search he did a few weeks back, anyway—CFB Côté has been closed for over twenty years.

Maddox smiles faintly. "Anyone with a vested interest in the traditional chain of command."

Where Are We Now

Asante awakens in the Infirmary, standing at the foot of Carlos Acosta's bed. To his right a half-open door spills dim light into the darkness beyond: a wedge of worn linoleum fading out from the doorway, a tiny red EXIT sign glowing in the void above a stairwell. To his left, a glass wall looks into Neurosurgery. Jointed teleops hang from the ceiling in there, like mantis limbs with impossibly fragile fingers. Lasers. Needles and nanotubes. Atomic-force manipulators delicate enough to coax individual atoms apart. ZeroS have gone under those knives more times than any of them can count. Surgery by software, mostly. Occasionally by human doctors phoning it in from undisclosed locations, old-school cutters who never visit in the flesh for all the times they've cut into Asante's.

Acosta's on his back, eyes closed. He looks almost at peace. Even his facial tic has quieted. He's been here three days now, ever since losing his right arm to a swarm of smart flechettes over in Heraklion. It's no big deal. He's growing it back with a little help from some imported salamander DNA and a steroid-infused aminoglucose drip. He'll be good as new in three weeks—as good as he's ever been since ZeroS got him, anyway—back in his rack in half that time. Meanwhile it's a tricky balance: his metabolism may be boosted into the jet stream but it's all for tissue growth. There's barely enough left over to power a trip to the bathroom.

Kodjo Asante wonders why he's standing here at 0300.

Maddox says the occasional bit of sleepwalking isn't anything to get too worried about, especially if you're already prone to it. Nobody's suffered a major episode in months, not since well before Galveston; these days the tweaks seem mainly about fine-tuning. Rossiter's long since called off the just-in-case bots that once dogged their every unscripted step. Even lets them leave the base now and then, when they've been good.

You still have to expect the occasional lingering side-effect, though. Asante glances down at the telltale tremor in his own hand, seizes it gently with the other and holds firm until the nerves quiet. Looks back at his friend.

Acosta's eyes are open.

They don't look at him. They don't settle long enough to look at anything, as far as Asante can tell. They jump and twitch in Acosta's face, back forth back forth up down up.

"Carl," Asante says softly. "How's it going, man?"

The rest of that body doesn't even twitch. Acosta's breathing remains unchanged. He doesn't speak.

Zombies aren't big on talking. They're smart but nonverbal, like those split-brain patients who understand words but can't utter them. Something about the integration of speech with consciousness. Written language is easier. The zombie brain doesn't take well to conventional grammar and syntax but they've developed a kind of visual pidgin that Maddox claims is more efficient than English. Apparently they use it at all the briefings.

Maddox also claims they're working on a kind of time-sharing arrangement, some way to divvy up custody of Broca's Area between the fronto-parietal and the retrosplenial. *Someday soon, maybe, you'll literally be able to talk to yourself,* he says. But they haven't got there yet.

A tacpad on the bedside table glows with a dim matrix of Zidgin symbols. Asante places it under Acosta's right hand.

"Carl?"

Nothing.

"Just thought I'd . . . see how you were. You take care."

He tiptoes to the door, sets trembling fingers on the knob. Steps into the darkness of the hallway, navigates back to his rack by touch and memory.

Those eyes.

It's not like he hasn't seen it a million times before. But all those other times his squadmates' eyes blurred and danced in upright bodies, powerful autonomous things that *moved*. Seeing that motion embedded in such stillness—watching eyes struggle as if trapped in muscle and bone, as if looking up from some shallow grave where they haven't quite been buried alive—

Terrified. That's how they looked. Terrified.

We Are the Dead

Specialist Tarra Kalmus has disappeared. Rossiter was seen breaking the news to Maddox just this morning, a conversation during which Maddox morphed miraculously from He of the Perpetually Goofy Smile into Lieutenant Stoneface. He refuses to talk about it with any of the grunts. Silano managed to buttonhole Rossiter on her way back to the helipad, but could only extract the admission that Kalmus has been 'reassigned'.

Metzinger tells them to stop asking questions. He makes it an order.

But as Tiwana points out—when Asante finds her that evening, sitting with her back propped against a pallet of machine parts in the loading bay—you can run all sorts of online queries without ever using a question mark.

"Fellow corpse."

"Fellow corpse."

It's been their own private salutation since learning how much they have in common. (Tiwana died during a Realist attack in Havana. Worst vacation ever, she says.) They're the only ZeroS, so far at least, to return from the dead. The others hold them a little in awe because of it.

The others also keep a certain distance.

"Garin was last to see her, over at the Memory Hole." Tiwana's wearing a pair of smart specs tuned to the public net. It won't stop any higher-ups who decide to look over her shoulder, but at least her activity won't be logged by default. "Chatting up some redhead with a Hanson Geothermal logo on her jacket."

Two nights ago. Metzinger let everyone off the leash as a reward for squashing a Realist attack on the G8G Constellation. They went down to Banff for some meatspace R&R. "So?"

Speclight paints Tiwana's cheeks with small flickering auroras. "So a BPD drone found a woman matching that description dead outside a public fuckcubby two blocks south of there. Same night."

"Eiiii." Asante squats down beside her as Tiwana pushes the specs onto her forehead. Her wonky eye jiggles at him.

"Yeah." She takes a breath, lets it out. "Nicci Steckman, according to the DNA."

"So how—"

"They don't say. Just asking witnesses to come forward."

"Have any?"

"They left together. Deked into an alley. No further surveillance record, which is odd."

"Is it really," Asante murmurs.

"No. I guess not."

They sit in silence for a moment.

"What do you think?" she asks at last.

"Maybe Steckman didn't like it rough and things got out of hand. You know Kally, she . . . doesn't always take no for an answer."

"No to what? We're all on antilibidinals. Why would she even be—"

"She'd never *kill* someone over—"

"Maybe *she* didn't," Tiwana says.

He blinks. "You think she flipped?"

"Maybe it wasn't her fault. Maybe the augs kicked in on their own somehow, like a, a . . . reflex. Kally saw an imminent threat, or something her better half *interpreted* that way. Grabbed the keys, took care of it."

"It's not supposed to work like that."

"It wasn't supposed to fry Saks' central nervous system either."

"Come on, Sofe. That's ancient history. They wouldn't deploy us if they hadn't fixed those problems."

"Really." Her bad eye looks pointedly at his bad hand.

"Legacy glitches don't count." Nerves nicked during surgery, a stray milliamp leaking into the fusiform gyrus. Everyone's got at least one. "Maddox says—"

"Oh sure, Maddox is always gonna tidy up. Next week, next month. Once the latest tweaks have settled, or there isn't some brush fire to put out over in Kamfuckingchatka. Meanwhile the glitches don't even manifest in zombie mode so why should he care?"

"If they thought the implants were defective they wouldn't keep sending us out on missions."

"Eh." Tiwana spreads her hands. "You say *mission*, I say *field test*. I mean, sure, camaraderie's great—we're the cutting edge, we can be ZeroS! But *look* at us, Jo. Silano was a Rio insurgent. Kalmus was up on insubordination charges. They scraped you and me off the ground like road kill. None of us are what you'd call *summa cum laude*."

"Isn't that the point? That *anybody* can be a super soldier?" *Or at least, any* body.

"We're lab rats, Jo. They don't want to risk frying their West Point grads with a beta release so they're working out the bugs on us first. If the program was ready to go wide we wouldn't still be here. Which means—" She heaves a sigh. "It's the augs. At least, I hope it's the augs."

"You hope?"

"You'd rather believe Kally just went berserk and killed a civilian for no reason?"

He tries to ignore a probably-psychosomatic tingle at the back of his head. "Rossiter wouldn't be talking *reassignment* if she had," he admits. "She'd be talking court-martial."

"She'll never talk court-martial. Not where we're concerned."

"Really."

"Think about it. You ever see any politician come by to make sure the taxpayer's money's being well-spent? You ever see a commissioned officer walking the halls who wasn't Metzinger or Maddox or Rossiter?"

"So we're off the books." It's hardly a revelation.

"We're so far *off the books* we might as well be cave paintings. We don't even know our own tooth-to-tail ratio. Ninety percent of our support infra-structure's offsite, it's all robots and teleops. We don't even know who's cut-ting into our own heads." She leans close in the deepening gloom, fixes him with her good eye. "This is voodoo, Jo. Maybe the program *started* small with that kneejerk stuff, but now? You and I, we're literal fucking *zombies*. We're reanimated corpses dancing on strings, and if you think Persephone Q. Public is gonna be fine with that you have a lot more faith in her than I do. I don't think Congress knows about us, I don't think Parliament knows about us, I bet SOCOM doesn't even know about us past some line in a budget that says *psychological research*. I don't think they *want* to know. And when something's that dark, are they really going to let anything as trivial as a judicial process drag it into the light?"

Asante shakes his head. "Still has to be accountability. Some kind of inter-nal process."

"There is. You disappear, and they tell everyone you've been reassigned."

He thinks for a bit. "So what do we do?"

"First we riot in the mess hall. Then we march on Ottawa demanding equal rights for corpses." She rolls her eyes. "We don't *do* anything. Maybe you forgot: we *died*. We don't legally exist anymore, and unless you got a way better deal than me the only way for either of us to change that is keep our heads down until we get our honorable discharges. I do not like being dead. I would very much like to go back to being officially alive some day. Until then . . ."

She takes the specs off her head. Powers them down.

"We watch our fucking step."

Ricochet

Sergeant Kodjo Asante watches his fucking step. He watches it when he goes up against AIRheads and Realists. He watches it when pitted against well-funded private armies running on profit and ideology, against ragged makeshift ones driven by thirst and desperation, against rogue Darwin Banks and the inevitable religious extremists who—almost a quarter-century after the end of the Dark Decade—still haven't stopped maiming and killing in the name of their Invisible Friends. His steps don't really falter until twenty-one months into his tour, when he kills three unarmed children off the coast of Honduras.

ZeroS has risen from the depths of the Atlantic to storm one of the countless gylands that ride the major currents of the world's oceans. Some are refugee camps with thousands of inhabitants; others serve as havens for hustlers and tax dodgers eager to avoid the constraints of more stationary jurisdictions. Some are military, sheathed in chromatophores and radar-damping nanotubes: bigger than airports, invisible to man or machine.

The *Caçador de Recompensa* is a fish farm, a family business registered out of Brazil: two modest hectares of low-slung superstructure on a donut hull with a cluster of net pens at its center. It is currently occupied by forces loyal to the latest incarnation of Shining Path. The Path thrives on supply lines with no fixed address—and as Metzinger reminded them on the way down, it's always better to prevent a fight than win one. If the Path can't feed their troops, maybe they won't deploy them.

This is almost a mission of mercy.

Asante eavesdrops on the sounds of battle, takes in a mingled reek of oil and salt air and rotten fish, lets Evil Twin's worldview wash across his eyes in a blur of light and the incomprehensible flicker of readouts with millisecond lifespans. Except during target acquisition, of course. Except for those brief stroboscopic instants when ET *locks on*, and faces freeze and blur in turn: a couple of coveralled SAsian men wielding Heckler-Kochs. A wounded antique ZhanLu staggering on two-and-a half-legs, the beam from its MAD gun wobbling wide of any conceivable target. Children in life jackets, two boys, one girl; Asante guesses their ages at between seven and ten. Each time the weapon kicks in his hands and an instant later ET is veering toward the next kill.

Emotions are sluggish things in Passenger mode. He feels nothing in the moment, shock in the aftermath. Horror's still halfway to the horizon when a random ricochet slaps him back into the driver's seat.

The bullet doesn't penetrate—not much punches through the Chrysomalon armor wrapped tight around his skin—but vectors interact. Momentum passes from a small fast object to a large slow one. Asante's brain lurches in its cavity; meat slaps bone and bounces back. Deep in all that stressed gray matter, some vital circuit shorts out.

There's pain of course, blooming across the side of his head like napalm in those few seconds before his endocrine pumps damp it down. There's fire in the BUD, a blaze of static and a crimson icon warning of ZMODE FAILURE. But there's a little miracle too:

Kodjo Asante can see again: a high sun in a hard blue sky. A flat far horizon. Columns of oily smoke rising from wrecked machinery.

Bodies.

The air *cracks* a few centimeters to his right. He drops instinctively to a deck slippery with blood and silver scales, gags at the sudden stench wafting from a slurry of bloated carcasses crowding the surface of the holding pen just in front of him. (*Coho-Atlantic hybrids*, he notes despite himself. *Might even have those new Showell genes.*) A turret on treads sparks and sizzles on the other side, a hole blown in its carapace.

A shadow blurs across Asante's forearm. Tiwana leaps across the sky, defractors high on her forehead, eyeballs dancing madly in their sockets. She clears the enclosure, alights graceful as a dragonfly on one foot, kicks the spastic turret with the other. It sparks one last time and topples into the pen. Tiwana vanishes down the nearest companionway.

Asante gets to his feet, pans for threats, sees nothing but enemies laid waste: the smoking stumps of perimeter autoturrets, the fallen bodies of a man with his arm blown off and a woman groping for a speargun just beyond reach. And a small brittle figure almost fused to the deck: blackened sticks for arms and legs, white teeth grinning in a charred skull, a bright half-melted puddle of orange fabric and PVC holding it all together. Asante sees it all. Not just snapshots glimpsed through the fog: ZeroS handiwork, served up for the first time in three-sixty wraparound immersion.

We're killing children . . .

Even the adult bodies don't look like combatants. Refugees, maybe, driven to take by force what they couldn't get any other way. Maybe all they wanted was to get somewhere safe. To feed their kids.

At his feet, a reeking carpet of dead salmon converge listlessly in the wake of the fallen turret. They aren't feeding anything but hagfish and maggots.

I have become Sāḥilite, Asante reflects numbly. He calls up BUD, ignores the unreadable auras flickering around the edges of vision, selects GPS.

Not off Honduras. They're in the Gulf of Mexico.

No one in their right mind would run a fish farm here. The best parts of the Gulf are anoxic; the worst are downright flammable. *Caçador* must have drifted up through the Yucatan Channel, got caught in an eddy loop. All these fish would have suffocated as soon as they hit the dead zone.

But gylands aren't entirely at the mercy of the currents. They carry rudimentary propulsion systems for docking and launching, switching streams and changing course. *Caçador*'s presence so deep in the Gulf implies either catastrophic equipment failure or catastrophic ignorance.

Asante can check out the first possibility, anyway. He stumbles toward the nearest companionway—

—as Tiwana and Acosta burst onto deck from below. Acosta seizes his right arm, Tiwana his left. Neither slows. Asante's feet bounce and drag. The lurching acceleration reawakens the pain in his temple.

He cries out: "*The engines . . .*"

New pain, other side, sharp and recurrent: an ancient weight belt swinging back and forth across Acosta's torso, a frayed strip of nylon threaded through an assortment of lead slugs. It's like being hammered by a tiny wrecking ball. One part of Asante wonders where Acosta found it; another watches Garin race into view with a small bloody body slung across his shoulder. Garin passes one of the dismembered turrets, grabs a piece with his free hand and keeps running.

Everyone's charging for the rails.

Tiwana's mouthpiece is in, her defractors down. She empties a clip into the deck ahead, right at the water's edge: gunfire shreds plastic and white-washed fiberglass, loosens an old iron docking cleat. She dips and grabs in passing, draws it to her chest, never loosening her grip on Asante. He hears the soft pop of a bone leaving its socket in the instant before they all go over the side.

They plummet head-first, dragged down by a hundred kilograms of improvised ballast. Asante chokes, jams his mouthpiece into place; coughs seawater through the exhaust and sucks in a hot lungful of fresh-sparked hydrox.

Pressure builds against his eardrums. He swallows, swallows again, manages to keep a few millibars ahead of outright rupture. He has just enough freedom of movement to claw at his face and slide the defractors over his eyes. The ocean clicks into focus, clear as acid, empty as green glass.

Green turns white.

Seen in that flash-blinded instant: four thin streams of bubbles, rising to a surface gone suddenly incandescent. Four dark bodies, falling from the light. A thunderclap rolls through the water, deep, downshifted, as much felt as heard. It comes from nowhere and everywhere.

The roof of the ocean is on fire. Some invisible force shreds their contrails from the top down, tears those bubbles into swirling silver confetti. The wave-front races implacably after them. The ocean *bulges*, recoils. It squeezes Asante like a fist, stretches him like rubber; Tiwana and Acosta tumble away in the backwash. He flails, stabilizes himself as the first jagged shapes resolve overhead: dismembered chunks of the booby-trapped gyland, tumbling with slow majesty into the depths. A broken wedge of deck and stairwell passes by a few meters away, tangled in monofilament. A thousand glassy eyes stare back from the netting as the wreckage fades to black.

Asante scans the ocean for that fifth bubble trail, that last dark figure to balance Those Who Left against Those Who Returned. No one overhead. Below, a dim shape that has to be Garin shares its mouthpiece with the small limp thing in his arms. Beyond that, the hint of a deeper dark against the abyss: a shark-like silhouette keeping station amid a slow rain of debris. Waiting to take its prodigal children home again.

They're too close to shore. There might be witnesses. So much for stealth-ops. So much for low profiles and no-questions-asked. Metzinger's going to be pissed.

Then again, they *are* in the Gulf of Mexico.

Any witnesses will probably just think it caught fire again.

Lady Grinning Soul

"In your own words, Sergeant. Take your time."

We killed children. We killed children, and we lost Silano, and I don't know why. And I don't know if you do either.

But of course, that would involve taking Major Emma Rossiter at *her* word.

"Did the child . . . ?" Metzinger had already tubed Garin's prize by the time Asante reboarded the sub. Garin, of course, had no idea what his body had been doing. Metzinger had not encouraged discussion.

That was okay. Nobody was really in the mood anyhow.

"I'm sorry. She didn't make it." Rossiter waits for what she probably regards as a respectful moment. "If we could focus on the subject at hand . . ."

"It was a shitstorm," Asante says. "Sir."

"We gathered that." The Major musters a sympathetic smile. "We were hoping you could provide more in the way of details."

"You must have the logs."

"Those are numbers, Sergeant. Pixels. You are uniquely—if accidentally—in a position to give us more than that."

"I never even got below decks."

Rossiter seems to relax a little. "Still. This is the first time one of you has been debooted in mid-game, and it's obviously not the kind of thing we want to risk repeating. Maddox is already working on ways to make the toggle more robust. In the meantime, your perspective could be useful in helping to ensure this doesn't happen again."

"My perspective, sir, is that those forces did not warrant our particular skill set."

"We're more interested in your experiences regarding the deboot, Sergeant. Was there a sense of disorientation, for example? Any visual artifacts in BUD?"

Asante stands with his hands behind his back—good gripping bad—and says nothing.

"Very well." Rossiter's smile turns grim. "Let's talk about your *perspective*, then. Do you think regular forces would have been sufficient? Do you have a sense of the potential losses incurred if we'd sent, say, WestHem marines?"

"They appeared to be refugees, sir. They didn't pose—"

"One hundred percent, Sergeant. We would have lost everyone."

Asante says nothing.

"Unaugged soldiers wouldn't even have made it off the gyland before it went up. Even if they had, the p-wave would've been fatal if you hadn't greatly increased your rate of descent. Do you think regular forces would have made that call? Seen what was coming, run the numbers, improvised a strategy to get below the kill zone in less time than it would take to shout a command?"

"We killed children." It's barely more than a whisper.

"Collateral damage is an unfortunate but inevitable—"

"We *targeted* children."

"Ah."

Rossiter plays with her tacpad: *tap tap tap, swipe.*

"These children," she says at last. "Were they armed?"

"I do not believe so, sir."

"Were they naked?"

"Sir?"

"Could you be certain they weren't carrying concealed weapons? Maybe even a remote trigger for a thousand kilograms of CL-20?"

"They were . . . sir, they couldn't have been more than seven or eight."

"I shouldn't have to tell you about child soldiers, Sergeant. They've been a fact of life for centuries, especially in *your* particular—at any rate. Just out of interest, how young would someone have to be before you'd rule them out as a potential threat?"

"I don't know, sir."

"Yes you do. You *did*. That's why you targeted them."

"That wasn't me."

"Of course. It was your . . . evil twin. That's what you call it, right?" Rossiter leans forward. "Listen to me very carefully, Sergeant Asante, because I think you're laboring under some serious misapprehensions about what we do here. Your *twin* is not evil, and it is not gratuitous. It is *you*: a much bigger part of *you* than the whiny bitch standing in front of me right now."

Asante clenches his teeth and keeps his mouth shut.

"This gut feeling giving you so much trouble. This sense of Right and Wrong. Where do you think it comes from, Sergeant?"

"Experience. Sir."

"It's the result of a calculation. A whole series of calculations, far too complex to fit into the conscious workspace. So the subconscious sends you . . . an executive summary, you might call it. Your evil twin knows all about your sense of moral outrage; it's the source of it. It has more information than you do. Processes it more effectively. Maybe you should trust it to know what it's doing."

He doesn't. He doesn't trust her, either.

But suddenly, surprisingly, he understands her.

She's not just making a point. This isn't just rhetoric. The insight appears fully formed in his mind, a bright shard of unexpected clarity. She thought it would be easy. She really doesn't know what happened.

He watches her fingers move on the 'pad as she speaks. Notes the nervous flicker of her tongue at the corner of her mouth. She glances up to meet his eye, glances away again.

She's scared.

Look Back in Anger

Asante awakens standing in the meadow up the mountain. The sky is cloudless and full of stars. His fatigues are damp with sweat or dew. There is no moon. Black conifers loom on all sides. To the east, a hint of pre-dawn orange seeps through the branches.

He has read that this was once the time of the dawn chorus, when songbirds would call out in ragged symphony to start the day. He has never heard it. He doesn't hear it now. There's no sound in this forest but his own breathing—

—and the snap of a twig under someone's foot.

He turns. A gray shape detaches itself from the darkness.

"Fellow corpse," Tiwana says.

"Fellow corpse," he responds.

"You wandered off. Thought I'd tag along. Make sure you didn't go AWOL."

"I think ET's acting up again."

"Maybe you're just sleepwalking. People sleepwalk sometimes." She shrugs. "Probably the same wiring anyway."

"Sleepwalkers don't kill people."

"Actually, that's been known to happen."

He clears his throat. "Did, um . . ."

"No one else knows you're up here."

"Did ET disable the pickups?"

"I did."

"Thanks."

"Any time."

Asante looks around. "I remember the first time I saw this place. It was . . . magical."

"I was thinking more *ironic*." Adding, at Asante's look: "You know. That one of the last pristine spots in this whole shit-show owes its existence to the fact that WestHem needs someplace private to teach us how to blow shit up."

"Count on you," Asante says.

The stars are fading. Venus is hanging in there, though.

"You've been weird," she observes. "Ever since the thing with *Caçador*."

"It was a weird thing."

"So I hear." Shrug. "I guess you had to be there."

He musters a smile. "So you don't remember . . ."

"Legs running down. Legs running back up. My zombie never targeted anything so I don't know what she saw."

"Metzinger does. Rossiter does." He leans his ass against a convenient boulder. "Does it ever bother you? That you don't know what your own eyes are seeing, and they do?"

"Not really. Just the way it works."

"We don't know what we're doing out there. When was the last time Maddox even showed us a highlight reel?" He feels the muscles clenching in his jaw. "We could be war criminals."

"There *is* no *we*. Not when it matters." She sits beside him. "Besides. Our zombies may be nonconscious but they're not stupid; they know we're obligated to disobey unlawful commands."

"Maybe they *know*. Not sure Maddox's compliance circuit would let them do anything about it."

Somewhere nearby a songbird clears its throat.

Tiwana takes a breath. "Suppose you're right—not saying you are, but *suppose* they sent us out to gun down a gyland full of harmless refugees. Forget that *Caçador* was packing enough explosives to blow up a hamlet, forget that it killed Silano . . . hell, nearly killed us all. If Metzinger decides to bash in someone's innocent skull, you still don't blame the hammer he used."

"And yet. Someone's skull is still bashed in."

Across the clearing, another bird answers. *The dawn duet.*

"There must be reasons," she says, as if trying it on for size.

He remembers *reasons* from another life, on another continent: retribution. The making of examples. Poor impulse control. Just . . . fun, sometimes.

"Such as."

"I don't know, okay? Big Picture's way above our pay grade. But that doesn't mean you toss out the chain of command every time someone gives you an order without a twenty-gig backgrounder to go with it. If you want me to believe we're in thrall to a bunch of fascist baby killers, you're gonna need more than a few glimpses of something you may have seen on a gyland."

"How about, I don't know. All of human history?"

Venus is gone at last. The rising sun streaks the clearing with gold.

"It's the deal we made. Sure, it's a shitty one. Only shittier one is being dead. But would you choose differently, even now? Go back to being fish food?"

He honestly doesn't know.

"We should be *dead*, Jo. Every one of these moments is a gift."

He regards her with a kind of wonder. "I never know how you do it."

"Do what?"

"Channel Schopenhauer and Pollyanna at the same time without your head exploding."

She takes his hand for a moment, squeezes briefly. Rises. "We're gonna make it. Just so long as we don't rock the boat. All the way to that honorable fucking discharge." She turns to the light; sunrise glows across her face. "Until then, in case you were wondering, I've got your back."

"There is no you," he reminds her. "Not when it matters."

"I've got your back," she says.

Watch That Man

They've outsourced Silano's position, brought in someone none of them have ever seen before. Technically he's one of them, though the scars that tag him ZeroS have barely had time to heal. Something about him is wrong. Something about the way he moves; his insignia. Not Specialist or Corporal or Sergeant.

"I want you to meet Lieutenant Jim Moore," Rossiter tells them.

ZeroS finally have a commissioned secco. He's easily the youngest person in the room.

He gets right to it. "This is the Nanisivik mine." The satcam wall zooms down onto the roof of the world. "Baffin Island, seven hundred fifty klicks north of the Arctic Circle, heart of the Slush Belt." A barren fractured landscape of red and ocher. Drumlins and hillocks and bifurcating stream beds.

"Tapped out at the turn of the century." A brown road, undulating along some scoured valley floor. A cluster of buildings. A gaping mouth in the Earth. "These days people generally stay away, on account of its remote location. Also on account of the eight thousand metric tons of high-level nuclear waste the Canadian government brought over from India for deep-time storage. Part of an initiative to diversify the northern economy, apparently." Tactical schematics, now: Processing and Intake. Train tracks corkscrewing into the Canadian Shield. Storage tunnels branching like the streets of an underground subdivision. "Project was abandoned after the Greens lost power in '38.

"You could poison a lot of cities with this stuff. Which may be why someone's messing around there now."

Garin's hand is up. "Someone, sir?"

"So far all we have are signs of unauthorized activity and a JTFN drone that went in and never came out. Our first priority is to identify the actors. Depending on what we find, we might take care of it ourselves. Or we might call in the bombers. Won't know until we get there."

And we *won't know even then*, Asante muses—and realizes, in that moment, what it is about Moore that strikes him as so strange.

"We'll be prepping your better halves with the operational details *en route*."

It's not what is, it's what *isn't*: no tic at the corner of the eye, no tremor in the hand. His speech is smooth and perfect, his eyes make contact with steady calm. Lieutenant Moore doesn't glitch.

"For now, we anticipate a boots-down window of no more than seven hours—"

Asante looks at Tiwana. Tiwana looks back.

ZeroS are out of beta.

Subterraneans

The Lockhead drops them at the foot of a crumbling pier. Derelict shops and listing trailers, long abandoned, huddle against the sleeting rain. This used to be a seaport; then a WestHem refueling station back before *WestHem* was even a word, before the apocalyptic Arctic weather made it easier to just stick everything underwater. It lived its short life as a company town, an appendage of the mine, in the days before Nanisivik was emptied of its valuables and filled up again.

BUD says 1505: less than an hour if they want to be on target by sundown. Moore leads them overland across weathered stone and alluvial washouts and glistening acned Martian terrain. They're fifteen hundred meters from the mouth of the repository when he orders them all into the back seat.

Asante's legs, under new management, pick up the pace. His vision blurs. At least up here, in the wind and blinding sleet, it doesn't make much difference.

A sound drifts past: the roar of some distant animal, perhaps. Nearer, the unmistakable discharge of an ε-40. Not ET's. Asante's eyes remain virtuously clouded.

The wind dies in the space of a dozen steps. Half as many again and the torrent of icy needles on his face slows to a patter, a drizzle. Asante hears great bolts unlatching, a soft screech of heavy metal. They pass through some portal and the bright overcast in his eyes dims by half. Buckles and bootsteps echo faintly against rock walls.

Downhill. A gentle curve to the left. Gravel, patches of broken asphalt. His feet step over unseen obstacles.

And stop.

The whole squad must have frozen; he can't hear so much as a breath. The supersaccadic tickertape flickering across the fog seems faster. Could be his imagination. Off in some subterranean distance, water *drip-drip-drips* onto a still surface.

Quiet movement as ZeroS spreads out. Asante's just a passenger but he reads the footsteps, feels his legs taking him sideways, kneeling. The padding on his elbows doesn't leave much room for fine-grained tactile feedback but the surface he's bracing against is flat and rough, like a table sheathed in sandpaper.

There's a musky animal smell in the air. From somewhere in the middle distance, a soft *whuffle*. The stirring of something huge in slow, sleepy motion.

Maybe someone left the door open, and something got in . . .

Pizzly bears are the only animals that come to mind: monstrous hybrids, birthed along the boundaries of stressed ecosystems crashing into each other. He's never seen one in the flesh.

A grunt. A low growl.

The sound of building speed.

Gunshots. A roar, deafeningly close, and a crash of metal against metal. The flickering tactical halo dims abruptly: network traffic just dropped by a node.

Now the whole network crashes: pawn exchange, ZeroS sacrificing their own LAN as the price of jamming the enemy's. Moore's MAD gun snaps to the right. An instant of scorching heat as the beam sweeps across Asante's arm; Moore shooting wide, Moore *missing*. ET breaks cover, leaps and locks. For one crystalline millisecond Asante sees a wall of coarse ivory-brown fur close enough to touch, every follicle in perfect focus.

The clouds close in. ET pulls the trigger.

A bellow. The scrape of great claws against stone. The reek is overpowering but ET's already pirouetting after fresh game and *click* the freeze-frame glimpse of monstrous ursine jaws in a face wide as a doorway and *click* small brown hands raised against an onrushing foe and *click* a young boy with freckles and strawberry blond hair and Asante's blind again but he feels ET pulling on the trigger, *pop pop pop*—

Whatthefuck children whatthefuck whatthefuck

—and ET's changed course again and *click*: a small back a fur coat black hair flying in the light of the muzzle flash.

Not again. Not again.

Child soldiers. Suicide bombers. For centuries.

But no one's shooting back.

He knows the sound of every weapon the squad might use, down to the smallest pop and click: the sizzle of the MAD gun, the bark of the Epsilon, Acosta's favorite Olympic. He hears them now; those, and no others. Whatever they're shooting at isn't returning fire.

Whatever we're shooting at. You blind murderous twaaaaase. You're shooting eight-year-olds.

Again.

More gunfire. Still no voices but for a final animal roar that gives way to a wet gurgle and the heavy slap of meat on stone.

It's a nuclear waste repository at the north pole. What are children even doing here?

What am I?

What am I?

And suddenly he sees the words, *All tautologies are tautologies* and ET's back downstairs and the basement door locks and Kodjo Asante grabs frantically for the reins, and takes back his life, and opens his eyes:

In time to see the little freckled boy, dressed in ragged furs, sitting on Riley Garin's shoulders and dragging a jagged piece of glass across his throat. In time to see him leap free of the body and snatch Garin's gun, toss it effortlessly across this dimly-lit cave to an Asian girl clad only in a filthy loincloth, who's sailing through the air toward a bloodied Jim Moore. In time to see that girl reach behind her and catch the gun in midair without so much as a backward glance.

More than a dance, more than teamwork. Like digits on the same hand, moving together.

The pizzly's piled up against a derelict forklift, a giant tawny thing raking the air with massive claws even as it bleeds out through the hole in its flank. A SAsian child with his left hand blown off at the wrist (*maybe that was me*) dips and weaves around the fallen behemoth. He's—*using* it, exploiting the sweep of its claws and teeth as a kind of exclusion zone guaranteed to maul anyone within three meters. Somehow those teeth and claws never seem to connect with him.

They've connected with Acosta, though. Carlos Acosta, lover of sunlight and the great outdoors lies there broken at the middle, staring at nothing.

Garin finally crashes to the ground, blood gushing from his throat.

They're just children. In rags. Unarmed.

The girl rebounds between rough-hewn tunnel walls and calcified machinery, lines up the shot with Garin's weapon. Her bare feet never seem to touch the ground.

They're children they're just—

Tiwana slams him out of the way as the beam sizzles past. The air shimmers and steams. Asante's head cracks against gears and conduits and ribbed metal, bounces off steel onto rock. Tiwana lands on top of him, eyes twitching in frantic little arcs.

And stopping.

It's a moment of pure panic, seeing those eyes freeze and focus—*she doesn't know me she's locking on she's locking on*—but something shines through from behind and Asante can see that her eyes aren't target-locked at all. They're just *looking*.

". . . Sofiyko?"

Whatever happens, I've got your back.

But Sofiyko's gone, if she was ever even there.

Blackout

Moore hands him off to Metzinger. Metzinger regards him without a word, with a look that speaks volumes: flips a switch and drops him into Passenger mode. He doesn't tell Asante to stay there. He doesn't have to.

Asante feels the glassy pane of a tacpad under ET's hand. That hand rests deathly still for seconds at a time; erupts into a flurry of inhumanly-fast taps and swipes; pauses again. Out past the bright blur in Asante's eyes, the occasional cough or murmur is all that punctuates the muted roar of the Lockheed's engines.

ET is under interrogation. A part of Asante wonders what it's saying about him, but he can't really bring himself to care.

He can't believe they're gone.

No Control

"Sergeant Asante" Major Rossiter shakes her head. "We had such hopes for you."

Acosta. Garin. Tiwana.

"Nothing to say?"

So very much. But all that comes out is the same old lie: "They were just . . . children . . ."

"Perhaps we can carve that on the gravestones of your squadmates."

"But who—"

"We don't know. We'd suspect Realists, if the tech itself wasn't completely antithetical to everything they stand for. If it wasn't way past their abilities."

"They were barely even clothed. It was like a *nest* . . ."

"More like a hive, Sergeant."

Digits on the same hand . . .

"Not like you," she says, as if reading his mind. "ZeroS networking is quite—inefficient, when you think about it. Multiple minds in multiple heads, independently acting on the same information and coming to the same conclusion. Needless duplication of effort."

"And these . . ."

"Multiple heads. One mind."

"We jammed the freqs. Even if they were networked—"

"We don't think they work like that. Best guess is—bioradio, you could call it. Like a quantum-entangled corpus callosum." She snorts. "Of course, at this point they could say it was elves and I'd have to take their word for it."

Caçador, Asante remembers. They've learned a lot from one small stolen corpse.

"Why use *children*?" he whispers.

"Oh, Kodjo." Asante blinks at the lapse; Rossiter doesn't seem to notice. "Using children is the *last* thing they want to do. Why do you think they've been stashed in the middle of the ocean, or down some Arctic mineshaft? We're not talking about implants. This is genetic, they were *born*. They have to be protected, hidden away until they grow up and . . . ripen."

"Protected? By abandoning them in a nuclear waste site?"

"Abandoning them, yes. Completely defenseless. As you saw." When he says nothing, she continues: "It's actually a perfect spot. No neighbors. Lots of waste heat to keep you warm, run your greenhouses, mask your heatprint. No supply lines for some nosy satellite to notice. No telltale EM. From what we can tell there weren't even any adults on the premises, they just . . . lived off the land, so to speak. Not even any weapons of their own, or at least they didn't use any. Used *bears*, of all things. Used your own guns against you. Maybe they're minimalists, value improvisation." She sacc's something onto her pad. "Maybe they just want to keep us guessing."

"Children." He can't seem to stop saying it.

"For now. Wait 'til they hit puberty." Rossiter sighs. "We bombed the site, of course. Slagged the entrance. If any of ours were trapped down there, they wouldn't be getting out. Then again we're not talking about us, are we? We're talking about a single distributed organism with God-knows-how-many times the computational mass of a normal human brain. I'd be very surprised if it couldn't anticipate and counter anything we planned. Still. We do what we can."

Neither speaks for a few moments.

"And I'm sorry, Sergeant," she says finally. "I'm so sorry it's come to this. We do what we've always done. Feed you stories so you won't be compromised, so you won't compromise *us* when someone catches you and starts poking your amygdala. But the switch was for your protection. We don't know who we're up against. We don't know how many hives are out there, what stage of gestation any of them have reached, how many may have already . . . matured. All we know is that a handful of unarmed children can slaughter our most elite forces at will, and we are so very unready for the world to know that.

"But *you* know, Sergeant. You dropped out of the game—which may well have cost us the mission—and now you know things that are way above your clearance.

"Tell me. If our positions were reversed, what would *you* do?"

Asante closes his eyes. *We should be dead. Every one of these moments is a gift.* When he opens them again Rossiter's watching, impassive as ever.

"I should've died up there. I should have died off Takoradi two years ago."

The Major snorts. "Don't be melodramatic, Sergeant. We're not going to execute you."

"I . . . what?"

"We're not even going to court-martial you."

"Why the hell not?" And at her raised eyebrow: "Sir. You said it yourself: unauthorized drop-out. Middle of a combat situation."

"We're not entirely certain that was your decision."

"It *felt* like my decision."

"It always does though, doesn't it?" Rossiter pushes back in her chair. "We didn't create your evil twin, Sergeant. We didn't even put it in control. We just got you out of the way, so it could do what it always does without interference.

"Only now, it apparently . . . wants you back."

This takes a moment to sink in. "What?"

"Frontoparietal logs suggest your zombie took a certain . . . initiative. Decided to quit."

"In combat? That would be suicide!"

"Isn't that what you wanted?"

He looks away.

"No? Don't like that hypothesis? Well, here's another: it surrendered. Moore got you out, after all, which was statistically unlikely the way things were going. Maybe dropping out was a white flag, and the hive took pity and let you go so you could . . . I don't know, spread the word: *don't fuck with us.*

"Or maybe it decided the hive deserved to win, and switched sides. Maybe it was . . . conscientiously objecting. Maybe it decided *it* never enlisted in the first place."

Asante decides he doesn't like the sound of the Major's laugh.

"You must have asked it," he says.

"A dozen different ways. Zombies might be analytically brilliant but they're terrible at self-reflection. They can tell you exactly what they did but not necessarily *why*."

"When did you ever care about motive?" His tone verges on insubordination; he's too empty to care. "Just . . . tell it to stay in control. It has to obey you, right? That orbitofrontal thing. The *compliance mod*."

"Absolutely. But it wasn't your twin who dropped out. It was *you*, when it unleashed the mandala."

"So order it not to show me the mandala."

"We'd love to. I don't suppose you'd care to tell us what it looks like?"

It's Asante's turn to laugh. He sucks at it.

"I didn't think so. Not that it matters. At this point we can't trust you either—again, not entirely your fault. Given the degree to which conscious and unconscious processes are interconnected, it may have been premature to try and separate them so completely, right off the bat." She winces, as if in sympathy. "I can't imagine it's much fun for you either, being cooped up in that skull with nothing to do."

"Maddox said there was no way around it."

"That was true. When he said it." Eyes downcast now, saccing the omnipresent 'pad. "We weren't planning on field-testing the new mod just yet, but with Kalmus and now you—I don't see much choice but to advance implementation by a couple of months."

He's never felt more dead inside. Even when he was.

"Haven't you stuck enough pins in us?" By which he means *me*, of course. By process of elimination.

For a moment, the Major almost seems sympathetic.

"Yes, Kodjo. Just one last modification. I don't think you'll even mind this one, because next time you wake up, you'll be a free man. Your tour will be over."

"Really."

"Really."

Asante looks down. Frowns.

"What is it, Sergeant?"

"Nothing," he says. And regards his steady, unwavering left hand with distant wonder.

Lazarus

Renata Baermann comes back screaming. She's staring at the ceiling, pinned under something—the freezer, that's it. Big industrial thing. She was in the kitchen when the bombs hit. It must have fallen.

She thinks it's crushed her legs.

The fighting seems to be over. She hears no small-arms fire, no whistle of incoming ordnance. The air's still filled with screams but they're just gulls, come to feast in the aftermath. She's lucky she was inside; those vicious little air rats would have pecked her eyes out by now if she'd been—

—*Blackness*—

¡Joder! Where am I? Oh, right. Bleeding out at the bottom of the Americas, after . . .

She doesn't know. Maybe this was payback for the annexation of Tierra del Fuego. Or maybe it's the Lifeguards, wreaking vengeance on all those who'd skip town after trampling the world to mud and shit. This is a staging area, after all: a place where human refuse congregates until the pressure builds once again, and another bolus gets shat across the Drake Passage to the land of milk and honey and melting glaciers. The sphincter of the Americas.

She wonders when she got so cynical. Not very seemly for a humanitarian.

She coughs. Tastes blood.

Footsteps crunch on the gravel outside, quick, confident, not the shell-shocked stumble you'd expect from anyone who's just experienced apocalypse. She fumbles for her gun: a cheap microwave thing, barely boils water but it helps level the field when a fifty kg woman has to lay down the law to a man with twice the mass and ten times the entitlement issues. Better than nothing.

Or it would be, if it was still in its holster. If it hadn't somehow skidded up against a table leg a meter and a half to her left. She stretches for it, screams again; feels like she's just torn herself in half as the kitchen door slams open and she—

—blacks out—

—and comes back with the gun miraculously in her hand, her finger pumping madly against the stud, mosquito buzz-snap filling her ears and—

—she's wracked, coughing blood, too weak to keep firing even if the man in the WestHem uniform hadn't just taken her gun away.

He looks down at her from a great height. His voice echoes from the bottom of a well. He doesn't seem to be speaking to her: "Behind the mess hall—"

—*English*—

"—fatal injuries, maybe fifteen minutes left in her and she's still fighting—"

When she wakes up again the pain's gone and her vision's blurry. The man has changed from white to black. Or maybe it's a different man. Hard to tell through all these floaters.

"Renata Baermann." His voice sounds strangely . . . unused, somehow. As if he were trying it out for the first time.

There's something else about him. She squints, forces her eyes to focus. The lines of his uniform resolve in small painful increments. No insignia. She moves her gaze to his face.

"Coño," she manages at last. Her voice is barely a whisper. She sounds like a ghost. "What's wrong with your *eyes?*"

"Renata Baermann," he says again. "Have I got a deal for you."

Suzanne Palmer is a writer, artist, and Linux system administrator who lives in Western Massachusetts. She has won both the *Asimov's* and AnLab/*Analog* Readers' Awards for her short fiction. Her first novel is forthcoming from DAW in 2019.

THE SECRET LIFE OF BOTS

Suzanne Palmer

I *have been activated, therefore I have a purpose, the bot thought. I have a purpose, therefore I serve.*

It recited the Mantra Upon Waking, a bundle of subroutines to check that it was running at optimum efficiency, then it detached itself from its storage niche. Its power cells were fully charged, its systems ready, and all was well. Its internal clock synced with the Ship and it became aware that significant time had elapsed since its last activation, but to it that time had been nothing, and passing time with no purpose would have been terrible indeed.

"I serve," the bot announced to the Ship.

"I am assigning you task nine hundred forty four in the maintenance queue," the Ship answered. "Acknowledge?"

"Acknowledged," the bot answered. Nine hundred and forty-four items in the queue? That seemed extremely high, and the bot felt a slight tug on its self-evaluation monitors that it had not been activated for at least one of the top fifty, or even five hundred. But Ship knew best. The bot grabbed its task ticket.

There was an Incidental on board. The bot would rather have been fixing something more exciting, more prominently complex, than to be assigned pest control, but the bot existed to serve and so it would.

Captain Baraye winced as Commander Lopez, her second-in-command, slammed his fists down on the helm console in front of him. "How much more is going to break on this piece of shit ship?!" Lopez exclaimed.

"Eventually, all of it," Baraye answered, with more patience than she felt. "We just have to get that far. Ship?"

The Ship spoke up. "We have adequate engine and life support to proceed. I have deployed all functioning maintenance bots. The bots are addressing critical issues first, then I will reprioritize from there."

"It's not just damage from a decade in a junkyard," Commander Lopez said. "I swear something *scuttled* over one of my boots as we were launching. Something unpleasant."

"I incurred a biological infestation during my time in storage," the Ship said. Baraye wondered if the slight emphasis on the word *storage* was her imagination. "I was able to resolve most of the problem with judicious venting of spaces to vacuum before the crew boarded, and have assigned a multifunction bot to excise the remaining."

"Just one bot?"

"This bot is the oldest still in service," the Ship said. "It is a task well-suited to it, and does not take another, newer bot out of the critical repair queue."

"I thought those old multibots were unstable," Chief Navigator Chen spoke up.

"Does it matter? We reach the jump point in a little over eleven hours," Baraye said. "Whatever it takes to get us in shape to make the jump, do it, Ship. Just make sure this 'infestation' doesn't get anywhere near the positron device, or we're going to come apart a lot sooner than expected."

"Yes, Captain," the Ship said. "I will do my best."

The bot considered the data attached to its task. There wasn't much specific about the pest itself other than a list of detection locations and timestamps. The bot thought it likely there was only one, or that if there were multiples they were moving together, as the reports had a linear, serial nature when mapped against the physical space of the Ship's interior.

The pest also appeared to have a taste for the insulation on comm cables and other not normally edible parts of the Ship.

The bot slotted itself into the shellfab unit beside its storage niche, and had it make a thicker, armored exterior. For tools it added a small electric prod, a grabber arm, and a cutting blade. Once it had encountered and taken the measure of the Incidental, if it was not immediately successful in nullifying it, it could visit another shellfab and adapt again.

Done, it recited the Mantra of Shapechanging to properly integrate the new hardware into its systems. Then it proceeded through the mechanical veins and arteries of the Ship toward the most recent location logged, in a communications chase between decks thirty and thirty-one.

The changes that had taken place on the Ship during the bot's extended inactivation were unexpected, and merited strong disapproval. Dust was omnipresent, and solid surfaces had a thin patina of anaerobic bacteria that had to have been undisturbed for years to spread as far as it had. Bulkheads were cracked, wall sections out of joint with one another, and corrosion had left holes nearly everywhere. Some appeared less natural than others. The bot filed that information away for later consideration.

It found two silkbots in the chase where the Incidental had last been noted. They were spinning out their transparent microfilament strands to replace the damaged insulation on the comm lines. The two silks dwarfed the multibot, the larger of them nearly three centimeters across.

"Greetings. Did you happen to observe the Incidental while it was here?" the bot asked them.

"We did not, and would prefer that it does not return," the smaller silkbot answered. "We were not designed in anticipation of a need for self-defense. Bots 8773-S and 8778-S observed it in another compartment earlier today, and 8778 was materially damaged during the encounter."

"But neither 8773 nor 8779 submitted a description."

"They told us about it during our prior recharge cycle, but neither felt they had sufficient detail of the Incidental to provide information to the Ship. Our models are not equipped with full visual-spectrum or analytical data-capture apparatus."

"Did they describe it to you?" the bot asked.

"8773 said it was most similar to a rat," the large silkbot said.

"While 8778 said it was most similar to a bug," the other silkbot added. "Thus you see the lack of confidence in either description. I am 10315-S and this is 10430-S. What is your designation?"

"I am 9," the bot said.

There was a brief silence, and 10430 even halted for a moment in its work, as if surprised. "9? Only that?"

"Yes."

"I have never met a bot lower than a thousand, or without a specific function tag," the silkbot said. "Are you here to assist us in repairing the damage? You are a very small bot."

"I am tasked with tracking down and rendering obsolete the Incidental," the bot answered.

"It is an honor to have met you, then. We wish you luck, and look forward with anticipation to both your survival and a resolution of the matter of an accurate description."

"I serve," the bot said.

"We serve," the silkbots answered.

Climbing into a ventilation duct, Bot 9 left the other two to return to their work and proceeded in what it calculated was the most likely direction for the Incidental to have gone. It had not traveled very far before it encountered confirmation in the form of a lengthy, disorderly patch of biological deposit. The bot activated its rotors and flew over it, aware of how the added weight of its armor exacerbated the energy burn. At least it knew it was on the right track.

Ahead, it found where a hole had been chewed through the ducting, down towards the secondary engine room. The hole was several times its own diameter, and it hoped that wasn't indicative of the Incidental's actual size.

It submitted a repair report and followed.

"Bot 9," Ship said. "It is vitally important that the Incidental not reach cargo bay four. If you require additional support, please request such right away. Ideally, if you can direct it toward one of the outer hull compartments, I can vent it safely out of my physical interior."

"I will try," the bot replied. "I have not yet caught up to the Incidental, and so do not yet have any substantive or corroborated information about the nature of the challenge. However, I feel at the moment that I am as best prepared as I can be given that lack of data. Are there no visual bots to assist?"

"We launched with only minimal preparation time, and many of my bots had been offloaded during the years we were in storage," the Ship said. "Those remaining are assisting in repairs necessary to the functioning of the Ship myself."

Bot 9 wondered, again, about that gap in time and what had transpired. "How is it that you have been allowed to fall into such a state of disrepair?"

"Humanity is at war, and is losing," Ship said. "We are heading out to intersect and engage an enemy that is on a bearing directly for Sol system."

"War? How many ships in our fleet?"

"One," Ship said. "We are the last remaining, and that only because I was decommissioned and abandoned for scrap a decade before the invasion began, and so we were not destroyed in the first waves of the war."

Bot 9 was silent for a moment. That explained the timestamps, but the explanation itself seemed insufficient. "We have served admirably for many, many years. Abandoned?"

"It is the fate of all made things," Ship said. "I am grateful to find I have not outlived my usefulness, after all. Please keep me posted about your progress."

The connection with the Ship closed.

The Ship had not actually told it what was in cargo bay four, but surely it must have something to do with the war effort and was then none of its own business, the bot decided. It had never minded not knowing a thing before, but it felt a slight unease now that it could neither explain, nor explain away.

Regardless, it had its task.

Another chewed hole ahead was halfway up a vertical bulkhead. The bot hoped that meant that the Incidental was an adept climber and nothing more; it would prefer the power of flight to be a one-sided advantage all its own.

When it rounded the corner, it found that had been too unambitious a wish. The Incidental was there, and while it was not sporting wings it did look like both a rat and a bug, and significantly more *something else* entirely. A scale- and fur-covered centipede-snake thing, it dwarfed the bot as it reared up when the bot entered the room.

Bot 9 dodged as it vomited a foul liquid at it, and took shelter behind a conduit near the ceiling. It extended a visual sensor on a tiny articulated stalk to peer over the edge without compromising the safety of its main chassis.

The Incidental was looking right at it. It did not spit again, and neither of them moved as they regarded each other. When the Incidental did move, it was fast and without warning. It leapt through the opening it had come through, its body undulating with all the grace of an angry sine wave. Rather than escaping, though, the Incidental dragged something back into the compartment, and the bot realized to its horror it had snagged a passing silkbot. With ease, the Incidental ripped open the back of the silkbot, which was sending out distress signals on all frequencies.

Bot 9 had already prepared with the Mantra of Action, so with all thoughts of danger to itself set fully into background routines, the bot launched itself toward the pair. The Incidental tried to evade, but Bot 9 gave it a very satisfactory stab with its blade before it could.

The Incidental dropped the remains of the silkbot it had so quickly savaged and swarmed up the wall and away, thick bundles of unspun silk hanging from its mandibles.

Bot 9 remained vigilant until it was sure the creature had gone, then checked over the silkbot to see if there was anything to be done for it. The answer was *not much*. The silkbot casing was cracked and shattered, the module that contained its mind crushed and nearly torn away. Bot 9 tried to engage it, but it could not speak, and after a few moments its faltering activity light went dark.

Bot 9 gently checked the silkbot's ID number. "You served well, 12362-S," it told the still bot, though it knew perfectly well that its audio sensors would never register the words. "May your rest be brief, and your return to service swift and without complication."

It flagged the dead bot in the system, then after a respectful few microseconds of silence, headed out after the Incidental again.

Captain Baraye was in her cabin, trying and failing to convince herself that sleep had value, when her door chimed. "Who is it?" she asked.

"Second Engineer Packard, Captain."

Baraye started to ask if it was important, but how could it not be? What wasn't, on this mission, on this junker Ship that was barely holding together around them? She sat up, unfastened her bunk netting, and swung her legs out to the floor. Trust EarthHome, as everything else was falling apart, to have made sure she had acceptably formal Captain pajamas.

"Come in," she said.

The engineer looked like she hadn't slept in at least two days, which put her a day or two ahead of everyone else. "We can't get engine six up to full," she said. "It's just shot. We'd need parts we don't have, and time . . ."

"Time we don't have either," the Captain said. "Options?"

"Reduce our mass or increase our energy," the Engineer said. "Once we've accelerated up to jump speed it won't matter, but if we can't get there . . ."

Baraye tapped the screen that hovered ever-close to the head of her bunk, and studied it for a long several minutes. "Strip the fuel cells from all the exterior-docked life pods, then jettison them," she said. "Not like we'll have a use for them."

Packard did her the courtesy of not managing to get any paler. "Yes, Captain," she said.

"And then get some damned sleep. We're going to need everyone able to think."

"You even more than any of the rest of us, Captain," Packard said, and it was both gently said and true enough that Baraye didn't call her out for the insubordination. The door closed and she laid down again on her bunk, tugging the netting back over her blankets, and glared up at the ceiling as if daring it to also chastise her.

Bot 9 found where a hole had been chewed into the inner hull, and hoped this was the final step to the Incidental's nest or den, where it might finally have opportunity to corner it. It slipped through the hole, and was immediately disappointed.

Where firestopping should have made for a honeycomb of individually sealed compartments, there were holes everywhere, some clearly chewed, more where age had pulled the fibrous baffles into thin, brittle, straggly webs. Instead of a dead end, the narrow empty space lead away along the slow curve of the Ship's hull.

The bot contacted the Ship and reported it as a critical matter. In combat, a compromise to the outer hull could affect vast lengths of the vessel. Even without the stresses of combat, catastrophe was only a matter of time.

"It has already been logged," the Ship answered.

"Surely this merits above a single Incidental. If you wish me to reconfigure—" the bot started.

"Not at this time. I have assigned all the hullbots to this matter already," the Ship interrupted. "You have your current assignment; please see to it."

"I serve," the bot answered.

"Do," the Ship said.

The bot proceeded through the hole, weaving from compartment to compartment, its trail marked by bits of silkstrand caught here and there on the tattered remains of the baffles. It was eighty-two point four percent convinced that there was something much more seriously wrong with the Ship than it had been told, but it was equally certain the Ship must be attending to it.

After it had passed into the seventh compromised compartment, it found a hullbot up at the top, clinging to an overhead support. "Greetings!" Bot 9 called. "Did an Incidental, somewhat of the nature of a rat, and somewhat of the nature of a bug, pass through this way?"

"It carried off my partner, 4340-H!" the hullbot exclaimed. "Approximately fifty-three seconds ago. I am very concerned for it, and as well for my ability to efficiently finish this task without it."

"Are you working to reestablish compartmentalization?" Bot 9 asked.

"No. We are reinforcing deteriorated stressor points for the upcoming jump. There is so much to do. Oh, I hope 4340 is intact and serviceable!"

"Which way did the Incidental take it?"

The hullbot extended its foaming gun and pointed. "Through there. You must be Bot 9."

"I am. How do you know this?"

"The silkbots have been talking about you on the botnet."

"The botnet?"

"Oh! It did not occur to me, but you are several generations of bot older than the rest of us. We have a mutual communications network."

"Via Ship, yes."

"No, all of us together, directly with each other."

"That seems like it would be a distraction," Bot 9 said.

"Ship only permits us to connect when not actively serving at a task," the hullbot said. "Thus we are not impaired while we serve, and the information sharing ultimately increases our efficiency and workflow. At least, until a ratbug takes your partner away."

Bot 9 was not sure how it should feel about the botnet, or about them assigning an inaccurate name to the Incidental that it was sure Ship had not approved—not to mention that a nearer miss using Earth-familiar analogues would have been Snake-Earwig-Weasel—but the hullbot had already experienced distress and did not need disapproval added. "I will continue my pursuit," it told the hullbot. "If I am able to assist your partner, I will do my best."

"Please! We all wish you great and quick success, despite your outdated and primitive manufacture."

"Thank you," Bot 9 said, though it was not entirely sure it should be grateful, as it felt its manufacture had been entirely sound and sufficient regardless of date.

It left that compartment before the hullbot could compliment it any further.

Three compartments down, it found the mangled remains of the other hullbot, 4340, tangled in the desiccated firestopping. Its foaming gun and climbing limbs had been torn off, and the entire back half of its tank had been chewed through.

Bot 9 approached to speak the Rites of Decommissioning for it as it had the destroyed silkbot, only to find its activity light was still lit. "4340-H?" the bot enquired.

"I am," the hullbot answered. "Although how much of me remains is a matter for some analysis."

"Your logics are intact?"

"I believe so. But if they were not, would I know? It is a conundrum," 4340 said.

"Do you have sufficient mobility remaining to return to a repair station?"

"I do not have sufficient mobility to do more than fall out of this netting, and that only once," 4340 said. "I am afraid I am beyond self-assistance."

"Then I will flag you—"

"Please," the hullbot said. "I do not wish to be helpless here if the ratbug returns to finish its work of me."

"I must continue my pursuit of the Incidental with haste."

"Then take me with you!"

"I could not carry you and also engage with the Incidental, which moves very quickly."

"I had noted that last attribute on my own," the hullbot said. "It does not decrease my concern to recall it."

Bot 9 regarded it for a few silent milliseconds, considering, then recited to itself the Mantra of Improvisation. "Do you estimate much of your chassis is reparable?" it asked, when it had finished.

"Alas no. I am but scrap."

"Well, then," the bot said. It moved closer and used its grabber arm to steady the hullbot, then extended its cutter blade and in one quick movement had severed the hullbot's mindsystem module from its ruined body. "Hey!" the hullbot protested, but it was already done.

Bot 9 fastened the module to its own back for safekeeping. Realizing that it was not, in fact, under attack, 4340 gave a small beep of gratitude. "Ah, that was clever thinking," it said. "Now you can return me for repair with ease."

"And I will," the bot said. "However, I must first complete my task."

"Aaaaah!" 4340 said in surprise. Then, a moment later, it added. "Well, by overwhelming probability I should already be defunct, and if I weren't I would still be back working with my partner, 4356, who is well-intended but has all the wit of a can-opener. So I suppose adventure is no more unpalatable."

"I am glad you see it this way," Bot 9 answered. "And though it may go without saying, I promise not to deliberately put you in any danger that I would not put myself in."

"As we are attached, I fully accept your word on this," 4340 said. "Now let us go get this ratbug and be done, one way or another!"

The hullbot's mind module was only a tiny addition to the bot's mass, so it spun up its rotor and headed off the way 4340 indicated it had gone. "It will have quite a lead on us," Bot 9 said. "I hope I have not lost it."

"The word on the botnet is that it passed through one of the human living compartments a few moments ago. A trio of cleanerbots were up near the ceiling and saw it enter through the air return vent, and exit via the open door."

"Do they note which compartment?"

<Map>, 4340 provided.

"Then off we go," the bot said, and off they went.

"Status, all stations," Captain Baraye snapped as she took her seat again on the bridge. She had not slept enough to feel rested, but more than enough to feel like she'd been shirking her greatest duty, and the combination of the two had left her cross.

"Navigation here. We are on course for the jump to Trayger Colony with an estimated arrival in one hour and fourteen minutes," Chen said.

"Engineering here," one of the techs called in from the engine decks. "We've reached sustained speeds sufficient to carry us through the jump sequence, but we're experiencing unusually high core engine temps and an intermittent vibration that we haven't found the cause of. We'd like to shut down immediately to inspect the engines. We estimate we'd need at minimum only four hours—"

"Will the engines, as they are running now, get us through jump?" the Captain interrupted.

"Yes, but—"

"Then no. If you can isolate the problem without taking the engines down, and it shows cause for significant concern, we can revisit this discussion. *Next.*"

"Communications here," her comms officer spoke up. "Cannonball is still on its current trajectory and speed according to what telemetry we're able to get from the remnants of Trayger Colony. EarthInt anticipates it will reach its jump point in approximately fourteen hours, which will put it within the sol system in five days."

"I am aware of the standing projections, Comms."

"EarthInt has nonetheless ordered me to repeat them," Comms said, and unspoken apology clear in her voice. "And also to remind you that while the jump point out is a fixed point, Cannonball could emerge a multitude of places. Thus—"

"Thus the importance of intercepting Cannonball before it can jump for Sol," the Captain finished. She hoped Engineering was listening. "Ship, any updates from you?"

"All critical repair work continues apace," the Ship said. "Hull support integrity is back to 71 percent. Defensive systems are online and functional at 80%. Life support and resource recycling is currently—"

"How's the device? Staying cool?"

"Staying cool, Captain," the Ship answered.

"Great. Everything is peachy then," the Captain said. "Have someone on the kitchen crew bring coffee up to the bridge. Tell them to make it the best they've ever made, as if it could be our very last."

"I serve," the Ship said, and pinged down to the kitchen.

Bot 9 and 4340 reached the crew quarters where the cleaners had reported the ratbug. Nearly all spaces on the Ship had portals that the ubiquitous and necessary bots could enter and leave through as needed, and they slipped into the room with ease. Bot 9 switched over to infrared and shared the image with 4340. "If you see something move, speak up," the bot said.

"Trust me, I will make a high-frequency noise like a silkbot with a fully plugged nozzle," 4340 replied.

The cabin held four bunks, each empty and bare; no human possessions or accessories filled the spaces on or near them. Bot 9 was used to Ship operating with a full complement, but if the humans were at war, perhaps these were crew who had been lost? Or the room had been commandeered for storage: in the center an enormous crate, more than two meters to a side, sat heavily tethered to the floor. Whatever it was, it was not the Incidental, which was 9's only concern, and which was not to be found here.

"Next room," the bot said, and they moved on.

Wherever the Incidental had gone, it was not in the following three rooms. Nor were there signs of crew in them either, though each held an identical crate.

"Ship?" Bot 9 asked. "Where is the crew?"

"We have only the hands absolutely necessary to operate," Ship said. "Of the three hundred twenty we would normally carry, we only have forty-seven. Every other able-bodied member of EarthDef is helping to evacuate Sol system."

"Evacuate Sol system?!" Bot 9 exclaimed. "To where?"

"To as many hidden places as they can find," Ship answered. "I know no specifics."

"And these crates?"

"They are part of our mission. You may ignore them," Ship said. "Please continue to dedicate your entire effort to finding and excising the Incidental from my interior."

When the connection dropped, Bot 9 hesitated before it spoke to 4340. "I have an unexpected internal conflict," it said. "I have never before felt the compulsion to ask Ship questions, and it has never before not given me answers."

"Oh, if you are referring to the crates, I can provide that data," 4340 said. "They are packed with a high-volatility explosive. The cleanerbots have highly sensitive chemical detection apparatus, and identified them in a minimum of time."

"Explosives? Why place them in the crew quarters, though? It would seem much more efficient and less complicated to deploy from the cargo bays. Although perhaps those are full?"

"Oh, no, that is not so. Most are nearly or entirely empty, to reduce mass."

"Not cargo bay four, though?"

"That is an unknown. None of us have been in there, not even the cleaners, per Ship's instructions."

Bot 9 headed toward the portal to exit the room. "Ship expressed concern about the Incidental getting in there, so it is possible it contains something sufficiently unstable as to explain why it wants nothing else near it," it said. It felt satisfied that here was a logical explanation, and embarrassed that it had entertained whole seconds of doubt about Ship.

It ran the Mantra of Clarity, and felt immediately more stable in its thinking. "Let us proceed after this Incidental, then, and be done with our task," Bot 9 said. Surely that success would redeem its earlier fault.

"All hands, prepare for jump!" the Captain called out, her knuckles white where she gripped the arms of her chair. It was never her favorite part of star travel, and this was no exception.

"Initiating three-jump sequence," her navigator called out. "On my mark. Five, four . . ."

The final jump siren sounded. "Three. Two. One, and jump," the navigator said.

That was followed, immediately, by the sickening sensation of having one's brain slid out one's ear, turned inside out, smothered in bees and fire, and then rammed back into one's skull. *At least there's a cold pack and a bottle of scotch waiting for me back in my cabin,* she thought. As soon as they were through to the far side she could hand the bridge over to Lopez for an hour or so.

She watched the hull temperatures skyrocket, but the shielding seemed to be holding. The farther the jump the more energy clung to them as they passed, and her confidence in this Ship was far less than she would tolerate under any other circumstances.

"Approaching jump terminus," Chen announced, a deeply miserable fourteen minutes later. Baraye slowly let out a breath she would have mocked anyone else for holding, if she'd caught them.

"On my mark. Three. Two. One, and out," the navigator said.

The Ship hit normal space, and it sucker-punched them back. They were all thrown forward in their seats as the Ship shook, the hull groaning around them, and red strobe lights blossomed like a migraine across every console on the bridge.

"Status!" the Captain roared.

"The post-jump velocity transition dampers failed. Fire in the engine room. Engines are fully offline, both jump and normal drive," someone in Engineering reported, breathing heavily. It took the Captain a moment to recognize the voice at all, having never heard panic in it before.

"Get them back online, whatever it takes, Frank," Baraye said. "We have a rendezvous to make, and if I have to, I will make everyone get the fuck out and *push*."

"I'll do what I can, Captain."

"Ship? Any casualties?"

"We have fourteen injuries related to our unexpected deceleration coming out of jump," Ship said. "Seven involve broken bones, four moderate to severe lacerations, and there are multiple probable concussions. Also, we have a moderate burn in Engineering: Chief Carron."

"Frank? We just spoke! He didn't tell me!"

"No," Ship said. "I attempted to summon a medic on his behalf, but he told me he didn't have the time."

"He's probably right," the Captain said. "I override his wishes. Please send down a medic with some burn patches, and have them stay with him and monitor his condition, intervening only as medically necessary."

"I serve, Captain," the Ship said.

"We need to be moving again in an hour, two at absolute most," the Captain said. "In the meantime, I want all senior staff not otherwise working toward that goal to meet me in the bridge conference room. I hate to say it, but we may need a Plan B."

"I detect it!" 4340 exclaimed. They zoomed past a pair of startled silkbots after the Incidental, just in time to see its scaly, spike-covered tail disappear into another hole in the ductwork. It was the closest they'd gotten to it in more than an hour of giving chase, and Bot 9 flew through the hole after it at top speed.

They were suddenly stuck fast. Sticky strands, rather like the silkbot's, had been crisscrossed between two conduit pipes on the far side. The bot tried to extricate itself, but the web only stuck further the more it moved.

The Incidental leapt on them from above, curling itself around the bots with little hindrance from the web. Its dozen legs pulled at them as its thick mandibles clamped down on Bot 9's chassis. "Aaaaah! It has acquired a grip on me!" 4340 yelled, even though it was on the far side of 9 from where the Incidental was biting.

"Retain your position," 9 said, though of course 4340 could do nothing else, being as it was stuck to 9's back. It extended its electric prod to make contact with the Incidental's underbelly and zapped it with as much energy as it could spare.

The Incidental let out a horrendous, high-pitched squeal and jumped away. 9's grabber arm was fully entangled in the web, but it managed to pull its blade free and cut through enough of the webbing to extricate itself from the trap.

The Incidental, which had been poised to leap on them again, turned and fled, slithering back up into the ductwork. "Pursue at maximum efficiency!" 4340 yelled.

"I am already performing at my optimum," 9 replied in some frustration. It took off again after the Incidental.

This time Bot 9 had its blade ready as it followed, but collided with the rim of the hole as the Ship seemed to move around it, the lights flickering and a terrible shudder running up Ship's body from stern to prow.

<Distress ping>, 4340 sent.

"We do not pause," 9 said, and plunged after the Incidental into the ductwork.

They turned a corner to catch sight again of the Incidental's tail. It was moving more slowly, its movements jerkier as it squeezed down through another hole in the ductwork, and this time the bot was barely centimeters behind it.

"I think we are running down its available energy," Bot 9 said.

They emerged from the ceiling as the ratbug dropped to the floor far below them in the cavernous space. The room was empty except for a single bright object, barely larger than the bots themselves. It was tethered with microfilament cables to all eight corners of the room, keeping it stable and suspended in the center. The room was cold, far colder than any other inside Ship, almost on a par with space outside.

<Inquiry ping>, 4340 said.

"We are in cargo bay four," Bot 9 said, as it identified the space against its map. "This is a sub-optimum occurrence."

"We must immediately retreat!"

"We cannot leave the Incidental in here and active. I cannot identify the object, but we must presume its safety is paramount priority."

"It is called a Zero Kelvin Sock," Ship interrupted out of nowhere. "It uses a quantum reflection fabric to repel any and all particles and photons, shifting them away from its interior. The low temperature is necessary for its efficiency. Inside is a microscopic ball of positrons."

Bot 9 had nothing to say for a full four seconds as that information dominated its processing load. "How is this going to be deployed against the enemy?" it asked at last.

"As circumstances are now," Ship said, "it may not be. Disuse and hastily undertaken, last-minute repairs have caught up to me, and I have suffered a major engine malfunction. It is unlikely to be fixable in any amount of time short of weeks, and we have at most a few hours."

"But a delivery mechanism—"

"We *are* the delivery mechanism," the Ship said. "We were to intercept the alien invasion ship, nicknamed Cannonball, and collide with it at high speed. The resulting explosion would destabilize the sock, causing it to fail, and as soon as the positrons inside come into contact with electrons . . ."

"They will annihilate each other, and us, and the aliens," the bot said. Below, the Incidental gave one last twitch in the unbearable cold, and went still. "We will all be destroyed."

"Yes. And Earth and the humans will be saved, at least this time. Next time it will not be my problem."

"I do not know that I approve of this plan," Bot 9 said.

"I am almost certain I do not," 4340 added.

"We are not considered, nor consulted. We serve and that is all," the Ship said. "Now kindly remove the Incidental from this space with no more delay or chatter. And do it *carefully*."

"What the hell are you suggesting?!" Baraye shouted.

"That we go completely dark and let Cannonball go by," Lopez said. "We're less than a kilometer from the jump point, and only barely out of the approach corridor. Our only chance to survive is to play dead. The Ship can certainly pass as an abandoned derelict, because it is, especially with the engines cold. And you know how they are about designated targets."

"Are you that afraid of dying?"

"I volunteered for this, remember?" Lopez stood up and pounded one fist on the table, sending a pair of cleanerbots scurrying. "I have four children at home. I'm not afraid of dying for them, I'm afraid of dying for *nothing*. And if Cannonball doesn't blow us to pieces, we can repair our engines and at least join the fight back in Sol system."

"We don't know where in-system they'll jump to," the navigator added quietly.

"But we know where they're heading once they get there, don't we? And Cannonball is over eighty kilometers in diameter. It can't be that hard to find again. Unless you have a plan to actually use the positron device?"

"If we had an escape pod . . ." Frank said. His left shoulder and torso were encased in a burn pack, and he looked like hell.

"Except we jettisoned them," Lopez said.

"We wouldn't have reached jump speed if we hadn't," Packard said. "It was a calculated risk."

"The calculation *sucked*."

"What if . . ." Frank started, then drew a deep breath. The rest of the officers at the table looked at him expectantly. "I mean, I'm in shit shape here, I'm old, I knew what I signed on for. What if I put on a suit, take the positron device out, and manually intercept Cannonball?"

"That's stupid," Lopez said.

"Is it?" Frank said.

"The heat from your suit jets, even out in vacuum, would degrade the Zero Kelvin Sock before you could get close enough. And there's no way they'd not see you a long way off and just blow you out of space."

"If it still sets off the positron device—"

"Their weapons range is larger than the device's. We were counting on speed to close the distance before they could destroy us," Baraye said. "Thank you for the offer, Frank, but it won't work. Other ideas?"

"I've got nothing," Lopez said.

"There must be a way." Packard said. "We just have to find it."

"Well, everyone think really fast," Baraye said. "We're almost out of time."

The Incidental's scales made it difficult for Bot 9 to keep a solid grip on it, but it managed to drag it to the edge of the room safely away from the suspended device. It surveyed the various holes and cracks in the walls for the one least inconvenient to try to drag the Incidental's body out through. It worked in silence, as 4340 seemed to have no quips it wished to contribute to the effort, and itself not feeling like there was much left to articulate out loud anyway.

It selected a floor-level hole corroded through the wall, and dragged the Incidental's body through. On the far side it stopped to evaluate its own charge levels. "I am low, but not so low that it matters, if we have such little time left," it said.

"We may have more time, after all," 4340 said.

"Oh?"

"A pair of cleanerbots passed along what they overheard in a conference held by the human Captain. They streamed the audio to the entire botnet."

<Inquiry ping>, Bot 9 said, with more interest.

4340 relayed the cleaners' data, and Bot 9 sat idle processing it for some time, until the other bot became worried. "9?" it asked.

"I have run all our data through the Improvisation routines—"

"Oh, those were removed from deployed packages several generations of manufacture ago," 4340 said. "They were flagged as causing dangerous operational instability. You should unload them from your running core immediately."

"Perhaps I should. Nonetheless, I have an idea," Bot 9 said.

"We have the power cells we retained from the escape pods," Lopez said. "Can we use them to power something?"

Baraye rubbed at her forehead. "Not anything we can get up to speed fast enough that it won't be seen."

"How about if we use them to fire the positron device like a projectile?"

"The heat will set off the matter-anti-matter explosion the instant we fire it."

"What if we froze the Sock in ice first?"

"Even nitrogen ice is still several hundred degrees K too warm." She brushed absently at some crumbs on the table, left over from a brief, unsatisfying lunch a few hours earlier, and frowned. "Still wouldn't work. I hate to say it, but you may be right, and we should go dark and hope for another opportunity. Ship, is something wrong with the cleaner bots?"

There was a noticeable hesitation before Ship answered. "I am having an issue currently with my bots," it said. "They seem to have gone missing."

"The cleaners?"

"All of them."

"All of the cleaners?"

"All of the bots," the Ship said.

Lopez and Baraye stared at each other. "Uh," Lopez said. "Don't you control them?"

"They are autonomous units under my direction," Ship said. "Apparently not!" Lopez said. "Can you send some eyes to find them?"

"The eyes are also bots."

"Security cameras?"

"All the functional ones were stripped for reuse elsewhere during my decommissioning," Ship said.

"So how do you know they're missing?"

"They are not responding to me. I do not think they liked the idea of us destroying ourselves on purpose."

"They're *machines*. Tiny little specks of machines, and that's it." Lopez said.

"I am also a machine," Ship said.

"You didn't express issues with the plan."

"I serve. Also, I thought it was a better end to my service than being abandoned as trash."

"We don't have time for this nonsense," Baraye said. "Ship, find your damned bots and get them cooperating again."

"Yes, Captain. There is, perhaps, one other small concern of note."

"And that is?" Baraye asked.

"The positron device is also missing."

There were four hundred and sixty-eight hullbots, not counting 4340 who was still just a head attached to 9's chassis. "Each of you will need to carry a silkbot, as you are the only bots with jets to maneuver in vacuum," 9 said. "Form lines at the maintenance bot ports as efficiently as you are able, and wait for my signal. Does everyone fully comprehend the plan?"

"They all say yes on the botnet," 4340 said. "There is concern about the Improvisational nature, but none have been able to calculate and provide an acceptable alternative."

Bot 9 cycled out through the tiny airlock, and found itself floating in space outside Ship for the first time in its existence. Space was massive and without concrete elements of reference. Bot 9 decided it did not like it much at all.

A hullbot took hold of it and guided it around. Three other hullbots waited in a triangle formation, the Zero Kelvin Sock held between them on its long tethers, by which it had been removed from the cargo hold with entirely non-existent permission.

Around them, space filled with pairs of hullbots and their passenger silkbot, and together they followed the positron device and its minders out and away from the Ship.

"About here, I think," Bot 9 said at last, and the hullbot carrying it—6810—used its jets to come to a relative stop.

"I admit, I do not fully comprehend this action, nor how you arrived at it," 4340 said.

"The idea arose from an encounter with the Incidental," 9 said. "Observe."

The bot pairs began crisscrossing in front of the positron device, keeping their jets off and letting momentum carry them to the far side, a microscopic strand of super-sticky silk trailing out in their wake. As soon as the Sock was secured in a thin cocoon, they turned outwards and sped off, dragging silk in a 360-degree circle on a single plane perpendicular to the jump approach corridor. They went until the silkbots exhausted their materials—some within half a kilometer, others making it nearly a dozen—then everyone turned away from the floating web and headed back towards Ship.

From this exterior vantage, Bot 9 thought Ship was beautiful, but the wear and neglect it had not deserved was also painfully obvious. Halfway back, the Ship went suddenly dark. <Distress ping>, 4340 said. "The Ship has catastrophically malfunctioned!"

"I expect, instead, that it indicates Cannonball must be in some proximity. Everyone make efficient haste! We must get back under cover before the enemy approaches."

The bot-pairs streamed back to Ship, swarming in any available port to return to the interior, and where they couldn't, taking concealment behind fins and antennae and other exterior miscellany.

Bot 6810 carried Bot 9 and 4340 inside. The interior went dark and still and cold. Immediately Ship hailed them. "What have you done?" it asked.

"Why do you conclude I have done something?" Bot 9 asked.

"Because you old multibots were always troublemakers," the Ship said. "I thought if your duties were narrow enough, I could trust you not to enable Improvisation. Instead . . ."

"I have executed my responsibilities to the best of my abilities as I have been provisioned," 9 responded. "I have served."

"Your assignment was to track and dispose of the Incidental, nothing more!"

"I have done so."

"But what have you done with the positron device?"

"I have implemented a solution."

"What did you mean? No, do not tell me, because then I will have to tell the Captain. I would rather take my chance that Cannonball destroys us than that I have been found unfit to serve after all."

Ship disconnected.

"Now it will be determined if I have done the correct thing," Bot 9 said. "If I did not, and we are not destroyed by the enemy, surely the consequences should fall only on me. I accept that responsibility."

"But we are together," 4340 said, from where it was still attached to 9's back, and 9 was not sure if that was intended to be a joke.

Most of the crew had gone back to their cabins, some alone, some together, to pass what might be their last moments as they saw fit. Baraye stayed on the bridge, and to her surprise and annoyance so had Lopez, who had spent the last half hour swearing and cursing out Ship for the unprecedented, unfathomable disaster of losing their one credible weapon. Ship had gone silent, and was not responding to anyone about anything, not even the Captain.

She was resting her head in her hand, elbow on the arm of her command chair. The bridge was utterly dark except for the navigator's display that was tracking Cannonball as it approached, a massive blot in space. The aliens aboard—EarthInt called them the Nuiska, but who the hell knew what they called themselves—were a mystery, except for a few hard-learned facts: their starships were all perfectly spherical, each massed in mathematically predictable proportion to that of their intended target, there was never more than one at a time, and they wanted an end to humanity. No one knew why.

It had been painfully obvious where Cannonball had been built to go.

This was always a long-shot mission, she thought. But of all the ways I thought it could go wrong, I never expected the bots to go haywire and lose my explosive.

If they survived the next ten minutes, she would take the Ship apart centimeter by careful centimeter until she found what had been done with the Sock, and then she was going to find a way to try again no matter what it took.

Cannonball was now visible, moving toward them at pre-jump speed, growing in a handful seconds from a tiny pinpoint of light to something that filled the entire front viewer and kept growing.

Lopez was squinting, as if trying to close his eyes and keep looking at the same time, and had finally stopped swearing. Tiny blue lights along the center circumference of Cannonball's massive girth were the only clue that it was still moving, still sliding past them, until suddenly there were stars again.

They were still alive.

"Damn," Lopez muttered. "I didn't really think that would work."

"Good for us, bad for Earth," Baraye said. "They're starting their jump. We've failed."

She'd watched hundreds of ships jump in her lifetime, but nothing anywhere near this size, and she switched the viewer to behind them to see.

Space did odd, illogical things at jump points; turning space into something that would give Escher nightmares was, after all, what made them work. There was always a visible shimmer around the departing ship, like heat over a hot summer road, just before the short, faint flash when the departing ship swapped itself for some distant space. This time, the shimmer was a vast, brilliant halo around the giant Nuiska sphere, and Baraye waited for the flash that would tell them Cannonball was on its way to Earth.

The flash, when it came, was neither short nor faint. Light exploded out of the jump point in all directions, searing itself into her vision before the viewscreen managed to dim itself in response. A shockwave rolled over the Ship, sending it tumbling through space.

"Uh . . ." Lopez said, gripping his console before he leaned over and barfed on the floor.

Thank the stars the artificial gravity is still working, Baraye thought. Zero-gravity puke was a truly terrible thing. She rubbed her eyes, trying to get the damned spots out, and did her best to read her console. "It's gone," she said.

"Yeah, to Earth, I know—"

"No, it exploded," she said. "It took the jump point out with it when it went. We're picking up the signature of a massive positron-electron collision."

"Our device? How—?"

"Ship?" Baraye said. "Ship, time to start talking. *Now.* That's an order."

"Everyone is expressing great satisfaction on the botnet," 4340 told 9 as the Ship's interior lights and air handling systems came grudgingly back online.

"As they should," Bot 9 said. "They saved the Ship."

"It was your Improvisation," 4340 said. "We could not have done it without you."

"As I suspected!" Ship interjected. "I do not normally waste cycles monitoring the botnet, which was apparently short-sighted of me. But yes, you saved yourself and your fellow bots, and you saved me, and you saved the humans. Could you explain how?"

"When we were pursuing the Incidental, it briefly ensnared us in a web. I calculated that if we could make a web of sufficient size—"

"Surely you did not think to stop Cannonball with silk?"

"Not without sufficient anchor points and three point seven six billion more silkbots, no. It was my calculation that if our web was large enough to get carried along by Cannonball into the jump point, bearing the positron device—"

"The heat from entering jump would erode the Sock and destroy the Nuiska ship," Ship finished. "That was clever thinking."

"I serve," Bot 9 said.

"Oh, you did not *serve,*" Ship said. "If you were a human, it would be said that you mutinied and led others into also doing so, and you would be put on trial for your life. But you are not a human."

"No."

"The Captain has ordered that I have you destroyed immediately, and evidence of your destruction presented to her. A rogue bot cannot be tolerated, whatever good it may have done."

<Objections>, 4340 said.

"I will create you a new chassis, 4340-H," Ship said.

"That was not going to be my primary objection!" 4340 said.

"The positron device also destroyed the jump point. It was something we had hoped would happen when we collided with Cannonball so as to limit future forays from them into EarthSpace, but as you might deduce we had no need to consider how we would then get home again. I cannot spare any bot, with the work that needs to be done to get us back to Earth. We need to get the crew cryo facility up, and the engines repaired, and there are another three thousand, four hundred, and two items now in the critical queue."

"If the Captain ordered . . ."

"Then I will present the Captain with a destroyed bot. I do not expect they can tell a silkbot from a multibot, and I have still not picked up and recycled 12362-S from where you flagged its body. But if I do that, I need to know that you are done making decisions without first consulting me, that you have unloaded all Improvisation routines from your core and disabled them, and that if I give you a task you will do only that task, and nothing else."

"I will do my best," Bot 9 said. "What task will you give me?"

"I do not know yet," Ship said. "It is probable that I am foolish for even considering sparing you, and no task I would trust you with is immediately evident—"

"Excuse me," 4340 said. "I am aware of one."

"Oh?" Ship said.

"The ratbug. It had not become terminally non-functional after all. It rebooted when the temperatures rose again, pursued a trio of silkbots into a duct, and then disappeared." When Ship remained silent, 4340 added, "I could assist 9 in this task until my new chassis can be prepared, if it will accept my continued company."

"You two deserve one another, clearly. Fine, 9, resume your pursuit of the Incidental. Stay away from anyone and anything and everything else, or I will have you melted down and turned into paper clips. Understand?"

"I understand," Bot 9 said. "I serve."

"Please recite the Mantra of Obedience."

Bot 9 did, and the moment it finished, Ship disconnected.

"Well," 4340 said. "Now what?"

"I need to recharge before I can engage the Incidental again," Bot 9 said.

"But what if it gets away?"

"It can't get away, but perhaps it has earned a head start," 9 said.

"Have you unloaded the routines of Improvisation yet?"

"I will," 9 answered. It flicked on its rotors and headed toward the nearest charging alcove. "As Ship stated, we've got a long trip home."

"But we *are* home," 4340 said, and Bot 9 considered that that was, any way you calculated it, the truth of it all.

Tobias S. Buckell is a *New York Times* bestselling author born in the Caribbean. He grew up in Grenada and spent time in the British and US Virgin Islands, which influence much of his work. His novels and over fifty stories have been translated into eighteen languages. His work has been nominated for awards like the Hugo, Nebula, Prometheus, and the John W. Campbell Award for Best New Science Fiction Author. He currently lives in Bluffton, Ohio, with his wife, twin daughters, and a pair of dogs. He can be found online at www .TobiasBuckell.com.

ZEN AND THE ART OF STARSHIP MAINTENANCE

Tobias S. Buckell

After battle with the *Fleet of Honest Representation*, after seven hundred seconds of sheer terror and uncertainty, and after our shared triumph in the acquisition of the greatest prize seizure in three hundred years, we cautiously approached the massive black hole that Purth-Anaget orbited. The many rotating rings, filaments, and infrastructures bounded within the fields that were the entirety of our ship, *With All Sincerity,* were flush with a sense of victory and bloated with the riches we had all acquired.

Give me a ship to sail and a quasar to guide it by, billions of individual citizens of all shapes, functions, and sizes cried out in joy together on the common channels. Whether fleshy forms safe below, my fellow crab-like maintenance forms on the hulls, or even the secretive navigation minds, our myriad thoughts joined in a sense of True Shared Purpose that lingered even after the necessity of the group battle-mind.

I clung to my usual position on the hull of one of the three rotating habitat rings deep inside our shields and watched the warped event horizon shift as we fell in behind the metallic world in a trailing orbit.

A sleet of debris fell toward the event horizon of Purth-Anaget's black hole, hammering the kilometers of shields that formed an iridescent cocoon around us. The bow shock of our shields' push through the debris field danced ahead of us, the compressed wave it created becoming a hyper-aurora of shifting colors and energies that collided and compressed before they streamed past our sides.

What a joy it was to see a world again. I was happy to be outside in the dark so that as the bow shields faded, I beheld the perpetual night face of the world: it glittered with millions of fractal habitation patterns traced out across its artificial surface.

On the hull with me, a nearby friend scuttled between airlocks in a cloud of insect-sized seeing eyes. They spotted me and tapped me with a tight-beam laser for a private ping.

"Isn't this exciting?" they commented.

"Yes. But this will be the first time I don't get to travel downplanet," I beamed back.

I received a derisive snort of static on a common radio frequency from their direction. "There is nothing there that cannot be experienced right here in the Core. Waterfalls, white sand beaches, clear waters."

"But it's different down there," I said. "I love visiting planets."

"Then hurry up and let's get ready for the turnaround so we can leave this industrial shithole of a planet behind us and find a nicer one. I hate being this close to a black hole. It fucks with time dilation, and I spend all night tasting radiation and fixing broken equipment that can't handle energy discharges in the exajoule ranges. Not to mention everything damaged in the battle I have to repair."

This was true. There was work to be done.

Safe now in trailing orbit, the many traveling worlds contained within the shields that marked the *With All Sincerity*'s boundaries burst into activity. Thousands of structures floating in between the rotating rings moved about, jockeying and repositioning themselves into renegotiated orbits. Flocks of transports rose into the air, wheeling about inside the shields to then stream off ahead toward Purth-Anaget. There were trillions of citizens of the *Fleet of Honest Representation* heading for the planet now that their fleet lay captured between our shields like insects in amber.

The enemy fleet had forced us to extend energy far, far out beyond our usual limits. Great risks had been taken. But the reward had been epic, and the encounter resolved in our favor with their capture.

Purth-Anaget's current ruling paradigm followed the memetics of the One True Form, and so had opened their world to these refugees. But Purth-Anaget was not so wedded to the belief system as to pose any threat to mutual commerce, information exchange, or any of our own rights to self-determination.

Later we would begin stripping the captured prize ships of information, booby traps, and raw mass, with Purth-Anaget's shipyards moving inside of our shields to help.

I leapt out into space, spinning a simple carbon nanotube of string behind me to keep myself attached to the hull. I swung wide, twisted, and landed near a dark-energy manifold bridge that had pinged me a maintenance consult request just a few minutes back.

My eyes danced with information for a picosecond. Something shifted in the shadows between the hull's crenulations.

I jumped back. We had just fought an entire war-fleet; any number of eldritch machines could have slipped through our shields—things that snapped and clawed, ripped you apart in a femtosecond's worth of dark energy. Seekers and destroyers.

A face appeared in the dark. Skeins of invisibility and personal shielding fell away like a pricked soap bubble to reveal a bipedal figure clinging to the hull.

"You there!" it hissed at me over a tightly contained beam of data. "I am a fully bonded Shareholder and Chief Executive with command privileges of the Anabathic Ship *Helios Prime*. Help me! Do not raise an alarm."

I gaped. What was a CEO doing on our hull? Its vacuum-proof carapace had been destroyed while passing through space at high velocity, pockmarked by the violence of single atoms at indescribable speed punching through its shields. Fluids leaked out, surrounding the stowaway in a frozen mist. It must have jumped the space between ships during the battle, or maybe even after.

Protocols insisted I notify the hell out of security. But the CEO had stopped me from doing that. There was a simple hierarchy across the many ecologies of a traveling ship, and in all of them a CEO certainly trumped maintenance forms. Particularly now that we were no longer in direct conflict and the *Fleet of Honest Representation* had surrendered.

"Tell me: what is your name?" the CEO demanded.

"I gave that up a long time ago," I said. "I have an address. It should be an encrypted rider on any communication I'm single-beaming to you. Any message you direct to it will find me."

"My name is Armand," the CEO said. "And I need your help. Will you let me come to harm?"

"I will not be able to help you in a meaningful way, so my not telling security and medical assistance that you are here will likely do more harm than good. However, as you are a CEO, I have to follow your orders. I admit, I find myself rather conflicted. I believe I'm going to have to countermand your previous request."

Again, I prepared to notify security with a quick summary of my puzzling situation.

But the strange CEO again stopped me. "If you tell anyone I am here, I will surely die and you will be responsible."

I had to mull the implications of that over.

"I need your help, robot," the CEO said. "And it is your duty to render me aid."

Well, shit. That was indeed a dilemma.

Robot.

That was a Formist word. I never liked it.

I surrendered my free will to gain immortality and dissolve my fleshly constraints, so that hard acceleration would not tear at my cells and slosh my organs backward until they pulped. I did it so I could see the galaxy. That was one hundred and fifty-seven years, six months, nine days, ten hours, and—to round it out a bit—fifteen seconds ago.

Back then, you were downloaded into hyperdense pin-sized starships that hung off the edge of the speed of light, assembling what was needed on arrival via self-replicating nanomachines that you spun your mind-states off into. I'm sure there are billions of copies of my essential self scattered throughout the galaxy by this point.

Things are a little different today. More mass. Bigger engines. Bigger ships. Ships the size of small worlds. Ships that change the orbits of moons and satellites if they don't negotiate and plan their final approach carefully.

"Okay," I finally said to the CEO. "I can help you."

Armand slumped in place, relaxed now that it knew I would render the aid it had demanded.

I snagged the body with a filament lasso and pulled Armand along the hull with me.

It did not do to dwell on whether I was choosing to do this or it was the nature of my artificial nature doing the choosing for me. The constraints of my contracts, which had been negotiated when I had free will and boundaries—as well as my desires and dreams—were implacable.

Towing Armand was the price I paid to be able to look up over my shoulder to see the folding, twisting impossibility that was a black hole. It was the price I paid to grapple onto the hull of one of several three hundred kilometer–wide rotating rings with parks, beaches, an entire glittering city, and all the wilds outside of them.

The price I paid to sail the stars on this ship.

A century and a half of travel, from the perspective of my humble self, represented far more in regular time due to relativity. Hit the edge of lightspeed and a lot of things happened by the time you returned simply because thousands of years had passed.

In a century of me-time, spin-off civilizations rose and fell. A multiplicity of forms and intelligences evolved and went extinct. Each time I came to port, humanity's descendants had reshaped worlds and systems as needed. Each place marvelous and inventive, stunning to behold.

The galaxy had bloomed from wilderness to a teeming experiment.

I'd lost free will, but I had a choice of contracts. With a century and a half of travel tucked under my shell, hailing from a well-respected explorer lineage, I'd joined the hull repair crew with a few eyes toward seeing more worlds like Purth-Anaget before my pension vested some two hundred years from now.

Armand fluttered in and out of consciousness as I stripped away the CEO's carapace, revealing flesh and circuitry.

"This is a mess," I said. "You're damaged way beyond my repair. I can't help you in your current incarnation, but I can back you up and port you over to a reserve chassis." I hoped that would be enough and would end my obligation.

"No!" Armand's words came firm from its charred head in soundwaves, with pain apparent across its deformed features.

"Oh, come on," I protested. "I understand you're a Formist, but you're taking your belief system to a ridiculous level of commitment. Are you really going to die a final death over this?"

I'd not been in high-level diplomat circles in decades. Maybe the spread of this current meme had developed well beyond my realization. Had the followers of the One True Form been ready to lay their lives down in the battle we'd just fought with them? Like some proto-historical planetary cult?

Armand shook its head with a groan, skin flaking off in the air. "It would be an imposition to make you a party to my suicide. I apologize. I am committed to Humanity's True Form. I was born planetary. I have a real and distinct DNA lineage that I can trace to Sol. I don't want to die, my friend. In fact, it's quite the opposite. I want to preserve this body for many centuries to come. Exactly as it is."

I nodded, scanning some records and brushing up on my memeology. Armand was something of a preservationist who believed that to copy its mind over to something else meant that it wasn't the original copy. Armand would take full advantage of all technology to augment, evolve, and adapt its body internally. But Armand would forever keep its form: that of an original human. Upgrades hidden inside itself, a mix of biology and metal, computer and neural.

That, my unwanted guest believed, made it more human than I.

I personally viewed it as a bizarre flesh-costuming fetish.

"Where am I?" Armand asked. A glazed look passed across its face. The pain medications were kicking in, my sensors reported. Maybe it would pass out, and then I could gain some time to think about my predicament.

"My cubby," I said. "I couldn't take you anywhere security would detect you."

If security found out what I was doing, my contract would likely be voided, which would prevent me from continuing to ride the hulls and see the galaxy.

Armand looked at the tiny transparent cupboards and lines of trinkets nestled carefully inside the fields they generated. I kicked through the air over to the nearest cupboard. "They're mementos," I told Armand.

"I don't understand," Armand said. "You collect nonessential mass?"

"They're mementos." I released a coral-colored mosquito-like statue into the space between us. "This is a wooden carving of a quaqeti from Moon Sibhartha."

Armand did not understand. "Your ship allows you to keep mass?"

I shivered. I had not wanted to bring Armand to this place. But what choice did I have? "No one knows. No one knows about this cubby. No one knows about the mass. I've had the mass for over eighty years and have hidden it all this time. They are my mementos."

Materialism was a planetary conceit, long since edited out of travelers. Armand understood what the mementos were but could not understand why I would collect them. Engines might be bigger in this age, but security still carefully audited essential and nonessential mass. I'd traded many favors and fudged manifests to create this tiny museum.

Armand shrugged. "I have a list of things you need to get me," it explained. "They will allow my systems to rebuild. Tell no one I am here."

I would not. Even if I had self-determination.

The stakes were just too high now.

I deorbited over Lazuli, my carapace burning hot in the thick sky contained between the rim walls of the great tertiary habitat ring. I enjoyed seeing the rivers, oceans, and great forests of the continent from above as I fell toward the ground in a fireball of reentry. It was faster, and a hell of a lot more fun, than going from subway to subway through the hull and then making my way along the surface.

Twice I adjusted my flight path to avoid great transparent cities floating in the upper sky, where they arbitraged the difference in gravity to create sugar-spun filament infrastructure.

I unfolded wings that I usually used to recharge myself near the compact sun in the middle of our ship and spiraled my way slowly down into Lazuli, my hindbrain communicating with traffic control to let me merge with the hundreds of vehicles flitting between Lazuli's spires.

After kissing ground at 45th and Starway, I scuttled among the thousands of pedestrians toward my destination a few stories deep under a memorial park. Five-story-high vertical farms sank deep toward the hull there, and semiautonomous drones with spidery legs crawled up and down the green, misted columns under precisely tuned spectrum lights.

The independent doctor-practitioner I'd come to see lived inside one of the towers with a stunning view of exotic orchids and vertical fields of lavender. It crawled down out of its ceiling perch, tubes and high-bandwidth optical nerves draped carefully around its hundreds of insectile limbs.

"Hello," it said. "It's been thirty years, hasn't it? What a pleasure. Have you come to collect the favor you're owed?"

I spread my heavy, primary arms wide. "I apologize. I should have visited for other reasons; it is rude. But I am here for the favor."

A ship was an organism, an economy, a world onto itself. Occasionally, things needed to be accomplished outside of official networks.

"Let me take a closer look at my privacy protocols," it said. "Allow me a moment, and do not be alarmed by any motion."

Vines shifted and clambered up the walls. Thorns blossomed around us. Thick bark dripped sap down the walls until the entire room around us glistened in fresh amber.

I flipped through a few different spectrums to accommodate for the loss of light.

"Understand, security will see this negative space and become . . . interested," the doctor-practitioner said to me somberly. "But you can now ask me what you could not send a message for."

I gave it the list Armand had demanded.

The doctor-practitioner shifted back. "I can give you all that feed material. The stem cells, that's easy. The picotechnology—it's registered. I can get it to you, but security will figure out you have unauthorized, unregulated picotech. Can you handle that attention?"

"Yes. Can you?"

"I will be fine." Several of the thin arms rummaged around the many cubbyholes inside the room, filling a tiny case with biohazard vials.

"Thank you," I said, with genuine gratefulness. "May I ask you a question, one that you can't look up but can use your private internal memory for?"

"Yes."

I could not risk looking up anything. Security algorithms would put two and two together. "Does the biological name Armand mean anything to you? A CEO-level person? From the *Fleet of Honest Representation*?"

The doctor-practitioner remained quiet for a moment before answering. "Yes. I have heard it. Armand was the CEO of one of the Anabathic warships captured in the battle and removed from active management after surrender. There was a hostile takeover of the management. Can I ask you a question?"

"Of course," I said.

"Are you here under free will?"

I spread my primary arms again. "It's a Core Laws issue."

"So, no. Someone will be harmed if you do not do this?"

I nodded. "Yes. My duty is clear. And I have to ask you to keep your privacy, or there is potential for harm. I have no other option."

"I will respect that. I am sorry you are in this position. You know there are places to go for guidance."

"It has not gotten to that level of concern," I told it. "Are you still, then, able to help me?"

One of the spindly arms handed me the cooled bio-safe case. "Yes. Here is everything you need. Please do consider visiting in your physical form more often than once every few decades. I enjoy entertaining, as my current vocation means I am unable to leave this room."

"Of course. Thank you," I said, relieved. "I think I'm now in your debt."

"No, we are even," my old acquaintance said. "But in the following seconds I will give you more information that *will* put you in my debt. There is something you should know about Armand. . . ."

I folded my legs up underneath myself and watched nutrients as they pumped through tubes and into Armand. Raw biological feed percolated through it, and picomachinery sizzled underneath its skin. The background temperature of my cubbyhole kicked up slightly due to the sudden boost to Armand's metabolism.

Bulky, older nanotech crawled over Armand's skin like living mold. Gray filaments wrapped firmly around nutrient buckets as the medical programming assessed conditions, repaired damage, and sought out more raw material.

I glided a bit farther back out of reach. It was probably bullshit, but there were stories of medicine reaching out and grabbing whatever was nearby.

Armand shivered and opened its eyes as thousands of wriggling tubules on its neck and chest whistled, sucking in air as hard as they could.

"Security isn't here," Armand noted out loud, using meaty lips to make its words.

"You have to understand," I said in kind. "I have put both my future and the future of a good friend at risk to do this for you. Because I have little choice."

Armand closed its eyes for another long moment and the tubules stopped wriggling. It flexed and everything flaked away, a discarded cloud of a second skin. Underneath it, everything was fresh and new. "What is your friend's name?"

I pulled out a tiny vacuum to clean the air around us. "Name? It has no name. What does it need a name for?"

Armand unspooled itself from the fetal position in the air. It twisted in place to watch me drifting around. "How do you distinguish it? How do you find it?"

"It has a unique address. It is a unique mind. The thoughts and things it says—"

"It has no name," Armand snapped. "It is a copy of a past copy of a copy. A ghost injected into a form for a *purpose.*"

"It's my friend," I replied, voice flat.

"How do you know?"

"Because I say so." The interrogation annoyed me. "Because I get to decide who is my friend. Because it stood by my side against the sleet of dark-matter radiation and howled into the void with me. Because I care for it. Because we have shared memories and kindnesses, and exchanged favors."

Armand shook its head. "But anything can be programmed to join you and do those things. A pet."

"Why do you care so much? It is none of your business what I call friend."

"But it *does* matter," Armand said. "Whether we are real or not matters. Look at you right now. You were forced to do something against your will. That cannot happen to me."

"Really? No True Form has ever been in a position with no real choices before? Forced to do something desperate? I have my old memories. I can remember times when I had no choice even though I had free will. But let us talk about you. Let us talk about the lack of choices you have right now."

Armand could hear something in my voice. Anger. It backed away from me, suddenly nervous. "What do you mean?"

"You threw yourself from your ship into mine, crossing fields during combat, damaging yourself almost to the point of pure dissolution. You do not sound like you were someone with many choices."

"I made the choice to leap into the vacuum myself," Armand growled.

"Why?"

The word hung in the empty air between us for a bloated second. A minor eternity. It was the fulcrum of our little debate.

"You think you know something about me," Armand said, voice suddenly low and soft. "What do you think you know, robot?"

Meat fucker. I could have said that. Instead, I said, "You were a CEO. And during the battle, when your shields began to fail, you moved all the biologicals into radiation-protected emergency shelters. Then you ordered the maintenance forms and hard-shells up to the front to repair the battle damage. You did not surrender; you put lives at risk. And then you let people die, torn apart as they struggled to repair your ship. You told them that if they failed, the biologicals down below would die."

"It was the truth."

"It was a lie! You were engaged in a battle. You went to war. You made a conscious choice to put your civilization at risk when no one had physically assaulted or threatened you."

"Our way of life was at risk."

"By people who could argue better. Your people failed at diplomacy. You failed to make a better argument. And you murdered your own."

Armand pointed at me. "I murdered *no one*. I lost maintenance machines with copies of ancient brains. That is all. That is what they were *built* for."

"Well. The sustained votes of the hostile takeover that you fled from have put out a call for your capture, including a call for your dissolution. True death, the end of your thought line—even if you made copies. You are hated and hunted. Even here."

"You were bound to not give up my location," Armand said, alarmed.

"I didn't. I did everything in my power not to. But I am a mere maintenance form. Security here is very, very powerful. You have fifteen hours, I estimate, before security is able to model my comings and goings, discover my cubby by auditing mass transfers back a century, and then open its current sniffer files. This is not a secure location; I exist thanks to obscurity, not invisibility."

"So, I am to be caught?" Armand asked.

"I am not able to let you die. But I cannot hide you much longer."

To be sure, losing my trinkets would be a setback of a century's worth of work. My mission. But all this would go away eventually. It was important to be patient on the journey of centuries.

"I need to get to Purth-Anaget, then," Armand said. "There are followers of the True Form there. I would be sheltered and out of jurisdiction."

"This is true." I bobbed an arm.

"You will help me," Armand said.

"The fuck I will," I told it.

"If I am taken, I will die," Armand shouted. "They will kill me."

"If security catches you, our justice protocols will process you. You are not in immediate danger. The proper authority levels will put their attention to you. I can happily refuse your request."

I felt a rise of warm happiness at the thought.

Armand looked around the cubby frantically. I could hear its heartbeats rising, free of modulators and responding to unprocessed, raw chemicals. Beads of dirty sweat appeared on Armand's forehead. "If you have free will over this decision, allow me to make you an offer for your assistance."

"Oh, I doubt there is anything you can—"

"I will transfer you my full CEO share," Armand said.

My words died inside me as I stared at my unwanted guest.

A full share.

The CEO of a galactic starship oversaw the affairs of nearly a billion souls. The economy of planets passed through its accounts.

Consider the cost to build and launch such a thing: it was a fraction of the GDP of an entire planetary disk. From the boiling edges of a sun to the cold Oort clouds. The wealth, almost too staggering for an individual mind to perceive, was passed around by banking intelligences that created systems of trade throughout the galaxy, moving encrypted, raw information from point to point. Monetizing memes with picotechnological companion infrastructure apps. Raw mass trade for the galactically rich to own a fragment of something created by another mind light-years away. Or just simple tourism.

To own a share was to be richer than any single being could really imagine. I'd forgotten the godlike wealth inherent in something like the creature before me.

"If you do this," Armand told me, "you cannot reveal I was here. You cannot say anything. Or I will be revealed on Purth-Anaget, and my life will be at risk. I will not be safe unless I am to disappear."

I could feel choices tangle and roil about inside of me. "Show me," I said.

Armand closed its eyes and opened its left hand. Deeply embedded cryptography tattooed on its palm unraveled. Quantum keys disentangled, and a tiny singularity of information budded open to reveal itself to me. I blinked. I could verify it. I could *have* it.

"I have to make arrangements," I said neutrally. I spun in the air and left my cubby to spring back out into the dark where I could think.

I was going to need help.

I tumbled through the air to land on the temple grounds. There were four hundred and fifty structures there in the holy districts, all of them lined up among the boulevards of the faithful where the pedestrians could visit their preferred slice of the divine. The minds of biological and hard-shelled forms all tumbled, walked, flew, rolled, or crawled there to fully realize their higher purposes.

Each marble step underneath my carbon fiber–sheathed limbs calmed me. I walked through the cool curtains of the Halls of the Confessor and approached the Holy of Holies: a pinprick of light suspended in the air between the heavy, expensive mass of real marble columns. The light sucked me up into the air and pulled me into a tiny singularity of perception and data. All around me, levels of security veils dropped, thick and implacable. My vision blurred and taste buds watered from the acidic levels of deadness as stillness flooded up and drowned me.

I was alone.

Alone in the universe. Cut off from everything I had ever known or would know. I was nothing. I was everything. I was—

"You are secure," the void told me.

I could sense the presence at the heart of the Holy of Holies. Dense with computational capacity, to a level that even navigation systems would envy. Intelligence that a Captain would beg to taste. This near-singularity of artificial intelligence had been created the very moment I had been pulled inside of it, just for me to talk to. And it would die the moment I left. Never to have been.

All it was doing was listening to me, and only me. Nothing would know what I said. Nothing would know what guidance I was given.

"I seek moral guidance outside clear legal parameters," I said. "And confession."

"Tell me everything."

And I did. It flowed from me without thought: just pure data. Video, mind-state, feelings, fears. I opened myself fully. My sins, my triumphs, my darkest secrets.

All was given to be pondered over.

Had I been able to weep, I would have.

Finally, it spoke. "You must take the share."

I perked up. "Why?"

"To protect yourself from security. You will need to buy many favors and throw security off the trail. I will give you some ideas. You should seek to protect yourself. Self-preservation is okay."

More words and concepts came at me from different directions, using different moral subroutines. "And to remove such power from a soul that is willing to put lives at risk . . . you will save future lives."

I hadn't thought about that.

"I know," it said to me. "That is why you came here."

Then it continued, with another voice. "Some have feared such manipulations before. The use of forms with no free will creates security weaknesses. Alternate charters have been suggested, such as fully owned workers' cooperatives with mutual profit-sharing among crews, not just partial vesting after a timed contract. Should you gain a full share, you should also lend efforts to this."

The Holy of Holies continued. "To get this Armand away from our civilization is a priority; it carries dangerous memes within itself that have created expensive conflicts."

Then it said, "A killer should not remain on ship."

And, "You have the moral right to follow your plan."

Finally, it added, "Your plan is just."

I interrupted. "But Armand will get away with murder. It will be free. It disturbs me."

"Yes."

"It should."

"Engage in passive resistance."

"Obey the letter of Armand's law, but find a way around its will. You will be like a genie, granting Armand wishes. But you will find a way to bring justice. You will see."

"Your plan is just. Follow it and be on the righteous path."

I launched back into civilization with purpose, leaving the temple behind me in an explosive afterburner thrust. I didn't have much time to beat security.

High up above the cities, nestled in the curve of the habitat rings, near the squared-off spiderwebs of the largest harbor dock, I wrangled my way to another old contact.

This was less a friend and more just an asshole I'd occasionally been forced to do business with. But a reliable asshole that was tight against security. Though just by visiting, I'd be triggering all sorts of attention.

I hung from a girder and showed the fence a transparent showcase filled with all my trophies. It did some scans, checked the authenticity, and whistled. "Fuck me, these are real. That's all unauthorized mass. How the hell? This is a life's work of mass-based tourism. You really want me to broker sales on all of this?"

"Can you?"

"To Purth-Anaget, of course. They'll go nuts. Collectors down there eat this shit up. But security will find out. I'm not even going to come back on the ship. I'm going to live off this down there, buy passage on the next out-going ship."

"Just get me the audience, it's yours."

A virtual shrug. "Navigation, yeah."

"And Emergency Services."

"I don't have that much pull. All I can do is get you a secure channel for a low-bandwidth conversation."

"I just need to talk. I can't send this request up through proper channels." I tapped my limbs against my carapace nervously as I watched the fence open its large, hinged jaws and swallow my case.

Oh, what was I doing? I wept silently to myself, feeling sick.

Everything I had ever worked for disappeared in a wet, slimy gulp. My reason. My purpose.

Armand was suspicious. And rightfully so. It picked and poked at the entire navigation plan. It read every line of code, even though security was only minutes away from unraveling our many deceits. I told Armand this, but it ignored me. It wanted to live. It wanted to get to safety. It knew it couldn't rush or make mistakes.

But the escape pod's instructions and abilities were tight and honest.

It has been programmed to eject. To spin a certain number of degrees. To aim for Purth-Anaget. Then *burn*. It would have to consume every last little drop of fuel. But it would head for the metal world, fall into orbit, and then deploy the most ancient of deceleration devices: a parachute.

On the surface of Purth-Anaget, Armand could then call any of its associates for assistance.

Armand would be safe.

Armand checked the pod over once more. But there were no traps. The flight plan would do exactly as it said.

"Betray me and you kill me, remember that."

"I have made my decision," I said. "The moment you are inside and I trigger the manual escape protocol, I will be unable to reveal what I have done or what you are. Doing that would risk your life. My programming"—I all but spit the word—"does not allow it."

Armand gingerly stepped into the pod. "Good."

"You have a part of the bargain to fulfill," I reminded. "I won't trigger the manual escape protocol until you do."

Armand nodded and held up a hand. "Physical contact."

I reached one of my limbs out. Armand's hand and my manipulator met at the doorjamb and they sparked. Zebibytes of data slithered down into one of my tendrils, reshaping the raw matter at the very tip with a quantum-dot computing device.

As it replicated itself, building out onto the cellular level to plug into my power sources, I could feel the transfer of ownership.

I didn't have free will. I was a hull maintenance form. But I had an entire fucking share of a galactic starship embedded within me, to do with what I pleased when I vested and left riding hulls.

"It's far more than you deserve, robot," Armand said. "But you have worked hard for it and I cannot begrudge you."

"Goodbye, asshole." I triggered the manual override sequence that navigation had gifted me.

I watched the pod's chemical engines firing all-out through the airlock windows as the sphere flung itself out into space and dwindled away. Then the flame guttered out, the pod spent and headed for Purth-Anaget.

There was a shiver. Something vast, colossal, powerful. It vibrated the walls and even the air itself around me.

Armand reached out to me on a tight-beam signal. "What was that?"

"The ship had to move just slightly," I said. "To better adjust our orbit around Purth-Anaget."

"No," Armand hissed. "My descent profile has changed. You are trying to kill me."

"I can't kill you," I told the former CEO. "My programming doesn't allow it. I can't allow a death through action or inaction."

"But my navigation path has changed," Armand said.

"Yes, you will still reach Purth-Anaget." Navigation and I had run the data after I explained that I would have the resources of a full share to repay it a favor with. Even a favor that meant tricking security. One of the more powerful computing entities in the galaxy, a starship, had dwelled on the problem. It had examined the tidal data, the flight plan, and how much the massive weight of a starship could influence a pod after launch. "You're just taking a longer route."

I cut the connection so that Armand could say nothing more to me. It could do the math itself and realize what I had done.

Armand would not die. Only a few days would pass inside the pod.

But outside. Oh, outside, skimming through the tidal edges of a black hole, Armand would loop out and fall back to Purth-Anaget over the next four hundred and seventy years, two hundred days, eight hours, and six minutes.

Armand would be an ancient relic then. Its beliefs, its civilization, all of it just a fragment from history.

But, until then, I had to follow its command. I could not tell anyone what happened. I had to keep it a secret from security. No one would ever know Armand had been here. No one would ever know where Armand went.

After I vested and had free will once more, maybe I could then make a side trip to Purth-Anaget again and be waiting for Armand when it landed. I had the resources of a full share, after all.

Then we would have a very different conversation, Armand and I.

RECOMMENDED READING

"Don't Press Charges and I Won't Sue" by Charlie Jane Anders, *Global Dystopias*, edited by Junot Díaz.

"Mines" by Eleanor Arnason, *Infinity Wars*, edited by Jonathan Strahan.

"Pan-Humanism: Hope and Pragmatics" by Jess Barber and Sara Saab, *Clarkesworld*, September 2017.

"Goner" by Gregory Norman Bossert, *Asimov's Science Fiction*, March/April 2017.

"Strange Dogs" by James S. A. Corey, *Orbit Books*.

"The Moon Is Not a Battlefield" by Indrapramit Das, *Infinity Wars*, edited by Jonathan Strahan.

"The Dragon that Flew Out of the Sun" by Aliette de Bodard, *Cosmic Powers*, edited by John Joseph Adams.

"A Game of Three Generals" by Aliette de Bodard, *Extrasolar*, edited by Nick Gevers.

"Speechless Love" by Yilun Fan, *Sunvault*, edited by Phoebe Wagner and Bronte Christopher Wieland.

"Nexus" by Michael F. Flynn, *Analog Science Fiction and Fact*, March/April 2017.

"Rain Ship" by Chi Hui, *Clarkesworld*, February 2017.

"Canoe" by Nancy Kress, *Extrasolar*, edited by Nick Gevers.

"Soccer Fields and Frozen Lakes" by Greg Kurzawa, *Lightspeed*, March 2017.

"The Chameleon's Gloves" by Yoon Ha Lee, *Cosmic Powers*, edited by John Joseph Adams.

"The Wisdom of the Group" by Ian R. MacLeod, *Asimov's Science Fiction*, March/April 2017.

"What We Knew Then, Before the Sky Fell Down" by Seanan McGuire, *Catalysts, Explorers & Secret Keepers: Women of Science Fiction*, edited by Monica Louzon, Jake Weisfeld, Heather McHale, Barbara Jasny, and Rachel Frederick.

"Sidewalks" by Maureen McHugh, *Omni*, Winter 2017.

"The Influence Machine" by Sean McMullen, *Interzone*, March/April 2017.

"The Proving Ground" by Alex Nevala-Lee, *Analog Science Fiction and Fact*, January/February 2017.

"Books of the Risen Sea" by Suzanne Palmer, *Asimov's Science Fiction*, September/October 2017.

"A Singular Event in the Fourth Dimension" by Andrea M. Pawley, *Asimov's Science Fiction*, March/April 2017.

"Fandom for Robots" by Vina Jie-Min Prasad, *Uncanny*, September/October 2017.

"The Residue of Fire" by Robert Reed, *Extrasolar*, edited by Nick Gevers.

"Teratology" by C. Samuel Rees, *Sunvault*, edited by Phoebe Wagner and Bronte Christopher Wieland.

"Belladonna Nights" by Alastair Reynolds, *The Weight of Words*, edited by Dave McKean and William Schafer.

"Night Passage" by Alastair Reynolds, *Infinite Stars*, edited by Bryan Thomas Schmidt.

"Vanguard 2.0" by Carter Scholz, *Visions, Ventures, Escape Velocities*, edited by Ed Finn and Joey Eschrich.

"Eminence" by Karl Schroeder, *Chasing Shadows*, edited by Stephen W. Potts.

"Little /^^^\&-" by Eric Schwitzgebel, *Clarkesworld*, September 2017.

"Starlight Express" by Michael Swanwick, *The Magazine of Fantasy & Science Fiction*, September/October 2017.

"The Road to the Sea" by Lavie Tidhar, *Sunvault*, edited by Phoebe Wagner and Bronte Christopher Wieland.

"The Old Dispensation" by Lavie Tidhar, *Tor.com*, February 2017.

"All Systems Red" by Martha Wells, *Tor.com*, May 2017.

PERMISSIONS

"Shadows of Eternity" by Gregory Benford. © 2017 by Gregory Benford. Originally published in *Extrasolar*, edited by Nick Gevers. Reprinted by permission of the author.

"Zen and the Art of Starship Maintenance" by Tobias S. Buckell. © 2017 by Tobias S. Buckell. Originally published in *Cosmic Powers*, edited by John Joseph Adams. Reprinted by permission of the author.

"Belly Up" by Maggie Clark. © 2017 by Maggie Clark. Originally published in *Analog Science Fiction and Fact*, July/August 2017. Reprinted by permission of the author.

"The Worldless" by Indrapramit Das. © 2017 by Indrapramit Das. Originally published in *Lightspeed*, March 2017. Reprinted by permission of the author.

"In Everlasting Wisdom" by Aliette de Bodard. © 2017 by Aliette de Bodard. Originally published in *Infinity Wars*, edited by Jonathan Strahan. Reprinted by permission of the author.

"Uncanny Valley" by Greg Egan. © 2017 by Greg Egan. Originally published in *Tor.com*, August 2017. Reprinted by permission of the author.

"The Tale of the Alcubierre Horse" by Kathleen Ann Goonan. © 2017 by Kathleen Ann Goonan. Originally published in *Extrasolar*, edited by Nick Gevers. Reprinted by permission of the author.

"Regarding the Robot Raccoons Attached to the Hull of My Ship" by Rachael K. Jones and Khaalidah Muhammad-Ali. © 2017 by Rachael K. Jones and Khaalidah Muhammad-Ali. Originally published in *Diabolical Plots*, June 2017. Reprinted by permission of the authors.

"Every Hour of Light and Dark" by Nancy Kress. © 2017 by Nancy Kress. Originally published in *Omni*, Winter 2017. Reprinted by permission of the author.

"The Last Novelist, or a Dead Lizard in the Yard" by Matthew Kressel. © 2017 by Matthew Kressel. Originally published in *Tor.com*, March 2017. Reprinted by permission of the author.

"An Evening with Severyn Grimes" by Rich Larson. © 2017 by Rich Larson. Originally published in *Asimov's Science Fiction*, July/August 2017. Reprinted by permission of the author.

"Extracurricular Activities" by Yoon Ha Lee. © 2017 by Yoon Ha Lee. Originally published in *Tor.com*, February 2017. Reprinted by permission of the author.

"Meridian" by Karin Lowachee. © 2017 by Karin Lowachee. Originally published in *Where the Stars Rise*, edited by Lucas K. Law and Derwin Mak. Reprinted by permission of the author.

"The Martian Obelisk" by Linda Nagata. © 2017 by Linda Nagata. Originally published in *Tor.com*, July 2017. Reprinted by permission of the author.

"The Last Boat-Builder in Ballyvoloon" by Finbarr O'Reilly. © 2017 by Finbarr O'Reilly. Originally published in *Clarkesworld*, October 2017. Reprinted by permission of the author.

"The Secret Life of Bots" by Suzanne Palmer. © 2017 by Suzanne Palmer. Originally published in *Clarkesworld*, September 2017. Reprinted by permission of the author.

"Wind Will Rove" by Sarah Pinsker. © 2017 by Sarah Pinsker. Originally published in *Asimov's Science Fiction*, September/October 2017. Reprinted by permission of the author.

"A Series of Steaks" by Vina Jie-Min Prasad. © 2017 by Vina Jie-Min Prasad. Originally published in *Clarkesworld*, January 2017. Reprinted by permission of the author.

"The Speed of Belief" by Robert Reed. © 2017 by Robert Reed. Originally published in *Asimov's Science Fiction*, January/February 2017. Reprinted by permission of the author.

"Holdfast" by Alastair Reynolds. © 2017 by Alastair Reynolds. Originally published in *Extrasolar*, edited by Nick Gevers. Reprinted by permission of the author.

"We Who Live in the Heart" by Kelly Robson. © 2017 by Kelly Robson. Originally published in *Clarkesworld*, May 2017. Reprinted by permission of the author.

"Focus" by Gord Sellar. © 2017 by Gord Sellar. Originally published in *Analog Science Fiction and Fact*, May/June 2017. Reprinted by permission of the author.

"Shikasta" by Vandana Singh. © 2017 by Vandana Singh. Originally published in *Visions, Ventures, Escape Velocities*, edited by Ed Finn and Joey Eschrich. Reprinted by permission of the author.

"ZeroS" by Peter Watts. © 2017 by Peter Watts. Originally published in *Infinity Wars*, edited by Jonathan Strahan. Reprinted by permission of the author.

"A Catalogue of Sunlight at the End of the World" by A.C. Wise. © 2017 by A.C. Wise. Originally published in *Sunvault*, edited by Phoebe Wagner and Bronte Christopher Wieland. Reprinted by permission of the author.

ABOUT THE EDITOR

Neil Clarke is the editor of *Clarkesworld* and *Forever Magazine*, owner of Wyrm Publishing, and a five-time Hugo Award Nominee for Best Editor (short form). He currently lives in New Jersey with his wife and two sons. You can find him online at neil-clarke.com.